Manhunter
&
Bloody Hand

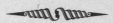

Manhunter

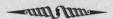

MATT BRAUN

St. Martin's Paperbacks

OTHER TITLES BY MATT BRAUN

TOMBSTONE
THE SPOILERS

EL PASO
THE WILD ONES

KINCH RILEY
INDIAN TERRITORY

HANGMAN'S CREEK
JURY OF SIX

DODGE CITY
DAKOTA
A DISTANT LAND
WINDWARD WEST
CROSSFIRE
THE HIGHBINDERS
THE WARLORDS
THE SPOILERS
HICKOK AND CODY
THE OVERLORDS
TOMBSTONE
RIO GRANDE
THE BRANNOCKS
THE GAMBLERS
RIO HONDO
THE SAVAGE LAND
NOBLE OUTLAW
CIMARRON JORDAN
LORDS OF THE LAND
ONE LAST TOWN
TEXAS EMPIRE
JURY OF SIX

AVAILABLE FROM ST. MARTIN'S PAPERBACKS

Manhunter

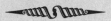

This is a work of fiction. All of the characters, organizations, and events portrayed in this novel are either products of the author's imagination or are used fictitiously.

MANHUNTER / BLOODY HAND

Manhunter copyright © 1981 by Matthew Braun.
Bloody Hand copyright © 1975 by Matt Braun.

For information address St. Martin's Press, 175 Fifth Avenue, New York, NY 10010.

ISBN: 978-1-250-21470-6

Our books may be purchased in bulk for promotional, educational, or business use. Please contact your local bookseller or the Macmillan Corporate and Premium Sales Department at 1-800-221-7945, ext. 5442, or by e-mail at MacmillanSpecialMarkets@macmillan.com.

Printed in the United States of America

Manhunter St. Martin's Paperbacks edition / March 2003
Bloody Hand St. Martin's Paperbacks edition / May 1996

St. Martin's Paperbacks are published by St. Martin's Press, 175 Fifth Avenue, New York, NY 10010.

10 9 8 7 6 5 4 3 2 1

To Bess and Paul
whose belief and support
are beyond measure

Author's Note

The Old West produced a unique collection of rogues and rascals.

Outlaws and grifters, gunfighters and gamblers, they formed a roll call unsurpassed for shady exploits. Certain of these men were supreme egotists, actively courting fame and glory. They manipulated the media of the day, and the media, with a public clamouring for larger-than-life heroes, was delighted to oblige. Dime novelists, abetted by newspapers and periodicals, transformed these rogues and rascals into the stuff of legend. Later, with a remarkable disdain for the facts, movies and television added their own brand of hype to an already false mythology. The end result was a pantheon of stalwart gunmen and chivalrous desperadoes.

For the most part, it was folklore founded on invention and lies. And it was sold to America by hucksters with an uncanny knack for distorting the truth.

Jesse James was one of the myths fobbed off on a gullible public. Far from the Robin Hood of legend, he was a paranoid outcast who robbed banks and trains rather than work for a living. He was also a master of propaganda. Throughout his career as an outlaw, he wrote articulate and persuasive letters to the editors of several midwestern newspapers. The letters were duly reprinted, and accounted, in large measure, for the belief that he "robbed the rich and gave to the poor." In reality, he was something less than charitable; there is no documented instance of his assisting the needy or championing the cause of oppressed people. He was, moreover, a sadistic killer without mercy or remorse. Still Jesse James captured the public's imagination, and he did it with a certain flair. He was his own best press agent.

Yet every myth has some foundation in fact. The Old West produced many mankillers who were both honourable and courageous. For the most part, however, they shunned the limelight. Because they weren't seeking fame or immortality, they made poor source material for dime novelists and hack journalists. The upshot was that their attributes were grafted onto the rogues and rascals. America, as a result, ended up revering men who deserved no place in our folklore. The truly legendary characters of the era became little more than footnotes in the pages of history.

Luke Starbuck was one such man. His character is a composite of several Old West detectives, who were the most feared mankillers of the day. They worked undercover—generally in disguise—and thus their exploits are not widely known. In *The Manhunter* Starbuck accepts an assignment that pits him against Jesse James. Though the events depicted are historically accurate, certain liberties have been taken regarding time and place. Yet the characters are real, and the revelations unearthed by Starbuck are fact, not fiction. His investigation at last brings to light the truth about Jesse James. A hundred years overdue, it is nonetheless a story that needs telling.

The Manhunter also reveals Starbuck's role in the

death of Jesse James. A compelling tale, it was until now shrouded in mystery. Luke Starbuck told no one of the part he played. For he was a man of many parts and many faces. None of them his own.

CHAPTER 1

The men rode into town from the north. Their horses were held to a walk and they kept to the middle of the street. Unhurried, with three riders out front and two more trailing behind, they proceeded towards the centre of town. No one spoke.

The community, like many midwestern farm towns, was bisected by a main thoroughfare. The business district, small but prosperous, consisted of four stores, a saloon and a blacksmith shop, and one bank. There were few people about and little activity in the downtown area. A typical Monday morning, it was the slowest time of the week. Which, in part, accounted for the five riders. Their business was better conducted in confidence and without crowds.

The men were unremarkable in appearance. Neatly dressed, they wore drab woolen suits and slouch hats. Three were clean-shaven and the other two sported well-trimmed beards. All of them were above average height, but only one, somewhat large and burly, was noticeable for his size. Their mounts were an altogether different matter. At first glance, the animals appeared to be common saddle stock. On closer examination, however, a uniform sleekness and conformation became apparent. The horses were built for endurance and stamina, staying power over long distances.

In the centre of town, the riders wheeled to the left and halted before the bank. There was a military precision to their movements, smooth and coordinated, somehow practiced. The two bearded men stepped down and handed their reins to the third man in the front rank. Without hesitation, the two riders in the rear positioned their mounts to cover the street in both directions. A moment passed while one of the bearded men took a long look around. His bearing was that of a field commander and he subjected the whole of the business district to a slow, careful scrutiny. Then, followed by his companion, he turned and entered the bank.

Inside the door, he stopped and quickly scanned the room. The cashier's window and the vault were to the rear. He noted that the vault door was closed and, to all appearances, locked. To his immediate left, seated behind a desk, the bank president was engaged in conversation with three middle-aged men. By their dress and manner of speech, they were gentlemen landowners and therefore no threat. He pulled a .45 Smith & Wesson revolver from a shoulder holster inside his suit jacket.

"Get your hands up! Keep 'em up and you won't get hurt!"

There was an instant of leaden silence. The cashier froze, watching him intently. At the desk, the president stared at him with disbelief, and the three customers swiveled around in unison. Suddenly, eyes wide with terror, one of them panicked and bolted from his chair.

"Robbers! The bank's being robbed!"

A gun exploded and the man staggered, clutching at his arm. His face went ashen, then he passed out, collapsing at the knees, and dropped to the floor. One eye on the cashier, the gang leader glanced over his shoulder. His companion, standing just inside the doorway, held a pistol trained on the men at the desk. A wisp of smoke curled upward from the barrel.

"Goddamnit!" he said gruffly. "Did you have to shoot him?"

"Seemed like the thing to do. Leastways it made him close his trap."

"Maybe so," the gang leader snapped. "But that gunshot will draw a crowd just sure as hell."

"I don't recollect that ever stopped you before."

"All right, forget it! Keep them birds covered while I tend to business."

With that, he walked to the rear of the bank and stopped before the cashier's window. He casually rested the butt of the Smith & Wesson on the counter, and nodded to the cashier.

"What's your name?"

"Martin," the cashier muttered. "Robert Martin."

"Well, Mr. Martin, how would you like to make it home to supper tonight?"

"I'd like that."

"Then get busy and open that vault. No fool tricks or I'll blow your head off. Hop to it!"

Martin eyed him steadily a moment, then turned towards the vault. A roar of gunfire, several shots in rapid succession, suddenly sounded from outside. The gang leader looked around and saw his companion peering out the door.

"What's all that about?"

"Nothin' serious. Some of the locals got nosy and the boys warned them to stay off the street."

"Keep a sharp lookout."

Turning back, he started and let loose a harsh grunt. Robert Martin had the cash drawer open and was clawing frantically at a revolver hidden beneath a stack of bills. The gang leader pulled the trigger and his Smith & Wesson spat a sheet of flame. The slug punched through Martin's forehead and tore out the back of his skull. A halo of bone and brain matter misted the air around his head, and he stood there a moment, dead on his feet. Then he folded at the waist and slumped to the floor.

"Dumb bastard!" the gang leader cursed savagely. "Told you I'd blow your head off!"

Leaning across the counter, he began scooping bills out of the cash drawer and stuffing them into his pockets. Once the drawer was empty, he wheeled about and marched towards the front of the bank. He signalled the bearded man at the door.

"Let's go! We're all done here."

"What about the vault?"

"No time! Another couple of minutes and the whole town'll be up in arms."

"The boys won't like it. They rode a long ways for a payday."

"Tough titty!" he barked. "You should've thought of that before you got an itchy trigger finger. C'mon, let's clear out!"

The din of gunfire swelled as they moved through the door. Still mounted, the gang members outside were winging random shots through store windows along the street. The merchants and townspeople had taken cover, and as yet there was no return fire. Crossing the broadwalk, the bearded men hastily swung into their saddles. Then, with everyone mounted, the robbers reined about and rode north out of town.

A short distance upstreet the gang leader abruptly brought his horse to a halt. Where the business district ended, the residential area began, and both sides of the street were lined with modest homes. Outside one house, a teenage boy stood at the edge of the yard. His eyes were filled with a mix of fear and youthful curiosity. He watched with wonder as the rest of the robbers skidded to a stop and turned their mounts. The gang leader calmly drew his pistol and extended it to arm's length. He stared down the sights at the boy.

"Come out to get an eyeful, did you?"

The youngster swallowed, licked his lips. "I didn't mean no harm, mister."

"Your mama should've taught you better manners."

Thumbing the hammer on his pistol, the gang leader sighted quickly and fired. A brilliant red splotch appeared on the pocket of the boy's shirt. He reeled backward, then suddenly went limp and fell spread-eagled in the yard. As he hit the ground, the other bearded robber kneed his horse forward, blocking the gang leader.

"Why'd you do that? Why'd you kill him?"

"I felt like it."

"For God's sake, he's just a kid!"

"So what."

"*So what!* You took your spite out on a kid. That's what!"

"Watch your mouth."

"The hell I will!"

The burly rider reined his horse closer. "What's the matter, Frank?"

"Ask Jesse."

"I'm askin' you."

"We didn't finish the job! Jesse said there wasn't time to clean out the vault, and now he's mad at himself."

"Wasn't time?" The large man scowled, turned his gaze on the gang leader. "Then how come you had time to stop and kill that kid?"

"Don't push me, Cole."

"And don't you try throwin' your weight around! We didn't ride to hell and gone just to come away with chicken feed."

"I told you to lay off! I won't tell you again."

"Well, I'll damn sure tell you something! Me and the boys are gonna go back and empty that vault. You can come or stay as you please."

"I'm warning you—!"

"Jesse, one of these days you're gonna warn me once too often."

A shot cracked and they instinctively ducked as a slug whizzed past their heads. Looking around, they saw a man standing in the middle of the street downtown. He had a rifle thrown to his shoulder, and as he fired the second time other men rushed to join him. The gang leader booted his horse and rapped out a sharp command.

"Too late now! Let's ride!"

A barrage from downtown settled the matter. With lead whistling around their ears, the robbers bent low and kicked their mounts into a headlong gallop. Moments later they cleared the edge of town and thundered north along a rutted wagon road.

Their leader, well out in front, never once looked back.

CHAPTER 2

Starbuck wiped his razor dry and walked from the bathroom. He selected a fresh linen shirt from the bureau, then took a conservative brown suit from the wardrobe. After knotting his tie, he slipped into a suit jacket and checked himself in the mirror. No dandy, he was nonetheless particular about his appearance.

Turning from the mirror, he moved to the bed and took a .45 Colt from beneath the pillow. He shoved the gun into a crossdraw holster worn on his left side, positioned directly above the pants pocket. The holster was hand sewn and wet-moulded to the Colt, crafted in such a manner that his belt snugged it flat against his body. The natural drape of his jacket concealed the entire rig and eliminated any telltale bulge. Only those who knew him well were aware that he went armed at all times.

Fully dressed, he walked towards the door leading to the sitting room. His suite in the Brown Palace Hotel was comfortable, though modest in size, and handsomely appointed. Off and on, after establishing headquarters in Denver, he had debated buying a house. His detective business kept him on the move—often for months at a stretch—and the cost of maintaining a suite on a permanent basis sometimes seemed exorbitant. Yet a house would have tied him down, and he wasn't a man who formed attachments easily. Besides, the hotel provided room service and laundry, not to mention a certain freedom of movement. All things considered, he was satisfied with the arrangement. It somehow suited his style.

Entering the sitting room, he nodded to the girl and took a seat beside her on the sofa. A singer, her stage name was Lola Montana, and she was the star attraction at the Alcazar Variety Theater. She was also his current bed partner, and for the past few weeks she had slept over almost every night. Still, in his view, she was a pleasant arrangement, with no strings attached.

A room-service cart was positioned beside the sofa. Earlier, they had shared a breakfast of ham and eggs, topped off with sourdough biscuits and wild honey. Now, luxuriating over a cup of coffee, Lola sat with her legs tucked under the folds of a filmy peignoir. The swell of her breasts was visible through the sheer fabric and she noted his appreciative glance. She vamped him with an engaging smile.

"You look real spiffy this morning, lover."

"I sort of like your getup, too. Hides just enough to give a fellow ideas."

"Ooo?" She slowly batted her eyelashes. "I thought by now you knew all my secrets."

"Let's just say you showed me a few surprises last night."

She laughed a low, throaty laugh. "The way I remember it, you rang the bell a couple of times yourself."

"Worked out even, then, didn't it?"

"How so?"

" 'Cause you rung the ding-dong clean out of mine."

His bantering tone delighted her. Normally reserved, he was a man of caustic wit but little natural humour.

Like everyone else in Denver, she knew he was a man-hunter—by some accounts, a mankiller—and a detective of formidable reputation. Danger intrigued her, and from the outset she'd been captivated by the fact that he looked the part as well. Corded and lean, with wide shoulders and a muscular build, he stood six feet tall. His eyes were pale blue, framed by a square jaw and light chestnut hair, and he gave the uncanny impression of seeing straight through another person. She thought his look not so much cold as simply devoid of emotion. The quiet, impersonal look of a man who would kill quickly, and without regret.

Today, however, his manner seemed light, almost chipper. She took that as a good sign, and wondered if he'd decided to unbend a little, let her have a glimpse of the man beneath the hard exterior. She felt no real conviction that it was true, and yet . . . a girl could always wish.

"Why not take the day off?" She stretched like a cat, and gave him a beguiling grin. "We could just loaf around, and who knows—maybe I'd show you some more surprises."

"Don't tempt me," Starbuck said genially. "The day's already half gone, and I've got some errands that won't wait."

"You know what they say, all work and no play."

"That's a laugh! You've kept me so busy, I haven't hardly had time to tend to business."

"Detective business?" she inquired innocently. "Or monkey business?"

Starbuck cocked one ribald eye at her. "I'll give you three guesses, and the first two don't count."

"Mr. Mysterious himself!" She mocked him with a minxlike look. "Got a hot case cooking, honeybun? C'mon, you can tell Lola."

"Strictly back burner," Starbuck said vaguely. "Nothing worth the telling."

She laughed spontaneously, in sheer delight. "You're one of a kind. Luke! I've just been told to butt out and damned if you didn't make me like it. That's real talent!"

"Ask me no questions and I'll tell you no lies."

Starbuck understood it was a game, lighthearted and meant in jest. Unlike many women he'd known, she wanted nothing of him. A good time and a few laughs—along with their romps in bed—were all she sought from the liaison. She possessed a kind of bursting vitality, and she seemed to have discovered the instant recipe for fun. Then, too, there were her physical attributes, which amounted to an altogether stunning package. She was smallish and compact, with coltish grace and a dazzling figure. Her features were mobile and animated, with a wide, sensual mouth, and her hair hung long and golden. She was impudent and puckish, with a sort of mischievous verve, and the tricks she brought to his bed never failed to amaze him. All in all, she was his kind of woman, sportive and undemanding, with no claims on tomorrow or the future. He thought it might last awhile.

"All right, lover," she said cheerfully. "Off to the races! Get your business done and we'll save our playtime for tonight."

"That sounds like a proposition."

"There's one way to find out."

"Then I reckon I'd better drop around to the theatre tonight."

"You miss my show and you'll never find out! How's that for a proposition?"

"Best offer I've had today."

She leaned forward and brushed his lips with a kiss. "See you there?"

"Count on it."

Starbuck rose and walked to the foyer. He took a wide-brimmed Stetson from the closet, jammed it on his head, and then shrugged into his overcoat. When he stepped into the hall, Lola poured herself another cup of coffee and lounged back on the sofa. A slow kittenish smile touched the corners of her mouth.

Outside the hotel Starbuck turned onto Larimer Street. It was a bitter cold day, with savage winds howling down from the northwest. A metallic sky rolled overhead and snow flurries peppered his face. As he passed the police station, he pulled up the collar of his coat and stuck his hands in his pockets. With the wind pushing him along, he rounded the corner and headed directly across town.

Several minutes later he crossed Blake Street. His destination was a small shop wedged between a pool hall and a hardware store. On the window was a neatly lettered sign, chipped and fading with age.

DANIEL CAMERON
GUNSMITH
PISTOLS—RIFLES—SHOTGUNS

An overhead bell jing-a-linged as Starbuck hurried through the door. The walls along both sides of the shop were lined with racks of long guns, and towards the rear a glass showcase was filled with pistols. Beyond the showcase, a grey-haired man turned from a workbench at the sound of the bell. Starbuck brushed snow off his coat and moved down the aisle.

"Afternoon, Daniel."

"Well, Luke!" Cameron warmly shook his hand. "I was beginning to think you'd forgotten our project."

"No," Starbuck said equably. "Too many irons in the fire, that's all."

"So I've heard." Cameron let a sly smile cross his face. "Apparently Lola Montana is a full-time . . . avocation."

Starbuck grinned. "If that means she keeps me busy, you're right. Course, I wouldn't exactly call it a chore."

"No need to explain." Cameron lifted his hands in an exaggerated gesture. "A man needs diversion! Enjoy it while you're young."

"I'm doing my damnedest," Starbuck said with heavy good humour. "How're things with you? Any luck?"

"Luke, I think I'm onto something. Not precisely what we're after, but close. Very close."

"Tell me about it."

"I'll do better than that. Come along and judge for yourself."

A master gunsmith, Cameron possessed an innovative mind and an unquenchable thirst to explore. Always receptive to a challenge, he had agreed to tackle a problem posed by Starbuck. The bullets commonly available were efficient killers but poor manstoppers. An outlaw, though mortally wounded in a gunfight, would often live long enough to empty his pistol. What Starbuck wanted was a bullet that would stop the other man instantly, neutralise him on the spot and take him out of the fight. For the past several weeks, engrossed in the project, Cameron had experimented with radical new bullet designs. Today, he proudly demonstrated the end result.

In the back room of the shop, Cameron lined up three Colt .45 shells on a table. The first was a factory loading, with the standard round pug-nosed bullet. The next shell, loaded with Cameron's new design, had a slug with shoulders which gradually tapered to a flat nose. The last shell was unlike anything Starbuck had ever seen. In effect, Cameron had turned his new slug upside down and loaded it backwards. The nose of the slug was now inside the casing, and the base, which was blunt and truncated, was now seated in the forward position. After a brief explanation, Cameron loaded the shells into a Colt sixgun.

Along the rear wall were arranged three bales of wet newspaper that had been tightly bound with rope. The distance was less than five yards, and each of the bales was marked with a bold X in the centre. Cameron aimed and fired, shifting from one bale to another, splitting the X with each shot. Then he walked forward, followed by Starbuck, and cut the bales open with a jackknife. The experiment spoke for itself.

The standard pug-nosed bullet had penetrated three-quarters of the way through the first bale. The bullet was virtually unmarred and still retained its original shape. The flat-nose slug, which was slightly deformed, had penetrated more than halfway through the second bale. Within the third bale, the reverse-loaded slug had penctrated scarcely one-third of the way through the wet newspaper. Yet the truncated base, upon impact with the bale, had been deformed beyond recognition. The entire slug had expanded, squashed front to rear, and emerged a mushroom-shaped hunk of lead.

"Quite an improvement," Cameron said, holding the slug between his fingertips. "The factory load expended all its energy drilling through the bale. Even my new design did much the same thing. But the reverse load! As you can see, the mushroom effect caused the bullet to impart its energy quickly and with massive shock."

Starbuck was impressed. "Would it work the same way on a man?"

"Much better," Cameron assured him. "The shock effect on human tissue would be far greater than it is on wet newsprint."

"Would it stop him cold?" Starbuck persisted. "Dead in his tracks?"

"Good question." Cameron's expression was abstracted. "I suppose we won't know that until you shoot someone, will we?"

"What about accuracy?"

"Now there we have a slight hitch. At long range, it's not as accurate as a factory load. On the other hand, most of your work is fairly close up. What would you estimate . . . five yards, ten at the outside?"

"I reckon it'd average that or less."

"Then you have no problem." Cameron tossed him the slug. "Go try it on someone, Luke! I'm willing to bet it's a manstopper."

Starbuck left the shop with a box of the new shells in his overcoat pocket. His faith in Daniel Cameron, however, rode in the crossdraw holster on his belt. The Colt was now loaded with blunt-nosed slugs.

Starbuck's next stop was his office. Located around the corner from the Windsor Hotel, the office was a second-floor cubbyhole, with no sign on the door and spartan as a monk's cell. Essentially it was a clearinghouse, with a secretary to handle correspondence and light bookkeeping chores. All else, especially matters of a confidential nature, Starbuck committed to memory.

His secretary, Verna Phelps, greeted him with prune-faced civility. Her desk and chair, along with a battered file cabinet, were the only furnishings in the room. Her cool manner stemmed from the fact that she hadn't seen Starbuck in almost two weeks. Though Denver was a cosmopolitan city—with a population approaching 100,000—one of the holdovers from its frontier days was an active and highly efficient gossip mill. Almost from the start, she had known the unsavory details of Starbuck's latest dalliance. And in her most charitable moments she considered Lola Montana nothing short of a wanton hussy.

With no great urgency, Starbuck sifted through a stack of mail now several days old. One by one he dropped letters from various railroads, stagecoach lines, and mining companies on the desk. A man of means— with investments in commercial real estate and a portfolio of major stocks—he had no compelling financial need to work. Then, too, his reputation allowed him to accept only those assignments that piqued his interest.

Several of his previous cases were celebrated for the notoriety of the outlaws involved. He had been instrumental in ridding New Mexico of Billy the Kid and largely through his efforts Wyatt Earp had been run out of Arizona. Apart from his eminence as a detective, he was also noted as a mankiller. By rough calculation— since he never discussed the topic—journalists estimated he had killed at least eighteen men. As a result, his fame had spread across the West, and he could now pick and choose from among the jobs offered. Yet fame, with the attendant publicity and newspaper photos, had destroyed the anonymity he'd once enjoyed. These days, he operated undercover, and always in disguise.

One letter caught his interest. Postmarked St. Louis, it was signed by the president of the International Bankers Association. Short and somewhat cryptic in tone, it requested his presence in St. Louis at the earliest possible date. He studied the letter a moment, then stuck it into his pocket. Looking up, he indicated the stack of mail he'd dropped on the desk.

"Write those outfits and tell them I'm unavailable till further notice."

A spinster, Verna Phelps had plain dumpling features and her hair was pulled severely away from her face into a tight chignon. She heartily applauded Starbuck's work as a detective, and took a certain grim satisfaction in the number of outlaws he'd killed. Yet she disapproved of his personal life, and viewed his conduct with women as reprehensible. Now, with a dour nod, she shuffled the letters into a neat pile.

"Are you accepting the St. Louis offer?"

"Maybe," Starbuck said noncommittally. "All depends on what they've got in mind."

"How long will you be gone?"

Starbuck shrugged. "Look for me when you see me."

"Very well." Her voice was tinged with reproach. "And the hotel suite? Shall I look after it as usual, or will your lady friend be staying on while you're gone?"

"Never give up, do you, Verna?" Starbuck smiled, and shook his head. "Follow the usual routine. Have the suite spruced up and tell the desk to send any messages over to you."

"Just as you wish, Mr. Starbuck."

"Hold down the fort." Starbuck waved, turning towards the door. "I'll be in touch."

Verna Phelps gave a rabbity sniff and watched him out the door. She marvelled at his devilish ways and his taste for cheap, tawdry women. Then, blushing beet red, she was jolted by a sudden thought.

She wondered how it might have been . . . if she were younger.

Starbuck arrived at the Alcazar Variety Theater late that evening. The owner greeted him warmly, and escorted him to his usual table down front. A complimentary bottle of champagne materialised, and he settled back to enjoy the show.

Several men, seated at nearby tables, exchanged friendly nods. But no one attempted to approach Starbuck, or engage him in conversation. A private man, he tolerated few questions. Nor would he indulge drunks or the idly curious. He was known on sight, and what he did for a living was no secret. Still, though he was widely admired, he never spoke of his business to anyone. That too was known, and while some people considered it eccentric, his wishes were respected. The sporting crowd of Denver had long ago learned to take him on his own terms. Or not at all. Which suited him all the way around. He was alone even in the largest crowd.

Tonight, a solitary figure lost in his own thoughts, his mind centred wholly on the moment. Tomorrow he would entrain for St. Louis, and whatever happened would happen, all in good time. Before tomorrow, there was one last night with Lola, and not an hour to be wasted. His anticipation was heightened all the more as the curtain rose and the orchestra struck up a catchy tune. Lola went prancing across the stage, her legs flashing and her breasts jiggling over the top of a peekaboo gown. The audience roared and she gave them a dazzling smile. Then her husky alto voice belted out across the hall.

> *"Oh, don't you remember sweet Betsy from Pike,*
> *Crossed the great mountains with her lover Ike,*
> *With two yoke of oxen, a large yellow dog,*
> *A tall shanghai rooster and one spotted hog!"*

CHAPTER 3

St. Louis itself was worth the trip.

Starbuck arrived on a blustery January evening. From Union Station, he took a hansom cab to one of the fashionable hotels on Olive Street. There he registered under an assumed name and gave San Antonio as his hometown. To all appearances, he was a well-to-do Texan visiting the big city on business.

A precautionary measure, the deception had by now become second nature. Only a couple of months past, the *Police Gazette* had done an article that labelled Starbuck the foremost mankiller of the day. He had no idea whether his notoriety extended as far eastward as Missouri. Yet he was a man who played the odds, and assumed nothing. Outside Denver, he always travelled under an alias.

After supper in the hotel dining room, he went for a stroll. St. Louis, with a population exceeding the half-million mark, was the largest city he'd ever visited. The downtown district was a hub of culture and commerce. Theatres and swank hotels, office buildings and banks and business establishments occupied several square blocks between Market Street and Delmar Boulevard. A sprawling industrial section, which had gravitated early to the riverfront, lay stretched along the levee. Steamboats were rapidly losing ground to railroads, and the city had developed into a manufacturing centre for clothing, shoes, and various kinds of machinery. Still, for all its advancement, St. Louis remained a major market for hides and wool, horses and mules, and a wide assortment of farm produce. However cosmopolitan, it had not yet fully made the transition from its frontier origins.

On the waterfront, Starbuck stood for a long while staring out across the Mississippi. The Eads Bridge, completed only eight years before, spanned the great river like a steel monolith. Far in the distance, he saw the lights of towns ranged along the Illinois shoreline. Not easily impressed, he was nonetheless taken with the sight. He had travelled the West from the Gulf of Mexico to the Pacific Coast, but he'd never had occasion to look upon the Mississippi. The breadth of the river, with girded steel linking one bank to the other, seemed to him a marvel almost beyond comprehension. He thought back to his days on the Rio Grande, and slowly shook his head. Age and experience, he told himself, altered a man's perception of things.

A nomadic westerner, Starbuck had grown to manhood in Texas. The Civil War, which had left him without family or roots, taught him that killing was a matter of expediency. Thereafter, he accepted abuse from no man, and quickly accommodated those who overstepped themselves. For a time he drifted from ranch to ranch, a saddletramp beckoned onward by wanderlust. Then, all within a period of a few years, he went from trailhand to ranch foreman to range detective. Quite by coincidence, one job leading to another, he discovered his niche in life.

Once his reputation as a manhunter spread, Starbuck

branched out from chasing horse thieves and common
rustlers. Offers from stagelines and railroads afforded
greater challenge, and there he came into his own as a
detective. Despite his renown, however, he was never
really satisfied with yesterday's accomplishments. He
enjoyed what he did for a livelihood, and he took pride
in his work. Yet something of the old wanderlust still
remained. He forever sought greater challenges, and he
was cursed with an itch to move on to the next case. A
blooded hunter, his quarry was man. And only when the
chase was joined was he truly content.

Now, his gaze fixed on the Mississippi, he wondered
what tomorrow would bring. His wire had confirmed the
time and place for the meeting. Otis Tilford, president
of the International Bankers Association, was expecting
him first thing in the morning. An assessment would be
made, and assuming he passed muster, an assignment
would be offered. The only imponderable was whether
or not he would accept. He was looking for tomorrows,
not yesterdays, and nothing else would turn the trick.
Nothing and no-damn-body.

He turned from the wharves and walked towards his
hotel.

The Merchants & Farmers Bank Building stood on the
corner of Fourth and Delmar. Starbuck entered the lobby
shortly before nine o'clock and took an elevator to the
third floor. At the end of the hall, he spotted a door with
frosted glass and gilt lettering. He moved directly along
the corridor, observant and suddenly alert. The lettering
on the door was sparkling fresh.

Inside the waiting room he closed the door and doffed
his hat. A mousy-looking woman, with grey hair and
granny glasses, sat behind a reception desk. She looked
him over, stern as a drill sergeant, and nodded.

"May I help you?"

"I'm Luke Starbuck. I have an appointment with Mr. Tilford."

"Yes, of course." She rose, bustling around the desk. "Please have a seat, Mr. Starbuck. I'll inform Mr. Tilford you're here."

Starbuck watched as she hurried down a hallway. Then, still standing, he slowly inspected the waiting room. All the furniture, including the receptionist's desk and a couple of wingbacked chairs, looked as though it had been delivered only that morning. A door on the opposite side of the room was open, and through it he saw several clerks in what appeared to be a general office. Their desks and a row of file cabinets along the far wall also looked fresh off a showroom floor. Whatever he'd expected, something about the layout put him on guard. He made mental note to do lots of listening, play it close to the vest. And volunteer nothing.

The receptionist reappeared, motioning him forward. "Will you come this way? Mr. Tilford can see you now."

"Much obliged," Starbuck said pleasantly. "I was just admiring your offices. Got a real handsome setup."

"Thank you."

"Been here long?"

"I beg your pardon?"

"Well, everything looks so new and all. I thought maybe you'd just opened for business?"

"No." She did not elaborate. "This way, Mr. Starbuck."

Starbuck followed her down the hall. She ushered him into a spacious office and stepped aside. The room was panelled in dark wood, with ornately carved furniture and a plush carpet underfoot. A coal-burning fireplace glowed cherry red, and directly opposite was an imposing walnut desk. Behind it, seated in a tall judge's chair, was a man who looked like a frog perched on a toad-stool. He was completely bald, with a wattled neck and beady eyes, and his oval face was peppered with liver spots. When he rose, extending his hand, his posture was shrunken and stooped. Yet, oddly enough, his voice was firm and lordly.

"Welcome to St. Louis, Mr. Starbuck."

"Pleasure's all mine, Mr. Tilford."

"Please be seated." Tilford let go his hand, and dropped into the judge's chair. "I trust your trip was without incident."

"More or less." Starbuck took an armchair before the desk. "One train ride's pretty much like another."

"No doubt." Tilford appeared to lose interest in the subject. "I appreciate your quick response to our request."

"When a man says 'urgent,' I take him at his word."

"Commendable," Tilford said, no irony in his tone. "All the more so since your services are much in demand these days."

"Don't believe everything you read in the *Police Gazette*."

Tilford's laugh was as false as an old maid's giggle. "On the contrary, Mr. Starbuck! I found the article most informative. Few men have your zeal."

"Oh?" Starbuck asked casually. "How so?"

"Once you accept a case, you display a remarkable tendency to see it through to a conclusion. Would you consider that a fair statement?"

"I generally finish what I start."

"Precisely." Tilford gave him an evaluating glance. "And more often than not you finish it permanently. Correct?"

Starbuck regarded him thoughtfully, "Why do I get

the feeling you know the answer before you ask the question?"

"I too am a man of zeal," Tilford replied loftily. "I had you checked out thoroughly before sending that wire."

"Sounds reasonable." Starbuck smiled humourlessly. "Hope you got your money's worth."

"The queries were of a personal nature. A man in my position develops certain alliances, and we often exchange information. All on a confidential basis, of course."

"Anyone I know?"

"What's in a name?" Tilford spread his hands in a bland gesture. "Suffice it to say you come highly recommended by the Central Pacific and Wells Fargo."

"I reckon they had no room for complaint."

"Indeed!" Tilford wagged his head. "You are too modest by far, Mr. Starbuck. I am reliably informed that you have no equal when it comes to meting out justice to outlaws."

"There's all kinds of justice."

"True." Tilford pursed his lips and nodded solemnly. "But only one kind of any lasting value. Wouldn't you agree, Mr. Starbuck?"

Starbuck took out the makings and rolled himself a smoke. He struck a match, all the while watching Tilford, and lit the cigarette. Then, inhaling deeply, he settled back in his chair.

"Suppose we get down to cases?"

"By all means." Tilford leaned forward, stared earnestly at him. "I presume you are familiar with the James-Younger gang?"

Starbuck looked at him without expression. "Jesse James?"

Tilford made a small nod of acknowledgement. "Over

the last seventeen years James and his gang have robbed dozens of banks and trains—"

"So I've heard."

"—and killed at least a score of innocent people."

"I wouldn't argue the figure."

"And yet," Tilford said in an aggrieved tone, "they are free to come and go as they please throughout Missouri."

"I understood," Starbuck observed neutrally, "that the Pinkertons had been brought in on the case."

"Quite true." Tilford's eyelids drooped scornfully. "Some eight years ago the Pinkerton Agency was retained for the express purpose of putting a halt to these depredations."

"That long?" Starbuck blew a plume of smoke into the air. "Guess they've had a run of bad luck."

"You're too charitable," Tilford said, not without bitterness. "To put it bluntly, Allan Pinkerton has accomplished nothing—absolutely nothing!—and he has been paid very handsomely for doing it."

"Nobody's perfect," Starbuck commented dryly. "Maybe it's time for the worm to turn."

"I seriously doubt it." Tilford shook his head in exasperation. "A coalition of banks and railroads still has Pinkerton under retainer. In my view, however, it's a waste of money. Given another eight years, he would be no closer than he is today."

"Sounds like you hold the Pinkertons in pretty low opinion."

"Unless I'm mistaken"—Tilford watched him carefully—"that is an opinion we share, Mr. Starbuck."

Starbuck flipped a hand back and forth. "Let's just say I think they're a little bit overrated."

"How would you like an opportunity to prove your point?"

"Try me and see."

"Very well." Tilford's voice dropped. "We wish to retain your services, Mr. Starbuck. Within reasonable limits, you can name your own price."

"Exactly what services did you have in mind?"

Tilford's face took on a sudden hard cast. "We want Jesse James killed."

Starbuck's gaze was direct now, his ice-blue eyes alert. "Who is 'we?' "

"Why, the International Bankers Association. I thought you understood—"

"Try another tune." Starbuck fixed him with that same disquieting stare. "The lettering on your door looks like the paint's hardly had time to dry. Every stick of furniture in your office is brand new, and unless I miss my guess, so's your association." He paused, his eyes cold and questioning. "I'll ask you again, and this time I want some straight talk. Who is 'we?' "

A shadow of irritation crossed Tilford's features. "You are a very discerning man, Mr. Starbuck. I commend you on your powers of observation. However, I am not in the habit of being interrogated. Nor do I appreciate your rather cavalier manner."

"That's your problem," Starbuck said woodenly. "Either I get an explanation or we don't do business. Take your pick."

Tilford reflected a moment. "Very well," he answered at length. "A number of bankers around the Midwest deplore Pinkerton's lack of results. We have severed our ties with the railroad and banking coalition, and formed our own organisation. Our purpose is legitimate and quite straightforward. We intend to eradicate Jesse James and those of a similar persuasion."

"How do you fit into the picture?"

"I am president and chief stockholder of the Merchants & Farmers Bank. In short, I own the bank down-stairs and the building in which we are seated."

Starbuck played a hunch. "From what I've heard, James normally concentrates on small-town banks. So that lets you out, unless you've got some personal score to settle. Suppose you tell me about it?"

"Are you a mind reader as well as a detective, Mr. Starbuck?"

"Tricks of the trade," Starbuck said flatly. "I'm waiting for an answer."

Tilford regarded him somberly. "Last July the evening train out of Kansas City was robbed. The conductor and a passenger by the name of McMillan were murdered in cold blood. Jesse James, and his brother Frank, were positively identified as the killers. Frank McMillan was my son-in-law."

"Tough break." Starbuck stubbed out his cigarette in an ashtray. "Any special reason you took it so personal?"

"I sent Frank to Kansas City on business. He was an officer of this bank, the husband of my only daughter, and the father of my grandchildren. As should be obvious, I feel responsible for his death."

"In other words," Starbuck ventured, "you want an eye for an eye. You formed the association—and gave it a high-sounding name—in order to put a legitimate front on personal vengeance."

"Not altogether," Tilford countered. "By ridding society of Jesse James, I am also performing a public service. I see those as compatible goals—a worthy endeavour!"

"Why kill him?" Starbuck inquired. "Why not bring him to trial and let him hang? That way the state executes him . . . instead of you."

"He must be killed!" Tilford's voice was heated and vindictive. "No jury in this state would convict Jesse

James. Nor would any court dare impose the death penalty."

"What makes you so sure?"

Tilford rose and moved to the wall directly behind him. With some effort, he lifted a large leather satchel off the floor and dropped it on his desk. Then, his expression grim, he resumed his chair.

"Inside that satchel you will find the Pinkerton file—eight years of investigation and surveillance—on the James-Younger gang. I obtained a duplicate of the file in the hope it would speed your own investigation. Aside from that, it will also convince you that Jesse James can never be convicted in the state of Missouri."

"Out of curiosity"—Starbuck gave him a quizzical look—"how did you come by it?"

"A friend," Tilford explained. "One who owns a railroad and contributes large sums to the settlement of Allan Pinkerton's fee."

Starbuck studied the satchel, thoughtful. For most of his professional career he had lived in the shadow of the world's most famous detective agency. The idea of going head to head with the Pinkertons—and beating them—was a challenge he found too tempting to resist. At last, with an overdrawn gesture, he looked up at Tilford.

"I don't work cheap."

"Ten thousand now," Tilford said gravely, "and ten thousand more when the job is completed. With one added proviso."

"Which is?"

"You are to kill Frank James as well."

"Want your pound of flesh, don't you?"

"I want them dead, Mr. Starbuck! Dead and buried—and forgotten."

"Hell, why not?" Starbuck shrugged. "I reckon one deserves it as much as the other."

"Then we have an agreement?"

"You ante up and we're in business. Two for the price of one, delivery guaranteed."

"Where will you start?"

Starbuck smiled cryptically. "Where Pinkerton should have started."

"Oh?" Tilford appeared bemused. "Where might that be?"

"Let's just say it won't be out in the open."

CHAPTER 4

The Pinkerton file was compelling stuff. Starbuck found himself fascinated almost from the first field report, which was dated January 23, 1874. He also found confirmation of what he'd suspected all along.

Jesse James was no garden-variety outlaw.

For three days and nights, Starbuck holed up in his hotel room. The file, he determined early on, could not be let out of his sight. One look by a snooper would jeopardise the need for secrecy, and pose the even greater threat of a leak to the press. Accordingly, he refused to allow the maids inside, and he himself never set foot outside. All his meals were ordered from room service, and on the first night he sent a bellman to fetch a quart of whiskey. Like a monk sequestered in a cell, he was alone with himself. And the file.

His first chore was to devise some system of organisation. The file was voluminous, and from the outset it was apparent that Allan Pinkerton had a fondness for long, rambling memos. The agency's founder exhorted everyone in his employ—from division chiefs to field operatives—with page after page of detailed instructions regarding the investigation. The flow of paperwork was compounded by the sheer number of personnel involved in the case. Apart from Pinkerton's two sons, who were responsible for field operations, there were a dozen or more investigators active at all times. The avalanche of reports and memos, generated from different parts of the country, was stupefying to contemplate. A method was needed to separate the chaff from the wheat.

Starbuck broke the material down into categories. Allan Pinkerton's directives, which contained little of value, were consigned to an ever-growing pile. Speculative reports were next in line, and armchair analyses by division chiefs formed still another stack. On-the-scene reports, written by field operatives, were divided into those dealing with conjecture and those that dealt in hard intelligence. The latter category, scarcely to Starbuck's surprise, made up the smallest pile. Nevertheless, taken as a whole, the file provided an absorbing overview. Chronicled there was the violent history of the James-Younger gang.

Like many men brutalised by the Civil War, Jesse and Frank James found it difficult to adjust to peacetime. During the hostilities they had ridden with Quantrill's guerrillas, and those savage years had instilled in them a taste for action. Bored and restless, they avoided the family farm and made no effort to earn an honest livelihood. Quickly enough, they developed a reputation as the chief troublemakers of Clay County.

To make matters worse, the Federal occupation forces sought retribution against their defeated enemies. Yet the James brothers were in no greater danger of reprisals than the balance of Quantrill's ex-guerrillas. The vast majority of former Confederates settled down and went to work, determined to put the war behind them. Other men, however, felt society had turned on them, and that a life of robbery and murder was justified. Such was the backdrop against which Jesse and Frank James took the outlaw trail.

At the time, Jesse James was eighteen years of age. Still, for all his youth, he was a blooded veteran and an experienced leader of men. Headstrong, with magnetic force of character, he dominated Frank, who was three years his senior. The Younger brothers, who were boyhood friends and former comrades under Quantrill, were recruited into the gang. Cole Younger, the eldest of the four brothers, was the same age as Frank James. Yet, like Frank, he submitted to the will of a fiery young hothead. By late winter of 1865, the gang was formed, all of them ex-guerrillas and stone-cold killers. Their leader was Jesse James.

Only ten months after the Civil War ended, the long string of depredations committed by the James-Younger gang began. On the morning of February 3, 1866, they rode into Liberty, Missouri, and robbed the Clay County Savings Association of $70,000. It was the first daylight bank robbery in American history, and created a furor in the nation's press. It also served as the template by which the gang would operate over the years ahead. In the course of the holdup, the bank teller and an innocent bystander were callously murdered. The only shots fired were those fired by the gang, and they escaped unharmed. The scene would be repeated time and time again.

For the next eight years the gang roamed the Midwest, robbing trains and looting banks. Their raids were conducted with military precision, and ranged over an area encompassing Missouri, Kansas, Arkansas, Kentucky, and Iowa. The dead littering their backtrail grew in number with each holdup, yet pursuit was rare. Even though the law knew their names, no concerted effort was made to track them to their homeground in Missouri. Like will-o'-the-wisps they appeared from no-where—hitting fast and hard—then vanished without a trace. And the bloodletting went on unabated.

Early in 1874 the Pinkerton agency entered the case. Their failure was monumental, and resulted in an im-mediate loss of prestige. One of their agents, operating undercover, was captured in Clay County. With his hands tied behind his back, he was executed personally by Jesse James. As an added humiliation—and a warn-ing to all lawmen—his body was left to be savaged by wild hogs. The incident kindled in Allan Pinkerton an unyielding hatred for the outlaws. His memos thereafter took on the fervour and tone of a holy war.

A few months later Pinkerton suffered yet another loss of face. On a brisk March day, two operatives, ac-companied by a deputy sheriff, were surprised by Jim and John Younger. The encounter occurred on a back-country road, and in the ensuing shootout both Youngers were wounded. One of the detectives and the deputy sheriff were killed on the spot. The second Pinkerton escaped during the confusion, and thus lived to tell the tale. While John Younger ultimately died of his wounds, the message quickly made the rounds among peace of-ficers. Any outsider who ventured into Clay County—whether Pinkerton or lawman—would be made to pay the price. And then left to the wild hogs.

In the end a combination of partisan politics and the terror inspired by the gang defeated the Pinkertons. If a group of former Quantrill raiders held up a bank or robbed a train, the common wisdom was that no great harm had been done. Bankers and railroad barons, who were considered thieves themselves, could easily afford the loss.

Friends and relatives, moreover, were always willing to hide the outlaws. Of no less significance, they also provided the gang with an efficient and highly reliable intelligence network. No stranger entered the backwoods of Clay County without arousing comment, and word swiftly found its way to those who supported the robbers. Those who were unsympathetic simply tended their own business and made every effort to remain neutral. Forced to choose, few would have taken sides with Yankee detectives in any event. A veil of silence hung like a wintry cloud over all of Clay County.

After losing two operatives, Allan Pinkerton waited almost a year before he again challenged the James boys on homeground. On the night of January 25, 1875, a squad of Pinkerton agents surrounded the home at the family farm. Jesse and Frank, with several members of the gang, had ridden away only hours before. Inside the house were Jesse's mother, his stepfather, Dr. Reuben Samuel, and his young half brother, Archie Samuel. A servant, awakened when the operatives pried open a window shutter, sounded the alarm.

The Pinkertons, determined to capture or kill the James boys, immediately tossed a large iron bomb through the window. While the family stumbled about in the dark, the bomb exploded. A piece of shrapnel struck Jesse's mother and tore off her right arm below the elbow. Across the room, young Archie was hit in the chest by another jagged shard and died instantly. Only the quick thinking of Dr. Samuel, who hastily applied a tourniquet to his wife's arm, saved her from bleeding to death.

With the house ablaze, and no sign of the James boys, the detectives panicked and fled. Later the Pinkerton agency denied that the object hurled through the window was a bomb. By then, however, the damage was done. Censure from the community and several prominent politicians forced Allan Pinkerton to withdraw his operatives from Clay County. Thereafter the Pinkertons were vilified as assassins and child killers. And the legend of Jesse James took on a whole new dimension.

Oddly enough, that aspect of the case stirred Starbuck's admiration. The Pinkerton file documented beyond question that Jesse James was a social misfit with a deep-rooted persecution complex. Nor was there any doubt that he was a mad-dog killer—lacking mercy or remorse—who dispatched his victims with cold ferocity. Yet he was also a master of propaganda. With cunning and calculation, he had captured the public's imagination and transformed himself into a heroic figure. In a very real sense, he was his own best press agent, and one with a certain flair for words. However grudgingly, Starbuck had to admit he'd done a slam-bang job of whitewashing himself and his murderous deeds.

Throughout the years, James had written articulate and persuasive letters to the editors of influential midwestern newspapers. The letters were duly reprinted, and accounted, in large measure, for the myth that "he robbed the rich and gave to the poor." Comparisons were drawn between Jesse James and Robin Hood, the legendary outlaw of Sherwood Forest. Not entirely in jest, newspaper editorials made reference to "Jesse and his merry band of robbers."

Apocryphal tales were widely circulated with regard to his charitable nature and his compassion for the poor. One story, typical of many, credited Jesse with donating a bag of gold to help establish a school for Negro children in Missouri. The gold, naturally, was reported to have been liberated from the coffers of a money-grabbing banker. In time, with such tales multiplying, Jesse became known as a champion of the oppressed and downtrodden. To backwoods Missourians and gullible Easterners alike he came to represent a larger-than-life figure. A Robin Hood reborn—who wore a sixgun and puckishly thumbed his nose at the law.

In Starbuck's view, the fault could be traced directly to the Pinkertons. Had they done their job, Jesse James would have been tried and hanged, and long forgotten. Instead they had botched the assignment from beginning to end. By hounding James for eight years they had turned themselves into the villains of the piece and transformed him into the underdog. Their abortive raid on the family farm had merely capped an already miserable performance. A child's death, and the horror of an innocent woman losing her arm, had been perceived by the public as unconscionable. That one act had stamped the Pinkertons as skulking cowards, somehow more outside the law than the man they hunted. And Jesse James, mindful of public reaction, had quickly seized on the opportunity. Without the Pinkertons, he would have been just another outlaw, foxier than most but nothing to rate front-page headlines. With the Pinkertons, he had become a mythical creature and a national sensation. A legend.

On the evening of the third day Starbuck finally put the file aside. His eyes were bloodshot from reading and his head felt like an oversoaked sponge. He poured himself a stiff shot of whiskey and slugged it back in a single motion. Then he stretched out on the bed, hands locked behind his head, and stared at the ceiling. Slowly, with infinite care, he examined what he'd gleaned from the file.

Several things were apparent now. Foremost among them was the fact that Otis Tilford had given him the straight goods. Nowhere in Missouri could Jesse James be tried in a court of law and found guilty. Even in the event he were captured, there was little likelihood of securing an indictment. The time for that was long past, and would never again return. Underdogs who became living legends were immune to the laws that governed lesser men. So the alternative was obvious, and precisely as Tilford had stated. Jesse James had to be killed.

Insofar as the job itself was concerned, Starbuck realised he faced a formidable task. All the obstacles that had defeated the Pinkertons would likewise hinder his own investigation. The people of Clay County were clannish, openly suspicious of any stranger, and would doubtless prove none too talkative. To compound the problem, they were rightfully fearful of the James-Younger gang, and aware of the consequences to anyone who spoke out of school. The reasonable conclusion, then, was that he would make little headway in Clay County itself. Without solid information—a lead of some sort—it would be a waste of time and effort. Not to mention the great probability he'd wind up bush-whacked on a back-country road some dark night.

Still, based on what he'd read in the file, there was a definite pattern to the gang's activities. After pulling a job every six months or so, they always vanished without a trace. Generally a month or longer would pass before they were again reported in Clay County. Which meant they went to ground and laid low following a holdup. The Pinkertons, even with their bureaucratic mentality, had tumbled to the pattern.

Yet, at the same time, the Pinkertons had overlooked what seemed a salient point. A passing comment in one of the reports noted that Cole Younger had sired a daughter by Belle Starr. Almost as an afterthought, the report indicated that Belle Starr was now living in Indian Territory. No other connection had been made regarding the gang, particularly with respect to Jesse James. Nor had it occurred to the Pinkertons to check it out further. Either Indian Territory wasn't their cup of tea, or else they considered the item a worthless bit of trivia. Whichever, it seemed to Starbuck an oversight.

There was a link, however tenuous, between Cole Younger and his former lady love. Coupled with the fact that the gang vanished after every job, it made for interesting speculation. Moreover, from the standpoint of a robber, it was a link that made eminent good sense. A hideout in Indian Territory would be damn hard to beat. Not only was it a sanctuary for outlaws, but the nearest law was the U.S. marshal's office at Fort Smith. No better place existed for a man to lose himself until the dust settled. And taken to its logical conclusion, the thought was equally true for an entire gang. Perhaps more so.

Starbuck had no idea whether Cole Younger and Belle Starr were still on speaking terms. That Jesse James and the gang used her place as a hideout was an even greater question mark. Yet the link existed, and thus far it was his only lead. A place to start.

CHAPTER 5

Starbuck stepped off the train at a whistle-stop in Indian Territory. A way station for travellers and freight, the depot was located on the west bank of the Arkansas River. On the opposite shore stood Fort Smith.

Hefting his warbag, Starbuck walked towards the ferry landing. No stranger to Indian Territory, he was reminded of an assignment that now seemed a lifetime ago. Some seven years past, on his first job as a range detective, he had trailed a band of horse thieves through the Nations. The homeland of the five Civilised Tribes—Cherokee, Chickasaw, Choctaw, Creek, and Seminole—it was so named because they had chosen to follow the white man's path. Bounded by Texas, Kansas and Arkansas, the Nations were still a long way from civilised.

No less ironic, in Starbuck's view, was the name of the railroad line. The Little Rock & Fort Smith Railroad extended to the depot on the western shoreline, and the river roughly paralleled the boundary separating Arkansas and Indian Territory. But there was no bridge spanning the river, and thus the railroad stopped short of its namesake. Ferryboats were the sole means of conveying freight and passengers from the depot to Fort Smith. As a practical matter, the railroad terminus was on Indian land, and separated from the white man's world by far more than a river. From the depot westward there was a sense of having taken a step backward in time.

Now, standing on the foredeck of the ferry, Starbuck stared across the river at Fort Smith. Originally an army post, the town was situated on a sandstone bluff overlooking the juncture of the Arkansas and Poteau rivers. With time, it had become a centre of commerce and trade, serving much of Western Arkansas and a good part of Indian Territory. Warehouses crowded the waterfront, and in the distance the town itself looked to be a prosperous frontier community. The largest settlement bordering the Nations, it boasted four newspapers, one bank, and thirty saloons which enjoyed a captive trade from transients bound for the great Southwest. By federal law, the sale of firewater was banned throughout Indian Territory.

When the ferry docked, Starbuck inquired directions to the U.S. marshal's office. From the wharf, he followed Garrison Avenue, the main street that ran through the centre of town. On the far side of the business district, he approached the garrison of the old army post. Abandoned some years before by the military, the compound was now headquarters for the Federal District Court of Western Arkansas. And the indisputable domain of Judge Isaac Charles Parker—the Hanging Judge.

Starbuck, like most Westerners, thought Judge Parker had been slandered by the Eastern press. His jurisdiction covered Western Arkansas and all of Indian Territory, a wilderness area which encompassed some 74,000 square miles. To enforce his orders, he was assigned two hundred U.S. deputy marshals, and the almost impossible task of policing a land virtually devoid of law. Four months after taking office, he had sentenced six convicted murderers to be hanged simultaneously.

The thud of the gallows trap that day called the attention of all America to Judge Parker. Newspapermen poured into Fort Smith, and a crowd of more than 5,000 gathered to witness the executions. The press immediately tagged him the Hanging Judge, and decried the brutality of his methods. In the furor, the purpose of his object lesson was completely lost. Yet the reason he'd hung six men that day—and went on to hang eighteen more in the next six years—lay just across the river.

Gangs, of white outlaws made forays into Kansas, Missouri and Texas, and then retreated into Indian Territory. There they found perhaps the oddest sanctuary in the history of crime. Though each tribe had its own sovereign government, with courts and Light Horse Police, their authority extended only to Indian citizens. White men were untouchable, exempt from all prosecution except that of a federal court. Yet there were no extradition laws governing the Nations; federal marshals had to pursue and capture the wanted men; and in time the country became infested with hundreds of fugitives from justice. Curiously enough, the problem was compounded by the Indians themselves.

The red man had little use for the white man's laws, and the marshals were looked upon as intruders in the Nations. All too often the Indians connived with the outlaws, offering them asylum; and the chore of ferreting out entire gangs became a murderous task. It was no job for the faint of heart, as evidenced by the toll in lawmen. Over the past six years nearly thirty federal marshals had been gunned down in Indian Territory.

The old military garrison was a grim setting for the grim work carried out by Judge Parker and his staff. A bleak two-storey building housed the courtroom and offices for the federal prosecutors. As many as ten cases a day were tried, and few men were acquitted. The majority were given stiff sentences—all the law would allow—and quickly transported to federal prisons. Convicted murderers were allowed one last visit with immediate family. Then they were hung.

Another stone building, formerly the post commissary, was situated across the old parade ground. A low one-storey affair, it was headquarters for the U.S. marshal and his complement of deputies. In the centre of the compound, within clear view of both buildings, stood the gallows. Constructed of heavy timbers, it had four trapdoors, each three feet wide and twenty feet long. If occasion demanded, there was adequate space for twelve men to stand side by side and plunge to oblivion on the instant. The structure was roofed and walled, so that executions could be performed even in bad weather. Judge Parker, among other things, believed that justice should be swift—and timely.

Crossing the compound, Starbuck observed activity near the gallows. A crowd, growing larger by the minute, was gathering outside a roped-off area which formed a horseshoe around three sides of the structure. The onlookers were composed of townspeople and farmers, their wives and children, and a collection of travellers distinguishable by their dress. A holiday atmosphere seemed to prevail, and an excited murmur swept over them as a bearded man slowly mounted the stairs. Hushed, the spectators watched as he walked to the centre trap and began testing the knotted hemp nooses. All business, he went about his work with an air of professional detachment.

Starbuck figured it was his lucky day. From the looks of things, he would get to see the Western District Court in action. With one last glance, he went up the steps to the old commissary building. Inside, directly off the hallway, he entered what appeared to be the main office. A man was seated at a battered rolltop desk, hunched forward over a litter of paperwork. He looked up without expression, and waited.

"Afternoon," Starbuck said amiably. "I'd like to see the U.S. marshal."

"You've found him," the man replied, rising from his chair. "I'm Jim Fagan."

Starbuck accepted his handshake. "Luke Starbuck."

Fagan was bearish in appearance, with square features and a shaggy mane of hair. Yet there was a rocklike simplicity in his manner, open and unassuming. He let go Starbuck's hand, cocked his head to one side.

"Starbuck." he repeated aloud. "Why, hell, yes! You're the detective fellow, aren't you? The one that got his picture in the *Police Gazette*."

"Wish to Christ I hadn't," Starbuck admitted unhappily. "In my line of work, it don't pay to have your face plastered all over the country."

"Take a load off your feet." Fagan gestured to a chair beside the desk. "Not often we get a look at a real-live detective."

Starbuck seated himself. "Don't believe everything you read. Lots of that stuff was hogwash, pure and simple."

"Now you're gonna spoil my day! Near as I recollect, that article said you had a hand in puttin' the skids to Wyatt Earp and Billy the Kid. You mean to tell me it's not so?"

"No," Starbuck conceded. "I'm just saying reporters invent about half of what they write. Never known one yet that stuck to the straight facts."

"Guess you got a point." Fagan leaned back in his chair, suddenly earnest. "Well, now, what brings you to Fort Smith? Hot on a case, are you?"

"After a fashion," Starbuck commented. "Wondered what you could tell me about Belle Starr."

"What's to tell?" Fagan said with mild contempt. "Her and Sam Starr—that's her husband—rustle livestock and pull penny-ante holdups. Strictly small-time."

"What kind of holdups?"

"Nuisance stuff," Fagan observed. "Trading posts, backwoods stores . . . every now and then they smuggle a load of whiskey into the Nations. Between them, they haven't got brains enough to take on a bank or train."

"Why haven't you arrested them?"

"We've got our hands full with the *real* hardcases. Course, that don't mean their number won't show. One of these days we'll gct 'em for horse stealing or some such—only a matter of time."

"So there's nothing hanging over their heads right now?"

"Nothing particular." Fagan's gaze sharpened. "What's your interest in Miz Belle? She's a slut, common as dirt. Otherwise she wouldn't have married herself off to a reformed dog-eater."

"Her husband's an Indian?"

Fagan nodded. "Full-blooded Cherokee."

"I understand they've got a place over in the Nations."

"On the Canadian River," Fagan affirmed. "Way the hell back in the middle of nowhere. Not marked on any map, but it's called Younger's Bend."

Starbuck looked startled. "Younger's Bend?"

"Well, so the story goes, Belle had herself a kid by Cole Younger. That was some years ago, but apparently she's not one to forget an old sweetheart."

"You're saying she named her place after Cole Younger?"

Fagan slowly shook his head. "I can see how you

made your mark as a detective. You've got a knack for askin' all the questions—without answering any yourself."

"No offence," Starbuck said, smiling faintly. "Old habits are hard to break."

"Suppose we try," Fagan said in a firm voice. "You dodged it a minute ago, so I'll ask again. What's your interest in Belle Starr?"

Starbuck gave him a thoughtful stare. "Anything I say would have to be off the record."

Fagan unpinned his badge and tossed it on the desk. "Shoot."

"I'm after Jesse and Frank James. I've got reason to believe they're using Belle Starr's place as a hideout."

"The hell you say!" Fagan looked at him with some surprise. "Where'd you get a notion like that?"

"A word here, a word there," Starbuck said evasively. "Nothing solid, but a man plays his best hunch."

"One way to find out," Fagan informed him. "I've got a chief deputy that sort of oversees the Cherokee Nation. Want me to call him in?"

"Will he keep his lip buttoned?"

"I'll guarantee it." Fagan threw back his head and roared. "Heck Thomas! Get your dusty butt in here— now!"

A moment passed, then the sound of footsteps drifted in from the hallway. The man who appeared through the door was tall and rangy, with close-cropped hair and a wide handlebar moustache. His eyes were grey and impersonal, and his features were set in the stern expression befitting a church deacon. Starbuck marked him as a mankiller, which immediately put them on common ground.

After a round of introductions, Fagan briefly explained the situation. Heck Thomas listened impassively, arms folded across his chest, saying nothing. At last, when his boss concluded, his gaze shifted to Starbuck.

"Belle and Sam aren't too high on our list, you understand?"

"So Marshal Fagan told me."

"Anything I pass along would be mostly hearsay and rumour."

"No harm in listening."

"Well—" Thomas paused, lifted his shoulders in a shrug. "Every now and then I get word that a bunch of strangers have been seen at Belle's place. Just that—a bunch of strangers—no names, no descriptions."

"You never had reason to check it out?"

"Nope," Thomas said simply. "Belle's probably screwed half the male population of Indian Territory. So it don't spark much curiosity when we hear there's strange men hangin' around her place."

"These strangers," Starbuck inquired, "were they white men?"

"I don't remember anybody sayin' one way or the other."

"How often have you heard they were there?"

"Oh, once or twice a year. Course, keep in mind, I never heard it was the same men every time. Like I said, no names, no descriptions . . . nothin'."

Starbuck thought it was far from nothing. The appearance of strangers at Belle Starr's place—once or twice a year—dovetailed very neatly with the disappearance of the James gang following their periodic holdups. The information was promising, and substantiated what until now had been a shot in the dark. His instinct told him he was on the right track.

For the next few minutes, he questioned Thomas at length about Belle Starr. The lawman required little prompting, and gave him an earful regarding the lady

bandit's tawdry personal life. Then, moving to a large
wall map, Thomas traced the route to Younger's Bend.
He allowed it was an easy two days' ride, but cautioned
Starbuck to keep his eyes open. The Nations was no
place for a man to get careless. And that applied most
especially, he added, to a lawman.

Starbuck inquired the best place to buy a horse, and
Fagan directed him to a stable on the south side of town.
After a few parting remarks, he shook the marshal's
hand and thanked him for his assistance. Thomas, waiting near the door, motioned him into the hallway and
walked him outside.

On the steps they halted and looked towards the gallows. The death warrant had been read and a minister
was intoning a final prayer. Four condemned men stood
positioned on the centre trap, their hands tied behind
their backs and black hoods fitted over their heads. The
bearded man Starbuck had seen earlier moved down the
line, snugging each noose tight, careful to centre the knot
below the left ear. Then he turned and walked directly
to a wooden lever behind the prisoners. The crowd, mor-
bidly curious, edged closer to the scaffold.

"Who's the hangman?"

"Name's George Maledon," Thomas said stolidly.
"Takes pride in his work. Likes to brag he's never let a
man strangle to death. Always breaks a fellow's neck
first crack out of the box."

"How many men has he hung?"

"That bunch'll make twenty-eight."

A loud *whump* suddenly sounded from the gallows.
The four men dropped through the trapdoor and hit the
end of the ropes with an abrupt jolt. Their necks snapped
in unison, and their heads, crooked at a grotesque angle,
flopped over their right shoulders. The spectators, staring
bug-eyed at the scaffold, seemed to hold their breath.

Hanging limp, the dead men swayed gently, the scratchy creak of taut rope somehow deafening in the stillness. One eye on his watch, the executioner finally nodded to the prison physician. Working quickly, the doctor moved from body to body, testing for a heartbeat with his stethoscope. A moment later he pronounced the four men officially dead.

Starbuck grunted softly to himself. "Damn shame Judge Parker's not running the whole country."

"How so?"

"Well, from what I've seen, there're more men that deserve hanging than gets hung. Jesse James and his crowd would be prime examples."

"Ain't it a fact!" Thomas paused, then laughed. "Sure you don't want a job? We could use a man with your style over in the Nations."

"Thanks all the same." Starbuck turned, his hand outstretched. "I'll stick to Judge Colt. Never have to worry about the verdict that way."

"Hallelujah!" Thomas grinned and pumped his arm with vigour. "Good huntin' to you, Luke."

Starbuck nodded and walked off in the direction of the street. Heck Thomas watched him a moment, wondering on the outcome with Belle Starr and her Cherokee lapdog. Then, as the spectators began dispersing, his attention was drawn to the gallows. The hanged men, one by one, were being unstrung. Somehow, though Thomas wasn't all that superstitious, it seemed prophetic. A favourable sign.

Starbuck ought to have himself a whale of a time at Younger's Bend.

CHAPTER 6

By late afternoon of the following day Starbuck was some fifty miles west of Fort Smith. The horse he'd bought was a roan gelding with an easy gait and an even disposition. Along with a secondhand saddle and worn range clothes from his warbag, he looked every inch the fiddle-footed cowhand. Which was precisely the role he'd chosen to play at Younger's Bend.

Early on in his career Starbuck had discovered something in himself that went hand in hand with the detective business. He possessed a streak of the actor, and seemed to have a natural flair for disguise. Every assignment differed, and the range of roles he'd played would have challenged a veteran thespian. Over the past few years he had posed as a saddletramp and stockbuyer, con man and grifter, tinhorn gambler and sleazy whoremonger. Experience had taught him that outward appearance fooled most folks most of the time. The balance of the deception required the proper lingo and a working knowledge of the character he portrayed. For that, he had developed the habit of studying other people's quirks of speech and their mannerisms. Operating undercover, his very survival rested on the skill of his performance. So it was he'd honed the trick of transforming himself, both outwardly and inwardly, into someone else. Once he assumed a disguise, he simply ceased to be Luke Starbuck.

For Younger's Bend, he already had a pip of a cover story in mind. All day, riding west from Fort Smith, he'd added a touch here and a touch there. Based on past assignments—the trial and error of mastering his craft—he knew that a credible cover story must always strike a delicate balance. A general rule was the simpler the better, with a guileless, straightforward approach. Yet an element of the outlandish—even something bizarre—added icing to the cake. A happy-go-lucky character who was half fool and half daredevil was the most convincing character of all. Somehow people never suspected a jester whose sights were set on the brass ring. A combination of down-at-the-heels cowhand turned bank robber seemed to Starbuck a real lulu for the task ahead. He thought it would play well at Younger's Bend.

Shortly before sundown Starbuck approached the juncture of the Arkansas and Canadian rivers. Farther west lay the Creek Nation and some distance south lay the Chocktaw Nation. Younger's Bend, which was on the fringe of the Cherokee Nation, was ideally situated to the boundary lines of all three tribes. By rough calculation, he estimated Belle Starr's place was some forty miles upstream along the Canadian. The general direction was southwest, and with no great effort he would arrive there around suppertime tomorrow evening. That fitted perfectly with his plan, for it was essential that he be invited to stop over at least one night. With no reason to travel farther, he decided to pitch camp on the banks of the Arkansas.

A stand of trees was selected for a campsite. There, with deadwood close to hand, a fire would be no prob-

lem. Along with a Winchester carbine he'd bought in
Fort Smith, Starbuck dropped his saddlebags and blanket
roll at the base of a tree. After being unsaddled, the roan
was hobbled and turned loose to graze on a grassy
stretch near the riverbank. A fire was kindled, and as
dusk fell a cheery blaze lighted the grove.

All in keeping with his role, Starbuck was travelling
without camp gear or victuals. He dined on a cold supper
of hardtack, store-bought beef jerky, and river water. An
hour or so after dark, he picketed the roan between a
couple of trees at the edge of the grove. Afterwards, with
an eye to comfort, he spread his blankets near the fire
and covered them with a rain slicker. By then a damp
chill had settled over the land, and he decided to call it
a night. With his saddle for a pillow, he crawled between
the blankets and turned up the collar of his mackinaw.
Overhead the indigo sky was clear and flecked through
with a zillion stars.

Unable to sleep, he soon tired of counting stars. His
thoughts drifted to Younger's Bend, and the reception
he might reasonably expect. Then, item by item, he began a mental review of all he'd learned about Belle Starr.
With everything contained in the Pinkerton file, added
to the rundown by Heck Thomas, it made a hefty package. None of it was good—a sorry account of an even
sorrier woman—but revealing all the same. And damned
spicy in spots.

Myra Belle Shirley was born in Jasper County, Missouri. Her father, who owned a blacksmith shop and livery stable, was widely respected and prominent in
politics. At the proper age, like all proper young ladies,
Myra Belle was enrolled in the Carthage Female Academy. There she was taught grammar and deportment,
and learned to play a passable tune on the piano. But
she was something of a tomboy, and more interested in

horses and guns than ladylike refinement. By the time abolitionist Kansas and pro-slavery Missouri went to war, she was an accomplished horsewoman and no slouch with a pistol.

The border states were savaged during the Civil War, at the mercy of guerrilla bands on both sides. Only fifteen when Quantrill pillaged and burned Lawrence, Kansas, Myra Belle was impressed by the way he had raised a band of volunteers and turned them into a small army of bloodthirsty raiders. Among them was her idol and secret lover, Cole Younger.

In 1863, Myra Belle's older brother was killed when federal troops razed Carthage. Wild with grief, she fled home and rode off to join Cole and the guerrillas. For the balance of the war, crazed with revenge, she served as an informant and spy for Quantrill. Then, with the South's surrender, Cole and the James boys took off on their own. She had no choice but to return to her family.

The summer of 1865 Myra Belle's father pulled up roots and moved the family to Texas. Outside Dallas, he bought a farm and dabbled in horse trading. Once more enrolled in school, Myra Belle seemed to have settled down and lost her taste for excitement. Then, early in 1866, Cole Younger rode into the farm with his three brothers and the James boys. Fresh from their first bank robbery, they were flush with money and lavished extravagant gifts on the family. A month or so later, when the gang rode back to Missouri, Cole left an even more lasting memento of the visit. Myra Belle, now a ripe eighteen, was pregnant.

When the child was born out of wedlock, the scandal rocked the farm community. Branded a hussy, Myra Belle left her daughter with her parents and fled to Dallas. There, working as a dance-hall girl, she dropped Myra from her name and became known simply as Belle.

There, too, she met and married a young horse thief named Jim Reed. Several years were spent on the run, flitting about from Texas to California, with the law always one step behind. At last, with no place to turn, Reed sought refuge in Indian Territory. Belle shortly joined him, and her career as a lady bandit began in earnest.

The Reeds were given sanctuary by Tom Starr, a full-blood Cherokee. Starr and his eight sons were considered the principal hell-raisers of the Cherokee Nation. Their land was located on a remote stretch of the Canadian River, and considered unsafe for travel by anyone not directly related to the Starr clan. Nonetheless, those who rode the owlhoot were welcome, and even white outlaws found haven there. Belle, the only white woman present, was accorded royal treatment by the Starrs. Then, in the summer of 1874, she abruptly became a widow. Jim Reed, trapped following a stagecoach robbery in Texas, was slain by lawmen.

Never daunted, Belle soon shed her widow's weeds and married Sam Starr. The fact that Sam was a full-blood gave Belle no pause whatever. By the marriage, she gained dower rights to her husband's share in the communal lands of the Cherokee Nation. For the first time in her life she was a woman of property; being white, she was also queen bee of the ruffians who found refuge with the Starr clan. Together she and Sam formed a gang comprising renegade Indians and former cowboys. All were misfits, none of them too bright, and Belle easily dominated the entire crew, her husband included. She promptly dubbed their base of operations Younger's Bend.

The eldest of Old Tom Starr's sons, Sam had a parcel of land located farther downstream on the Canadian. From here, the gang rustled livestock, robbed backwoods stores, and occasionally ran illegal whiskey across the border. Belle was the planner—the brains—and shrewdly brought the men together only when a job was imminent. Afterwards, the gang members scattered to Tulsa and other railroad towns to squander their loot. Meanwhile, back at Younger's Bend, Belle and Sam were virtually immune to arrest. Their home was surrounded by wilderness and mountains, and the only known approach was along a canyon trail rising steeply from the river. So inaccessible was the stronghold that lawmen—both Light Horse Police and federal marshals—gave it a wide berth. After ten years in Indian Territory, Belle was riding high and in no great danger of a fall. She was living the life Myra Belle Shirley had sought since girlhood. And she gloried in the notoriety accorded the Nation's one and only lady bandit, Belle Starr.

To Starbuck, it was a challenge with an unusual twist. Yet tonight, warmed by the embers of the fire, he concluded the lady bandit was vulnerable on several counts. Aside from the vanity normal to any woman, there was the added vanity of a woman who had made her mark in a man's world. A woman who ruled her own robbers' roost and considered herself the femme fatale of the James-Younger gang. Such a woman, unless he missed his guess, was likely to have chapped lips from kissing cold mirrors. And a man who played on her vanity might very easily induce her to brag a little. Or maybe a lot, particularly where it concerned an old beau and lingering sentiment. A sentiment expressed in the name itself—Younger's Bend.

Worming deeper into his blankets, Starbuck turned his backside to the fire. He closed his eyes and drifted towards sleep, thinking of tomorrow. And the lady who was no lady.

. . .

In the lowering dusk Starbuck emerged from the canyon trail. Before him, surrounded by dense woods, lay a stretch of level ground. Not fifty yards away, a log house stood like a sentinel where the trail ended. One window was lighted by a lamp.

A flock of crows cawed and took wing as he rode forward. From the house a pack of dogs joined the chorus, and he smiled to himself. On horseback or on foot, there was little chance anyone would approach Younger's Bend unannounced. He noted as well that trees had been felled in a wide swath from the clearing around the house to the mouth of the canyon. The purpose—an unobstructed field of fire—was obvious. He felt a bit like a duck in a shooting gallery.

The door of the house opened and a woman stepped onto the porch. Her features were indistinct, but the lines of her figure and the flow of her dress were silhouetted against lamplight from inside. She hushed the dogs with a sharp command, and stood waiting with her hands on her hips. Starbuck reined to halt in the yard, mindful he wasn't to dismount unless invited. He smiled politely and touched the brim of his hat.

"Evenin', ma'am."

"Evening."

"You'd likely to be Miz Starr."

"Who's asking?"

"Clyde Belden."

"I don't recall we've met, Mr. Belden."

"No, ma'am," Starbuck said briskly. "I was steered to you by a mutual friend."

"Would this friend have a name?"

"Sure does," Starbuck said with the slow whang of a born Missourian. "None other than Jim Younger hisself."

There was the merest beat of hesitation. "Come on

inside, Mr. Belden. Just be careful to keep your hands in plain sight."

"Anything you say, Miz Starr."

Starbuck stepped down out of the saddle and left the gelding ground-reined. From the corner of the house, a man materialised out of the shadows. He moved forward, holding a double-barrel shotgun at hip level. In the spill of light from the window, Starbuck immediately pegged him as Sam Starr. He was lithely built, with bark-dark skin, muddy eyes, and sleek, glistening hair. His pinched face had an oxlike expression, and he silently followed along as Starbuck crossed the porch and entered the house. Lagging back, he stopped halfway through the door, the shotgun still levelled.

When Belle Starr turned, Starbuck got the shock of his life. Based on her long string of lovers, he'd expected at the very least a passably attractive woman. Instead, she was horsefaced, with a lantern jaw and bloodless lips and beady close-set eyes. Her figure was somehow mannish, with wide hips and shoulders, and almost no breasts beneath her drab woolen dress. While his expression betrayed nothing, Starbuck thought she looked like a cross between ugly and uglier. He'd seen worse, but only in a circus tent show.

Inspecting him, Belle's eyes were guarded. He figured the chances of being recognised were slight. It was unlikely the *Police Gazette* had any wide readership in the Nations; only through a fluke would she have seen the issue bearing his photo. Then, too, his face was now covered with bearded stubble, which tended to alter his appearance. At length, watching him closely, she put him to the test.

"What makes you think I know Jim Younger?"

"He told me so!" Starbuck beamed. "Course, I haven't seen him in a spell, but that don't make no nevermind. The day I headed west he told me all about you and Younger's Bend."

"Then you're from Missouri?"

"Born and bred," Starbuck said with cheery vigour. "All us Beldens come from over around Sedalia way."

Belle gave him a veiled but searching look. "I suppose you rode with Jim during the war?"

"No such luck! I got called up and served with the regulars. Jim and me didn't make acquaintance till after the shootin' stopped."

"You mean you rode with him afterwards?"

"Naw," Starbuck said sheepishly. "Jim and me was just drinkin' pals. He used to talk to me about it some, but I didn't have the sand for it in them days."

"So how did he come to mention me?"

"Well, like I said, I decided to cut loose and head west. Wanted to be a cowboy, and I shore got my wish! Been up the trail from Texas ever' year since the summer of '78."

"You left out the part about Jim."

"Ain't that just like me!" Starbuck rolled his eyes with a foolish smile. "I get started talkin'—well, anyway, Jim told me if I ever got in a tight fix to look you up. So here I am!"

Belle studied him in silence a moment. "What sort of fix?"

"Robbed me a bank!" Starbuck lied heartily. "Walked in all by my lonesome and cleaned 'em out!"

"Where?"

"Vernon," Starbuck informed her. "That's a little burg on the Texas side of the Red River. Figgered it was a good place to get my feet wet."

"Wait a minute." Belle blinked and looked at him. "Are you saying that was your first job?"

"Shore was." Starbuck gave her a lopsided grin.

"Pulled it off slicker'n a whistle, too. Got pretty near two thousand in cold cash!"

"Why now?" Belle appeared bemused. "After all this time what changed your mind?"

"Got tired of workin' for thirty a month and found. Thought it over and decided ol' Jim was right. There's easier ways to make a livin', lots easier."

"So what brings you here?"

"By jingo!" Starbuck boomed out jovially. "Where's a better place to lose yourself? The way Jim talked, you're the soul of Christian charity. I just figgered I'd hightail it into the Nations and make your acquaintance. Better late than never!"

Belle seemed to thaw a little. "Clyde, I'd say you've got more sand than you gave yourself credit for."

"Why, thank you, ma'am." Starbuck swept his hat off. "Comin' from you, I take that as a puredee compliment."

"Do you now?" Belle sounded flattered. "What makes you say that?"

"Why, you're famous, Miz Belle! Ole Jimbo thinks the sun rises and sets right where you stand. And it ain't just him either! I've heard Jesse and Cole brag on you till they plumb run out of wind. That's gospel fact!"

"Ooo, go on!" Belle cracked a smile. "I don't believe a word of it!"

"Miz Belle, I do admire a modest lady. You make me proud to say I'm an ol' Missouri boy. Yessir, you shorely do!"

From the doorway Sam Starr cleared his throat. Belle glanced in his direction and he jerked his head outside. Then he backed away and turned out of the lamplight spilling through the door. Belle frowned, clearly displeased by her husband's presumptuous manner. After a moment, her gaze shifted to Starbuck and she smiled.

"Have a seat." She waved him to a crude dining table. "I'll be with you in a minute."

"Thank you kindly." Starbuck took a chair and tossed his hat on the table. "Don't rush on my account, Miz Belle. I got time to spare."

Belle merely nodded and walked swiftly from the room. Outside, she wheeled right and strode to the end of the porch. Sam was stationed where he could watch the door, the shotgun cradled over one arm. His view through the window was partially obstructed by the angle, but he could see the edge of the dining table and Starbuck's hat. Belle stopped, fixing him with an annoyed squint. Her voice was harsh, cutting.

"What the fuck's your problem?"

"Not me," Sam grunted coarsely. "That feller in there's the problem."

"If you've got something to say, why don't you just spit it out?"

"You ain't gonna like it."

"Try me and see."

"We got to kill him, Belle. Kill him now!"

CHAPTER 7

Starbuck sat stock-still. He listened as Belle's footsteps rapidly crossed the porch, then there was silence. His smile vanished and his eyes flicked around the room.

The interior of the house was smaller than it appeared from outside. Stoutly built, with chinked log walls, it consisted of a central living area and a separate bedroom. The battered table and chairs stood before an open fireplace with a mud chimney. A commode with a faded mirror occupied the wall beside the bedroom door. An ancient brass bed, visible through the door, gleamed in the flames from the fireplace. To the rear of the main room was a wood cooking stove and rough-hewn shelves packed with canned goods. A jumble of odds and ends was piled in the far corner.

On the whole, it was sparse on comfort and smelled like a wolf den. Yet Starbuck wasn't concerned with tidiness or the accommodations. He was looking for a backdoor—all too aware his Colt was no match for a shotgun at close quarters, and suddenly uncomfortable that the only exit was the door through which he had entered. His attention turned to the powwow under way on the front porch. There was no question he was the topic of conversation, but considerable doubt existed as to the verdict. He subscribed to the theory of "shoot first and talk about it later," and a vantage point nearer the door seemed eminently advisable. Then, too, a bit of eavesdropping might very well improve his odds.

Quietly, Starbuck rose and moved to the fireplace. He stood with his hands outstretched to the flames, one eye on the window. No one was watching him—nor was there any sound from outside—and he concluded they were still huddled at the end of the porch. Hugging the wall, he ghosted towards the front of the house. There, he flattened himself beside the windowsill and pressed his ear to the logs. The chinking was old and cracked, seeping air between small gaps, and through it he heard the drone of voices. A heated argument was under way.

"I don't give a good goddamn what you think!"

"You'd better," Sam grumbled. "I got a nose for those things."

"Heap big Injun!" Belle mocked him. "You'd starve to death if somebody hadn't invented tinned goods!"

"You got no call to say that."

"Oh, no? When's the last time you and your mangy pack of brothers shot a deer—or a rabbit—or even a squirrel, for Chrissakes? You've got a hunter's nose like I've got warts on my ass!"

"I'm warnin' you now! You leave my brothers outta this!"

"Awww, dry up," Belle said in a waspish tone. "The whole bunch of you couldn't hold a candle to a cigar-store Indian. Your pa's the only one with any balls—and it sure as hell didn't get passed along to you!"

"How come you're always throwin' the old man up in my face?"

"Because nobody ever pulled his tail feathers. Go on,

admit it! You're full-grown and you still wet your pants anytime he looks cross-eyed at you."

"Mebbe you should've married him 'stead of me."

"Maybe!" Belle crowed. "Jesus Christ, no maybe about it! At least he's still got some red-hot Injun blood left in him. Which is more than I can say for you and your butthole brothers."

Sam laughed without mirth. "Won't work, Belle! I ain't gonna get mad."

"Talk sense! What the Sam Hill's that got to do with anything?"

" 'Cause you're tryin' to throw me off the scent and we both know it."

"Here we go again," Belle gibed. "You and your track-'em-through-the-woods nose!"

"I know a lawdog when I smell one."

"Sam, you poor sap! You couldn't smell a fart if somebody caught it in a bottle and let you have the first sniff."

"I am warnin' you, woman. That feller's no bank robber! I'll betcha he don't know Jim Younger nor none of the others either."

"Judas Priest," Belle groaned. "You heard me question him! You were standing there the whole time and I didn't trip him up once. How do you explain that?"

"I didn't say he was dumb," Sam reminded her. "I said he was a lawdog! So it just naturally figgers he'd have all the right answers. Any fool oughta see that."

"Are you calling me a fool, Sam Starr?"

"No, I ain't. I'm only tryin' to talk some sense into your head."

"Well, you can talk till you're blue in the face and it won't change a thing. I told you once and I'm telling you again! I won't let you kill him."

"Too bad your brains ain't where they're supposed to be."

"What the hell does that mean?"

"It means you've got hot drawers, that's what it means."

"You're crazy as a loon!"

"Yeah?" Sam bristled. "You think I don't know the sign when I see it? You got your mind set on him humpin' you, and you ain't gonna listen to reason till he forks you good and proper."

"That's a dirty goddamn lie!"

"Belle, how many men you humped since we got married? Mebbe you lost count, but I haven't. I watched it happen enough times I know what I'm talkin' about. You don't want me to kill him 'cause you got hot drawers. So don't tell me different."

"Well, so what?" Belle lashed out. "I go to bed with any damn body I please. I don't need your permission!"

"Never said otherwise," Sam conceded. "All I'm sayin' is, we'd be better off with him dead. So I'll wait till after you're done and then kill him. How's that?"

"No deal," Belle said sternly. "I will budge a little, though. We'll let him spend the night and then send him on his way. Fair enough?"

"I wish you'd believe me when I tell you he's a lawman. Probably sent personal by the Hangin' Judge hisself."

"You think I don't know a Missouri boy when I see one? He's no more a marshal than you are. Hell's bells, I'm a better judge of character than that!"

"So go on and suit yourself. You always do anyway."

"Sam?"

"Yeah?"

"Don't get any wiseass notions about killing him after he leaves here. You do and I'll wait till you're asleep some night—and then I'll cut your goddamn tally-whacker clean off! You hear me, Sam?"

"I hear you."

Starbuck heard her, too. He was again seated at the dining table when Belle led her husband through the door. Several things were apparent to him from their conversation. Foremost was that he would have only one night to squeeze Belle dry of information. Another factor, which might serve to loosen her tongue, was that she'd bought his story about Jim Younger. Yet, like an alley cat in heat, she had designs on his body, and big plans for the night ahead. One look at her gargoyle face and he began having second thoughts about the detective business. He wasn't sure he could get it up—much less romance her—even in the cause of law and order.

Sam halted near the door and Belle moved directly to the table. Watching her, Starbuck wondered how it would work with a sack over her head. He thought it an idea worth exploring.

"Forgot to introduce you boys," Belle said, gesturing towards the door. "Clyde, want you to meet my husband Sam Starr."

"Howdy, Sam." Starbuck nodded amiably. "Pleasure's all mine."

Sam muttered something unintelligible, and Belle quickly resumed. "How would you like to stay to supper and spend the night?"

"Why, I'd be most obliged, Miz Belle."

"We'd ask you to stay longer, but it wouldn't work out just now. We've got a business deal of our own that won't keep."

"No problem," Starbuck said agreeably. I was just passin' through, anyhow. Only stopped off to pay my respects."

"Too bad in a way." Belle feigned a rueful look. "You

and Sam would probably get a kick out of chewing the fat. But he's got to run over to his pa's place and tend to that business deal. Don't you, Sam?"

"Yeah, sure." Sam gave her a disgruntled scowl, then turned towards the door. "See you in the mornin'."

A few minutes later, Belle watched from the porch while her husband led a horse from the barn and mounted. When the hoofbeats faded into the night, she stepped back inside and closed the door. She smiled like a tigress stalking a goat.

Starbuck, cast in the role of the goat, had a sudden sinking feeling. It looked to be a long night.

Whatever else she was, Belle Starr was no cook. She served Starbuck sowbelly and beans, a pasty hominy gruel, and cornbread baked hard as sandstone. He wolfed it down with gusto—grinning all the while—and topped off the performance with an appreciative belch. The belch was the easiest part, and required no strain. He felt gassy as a bloated hog.

After clearing the table, Belle brought out a couple of tin cups and a quart of rotgut. The whiskey had a bite like molten lead, and tasted as though it had been aged in a turpentine barrel. No sipper, Belle was clearly a lady who enjoyed her liquor. She poured with the regularity of a metronome, and slugged it down without batting an eye. Starbuck, sensing opportunity, matched her shot for shot. She wanted his body and he wanted information, and it all boiled down to who got crocked first. Unless she had a hollow leg, he thought there was a reasonable chance he could outlast her.

In passing, Starbuck noted that he'd been dead on the mark regarding her vanity. She was a woman with a high opinion of herself, and not above putting on airs. Earlier, on the porch with Sam, she had displayed the foul mouth of a veteran muleskinner. Yet with Starbuck, her language bordered on the ladylike, sweeter than sugar and twice as nice. The more she drank, the more he had to admire her style. For a virtuoso of four-letter words, it took considerable restraint to hobble her tongue. He mentally applauded the effort, and bided his time waiting for her to slip back into character. Only then would he make his move.

Along towards midnight, Starbuck's patience was rewarded. The bottle of popskull was approaching empty, and Belle's eyes were fixed in a glassy stare that seemed vaguely out of focus. She wasn't ossified, but her tolerance to snakebite would last well into next week. Starbuck was feeling a little numb himself, warmed by a tingling sensation that extended to his hair roots. Yet he still had his wits about him, and it appeared he'd won the drinking bout. The lady bandit suddenly reverted to her true self. And her choice of words was all the tipoff he needed.

"You know something, Clyde?" Her mouth curled in a coy smile. "For an old Missouri boy, you're a goddamn sweet-looking man."

"Well, Miz Belle"—Starbuck grinned, suppressing his revulsion, and plunged ahead—"you're pretty easy on the eyes yourself."

"Forget that Miz Belle shit. I'm not your mama and you're not wet behind the ears. You follow me?"

Starbuck's grin turned to a suggestive leer. "What'd you have in mind?"

"When I was a girl—" Belle burst out in a bawdy horselaugh. "All the prissy-assed little buttermouths at the Female Academy called it the birds and the bees. Once I took up with boys, I learned it was better known as stink finger and hide the weenie. That answer your question?"

"Sounds the least bit like an invitation."

"I never was one to mince words. A woman's got the same needs as a man."

"Some folks call it horny."

"By God, Clyde, you're a card! Always was partial to a man with a sense of humour."

"What about Sam?" Starbuck jerked his chin at the door. "I'd hate to have him come bustin' in here with that shotgun just when I was all set to flush the birds out of your nest."

"Wooiee!" Belle leaned forward, grabbing his head in both hands, and planted one smack on his lips. "Flush the birds out of my nest! Goddamn, that's rich, Clyde. I do like the sound of it!"

Starbuck felt like he'd been kissed by a dragon. "Not to put a damper on things, but I'd shore like to hear your answer about Sam."

"Who gives a fuck?" Belle gave him a sly and tipsy look. "I sent Sam packing for the night, and that's that! You just rest easy, sport."

Starbuck paused, then smoothly laid the trap. "Well, now, I dunno. Jim told me about you and Cole, but I just naturally figgered—"

"What about Cole?"

"Why, that you was sweet on him. The way Jim talked it went back long before the war."

Belle poured herself a stiff shot and knocked it back. "What else did he tell you?"

"Say, look here—Starbuck broke off with a troubled frown. "I don't want to step on nobody's toes. Maybe I'd best let it drop there."

"No, you don't!" Belle demanded. "You started it, now finish it!"

"Listen, Belle, me and Jim go way back. I shore wouldn't wanna get him in Dutch."

"Oh, for God's sake!" Belle drunkenly waved the objection aside. "I won't hold it against Jim. Now stop dancing around and spill it! What'd he tell you?"

"Nothin' much, really." Starbuck's tone was matter-of-fact. "Only that you let Cole and the boys hide out here after they'd pulled a job. I seem to recollect he mentioned Jesse and Frank, too."

The effects of her last drink suddenly overtook Belle. She squinted owlishly and her speech slurred. "How about Ruston's place?"

Starbuck held his breath. "You mean the other hideout?"

"Yeah."

"Wait a minute!" Starbuck wrinkled his brow in concentration. "Why, shore, Ruston! Near as I recall, Jim said he'd served with 'im under Quantrill. Now what the blue-billy-hell was his first name? Got it right on the tip of my tongue!"

"Tom," Belle mumbled. "Good ol' Tom Ruston. Wish I had his spread and he had a feather up his ass! We'd both be tickled pink."

Starbuck played along. "Jim said it was some layout."

"One of the biggest." Belle nodded. "And on the Pecos, that's saying a lot! Nothing small-time about Texans."

"You're tellin' me!" Starbuck laughed. "I reckon I've trailed enough cows outta Texas to have a pretty fair idea." He hesitated, choosing his words. "Well, maybe I'll run acrost Jim down there one of these days."

"Not likely." Belle sloshed whiskey into her cup, wholly unaware she had emptied the bottle. "Long as they're safe here, they got no reason to bother Ruston."

Starbuck decided not to press it further. The last piece of the puzzle was now clear, and all that remained was to fit the parts together. With a broad grin, he lifted his cup in a toast. "Here's to the Youngers! Ol' King Cole and the best damn brothers any man could ask for."

"I'll drink to that!"

Belle drained her cup in a long swallow and lowered it to her lap. Whiskey dribbled down her chin and she burped, clapping her hand to her mouth with a foolish giggle. She gave Starbuck a dopey smile and reached for his hand. Then a wave of dizziness rocked her, and her eyes suddenly glazed. The cup clattered to the floor and her head thumped forward onto the table.

Starbuck lifted her from her chair and carried her to the bedroom. She was out cold and lay like a corpse while he undressed her. Unmoved by her nakedness, he pulled the covers up to her chin and turned away. At the door, he glanced back and let go a heavy sigh of relief.

He felt like a condemned man with a last-minute re-prieve.

Late the next morning Starbuck led his horse from the barn and halted before the house. Belle, suffering from a monumental hangover, stood on the porch. He gave her a lewd wink and playfully patted her on the thigh.

"You're some woman, Miz Belle Starr. One of a kind!"

Belle's eyes were bloodshot, vaguely disoriented. "Clyde, tell me something. How'd things work out last night?"

"You don't remember?"

"Not just exactly. Did you—uh—flush the birds out of the nest?"

"Did I ever!" Starbuck whooped. "Scattered 'em all to hell and gone!"

"Yeah?" Belle seemed bemused. "Well, how was it?"

"Never had none better! You plumb tuckered me out, and that's the gospel truth."

Belle brightened visibly. "You Missouri boys always was hot-blooded."

"Godalmightybingo! Stink finger and hide the weenie! Wouldn't have missed it for the world, Miz Belle!"

Starbuck tossed her a roguish salute and stepped into the saddle. He turned the gelding out of the yard and gigged him into a prancing trot. At the mouth of the canyon, he twisted around and waved his hat high overhead. Belle, looking fluttery as a schoolgirl, threw him a kiss.

The performance ended as Starbuck rode towards the river. His jaw hardened and his mouth set in a tight line. For the moment, Indian Territory was a washout, and he saw nothing to be gained in scouting the ranch on the Pecos. All of which meant he'd exhausted his options. Jesse James would have to be hunted down on homeground.

He forded the river and headed north, towards Missouri. And Clay County.

CHAPTER 8

A cold blue dusk settled over the winter landscape.

Lamar Hudspeth waited in the shadows of the barn. With his son at his side, he watched three riders approach along the rutted wagon road. A snowfall, followed by a brief warm spell, had turned the road into a boggy quagmire. The horses slogged through the mud, heads bowed against a brisk wind, snorting frosty clouds of vapour. Their riders reined off the road and proceeded towards the barn at a plodding walk. Hudspeth stepped out of the shadows.

"Cole." He greeted the men by name as they dismounted. "Jim, you're lookin' fit. Evenin', Bob."

"How do, Lamar."

Cole Younger merely bobbed his head. "Jesse here yet?"

"Nope," Hudspeth replied with a shrug. "He'll be along directly though. Probably waitin' till it gets full dark."

"Horseshit!" Cole loosed a satiric laugh. "He's waitin' to see if we get ourselves ambushed. Jesse always was good at lettin' somebody else bird-dog for him."

"You got no call to talk that way, Cole."

"Think not? Then how come we're the first ones here when it's him that called the meetin'? Go on, answer me that!"

"I 'spect he's got his reasons."

"Lamar, there's none your equal when it comes to stickin' by kinfolk. I'll hand you that."

"Speakin' of kin," Hudspeth said, easing into another subject, "I made the rounds today. Stopped by Miz Samuel's place, just to make sure there wasn't no outsiders nosin' about."

"We done the same," Cole remarked, motioning to his brothers. "All of us snuck in to see our women last night. Things appear to be pretty quiet."

"So Miz Samuel said," Hudspeth acknowledged. "She ain't seen hide nor hair of anybody that looks like a Pinkerton."

"Jesse's wife still stayin' with his ma?"

"Well, her being in a family way and all, I 'spect she'll stay there till her time comes."

"Leastways Jesse don't need no bird dog there. One way or another, he manages to sire his own pups."

"Iffen it was me, I wouldn't let Jesse hear you say a thing like that."

"Before the night's over, he's gonna hear lots worse. I got a bellyful, and I aim to speak my piece."

"I reckon you're full-growed." Hudspeth gestured to his son. "The boy'll put your horses in the barn. There's coffee on the stove and angel cake for them that wants it."

"Your woman's braver'n most, Lamar."

"How's that?"

"Bakin' an angel cake for this crew? Damnation, she's liable to get your house struck by lightning!"

Cole laughed and walked off with his brothers. The Hudspeth boy, flushed with shame for his father, led their horses into the barn. For his part, Lamar Hudspeth took no offence at the crude humour. His one concern was that there would be no spillover of animosity tonight. Yet, from all indications, he sensed that it wasn't to be. Cole Younger was plainly looking for an excuse to start trouble.

The Hudspeth farm was located some miles outside the town of Kearney. Hudspeth himself was a law-abiding family man, a deacon in the Baptist church, and modestly active in Clay County politics. He was also a second cousin of Jesse and Frank James. Though he abhorred their methods—for he was a fundamentalist who took the Scriptures literally—he nonetheless believed they were being persecuted by shylock bankers and unscrupulous railroad barons. Like many people, he assisted the James boys and the Youngers at every turn. Since their own homes were unsafe, the gang members found shelter with friends and relatives; constantly on the move, they seldom spent more than a couple of nights in any one spot. The system baffled the law and allowed the robbers to visit their wives and children on a sporadic basis.

After nearly seventeen years, the people of Clay County had grown accustomed to a climate of conspiracy and distrust. Their efforts on behalf of the gang were now commonplace, an everyday part of life. Not unlike measles or whooping cough, it was accepted as the natural order of things.

Lamar Hudspeth, no different from his neighbours, would have scoffed at the notion that he was aiding and abetting outlaws. The James boys were kinsmen, and the Youngers, with the possible exception of Cole, were old and valued friends. Honour dictated that he shield them from harm and forever take their part in the struggle against the Pinkertons. Tonight, as he had on past occasions, he had consented to let them meet in his home. He recognised the danger and gave it no more than passing consideration. They were, after all, family.

A short while after dark Jesse and Frank emerged from the woods north of the house. Hudspeth wasn't surprised, and while he'd denied it earlier, he knew Cole Younger was right all along. Jesse was a cautious man, forever leery of a trap; it was no accident he hadn't arrived on time for the meeting. Instead, waiting in the trees, he had probably watched the house since well before dusk. Hudspeth thought it a sensible precaution, if not altogether admirable. Yet there was no condemnation in the thought. He never judged a kinsman.

Jesse reined to a halt and swung down out of the saddle. He was lean, with stark features and a cleft chin and cold slate-coloured eyes. His beard was neatly trimmed, and he carried himself with the austere, straight-backed posture that bordered on arrogance. He was a man of dour moods and he seldom smiled. His natural expression was rocklike, wholly devoid of sentiment.

By contrast, Frank was courteous and thoughtful, with a warm smile and an affable manner. Quietly studious, he was self-educated and an ardent reader, especially partial to the works of Shakespeare. To the dismay of the other gang members, he liberally quoted the Bard whenever the occasion permitted. Among friends and family, it was an open secret that he supplied the wording for Jesse's articulate letters to the newspaper editors. Except for the dominance of his brother, he might have been a scholar, or a man of the cloth. He was, instead, an outlaw with a price on his head.

After a round of handshakes, Jesse cut his eyes towards the house. "Cole and the boys inside?"

Hudspeth nodded. "Cole's some put out 'cause you

wasn't here first. Hope there won't be any trouble."

"Cole's all wind and no whistle. He just likes to hear himself talk."

"Maybe so," Hudspeth said, without conviction. "He's on a tear tonight, though. Told me he'd had a bellyful and meant to get it out in the open."

"Bellyful of what?"

"Search me," Hudspeth responded. "I just listen, Jesse. I don't meddle."

"One of these days," Jesse said crossly, "I'm gonna fix his little red wagon for good."

"C'mon now, Jess," Frank gently admonished. "Cole doesn't mean any harm. He just flies off the handle every now and then, that's all. Besides, it wouldn't do to forget . . . you need him and the boys."

The men stood for a moment in a cone of silence. Then, to no one in particular, Hudspeth spoke. "Saw your ma today."

"Figured you might." Jesse's expression mellowed slightly. "She all right?"

"Tolerable," Hudspeth allowed. "Got herself a touch of rheumatism, and that's slowed her up some. Course, she ain't one to complain."

"No, it's not her way. How's Zee?"

Hudspeth looked down and studied the ground. "She asked me to pass along a message."

"Yeah?"

"She ain't happy with your ma, Jesse. One woman under another woman's roof puts a strain on everybody concerned. She asked me to tell you she wants a place of her own."

Jesse acted as though he hadn't heard. "Well," he said, after a measurable pause, "I guess we'd best get the meeting started. What with one thing and another, it's liable to take awhile."

Hudspeth pursed his lips, on the verge of saying something more. Then, reluctant to meddle, his gaze shifted to Frank. "Sorry I didn't get by to see Annie. Between chores and all, there just wasn't time enough."

"In our line of work," Frank said with a rueful smile, "wives learn to take catch as catch can. All the same, I'm planning to slip into home tonight when we're done here. I'll tell her you asked after her."

"Let's get on with it." Jesse started off, then turned back. "Lamar, you aim to keep a lookout while we're inside?"

"No need to fret," Hudspeth assured him. "Anybody comes along, I'll send the boy to fetch you lickety-split."

"What about Sarah?"

"She knows to stay in the kitchen. If you'll recollect, she never wanted to hear nothin' about your business anyhow."

With a querulous grunt, Jesse trudged off in the direction of the house. Frank traded glances with Hudspeth, then tagged along on his brother's heels. Upon entering the house, they found the Youngers seated around the parlour. Bob and Jim greeted them civilly enough, but Cole opted for brooding silence. An air of tension seemed to permeate the room.

No one spoke as Jesse hung his coat and hat on a wall peg beside the entrance. Without a word, he crossed the parlour and closed a door leading to the kitchen. Frank, fearing the worst, lowered himself into a rocker and began stuffing his pipe. Then, once more crossing the room, Jesse took a chair directly across from Cole. His eyes were metallic.

"I understand you've got your bowels in an uproar?"

"You understand right."

"Then spit it out, and be damn quick about it!"

Cole reddened, stung by his tone. An oak of a man,

with brutish features and a square jaw, the eldest of the Younger brothers was ruled by a volatile temper. Yet, where Jesse was concerned, his outbursts were generally of short duration. For years he had allowed himself to be intimidated by the gang leader's autocratic manner. His deference, though he had never admitted it to anyone, was due in no small part to fear. He knew Jesse would kill without pretext or provocation, the way a fox mindlessly slaughters a coop full of chickens. Tonight, however, he was determined to stand his ground. His jaw set in a bulldog scowl, and his gaze was steady.

"Me and the boys"—he motioned to his brothers—"are fed up! We want a bigger say in how this outfit's run. All the more so since you likely called us together to plan a job."

Jesse nailed him with a corrosive stare. "Suppose we leave Bob and Jim out of it. You're the one that's got a hair across his ass! So let's just keep it between ourselves."

"That ain't so," Cole corrected him. "We talked it out and we're of a mind. We've got to have more say so in how things are done."

"Don't make me laugh," Jesse's voice was alive with contempt. "The three of you together don't have brains enough to pour piss out of a boot. Without me to do your thinking for you, you'd starve to death in nothing flat."

"Bullfeathers!" Cole said defiantly. "We ain't been doing so hot with you! Our last couple of jobs was nickel-and-dime stuff. Keep on that way and we'll have to take up honest work to make a livin'."

"Quit bellyaching! You and the boys have done all right for yourselves."

"No, we ain't neither! You bollixed our last bank job and that train holdup last summer was a regular gawddamn disaster. All we done was kill a lot of people! And in case it slipped your mind, that ain't exactly the purpose in pullin' a robbery."

An evil light began to dance in Jesse's eyes. He glanced at Bob and Jim, and they seemed to cower before the menace in his gaze. Neither of them spoke, and their hangdog expressions evidenced little support for their brother. At length, Jesse swung back to Cole.

"Sounds like you've got some idea of moving me aside and stepping into my boots."

"Never said that," Cole protested. "All I'm sayin' is that we want a vote in the way things are handled."

"A vote!" Jesse fixed him with a baleful look. "We don't operate by ballot. Only one man around here calls the shots—and that's me!"

"Confound it, Jesse!" Cole said explosively. "That won't cut the ice no more. We're done takin' orders like we was a bunch of ninnies! Either you treat us square or else—"

"Don't threaten me." Jesse's tone was icy. "You do, and I'm liable to forget your name's Younger."

"Whoa back now!" Frank struck into the argument with a gentle rebuke. "You two keep on that way and we'll all wind up losers. Jesse, it wouldn't hurt anything to listen. Why not let Cole have his say?"

"Are you taking sides against me?"

Frank appraised his brother with a shrewd glance. "You ought to know better than to even ask such a thing. I'm just trying to get you to listen, that's all. We have to divvy up the same bone—so where's the harm?"

"Well . . ." Jesse said doubtfully. "I don't mind listening. I just don't want anybody telling me I don't know my business."

"Never said that either," Cole insisted. "But Frank hit the nail on the head. We ain't had a decent payday in a long gawddamn time, and it wouldn't hurt to take a new slant on things."

"A new slant?" Jesse repeated stiffly. "What's that supposed to mean?"

"For one thing," Cole explained, "we've got to give a little more thought to the Pinkertons. The way I see it, they pretty well got us euchred."

"Awww, for God's sake," Jesse said with heavy sarcasm. "You're crazy as a hoot owl! How long's it been since a Pinkerton set foot in Clay County?"

"Fat lotta good that does us! They've figured out we only operate in certain states and they've got everybody nervy as a cat in a roomful of rockers. We haven't hit one bank or one train in the last year that wasn't halfway expectin' to be robbed."

"So what's your idea? Should we start robbing poor boxes, candy stores—what?"

"No," Cole said with an unpleasant grunt. "I think we ought to consider explorin' new territory."

"Don't tell me," Jesse taunted him. "Let me guess. You've got just the place picked out—am I right?"

"Now that you mention it," Cole noted with vinegary satisfaction, "I stumbled across a real humdinger. A friend had some kinfolk move up there, and the way their letters read, the streets are paved with gold."

"Up where?"

"Minnesota," Cole informed him. "Northfield, Minnesota."

"You are nuts!" Jesse snorted. "What the hell's in Minnesota worth robbing?"

"A bank," Cole replied in a sandy voice. "I had my friend write his relatives—all nice and casual—and it turns out Northfield's smack-dab in the centre of things up that way. And there's only *one* bank. A big bank!"

"There's lots of big banks, and lots closer, too. Hell's

fire, Minnesota must be three hundred miles away, maybe more."

"I checked," Cole said without expression. "Northfield's right at four hundred miles from where we're sittin'."

"That corks it!" Jesse said, almost shouting. "Why in Christ's name would we ride four hundred miles to rob a bank?"

"Because it's the last place on earth the Pinkertons would expect us to hit. So far as I'm concerned, that's about the best reason there is. You stop and think on it, and you'll see I'm right."

A thick silence settled over the room. Jesse caught Frank's eye, and they exchanged a long, searching stare. Then, with a sombre look, Frank slowly bobbed his head.

"It makes sense, Jess. I never heard of Northfield, and I doubt that the Pinkertons have either. Matter of fact, it's so far out of our usual territory, they'd probably blame the job on someone else."

Jesse heaved himself to his feet. He began to pace around the parlour, hands stuffed in his pockets. No one spoke, and the tread of his footsteps seemed somehow oppressive in the stillness. After a time, he stopped, his head bowed, studying the floor. At last, as though to underline the question, he raised his head and looked Frank squarely in the eye.

"Are you voting with Cole?"

"Jesse—" Frank paused, weighing his words. "I couldn't vote one way or the other, not till we've got more details. I'm only saying the idea itself sounds good."

"All right," Jesse said in a resigned voice. "Here's the way we'll work it. Since Bob's the best scout we've got, he goes to Northfield to check the layout. I want to know everything there is to know about the bank and the town. And most especially, I want you to map out a step-by-step escape route to Belle Starr's place. You got that straight, Bob?"

"Sure do, Jesse." Bob grinned, sitting erect in his chair. "I'll leave first thing in the mornin'."

Jesse considered a moment. "I figure two weeks ought to do it. That'll push you a little, but not too bad. So unless I send word to the contrary, we'll all meet back here two weeks from tonight. Any questions?"

There were no questions. Jesse looked around the room, and his eyes were suddenly stern, commanding. "One last thing. Lay low and stay out of trouble. We don't want to draw attention to ourselves just before we pull a job." He paused, and added a blunt afterthought. "Cole, that goes for you more than the others. None of your monkeyshines down at Ma Ferguson's."

Cole darted a glance at Frank, then shrugged. "No nookie for two weeks? That's a pretty tall order."

"Tie a string on it and keep it in your pants."

"We ain't all got your willpower, Jesse."

"You've argued with me enough for one night. Just do like I say."

"Well, I'll give 'er a try. Yessir, I shore will!"

Jesse stared at him a moment. Then, nodding to Frank, he turned towards the door. With no word of parting, he shrugged into his coat and stepped into the night. Frank, trading one last look with Cole, dutifully tagged along.

The parlour suddenly seemed ominously quiet.

CHAPTER 9

Starbuck rode into Clay County on a bleak February evening. The sky was heavy with clouds and beneath it the frozen trees swayed in a polar wind. His destination was Ma Ferguson's roadhouse.

Upon returning from Indian Territory, he had laid over several days in Kansas City. The delay, though it had grated on him, was unavoidable. He'd needed time to perfect a disguise, and assume yet another identity. There was every reason to believe that the *Police Gazette*—which frequently carried articles about the James-Younger gang—was widely read in Clay County. His photo, which had appeared in the same publication, would have proved a dead giveaway. The upshot, were he to be recognised, was none too pleasant to contemplate. He wisely undertook a transformation in his appearance.

A theatrical supplier was his first stop. Kansas City was a crossroads for show companies, and the supplier stocked all manner of props and costumes. There, Starbuck obtained a bottle of professional hair dye, choosing dark nut-brown as a suitable contrast to his light chestnut mane. The proprietor assured him a dye job would last several weeks, barring a hard rain or any great penchant for hot baths. As an added touch, Starbuck also bought a spit-curled moustache of the same colour. Though fake, the moustache was quality work; even on close examination it looked to be the genuine article. A liberal application of spirit gum guaranteed it would remain glued to his upper lip.

While arranging the disguise, Starbuck had reviewed his mental catalogue on Clay County. From the Pinkerton file, he recalled that the Younger brothers were notorious womanisers. The James boys, for all their quickness with a gun, were faithful husbands and devoted family men. But the Youngers, particularly Cole, were known to frequent a brothel operated by one Ma Ferguson. Located outside the town of Liberty, the bawdy house was situated in the southwestern tip of the county, and apparently catered to the rougher element. Somewhat remote, lying on a back-country road between Kearney and Liberty, it was a place to be avoided by strangers. According to the Pinkerton file, it was considered a certain-death assignment for both law officers and private investigators. No undercover operative had ever attempted to infiltrate Ma Ferguson's cathouse.

Starbuck thought it the most likely place to start. For one thing, he would arouse less suspicion simply because the Pinkertons, for the last eight years, had steered clear of the dive. For another, it would allow him to observe the gang—perhaps strike up an acquaintance—when they were most vulnerable. Men intent on swilling booze and rutting with whores were almost certain to lower their guard. Then, too, the easygoing atmosphere of a brothel fitted nicely with his overall plan. Ma Ferguson's was but an initial step, a matter of establishing himself and gaining the confidence of the girls who worked there. His ultimate goal was to infiltrate the James-Younger gang itself.

Starbuck had devised a cock-and-bull story that was entirely plausible. He would pose as a horse thief—operating out of Dodge City—who was now on the run from Kansas lawmen. Dodge City, billing itself as the Queen of Cowtowns, was also the current horseflesh capital of the West. Along with the longhorn herds driven to railhead, thousands of horses were trailed up each year from Texas. Some were sold there; others were moved north, to distant markets in Montana and Wyoming. Horse thieves, like wolves sniffing fresh scent, had made Dodge City their headquarters. And therein lay his cover story. One thief, forced to take the owlhoot, would draw little in the way of curiosity. It was an occupational hazard, all part of the game. So common, in fact, that wanted posters were no longer circulated on horse thieves.

All that remained was to attract the attention of the Younger brothers. A high roller, throwing his money to the winds, would do for openers. Then, somewhere along the line, he would find a way to impress them, and gain their favour. Only then would they accept him as a thief who aspired to greater things, one who deserved their consideration. And only then, when he'd wormed his way into their ranks, would he get the chance he sought. A shot at Jesse James.

The plan entailed a high degree of risk. One slip—the slightest miscue—and he was a dead man. Yet, at the same time, his charade would represent the safest possible approach. The Youngers would never suspect that a private detective, alone and unaided, would invade their favourite whorehouse. Nor would they guess that his audacity was less invention than necessity. Try as he might, he'd thought of nothing else that would work in Clay County.

Shortly after nightfall, Starbuck rode into the yard of Ma Ferguson's place. The house was a large two-storey structure, brightly lighted and painted a dazzling white. He thought the colour an ironic choice—one seldom associated with ladies of negotiable virtue—and instantly pegged Ma Ferguson for a woman with a sense of humour. Stepping down from the saddle, he loosened the cinch and left the roan tied to a hitch rack out front. Then, dusting himself off, he strode boldly into the house.

The front room, as in most bordellos, was fashioned on the order of a parlour. Sofas and chairs were scattered at random, with a small bar in one corner and an upright piano along the far wall. The hour was still early, and only two customers, townsmen by their dress, were in evidence. The girls, nearly a dozen in number, lounged on the sofas while a black man with pearly teeth pounded out a tune on the piano. Ma Ferguson, a large, heavyset woman in her forties, was seated in an overstuffed armchair. She gave Starbuck's range clothes a slow once-over, then smiled and waved him to the bar.

"First one's on the house, dearie!"

"Thank you, ma'am." Starbuck doffed his Stetson and hooked it on a hatrack. "Don't mind if I do."

Walking forward, he halted at the bar and ordered rye. Before the barkeep finished pouring, a girl appeared at his elbow. Her eyelids were darkened with kohl and her cheeks were bright with rouge. She smiled a bee-stung smile.

"Hello there, handsome."

"Hello yourself." Starbuck gave her a burlesque leer. "Buy you a drink?"

"My mama taught me to never say no."

Starbuck laughed, his face wreathed in high good humour. "I shore hope that don't apply just to drinks."

"Why, honeybunch, you can bet your boots on it!"

The girl was a pocket Venus. She was small and saucy, with a gamine quality that was compellingly attractive. Her delicate features were framed by ash-blonde hair, and her wraparound housecoat fitted snuggly across fruity breasts and tightly rounded buttocks. She fixed him with a smile that would have melted the heart of a drill sergeant.

"Let me guess." Her eyes sparkled with suppressed mirth. "You're a cowboy, aren't you?"

"Close," Starbuck said with a waggish grin. "You might say I'm a horse trader."

"Nooo," she breathed. "Really?"

"Sometimes." Starbuck's grin broadened. "Course, it all depends."

"On what?"

"On whose horses we're tradin'."

She threw back her head and laughed. "Sweetie, I do like a man who likes a joke!"

"Well, little lady, I've got a hunch you're gonna like me lots."

"I'm Alvina." She leaned closer, squashing a breast against his arm. "What's your name . . . horse trader?"

"Floyd Hunnewell." Starbuck cocked one eye askew. "Fresh from Kansas and hot to trot."

"Then you've come to the right place, Floyd."

"Alvina, you shore know how to make a feller feel welcome."

"Honey, you haven't seen nothing yet!"

For the next two nights Starbuck played the braggart. He took a room at the hotel in Liberty; but he saw it only during daylight hours. By dark each evening, he was

Johnny-on-the-spot at Ma Ferguson's bordello. And his nights were spent in Alvina's bed.

Starbuck drank heavily, and flung money around as if he owned a printing press. The effect, considering the mercenary nature of his hostess, was somewhat predictable. Ma Ferguson accorded him the deferential treatment reserved for big spenders, and saw to it that his glass was never empty. She also allowed him to monopolise Alvina. The charge, which included sleeping over, was a mere twenty dollars a night.

Outwardly bluff and hearty, Starbuck acted the part with a certain panache. Sober, he appeared to be a happy-go-lucky drifter, with some mysterious, and inexhaustible, source of funds. With several drinks under his belt, he then turned garrulous, pretending the loose tongue of an amiable drunk. Whores were accustomed to braggarts who seemed possessed of some irresistible urge to toot their horn and confide their innermost secrets. So Alvina found nothing unusual in Floyd Hunnewell's boastful manner, and she dutifully portrayed the spellbound listener. He told her a tale of outlandish proportions.

Improvising as he went along, Starbuck intertwined fact with fabrication. His story, unfolding in bits and pieces, was recounted with an air of drunken self-importance. A Texan born and bred, he'd worked as a cowhand since boyhood. Over the years, he had trailed herds to every cowtown on the Kansas plains. Then, after last summer's drive to Dodge City, he awoke to the fact that he was getting no younger, and no richer. Determined to make something of himself, he looked over the field and decided that horse stealing was an enterprise with real potential. For the past seven months, he had averaged better than fifty head a month, and it was all profit. In total, he had cleared more than ten thousand

and no end in sight. A minor error in judgement had put the law on his tail, but that was no great calamity. He could afford to lie low and let the dust settle. Meanwhile, he was scouting around for a new venture, something befitting a man of his talents. Horse stealing, he'd decided, was too easy. A fellow who wanted to get ahead had to raise his sights—aim higher!

Alvina bought the story. It was, after all, no great shocker. Cowhands turned outlaw were fairly commonplace, and a horse thief in her bed was no cause for excitement. She'd slept with worse—lots worse—and never given it a thought. Yet she hadn't slept with anyone lately who was as much fun as Floyd Hunnewell. For all his crowing and cocksure conceit, he was damned likable. And to her surprise, he was a regular ball of fire in bed. The last couple of nights, she'd actually found herself enjoying it. Which was something to ponder.

To Starbuck, it was all in a day's work. Alvina was good company—gullible like most whores—and he was pleased that she'd swallowed his fairy tale so readily. But that wasn't the reason he had selected her over the other girls, and stuck with her for two nights running. Instead, he'd zeroed in on her because she was by far the prettiest girl in Ma Ferguson's henhouse. Some gut instinct told him that her pert good looks would make her the favourite of one or more of the Younger brothers. By and by, he meant to turn that to advantage.

Late the third evening, Starbuck was seated on one of the sofas with Alvina. They were talking quietly, sipping whiskey, but his mind was elsewhere. The thought occurred that he might be in for a long wait. So far there had been no sign of the Youngers, and he'd heard no mention of their name. For all he knew, they might have taken their trade to another whorehouse. Or even worse, they could be off robbing a bank—and ready to hightail it for the Nations. By his count, they were already some months overdue at Belle Starr's. Still, there was nothing for it but to curb his impatience and wait it out. Time would tell, and meanwhile Alvina was a pleasant enough diversion. A damn sight more pleasant than that axe-faced bitch he'd wooed at Younger's Bend.

Alvina suddenly stiffened. She caught her breath in a sharp gasp and stared past him towards the door. He turned and saw three men enter the parlour. Though no photographs or drawings existed, the men fitted the general description of the Younger brothers. One of them separated, walking in the direction of the sofa while the other two continued on to the bar. He was powerfully built, with a pockmarked face, coarse sandy hair, and the bulge of a pistol beneath his coat. He halted, nodding to Alvina.

"How's things?"

"Fine." Alvina appeared flustered. "You haven't been around much lately."

"Well, I'm here now. C'mon, we'll have a drink and get ourselves caught up."

"Cousin," Starbuck interrupted politely. "You've done stopped at the wrong pew. The lady's taken for the night."

"Who says?"

"I reckon I do." Starbuck uncoiled slowly and got to his feet. " 'Specially since I paid for the privilege."

"The night's young. You just get in line, and when I'm done, she's all yours."

Starbuck sensed opportunity, and seized it. "Cousin, you must've heard wrong—"

"I've heard all I wanna hear! Close your trap or I'll close it for you."

"Say, looky here." A cocked sixgun emerged like a magician's dove from inside Starbuck's jacket. He scowled, and wagged the tip of the barrel. "I don't much cotton to threats. Suppose you just haul it out of here before I get tempted to make your asshole wink."

"Omigawd!" Alvina jumped to her feet. "Floyd, put it away! Please, honey, I'm asking—"

"Why the hell should I?"

"Because," Alvina whispered, touching his arm. "That's Jim Younger! The big one at the bar is Cole Younger, and the other one is Clell Miller. They'll kill you if you don't back off!"

"Younger?" Starbuck gave her a look of walleyed amazement. "Are you talkin' about *the* Younger brothers?"

"In the flesh," Alvina acknowledged. "Now cool down and play it smart! Like he told you, the night's young."

Starbuck shook his head in mock wonder. Then he lowered the hammer and slowly holstered the Colt. With a lame smile, he glanced at Jim Younger.

"Any friend of Alvina's is a friend of mine."

Younger grunted, and roughly pushed Alvina towards the door. Without a word, she led the way into the hall and they mounted the stairs to the second floor. Starbuck watched after them a moment, trying his damnedest to look unnerved and properly chastised. After a time his gaze shifted to the bar, and he found himself pinned by Cole Younger's stare. He grinned weakly and walked forward, halting a pace away.

"No offence." He stuck out his hand. "Name's Floyd Hunnewell, and I shore don't want no trouble with the Youngers."

Cole ignored the handshake. "You're pretty sudden with a gun."

"Wisht I wasn't sometimes."

Cole regarded him evenly. "You keep pullin' guns on

people and somebody's liable to give you a try."

"Hope there's no hard feelings." Starbuck looked painfully embarrassed. "I'd shore admire to buy you a drink, Mr. Younger."

"I guess not," Cole said bluntly. "We're sort of choosy about who we drink with."

"Well, maybe another time. I wouldn't want you to think I was unsociable, Mr. Younger."

"I'll keep it in mind."

Starbuck turned and walked back to the sofa. He was conscious of Ma Ferguson's beady glare and an almost palpable sense of tension among the girls. With a hang-dog expression, he took out the makings and began rolling a smoke. He made a show of nervously spilling tobacco, and took two tries to light a match. Yet inside he was laughing, positively jubilant.

By sheer outhouse luck, he'd made an impression the Youngers would never forget. The suddenness of his draw—his willingness to resort to gunplay—all that would stick in their minds. Then, too, there was Alvina. Even now, she was probably spilling his story to Jim Younger. And soon enough the word would circulate. Floyd Hunnewell was a wanted man, a horse thief with his eye on bigger things.

All in all, Starbuck thought he'd made a helluva start.

CHAPTER 10

"We've got ourselves a real stem-winder this time!"

"Why's that?"

"Have a look and you'll see."

Bob Younger, recently returned from Minnesota, unfolded a hand-drawn map. The men were gathered around the dining table in the Hudspeth home. Jesse and Frank sat at opposite ends of the table, with Cole on one side and Bob, flanked by Jim, on the other. Bob spread the map in the middle of the table, and everyone leaned forward for a better look. A series of lines, radiating outward like spokes in a wheel, converged on a central spot. He pointed with his finger.

"Here's Northfield. This wavy line's the Cannon River. Whoever named it ought've called it the curlycue. Crookedest sonovabitch you ever saw!"

Jesse glanced up. "What's so important about a river?"

"Oh, nothin' much." Bob smiled lazily. "It just splits Northfield clean down the middle, that's all."

"You're saying the town's divided by the river?"

"See that mark?" Bob indicated two parallel lines. "That's the Northfield Bridge. The river runs roughly north-south and the bridge crosses it east to west. Separates the town pretty near half and half."

"So how's the town laid out?"

"Well, it's mostly houses on the west side of the bridge. Then you cross the bridge headed east and you come out smack-dab on the town square. That's the main business centre, with a few stores and some such off on these side streets. On beyond that, there's more houses."

"Sounds like a fair-sized town."

"You ain't whistlin' Dixie!" Bob's mouth curled. "I had a few drinks in one of the bars, and got cosy with some of the locals. They told me the town's pushin' five thousand and still growin' strong."

No one spoke for several moments. Cole Younger, already briefed by his brother, sat without expression, waiting. Frank shot him a sidewise glance, then quickly looked away. Jesse stared at the map a long while, his features unreadable. Then, almost to himself, he finally broke the silence.

"That's considerable bigger than anything we ever tackled before."

"Bigger haul, too!" Cole said stoutly. "Wait'll Bob tells you about the bank."

"What about it?"

Bob leaned back, thumbs hooked importantly in his suspenders. "Them locals I talked to was regular civic boosters. Told me the bank was just about the biggest in southern Minnesota. Hell, it's even got a highfalutin name—the First National Bank!"

"Forget the name." Jesse gave him a sour look. "How's it fixed for money?"

"Plumb loaded!" Bob let loose a hoot of laughter. "Them barflies said it's got a vault the size of a barn. And they wasn't lyin' either! I meandered over and had a look for m'self."

"You checked out the bank?"

"Figgered I might as well. It was a Saturday, and the town was crawlin' with farmers and their families. I just joined the crowd and waltzed in there nice as you please."

"Tell him about the vault," Cole prompted. "What you saw."

"Well, now!" Bob snapped his suspenders and grinned. "The people was lined up three deep and depositin' money hand over fist. Seems like Saturday is the day all the farmers and folks from neighbourin' towns does their business. You never saw nothin' like it in all your born days!"

"The vault," Jesse reminded him. "Did you get a look or not?"

"I did for certain! The door was standin' wide open, and you could've drove a wagon through the inside with room to spare. Ever' wall was lined with shelves and drawers, and the whole kit 'n' caboodle was stacked knee deep with money. Goddamnedest sight I ever laid eyes on!"

"How much would you estimate?" Jesse eyed him keenly. "Just a rough calculation?"

"Well, don't you see—" Bob spread his hands in an expansive gesture. "Folks come from all over to do their bankin' there 'cause it'd take a cannon to blow the door off that vault. The locals told me nobody'd ever tried a holdup. Not once!"

"Answer the question," Cole said with weary tolerance. "You done told me and Jim. Now tell Jesse. How much?"

Bob swallowed, licked his lips. "I'd judge two hundred thousand. As God's my witness, Jesse—not a penny less!"

Jesse shoved his chair from the table. He rose and

without a word walked to the parlour, where he began pacing back and forth in front of the fireplace. Silence thickened at the table, and the men tracked him to and fro with their eyes. His head was bowed, thinking private thoughts, and a minute or longer passed before he suddenly stopped. Then he turned and moved once more to the table, standing behind his chair. His expression was sombre, and determined.

"I don't like it." He punctuated the statement with a vigorous gesture. "There's got to be a reason that bank's never been robbed. Somebody would've tried—especially with all that money layin' around—unless there was a damn good reason. I say we scotch the idea right here and now."

"No!" Cole's jaw jutted stubbornly. "We've waited a lifetime for this kind of payday. Just because nobody else has busted that bank don't mean it can't be done. And that sure as hell ain't no reason for us not to try!"

Jesse was very quiet, eyes boring into him. "Cole, I've spoke my piece. I say it's a washout, and that's that."

Cole's bushy eyebrows seemed to hood his gaze. "Last time we met, I told you the Youngers wouldn't play tin soldier no more. That goes double after hearin' what Bob saw at Northfield."

"Suppose you spell that out a little plainer?"

"Since you asked—" Cole smiled with veiled mockery. "We're fed up with nickel-and-dime jobs, and we're through playin' it safe. If you haven't got the stomach for Northfield, then we'll handle it our own selves."

A stony look settled on Jesse's face. "You sorry goddamn ingrate! I ought to kill you where you sit."

"Maybe you ought to," Cole challenged him, "but you won't. The way it stands now, you'd have to fight all us Youngers—not just one."

"Don't tempt me! Haulin' your ashes might make it worth it!"

Cole flipped his hand in scorn. "You love yourself too much for that, Jesse. So I don't guess I'm gonna lose any sleep over it."

"By Christ—!"

"Not Christ," Frank interrupted, clearing his throat. "To quote the Bard: 'Hell is empty and all the devils are here.' You two make the line sound prophetic."

Jesse and Cole stared at him blankly. When neither of them responded, he went on. "Why in thunder do you have to fight? We've got enough enemies without turning on one another." He paused, then continued in a temperate voice. "Jess, I'm not taking sides; but you have to face the facts. Unless you bend a little, Cole and the boys will take off on their own. Once it comes to that, we'll likely never get it healed. So maybe you ought to make allowances. We've been together a long time."

Jesse was white around the mouth, his temples knotted. Yet he held his temper, avoiding Frank's steady look, and gave the matter some thought. "All right," he said finally, squaring himself up. "We'll lay out the job and get on with it. But once we're in Northfield—if it don't smell right or anything looks queer, I'll call it off and no questions asked. That's as far as I'm willin' to bend, no farther. So take it or leave it."

The Younger brothers swapped quick glances among themselves. At length, Cole nodded and swivelled his head just far enough to meet Jesse's venomous glare. "I guess we could go along with that. You always said Bob was the best scout in the bunch, and Northfield didn't give him the willies. Don't expect it will you either. Specially when you get a gander at the vault."

"If we get that far," Jesse said, watching him with

undisguised hostility. "Just remember, once we're there, I call the tune as to whether or not we hit the bank. That's the deal."

"You want a blood oath?" Cole cracked a smile. "Or will my word do?"

Jesse let the remark pass. He seated himself, then reached out and pulled the map closer. "Bob, show me the layout. Let's start with the bank."

"Sure thing, Jesse." Bob leaned forward, explaining various marks on the map. "The bank's over here at the east end of the square. Sits right on a corner, where the square leads into Division Street. I figgered the best approach was to come into town from the east—that means we'd be headed west on Division Street—and stop right in front of the bank. That way we can cover the square without exposing ourselves, and we've got nothin' behind us but a few stores. When the job's done, we just turn around and ride out the same way we came in. It's the shortest and safest route, near as I could tell."

"The shortest, maybe." Jesse studied the map with a critical eye. "Not necessarily the safest."

"I don't follow you."

"Your way we've only got one line of retreat. If we were discovered—and these shopkeepers back here on Division Street got up in arms—then we'd be caught between them and the ones on the square. In other words, they'd have us trapped in a bottleneck. I can't say I'd care too much for that idea."

"By gum, you got a point there."

"Where's the town marshal's office?"

"Over here." Bob pointed with a dirty fingernail. "Off the south side of the square, just round the corner."

"Which means he steps out his door and he's roughly kitty-corner to the bank."

"Yeah, I reckon it does."

"What's along the other sides of the square?"

"Oh, just the general run of business and shops. Couple of cafés and that saloon I mentioned. A hotel over on the north side, right about in the middle of the block. Course, down here, on the west side, there's not much of anything. Don't you see, that leads directly to the bridge."

"How wide is the bridge?"

"Well, it'll take two wagons abreast. Looked like they built it specially for the farm trade."

"Across the river"—Jesse directed his attention to the western shoreline—"you show a road headed south. What's down that way?"

"Nothin' much. The road generally follows the river, and a couple of miles south there's a crossroads called Dundas. After that, you hit a long stretch of woods. Then maybe ten miles south there's a fair-sized town called Faribault."

"What's west of those woods?"

"I brought back maps of Minnesota and Iowa. You want me to show you in detail?"

"Later," Jesse said shortly. "For now, just tell me about those woods."

"To the west, there's more of the same. Broken woods, with marshy terrain and lots of small lakes. Due west—maybe thirty miles—there's a town called St. Peter and southwest there's one called Mankato."

Jesse abruptly switched back to the Northfield Bridge. "From here, are there any telegraph lines runnin' south?"

"No, there ain't." Bob pondered a moment. "I guess the towns are too small down that way. Near as I recollect, the poles all took a northerly direction—to Minneapolis."

"Thought so," Jesse said, almost to himself. "Now tell me about the bank. How's it laid out inside?"

Bob took a stub pencil from his coat pocket. Turning the map over, he began sketching a diagram on the opposite side. Watching them, Cole marvelled at Jesse's tactical genius. Always the guerrilla commander, he saw any job along the lines of a military raid. Before an actual date was set for the job, he would have worked out every detail, including their route to Minnesota and the order of retreat once they'd robbed the bank. However grudgingly, Cole had to admit there were none the equal of Jesse James when it came to planning a holdup. The end result would be a textbook study in how to rob a bank and make a clean getaway. All without losing a man or exposing themselves to unnecessary risk.

After studying the floor plan of the bank, Jesse flipped over to the map. He briefly scanned the drawing of Northfield, then nodded to himself in affirmation.

"Here's the way I see it." His finger stabbed out at the map. "That bridge is the key point. Once we occupy it and hold it, we have a clear field of fire that covers the entire square. On top of that, our best line of retreat is south along the road to that stretch of woods. So everything hinges on taking control of the bridge."

"Lemme understand," Cole said, hunching forward for a look at the map. "You're sayin' somebody posted at the bridge could keep the townspeople pinned down while we're in the bank. Is that it?"

"Yeah, that's the first step. Course, we'll also need covering fire when we leave the bank and head back across the square. So like I said—that bridge has got to be held the whole time."

"No question there," Cole agreed. "What about the bank itself?"

"We'll split up into groups." Jesse tapped the map with his finger. "One at the bridge and another outside the bank. Between them, they'll have the square covered in a crossfire from one end to the other. Once they're in place, the third group will enter the bank and pull the job."

"Hold on!" Cole protested. "That'll split us up pretty thin, won't it?"

"Normally it would," Jesse said levelly. "Except I'm figurin' on eight men altogether. Three at the bridge, two outside the bank, and three more inside. With the size of the town, and the way it's laid out, I wouldn't try it with any less."

"So you're talkin' about three more besides ourselves?"

"That's the general idea."

"Well, I don't like it! That means we're gonna have to divvy out eight shares instead of five."

"Either we do it right or we don't do it at all. It'll take eight men to make certain we hold that bridge. And without the bridge—I'm not settin' foot in Northfield!"

"Whereabouts you figure to get 'em? There ain't a helluva lot of men I'd trust to cover my backsides."

"What about Clell Miller?" Bob suggested. "He pulled his weight on that last train job."

"Don't forget Charlie Pitts," Jim added quickly. "He's no slouch either."

"I suppose they'll do," Cole grumbled. "Now try thinkin' of another one that's worth his salt! All the good ones are dead or else they've turned tame as tabby cats."

"Not all," Frank said with a slow grin. "The way Jim tells it, there's a fellow down at Ma Ferguson's who acts more like a bobcat."

"Awww, hell, Frank!" Jim groaned. "I told you that private. Besides, he sucked wind quick enough when push came to shove."

"Only because you had Cole and Clell Miller to back your play."

"Wait a minute," Jesse broke in. "Who're you talkin' about?"

"Some stranger." Jim shrugged it off. "Him and me got into it over a girl, and he pulled a gun. Wasn't all that much to it."

"Tell me anyway," Jesse persisted. "Who is he? What d'you know about him?"

"He's a small-time horse thief. Alvina, that's the girl, told me the law run him out of Kansas. Way he acts, he's had lots of experience runnin'."

"Bullfeathers!" Frank laughed. "You told me he got the drop on you so fast you never knew what happened. Anybody that handy with a gun, maybe we ought to consider him for the third man."

"God a'mighty!" Cole blustered. "You got rocks in your head, Frank. The man's an outsider."

"Cole, answer me this," Jesse said in a cold, dry manner. "What were you doing at Ma Ferguson's in the first place? I thought we agreed you'd stay clear of there."

"No such thing!" Cole muttered. "I told you I'd stay out of trouble—and I did!"

"The hell you did! A man pullin' a gun sounds like the kind of trouble we could do without."

"Jesus Christ! He pulled on Jim, not me!"

Jesse eyed him in disgust. "Maybe Frank's right. We could use some new blood in this outfit. 'Specially a rooster that'd pull on the Youngers."

"Whoa back, Jesse." Frank gave a troubled look. "I was only joking around. Why take it out on Cole?"

"Why not?" Jesse said with heavy sarcasm. "Anybody Cole don't like probably deserves a second look. You go on down to Ma Ferguson's and check out this horse thief. He might be just the man we need."

"You're makin' a mistake," Cole said sullenly. "And

you know goddamn well you're only doing it to spite me."

"C'mon now!" Jesse mocked him. "You mean to say you don't trust Frank's judgement?"

"That ain't what we're talkin' about here."

"What are we talkin' about, then?"

"The same old thing." Cole's jaw muscles worked. "Who beats the drum and who winds up playin' tin soldier."

"Cole, I do believe you got the message."

"You're liable to thump your drum one of these days and nobody'll answer muster."

A ferocious grin lit Jesse's face. "There's lots of tin soldiers, Cole. But I'm the only one that's got a drum . . . and I aim to keep it!"

CHAPTER 11

"You shouldn't be so impatient, lover."

"Hell, I need some action! Fun's fun, but a steady diet of it don't suit my style."

"Thanks a lot!" Alvina crinkled her nose in a pout. "You sure know how to make a girl feel special."

"Holy moly!" Starbuck rolled his eyes upward. "I done spent six nights in a row with you! If that don't make you special, I shore as the devil don't know what would."

"A little sweet talk wouldn't hurt. You were full of it up until tonight."

"Yeah, you're right." Starbuck's tone was grumpy, out of sorts. "It's just that a feller goes stale after a while. Not that you ain't good company! I got no complaints on that score, none a 'tall. But it's like I'm gettin' itchy—and don't know where to scratch."

"Ooo." Alvina clucked sympathetically, kissed him softly on the cheek. "Don't get down in the mouth, sweetie. I told you I'd talk to Jim, and I will. Cross my heart!"

"Probably won't do no good," Starbuck said glumly. "Them Youngers ain't the friendliest bunch I ever run acrost."

"You leave it to me," Alvina assured him brightly. "Jim Younger thinks more of me than he does his own wife! One way or another, I'll convince him to at least talk to you."

"Well, I shore as hell wisht he'd show again! I'm plumb tuckered out with sittin' on my duff."

Starbuck's gruff manner was no act. Seated beside Alvina on a sofa, he watched listlessly as the evening crowd began drifting into Ma Ferguson's. The ivory tickler was playing a melancholy tune on the piano, and it somehow suited his mood. For the past three nights— since the evening he'd braced Jim Younger—he had planted himself on the sofa and waited. Some inner conviction told him the Youngers would return, and he'd kept himself steeled to take the next step in his plan. Yet tonight his conviction was waning rapidly. Unless the outlaws put in an appearance soon, then it was all wishful thinking. Not a plan but rather a pipe dream. He dully wondered if he'd sold himself a bill of goods.

"Don't you worry, Floyd." Alvina lowered one eyelid in a bawdy wink. "Where Jim Younger's concerned, I'm the hottest stuff in Clay County! He couldn't stay away if his life depended on it."

"Looks like he's making a pretty good stab at it."

"Oh, pshaw! You know what my mama used to say?"

"What's that?"

"She used to say, 'Worry is the curse of those who borrow trouble.' "

"I ain't worried," Starbuck grumbled. "It's like I told you—I'm just tryin' to scratch that itch."

"Well, I can't see why you're so stuck on becoming a bank robber anyway. The notion probably wouldn't have occurred to you in a thousand years if you hadn't bumped into the Youngers the other night."

"Who knows? I was lookin' for a new line of work

and they just happened along at the right time. Nothing ventured, nothing gained."

"From what Jim tells me, they've ventured a lot and gained a little here lately. Talk about a bunch that needs a rabbit's foot!"

"He tells you all his secrets, does he?"

Alvina giggled and batted her eyelashes. "Honey, you just wouldn't believe it! I told you he was sweet on me."

"So their luck's turned sour, then?"

"Let's say they're not exactly rolling in clover."

"Hell, maybe you're right," Starbuck said guilefully. "Maybe robbin' banks ain't what it's cracked up to be."

"Feast or famine, that's the way it looks to me."

"I guess I could always go back to Kansas. Things have likely cooled off by now, and horse stealing ain't all that bad. Least it's regular work."

"Floyd!" Alvina looked wounded. "You said you liked it here!"

"I do," Starbuck said earnestly. "That's why I asked you to put in the word with Younger. But now, you sound like you're tryin' to talk me out of it."

"No, I'm not!" Alvina snuggled closer on the sofa. "You just put Kansas out of your mind. And stop worrying about Jim Younger! I'm one girl that doesn't go back on a promise."

Starbuck felt only a twinge of conscience. He had purposely set out to win her over, and six nights in her bed had proved adequate to the job. He'd treated her with gentleness and affection, and seen to it that their lovemaking was a thing of ardour rather than passionless rutting. All of which was like catnip to a working whore. She'd fallen for him very much in the manner of a schoolgirl surrendering her virginity. And recruiting her to his cause had been accomplished with surpassing ease.

Having failed in his approach to Cole Younger, he'd thought to hedge his bet with Alvina. Her assistance created a couple of intriguing possibilities. For openers, she was a veritable fund of information. As she herself had noted, men often confided more in whores than in their own wives. Apparently that was the case with Jim Younger, and whatever tidbits she gleaned would be a welcome addition to the file. Of greater import, she claimed some influence over Younger. In the event she persuaded him to vouch for Floyd Hunnewell, then the larger part of the problem would be resolved. One recommendation would lead to another, forming a daisy chain that would ultimately lead to Jesse James. From there, it would remain but a matter of time—and opportunity.

Starbuck by no means felt sanguine. Alvina might prove an asset, and then again her efforts might very well come to nothing. Yet, from his standpoint, there was everything to gain, with little or no risk of exposing his hand. She was an unwitting operative—undercover in every sense of the word—and more valuable for it. Should she prove ineffective, then it would have cost him nothing more than six nights of ardent lovemaking. And in all truth, the expenditure had required no labour. He'd thoroughly enjoyed himself.

"See!" Alvina suddenly hissed out of the corner of her mouth. "I told you he couldn't stay away!"

She popped off the sofa and hurried towards the door. As Starbuck watched, she greeted Jim Younger with an exuberant laugh and a teasing peck on the mouth. Behind him, crowding through the doorway, were Cole and two other men. One of them, not unlike the third pea in a pod, was clearly Bob Younger. The other newcomer was slimmer of build, somewhat gangling, with a determined jaw and a neatly trimmed beard. Something about him bothered Starbuck. A wisp of recognition that was at once familiar and elusive.

The men walked to the bar, with Alvina hanging on Jim Younger's arm. None of them so much as glanced at Starbuck, and he pretended to mind his own business. After a couple of drinks, Jim ordered a bottle from the barkeep; with Alvina in tow, he excused himself and led her towards the hallway. Cole, his voice loud and boisterous, subjected them to a coarse ribbing as they crossed the parlour. Arm in arm, ignoring his jibes, they disappeared up the stairs. Cole laughed uproariously and turned back to his companions. He whacked the bar, ordering a fresh round of drinks.

Several minutes later, the bearded man abruptly shoved away from the bar. He walked directly to the sofa and halted. His eyes were friendly but sharp, very sharp. He nodded to Starbuck.

"Mind if I sit down?"

"Help yourself, cousin. It's a free country."

Starbuck had a feral instinct for the truth. His every sense alerted, and he warned himself to play it loose. For some reason as yet unrevealed, he was about to be put to the test. He knew he dare not fail.

"I'm told," the man said tentatively, "you go by the name of Floyd Hunnewell?"

"You're told right," Starbuck said with a raffish smile. "Appears you've got the advantage on me."

"Most folks call me Frank."

"Well, I'll be jiggered!" Starbuck gave him a look of unalloyed amazement. "I ain't no mental wizard, but my ma didn't raise no dimdots neither. Something tells me you got a brother named Jesse."

Frank gazed at him for a long, speculative moment. "Let's talk about you. I understand you're from Kansas?"

"Now and then," Starbuck said, grinning. "The rest of the time I'm a Texican—and damn proud of it!"

"Strayed a mite far north, haven't you?"

Starbuck regarded him with an expression of amusement. "Women shore do talk, don't they?"

"How so?"

"Why don't we skip the guessin' game? Seems pretty clear Alvina spilled the beans to Jim Younger, and now he's put the bee in your ear. So it boils down to you askin' questions when you already know the answers."

"You're right." Frank smiled genially. "Your ma didn't raise any dimdots."

"Only one thing troubles me." Starbuck leaned back, legs casually stretched out before him. "Why're you askin' me any questions at all?"

"You could be a Pinkerton." Frank let the idea percolate a few moments. "A stranger appears out of nowhere and passes himself off as a horse thief. If you were in my boots—wouldn't that tend to make you leery?"

"*Pinkerton!*" Starbuck said wonderingly. "I been called lots of things in my time, but never nothin' that lowdown. Course, you wasn't exactly accusin' me"—he paused for effect—"or was you?"

Frank smiled in spite of himself. "Fast as you are with a gun, that'd be pushing my luck pretty far, wouldn't it?"

"Shore do regret that." Starbuck chuckled, stealing a glance at the bar. "Guess the Youngers was some put out, huh?"

"No harm done. Jim has a habit of crowding people when he shouldn't. Nobody faults you for pulling a gun . . . so long as you don't do it again."

"In that case—" Starbuck raised an uncertain eyebrow. "How come you and me are sittin' here playing ring-around-the-rosy?"

Frank cocked his head and studied Starbuck thoughtfully. "Jim was naturally curious, especially after you threw down on him so quick. He twisted Alvina's arm and she let it drop that you're on the run. Any truth to it?"

Starbuck wormed around on the sofa and flexed his shoulders. "I'll have to have m'self a talk with Alvina. Her arm twists a little too easy—regular goddamn blabbermouth!"

"She also said you're on the scout for a new line of work."

"So?"

"Wondered why," Frank said almost idly. "You seem to have done fairly well in the horse business."

"Simple enough," Starbuck said lightly. "I don't aim to scratch a poor man's ass all my life. There's ways to make lots more money—and lots faster, too!"

Frank gave him a swift, appraising glance. "Got anything particular in mind?"

"Why?" Starbuck asked, deadpan. "You offerin' me a job?"

"What if I was?"

"I'd still ask why. You don't know me from a hole in the ground, and I ain't exactly in your league. See what I mean?"

"Everybody has to start somewhere."

"That's a fact," Starbuck said slowly. "Howsoever, not everybody starts at the top. Sort of makes me wonder whether you're testin' the water—or what?"

The shadow of a question clouded Frank's eyes, then moved on. "Why don't you sit tight for a minute? I want to have a word with Cole."

Starbuck's expression revealed nothing. Yet he was

astonished by the turn of events, searching for a reason where none seemed to exist. Frank rose, nodding to him, and walked to the bar. The conversation with Cole Younger was short, and heated.

"I sounded him out," Frank commenced guardedly, "and he strikes me as being on the level."

Cole nailed him with a sharp, sidelong look. "You're not serious—are you?"

"Why not?" Frank temporised. "He's smart and he's had experience dodging the law. And you saw for yourself, he's no tyro with a gun."

"Come off it!" Cole demanded churlishly. "The bastard's an outsider! I don't want no part of it."

"Then why are we here?"

" 'Cause I didn't want no trouble with Jesse! Besides, it gimme me a chance to get my wick dipped."

Frank's face grew overcast. "I think you're being shortsighted, Cole. We could use a good man on this job, and Hunnewell seems to fit the ticket."

"No sale!" Cole's headshake was emphatic. "I won't work with a stranger. You give him the nod and you can count me out! That goes for the boys, too."

Cole turned away, ending the discussion. He signalled Bob, and in short order they had each selected a girl. Without another word to Frank, they stalked from the parlour, trailed by a couple of blowzy whores, and mounted the stairs. Frank appeared slightly bemused, staring after them for several seconds. Then, with a hopeless shrug, he walked back to the sofa.

"Sorry, Hunnewell." He rocked his head from side to side. " 'The nature of bad news infects the teller.' "

"Come again?"

"A line from Shakespeare." Frank lifted his hands with a sallow smile. "I thought we could find a spot for you, but it seems I was mistaken. Maybe next time."

"Next time?" Starbuck repeated, genuinely confused. "What's that supposed to mean?"

"A figure of speech," Frank said evasively. "There's always a next time and a time after that. See you around."

· On that cryptic note, Frank moved into the hallway and out the door. Starbuck simply sat there, stunned. He hadn't the least notion of what had transpired or why. Yet there was one thing about which he was utterly certain. He'd just been blackballed for membership in the James-Younger gang.

Late that night Alvina joined him in the parlour. The Younger brothers, drunk and raucous, had departed only a short while before. She looked some the worse for wear, sombre and somehow distracted. With a heavy sigh, she dropped beside him on the sofa.

"Well, lover." She smiled wanly. "How's things with you?"

"Slow." Starbuck's smile was equally bleak. "Mighty slow."

"Sorry," Alvina apologised. "I couldn't get rid of him. Usually he doesn't drink all that much; but there wasn't anything usual about tonight. He damn near killed that whole bottle."

"Forget it," Starbuck said darkly. "You got a job to do, and nobody's blamin' you for that."

Alvina studied his downcast face. "Aren't you going to ask me what happened?"

"Happened with what?"

"With Jim Younger," Alvina reminded him. "I was supposed to talk to him . . . remember?"

"Oh, yeah." Starbuck seemed to lose interest. "How'd it go?"

"It didn't! The bastard got drunk as a skunk and I never had a chance to sound him out."

"Don't matter," Starbuck said miserably. "Too late anyway."

"Too late?" Alvina parroted. "Too late for what?"

"Too late for me!" Starbuck's tone suddenly turned indignant. "Frank James halfway gave mc an invite to join up with 'em. Then Cole Younger put the quietus on it so fast it'd make your head swim. I was in and out before I knew what hit me!"

"Jeezus!" Alvina murmured. "You've had yourself some night, honeybun!"

"I suppose you could say that."

"Well, at least I know why Cole nixed you."

"You do?"

Alvina gave him a bright nod. "They're planning a job. That's why I couldn't get a word in edgewise with Jim. He got drunk and bragged himself blue in the face." She hesitated, put a hand on his arm. "Don't blame yourself, lover. As big as this job sounds, Cole wouldn't risk breaking in a new man."

"Just my luck." Starbuck suppressed a sudden jolt of excitement. "How big . . . or didn't he say?"

"Oh, he said all right! To hear him tell it, they'll all retire when this one's over."

"Sounds like an express-car job."

"No, it's a bank. A real *big* bank."

"Wouldn't you know it!" Starbuck cursed, slumped back on the sofa. "Whereabouts? Not that it matters a whole helluva lot."

An indirection came into Alvina's eyes. "North-something-or-other. I think he said Northfield. Or maybe Northville. Tell you the truth, I wasn't listening too close. What a girl don't know can't hurt her."

Starbuck chanced one last question. "Northfield? Hell,

that don't sound so big to me. Where's it at?"

"Search me, lover. He didn't say and I didn't ask! All night he just kept saying it was going to surprise the living bejesus out of the Pinkertons."

"Wonder what he meant by that?"

"Who knows?" Alvina murmured wearily. "You'll pardon my French . . . but I really don't give a fuck anyhow."

Starbuck knew then he would learn no more. Yet, with luck, he thought perhaps he'd learned enough. The germ of an idea took shape in his mind, and his pulse quickened. A bank, more so than most places, would make a fitting stage. And a final curtain for Jesse James.

He wondered if there was a morning train to St. Louis.

CHAPTER 12

Starbuck revised his plan. After sleeping on it overnight, he decided the delay of another day was of no great consequence. Speed, in the overall scheme of things, was less essential than maintaining his cover story.

He had no clear idea when the robbery would occur. Yet it seemed unlikely the gang would ride out within the next couple of days. The Youngers, after their binge of last night, would need time to recuperate. Then, too, Frank James had evidenced no sense of urgency in either his attitude or his curious offer. All that indicated the holdup would not take place for at least three days, perhaps more. And since Starbuck's own plan was based largely on guesswork, he felt the need to copper his bet.

For Floyd Hunnewell to disappear mysteriously would almost certainly arouse suspicion. All the more so in the light of Alvina's thoughtless revelations the night before. A bit of insurance seemed in order, and for the simplest of reasons. There was an outside possibility that Floyd Hunnewell would, by necessity, return to Ma Ferguson's. To do so—without getting killed in the process—would require that his credentials as a horse thief withstand scrutiny. On balance, then, it seemed wise to enlarge the original cover story with still another tapestry of lies.

To that end, Starbuck improvised a tale designed to touch a whore's heart. He appeared disgruntled, thoroughly crestfallen that he'd muffed his chance to join the James-Younger gang. A change of scenery, he explained, along with a little action, was needed to restore his spirits. He'd decided to return to his old haunts—a horse-stealing foray into Kansas which would last a week, perhaps longer, depending on circumstances. Then, with his funds replenished, he would hightail it straightaway back to Ma Ferguson's. It wasn't goodbye, he told Alvina, but merely a pause in the festivities. Upon his return, the party would resume right where they'd left off.

Alvina accepted the story at face value. She was sad, even a bit misty-eyed, but not without hope. When he departed around midmorning, she was convinced their separation would be of short duration. She peppered him with kisses, hugging him fiercely, and let go only when he stepped through the front door. Waving, bravely snuffling back her tears, she watched as he rode away. For a whore, whose memories were generally bereft of sentiment, it was a moment to be treasured. She was overcome by the old sensation of a woman sending her man off to battle.

Starbuck turned his attention to the task ahead. Kansas City was less than twenty miles from Ma Ferguson's, and he arrived there early that afternoon. He left the gelding at a livery stable, paying a week's charges in advance, and emerged onto the street. For the next hour he circled through the downtown area, frequently doubling back, always looking over his shoulder. At last, satisfied he hadn't been followed, he went to the train station and collected a suitcase he'd checked the week before. A short while later he stepped into one of the town's busier hotels. There, registering under a false name, he took a room.

Upstairs, Starbuck paused only long enough to deposit the suitcase in his room. Then he quickly took possession of the bathroom at the end of the hall. With all the modern conveniences, including hot and cold running water, he set to work. Standing before the lavatory mirror, he peeled off the fake moustache and carefully scrubbed spirit gum from his upper lip. After undressing, he drew a scalding bath and lowered himself into the tub. The water slowly turned dark brown as he alternately lathered and rinsed his hair. A final washing, with his head directly under the tap, removed the last of the dye. When he inspected himself in the mirror, the transformation was complete. Floyd Hunnewell had been laid to rest.

Late that afternoon, Starbuck emerged from the hotel by a side exit. He caught a hansom cab and went straight to the train station. After dropping his bag at the checkroom, he purchased a ticket; then he swiftly mingled with the crowd. Only by a fluke would he have been recognised by anyone from Clay County; he was attired in his Denver clothes, and his hair was once again light chestnut in colour. Still, there was always that off chance, and he'd learned long ago that too much caution was far healthier than too little. By train time, he felt reasonably confident he was in the clear. On the stroke of six he boarded the evening eastbound for St. Louis.

At the first stop, an hour or so down the line, Starbuck hopped off the train. He collared the station agent, handing him a scribbled message and a ten-dollar bill. The agent, impressed by his generosity, promised to send the wire the moment the train was under way.

The message was addressed to Otis Tilford.

• • •

Not long after sunrise the train pulled into St. Louis. Starbuck left the depot on foot and headed uptown. A walk in the brisk morning air took the kinks out of his muscles and revived him from a long night in the chair car. By the time he reached the corner of Olive and Fourth, he'd worked up an appetite.

A café catering for the early-morning breakfast trade caught his attention. He first used the washroom to splash sleep out of his eyes and scrub his teeth with soap and a thorny forefinger. Then he sat down to a plate of ham and eggs, with a side order of flapjacks. He topped off the meal with a cigarette and a steaming mug of black coffee. On the street again, he went looking for a barbershop.

By half past eight, he'd had a trim and a shave. He reeked of talcum powder and bay rum, and he felt positively chipper as he walked along Fourth towards Delmar. At the corner, he entered the Merchants & Farmers Bank Building. The elevator deposited him on the third floor, and a moment later he pushed through the door of the International Bankers Association. The receptionist, still masquerading as a drill sergeant, evidenced no surprise at his arrival. His wire had been slipped under the door early that morning and he was expected. She escorted him directly into Otis Tilford's office.

The banker was seated behind his desk. He smiled and beckoned Starbuck forward. His eyes were strangely alert and his handshake was cordial. He motioned to a chair.

"I must say I'm delighted to see you, Mr. Starbuck. There for a while I began to wonder if you had fallen victim to foul play."

"Nothing like that," Starbuck said, seating himself.

"I've been on the go since I left here, and not a whole lot to report. Up till now anyway."

"You have news, then?" Tilford leaned forward eagerly. "A break in the case?"

"Maybe," Starbuck allowed. "Maybe not. All depends on the next turn of the cards."

"I don't believe I follow you."

"Suppose I fill you in on what's happened?"

"Yes, by all means! Please do, Mr. Starbuck."

Starbuck began with the tenuous leads he'd unearthed from the Pinkerton file. From there, he briefly recounted his trip to Indian Territory and the night with Belle Starr. Then, touching only on salient details, he related how he had infiltrated Ma Ferguson's bordello. Apart from the cover story, he made no mention of the disguise or the alias he'd assumed. As a matter of security, he never revealed professional secrets to anyone, not even a client. He went on to tell of Alvina and the Youngers, and his gradual acceptance as a regular at the brothel. Then, finally, he spoke of his strange conversation with Frank James.

"I got close," he concluded. "But close don't count except in horseshoes. One word from Cole Younger put a damper on the whole works."

"Good Lord!" Tilford said, visibly impressed. "You were actually face to face with Frank James!"

"Closer than I am to you right now. With a little luck, I could've killed him and the Youngers there and then. Course, I never tried for the obvious reason. I figured you wanted Jesse or nobody."

"Quite correct," Tilford said briskly. "Nevertheless, you are to be commended, Mr. Starbuck. To my knowledge, no one—certainly no Pinkerton—has ever made personal contact with Frank James. Not to mention the Younger brothers—and all of them in the same room!"

"All of them except the one we're after."

"A masterful piece of work, nonetheless! How on earth were you able to gain their confidence?"

"The girl," Starbuck told him. "She was the key. Once I got her on my side, the rest just fell into place."

"I marvel that the Pinkertons never considered such an approach."

Starbuck gave him a cynical smile. "I'd guess the Pinks wouldn't talk the same language as whores."

"Perhaps not." Tilford appeared nonplussed, and quickly dropped the topic. "Well, now, Mr. Starbuck! Where do we proceed from here?"

"I need some information, and I need it today."

"Exactly what sort of information?"

"Alvina—she's the girl I mentioned—let slip that the gang has a holdup planned. She wasn't certain, but she thought the name of the town was either Northfield or Northville. We've got to determine which it is—and where."

"Where?"

"What state."

"Are you telling me she gave no indication as to the state?"

"She couldn't," Starbuck replied. "She didn't know."

"And she wasn't precise as to whether it's Northfield or Northville?"

"She leaned towards Northfield. All the same, she wouldn't have sworn to it."

"So, then, we're faced with a conundrum of sorts, aren't we?"

"If that means a head scratcher, then I'll grant you it's a lulu."

Tilford steepled his fingers, thoughtful. "A possible solution occurs to me. The American Bankers Association publishes a booklet listing all member banks. In addition, when we were organising the International Association, we compiled a list of virtually every bank in the Midwest. Between the two lists, we might very well find the answer."

"Sounds good," Starbuck observed. "How long will it take?"

"I have no idea." Tilford rose from his chair. "However, I will attend to the search personally. I daresay that will speed things along."

"Need some help?"

"Thank you, no." Tilford moved around his desk. "I'll put every available clerk on it immediately. Please make yourself comfortable, Mr. Starbuck."

With that, Tilford hurried out of the office. Starbuck took out the makings and began building himself a smoke. He creased a rolling paper, holding it deftly between thumb and forefinger, and sprinkled tobacco into it. Then he licked, sealing the length of the paper, and twisted the ends. He struck a match on his boot sole and lit the cigarette. Exhaling smoke, he snuffed the match and tossed it into an ashtray. He settled down to wait.

Several times over the next hour Tilford's receptionist popped in to check on him. She offered coffee, which he accepted, and refilled his cup on each trip. At last, with his kidneys afloat, he declined the fourth refill. A cup of coffee was nothing without a smoke, and he put a dent in his tobacco sack during the prolonged wait. He was lighting yet another cigarette as Tilford bustled through the door. In his hand, the banker held a single sheet of foolscap.

"I fear we've somewhat compounded the problem, Mr. Starbuck."

"Oh, how so?"

"See for yourself." Tilford seated himself, and placed

the paper on the desk between them. I regret to say the prefix 'North' is not all that uncommon."

Starbuck pulled his chair closer and scanned the paper. On it, printed in neat capital letters, was a list of five towns: NORTHFIELD, ILLINOIS. NORTHFIELD, MINNESOTA. NORTHVILLE, MICHIGAN. NORTH-RIDGE, OHIO. NORTHWOOD, IOWA. His eye was drawn to the top of the list, and he briefly considered the two Northfields. Then he took a long, thoughtful draw on his cigarette.

"Illinois and Minnesota." The words came out in little spurts of smoke. "Guess we could toss a coin and hope for the best."

"Let me pose a question." Tilford studied his nails a moment. "Is it possible the girl was confused, somehow got the name of the town wrong?"

"Anything's possible," Starbuck remarked. "What makes you ask?"

"You will note"—Tilford tapped the paper—"there are five states listed there. Of those states, the James-Younger gang has been active in only one, that state being Iowa."

"You're saying there's a connection?"

"Precisely!" Tilford intoned. "For all his robberies, Jesse James had limited himself to a very defined territory. If nothing else, the Pinkertons established that every robbery occurred either in Missouri or in a state contiguous to Missouri."

"I'm not much on four-bit words."

"Contiguous," Tilford elaborated, "simply means a bordering state. In short, the James-Younger gang had *never* been known to operate in a state which did not directly border Missouri."

Starbuck again scanned the list. "You're telling me we ought to forget Minnesota, Michigan, and Ohio?"

"I am indeed," Tilford affirmed. "I seriously question that Jesse James would cross Iowa to rob a bank in Minnesota. Nor would he cross Illinois and Indiana to rob a bank in Michigan. It flies in the face of a record established over a period of seventeen years."

Starbuck was silent for a time. "I take it you've got a theory all worked out?"

"Facts speak for themselves," Tilford said with exaggerated gravity. "I submit the robbery will take place in one of two towns. The logical choice—based on what the girl was told—is Northfield, Illinois. A distant second, at least in my opinion, would be Northwood, Iowa."

"Northwood's out," Starbuck said in a low voice. "She wasn't certain, but she only mentioned two names: Northfield and Northville." He paused, slowly stubbed out his cigarette in the ashtray. "Tell me about Northfield, Illinois. What size town is it?"

"Quite small. I believe the population is something less than five hundred."

"Which means the bank wouldn't be any great shakes. How about Northfield, Minnesota?"

"Considerably larger," Tilford admitted. "I would judge it at roughly five thousand."

"And the bank?"

"Old and very prosperous," Tilford said, frowning heavily. "One of the largest in the Midwest."

There was a moment of weighing and deliberation before Starbuck spoke. "Alvina told me it was a big job, bigger than anything the gang had ever pulled. So that pretty well eliminates the bank in Illinois. To my way of thinking, it narrows down to one candidate—Northfield, Minnesota."

"I strongly disagree," Tilford said sharply. "Why would Jesse James travel that far to rob a bank? There's no logic to it! Absolutely none!"

"Outlaws aren't noted for logic. Even if they were, I'd have to follow my hunch on this one. Jesse and his boys are out to make a killing, and it was Jim Younger himself who said so. That speaks lots louder to me than all your facts."

"Are you prepared to stake your reputation on a hunch, Mr. Starbuck?"

"Why not?" Starbuck said with sardonic amusement. "Except for hunches, I would've been dead a long time ago."

"And in the event logic prevails . . . what then?"

"Tell you what." Starbuck met his look squarely. "You alert the authorities at Northfield, Illinois. Meantime, I'll get myself on up to Minnesota. That way everybody's happy."

"Compromise was hardly what I had in mind."

"It's all you'll get," Starbuck said quietly. "I told you when I signed on . . . I do it my way or I don't do it at all."

There was an awkward pause. Tilford's features congested, and his mouth clamped in a bloodless line. "Very well," he conceded at length. "When will you leave?"

"First train out," Starbuck informed him. "I like to scout the terrain before I lay an ambush."

"Ambush!" Tilford looked upset. "Won't the authorities in Minnesota have something to say about that?"

"All depends."

"On what, may I ask?"

"On whether or not I tell them."

"Good God!" Tilford shook his head in stern disapproval. "Surely you don't intend to take on the entire gang—without assistance!"

"We'll see." Starbuck gave him a devil-may-care grin. "Sometimes it's easier to kill a man by operating alone. Northfield might be too civilised for *our* kind of justice."

Tilford could scarcely mistake the nature of the grin, or the words. He had, after all, hired a man to dispense summary justice. Northfield's wishes in the matter were wholly immaterial.

"Yes." His tone was severe. "You may very well have a point, Mr. Starbuck."

Starbuck unfolded slowly from his chair. He tugged his jacket smooth and walked to the door. Then, as he was about to step into the hall, he paused and looked back over his shoulder. A ghost of a smile touched his mouth.

"I'll let you know how it comes out."

CHAPTER 13

Starbuck stood on the veranda of the Dampier House Hotel. A cigar was wedged in the corner of his mouth and his hands were locked behind his back. Under a noonday sun, he puffed thick clouds of smoke and stared out across the square. His gaze was fixed on the First National Bank.

Only an hour before, upon arriving in town, Starbuck had checked into the hotel. He was posing as a sundries drummer, whose territory had recently been broadened to include Minnesota. Apart from the ubiquitous cigar, his attire was the uniform of virtually all travelling salesmen. He wore a derby hat and a snappy checkered suit with vest to match. A gold watch chain was draped across the vest, and a flashy diamond ring sparkled on his pinky. His physical appearance was unchanged, with the exception of an old standby.

A gold sleeve, crafted with uncanny workmanship, was fitted over his left front tooth. The overall effect, as with any subtle disguise, was principally one of misdirection. When he smiled, which was a drummer's stock in trade, people seldom saw his face. Their recollection was of a gold tooth and a steamy cigar. The man who called himself Homer Croydon was otherwise lost to memory.

Today, eyes squinted in concentration, Starbuck was performing a feat of mental gymnastics. A manhunter who survived soon acquired the knack of looking at things from an outlaw's perspective. Long ago, the trick had become second nature, and he was now able to step into the other fellow's boots almost at will. Visualising himself to be Jesse James, he pondered on a foolproof way to rob the bank.

Based on all he'd learned, Starbuck knew it would be a mistake to think in conventional terms. Jesse James, unlike most bank robbers, approached each job as though it were a military operation. The Pinkerton file rather conclusively demonstrated that the James-Younger gang was organised along the lines of a guerrilla band. Without exception, their holdups had been executed with a certain flair for hit-and-run. Surprise, as in any guerrilla raid, was the key element. Every step was orchestrated—planned with an eye to detail—and the gang generally made good their escape before anyone realised a robbery had occurred. That, too, indicated the meticulous preparation characteristic of each job. The retreat, and subsequent escape, was engineered with no less forethought than the holdup itself. And therein lay the mark of Jesse James' overall genius. In seventeen years, he had never been outfoxed. His trademark was a cold trail . . . leading nowhere.

Yet Northfield presented a unique tactical problem. Brooding on it, Starbuck slowly became aware that the situation was fraught with imponderables. The layout of the town did not lend itself to a hit-and-run raid. The square was open and broad, affording little in the way of concealment. On all sides, stores fronted the square; tradesmen and shopkeepers had a perfect view of the bank; any unusual activity would immediately draw their attention. The chances of discovery—before the job was completed—were therefore increased manyfold. In that event the odds also multiplied that the gang would be forced to fight its way out of Northfield. Because the river bisected the town, however, there were only two logical lines of retreat. One led eastward, along Division Street, which began on the corner where the bank was located. Yet, while Division Street was the quickest route of escape, any flight eastward would merely extend the line of retreat. Headed in the wrong direction, the gang would at some point be compelled to double back on a south-westernly course. For in the end, there was no question they would make a run for Indian Territory.

The other escape hole was westward, across the bridge. There, too, the tactical problem was apparent. To reach the bridge, the gang would have to traverse the entire length of the square. Should trouble arise, and the townspeople take arms, the outlaws would be forced to run a gauntlet of gunfire. At first glance, the hazards entailed seemed to rule out the bridge. Still, apart from surprise, the chief attribute of an experienced guerrilla leader was to do the unexpected when it was least expected. A calculated risk at best, the bridge might nonetheless offer the lesser of two evils. It led westward, the ultimate direction of escape, and it shortened the line of retreat by perhaps thirty or forty miles. On balance, then, the advantages might very well outweigh the hazards. No one would expect a gang of bank robbers to take the hard way out of town. Nor would they anticipate that the gang leader might deliberately—

Starbuck was rocked by a sudden premonition. He stepped off the veranda and crossed the block-long expanse of the square. At the bridge, he halted and stared for a moment at the houses on the opposite side of the river. Then, on the verge of turning, his eyes were drawn to the line of telegraph poles running north. His gaze shifted south—no telegraph poles!—and any vestige of doubt disappeared. Facing about, he subjected the square to cold scrutiny. From a tactical outlook, the bridge instantly became a key vantage point. The entire square, from end to end, was commanded by an unobstructed field of fire. There was, moreover, the element of the unexpected from where it was least expected. In the event fighting broke out, the townspeople would be looking towards the bank, not the bridge. And the outcome was easy to visualise.

Starbuck walked back to the hotel. Whether by deductive reasoning or swift-felt instinct, he knew he'd doped out the plan. Some inner certainty told him the holdup would proceed along the lines he'd envisioned. All that remained was to decide his own course of action. As he saw it, there were two options, both of which held merit. The critical factor was yet another of those imponderables.

To kill Jesse James all he had to do was bide his time. His room, which was on the second floor, fronted the hotel and directly overlooked the square. The range, from his window to the door of the bank, was roughly forty yards. No easy shot with a pistol, it was nonetheless one he had made many times before. By placing his gun hand on the windowsill—and holding high with the sights—he felt entirely confident of a kill shot. When the gang exited the bank, his shot was certain to go unnoticed in the ensuing gunfire.

Then, still posing as a drummer, he need only check out of the hotel and be on his way. Homer Croydon would be remembered by no one. Nor would anyone associate him with the death of Jesse James.

The alternative was to contact the town marshal.

However, that route would require discretion and an oath
of silence. Should the marshal prove the talkative sort—
and word of an impending robbery spread through
Northfield—then any hope of trapping the gang would
be gravely jeopardised. The risk was compounded by the
fact that others, by necessity, would be drawn into the
scheme. Quite properly, the marshal would insist on
alerting some of the townsmen. Extra guns, and men
willing to use them, would be needed against a band of
killers. Still, by stressing the need for secrecy, there was
every reason to believe the plan would work. The welfare of Northfield and its citizens would be at stake. And
trustworthy men, committed to the common good, could
be persuaded to hold their silence.

In the end, Starbuck's decision had little to do with
Northfield. He was concerned for the lives of innocent
bystanders, and he had no wish to see the square turned
into a battleground. Yet, for all that, his decision was a
matter of personal integrity. While he had killed many
men, he was no assassin. To hide, and shoot down a
man from his hotel window, somehow went against the
grain. His code in such matters was simple and pragmatic. He always gave the other man a chance, but he
tried never to give him the first shot.

On reflection, it was the way he preferred to kill Jesse
James. No stealth or potshots from hotel windows. He
would do it openly, face to face—on the street.

Shortly after the noon hour, Starbuck left the hotel
and crossed the square. Opposite the bank, he rounded
the corner and walked towards the marshal's office,
which was one door down. Northfield appeared to be a
peaceful town, with nothing more serious than an occasional fistfight or a rowdy drunk. Other than the marshal, he thought it unlikely the town would employ any
full-time officers. When he entered the office, his judge-

ment was confirmed. All the cell doors stood open, and except for the marshal, the place was deserted. Seated behind a battered desk, the lawman was idly cleaning his fingernails with a penknife.

"Afternoon."

"Yessir." The marshal gave his gold tooth and snappy outfit a quick once-over. "Do something for you?"

"Are you Marshal Wallace Murphy?"

"I am." Murphy closed the penknife and stuck it in his pocket. "What's the problem?"

"No problem, Marshal. I was instructed to call on you when I got into town."

"Don't say?" Murphy looked flattered. "Who by?"

"Mr. Otis Tilford," Starbuck lied. "President of the International Bankers Association."

"Oh, yeah! Now that you mention it, the name rings a bell. Formed not too long ago, wasn't it?"

"Last summer," Starbuck said with a note of pride. "We're headquartered in St. Louis."

"I take it you work for the association?"

"In a manner of speaking. I'm a private detective, Marshal." Starbuck grinned and tipped his derby. "This drummer's getup is strictly window dressing. I was hired as an undercover operative by Mr. Tilford."

"I don't believe I caught your name?"

"Luke Starbuck. Course, that's just between you and me. I'm registered at the hotel under the name of Homer Croydon."

Murphy was heavily built, with a square, thick-jowled face and a ruddy complexion. The chair squeaked under his weight as he leaned forward, elbows on the desk. He suddenly appeared attentive.

"Why all the secrecy?"

"Like I told you, I'm working undercover."

"So you did." Murphy eyed him with a puzzled frown. "What brings you to Northfield?"

"Well . . ." Starbuck let him hang a moment. "I need your word everything will be kept in the strictest confidence, Marshal. Otherwise I'm not at liberty to divulge the details of my assignment."

"I dunno." Murphy sounded uncertain. "If it's got to do with Northfield, that could put me in an awkward position."

Starbuck flashed his gold tooth. "I'd say it's more likely to make you the town hero. Hear me out and I think you'll agree I'm right."

Murphy nodded, digesting the thought. "Okay, fire away. Only I warn you—I won't be a party to anything that's not in the best interests of Northfield."

"Fair enough." Starbuck's expression turned solemn. "Sometime within the next week, the First National Bank will be robbed."

"Robbed!" Murphy stared at him, dumbstruck. "How the hell would you know a thing like that?"

"How I know isn't important—"

"Says you!" Murphy cut him short. "You walk in off the street and tell me the bank's about to be robbed? I'll have an explanation, mister. And I'll have it damned quick."

"Suit yourself." Starbuck read a certain disbelief in his face, and decided to embellish the truth. "I was hired to infiltrate a gang of bank robbers. I located their hangout—a whorehouse—and I managed to get on chummy terms with them. Three nights ago, one of them got drunk and spilled the beans. So I checked with Mr. Tilford and he ordered me to contact you on the double. Here I am."

Murphy looked at him with narrow suspicion. "How do I know you're on the level?"

"If you don't believe me," Starbuck said lightly, "then just hide and watch. They're on their way to Northfield right now."

"Who's they?"

"Jesse James and the Youngers."

Murphy's mouth popped open. "Did you say Jesse James—*the* Jesse James?"

"The one and only."

"That's impossible!" Murphy shook his head wildly. "Why would Jesse James come all the way to Minnesota to rob a bank? It doesn't make sense!"

"Pay close attention, Marshal." Starbuck's eyes went cold and impersonal. "I don't have time to waste arguing with you. They're headed in your direction and that's a rock-solid fact. Now, I can show you how to stop them from robbing the bank, not to mention covering yourself with glory." He paused, jerked a thumb over his shoulder. "Or I can walk out that door and leave you with egg on your face. I reckon it all depends on how much you like wearing a marshal's badge."

"What the hell do you mean by that?"

"Why, it's pretty simple," Starbuck said without expression. "The town fathers wouldn't look too kindly on a man who let Jesse James ride in here and empty out the bank. All the more so once they heard Mr. Otis Tilford sent a special representative to warn you in advance."

There was a stark silence. Wallace Murphy stared down at his hands, tight-lipped. He seemed to be struggling within himself, and several moments passed before he looked up. Then he dipped his head in affirmation.

"Go ahead, say your piece. I'm listening."

On impulse, Starbuck pressed the advantage. "One more thing. I call the shots from here on out. You can take all the credit, but I won't let you monkey with my plan. Understood?"

"Understood," Murphy agreed gingerly. "Only you better come up with something damn good."

"I already have," Starbuck said with an odd smile. "You see, Marshal—I know how they intend to pull the job."

"Big deal!" Murphy laughed uneasily. "What's to robbing a bank? You just walk in and pull a gun."

"Not Jesse James," Starbuck countered. "Him and his boys are old guerrilla fighters. So we're in for a military operation from start to finish."

"Would you care to spell that out?"

"For openers, a couple of the gang will post themselves somewhere near the bank door. They're the outside men, and their job is to keep the street clear. That way, there's less chance of trouble when it comes time for the getaway."

"In other words, they're the ones that'll show first?"

Starbuck nodded. "Once they're in position then Jesse and a couple more of the gang will enter the bank. We can depend on that. Jesse always handles the inside work himself."

"What's so unusual about that? Sounds fairly routine to me."

"There's an added touch," Starbuck said soberly. "At least two men, maybe more, will take control of the bridge. If trouble develops during the holdup, they'll keep everyone on the square pinned down with gunfire. Afterwards, they'll cover the withdrawal when the bunch at the bank starts back across the square. Their last job is to act as a rear guard; fight a holding action at the bridge. Once the others are across the river and in the clear, then they'll take off like scalded ducks."

"Damn!" Murphy suddenly grasped it. "That means

anybody who tangles with them would be caught in a crossfire. It'd be suicide to set foot on the square!"

"We'll let Jesse and his boys go right on thinking that. Meantime, we'll arrange a little surprise of our own."

"An ambush!" Murphy's eyes brightened. "By God, I like your style, Starbuck! How long you figure we've got?"

"Well, let's see." Starbuck pulled at his ear. "Tomorrow's Saturday, and they wouldn't risk it with the farm crowd in town. So I'd say the early part of the week, probably Monday."

"With seven or eight of them, we'll need some help with this ambush of yours."

"Not too many," Starbuck cautioned him. "The fewer involved, the less chance of word leaking out. Do you know three or four men who can be trusted to keep their mouths shut?"

"Oh, hell, yes!" Murphy chortled. "Half the men in Northfield would give their left nut for a crack at Jesse James."

"Hold it to three," Starbuck said firmly. "That's plenty for what I have in mind. And don't let the cat out of the bag! Arrange to get them together sometime tomorrow, and I'll explain the setup myself. I already know where I want them spotted."

"I guess that only leaves Fred Wilcox. He's the president of the bank. When do we give him the good news?"

"We don't."

"What?" Murphy went slack-jawed with amazement. "Fred's got to be warned! You can't let that gang of murderers walk in there cold!"

"I don't aim to." Starbuck regarded him with a level gaze. "But we can't risk a bunch of nervous Nellies tipping our hand. We'll hit the minute Jesse steps down out of the saddle. So don't work yourself into a sweat. He'll never make it inside the bank—I guarantee it."

"Kill him dead!" Murphy cackled. "Shoot him down like a mad dog! That's what you're saying, isn't it?"

Starbuck smiled. "If a man's worth shooting, then I reckon he's worth killing."

"Like I said, Starbuck." Murphy chuckled heartily. "I admire your style."

"One last thing," Starbuck advised him. "I fire the first shot. That'll be the signal for you and your men to cut loose; but I don't want anybody to get overeager. Agreed?"

"Agreed! You've got my word on it."

Wallace Murphy was tempted, but he let the question go unasked. He already knew the answer, and counted it no great surprise. Starbuck's presence in Northfield was explanation enough.

The first shot would be for Jesse James.

CHAPTER 14

On Monday morning, the First National Bank opened at the usual time. Fred Wilcox, the president and chief stockholder, arrived a minute or so before eight. Waiting for him were the bank tellers, Joseph Heywood and Alan Bunker. He unlocked the front door and the men filed inside. A moment later the shade snapped up on the wide plateglass window fronting the square.

Starbuck was seated on the veranda of the hotel. He pulled out his pocket watch and checked the time. The marshal had told him Wilcox was a punctual man, and he noted the window shade went up almost precisely on the stroke of eight. Around the square, following the banker's example, tradesmen began opening their doors. Northfield stirred and slowly came to life. To all appearances it was a typical Monday morning, unremarkable in any respect. The townspeople, suspecting nothing, went about the routine of another business day.

A cigar jutting from his mouth, Starbuck lazed back in the cane-bottomed rocker. His legs were outstretched, heels planted atop the veranda railing, and the derby was tipped low over his forehead. To passersby, he looked like a slothful drummer, sunning himself after a heavy breakfast. In truth, he was alert and observant, his eyes moving hawklike around the square. He set the rocker in motion, ticking off a mental checklist item by item.

The three men selected by Marshal Wallace Murphy were already in position. Their weapons were secreted, but close at hand, and there was nothing about them to draw undue attention. One, Arthur Manning, operated a dry-goods store, located two doors north of the bank. Another, Elias Stacey, was proprietor of the town pharmacy. His shop was on the southeast corner of the square, directly across Division Street from the bank. The third man, Dr. Henry Wheeler, was stationed in Starbuck's second-floor hotel room. A crack shot, widely known for his marksmanship, Doc Wheeler was armed with a breech-loading target rifle. The marshal, whose office was kitty-corner from the bank, kept a lookout from his window. His instructions were to stay off the street and out of sight.

Early Saturday morning, the three men had been summoned to the marshal's office. There, he had introduced them to Starbuck and briefed them on the forthcoming holdup attempt. The men had listened with dismay and shock, somewhat incredulous. Yet all three were veterans of the Civil War, and no strangers to bloodshed. Nor were they overawed that they were being asked to take arms against the James-Younger gang. They were, instead, filled with a sort of righteous indignation. Jesse James was vilified as a murderous blackguard, and each of them looked upon the defence of their town and their neighbours as a civic duty. To a man, they eagerly volunteered their services.

Starbuck had first sworn them to an oath of silence. He impressed on them the need for absolute secrecy, which included wives and friends and business acquaintances. Jesse James, he noted, would be on guard for anything out of the ordinary; it was entirely likely a member of the gang would reconnoitre the town one last time before the robbery. With the point made, Starbuck then went on to the ambush itself. Their primary objective was the group of robbers—four or five in number—who would assemble outside the bank. These men were to be killed on the spot, before they had time to react and turn the square into a battleground. The men at the bridge, so long as they made no attempt to cross the square, were secondary. By concentrating on the bank, a dual goal would be served. The majority of the gang would be wiped out and the robbery would be aborted on the instant.

From there, Starbuck had proceeded to the matter of individual assignments. Manning and Stacey, whose stores were in direct proximity to the bank, were to arm themselves with shotguns. Caught between them, the robbers would be neatly sandwiched in a crossfire; their shotguns would sweep the sidewalk immediately outside the bank with a barrage of lead. The marshal, armed with a repeating rifle, would fire from the doorway of his office. His principal concern would be the outside team of robbers; once the firing became general, however, he would be free to select targets of opportunity. Doc Wheeler, whose target rifle was equipped with peep sights, would be responsible for the bridge. The gang members there were to be killed or pinned down, and thus neutralised. In that manner, they would be effectively eliminated from the larger fight.

Starbuck next outlined his own role in the ambush. Several of the gang members—notably Frank James and the three Younger brothers—were known to him on sight. The odds dictated that one or more of these men would be part of the outside team, the first contingent to approach the bank. Upon spotting them, he would leave the hotel veranda and cross to the south side of the square. His movement would alert Manning, Stacey, and Doc Wheeler that the holdup attempt was under way. Once across the square, he would then turn east and stroll towards the corner. By timing it properly, he would arrive at the corner as the second contingent rode up to the bank. One of these men was certain to be Jesse James, and along with the inside team he would dismount at the hitch rack. The moment they were on the sidewalk, and moving towards the door of the bank, Starbuck would open fire. His shot would be the signal for Marshal Murphy and the others to cut loose. With luck, the whole affair would be concluded in a matter of seconds.

Summing up, Starbuck had stressed the importance of a dispassionate attitude. He reminded the men that the James-Younger gang was a band of cold-blooded murderers, prone to acts of savagery. He urged them to shoot to kill, and to continue firing until the last outlaw had been taken out of action. Any hesitation, any show of mercy, would only endanger innocent bystanders. To save the lives of friends and neighbours required that they kill quickly and efficiently. And with no regard for the aftermath.

Arthur Manning, perhaps having second thoughts, had then raised the issue of bystanders. In the event passersby happened along at the last moment or innocent parties got in the line of fire, he wondered if it might not be prudent to hold off, and let the gang rob the bank. At that point, he observed, when they were once again mounted and moving across the square, they could be ambushed in a relatively open area. Starbuck assured him that such a plan would result in random gunfire, and imperil the lives of everyone on the square. By containing the shooting to a limited zone—the front of the bank—there was less chance of someone catching a stray bullet. Doc Wheeler, whose usual business was saving lives, forcefully agreed. He advised Manning to leave tactics to Starbuck. The ambush, as laid out, was in his opinion their best hope. The others voiced assent, and the meeting had concluded on that note. Starbuck's plan would be followed to the letter.

To bolster their confidence, Starbuck had arranged a dry run later that afternoon. He waited until the farmers and their families began the trek homeward; with their departure, the Saturday crowds thinned out and the sidewalks became passable. Walking to the southwest corner of the square, he stopped and turned to face the bank. From there, he was in plain view of Doc Wheeler and the two tradesmen. He gave them the high sign, indicating he was satisfied with the arrangement. Then, cutting across the intersection on an oblique angle, he stepped off the distance to the bank entrance. By his stride, it was fourteen paces, roughly fifteen yards. He considered it an easy shot. One Jesse James would never hear.

Yet now, seated in the rocker, he wondered if today would be the day. Where Jesse James was concerned, there were few certainties, and a good deal of guesswork. Still, if a bank was to be robbed, then Monday was the ideal time. All morning, a steady stream of merchants and shopkeepers had trooped into the bank. Their receipts from Saturday's trade were heavy, and they were clearly anxious to get the money out of the stores and on deposit. Which made the bank a tempting target indeed. The vault would be stuffed with cash—and standing wide open.

As the noon hour approached, Starbuck experienced a moment of concern. If today was not the day, he knew he could expect problems with his squad of volunteers.

Wallace was a peace officer, and therefore somewhat accustomed to the vagaries of manhunting. The others, despite their wartime service, were newcomers to the game. A professional soon learned that patience and determination were essential in any match of wits with outlaws. Amateurs, on the other hand, were quick to lose their taste for killing. The excitement—that initial surge of blood lust—was short-lived. The longer the wait, the more time they had to think. And given enough time, most men would talk themselves out of the notion. Unless the gang struck today, that might easily happen in Northfield. For the three townsmen, the act of cold and premeditated killing would begin to weigh heavily. Tomorrow or the next day—

All at once Starbuck alerted. His pulse quickened as he spotted Cole Younger and the man named Clell Miller ride over the bridge. Unhurried, holding their horses to a walk, they proceeded on a direct line across the square. Their eyes moved constantly, searching the stores and the faces of people on the street. Anything out of the ordinary—empty stores or too few people abroad—would immediately put them on guard. For the job to go off as planned, the town had to appear normal, nothing unusual or out of kilter. Otherwise they would simply turn and ride back across the bridge.

Starbuck sat perfectly still. From beneath the brim of his derby, he watched them ride past and plod on in the direction of the bank. He casually stood, stretching himself, and yawned a wide, jaw-cracking yawn. Then he bit off the tip of a fresh cigar and lit it with the air of a man savouring a good smoke. Stuffing the cigar in his mouth, he went down the hotel steps and meandered across the square. On the sidewalk, he turned and strolled aimlessly towards the corner. Ahead, he saw the two outlaws rein to a halt before the bank and dismount.

Cole stooped down and pretended to tighten the saddle girth on his horse. Miller circled the hitch rack and stepped onto the sidewalk. With a look of bored indifference, he stood gazing out at the square.

Approaching the corner, Starbuck slowed his pace. Directly ahead, he spotted Stacey watching him through the window of the pharmacy. Out of the corner of his eye, he caught a glimpse of Manning leaning idly in the doorway of the dry-goods store. He stopped before a clothing emporium, playing for time, and made a show of peering at the window display. The hotel, now diagonally behind him, was mirrored in the reflection of the glass. He studied the window of his room, noting the lower pane was raised; through the gauzy curtains, the outline of Doc Wheeler was faintly visible. The men were in place and ready to act the instant he gave the signal. All that remained was for Jesse James to put in an appearance.

Starbuck puffed his cigar and bent closer to the window. He checked the bank in the reflection, troubled by what seemed an abnormal lapse of time. Cole and Clell Miller, still loafing outside the bank, were staring in the direction of the bridge. Starbuck turned his head slightly, and took a quick peek. His expression darkened, oddly bemused. Jim Younger, accompanied by two men unknown to him, cleared the east end of the bridge and reined their horses off to one side. They dismounted, reins gripped firmly, and stood as though waiting. Their eyes were fixed on the bank.

A sudden chill settled over Starbuck. Something about the setup was wrong, all turned around. The way he'd figured it, occupying the bridge was to have been the last step. Before then, both the outside team and the inside team should have been in position. Yet the rear guard had now taken control of the bridge and there were no more riders in sight. No sign of the inside team!

Then, suddenly, a tight fist of apprehension gripped his stomach. He wheeled away from the store window and froze, turned to stone. Frank James and Bob Younger, led by a third man, rounded the corner of Division Street and entered the bank. The man in the lead, like Frank, wore a beard, and carried himself with austere assurance. His identity was all too apparent.

Starbuck spat a low curse and flung his cigar into the gutter. He saw their horses tied to the hitch rack on Division Street, and too late he realised his mistake. While he was watching the bridge, he'd been outsmarted and outmanoeuvred. Jesse James, foxy to the end, had circled Northfield and entered town from the east. A clever ruse, wholly unexpected, and timed precisely when it was least expected. The trademark of an old guerrilla fighter—and brilliantly executed.

Before Starbuck could react, the situation went from bad to worse. The proprietor of a hardware store next to the bank boldly approached Cole Younger and Clell Miller. He looked them over, openly curious, then walked on towards the bank entrance. Miller drew a gun and brusquely ordered him to move along. The store owner obeyed, rounding the corner onto Division Street. Then he took off running, shouting at the top of his lungs.

"Bank robbers! The bank's being robbed!"

With the element of surprise gone, the gang moved swiftly. Cole fired a shot to alert the men at the bridge. In turn, they began winging shots across the square, warning passersby off the street. A townsman, seemingly befuddled by the commotion, was too slow to move, and a bullet dropped him where he stood. Starbuck, with lead whizzing all around him, jerked his Colt and hurried to the corner. There he ducked behind a lamppost and waited. His pistol was trained on the bank entrance.

From the pharmacy, Stacey fired a shotgun blast across the street. Birdshot peppered Miller's face just as he started to mount his horse. At the same instant, the marshal cut loose from his office window and drilled a slug through Cole's thigh. Then, from the opposite direction, Manning stepped out the door of the dry-goods store and triggered both barrels on his shotgun. The impact of a double-load struck Miller in the chest, and knocked him raglike off his feet. He dropped dead in the street.

Doc Wheeler, firing from the hotel window, quickly routed the rear guard. His first shot, slightly low, killed a horse and sent the rider tumbling to the ground. His next shot went high and struck the bridge, exploding splinters directly over Jim Younger's head. On the third shot, the physician found the range. The remaining outlaw took a bullet through the heart, and pitched headlong off his horse.

A shot sounded from within the bank and one of the tellers stumbled through the door. He lost his footing and fell face first on the sidewalk. On his heels, the three inside men burst out the door and ran for their horses. Frank was in the lead, followed by Jesse, and last in line was Bob Younger. Bunched together, they dodged and weaved, snapping off wild shots as they headed for the hitch rack. The marshal and Elias Stacey opened up on them in a rolling barrage. The bank window shattered and bullets pocked the wall of the building all around them. Younger's horse reared backward and toppled dead as he grabbed for the reins. Beside him, still in the middle, Jesse bent low under the hitch rack.

Starbuck, tracking them in his sights, had not yet fired. From the moment they darted out of the bank, he'd waited for a clear shot. His concentration was on Jesse, but the other men were in the way, spoiling his aim.

Then, as Younger's horse fell dead, he saw an opening. He touched off the trigger as Jesse rose from beneath the hitch rack. Bob Younger, scrambling away from his plunging horse, stepped into the line of fire. The slug plowed through his arm from hand to elbow. Jesse vaulted into the saddle, and Starbuck fired a hurried shot. The slug, only inches off target, blew the saddlehorn apart.

Out of nowhere, Cole galloped into the mêlée and swung Bob aboard his own horse. Once again Starbuck was blocked, and he waited as they turned and thundered in a tight phalanx through the intersection. Standing, he moved from behind the lamppost and brought the Colt to shoulder level. He was vaguely aware of the marshal halting at the corner, and distantly he heard the boom of shotguns. Yet he closed his mind to all else, his attention zeroed on a lone figure within the pack of horsemen. He was determined to make the shot count.

The riders hurtled past him and his arm traversed in a smooth arc. From the rear, the horses were separated by wider gaps, and his sights locked on the bearded figure. The Colt roared and he saw Jesse's hat float skyward. He quickly thumbed the hammer back and once more brought the sights into line. Then, on the verge of firing, the horsemen drifted together in a jumbled wedge and he lost his target. There was no time for a last shot.

The outlaws pounded across the bridge and turned south along the Dundas road. A moment slipped past, then they disappeared from view on the opposite side of the river. A pall of eerie silence descended on Northfield.

Starbuck cursed savagely and slowly lowered the hammer on the Colt. His eyes were rimmed with disgust.

CHAPTER 15

A crowd of townspeople stood clotted together outside the bank. Unmoving, they seemed paralysed in a kind of stilled tableau. Their faces were set in a curious attitude of horror and sullen disbelief. All ears, they listened intently as Fred Wilcox vented his outrage.

Only in the aftermath of the shootout had the full carnage become obvious. One outlaw lay sprawled in a welter of blood on the sidewalk. Another, his eyes staring sightlessly into the noonday sun, was spread-eagled on the ground near the bridge. A townsman, killed when he failed to take cover, was crumpled in a ball on the north side of the square. One of the tellers, wounded when he attempted to flee the bank, was now being attended by Doc Wheeler. The other teller, Joseph Heywood, was less fortunate. His throat slashed, he lay dead beside the bank vault. The vault door was closed and locked.

Fred Wilcox, the bank president, was unharmed. A short, fat man, his visage was somewhat like that of a bellicose pig. His lips were white and all the blood had leeched out of his face. He was shouting at Wallace Murphy in a loud, hectoring voice.

"You're the marshal! You're paid to protect the town—not to get people killed!"

"I know that." Murphy looked wretched. "Things went haywire, Mr. Wilcox. We planned to get 'em before they got inside the bank—"

"Damn your plan!" Wilcox said furiously. "Your job is to prevent such things from happening!"

"We tried to," Murphy answered with defensive gruffness. "That's what I keep telling you. We had an ambush all laid out. Then Jack Allen walked out of his hardware store and spoiled the whole thing. If he hadn't got so curious, we would've mowed 'em down right where they stood."

"Don't blame Allen! The fault is yours, and yours alone! Poor Heywood would still be alive if it weren't for your bumbling."

Wilcox made an agitated gesture with both hands. His glance shuttled across the room, where the teller's body lay slumped beside the vault door. The stench of death was still strong, and a puddle of blood stained the floor dark brown. He suddenly looked queasy and his voice trembled.

"My God." He passed a hand across his eyes and swallowed hard. "I'll never forget Heywood's face. When they put that knife to his throat . . ."

His voice trailed off, and Murphy nodded dumbly. "How'd the vault door come to be locked?"

"I—" Wilcox tried to speak, choked on his own terror, then started again. "It was almost noon. I always lock the vault before I go to lunch. Merely a precautionary measure, nothing more."

"The robbers didn't get anything, then?"

"No," Wilcox said hollowly. "Not a dime."

Standing nearby, Starbuck listened without expression. Outwardly stony, he was seething inside. Within him the full impact of his failure smouldered corrosively, shadowing his every thought. An innocent bystander dead and a bank teller brutally murdered. And Jesse James unscathed, still very much alive. All in all, he reflected, it was a sorry performance. He'd made a monstrous gaffe, underestimating the outlaw leader and attaching far too much weight to his own assessment of the robbers' plans. In effect, he had second-guessed a tactical wizard, and he'd guessed wrong. The fault was his own, not Wallace Murphy's. Here today, men had died needlessly, and it left a leaden feeling in his chest. A feeling of abject loathing for himself. And a sense of homicidal rage towards the man who had outwitted him.

"The money," Wilcox went on bitterly, "has no bearing on what's happened. Joe Heywood is dead"—his finger stabbed accusingly at the marshal—"and I hold you personally responsible!"

Murphy looked at him with dulled eyes. "Nobody feels any worse about it than me, Mr. Wilcox. I was only trying to do my duty."

"Your duty!" Wilcox thundered righteously. "You chowderheaded ass! I'll have your job! Before I'm through, the people of Northfield will ride you out of town on a rail. Do you hear me—a rail!"

There was a harried sharpness in the banker's words. He was strung up an octave too high, and Starbuck brought him down. Stepping forward, he fixed Wilcox with an inquisitorial stare.

"Tell me something." His voice was pitched to reach the onlookers crowding the doorway. "Why did they cut Heywood's throat?"

"I—" Wilcox blinked several times. "I beg your pardon?"

"You heard me." Starbuck's eyes hooded. "There must've been a reason. It had to happen before all the shooting started; so it's pretty clear they used a knife to avoid attracting attention. What's the reason?"

"The vault." Wilcox looked ill, suddenly averted his gaze. "They wanted the combination to the vault. When I . . ."

"When you refused," Starbuck finished it for him, "that's when Heywood got the knife. Then they started for the other teller—now that you knew they weren't bluffing—and he bolted for the door. Have I got it straight?"

Wilcox blanched, mumbled an inaudible reply. Starbuck studied him a moment, then added a casual afterthought. "Who used the knife? Which robber?"

"Ooo God!" Tears welled up in Wilcox's eyes. "It . . . it was . . . one of the bearded men."

"Which one?" Starbuck persisted. "The one about my height, or the taller one?"

"Your height." Wilcox pulled out a handkerchief and loudly honked his nose. "The one who gave the orders."

"It figures." Starbuck turned away, motioning to the marshal. "C'mon, Wally. We'll leave Mr. Wilcox to count his money. Let's go catch ourselves some robbers."

Wallace Murphy thrust out his jaw and gave the banker an ugly stare. Then he let out his breath between clenched teeth, and followed Starbuck towards the door. On the steps they halted and stood looking at the upturned faces of the crowd. Murphy's chest swelled and he appeared to grow taller. His eyes blazed with authority.

"I'm forming a posse!" he rumbled in a gravelly voice. "That gang of murderers killed Joe Heywood and poor ol' Nick Gustavson! I give you my solemn oath the bastards will be caught and brought to justice! Any man jack that wants a hand in running 'em down—step forward!"

Several men moved to the front of the crowd. Murphy began ticking off names and issuing orders. The posse members were to provide their own guns and their own horses, and report back to the marshal's office on the double. They were advised to bring along blankets and enough rations to last at least two days. The chase would end when it ended, Murphy shouted. And not a moment before!

An hour later Starbuck and Murphy led six grim-faced men across the bridge. They rode south on the Dundas road.

A hunter's moon slipped out from behind the clouds. The posse was halted some ten miles southwest of Dundas. The men were dismounted at the side of the road, and no one spoke. Gathered around Murphy, they waited with an air of suppressed tension.

Starbuck was squatted down on his haunches. In the spectral moonlight, he slowly scrutinised a crazy quilt of hoofprints on the dirt road. After a time he stood and carefully followed a set of tracks that led west, into a stand of woods. There he knelt and once more studied the sign. He touched a spot of ground which glistened wetly in the light, and smelled his fingers. He allowed himself a satisfied grunt, and climbed to his feet. Then he walked back to where the men waited. He nodded to Murphy, gesturing along the road.

"Five horses, six riders," he remarked. "That means we're on the right trail. Bob Younger was riding double with Cole when they took off."

"What was it you found at the side of the road?"

"Blood." Starbuck rubbed his fingers together. "Still pretty fresh too. I know for a fact Bob Younger was wounded. So the way it figures—he passed out and fell off the horse not long after dark. I'd guess they had to let him rest a spell before they moved on."

"Sounds reasonable." Murphy pointed off into the woods. "We're in big trouble if they headed that way. There's nothing out there but swamps and heavy timber. Probably thirty miles of wilderness between here and the next farm road."

Starbuck's eyes narrowed. "Only three horses went that way, and one of them was carrying double. I'd say it was the Younger brothers and that fourth man. The one Doc Wheeler missed at the bridge."

"You mean to tell me they split up?"

"That's the way I read it. Looks to me like the Youngers took to the brush and the James boys stuck to the road."

"Hell of a note!" Murphy groaned. "They're forcing us to choose. We sure as the devil can't follow both trails!"

"Tell you what, Wally." Starbuck's expression was wooden. "Why don't you and your men stick with the Youngers? I'll tend to the James boys myself."

Murphy returned his gaze steadily. "I never asked, but I suppose I knew all along. You want Jesse real bad, don't you?"

"Yeah." There was a hard edge to Starbuck's tone. "I want him so bad it makes my teeth hurt."

"Any special reason? Or am I overstepping my bounds by asking?"

"No." Starbuck's voice took on a peculiar abstracted quality. "Some men need killing, and his name heads the list. I reckon that's reason enough."

"I'd sure as hell second that motion!"

"Lots of people already beat you to it."

Murphy took his arm and walked him off to one side.

"Just in case we shouldn't meet again, there's something I want you to know."

"Fire away."

"I owe you for the way you stepped in with Wilcox back there at the bank. Except for you, I would've been finished in Northfield. You pulled my fat out of the fire, and I'm obliged."

Starbuck smiled. "Catch the Youngers and we'll call it even." He offered his hand. "Good luck, Wally."

Their handshake was strong, and for a moment they stood grinning at each other in the pale moonlight. Then Starbuck walked to his horse and mounted. He nodded to the other men, reined sharply about, and rode off down the road.

Wallace Murphy watched until he disappeared into the night.

Events of subsequent days proved both frustrating and tantalising. Starbuck's manhunt took him on a tortuous path full of blind ends and false leads. Yet he never entirely lost the trail. Nor was he discouraged by the snaillike pace of the search.

The trail led him first to Mankato, some fifty miles southwest of Northfield. From there, always inquiring about two bearded men on horseback, he tracked the James brothers to Sioux City. Located on the Iowa-Nebraska border, the town represented a point of departure for either Indian Territory or Missouri. A major trade centre, the sheer size of the town also delayed his progress.

Finally, after several days of investigation, he discovered that a bearded man had swapped two saddle horses, along with a hundred dollars cash, for a wagon and team. The switch to a wagon left him puzzled; all the more so when he was unable to turn up a new trail. Exhaustive inquiry at last provided the answer. A wagon, with one clean-shaven man driving, and another on a pallet in the back, had crossed the border into Nebraska. He concluded that one of the brothers, probably Frank James, had been wounded in the shootout at Northfield. The switch to a wagon indicated his condition had worsened over the gruelling flight.

By shaving their beards, the outlaws had cost Starbuck precious time. Once he uncovered the ruse, he set out in hot pursuit; but in the end, their lead was too great. Some two weeks after the chase began, he rode into Lincoln, Nebraska. There, in a maddening turnabout, the trail simply petered out. A day was consumed before he learned the wagon and team had been traded to a livestock dealer. The James boys had departed on horseback three days before his arrival, and no clue to the direction they'd taken. He was stymied.

There was, nonetheless, sensational news regarding the Youngers. The governor of Minnesota had declared a reward of $1,000 per man—dead or alive—and thereby sparked the most massive manhunt in the state's history. For the past two weeks, the outlaws had eluded capture by hiding out in the wilderness maze of southern Minnesota. Then, trapped by a posse, they had taken refuge in a dense swamp. The posse, led by Marshal Wallace Murphy, surrounded them, and a furious gun battle ensued. When the smoke cleared, the Youngers had been shot to ribbons. Bob had suffered three wounds, one of which shattered his jaw. Jim, with a slug through his right lung, had a total of five wounds. Cole, miraculously, had survived eleven wounds, none of which struck a vital organ. The fourth robber, identified as Charlie Pitts, had been killed in the shootout. The Younger brothers, after being loaded into farm wagons, had been carted to the town of Madelia. There, under a doctor's care, they were sequestered in the local hotel.

Upon reading the account in a newspaper, Starbuck boarded the next northbound train out of Lincoln. The trip, with a brief layover in Sioux City, consumed the better part of forty-eight hours. On the evening of the second day, bone-weary and covered with train soot, he arrived in Madelia. He inquired at the depot and learned that the Youngers were being held under guard at the Flanders Hotel. A short walk uptown brought him to the hotel, which was located in the heart of a small business district. He found Wallace Murphy seated in the lobby.

The marshal let out a whoop, amazed to see him and clearly delighted. For the next few minutes they swapped stories, with Starbuck offering congratulations and Murphy extending words of encouragement. On that note, Starbuck asked to speak privately with Cole Younger. At a dead end, he was hopeful that Younger would provide a lead to the whereabouts of Jesse James. There was no love lost between the two outlaws, and with proper interrogation, he thought Younger might be persuaded to talk. Murphy quickly agreed, escorting him to a room upstairs. A deputy, seated inside with the wounded outlaw, was ordered to wait in the hall. Starbuck, prepared for a hostile reception, entered alone.

Cole Younger was swathed in bandages. Still in some pain, and doped up with laudanum, he was staring groggily at the ceiling. Approaching the bed, Starbuck thought he'd never seen a better example of death warmed over.

"Evening, Cole."

Younger rolled his head sideways on the pillow. He batted his eyes, trying to bring Starbuck into focus. Then, somewhere deep in his gaze, a pinpoint of recognition surfaced.

"I know you." His mouth lifted in an ashen grin. "You

was standin' on the corner . . . that day in Northfield. Saw you shootin' at Jesse and the other boys."

"Not the others," Starbuck said softly. "Just Jesse."

"Yeah?" Younger sounded pleased. "Well, I'm sorry to say you missed. The bastard leads a charmed life."

On impulse, Starbuck took a gamble. "I sort of guessed you two might've had a falling out."

"What makes you think that?"

"Easy to figure," Starbuck said with a shrug. "Bob was wounded and slowing you down. Jesse split up so him and Frank could make better time. Wasn't that how it happened?"

"Shit!" Cole said viciously. "You don't know the half of it. He wanted to kill Bob and leave him! I told him he'd have to kill me first."

"Wasn't Frank wounded too?"

"Yeah, but he was able to ride. After Jesse and me had words, they took off. Sonovabitch! All he ever cared about was savin' his own neck."

"You reckon he's headed for Belle's place . . . Younger's Bend?"

Younger peered at him, one eye sharp and gleaming. "Who the hell are you anyway? How'd you know about Belle?"

"Let's just say I've got a powerful urge to see Jesse dead."

"Join the club." Younger gave him a ghastly smile. "You ain't gonna find him at Belle's, though. She wouldn't give him the time of day—not without me along!"

"How about Ruston's spread?" Starbuck watched his eyes. "Down on the Pecos?"

"Ain't nothin' you don't know, is there? Only thing is, you're barkin' up the wrong tree. Tom Ruston swears by Frank, but he's like me when it comes to Jesse. He wouldn't piss on him if his guts was on fire!"

"You tell me, then. Where should I look?"

"Why should I?" Younger said hoarsely. "You got Pinkerton written all over you."

"Guess again," Starbuck said without guile. "I was hired by someone who wants a personal score settled. It's got nothing to do with you or your brothers . . . only Jesse."

Younger regarded him a moment, then nodded. "Without Belle, Jesse's got no place to run this time. So I'd say your best bet's Clay County. He's partial to his wife, and sooner or later he'll show." His lips curled in a cunning, wrinkled grin. "Watch the bitch and the dog won't be far behind."

Starbuck's instinct told him he'd heard the truth. He thanked the outlaw and wished him a speedy recovery. Then, as he turned towards the door, Younger stopped him with one last remark.

"Damnedest thing! You put me in mind of another feller I used to know. Met him once in a whorehouse!"

"Well, Cole, I guess that just goes to show you. It's a small world, after all."

The door opened and closed, and Starbuck was gone. Younger thought about it for a time, his brow screwed up in a frown. At last, no student of irony, he closed his eyes and surrendered to the laudanum.

CHAPTER 16

Starbuck's return from Minnesota was anything but triumphant. In a very real sense, he had travelled full circle, and the knowledge did little to improve his humour. Still, like a crucible enveloped in flame, Northfield had tested his character. He emerged with a kind of steely resolve.

Now, more than ever before, he was determined to kill Jesse James. No longer a job, it was a personal matter. A contest between hunter and hunted.

A day's layover in St. Louis merely strengthened his resolve. Covering all bets, he first sent a wire to the U.S. marshal in Forth Smith. He requested verification as to whether or not a pair of strangers, both white men, had been reported at Younger's Bend. The reply was prompt and unequivocal. Belle Starr and her husband had been arrested and tried for horse stealing. Found guilty, they had been sentenced by Judge Parker to one year in prison. Only yesterday, under heavy guard, the Starrs had entrained for the federal penitentiary in Detroit. Informants in the Cherokee Nation reported that Younger's Bend was now deserted.

Upon reflection, Starbuck decided to scratch Indian

Territory from his list. With Belle Starr in prison, there was small likelihood the James boys would seek refuge at Younger's Bend. The chance seemed even more remote considering the nature of Belle's in-laws. The reward for Jesse and Frank now totalled $10,000—and old Tom Starr might find the temptation too great to resist. Trusting no one, least of all a renegade Cherokee, Jesse would give Younger's Bend a wide berth. As for Belle, Starbuck was mildly amused. He thought the guards at the federal prison were in for a rough time. Where the lady bandit was concerned, anything that wore pants was fair game.

Otis Tilford was Starbuck's next stop. He gave the banker a blow-by-blow account of the Northfield raid and the ensuing manhunt. He made no attempt to spare himself, and freely admitted he'd been snookered by the outlaw leader. Oddly enough, Tilford seemed encouraged. The Northfield incident, he pointed out, had decimated the James-Younger gang. Which was a good deal more than either the law or the Pinkertons had ever accomplished. By virtue of that fact, Jesse James had lost his aura of invincibility. And that made him vulnerable as never before. Tilford heartily approved Starbuck's immediate plan. A staked-out goat, he observed, rarely ever failed to entice a man-eating tiger into the open. Zee James seemed the perfect bait.

After their meeting, Starbuck caught the next train for Kansas City. There he collected his suitcase from the depot storage room, and once more checked into a hotel. A dye job on his hair, added to the spit-curled moustache, turned the trick. He emerged from the hotel in the guise of Floyd Hunnewell. Then, stowing his suitcase once again, he reclaimed his horse from the livery stable. Late that evening, only three days after departing Minnesota, he entered Clay County. His destination was Ma Ferguson's bordello.

Alvina treated his arrival somewhat like a homecoming. After nearly a month's absence, she'd lost any hope he would ever return. She was both amazed and overjoyed, and she smothered him with a childlike affection that was almost embarrassing. Starbuck spun a windy tale which left even Ma Ferguson enthralled. Over the past several weeks, he related, he'd stolen a herd of horses in Kansas, trailed them to Montana, and sold the lot for top dollar. His bankroll was replenished—big enough to choke a horse, he told them with a wry grin— and he was ready to celebrate. Ma Ferguson beamed mightily and the party got under way. Like the prodigal son returned, nothing was too good for Floyd Hunnewell.

Somewhere in the course of the festivities, Alvina broke the sad news about the debacle at Northfield. Starbuck was properly stunned, expressing just the right touch of morbid curiosity and maudlin regret. All of Clay County, Alvina revealed, was in a state of mourning, absolutely devastated. With a shudder, almost weepy, she told him to thank his lucky stars. Had he been accepted into the gang, he too would have ridden hell-bent for Northfield. And got his ass shot off—just like the Youngers!

Starbuck thought it a damn fine joke. Yet he nodded solemnly, and agreed that he was indeed a mighty lucky fellow. He'd count his blessings, and stick to what he knew best, horse stealing. Alvina squealed with delight and made him cross his heart. So he did, and she sealed their pact with another syrupy kiss. Then she hauled him off to bed and welcomed him home in her own inimitable style.

That night, the waiting game began.

• • •

A month passed.

On occasion, Starbuck despaired and silently cursed what seemed an ill-fated venture. At other times, his hopes soared and he rode the intoxicating wind of renewed conviction. His spirits were up and down so often he felt like a broncbuster working a raw string of mustangs.

Towards the end of the second week of his wait, Cole Younger proved to be a swami. One whose crystal ball was not only unclouded, but unerringly accurate. Precisely as he'd predicted, the dog was indeed not far behind its mate. Zee James mysteriously disappeared from Clay County.

Starbuck learned the details from a new drinking crony. Alvina, who was herself a fund of information, had introduced him to Ed Miller. An aspiring bandit, Ed was a distant relation of Lamar Hudspeth, and claimed to have an inside track with the James boys. He was also the brother of Clell Miller, who had been blown to smithereens outside the Northfield bank. That, in itself, lent a certain credence to his gossipy boasting.

A minor celebrity himself, Starbuck traded on his credentials as a thief. He cultivated Miller's friendship by commiserating with him over the loss of his brother. Then, playing the big spender, he treated Miller to a nightly round of drinks. With practised ease, he quickly wormed his way into the man's confidence. And Miller, who was a talkative drunk, repaid his largesse manyfold. A question here and a question there elicited all there was to know about the clannish inner workings of Clay County. In short, Ed Miller and hard liquor were an unbeatable combination.

A couple of nights after Zee James vanished, the investment produced a windfall dividend. Sloshed to the gills, Miller slyly unloaded the latest tidbit. Zee James, he related with conspiratorial bonhomie, had slipped away to join Jesse in Kansas City. Starbuck, who was a master of subtle interrogation, plied him with drinks and prompted him further. Before the night was out, Miller had told all, impressing his friend with details known only to trusted insiders. Later, when Miller staggered out of the bordello, Starbuck acted quickly. Apologising to Alvina, he complained of intestinal trouble, and begged off for the night. Then he rode like the hounds of hell for Kansas City.

Early the next morning, disguised as a rag-and-junk man, Starbuck trundled a cart down Woodland Avenue. Halfway along a quiet residential block, he stopped and rapped on the door of a modest frame house. His hat was doffed at waist level, and beneath it, his hand was wrapped around the butt of his pistol. According to Ed Miller, the master of the house went by the alias of T. J. Jackson. His real name was Jesse James.

When there was no answer, Starbuck went next door. He engaged the neighbour lady in conversation, and soon had the full story. The Jacksons, she informed him, had hastily packed and moved out late yesterday afternoon. She thought it a shame, for Mrs. Jackson, who had arrived only the day before with their children, seemed a perfect angel. As for T. J. Jackson, he'd always struck her as a bit unsociable, somehow preoccupied. Still, in all fairness, she had to admit he'd lived there not quite two weeks, and spent a good deal of time away from home. She surmised he was a travelling man, new to Kansas City. She thought it a reasonable assumption, for it was a furnished house. All of which reminded her to tell the landlord his new tenants had decamped like a band of gypsies. Without so much as a last goodbye.

Starbuck went away with his head buzzing. Everything fitted, down to the woman's physical description of T. J. Jackson. Yet the facts, like loose parts of a puzzle, made no sense. Assuming Miller had it correct—that Jackson was in truth Jesse James—then the sudden departure indicated panic. The natural question was why—after spiriting his wife and children into Kansas City—would the outlaw take flight. One day there, the next day gone, and seemingly without rhyme or reason. The whole thing beggared explanation.

That night, upon returning to Ma Ferguson's, Starbuck got both the explanation and the reason. Apparently Ed Miller had been wagging his tongue all over Clay County. A braggart, desperate to impress everyone he knew, he'd talked himself to death. Only that afternoon, Jesse James had called him out of his home and shot him down on his own doorstep. The killing, performed openly and in broad daylight, was a clear-cut warning. Those who spoke out of turn would speak no more—forever.

Starbuck found himself in the same old cul-de-sac. He'd been thwarted again—seemingly at the very last moment—by a queer juxtaposition of poor timing and bad luck. Worse, he'd lost his pipeline into the backwoodsy world of Clay County. Ed Miller, albeit unwittingly, had proved his most knowledgeable source to date. Now, with the pipeline shut off, he had no choice but to wait and keep his ear to the ground. Yet his patience was wearing thin, and the waiting sawed on his nerves.

For a week or so, Starbuck brooded around Ma Fersuson's. Alvina thought he was saddened by the death of Ed Miller, and he did nothing to dissuade her of the notion. In his view, no man was unkillable; though he was frank to admit some men possessed the proverbial longevity of a cat. Certainly Jesse James had expended nine lives and more over the years. Still, the outlaw was now encumbered by wife and children, a grave tactical error. A family reduced a man's mobility, and tended to anchor him closer to homeground. Some inner voice told Starbuck to sit tight. Clay County was the lodestone, and he felt reasonably confident Jesse James hadn't run far. Sooner or later, almost inevitably, the gossip mill would churn to life. And someone would talk.

The break virtually dropped into his lap. On a mild spring evening, a man unknown to Starbuck walked through the door of the bordello. He was big and fleshy, with the meaty nose and rheumy eyes of a hard drinker. Yet there was nothing to distinguish him from the other customers, and he normally wouldn't have rated a second glance. His furtive manner was the tip-off, and when he displayed no interest in the girls, that cinched it. Starbuck pegged him for a man on the dodge, with something or someone close on his back trail. And plainly terrified by the prospect.

After a couple of drinks, the man approached Ma Ferguson. She listened a moment, then levered herself out of her armchair and followed him into the hallway. A heated exchange ensued, with the man pleading and the madam of the house stubbornly shaking her head. An icy realist, Ma Ferguson was a woman of little charity. She provided a service, at a fair price, and studiously avoided any personal involvement with her clientele. The man was clearly asking a favour, and from Ma Ferguson's reaction, he'd picked the wrong whorehouse. His argument took on strength when he fished a wad of bills out of his pocket and pressed them into her hand. She wavered, locked in a struggle with avarice, and greed finally prevailed. The man was shown to a room upstairs; but the price apparently included only lodging. None of the girls was sent to join him.

Alvina, at Starbuck's request, soon pried the details out of Ma Ferguson. The man's name was Jim Cummins. A first cousin of Lamar Hudspeth—who in turn was related to the James boys—Cummins was privy to all the family secrets. Yet he was also a close friend of Ed Miller, and therefore guilty by association. Whether he had or had not talked out of turn was a moot point. Suspicion alone was enough to seal a man's death warrant, and he'd gotten the notice late that afternoon. Jesse James had appeared at his sister's house, where he was a full-time boarder and a sometime farmhand. The purpose of the visit was unmistakable.

His sister, when questioned, had denied any knowledge of his whereabouts. Understandably skeptical, the outlaw had bullied and threatened, but he'd done her no harm. Instead, he took her fourteen-year-old son into the woods and attempted to beat the truth out of him. When the boy refused to talk, Jesse James left him bloodied and senseless, and rode off in disgust. That evening, upon arriving home, Cummins realised he was in imminent danger. To run was an admission of guilt; to stay put, on the other hand, would merely get him killed. He needed refuge, and he needed it fast. He'd made a beeline for Ma Ferguson's place.

Starbuck sensed opportunity. Cummins' professed innocence had a false ring; anyone that close to the fire had to come away singed. The great likelihood was that Cummins knew too much for his own good, and the good of Jesse James. Starbuck thought he might be persuaded to talk.

Late that night, with Alvina asleep, Starbuck eased out of bed. He dressed in the dark and slipped quietly from the room. All the girls had retired an hour or so earlier, and the house was still. Fortunately, like all whorehouses, there were no locks on the doors, and that made his job simpler. He catfooted down the hall and let himself into Cummins' room. He waited a moment, listening to the even rise and fall of the man's breathing. Then he pulled his sixgun and crossed to the bed.

"Cummins." He stuck the snout of the pistol in Cummins' ear. "Wake up."

"What the hell!"

Cummins jerked and started to sit up. Starbuck pressed the muzzle deeper into his ear, forcing him down. His eyes were wide and white, bright ivory in the dark.

"Listen close," Starbuck said roughly. "I'm here to offer you a deal. So lay real still and pay attention."

"Who're you? How'd you know my name?"

"Who I am doesn't matter. The only thing that counts is what I've got to say."

"Awright," Cummins said stiffly. "I'm listenin'."

"You're going to tell me where Jesse's—"

"I ain't gonna tell you nothin'!"

"Shut up and listen!" Starbuck ordered. "You *will* tell me where Jesse's holed up. In return, I won't tell any of his kinfolks where you're hiding. That's the deal."

"I got no idea where Jesse's at! I swear it!"

"Too bad for you," Starbuck remarked. "That's the only thing that'll get you out of this fix alive."

"What d'you mean?"

"I mean you're no good to me unless you talk."

"You're bluffin'!" Cummins scoffed. "You wouldn't shoot a man just 'cause he don't know nothin'!"

"Think so?" Starbuck thumbed the hammer to full cock. "Try me and see."

Cummins took a deep breath, blew it out heavily. "Suppose I was to tell you? What happens then?"

"You go your way and I'll go mine. So far as anybody knows, we never met."

"Why you so set on findin' Jesse?"

"That's my business," Starbuck said deliberately. "Cough it up or get yourself a permanent earache. I'm fresh out of time."

"St. Joe," Cummins mumbled hastily. "Took Zee and the kids, and moved to St. Joseph. That's the straight goods!"

"What name's he going by?"

"Howard. Thomas Howard."

"Who told you so?"

"Lamar Hudspeth," Cummins said weakly. "He's my cousin, and he tried to do me a good turn. Jesse's puttin' a new gang together, and Lamar asked him to gimme a chance. I thought it was all set . . . up till today anyway."

"Who else got tapped to join?"

"Besides me, there's Dick Liddil, and Bob and Charley Ford. The Fords left for St. Joe yesterday. Liddil and me were supposed to leave tomorrow."

"What's he planning?" Starbuck pressed. "Another bank job?"

Cummins nodded. "Only nobody never told me when or where."

"St. Joe's a big place." Starbuck let the thought hang a moment. "Where would I find him . . . just exactly?"

"Search me," Cummins said lamely. "Lamar was gonna give me and Liddil the address just before we started out."

"One last thing," Starbuck said, his tone quizzical. "What made you think you'd be safe this close to home?"

"Hell, that's easy!" Cummins chuckled softly. "Jesse wouldn't be caught dead in a whorehouse. Safest place on earth!"

Starbuck marked again a phenomenon he'd noted before in certain outlaws. Family men, curiously God-fearing, they never blasphemed or cheated on their wives. Yet they thought nothing of robbery and cold-blooded murder. Their morality was not only selective, but took more twists than a pretzel. It was a paradox he'd never quite fathomed.

"You lay real still." Starbuck backed to the door. "One peep before I make it downstairs and you won't have to worry about Jesse. I'll fix your wagon myself."

"Wait a minute!" Cummins called out quickly. "Just for kicks, answer me a question. Who the hell are you, mister?"

"The name's Billy Pinkerton."

Starbuck smiled and stepped through the door.

CHAPTER 17

The train chugged into St. Joseph late the next afternoon. To the west, a brilliant orange sun dipped lower over the Missouri. The depot, which was situated above the waterfront, afforded a spectacular view of the river. Chuffing smoke, the locomotive rolled to a halt before the platform.

Starbuck stepped off the lead passenger coach. He was attired in a conservative grey suit and a dark fedora. His four-in-hand tie was funeral black, and a gold cross hung from the watch chain draped across his vest. He was clean-shaven, but his jaws were stuffed with large wads of cotton wool. The effect broke the hard line of his features and gave him the appearance of an amiable chipmunk. He was carrying a battered suitcase and a worn leather satchel. He looked very much like an itinerant preacher.

St. Joseph was located some forty miles northwest of Ma Ferguson's bordello. By horse, Starbuck could have ridden through the night and arrived early that morning. Yet he was confident that Jim Cummins—fearful of being branded a Judas—would reveal nothing of their conversation. With some leeway in time, he had walked from the bordello and ridden straight to Kansas City. There, in a whirlwind of activity, he had purchased all the paraphernalia necessary for a new disguise. Once more checking into a hotel, he'd rinsed the dye from his hair and temporarily laid Floyd Hunnewell to rest. By noontime, when he emerged onto the street, he was someone else entirely. After a quick lunch, he'd caught the afternoon train for St. Joseph. A milk run, the trip had consumed the better part of six hours.

Outside the depot, Starbuck paused and slowly inspected the town. A historic spot, St. Joseph was settled on the east bank of the Missouri River. Originally a trading post, it later became the jumping-off point for westward-bound settlers. Shortly before the Civil War, it served as the terminus for the Pony Express, with riders crisscrossing the continent between there and California. Following the war, it developed into a major rail centre, with one of the largest livestock and grain markets in Missouri. Now a hub of commerce, its population was approaching the thirty thousand mark. Which greatly compounded Starbuck's most immediate problem.

Before he could kill Jesse James, he must first locate a man named Thomas Howard. In a burgeoning metropolis the size of St. Joseph, that loomed as a task of no small dimensions.

All afternoon, staring out the train window, Starbuck had pondered the problem. However grudgingly, he'd felt a stirring of admiration for the outlaw. At best unpredictable, Jesse James had exhibited a whole new facet to his character. On the run, fresh from the defeat at Northfield, he'd performed a turnaround that was a marvel of ingenuity. By quitting the backwoods of Clay County, he had broken the pattern established over his long career of robbery and murder. And in the process, he'd left no trail, no clue to his whereabouts. Instead, displaying both imagination and flexibility, he had taken up residence in Kansas City. A clever ruse, it had all but turned him invisible. He'd simply stepped into the crowd, joined the hustle and bustle of city dwellers. And vanished.

Yet, for all his cleverness, Jesse James had been unable to sever the cord. He was bound to wife and children, family and friends, and seemingly to the very earth of Clay County itself. In the end, those ties had proved his undoing. For no man disappears unless he cuts the knot with his past.

Still, given the nature of the man, Starbuck was not all that surprised. Apart from wife and children, Jesse James had been drawn back for perhaps the most elemental of reasons. He was a robber, and since early manhood he'd known no other livelihood. Northfield had destroyed his gang; the Younger brothers, following their capture, had quickly pleaded guilty in return for a life sentence. Then, too, the disaster at Northfield had left the outlaw leader virtually penniless. He desperately needed funds, and for that he had no choice but to form a new gang. Under the circumstances, it was only natural that he would return to Clay County. There, among family and friends, he could recruit men who were eager to ride with the notorious Jesse James. Untested but trustworthy, they would provide the cadre for a new guerrilla band. And above all else, because they were Clay County men, they would follow him with blind loyalty. His roots were their roots, and no stronger bond existed.

Even now, standing outside the depot, Starbuck had to give the devil his due. St. Joseph, although smaller than Kansas City, was yet another shrewd stroke. By not drawing attention to themselves, the gang could assemble anywhere in the town, and no one the wiser. The fact that he knew the names of the new members—Dick Liddil and the Ford brothers—was informative but of no great value. Today only one name counted—Thomas Howard.

Hefting his bags, Starbuck strolled away from the train station. On the walk uptown, he mentally conditioned himself to undertake a new role. From childhood he dredged up long-forgotten quotes from the Scriptures, and silently practiced the orotund cadence of a zealous Bible-thumper. By the time he bustled through the door of the town's largest hotel, he was wholly in character. He positively glowed with a sort of beatific serenity.

"Praise the Lord!" His voice boomed across the lobby with sepulchral enthusiasm. "And a good afternoon to you, brother!"

Halting before the registration desk, he dropped his bags on the floor. His face was fixed in a jaunty smile. The room clerk looked him over like something that had fallen out of a tree.

"May I help you, sir?"

"Indeed you may!" Starbuck said affably. "I wish to engage accommodations. Nothing elaborate, but something nonetheless commodious. A corner room would do nicely."

"How long will you be staying with us, Mr.—?"

"Joshua Thayer," Starbuck informed him grandly. "Western representative for the Holy Writ Foundation."

"Beg pardon?"

"The Good Book!" Starbuck struck a theatrical pose. " 'I am not come to call the righteous, but rather the sinners to repentance!' "

"Oh." The clerk seemed unimpressed. "A Bible salesman."

Starbuck looked wounded. "We all labour in the vineyards, brother. Each in our own way."

"I guess." The clerk turned towards a key rack. "Would you care to sign the register, Mr. Thayer?"

"Delighted!" Starbuck dipped the pen in the inkwell, scribbled with a flourish. "I plan to stay the week, perhaps longer. Your fair town looks hospitable, and promising. Very promising, indeed!"

"We're not shy on sinners." The clerk handed him a key. "Room two-o-four, Mr. Thayer. Up the stairs and turn right. The bellboy's out on an errand just now. He'll be back directly if you care to wait."

" 'Pride goeth before the fall,' " Starbuck intoned. "I can manage quite well, thank you."

"Suit yourself."

"By the way." Starbuck spread his hands on the counter, leaned closer. "An old acquaintance resides in St. Joseph. I haven't his address, but perhaps you might know him. His name is Thomas Howard."

"Sorry." The clerk shook his head. "Doesn't ring any bells."

"A pity," Starbuck observed. "But, then, 'the grains of sand are beyond counting,' are they not?"

The clerk gave him a blank stare. "I'll take your word for it."

"One last question." Starbuck lowered his voice. "Where might I find a peaceful spot for a mild libation?"

"A saloon?" The clerk eyed him with a smug grin. "I wouldn't have thought a man in your line of work would take to demon rum."

"On the contrary!" Starbuck beamed. " 'Let us do evil, that good may come.' Romans, Chapter three, Verse eight."

"Well, the quietest place in town is O'Malley's. Out the door and turn right. Couple of blocks down, on the corner."

"By that, I take it you mean a respectable clientele?"

"You might say that."

"I thank you kindly for the advice."

"Don't mention it."

"Peace be with you, brother!"

Starbuck collected his bags and crossed the lobby. As he mounted the stairs, his mind turned to the evening ahead. Saloons were the gossip mills of any river town, and he doubted St. Joseph would prove the exception. A question here and a question there, and anything was possible. Even the present whereabouts of one Thomas Howard.

He thought it looked to be a long night.

Starbuck rose early the next morning. His head thumped, and he regretted now what had seemed a workable idea last night. From the uptown saloons to the waterfront dives, he had toured St. Joseph until the early morning hours. He'd talked with a succession of bartenders and townsmen, and everywhere he had posed the same question. The sum of his efforts was zero.

No one had ever heard of Thomas Howard.

Through the window, a bright April sun flooded the room. One hand shielding his eyes, Starbuck rolled out of bed and padded to the washstand. He vigorously scrubbed his teeth and took a quick birdbath. After emptying the basin, he laid out a straight razor and mug, and poured tepid water from the pitcher. Then, with dulled concentration, he lathered his face and began shaving. The image in the mirror was reflective, somehow faraway.

Somewhere in St. Joseph, he told himself, Jesse James was staring into a mirror and performing the same morning ritual. The outlaw, with his family to consider, would have rented a house in a quiet residential neighbourhood. A newcomer to town, travelling light, he would have likely rented a furnished house. His starting point would have been—

The newspaper! The classified ads. Houses for rent!

Starbuck's hand paused in midstroke. Then, careful not to nick himself, he finished shaving. Wiping his face dry, he next stuffed his jaws with fresh wads of cotton wool. Turning to the wardrobe, he dressed in his preacher's suit and clapped the fedora on his head. The Colt sixgun, fully loaded and riding snug in the cross-draw holster, was hidden by the drape of his jacket. A last check in the wardrobe mirror satisfied him all was in order. On his way out the door he collected the worn leather satchel.

By eight o'clock, Starbuck was standing in front of the St. Joseph *Herald*. He'd taken breakfast in a café down the street, and casual inquiry had produced the name of the newspaper's editor. Once inside, he by-passed a woman at the front counter with a chipper wave. Several men, reporters and clerks, looked up from their desks as he moved across the room. At the rear, he halted before a glass-enclosed office and straightened his tie. Then he plastered a grin on his face and barged through the door.

"Good morning, Brother Williams!"

Edward Williams was a frail man, with moist eyes and a sour, constipated expression. He laid a sheaf of foolscap on his desk, and frowned.

"Who are you?"

"Joshua Thayer," Starbuck said in high good humour. "I represent the Holy Writ Foundation, and discreet inquiry informs me that you are one of St. Joseph's more upstanding Christian gentlemen."

Williams nodded wisely. "Bible peddler, huh?"

"No indeedee!" Starbuck trumpeted. " 'I give light to them that sit in darkness.' "

"That a fact?"

"Allow me." Starbuck opened the satchel and took out a leather-bound, gilt-edged Bible. He placed it in front of Williams and stood back proudly. " 'Blessed are they which do hunger and thirst after righteousness!' Wouldn't you agree, Brother Williams?"

Williams studied the Bible. "If they do, I'll bet they pay an arm and a leg for it."

"According to Job," Starbuck said genially, " 'The price of wisdom is above rubies.' "

"Spare me the sermon." Williams tilted back in his chair. "What can I do for you, Mr. Thayer?"

"A small favour," Starbuck announced. "A good deed by which your fellow Christians will profit mightily."

"What sort of favour?"

"By chance, do you publish the names of newcomers to your fair city? A list—perhaps a column—devoted to some mention of those recently settled in St. Joseph?"

"Once a week," Williams replied. "People like to see their names in the paper; helps build circulation. We collect the information from realtors and landlords. Why would that interest you?"

Starbuck opened his hands in a pious gesture. "The lot of strangers in a strange city can oftentimes be lonesome. And I ask you, Brother Williams—what better solace for a troubled heart than the words of the Good Book?"

"In plain English," Williams said cynically, "you're drumming up a list of prospects to call on. Isn't that the idea?"

" 'Whatsoever a man soweth, that shall he also reap!' "

" 'Cast thy bread upon the waters, and wait for the fish to nibble.' Wouldn't that be more like it, Mr. Thayer?"

"You are a man of rare perception, Brother Williams."

"Save it for the sinners." Williams leaned forward. "I take it you'd like to look over our back issues and copy down the names?"

"Precisely." Starbuck gave him a disarming smile. "The last couple of weeks should do very nicely. And needless to say, I shan't reveal how I came by the names."

"You do and I'll have your larcenous butt run out of town!"

"Never fear!" Starbuck struck a pose. " 'Wisdom excelleth folly!' So sayeth the travelling man's almanac."

Williams grunted. "The lady at the counter will dig out the files for you. Good day . . . Brother Thayer."

A short while later Starbuck walked from the *Herald*. In his pocket was a list of names and addresses, and a map of the city. One address—1318 Lafayette Street— was circled with a bold scrawl. The occupant was Thomas Howard.

Walking across town, Starbuck quickly formulated a plan. He would knock on the door, posing as a Bible salesman, and attempt to gain entry. From there, assuming he positively identified the outlaw, he would play it by ear. So early in the morning, there was every likelihood Zee James would be present. Even worse, it was possible the Ford brothers were being quartered at the house. In that event, he would simply make his sales pitch and depart without incident. Sooner or later, Jesse James would go out for a stroll, perhaps wander downtown on an errand. Time enough then to brace him on the street. Shout his name, let him make his move—and end it.

On the other hand, it was entirely conceivable he would find the outlaw home alone. All things considered, that would present the simplest, and the quickest, solution. By identifying himself, with the edge of surprise, he would force the gang leader into blind reaction. The outcome was foreordained. He would kill Jesse James on the spot.

The general neighbourhood was situated on a hill east of the business district. As Starbuck had suspected, it was quiet and respectable, modestly affluent. From downtown, he walked uphill, checking house numbers block by block. Some three-quarters of the way up the grade, he spotted the house on the opposite side of the street. A one-storey affair, with a picket fence out front, it stood on the corner of 13th and Lafayette. Halting at the corner, he pulled out his list and made a show of checking off names. Then he angled across the street with a jaunty stride.

A gunshot suddenly sounded from within the house. Starbuck stopped in his tracks, stock-still and watchful. An instant later he heard a woman's shrill, piercing scream. Then the door burst open and two men rushed outside. Jamming on their hats, they pushed through the fence gate, and turned downhill. The one in the lead darted a glance at Starbuck, but quickly looked away. The gate slammed shut and they hurried off in the direction of the business district.

Starbuck swore under his breath. He immediately pegged the men as the Ford brothers, and he had a sinking feeling about the gunshot. His nerves stretched tight, he walked to the fence and eased through the gate. Then he dropped the satchel and warily approached the house. His gun hand slipped beneath the front of his jacket.

The door was open, and from inside he heard a low, keening moan. A step at a time, he edged slowly through the door. The children, a young boy and a little girl, were the first thing he saw. Across the parlour, standing frozen in the kitchen doorway, they stared with shocked round eyes. Their faces, like marble statuary, were drained of colour.

Starbuck's gaze shuttled from them to the woman. She was on her knees, caught in a shaft of sunlight from the front window. Her dress was splashed red with blood and her head arched back in a strangled sob. She cradled a man in her arms, rocking back and forth, holding him tightly to her breast. His feet were tangled in an over-turned chair, and on a nearby sofa lay a double shoulder rig, pistol butts protruding from the holsters. His left eye was an oozing dot and the back of his skull was blown apart directly behind the right ear. A stench of death filled the parlour.

Starbuck saw then he was too late. The woman crouched on the floor was Zee James. Her blood-soaked dress and her wailing cry were stark testament to a grisly truth.

The dead man in her arms was Jesse James.

CHAPTER 18

The coroner's inquest began the next morning.

News of Jesse James' death had created a national sensation. Accounts of the killing rated banner headlines from New York to Los Angeles. The stories, based on hearsay and preliminary reports, were sparse on details. Yet the overall theme of the stories reflected a universal sentiment. The Robin Hood of American outlaws had been laid low by a hired assassin.

The hearing room was packed with an overflow crowd. Newspaper reporters from as far away as Kansas City and St. Louis were seated down front. Behind them, wedged together in a solid mass, was a throng of spectators. The majority, citizens of St. Joseph, were drawn by morbid curiosity. Farmers and people from outlying towns were drawn by grief, and a compelling sense of outrage. They were there to look upon the man who was already being labelled "the dirty little coward."

Starbuck was seated in the front row. Outwardly composed, he was still in the guise of the Bible salesman, Joshua Thayer. Underneath, however, he was filled with a strange ambivalence. Jesse James was dead, and whether by his hand or that of Bob Ford, the result was the same. Yet he felt oddly cheated, almost bitter. Once again, as though some capricious power were at work, he had been thwarted at the very last moment. After months of investigation, added to the strain of operating undercover, the letdown was overwhelming. By his reasoning, he'd been robbed of a hard-won victory.

Still, for all that, his assignment was not yet completed. There was widespread speculation that Frank James would appear—at the risk of his own life—and take vengeance on his brother's killer. Starbuck considered it an improbable notion. Frank James, in his view, was too smart for such a dumb play. On the outside chance he was wrong, however, he waited. One day more hardly seemed to matter.

The inquest, thus far, had produced no startling revelations. Zee James, who was eight months pregnant, and reportedly still in a state of shock, had not been called to testify. Sheriff John Timberlake, summoned from Clay County, had earlier viewed the body in the town mortuary. Based on long personal acquaintance, he positively identified the dead man as Jesse James. Dick Liddil, collared at the last moment by Sheriff Timberlake, had been hauled along to St. Joseph. In corroborating the identification, he noted the deceased was missing a finger on the left hand. The outlaw leader was known to have suffered a similar loss during the Civil War.

Horace Heddens, the coroner, conducted the inquest like a ringmaster working a three-ring circus. He was on the sundown side of fifty, with thin hair and watery brown eyes. Yet his reedy voice was clipped with authority, and he brooked no nonsense from the spectators. When he called Bob Ford to the witness chair, the hearing room erupted in a gruff buzz of conversation. Heddens took up a gavel and quickly hammered the crowd into silence.

Starbuck, with clinical interest, studied the witness while he was being sworn. He thought he'd never seen a more unlikely looking killer. Under different circumstances, Bob Ford might have been a stage idol. He was painfully handsome, in his early twenties, with chiselled features and dark wavy hair. Only his eyes gave him away. He looked unsufferably taken with himself, somehow haughty. His demeanour was that of a celebrity.

The witness chair was centred between Heddens' desk and the jury box. As the coroner went through the preliminary questions, the jurors watched Ford with rapt attention. The effect was somewhat like people mesmerised by the snake rather than the snake charmer.

"Now, Mr. Ford." Heddens held up a long-barrelled revolver. "I direct your attention to this Smith & Wesson forty-four-calibre pistol. Do you recognise it?"

"I do," Ford said without hesitation. "It's the gun I used to kill Jesse James."

"For the record," Heddens said, placing the revolver on the desk. "You shot the deceased yesterday—April 3, 1882—at approximately nine o'clock in the morning. Is that correct?"

"Yessir," Ford smirked. "Shot him deader'n a door-nail."

Heddens laced his fingers together. "For the benefit of the jurors, would you elaborate as to your motive?"

"The reward," Ford said simply. "I did it for the money—ten thousand dollars."

"Were you acting on your own, or at the behest of someone else?"

"Oh, it was official," Ford assured him. "I went to Sheriff Timberlake a couple of weeks ago. Told him I had a once-in-a-lifetime chance to get Jesse."

"Exactly how did this 'chance' come about?"

"Well, like I said, it started a couple of weeks ago. Jesse's gang was all broke up, and he come to Clay County lookin' for new men. I'd known him off and on, and he'd always treated me decent. So I told him me and Charley—that's my brother—wanted to join up and be outlaws. He took to the idea right off, and said I'd get instructions where to meet him. Course, he never had no idea we'd play him false."

"What happened next?"

"That's when I contacted Sheriff Timberlake." Ford's mouth lifted in a sly smile. "Told him I'd deliver Jesse for the reward and a promise of immunity. He went to see the governor, and by the end of the week we had ourselves a deal."

"Thomas Crittenden?" Heddens prompted. "The governor of Missouri?"

"The one and only," Ford said smugly. "He authorised me to go ahead and do it the best way I saw fit."

"There was never any question of taking Jesse James alive? The plan, as sanctioned by Governor Crittenden, was to kill him in the most expedient manner. Is that essentially correct?"

"Naturally." Ford grinned, and wagged his head. "Only a fool would try to take him prisoner. It was either kill him or chuck the whole idea."

"Proceed," Heddens said sternly. "What next transpired?"

"Jesse brought me and Charley here to St. Joe. He had a bank job lined up, and we was to stay with him till the time come. So we moved in with him."

"You refer to the deceased's place of residence, on Lafayette Street?"

"That's right."

"Continue."

"Well, it was touch and go for a while. Jesse was always on guard, real leery. Never once saw him go out of the house during the day. After dark he'd go downtown and get the newspapers, 'specially the Kansas City *Times*. But mostly that just put him in a bad frame of mind, and spoiled our chances all the more."

"Are you saying the newspapers affected his mood?"

"Yeah." Ford gestured with his hands. "A few days ago there was a piece in the *Times*. It went on about how he was all washed up, called him a has-been outlaw. He got awful mad, and said he'd show 'em Jesse James wasn't done yet. Things like that kept him edgy, and just made it harder for us."

"Harder in what way?"

"He always went armed, even in the house. Carried two guns, a Colt and a Smith & Wesson, both forty-fives. Wore 'em in shoulder holsters he'd had made special. So we just never had a chance to get the drop on him. Not till yesterday anyway."

Heddens addressed him directly. "Why was yesterday any different than normal?"

"Jesse was all fired up," Ford replied. "He'd decided to pull the bank job next Monday, and that put him in high spirits. After breakfast, me and Charley followed him into the parlour. He spotted some dust on a picture hanging by the front window, and darned if he didn't go get himself a feather duster."

"He was still armed at that point?"

"Yeah, he was." Ford's expression turned to mild wonder. "Then he says something about how the neighbours might spot him through the window, wearing them guns. So I'm blessed if he don't slip out of the shoulder rig and lay it across a divan. I like to swallowed my tongue."

"So he was then completely disarmed?"

"That's the size of it." Ford nervously licked his lips. "Next thing I know, he stepped up on a straight-backed chair and commenced to dust the picture. Charley and me looked at each other, and we figured it was now or never."

"For the record," Heddens asked with a note of asperity, "Jesse James was standing on a chair—with his back to you—and he was unarmed. Is that your testimony?"

"Yessir, it is."

"Proceed."

A vein pulsed in Ford's forehead. "Well, it all happened pretty quick. Charley and me pulled our guns, and I cocked mine. Jesse must've heard it, because he turned his head like lightning. I fired and the ball struck him square in the left eye. Not one of us ever spoke a word. I just fired and he dropped dead at Charley's feet."

The hearing room went deathly still. The jurors were immobile, staring at Ford with open revulsion. A woman's sob, muffled by a handkerchief, was the only sound from the spectators. At length, with a look of utter contempt, Heddens spoke to the witness.

"What were your actions immediately following the shooting?"

"We cleared out," Ford muttered, lowering his eyes. "We went down to the telegraph office, and I wired Governor Crittenden and Sheriff Timberlake what we'd done. Then we turned ourselves over to the St. Joe police. That was it."

"Indeed?" Heddens' nostrils flared. "And what was the gist of your message to the governor and Sheriff Timberlake?"

"Five words." Ford looked oddly crestfallen. "I have got my man. Wasn't no question what I meant."

"I daresay." Heddens was glaring at him now, face

masked by anger. "Allow me to summarise, Mr. Ford. You capitalised on a man's trust in order to profit by his death. He took you into his home—under the same roof with his wife and family—and by your own admission, he treated you fairly. In return, you waited until he was defenceless, and then—with premeditation and in cold blood—you shot him down. In short, you are nothing more than a common assassin." He paused, drew a deep, unsteady breath. "Have you anything further to add to the record, Mr. Ford?"

"No, nothing," Ford said in a shaky voice. "Except I ain't ashamed of what I done. Somebody had to kill—"

Heddens banged his gavel. "Witness is dismissed!"

Bob Ford rose from the witness chair and darted a hangdog look at the jurors. Then two city policemen stepped forward and led him out by a rear door. There was a protracted interval of silence in the hearing room, and all eyes seemed fixed on Heddens. Finally, with a measure of composure, he consulted a list of names at his elbow. He looked up, searching the front row.

"Joshua Thayer?"

Starbuck jumped. "Here!"

"Please take the witness chair."

Somewhat astounded, Starbuck stood and walked forward. Following the shooting, he had stayed with Zee James and the children until the police arrived. Later, after he'd made a statement at police headquarters, he learned the Ford brothers had voluntarily surrendered. With the killer in custody and the unsavoury details already leaked to the press, it never occurred to Starbuck that he would be called to testify. Now, while the oath was being administered, he prepared himself to continue the charade. Any disclosure of his true identity would merely serve to alert Frank James. And vastly complicate his own life.

"Mr. Thayer." Heddens began, reading from an official document, "I have here your statement to the police. In it, you identify yourself as a Bible salesman. Is that correct?"

"Commissioned agent." Starbuck amended with an engaging smile. "The Holy Writ Foundation doesn't employ salesmen. The Good Book sells itself."

"I stand corrected," Heddens said with strained patience. "Nevertheless, while going about your duties, you were in the vicinity of the deceased's residence early yesterday morning. Would you please tell the jurors what you witnessed at that time?"

"A truly dreadful thing," Starbuck said with soft wonder. "I heard a gunshot, and then two men ran from the house and hurried off towards town. A woman was sobbing—most pitifully, I might add—so I took it upon myself to enter the house. I found a lady crouched over the man who had been shot. He was quite dead."

"At that time, you were unaware that the deceased was in fact Jesse James?"

"Oh, my, yes!" Starbuck's eyes widened in feigned astonishment. "I merely attempted to play the Good Samaritan."

"Very commendable," Heddens said dryly. "For the record, however, I wish to establish eyewitness identification. Do you now state that the men who ran from the house were in fact Charles and Robert Ford?"

"I do indeed," Starbuck affirmed. "Not one iota of doubt. I saw their faces quite clearly."

Heddens eyed him, considering. "One last question, Mr. Thayer. Did you attempt to stop these men from fleeing the scene?"

"Good heavens, no!"

"Did you order them to halt—call out for help from the neighbours—anything?"

"I would hardly have done that."

"Why not?"

" 'A living dog is better than a dead lion.' "

"I beg your pardon?"

"Ecclesiastes." Starbuck smiled in mock piety. "Chapter nine, Verse four."

"I see." Heddens frowned. "So you failed to act out of fear for your life. Is that it, Mr. Thayer?"

Starbuck gave him a sheepish look. "I am not a man of violence. 'Blessed are the meek; for they shall inherit—' "

"Very well, Mr. Thayer." Heddens rapped his gavel. "You're dismissed."

Starbuck nodded diffidently and returned to his scat. The inquest concluded with the testimony of Charley Ford. His story was a reprise of his brother's statement, and added nothing to the record. Late that afternoon the coroner's jury returned a verdict of justifiable homicide. Horace Heddens, in his closing remarks, laid the onus on Governor Thomas Crittenden. The Fords, however despicable their deed, were sanctioned by the highest authority of the state. The murder of Jesse James, he noted, was therefore a legal act. The verdict returned was the only verdict possible.

Then, ordering the Ford brothers released from custody, he adjourned the hearing. He refused all comment to reporters, and walked stiffly from the room.

The train bearing Jesse James' body departed St. Joseph that evening. The destination was Kearney, the slain outlaw's hometown. A short time later, Starbuck boarded a train bound for Kansas City. Upon arriving there, he immediately went through his chameleon routine. Joshua Thayer, Bible salesman, was quickly transformed into

Floyd Hunnewell, horse thief. By midnight, he was mounted and riding hard towards Clay County.

The following day he drifted into Kearney. The funeral was scheduled for late that afternoon, and by midmorning the town was swamped with several thousand people. Some were friends and neighbours, and many were heard to proclaim they had ridden with Jesse James during the war. But the majority were strangers, travelling great distances by wagon and horseback. They were brought there by some macabre compulsion, eager to look upon the casket of a man who had titillated them in life, and now in death. To the casual observer, there was something ghoulish in their manner. They had come not to mourn but rather to stare.

Starbuck, lost in the crowd, was there on business. With no great expectation, he was playing a long shot. He thought Frank James would be a fool to come anywhere near Kearney. Yet stranger things had happened. Grief was a powerful emotion, and it sometimes got the better of a man's judgement. He waited to see how it would affect the last of the James brothers.

A funeral service was held in the Baptist church. Afterwards, the casket was loaded onto a wagon, with the immediate family trailing behind in buggies. The cortege then proceeded to the family farm, some four miles outside town. Not all the crowd tagged along, but hundreds of spectators went to witness the burial. Beneath a large tree in the yard, the outlaw was laid to rest. Gathered around the grave were his wife and children, his mother and sister, and several close relatives. A last word was said by the preacher, then some of the men went to work with shovels. The women retreated to the house.

Frank James was not among the mourners.

The crowd slowly dispersed. Starbuck was among the

first to leave, and he passed through Kearney without stopping. All along, he'd somehow known Frank wouldn't show. As he rode south out of Kearney, he finally admitted what his instinct had told him in St. Joseph. Bob Ford, both at the police station and the inquest, had never mentioned the eldest James brother. And the obvious reason was at once the simplest explanation. Frank James was long gone to Texas.

By sundown, Starbuck arrived at Ma Ferguson's. The moment he walked through the door Alvina sensed something was wrong. He bought her a drink, and they sat for a while making small talk. She asked no questions, and he offered no explanation for his curious disappearance over the past four days. She appeared somewhat resigned, almost as though she had prepared herself for the inevitable. At last, with a look of genuine regret, Starbuck took her hand.

"Wish it wasn't so," he said quietly, "but it's time for me to move on."

"I know." She squeezed his hand. "You never was much of an actor, honeybunch. It's written all over your face."

Starbuck permitted himself a single ironic glance. "Guess some things are harder to hide than others."

Alvina gave him a fetching smile. "You're a sport, Floyd Hunnewell. I won't forget you—not anytime soon."

"That goes both ways."

Starbuck kissed her lightly on the mouth. Then, with an offhand salute, he rose and walked towards the door. Outside he stepped into the saddle and reined his horse out of the yard.

His thoughts turned to tomorrow, and St. Louis. And beyond that . . . Texas.

CHAPTER 19

"Good afternoon, Luke!"

"Mr. Tilford."

Otis Tilford rose from behind his desk. He was beaming like a mischievous leprechaun. His handshake was warm and cordial, and he appeared genuinely delighted to see Starbuck. He motioned to a chair.

"You made good time."

"Not too bad," Starbuck allowed, seating himself. "Caught the morning train out of Kansas City."

Tilford tapped a newspaper on his desk. "I've been reading about the funeral. I presume you were there?"

"You might say that."

"Of course!" Tilford chortled slyly. "Incognito, as it were! Hmmm?"

Starbuck shrugged. "Just a face in the crowd. Nothing worth talking about."

"The newspapers estimated the crowd at several thousand. Is that true?"

"Close enough." Starbuck took out the makings and began rolling a smoke. "It was sort of a cross between an anthill and a circus."

"Indeed!" Tilford snorted. "I must say I find it a rather

disgusting spectacle. All those people congregating to pay homage to a murderous killer! One wonders what the world is coming to."

"Folks need heroes." Starbuck lit his cigarette, exhaled slowly. "Jesse got canonised long before he died. Course, the way he died turned him into a regular martyr. I understand there's already a ballad out about how Bob Ford backshot him."

"Utter nonsense!" Tilford said angrily. "In my opinion, Ford richly deserves a medal."

"I got the impression he preferred the money."

"I was right, then." Tilford eyed him with a shrewd look. "You attended the inquest, didn't you?"

"What gave you that idea?"

"I read about a Bible salesman who testified. The news stories placed him on the scene immediately after the Ford brothers fled. I gather he was the first one inside the house . . . following the killing."

"You couldn't prove it by me."

"No?" Tilford searched his face. "Wouldn't you agree that it strains the laws of coincidence? A Johnny-on-the-spot Bible salesman—working that particular neighbourhood—on that particular morning?"

Starbuck took a long drag on his cigarette. "I wouldn't hazard a guess one way or the other."

"Good grief!" Tilford laughed. "I'm not asking you to compromise professional secrets. I simply wanted a firsthand account of what happened." He paused, watching Starbuck closely. "You were there—when Jesse James died—weren't you?"

"The Bible peddler was," Starbuck said evasively. "For the sake of argument, let's suppose I could tell you what he saw. Anything special you wanted to know?"

"I read an account of Ford's testimony at the inquest.

Several newspapers, however, still claim he shot James in the back. Which version is true?"

"Half and half," Starbuck commented. "James turned his head just as Ford fired. So he got it straight on—clean through the eye."

"How can you be certain?"

"A gunshot wound pretty much tells its own story. In this case the eye was punched inward, like somebody had jabbed him with a sharp stick. The exit wound was bigger, and messier. Tore out the back of his skull and splattered brains all over the wall. No other way it could've happened."

"Then he died quickly?"

"Instantaneous," Starbuck explained. "Lights out before he knew what hit him."

"A pity." Tilford's mouth zigzagged in a cruel grimace. "He deserved to die harder."

Starbuck regarded him impassively. "Dead's dead."

"Perhaps," Tilford said without conviction. "On the other hand, a quick and painless death is no great punishment. A man with so many sins on his head should be made to suffer in *this* life."

"Nail him to the cross and let him die slow. That the general idea?"

"Precisely!" Tilford said with a clenched smile. "The Romans employed crucifixion to great effect. I daresay it was one of history's more lasting object lessons."

"I hear they also fed people to lions."

"Even better!" Tilford's eyes blazed. "I would have taken a front-row seat to watch Jesse James being devoured by a lion."

Starbuck examined the notion. "Some folks got stronger stomachs than others."

"Come now!" Tilford insisted. "Compassion hardly

seems your strong suit. Not after all of those men you've
. . . sent to the grave."

"You ever kill a man?"

"I—no, I haven't."

"Thought not." Starbuck fixed him with a pale stare.
"The killing's no problem. After the first couple of
times, you get used to it. But once you've shot a man
and watched him suffer, you sort of lose your taste for
slow death." His expression was stoic, and cold. "You
learn to kill them fast, *muy* goddamn *pronto*! Otherwise
you don't sleep so good at night."

Tilford looked at him, unable to guess what might lie
beneath the words. He sensed he'd somehow offended
Starbuck, yet the reason eluded him. He couldn't imagine that a manhunter would harbour ethics about killing.
Still, by reading between the lines, a rather primeval
code had been expressed. A code common to all the
great predators. Kill swiftly and cleanly, and do it well.
Sudden death.

"To be absolutely truthful," Tilford said at length, "I
haven't the stomach for it in any form or fashion. But
then, I suspect you knew that all along."

"I never gave it much thought."

"Well, now," Tilford said tactfully, "on to other
things. Where do we go from here?"

Starbuck stubbed out his cigarette in an ashtray. "I
just stopped off to say goodbye."

"Goodbye!" Surprise washed over Tilford's face.
"I'm afraid I don't understand."

"Simple enough," Starbuck remarked. "You hired me
to do a job, and I flubbed it up six ways to Sunday. So
I'm—"

"On the contrary," Tilford interrupted. "You've performed brilliantly, Luke! Without you, I daresay Jesse

James would not have been buried yesterday—or any other day!"

"No thanks to me," Starbuck reminded him. "Bob Ford's the one that got him. I was strictly a spectator."

"Nonsense!" Tilford scoffed. "You routed the gang! If it weren't for that, Ford would never have gotten anywhere near Jesse James. Perhaps you didn't fire the shot, but that's immaterial. Only the end result counts!"

"The fact remains, it was Ford who pulled the trigger. I don't take pay when somebody else does my job."

"That's absurd!" Tilford protested. "I'm the judge of what you did or did not do, and I say you earned the money. I won't hear of your returning one red cent!"

Starbuck gave him a tight, mirthless smile. "I never said anything about returning it."

"I fail to see the distinction."

"I'm trying to tell you I won't take any pay for Jesse."

"Then you're not quitting?"

"No." Starbuck grinned crookedly. "Not till the job's done."

"I see." Tilford looked relieved. "I take it you're referring to Frank James?"

"Only if you still want him."

"Indeed I do! He's no less guilty than his brother."

"Then I'll leave tonight. But I want it understood— you don't owe me another dime. I'll get Frank and then we're even steven. All accounts squared."

"Come now, Luke," Tilford admonished him. "That's carrying integrity a bit far, don't you think?"

"Take it or leave it," Starbuck countered. "I won't have it any other way."

"Very well," Tilford conceded. "Where will your search begin?"

"No search to it," Starbuck told him. "I know where he's hiding, and I'll be there by the end of the week. So you just go ahead and consider him dead."

"Luke, why do I get the impression I won't see you again?"

"No reason you should. Where I'm headed, I'll be closer to Denver than here. Once it's over, I reckon I'll head on home."

"Quite understandable," Tilford said, troubled. "But how will I know for certain Frank James is dead?"

"When it's done, I'll send you a wire."

"Oh?" Tilford pondered a moment. "I wouldn't have thought you'd put it in writing."

"Nothing fancy." Starbuck flipped a palm back and forth. "I'll just say 'assignment completed' and let it go at that."

"How will I know the wire was sent by you?"

"I'll sign it Floyd Hunnewell."

"Does that name have some special significance?"

Starbuck smiled. "Only to horse thieves and whores."

The trip south was long and boring. The train passed through Kansas and Indian Territory, and finally crossed into Texas. With nothing to do but stare out the window, Starbuck found that time weighed heavily. His thoughts, oddly enough, turned inward.

By nature, Starbuck was not given to introspection. He was at peace with himself, and he seldom examined his own motives. Sometimes too cynical, he tended to view the world through a prism of cold reality. Any illusions about other men—and their motives—were long since shattered. Saints and sinners, in his experience, all walked the same tightrope. None were perfect, and he often thought that blind luck, rather than circumstance, dictated which ones lost their balance. In the end, only a hairline's difference separated the upright from the downfallen. There was nothing charitable in his outlook, for he'd discovered that rose-tinted glasses merely distorted the truth. His cynicism was simply a by-product of unclouded observation.

Yet, with time to reflect, he was struck by a queer sentiment. The more he examined it, the more he realised it was wholly out of character. He survived at his trade by virtue of the fact that he gave no man the benefit of the doubt. Still, however sardonic his attitude, a worm of doubt had begun gnawing at his certainty. He was having second thoughts about Frank James.

Not at all comfortable with the feeling, he found it growing more acute as the train rattled towards Fort Worth. He ruminated on their one meeting, a brief exchange of words at Ma Ferguson's whorehouse. He'd sensed that Frank James was a man of some decency. Even then, under the strained circumstances, the eldest James brother had seemed curiously unlike the other members of the gang. Some intangible quality—a mix of honour and conscience—had shown through the hard exterior. None of which fitted with the known facts. The man was an outlaw and a killer, one who lived by the gun. Quoting Shakespeare scarcely absolved him of his crimes.

All the same, Starbuck had found him eminently likable. And that was perhaps the most troubling aspect of the whole affair. His instincts told him Frank James hadn't slipped off the tightrope. Instead, he'd been pulled down by Jesse and the Youngers. Viewed from that perspective, he was a victim of blood relations and bad luck. Still, no man was victimised without his co-operation. Weakness of character was hardly an excuse for murder. Nor was it sufficient reason to grant the murderer a reprieve. And Frank James was known to have killed at least three men.

Stewing on it, Starbuck played the devil's advocate.

He argued both sides, and in the end he worked himself into a dicey position. On the one hand, the last survivor of the James-Younger gang most assuredly deserved killing. On the other, Starbuck was no longer certain he *wanted* to kill Frank James. His sense of duty was in sharp conflict with his personal feelings. Which was a pretty pickle for someone in the detective business. A manhunter with sentiment!

He finally laughed himself out of the notion. On the Pecos, there would be no time for such damn-fool nonsense. Otherwise the damn fool—not Frank James—would get himself killed. And that, indeed, was a personal sentiment.

With brief layovers in Fort Worth and San Angelo, Starbuck slowly worked his way westward. By the fifth day, he'd switched to horseback, and that evening he rode into Fort Stockton. There, posing as a saddletramp looking for work, he drifted into the local watering hole. His questions aroused no suspicions, and within the hour he struck pay dirt. Tom Ruston's ranch lay in the shadow of Table Top Mountain, along a winding stretch of the Pecos. He estimated it was less than a day's ride away.

By dusk the next evening, he had located the spread. Ruston used a Running R brand, and the cows on his range were easily spotted. The land was dotted with cholla cactus and prickly pear, and beyond the river a range of mountains jutted skyward like white-capped sentinels. Far to the northeast lay the Staked Plains, and some seventy miles south was the Rio Grande and the Mexican border. It was remote and isolated, literally out in the middle of nowhere. A perfect hideout for an outlaw from Missouri.

Starbuck camped that night within sight of the ranch compound. When dawn peeled back the darkness, he was squatted in an arroyo not thirty yards from the main

house. Off to one side, purple blemishes in the gathering
light, were a cook shack and a small bunkhouse. He
watched, curbing his impatience, while the outfit slowly
came to life. As the sun crested the distant mountains, a
man emerged from the main house and walked towards
the cook shack. He took the man to be Tom Ruston, and
that assumption was borne out several minutes later. The
rancher led a crew of cowhands from the cook shack,
and moved directly to a large corral. There, the men
roped ponies out of the remuda, and saddled up for the
day's work. With Ruston at the head of the column, they
mounted and rode south along the river. Apart from the
cook, that left no one on the place except Ruston's wife.
And Frank James.

Starbuck scrambled out of the arroyo and circled the
house from the rear. At the corner, he paused, searching
the compound one last time, and pulled his sixgun. Then
he edged cautiously along the front wall, and halted beside the door. Inside, he saw a dark-haired woman washing dishes at the sink. Beyond the living area, there was
a short hallway with doors opening onto two bedrooms.
No one else was in sight.

One eye on the hall, Starbuck stepped through the
door. He ghosted across the room, approaching the
woman from behind. Suddenly she turned, reaching out
for a dish towel, and saw him. She gasped, and her eyes
went wide with terror. Her mouth ovaled, on the verge
of a scream, and he had no choice. His left hand struck
out in a shadowy movement and clouted her upside the
jaw. She hit the sink, scattering dishes, and dropped to
the floor. He wheeled and strode swiftly to the hallway
entrance.

"Martha?"

A voice sounded from one of the bedrooms. Starbuck

stopped cold, hugging the wall. He thumbed the hammer on the Colt, and waited.

"Hey, Martha!" The voice was familiar, but strangely weak. "What's all the noise?"

Starbuck would later wonder what made him speak out. He could have waited until curiosity brought the outlaw through the door and ended it there. Instead, he called down the hallway. "Hello, Frank!"

There was a beat of hesitation. "Who's that?"

"The law," Starbuck answered. "I've come to take you in."

"You figure to manage that all by yourself?"

"No need to stall," Starbuck advised him. "Ruston and his boys already rode off. It's just you and me."

"What makes you think I'll go peaceable?"

"Because if you don't, I'll kill you."

"So what?" Frank shouted hoarsely. "I'd just as soon die here as get hung in Missouri!"

"Think on it a minute! With a slick lawyer—especially now that Jesse's dead—you might have a chance in court. With me, you've got no chance at all. It'll end here and now!"

"Mister, you're dreaming! I'd never make it to trial back home! Somebody would get me the same way they got Jesse—only easier!"

"No," Starbuck assured him earnestly, "I'll get you there in one piece, and I'll see to it you get a fair trial. You've got my word on it, Frank. No one will kill you!"

The intensity of Starbuck's voice gave his words a ring of prophecy. A leaden stillness descended over the house, and for a while he thought Frank wouldn't respond. Then, abruptly, a revolver sailed through the door and bounced across the floor.

"There's my gun! I've quit the fight!"

Starbuck eased down the hallway. He went to one

knee and took a quick peek through the door. Then he slowly rose and moved into the bedroom. He saw that his instinct hadn't played him false.

Frank James lay slack and unmoving on the bed. Ugly lines strained his face, and his eyes were oddly vacant. His breathing was laboured, lungs pumping like a bellows. He looked worn and haggard, older than his years.

"Frank." Starbuck nodded, quickly holstered the Colt. "What ails you? You look a little green around the gills."

"Don't worry." Frank tried to smile, a tortured smile. "I won't die on you. Got a touch of consumption, that's all."

"I'd say that's enough."

"Yeah, it wouldn't have been much of a fight, would it?"

Starbuck had a sudden vision of hell. He saw himself killing a bedridden invalid, not a bayed outlaw. The sight turned his guts to stone.

He silently blessed Frank James for throwing in the towel. And his gun.

CHAPTER 20

" 'Our virtues would be proud if our faults whipped them not.' "

Starbuck smiled. "Before we're finished, you'll have me spouting Shakespeare."

"It's like tobacco." Frank gestured with his pipe. "Once you've got the habit, it's hard to break."

"How'd you get the habit to start with?"

"Well, I never had much formal education. But I got a taste of Shakespeare in school, and I was always impressed by his eloquent way with words. He said things lots better than I ever could."

"Like the one you just quoted?"

"Yes." Frank stared out the train window, silent a moment. "Believe it or not, I've always considered myself a virtuous man. Does that sound strange, Luke?"

Starbuck considered the thought. Over the past month, he'd found Frank James to be a man of his word. After surrendering, the outlaw had convinced Tom Ruston to abide by his decision. The rancher acceded, and thereafter Starbuck had been treated like a guest. In time, Martha Ruston even forgave him the blow upside her jaw.

Their common concern was Frank James. For some years, he had been afflicted with a mild case of tuberculosis. His condition worsened after Northfield, aggravated by the desperate flight and a bullet wound in the leg. When captured by Starbuck, he'd still been weak and frail. Travel was out of the question, and Starbuck had agreed to wait until he'd recuperated. Another month of bed rest—and Martha Ruston's cooking—had put him back on his feet. He was wasted and stooped, a pale shadow of his former self; but he seemed somehow relieved that the running was over at last. Four days ago he had expressed the wish to get on with the business of formal surrender. Starbuck readily approved, and they had entrained for Missouri. Their destination was Jefferson City, the state capital.

Tonight, rattling across the Missouri countryside, Frank James had turned reflective. Starbuck detected a melancholy note in his voice, and sensed he was filled with mixed emotions. With relief, there was also the uncertainty of what lay ahead. Under the circumstances, it seemed natural he would look backward in time. Tomorrow would mark the beginning of the end.

"Virtue's a funny thing," Starbuck said at length. "I guess we all see something different when we look in a mirror."

"No need to ask how a jury will see it."

"Don't sell yourself short. I'd say the odds are fifty-fifty, maybe better."

Frank gave him a tired smile. "Well, however it works out, I'm just glad it's over. I haven't known a day of peace since the war ended. Always looking over my shoulder, afraid to sleep without a gun close at hand. No one could understand what that kind of life does to a man. Not unless he'd lived it himself."

"I've got a fair idea," Starbuck said slowly. "Course,

I was on the other side of the fence. So it's not exactly the same thing."

"God!" Frank laughed suddenly. "When I think back to that night at Ma Ferguson's! It's still hard to believe you and that walleyed horse thief are one and the same."

Starbuck shrugged it off. "All part of working under-cover . . . tricks of the trade."

"You fooled us good," Frank confessed. "After North-field, Jesse knew we'd been euchred somehow. But I wouldn't have suspected you in a thousand years."

"No hard feelings?" Starbuck inquired. "I reckon you know by now there wasn't anything personal involved."

"Perish the thought," Frank said, grinning. "You were hired to do a job, and you did it. I'm just glad you never joined the Pinkertons."

"No chance of that," Starbuck chuckled. "I'm not much for crowds."

"I'd be the first to admit you did very well on your own. I swore I'd never be taken alive—and look at me now!"

Starbuck nodded, watching him. "You're reconciled to it, then? No regrets?"

"Only one."

"What's that?"

"The Bard said it best." Frank's eyes took on a distant look. " 'For mine own part, I could be well content to entertain the lag-end of my life with quiet hours.' "

"Like I told you, the odds are fifty-fifty."

"I wish I believed that as much as you do, Luke."

There seemed nothing more to say. Frank slumped lower in his seat and soon drifted off in an uneasy sleep. Starbuck sat for a long while staring out the window.

Early next morning the train pulled into Jefferson City.

From the depot, Starbuck and Frank James took a hansom cab to the state capitol. A domed structure, the building stood on a bluff overlooking the Missouri River. The view was panoramic, and under different circumstances would have rated a second look. Neither of them paid the slightest attention. Together, they mounted the marble steps and entered the main corridor.

A capitol guard directed them to the second floor. Upstairs, they circled the rotunda and walked directly to the governor's office. An appointments secretary, seated at a desk in the anteroom, looked up as they entered. His smile was at once pleasant and officious.

"Good morning, gentlemen."

"Morning," Starbuck said, removing his hat. "I'd like to see Governor Crittenden."

"And your name, sir?"

"Luke Starbuck."

The man consulted his appointment book. "I'm sorry, Mr. Starbuck. I don't seem to find your name on today's calendar."

"He'll see me," Starbuck said firmly. "Tell him I've brought Frank James here to surrender."

The man's eyes darted to Frank, then back to Starbuck. "Are you serious?"

"Dead serious," Starbuck said with a steely gaze. "So hop to it—now!"

The man bolted from his chair and hurried through the door to an inner office. Several minutes elapsed, then the door creaked open. The appointments secretary poked his head into the anteroom.

"Mr. Starbuck," he said weakly. "The governor wants to know if Mr. James is armed?"

"No." Starbuck fanned his coat aside, revealing the holstered Colt. "But I am, and I know how to use it. Tell the governor he's in no danger."

"Very well." The door swung open. "You may come in."

Governor Thomas Crittenden was seated behind a massive walnut desk. A tall man, with glacial eyes and a hawklike nose, he appraised them with a cool look. Then he glanced past them, nodding to his appointments secretary. The door closed, and he motioned them closer.

"You should be informed," he said curtly, "that I have sent for the capitol guards. In the event you attempt violence, you will never leave this room alive."

Starbuck, with Frank at his side, halted in front of the desk. He fixed the governor with a wintry smile. "You can call off the dogs. Frank means you no harm."

"Are you a law officer, Mr. Starbuck?"

"Private detective," Starbuck said levelly. "I was hired to locate Frank."

"Indeed?" Crittenden sized him up with a lengthy stare. "By whom were you retained?"

"That's privileged information," Starbuck replied. "Let's just say I'm here as an intermediary."

"An intermediary on whose behalf?"

"On behalf of my client—" Starbuck paused for emphasis. "And on behalf of Frank James."

"Oh?" A puzzled frown appeared on Crittenden's face. "I understood you were here to effect a surrender."

"I am," Starbuck acknowledged. "So long as you agree to certain conditions."

"Conditions!" Crittenden repeated with a sudden glare. "What conditions?"

"For openers," Starbuck ventured, "you agree to announce that Frank surrendered voluntarily. I have his gun in my possession, and you can say he handed it over of his own free will. That ought to carry a little weight when he goes before a jury."

Crittenden made an empty gesture. "Next?"

"You agree that he'll be tried on only one charge. One murder, one bank job, or any combination thereof.

But it ends there, whatever the outcome. One trial—and that's it!"

"Anything else?"

"Nope." Starbuck dusted his hands. "Those are the conditions."

Crittenden shook his head from side to side. "Now tell me why I should honour your request?"

"I've got a better question." Starbuck gave him a straight hard look. "Why shouldn't you?"

"I don't bargain with murderers, Mr. Starbuck."

"You killed Jesse." Starbuck's voice was suddenly edged. "Don't you think the state's had its pound of flesh?"

"I killed no one!" Crittenden said abrasively. "Besides, I fail to see how that constitutes grounds for leniency."

"How about politics?" Starbuck suggested. "Would that get your attention?"

"Politics?" Crittenden appeared bewildered. "What earthly connection does that have with"—he flung out a hand at Frank—"a murderer?"

Starbuck eyed him with a steady, uncompromising gaze. "You lost lots of votes when you had Jesse assassinated. By giving Frank a square deal, it might just balance the ledger." He let the governor hang a moment, then went on. "Or aren't you interested in serving another term?"

Crittenden threw back his head and laughed. "Are you seriously suggesting that I would barter with a villainous killer merely to enhance my position at the polls?"

"Look at it this way, Governor. A practical man knows when to bend! Frank will be tried in a court of law, and a jury will decide his fate. Which means you've done your duty, and at the same time you've shown yourself to be a man of fairness and compassion. You'll come out smelling like a rose!"

There was no immediate reply. Starbuck sensed then he'd struck the right chord. Experience had taught him that all politicians justify unconscionable deeds in the name of noble ends. Thomas Crittenden was just such a man.

"Very well." Crittenden nodded with chill dignity. "I will instruct the attorney general to proceed accordingly."

"The people of Missouri won't forget you, Governor. It's a decision worthy of Solomon himself."

"One question, Mr. Starbuck." Crittenden studied him with a keen, sidewise scrutiny. "Why have you interceded on this man's behalf?"

Starbuck grinned ferociously. "I went out of my way to save his life. I figure it'd be a waste to let him hang now."

Words appeared to fail the governor. Starbuck turned and shook Frank James' hand with mock solemnity. He gave the outlaw a broad wink.

The charge was murder.

A trial date was set, with the proceedings to be held in the town of Gallatin. There, some thirteen years previously, the state alleged that Frank James had participated in looting the Gallatin Merchants' Bank. The actual date was December 7, 1869, and in the course of the robbery the bank cashier had been killed. Frank James was charged with having fired the fatal shot.

Missourians rallied to the cause. Though there was sharp disagreement about Jesse, the barometer of public opinion heavily favoured the elder brother. For an outlaw, Frank James was held in high regard and treated with singular respect. His mild manner and frail health evoked widespread sympathy, and there was an outcry to spare him the hangman's noose. Under the tightest security, he was taken by train from Jefferson City to Gallatin. Yet, at every stop along the way, the train was met by cheering crowds. The journey, duly reported by the press, was a triumph. The last of the James boys had come home.

Clay County led the way in establishing a defence fund. Contributions poured in from throughout the state, and the groundswell of support steadily gained momentum. Several attorneys volunteered their services; but Frank James shrewdly selected his own legal counsel. Heading the defence team was General Jo Shelby, a Confederate war hero reverently admired by all Missourians. The second member of the team, famed for both his courtroom oratory and his battlefield exploits, was Major John Edwards. The prosecutor, heavily outgunned, was Robert Spooner of Gallatin. His privately expressed opinion of Governor Thomas Crittenden was not fit for print. Publicly, he theorised that in the event of a conviction he himself might be lynched. The press agreed.

The case went to trial on a Monday morning. Prosecutor Spooner, vainly attempting to resurrect evidence, was handicapped from the outset. His only eyewitness to the killing was a former bank teller, William McDowell. Unfortunately for the state, McDowell had suffered a fatal stroke earlier in the year. By default, the star witness then became a local grocer, Fred Lewis. At the time of the robbery, Lewis was seventeen years old, and his memory had apparently dimmed with age. Upon hearing the gunshot, he testified, he had dashed into the bank and spotted two robbers exiting by the backdoor. Following close behind, he saw the men approach their horses, which were tethered in the alley. One robber was thrown to the ground when his horse bolted as he attempted to mount. He then swung up behind the other robber, and they galloped out of town on one horse. On direct examination, Lewis tentatively identified Frank James as the man who had taken the spill. On cross-examination, he admitted he'd been somewhat hysterical at the time of the holdup. He *thought* the robber was Frank James—but he couldn't be positive.

The second witness called to the stand was a farmer, Dan Smoot. On the morning of the holdup, he testified, he was riding into town as the robbers rode out. At gunpoint, they forced him to dismount and commandeered his horse. Then, with a polite goodbye, they thundered away and left him standing in the middle of the road. When asked to identify the accused, he squinted across the courtroom through store-bought spectacles. He finally muttered a reluctant "Maybe." On cross-examination, Major Edwards inquired whether he'd been wearing his glasses on the day of the robbery. With a look of profound relief, he admitted he hadn't. Major Edwards smiled knowingly at the jurors, and asked no further questions. On that note, the prosecution rested its case.

The defence called only two witnesses. The first was Frank James. He testified he'd taken no part in the robbery, and before being brought to Gallatin in irons, he had never set foot in the town. Prosecutor Spooner, attempting to rattle him on cross-examination, was unable to shake his testimony. Frank James left the witness stand to an ovation from the packed courtroom.

With order restored, Starbuck then took the stand. Presented as a character witness, his testimony was compelling stuff. Counsel for the defense wisely allowed him to tell his story in his own words. He recounted the highlights of his undercover work and the results of his investigation. He dwelled at length on the low morals of the Younger brothers and their general disregard for human life. Then he went on to testify that, in his opinion, Frank James was a man of high Christian principles and the most unlikely outlaw he'd ever encountered. He stated emphatically that Frank had welcomed the chance to surrender, and had freely embraced the opportunity to atone for his crimes. On cross-examination, he refused to divulge the name of his client. He admitted, however, that he had been hired to track down and kill the James boys. When asked why he had spared the life of Frank James, his reply left the spectators spellbound and all but reduced the jurors to tears.

"I could have killed him several times over and in each instance something stopped me. Some people would call it divine intervention, mercy accorded a merciful man. I simply believe Frank James was meant to live."

Final arguments produced the only real fireworks of the trial. Jo Shelby and John Edwards, old soldiers that they were, followed the maxim that the best defence is a good offence. Instead of defending Frank James, they attacked the state of Missouri. Their technique was to raise the spectre of Jesse James. In summation, Major Edwards addressed himself to the life and death of the outlaw leader. His style of oratory was florid, and devastatingly effective.

"There was never a more cowardly murder committed in all America than the murder of Jesse James. Not one among those on the hunt for blood money dared face him until he had disarmed himself and turned his back to his assassins!

"If Jesse James had been hunted down, and killed while resisting arrest, not a word would have been said to the contrary. In his death the majesty of the law would have been vindicated. But here the law itself becomes a murderer! It leagues with murderers. It hires murderers. It promises immunity and protection to murderers. It aids and abets murderers. It is itself a murder!

"What a spectacle! Missouri, with a hundred and seventeen sheriffs! Missouri, with a watchful and vigilant marshal in all her principal towns and cities! Yet Missouri had to ally with cutthroats so that the good name of the state might be saved from further reproach. *Saved!* Why, the whole state reeks today of infamy!

"Tear the two bears from the flag of Missouri! Put thereon, in their place, a thief blowing out the brains of an unarmed victim, and a brazen harlot—naked to the waist—and splashed to the brows in blood!"

The jury deliberated ten minutes, and the verdict was unanimous. Frank James was acquitted.

Starbuck called on Frank early the next morning. Seated in the outlaw's hotel room, they rehashed the trial and chuckled at the devious ways of politicians. Governor Thomas Crittenden had indeed delivered on his promise. The Gallatin case, of all those on the books, was the weakest of the lot. Acquittal translated into votes, and for a politician there was no more compelling motive. Those who fed at the public trough understood the nature of the game. Or perhaps, as Starbuck labelled it, the world's second oldest profession.

"I never asked," Frank said after a time. "But now that it's over . . . who hired you?"

"When all's said and done, does it matter?"

"I guess not." Frank massaged his nose, thinking. "Only you'll have a devil of a time explaining why you didn't kill me."

Starbuck smiled a cryptic smile. "The way it works out, I reckon he'll get his money's worth."

"Well, all the same, I owe you more than—"

"Your credit's good." Starbuck extended his hand. "Stick to the straight and narrow, Frank."

Frank grinned like a possum. " 'Read not my blemishes in the world's report; I have not kept the square, but that to come shall all be done by the rule.' You can bank on it, Luke."

"I already did." Starbuck shook his hand hard. "Down on the Pecos."

Outside the hotel, Starbuck crossed the street and stepped into the post office. He bought stamps and pasted them onto a letter. The envelope was addressed to Otis Tilford, and inside was a bank draft for $10,000. The accompanying message was short and succinct: "No delivery, no charge. Refund enclosed."

He smiled and dropped the letter through the slot. Then, whistling softly to himself, he strolled down to the depot. He caught the morning train for Kansas City and points west.

His assignment in Missouri was complete.

CHAPTER 21

The Alcazar Variety Theater was hushed and still. Starbuck stopped just inside the bat-wing doors. All eyes were fixed on the stage and the crowd appeared hypnotised. He joined them, thumbs hooked in his vest. A slow smile touched the corner of his mouth.

Lola Montana was bathed in the cider glow of a spotlight. She stood centre stage, her face lifted upward in a woeful expression. Her gown was teal blue and her hair was piled atop her head in golden ringlets. The overall effect was one of lost innocence, and smoky sensuality. Her clear alto voice filled the hall, pitched low and intimate. She sang a heartrending ballad of unrequited love. And her eyes were misty.

Starbuck watched her with a look of warm approval. Her performance was flawless, utterly believable. She acted out the song with poignant emotion, and her sultry voice somehow gave the lyrics a haunting quality. The audience was captivated, caught up in a tearjerker that was all the more sorrowful because of her beauty. She had them in the palm of her hand, and she played it for all it was worth. There was hardly a dry eye in the house, and even the pug-nosed bouncer looked a little weepy.

She held them enthralled to the very last note.

A moment slipped past, frozen in time. Then the crowd roared to life, the theatre vibrating to thunderous applause and wild cheers. Lola took a bow, then another and another, and still the house rocked with ovation. At last, she signalled the maestro and the orchestra segued into a rousing dance number. A line of chorus girls exploded out of the wings and went high-stepping across the stage. Lola raised her skirts, revealing a shapely leg, and joined them in a prancing cakewalk. The girls squealed and Lola flashed her underdrawers and the tempo of the music quickened. The audience went mad with exuberance.

Jack Brady, proprietor of the Alcazar, suddenly spotted Starbuck. He bulled through a throng of regulars at the bar and hurried towards the door. His bustling manner attracted attention, and other men turned to look. A low murmur swept back over the crowd as they recognised the manhunter. The threatre owner, enthusiasm written across his face, stuck out his hand. He gave Starbuck a nutcracker grin, and began pumping his arm.

"Welcome home, Luke!"

"Hello, Jack."

"By God, you're a sight for sore eyes! When did you hit town?"

"Couple of hours ago," Starbuck said pleasantly. "Came in on the evening train."

"No need to ask where from!" Brady laughed. "The whole town's buzzing about you. Newspapers have been full of it for the last week!"

"Don't believe everything you read."

"Go on with you!" Brady hooted. "You made the front page, Luke! Headlines and a story as long as your arm. The whole ball of wax!"

Starbuck looked uncomfortable. "Well, I reckon it's yesterday's news now."

"In a pigs eye! Every son-of-a-bitch in Denver wants to buy you a drink. You wait and see!"

"I guess I'll pass," Starbuck said matter-of-factly. "Got a table for me, Jack?"

"You damn betcha I do! Best table in the house!"

Brady wheeled about and cleared a path through the crowd. Starbuck tagged along, not at all pleased by the attention. Westbound on the train, he'd read news stories of the trial, which had created a furor in the nation's press. Worse, he had found his photo prominently displayed in the papers, alongside that of Frank James. The publicity was unwanted, and the photo would definitely prove a liability on future undercover assignments. Still, despite the sensationalism, he'd thought his privacy would be respected in Denver. Jack Brady's ebullient greeting dispelled that notion. An unobtrusive personal life appeared to be a thing of the past.

A spate of jubilant shouts erupted all around him. Men jostled and shoved, pushing forward to slap him on the back or try for a quick handshake. There was a curious note to their congratulations and the general tenor of the reception. For all his reputation as a mankiller, they perceived no weakness in the fact he'd spared Frank James. Instead, they were all the more awed, oddly fascinated and unable to hide it. There was something godlike in possessing the power to kill—within the law—and choosing instead to grant clemency. The very idea of it was scary and admirable, all rolled into one. To the sporting crowd of the Alcazar, it gave Starbuck even added stature. He was no longer merely a celebrity, the town's resident manhunter and detective. He was now a personage. A killer with class . . . and a touch of the invincible.

Onstage, Lola's attention was drawn to the commotion out front. She stared past the footlights and saw Jack Brady unctuously seating Starbuck at a ringside table. In the midst of the dance routine she waved and blew him a kiss. The crowd roared with delight, and Starbuck bobbed his head in an awkward nod. Then the orchestra thumped into the finale with a blare of trumpets and a clash of cymbals. The chorus line, in a swirl of flashing skirts and jiggling breasts, went cavorting into the wings. Lola bypassed the curtain call, moving directly to the side of the stage. She went down a short flight of steps and swiftly circled the orchestra pit.

Starbuck stood as she approached the table. Her china-blue eyes were fastened on him as if caught in something sweet and sticky. She threw herself into his arms and hugged him fiercely. Then, oblivious to the onlookers, she gave him a long and passionate kiss. Clapping and stamping their feet, the audience broke out in rowdy applause. For the first time in his life, Starbuck blushed. He finally got himself disengaged from her embrace, and managed to plant her in a chair. He sat down fast.

"Hello, lover," Lola said breathlessly. "Did I embarrass you?"

"Some," Starbuck replied with a shrug. "I'm not used to an audience."

"Who cares!" She wrinkled her nose with an impudent smile. "You looked too yummy to resist."

"Yeah." Starbuck's eyes dipped to the top of her peekaboo gown. "You might have a point there."

"Why, Mr. Starbuck!" She fluttered her eyelashes. "I do think you missed me . . . or did you?"

Starbuck chuckled. "You crossed my mind now and then. Couple of times, I even had trouble getting to sleep."

"I'll bet!" She sniffed, lifting her chin. "You probably tapped half the farm girls in Missouri!"

"Who, me?" Starbuck looked at her with mock indignation. "I was so busy chasing robbers it kept me worn down to the nubbin. Don't you read the papers?"

"Do I ever!" She threw her hand to her head with a theatrical shudder. "God, my heart was in my mouth when I read those stories. It's a wonder you weren't killed!"

"I can see you almost perished with worry."

"Well, seriously, lover." Her mood suddenly turned sombre. "Do me a favour and kill the bastard next time! I want you all in one piece."

"If it was anybody else—" Starbuck stopped, weighing his words. "Let's just say Frank James was a special case, and leave it at that."

A waiter appeared with a bottle of champagne. He poured, then tucked the bottle into an ice bucket and hurried off. Lola lifted her glass and leaned closer.

"A toast." Her voice went husky. "To you and me— and lots of long nights!"

"I'll drink to that." Starbuck sipped, then slowly lowered his glass. "Only we'll have to hold it to a couple of long nights."

"Ooo God!" She groaned. "Tell me it's not so!"

"Wouldn't lie to you," Starbuck said cheerily. "I stopped by the office and there was an urgent message."

"Just my luck," she marvelled. "All right, break it to me gently. Where are you off to now, lover?"

"Wyoming," Starbuck confided. "Some payroll robber named Cassidy was kind enough to leave his calling card. A client wants me to . . . return the favour."

"It's the story of my life." She stuck out her lip in a little-girl pout. "Here today, gone tomorrow."

"No," Starbuck said, a devilish glint in his eye. "Day after tomorrow."

"That's right!" She brightened, sat straighter. "You said a couple of nights—didn't you?"

"Play your cards right, and we might even squeeze in a matinée."

Lola Montana laughed a deep, throaty laugh. Starbuck poured champagne, and gave her a jolly wink. He thought it was good to be home.

EPILOGUE

New Orleans
May 14, 1903

Starbuck stepped off the trolley car on a warm spring evening. Crossing the street, he went through a turnstile and entered the fairgrounds. He walked towards a candy-striped circus tent.

The sticky humidity made him long for Denver. After two days in New Orleans, he was feeling a bit worn and frazzled. Age had begun to thicken his waistline, and he'd ruefully come to the conclusion that he no longer had much tolerance for heat. Yet, for all the passing years, he was nonetheless an imposing figure of a man. He was still sledge-shouldered, with solid features and the look of vigorous good health. His eyes were alert and quick, and the force of his pale blue gaze was undiminished by time. Nor had age dimmed his zest for his work and the challenge of the chase. He still hunted men.

These days, Starbuck seldom worked alone. Over the years, his reputation as a detective had brought him national attention. At last, with clients begging him to go on retainer, the caseload had become too much for one man. In 1890, he had begun an expansion programme, establishing branch agencies throughout the West. By the turn of the century, he had offices in Denver, San Francisco, Portland, and Tulsa. The agencies were staffed with former law officers, and he'd given each of the branch superintendents a high degree of autonomy. His own time was spent in the field, working directly with the operatives. No armchair general, he led by example and on-the-spot-training, rather than issuing directives. Sometimes, just for a change of pace, he took off on an assignment by himself. And that had brought him to New Orleans.

Last night, glancing through the newspaper, his eye had been drawn to an advertisement. The James-Younger Wild West Show was currently playing a limited engagement at the fairgrounds. Some months ago, he'd heard that Frank James and Cole Younger had formed a road company and were touring the country. Since the Gallatin trial in 1882, he and Frank had never crossed paths. Now, by happenstance, they were in New Orleans at the same time. His curiosity got the better of him.

Hopping a trolley, he'd gone to the evening performance. Like other Wild West extravaganzas, the show featured savage redskins and trick-shot artists and various specialty acts. The star attraction, however, was the two old outlaws. Between acts, they took turns lecturing the crowd. Frank spoke on the evils of crime, and recounted details of the life he'd led with his infamous brother. Cole spun windy tales about their outlaw days, and dwelled at length on the horrors of life in prison. The finale was a reenactment of the Northfield raid. Short on facts and long on melodrama, it dealt mainly with the bloody gun battle outside the bank. There were running horses and an earsplitting barrage of blank gun-fire and lots of dying men. The audience gave them a standing ovation.

Watching from the bleachers, Starbuck was struck by the men's general appearance. Neither of them had aged well, and theatrical makeup did little to hide the ravages of time. Frank was stooped and bony, almost cadaverous, with the mark of years etched in his features. Cole was little more than a bookmark of his former self. His colour was jaundiced and his jowls hung like wattle around his neck. Time lays scars on men, and in their case the journey had been a cruel one. Both of them looked long overdue for the old soldiers' home.

After the show, Starbuck went back to say hello. Frank was genuinely delighted to see him, eager to renew an old friendship. Cole's greeting was civil but cool, and he quickly excused himself. Later, seated in Frank's dressing room, the reason became obvious. Cole's outlook, Frank explained, had been darkened by nearly twenty years in prison. Then, too, he'd lost both his brothers. Bob, after contracting tuberculosis, had died a convict in 1889. Early in 1901, Cole and Jim had at last been paroled. But the next year, despondent and unable to find a job, Jim had locked himself in a hotel room and committed suicide. Thereafter, Cole had worked as a tombstone salesman and sold insurance, living from hand to mouth. Not until they'd teamed up and formed the Wild West Show had he begun to come out of his shell. He still had a long way to go.

As for himself, Frank had no quarrel with life. His wife had stuck by him, and he'd always managed to earn an honest livelihood. His notoriety had made him an attraction, and he'd had no qualms about cashing in on the James name. Down through the years, he had worked as a race starter at county fairs, lectured in theatres, and even tried his hand as an actor in travelling stock companies. At times he felt himself an oddity—something on the order of a circus freak—but all in all he had no complaints. His only regret was that he'd never had the gumption to kill Bob Ford. Someone else had done the job—gunning down Ford in 1892—and his one consolation was that the "dirty little coward" had got it in the back. As for the future, Frank was relatively sanguine. The Wild West Show was booked into next year, and the money was good. When it finally folded, he thought he might try horse breeding, or perhaps go back to farming. He was now sixty years old, and sometimes felt a hundred. Clay County beckoned, and a rocker on the porch of the family farm had a certain appeal. There were worse ways for an old outlaw to end his days.

Starbuck considered the statement a small pearl of wisdom. Upon reflection, after returning to his hotel last night, he'd come to the conclusion it was typical of the man. Frank James was no phony, and he never tried to fool himself or anyone else. Even in the old days, he had possessed that quality so rare among gunmen. He saw things in the cold light of truth, without distortion or whitewash. And he never deluded himself about the romantic nonsense published in penny dreadfuls and dime novels. He was brutally honest about the life he'd led, and his statement summed it up in a nutshell. There were, indeed, worse ways for an outlaw to end his days.

Tonight, the thought was very much on Starbuck's mind. As he walked towards the rear of the circus tent, he marked again the wisdom of some men and the folly of others. Late that afternoon he had concluded his business in New Orleans, and the outcome was anything but satisfactory. He would have preferred a different ending altogether. Something more along the lines of that day, nearly twenty years ago, down on the Pecos. Yet some

men, unlike Frank James, were bound and determined
to go out the hard way. He took no pleasure in the fact
that he was still able to accommodate them. Dead or
alive somehow seemed an anachronism. Not at all suited
to the twentieth century.

Frank's dressing room was located directly behind the
bandstand. Starbuck found him seated before a mirror,
applying stage makeup. He looked up with a sheepish
grin.

"You caught me!" He gave his face one last dab with
a makeup sponge. "Hiding all these wrinkles takes considerable work."

"Near as I recollect," Starbuck said affably, "you always had a secret yearning to tread the boards. Looks
like you got your wish."

" 'All the world's a stage!' " Frank said with an eloquent gesture. " 'And one man in his time plays many
parts!' "

Starbuck's smile broadened. "I've played a few myself . . . here and there."

"A few!" Frank laughed. "Luke, you're a born actor!
You could've made it big in the theatre."

"Well, like you said, all the world's a stage."

Frank waved him to a chair. Starbuck seated himself
and took out a pack of cigarettes. Some years ago he
had switched from roll-your-owns to the new tailor-
made variety. It was one of his few concessions to the
modern age; he still preferred, and used, ordinary kitchen
matches. He struck one on his thumbnail and lit the cigarette.

"Talking about rôles reminds me." Frank began stuffing an ancient briar pipe. "I meant to ask last night, and
it slipped my mind. You in town on business?"

"After a fashion." Starbuck took a long puff, and his
genial face toughened. "Fellow embezzled a bank out in

California. I got wind he was holed up somewhere in the French Quarter."

"Was?" Frank eyed him with a curious look. "You say that like he's not there anymore."

"Yeah, well—" Starbuck hesitated, a note of irritation in his voice. "I went to arrest him this afternoon. Damn fool decided to make a fight of it."

"He pulled on you?"

Starbuck nodded. "Had himself a little peashooter. One of those thirty-two-calibre jobs."

Frank regarded him sombrely. "So you killed him?"

"No choice," Starbuck explained. "I had the drop on him and he still went for his gun. A goddamn book-keeper, for Chrissake!"

Starbuck was not as sudden as he'd once been. Time had slowed his gun hand, but he now compensated by gaining the edge before he made his move. These days, the old .45 Colt, still carried in a crossdraw holster, was already in hand when the trouble commenced. If anything, he was more dangerous than ever.

"Too bad for him." Frank sucked on his pipe, his gaze speculative. "How many does that make? From what I've read, you must have better than thirty notches by now."

"Notches!" Starbuck repeated in a sardonic tone. "What a crock! Bat Masterson fed that hogwash to the papers and they swallowed it whole."

"I don't follow you."

"Well, last year he went to work as a sportswriter for the *Morning Telegraph* in New York. For my money, they ought to have him reporting on sporting houses. That and gambling was always his strong suit."

"Yeah?" Frank appeared puzzled. "So what's that got to do with this 'notches' business?"

"Once a tinhorn, always a tinhorn! He wanted to impress all his Eastern friends, and he needed an angle. So he bought himself an old Colt and cut notches in the handle. To be exact, twenty-six notches! Now he's got everybody convinced he tamed the West and killed all those badmen in gunfights. Spun himself a fairy tale and goddamn if they didn't buy it!"

"I take it you've got the straight goods on him?"

"For a fact!" Starbuck puffed smoke like an angry dragon. "I've known Masterson going on thirty years. He only killed one man in his whole life! And that was in a shootout over a whore. Course, nobody would believe the truth if you told them. He's set himself up as the he-wolf lawman of the frontier and it's all but carved in stone. I think back to marshals like Tilghman and Heck Thomas, and it flat turns my stomach. They're the ones that did the dirty work, and tinhorns like Masterson wind up with all the glory. Sorry bastard!"

"Life's funny." Frank wagged his head back and forth. "All this whiffledust about the old days ought to give people dizzy spells. Sometimes I think they prefer the lies—and the liars."

"Yeah, damned if they don't!" Starbuck considered a moment. "What's the reaction to these talks you and Cole give every night? Do the crowds believe you when you tell them how it really was with Jesse?"

"I tend to doubt it." Frank's eyes were suddenly faraway and clouded. "Legends die harder than men. Jesse was killed twenty-one years ago last month, and folks still believe what they want to believe. Hell, not long ago, even Teddy Roosevelt likened him to Robin Hood! And a president's never wrong. Anybody will tell you that."

"How about you?" Starbuck asked quietly. "When you look back . . . how do you see Jesse?"

Frank gave him a humourless smile. " 'Lord, Lord,

how subject we old men are to this vice of lying!' "

"Forget Shakespeare," Starbuck countered. "You're no liar, so tell me how Frank James feels."

"Luke, you heard my talk last night. I might have shaded the truth to add a touch of drama; but for the most part, it's what I say to every crowd, at every show. We robbed banks and trains because it was easy work. As for the poor and oppressed—we never robbed to help anybody but ourselves."

"And Jesse?"

"A hard man," Frank said with a distracted air. "Too hard for me to remember him with any real charity. I guess I just saw him kill too many people."

"I'd say that's epitaph enough."

"Let's turn it around," Frank said with a glint of amusement in his eyes. "How would you want your own epitaph to read?"

Starbuck looked stern, and then burst out laughing. "Tell you the truth, I don't give a good goddamn! I reckon I never did. Otherwise I would've chose a different line of work."

"You take that attitude and you'll wind up in the same boat with Tilghman and Heck Thomas. A hundred years from now nobody will know your name or anything about you. All they'll remember is Masterson and that crowd. The tinhorns who tooted their own trumpet!"

"No." Starbuck's weathered face split in a grin. "I'll be remembered. A whole crowd will turn out to greet me when I walk through the gates of hell."

"You call that an epitaph?"

"Why not?" Starbuck remarked softly. "I'm the one that sent them there."

"Do me a favour, will you?"

"Name it."

"When you get there"—Frank's mouth curled in an odd smile—"tell Jesse I said hello."

"Frank, you've got yourself a deal."

The old outlaw and the manhunter shook hands. Then Starbuck stood and walked to the door of the dressing room. There he turned, and gave the last of the James boys an offhand salute.

Outside the tent, a line was slowly gathering at the ticket booth. Starbuck skirted around them, idly wondering how large a crowd would attend the evening show. As he walked towards the fairgrounds entrance, it occurred to him that nothing had changed. Tonight merely confirmed what he'd always wanted to believe.

A lifetime ago he had followed his instincts and spared a wanted man. The gesture had cost him $10,000 and the everlasting enmity of a St. Louis banker. Now, looking back across the years, he thought he'd been repaid manyfold. Some men deserved to die and others deserved to live.

He was glad he hadn't killed Frank James.

Bloody Hand

MATT BRAUN

St. Martin's Paperbacks

Bloody Hand

This is a work of fiction. All of the characters, organizations, and events portrayed in this novel are either products of the author's imagination or are used fictitiously.

MANHUNTER / BLOODY HAND

Manhunter copyright © 1981 by Matthew Braun.
Bloody Hand copyright © 1975 by Matt Braun.

For information address St. Martin's Press, 175 Fifth Avenue, New York, NY 10010.

ISBN: 978-1-250-21470-6

Our books may be purchased in bulk for promotional, educational, or business use. Please contact your local bookseller or the Macmillan Corporate and Premium Sales Department at 1-800-221-7945, ext. 5442, or by e-mail at MacmillanSpecialMarkets@macmillan.com.

Printed in the United States of America

Manhunter St. Martin's Paperbacks edition / March 2003
Bloody Hand St. Martin's Paperbacks edition / May 1996

St. Martin's Paperbacks are published by St. Martin's Press, 175 Fifth Avenue, New York, NY 10010.

10 9 8 7 6 5 4 3 2 1

My books are the brook, and my sermons the stones,
My parson a wolf on a pulpit of bones

Anonymous

CHAPTER 1

They topped the last ridge and brought their horses to a halt in a knotted bunch. None of them said anything, but their eyes glinted and among them crackled a ripple of excitement. Below stretched the vast corridor of Cache Valley, surrounded by rock-studded mountains gone splotchy with springtime green. Spread over the valley in the deepening sunset, shimmering with gold-flecked streamers of polar blue, lay Bear Lake.

Frozen in their stillness like grizzled centaurs in smoked buckskin, the men stared down as if bedeviled by the sparkling water. Overhead a pair of mountain jays skimmed and dipped, bright flashes in a melting sun. The trappers started, shifting in their saddles, their spell broken by the beat of wings. Grinning tight, wooden grins, they slewed quick looks around at one another. Then, somewhat sheepishly, they broke out chuckling at the absurdity of the whole thing.

After all, it wasn't as if they hadn't seen a mountain before. Or a lake. *Waugh!* They'd seen their share and more. Enough to make any child shine. Still, they had seen none quite like this—or more precisely, none which offered the temptations awaiting them at Bear Lake. Not since Rendezvous a summer past at any rate.

The brigade had wintered in Snake River country, moving south as they trapped the creeks and freshets

with spring melt-off. Behind them trailed a string of
pack horses loaded with beaver pelts, and prime fur at
that. Sufficient to make even the sorriest among them a
wealthy man by mountain standards. Below, along the
southernmost shore of the lake, was the reason grown
men willingly waded icy streams the better part of a
year.

Rendezvous. The Mountain Man's Fair. Carnival and
orgy all rolled into one. Where trappers gathered each
spring with others of their breed and traded glossy
brown pelts for all manner of things, but mostly for
watered whiskey and pesky women. Sometimes on a
pony race or a throw of the bones. Occasionally even a
quick burial when the knives came out and a man's luck
ran short.

Unlike civilized jubilees, Rendezvous had a way of
being bloody as well as entertaining.

Gazing off across the valley, Davey Jackson regarded
the beehive encampment thrown up on a broad meadow
skirting the lake. Clearly the brigade he led was among
the last to reach Rendezvous. Which in itself meant little or nothing. The trading wouldn't begin—couldn't—
until he arrived. His partners would see to that.

Shifting, Jackson turned in the saddle to face his men.
"Boys, this coon's 'bout half froze to git his pole
greased. I don't reckon nobody'd object if we sashayed
on down and joined the fun."

The trappers hooted him down with coarse jeers.
They were primed and loaded for bear, and Jackson
damn well knew it. Every man in the brigade had slept
with a stiff pecker for longer than any of them cared to
recollect. Merely the thought of what awaited them below was enough to make a fellow's mouth go dry and
pasty.

Over the catcalls came a slurred gibe which set the
men to snickering. "Look hyar now, Cap'n, you figger
they gonna have any dark meat this time? This chile's

done humped so much red stuff he's near forgot what sweetmeat looks like."

Even without turning the trappers knew the voice. Among mountain men only two of their number spoke with that faintly brazen drawl, and the one named Rose had gone under a couple of years back. That left only Jim Beckwith. Not exactly the ace of spades, but darker than anybody would have expected of a mulatto. Beckwith had come to the mountains some six seasons past, hired straight off the St. Louis docks by Rocky Mountain Fur. He had never once looked back, or expressed any notion whatever of returning to civilization. Tall, with skin that had the flat sheen of charred rawhide, he was a gnarled-muscled, lynx-eyed sort of man. Though most of the trappers didn't especially take to him, they'd learned to overlook his highfalutin' manner.

Not that Beckwith was quarrelsome or brusque or even hot-tempered. He was just genuinely willing to accommodate anyone who didn't speak kindly of smart-mouthed niggers. Knives, guns, or fists, it made no difference to him, and the black man hadn't yet lost his topknot. Besides, he was damned handy with a Hawkens when the gut-eaters went on a rampage, and though it galled some, there weren't many his equal when it came to trapping beaver.

All things considered, Beckwith had made a place for himself among the mountain breed, and it was commonly held that his swaggering ways were best tolerated, leastways if a fellow didn't figure to lose a little skin in the bargain.

Davey Jackson merely smiled and shrugged, leaving the black man's question to answer itself. Reining about, he put his horse over the forward slope of the ridge and led the way down. The brigade trailed behind single file, their progress marked by the clatter of hooves and the musical jangle of saddlegear. Moments later the column disappeared into a towering spruce grove.

* * *

Towards dusk, some two hours later, Jackson and his men emerged from an aspen forest bordering the valley floor. They kneed their mounts into a ragged lope and made a beeline for Rendezvous. Drawing closer, they saw the lodges of three Indian villages, each erected somewhat apart from the other, and all set back away from the main encampment itself. The signs seemed to indicate that the Utes, Shoshones, and Crows had come to Rendezvous this year. Since the company actively sought trade alliances with mountain tribes, and only through traders could the Indians obtain the firearms and gewgaws they prized so highly, it was a constant wonder to the trappers that every Indian in Kingdom Come didn't turn up at Rendezvous.

But then, as mountain men often observed among themselves, there was no explaining a gut-eater. None a'tall. They were just downright peculiar, and having said that, a man had pretty near covered the subject.

Jackson's brigade rode into the encampment midst a chorus of barking dogs and shouting mountain men. They were jerked from their horses and embraced in crushing bear hugs by comrades they hadn't seen in close to a year. As they flung from man to man in the drunken crowd, the good-natured pummeling they took raised small billows of dust from their gritty buckskins. Even the Indians came running, drawn by the sheer exuberance of a mountain man reunion. For young warriors who had never before attended a Rendezvous, the swirl of back-slapping and hand-pumping merely confirmed the wisdom of their tribal elders.

White men, whatever their skills as hunters or fighters, were all demented, touched-by-the-Moon beings.

Beckwith was one of the first to be dragged down, snatched clean from his saddle by the massive paws of Doc Newell. The vinegary old trapper had taken him under wing back in the early days, instructing him in the ways of beaver and unsociable Indians, and all the little tricks that kept a man alive in the wilderness. While they seldom wintered together, they remained *companeros,* and for them both, Rendezvous was the high spot of the year.

Jim Beckwith was sledge-shouldered, with the lean flanks of a meat-eater, and by any yardstick he would have been classed a husky specimen. But Newell was immense as an ox, and with almost effortless ease, he shook the mulatto like a limply stuffed doll.

"Jim, ye miserable ol' hunk o' bear-bait! How be ye?" Brushing the black man's cap aside, Newell playfully ruffled his hair. "Goddamn me if ye ain't done it again! Come through with that kinky topknot still in place, didn't ye?"

"Course I come through. I'm standin' hyar right 'fore yore very eyes, ain't I?" Beckwith extracted himself from the older man's grip, gingerly flexing his arms to start the blood circulating again. Cocking his head at a critical angle, he rapped Newell in the midriff. " 'Pears ye wintered purty well yore own self. From the way ye tallowed out I'd judge the fixin's warn't nowhar on the lean side."

Newell's great belly bounced with rumbling laughter. "Christ A'mighty, I'm hyar to tell ye we had a year, Jimbo. Hump meat in the pot nigh onto ever' day, and more blasted beaver'n ye could beat off with a club. Yore lookin' at a rich man, young'n. Made'em come, I did!"

"Wal, braggin' ain't my specialty, ye'll recollect, but we didn't exactly pull up empty-handed our own selves. Davey Jackson ain't no one to share a cave with, but that coon shore outshines the rest of his bunch. Brung in twenty-three packs, we did, and nary a pelt among 'em won't go fer prime."

The old trapper blinked on that. There were a hundred pelts to a pack, which meant that Jackson's brigade had had a very good year indeed.

"Damned if ye ain't got a point thar, Jim." Newell's humor seemed to evaporate on the instant, and his

voice lowered to an angry growl. "Sublette wasted the
better part of the year struttin' his stuff back in St.
Louis, and Jed Smith jest about swapped ha'r fer ever'
pelt he took. Lost nine men out o' his brigade to Injuns,
and the way I hear it, warn't nothin' but the damn fool
hisself that brung it to pass."

Beckwith nodded soberly, but nothing in his face
changed. Hell, better them than him.

Not a year went by but what certain boneheads managed to get themselves killed off, and it wasn't likely to
change anytime soon. Besides, Newell was the only real
friend he had among the mountain brigades anyway, so
it didn't exactly call for sackcloth and ashes. Whatever
his own feelings, though, he could still appreciate the
older man's sense of loss.

"Wal, Doc, I guess they should'a had better luck."

Newell considered the thought a moment, then
ducked his chin. "Yeh, that's the way the stick floats
awright."

Neither of them felt the need to say more. What was
left unsaid required no explanation. Or comment.
Among mountain men there was a degree of fatalism
that bordered on the mystic. The living were obliged to
get on with the business at hand, taking care not to lose
their topknots in the process.

Crudely yet simply put, the dead should have had better luck.

The boys were having a whale of a time. After a winter
of battling icy streams and snowy mountain passes, Rendezvous was their chance to cut the wolf loose and let
him run. One week a year in which they could let their
hair down—without fear of losing it—and give themselves over to the pursuits of lust, liquor, and stomping
the bejesus out of all comers. Grain alcohol spiced with
raw peppers and tobacco juice went for five dollars a
pint, and worth every penny of it. There were no limits
to what a man could do once he was juiced up on fire-

water. It lent strength to his arms in the wrestling contests, made him invincible throwing the bones with the gut-eaters, and somehow even caused his Hawken to fire straighter in the shooting matches. Carousing and gambling rarely sufficed, though. The greater spectacle came when the brawls started. Fair fights, those sissified bare-knuckle events, were for the *mangeurs de lard*, newcomers fresh out from St. Louis. When mountain men collided the object of the game was to cripple and maim—eyes gouged, ears chewed off, bones snapped like kindling. Not without reason, then, the casualty list began to mount, even as Rendezvous of '29 awakened numbed and dazed to greet its second sunrise.

Walking through the encampment early that morning, Beckwith and Newell counted five men who looked like they ought to be dead, and a fifth about whom there was no doubt whatever. With hardly a break in pace, the deceased's comrades were dealing a four-handed game of euchre atop his corpse. Talking it over, the mulatto and his burly friend found it a very sensible idea: stiffened out properly, the dead man made a damn fine card table, much better than a sweaty horse blanket.

While deep in their own cups the night before, Beckwith and Newell had been spectators to one blood-splattered fracas after another. Yet neither of them were asked to join the fun. Not even the pugnacious bantam Kit Carson cared to test their sand, though he had laid three men out cold without hardly working up a sweat.

Seemingly, the volcanic nature of trade whiskey wasn't enough in itself to cloud a man's judgment past certain limits. Doc Newell, who bore a striking resemblance to a stone church, was just naturally the kind of fellow other people left to his own devices. Beckwith, on the other hand, had given lessons so often in rough-and-tumbles that everybody had simply sworn off ruffling his fur. When the cocky ones made their brag—declaring themselves half-horse, half-alligator—the black man and his ham-fisted *compadre* merely sat back and watched. The challenge hadn't been tossed out to them, and everyone in camp knew it.

Curiously, with every Rendezvous that rolled around, Beckwith found himself being drawn more and more toward the Indian games. They were inveterate gamblers, willing to stake everything they owned on a toss of the bones or the swiftness of a favorite pony. Not unlike the mountain men, the warriors were equally fascinated with tests of strength and skill—wrestling, foot races, knife-throwing, and the like. Sometimes they could even be goaded into a shooting match, although taken as a whole they were far more accurate with a bow than the cheap trade muskets sold by fur companies. Among the trappers it was commonly held that being shot by a gut-eater was closely akin to being struck by lightning: strictly an act of God, or perhaps the fickle bitch called Fate.

True or not, the black man had observed that Indian women more than compensated for the excesses of their men. Squaws were neither capricious nor inaccurate. They were doubtless the most mercenary females he had yet encountered, of whatever color, in a long and varied sampling of women. Certainly when a tribe departed from Rendezvous, it was the squaws who had turned the highest profit. On that score not even the warriors were inclined to disagree.

Though Crow women restricted their trade with mountain men to softly tanned shirts and moccasins, the squaws of other tribes dealt in a commerce where supply seldom exceeded demand. They sold themselves, and horny trappers stewed to the gills on panther juice rarely haggled over price.

Sometimes the women strode boldly through camp advertising their own wares, but more often it was the father, or even the husband, who made the arrangements. The squaws treated the whole affair with phlegmatic detachment, yet their performance was seldom under duress. The beads and rings, yard goods, and mirrors, bells, and bangles which they coveted so highly came far easier on a robe couch than in the bartering of buckskins. Besides, no one could equal the Crow women in tanning hides and it simply made more sense to sell what the trappers wanted most. The pay was higher, too, generally about twice the price of a pair of moccasins.

Beckwith had bedded his share of squaws at every Rendezvous, including a flat-nosed little squiggler just last night. But he always went away vaguely uneasy, somehow ungratified, as though he would have done just as well to spurt the stuff over a chokecherry bush. Granted the woman breathed, and if pinched in the right spot even moved on occasion, but the bush would have been no less passionless.

Still, on this particular morning, the mulatto's thoughts were far removed from lukewarm squaws. In league with Doc Newell he intended to outfox the Indian braves at their own game. Some trappers called it the Hand Game, while most simply referred to it as Bones. Yet by whatever name, it was sleight of hand that won the goodies. Anyone who seriously doubted that the hand was quicker than the eye could lose an entire season's earnings with an ill-timed blink.

Hashing it over, Beckwith and Newell had selected the Crows as their mark. It was the richest tribe in both horses and pelts, and therefore prime for skinning. What the Crows stood to lose, they were sure to gain, and if it was enough they might just tell Rocky Mountain Fur to take a swift peek at their dusty rumps. Though this sunrise call on the Crows might have seemed a trifle early to some, it made perfect sense to the two trappers. They had not yet been to bed, having consumed the better part of a gallon jug in the course of the night. From their fuzzy vantage point, catching the gut-eaters sleepy and unawares was nothing short of absolute genius.

Nearing the Crow camp, Beckwith laid it out one last

time for his partner. "Now remember, Doc, ye stand square behind me and watch their hands like a hawk. When they gits done mixin' things 'round ye signal me easy like with yore toe. We'll salt their guts quicker'n scat. Mebbe win ourselves a whole damn tribe."

Newell shot him a testy look. "Quit yore frettin', Jim. We'll nail 'em dead to rights. Hell, there ain't nary Injun alive that could outfox the both of us. Jest wait, ye'll see. Mark my words."

"Jest keep yore eyes open. That's all I'm sayin'. Prop 'em open if ye hafta, but don't let 'em flicker even a leetle bit. Otherwise we're gonna be walkin' away with our ass in our hands, 'stead of the other way 'round."

The black man halted in midstride and peered intently toward the Crow encampment. Bright sunlight was even then burning off the morning mist, but the far side of the village was still obscured in a murky haze. Beckwith blinked his eyes a couple of times and stared harder.

"Doc, lessen I'm goin' blind, there's a bunch of Blackfeet gittin' set to drive off that pony herd."

The words were no sooner out than both men instinctively bellied down on the ground. Across the way they could see movement where the Crow horses grazed west of the camp. After a moment Newell whistled softly between his teeth. "Goddamn me if ye ain't right. But why're the idjits raidin' in broad daylight? Whyn't they slip in last night like they had good sense?"

Beckwith snorted, shaking his head. "Y'know Bug's Boys. Allus got to show everybody they're meaner'n sin and twice as nervy."

Bug's Boys—the mountain men's name for the Blackfeet—was no mere jest. Among the Upper Missouri tribes, the Blackfeet had earned their niche as the most savage—the Devil's own. They warred on everyone about them with impunity.

Their sunrise raid on the Crow was but another demonstration of this supreme arrogance. While the other

tribes came to trade, the Blackfeet mocked their enemies, both red and white, with the sheer impudence of a
daylight raid. The fact that they had selected the Crow
pony herd was yet another sign of their contempt, for it
was commonly vouchsafed that the Crows were the
most superlative horse thieves ever to roam the earth.

Beckwith and Newell held their position as the Blackfeet began driving the herd north along the meadows
bordering Bear Lake. Visible now were the bodies of
the Crow night guards, who apparently had been stalked
and cut down sometime before dawn. Hanging back,
upwards of fifteen Blackfeet warriors walked their ponies toward the slumbering Crow village. Their purpose
was brutally clear. Just as the camp came awake, they
meant to conduct a murderous sweep through the
ringed lodges, killing everything that moved in one final
insult to their ancient foes.

Suddenly the door flap on a lodge flew back and a
squaw stepped out carrying a water skin. For a moment
she froze, eyes wide with terror, then her mouth opened
as she whirled to run. The scream died in her throat
with the rattling boom of several muskets, and the
Blackfeet instantly charged the village. Without a word
Beckwith and Newell came to their knees, tearing back
the hammers on their Hawkens in the same movement.
With the sharp crack of the rifles, two of Bug's Boys
pitched headlong from their ponies. Working fast, the
mountain men jerked wiping sticks and coolly commenced reloading. Even as they rammed home the balls
and struck fresh caps in place, Crow warriors began
boiling from their lodges.

Unnerved by the rifle fire from their flank, the Blackfeet reined their ponies around, milling about in some
confusion. Fighting bleary-eyed Crows was one thing.
But exposing their backs to the deadly Hawkens was
another matter entirely. Particularly since a swarm of
Crows were now dusting them from the front with trade
muskets. When one of the raiders' ponies went down

with a ball through the spine they hastily called it a day. Whipping their mounts into a lope, they took off after the retreating horse herd.

The mountain men jumped to their feet and swung the stubby Hawkens in a slow arc, tracking the fleeing warriors for a split second. Beckwith's rifle barked only an instant before Newell's, and through the smoke they saw a brace of Blackfeet topple backwards over their ponies' rumps.

Newell calmly began reloading, but his eyes gleamed as he darted a glance at the black man. "Ye made 'em come, Jimbo! Damn me if ye didn't. Never yet seen the chile that'd outshine ye when it got down to burnin' powder."

Beckwith grunted, holding back a grin. "Jest natural fer a Hawkens, Doc. Throws plumb center ever' time." When he saw the old trapper wince, he chuckled softly. " 'Sides, I had good l'arnin'. Ferget the feller's name. Some ol' goat that didn't hardly never miss neither."

After both men had reloaded—Newell's first lesson some years past had been that only fools and greenhorns walked around with unloaded rifles—they turned and strolled casually back toward the main encampment. The game of Bones with the Crow would have to wait. Somehow it didn't seem fitting to cheat a fellow when you'd just saved his fat from the fire.

Seated in his tent, William Ashley poured himself a dram of brandy. Unlike the mountain men, he had no taste for trade whiskey. Not that he objected to it— firewater added a considerable margin to his profits at Rendezvous—he was simply accustomed to finer things. The fact that he traded with grimy, unwashed trappers was hardly reason to lower himself to their level, whether in manner, dress, or drink.

Ashley was a man given to profound thoughts, as well as excellent liqueurs, a schemer of sorts, who dwelled much on outsized conspiracies that would have been lost on lesser men. While those of an uncharitable nature damned him as a blackguard and pirate, it was commonly accepted that without Ashley the mountain men would have been thrown to the wolves, the predators in this case being Hudson's Bay and the American Fur Company.

Not that Ashley was any saint, or pretended to be. Giving the other man a fair shake wasn't his idea of sharp trading. Though born to an old St. Louis family, his involvement in the fur trade stemmed from a motive as pragmatic and dispassionate as the man himself: *profit*. When outfitting trappers at the yearly Rendezvous, he deftly extracted his pound of flesh, and they never made any bones about the outrageous prices he charged.

Still, had it not been for William Ashley, there would have been no Rocky Mountain Fur Company. Back in '22 he had boldly led the first brigade into the mountain fastness, establishing a nucleus around which the company was to expand and grow. Before that time, Hudson's Bay to the north, and John Astor's American Fur to the east, had functioned solely as traders, relying on the Indians to trap the furs and transport them to far-flung company outposts. Some years later, when Ashley sold the trapping operation to three members of the original brigade—Jed Smith, Will Sublette, and Davey Jackson—the company had grown to three brigades, encompassing more than a hundred mountain men.

Thereafter, by an ironclad contract, Ashley had served as sole supplier to Rocky Mountain Fur. While the mountain men were doggedly individualistic, living in a land where every man was his own conscience, Ashley aptly perceived that they couldn't stand alone. Their lifeline was the trade route which connected them to the centers of commerce back east. Without a market for the furs, and the goods necessary to survival in the wilderness, the company would have folded within the span of a single season.

Ashley had also been the first to grasp a fundamental tenet of the fur trade. In the mountains, the trader was King of the Hill. Given the excessive cost of overland transport, beaver pelts bought in the mountains for $5 and sold in St. Louis for $8 resulted in a profit of roughly ninety cents, which was exactly the reason Ashley had sold out to the ambitious, if somewhat short-sighted, trio of Smith, Sublette, and Jackson.

Rendezvous in the years that followed had been a time of both merriment and considerable groaning. Because Ashley paid for pelts not in cash, but in trade goods set at his own valuation, he had the trappers in a hammerlock. The markup on merchandise rarely fell below four hundred percent and often exceeded that by a wide margin. Yet, cuss and storm as they would, the mountain men were powerless to combat the situation: Ashley had the only store in town.

Gunpowder and lead, which sold for seven cents a pound in St. Louis, went for $2 a pound in the mountains. Coffee, salt, and sugar, luxuries fully appreciated only by those who live in the wilderness, generally sold at far more exorbitant prices. Ashley's rule was to charge what the traffic would bear, plus another ten percent for good measure. The result was predictable, if not exactly popular. The trapper, with only one market for his catch, was forced to choose between his sweet tooth and enough lead to keep his hair intact through the winter.

What came to pass was that the outfitter—William Ashley—grew rich on the fur trade, while the mountain men barely eked out an existence. Yet even Ashley was preferable to Hudson's Bay or old Astor's pinch-penny outfit. Compared to them, the little man from St. Louis was absolutely magnanimous.

Still, empires founded on greed are shaky at best, as Ashley had only recently become aware. Ironically, his sand castle was being eroded by the very forces that had enabled him to build it.

Quietly, with hardly a ripple, an elaborate struggle for control of the fur trade had been undertaken. Outright deceit, treachery in some instances, were the rules of the game, and the mountain men themselves were cast in the role of pawns. Expendable pieces to be manipulated and sacrificed while the kings waged all-out war for a fortune in pelts.

Though the two companies were scarcely in league with one another, Hudson's Bay was infiltrating the mountains from the north at the exact moment American Fur was spreading its tentacles to enfold the Upper Missouri. Ashley had shown them the way—proved that white trappers could survive in the red man's domain—and both companies had astutely grasped the significance of his success. They meant to share in the spoils, devil take the hindmost, and from past dealings Ashley knew that no quarter would be asked or given. Intrigue and cutthroat tactics would shortly become the order of the day, and only the very crafty would emerge with whole skins.

After considerable soul-searching, Ashley had concluded that the situation called for extreme measures. He must execute some audacious and completely unexpected scheme which would leave the competition standing flat-footed. In short, he had to get the jump on them and make damned sure they were never given a chance to match his stride.

All of which had led him ultimately to a consideration of the Crows. While other tribes were stronger in number, perhaps even more warlike, none controlled the amount of territory claimed by these prodigious stealers of horses. They ruled from the Yellowstone in the north to the Platte in the south, a land mass roughly two hundred fifty miles square. Within its bounds lay the most fertile beaver country on the Continent. Yet the Crows had steadfastly refused to allow the mountain men to violate their hunting grounds. The solution to Ashley's problem was audacious to the extreme, almost biblical in concept, for it was predicated on the belief that certain fools will always walk in where wise men fear to tread.

Whoever gained the Crows' confidence, and the right to trap their mountain stronghold, would rule the fur trade for decades to come.

Yet the riddle might not be as sticky as it appeared at first glance. Only that morning the mulatto, the one called Beckwith, had sided with the Crows in a small skirmish. Everyone knew that Rotten Belly, the Crow chief, was partial to blacks—hadn't he allowed Ed Rose to winter in the Wind River Mountains? Of course, if Rose had not been chopped to ribbons by the Rees, he would have made the perfect stalking horse. But then, there was little to be gained in crying over spilt milk. Or dead niggers. Still, Jim Beckwith might do very nicely, very nicely indeed.

Ashley's train of thought was broken as Robert Campbell, *bourgeois* of his supply caravan, entered through the tent door. "You sent for me, Colonel?"

"Yes, Bob, I did. Sit down a moment." After Campbell had seated himself on the floor, the trader eyed him speculatively. "Tell me, what's being said about that little scrap this morning with the Blackfeet?"

Campbell pursed his lips, somewhat surprised by the question. "Nothin' much. The Crows pulled in a couple of hours ago. 'Pears they run the Blackfeet down and got their ponies back. Can't say as anybody in camp much cared one way or the other."

"I dare say," Ashley observed, leaning forward to light his pipe from the fire. "What about Beckwith's part in it? Perhaps there's been some talk of that."

The *bourgeois* wasn't put off by Ashley's casual manner. Something was in the wind, otherwise His Nibbs wouldn't be so inquisitive. "Aw, Bridger and some of the boys have been ribbin' Beckwith and Newell, but it don't amount to anything. Just the usual horsin' around." Campbell paused, rubbing the stubble along his jawline. "Now that I think on it, there is one thing. Word's around that Rotten Belly is plumb took with the way Beckwith and Newell pitched in this mornin'. Seems like that squaw that got killed turned out to be Rotten Belly's sister. What I hear, the old devil's gonna let them two boys take their pick out of his pony herd."

Something flickered in the trader's gaze and a small smile played at the corners of his mouth. "Bob, I sometimes think the hand of Providence plays a very curious part in the webs men weave. To be sure, the timing couldn't have been better. Ironic, isn't it?"

Campbell didn't know whether to nod or shake his head. "You sorta left me downtrail on that one, Colonel."

"Don't concern yourself too much. All in due time, my friend." Ashley puffed contentedly on his pipe, thoroughly enjoying himself now. Settling back, he stretched out on a silky buffalo robe and let his eyes drift off into space. "Bob, it occurs to me that our stout friend, Mr. James Beckwith, is about to discover a completely new side to his family tree. Now let me consider a moment. With that skin and kinky hair we couldn't say he was thoroughbred Crow. But if he happened to have a Comanche father—or better yet, Cheyenne—that might just turn the trick."

Springing erect, he paced across the tent and back again, his eyes sparkling with the mischief of it all. "That's it, by George! We'll give him a Crow mother and a Cheyenne father, and nobody the wiser. Why, it's as good as in the bag. A *fait accompli!*"

Robert Campbell watched his employer with a growing sense of befuddlement. Sometimes he thought himself a dullard for failing to comprehend the man's schemes more readily. Yet there were other times when he seriously considered William Ashley stark raving mad.

Who else could dream up the cock-and-bull story he had just heard?

After a moment, though, Campbell focused once more on the instructions being rattled off by Ashley. Idle speculation, he reminded himself, was dangerous ground for a mere *bourgeois*.

Better just to listen and do exactly as he was told, and along the way, of course, remember to act as if he knew what the hell was going on.

Beckwith wasn't exactly sober and he wasn't exactly drunk either. But the little men working on his skull with hammers made him wish he'd tapered off long before he had. Worse yet, his tongue felt coated with fur, and from the taste in his mouth, he might well have taken breakfast with a buzzard. All of which had his guts churning like a swarm of nervous butterflies.

When Robert Campbell had awakened him earlier he felt sure he was dead, or paralyzed at the very least. After testing his arms and legs, though, he had somehow crawled from his robes and managed to stagger off in the direction of the lake. There, with his head immersed in the icy mountain water, he had again rejoined the living, rising at last, spewing and snorting, like some great dusky whale from the ocean's depths.

Seated on the bank afterwards he dimly recollected some rhubarb with Old Gabe and that little shitheel Carson. Something about them ragging him and Doc over—damned if he could recall what. Still, it must have come to nothing, for he wasn't skinned up any, and while he felt stiff as a frozen turd, it sure as hell wasn't the result of fighting. Hazily he remembered calling it a night along about noonday and stumbling off to his robes like a blind pup. Then there was nothing but a merciful blank spot until Ashley's bootlicker had rousted him awake.

Ashley! That was it. The head wolf had sent Campbell out to fetch him. Wanted to talk to him, Campbell had said. Just that, no reason stated. But then, Ashley wasn't the kind to give reasons. Lots of orders—real high and

mighty he was—but damned shy on the whyfors. Well,
dip shit and bark at the moon, it made no never mind
anyway. Whatever it was, he'd find out soon enough.

Struggling to his feet, Beckwith ambled off through
the encampment toward Ashley's tent. Though his head
was still buzzing, and his pace a bit unsteady, he had the
distinct feeling he might just pull through. Not that he
would ever fully recover. Whatever that batch of firewater had in it—probably snakeheads—it had corroded
his innards like a dose of green meat. Idly, he speculated on the possibility that he'd been poisoned. Then
he discarded the idea after a moment's thought. Shit!
He'd been stung by rattlers, scorpions, even a couple of
cottonmouths when he was a kid. His old mammy had
fixed him up with enough voodoo hoodoo to last a lifetime. There weren't nothin' this side of the Jordan itself
he couldn't handle. Panther juice included!

Approaching Ashley's quarters, he gave the tent a
sideways scowl. The little bugger sure fancied himself
something fierce. Had everybody bowing and scraping,
and calling him Colonel, just because he'd served in the
militia once. Couldn't even use a skin lodge like regular
folks. Every year, come Rendezvous, up went that tent.
Just like one of them grand potentates, the ones Jed
Smith was always reading about, had come to visit the
riffraff.

What the hell, though! It wasn't no skin off nobody's
nose. Not when a fellow stood off and looked at it just
right. Some ways it was even funny. That scrawny little
mousefart rocking up on his toes so he wouldn't have to
look a man in the bellybutton.

The black man grinned, then winced. Christ, if it
wasn't for his head hurtin' so goddamn bad, it'd be
plumb laughable.

Stooping, he entered the tent and found Ashley
seated on a couch of buffalo robes, busily riffling
through a sheaf of foolscap. The trader looked up from
his papers and smiled amiably, too much so to suit

Beckwith. Sort of like a weasel when he's about to jump
his supper. It was plain to see, the Colonel was after
something. Though for the life of him, Beckwith
couldn't imagine what he had that would interest a
fancy-britches like Ashley.

"Sit down, Jim. Take a load off your feet." The
trader's waxy smile faded as he observed Beckwith gingerly squat and ease himself to the floor. Solicitous now,
he clucked softly, shaking his head. "Unless I'm mistaken, you've had a long night. Little too much liquor,
perhaps?"

"Too much or not 'nough. I ain't right sure which.
When yore budgeway woke me I was so thirsty I
could've drunk bear piss. Must've swallered half that
lake gettin' my bowels cooled down."

"Well, why not, Jim? Rendezvous only comes once a
year. A man's entitled to let himself go on occasion. Eat,
drink, and be merry, for tomorrow may not come. Don't
you agree?"

"Tell you the truth"—Beckwith paused and let fly a
gassy belch—"I ain't plumb sartain 'bout today."

Ashley's smile returned. "Jim, that's precisely why I
sent for you. I need your help on a matter of some
consequence, and tomorrow may well be too late. As a
matter of fact, today might be the best chance we'll ever
have. Perhaps the only chance."

The mulatto braced himself. Whatever the Colonel
had in mind, it was about to be unloaded on him. Still,
he didn't flicker so much as an eyelash throughout Ashley's oily discourse, taking it all in with the unruffled
calm of a sleepy owl. While the part about Hudson's
Bay and American Fur sounded like garbled nonsense
at first, he began to get the gist of the scheme once
Ashley worked around to the Crows. Whatever his personal feelings about the trader, he had to admire his
cunning. The man was slick as greased bear shit.

Ashley concluded on a stirring note of camaraderie.
"Working together, Jim, we can scuttle the opposition

for years to come. The way I envision it, you will become a Crow in every sense of the word. Through your influence, we can persuade them to trade only with Rocky Mountain Fur. Then, sometime later—when the time seems ripe, you understand—we'll negotiate an agreement allowing company men to trap south of the Yellowstone. Why, the effect on the fur trade could be staggering. Revolutionary even. Just think of it!"

Beckwith was doing just that, but along somewhat different lines. The idea appealed to him, touched a nerve that sent little jangles up his spine. Not even Ed Rose—sorry excuse for a nigger that he was—had pulled off anything like this. Nobody had.

Hell, chances were nobody could.

All the same, if he could swing it—somehow get the Crows to thinking his shit didn't stink—there'd be a whole passel of mountain men standing in line to kiss his ass.

The thought had a savor all its own, but it still wasn't enough. There had to be more, a little something extra to sweeten the pot. Something that would make Ashley himself squirm.

"Cap'n, if I git yore drift, ye figger fer me to go off and live with the Crows and someway bring 'em 'round to yore camp."

Ashley blinked at his sudden reduction in rank, but he let it pass. "Precisely, Jim. For a man of your talents, it shouldn't be any problem at all. Why, I venture to say you'll have them eating out of your hand before first snow flies."

"Mebbe. Course, that ain't sayin' I'll do it." Beckwith fixed his gaze on a spot somewhere over the trader's head and tried his damnedest to look shrewd. "Jest supposin' I did, though. Ain't hard to see how the company'd come up dippin' honey, but so far I don't calculate nothin' in it fer me."

Taken unawares, Ashley just stared at him. Clearly there were facets to this mulatto woods colt he had

never seen before. After a moment he smiled, trying for
a benign effect. "Yes, I see your point. And well taken,
too. Suppose we provide an inducement, Jim. Something on the order of say five percent of all pelt taken
from Crow territory. How would that strike you?"

"Nothin' personal, Cap'n, but it strikes me as sort o'
stingy. Make it ten and ye got yoreself a deal."

"Done. We'll shake on it. And let me congratulate
you, Jim. You drive a hard bargain, but fair. Very fair.
While I'm not normally given to predictions, I dare say
the pact we've struck today will make you a rich man.
Very rich indeed."

" 'Ceptin' fer a few things 'twixt here and there."
Beckwith pumped his hand a couple of times and let go,
then cocked an eyebrow. "Jest fer instance, Cap'n. D'ye
actual think them Crows are gonna swaller that doosie
'bout the Cheyennes swipin' my ma?"

"Why, they'll positively revel in it! Campbell is out
right now spreading the story. Once Rotten Belly gets
wind of it he'll go into conniption fits. Take my word for
it, Jim. After all, you are the man who avenged his murdered sister. What could be more fitting?"

Beckwith had to admit it was a good plan. Crafty
even. Maybe a little ripe here and there, but what the
hell? The Crows weren't any brighter than the rest of
the gut-eaters. They would doubtless gobble it down just
like Ashley said.

When the trader walked him to the door, they again
shook hands. Just for a moment, he caught a glint of
something in Ashley's eyes like a cat gloating over a tub
of cream. Then it passed and the little man graced him
once more with that wooden smile.

Striding back through the encampment, Beckwith
couldn't shake the feeling that he had just struck a bargain with Lucifer himself. Clearly Col. William Ashley
was playing for high stakes, in a game where one nigger
more or less wouldn't mean a hill of beans.

Which made him a man not to be taken lightly, or trusted.

Beckwith and Newell found the Crow village all but deserted, the streets empty and the lodges curiously silent. While they hadn't expected to be welcomed as conquering heroes, they also weren't prepared to be treated as lepers. The stillness was wholly out of place for an Indian camp, and somehow eerie, and both men had the prickly feeling of being watched by someone who remains unseen. Even the cooking fires had died down, though dusk was yet an hour away and the western mountains were still bathed in an orangy glow.

There was something spooky about it, unnatural, the icy tingle along a man's spine when fleeting things lurk and watch but keep themselves hidden. Like a graveyard, where the dead still walk and the living come unbidden only at great peril.

When the mountain men halted before Rotten Belly's lodge the *aciperirau* awaited them. Earlier that afternoon, speaking on behalf of the chief, he had extended an invitation to take supper with the most famed of Crow leaders. Presumably the summons stemmed from their part in the horse raid that morning. Yet an element of uncertainty manifested itself there, too. For the astounding tale of Beckwith's childhood had already galvanized the camp into an endless round of speculation and debate. The mountain brigades had greeted the story with a chorus of braying disbelief, wondering what trick the roguish black had up his sleeve this time.

What the Crows thought was anyone's guess. They hadn't ventured into the main encampment all afternoon, which in itself might mean nothing. Thus far, though, no one had been struck by any great urge to waltz over and pop the question.

Beckwith and Newell, then, would be the first to get the straight goods from the Crows themselves, which seemed profoundly fair to the rest of the trappers, since by now it was generally accepted that the mulatto had rigged the whole affair for some murky purpose all his own.

When the *aciperirau* ushered Beckwith and Newell into the lodge, they found Rotten Belly seated alone before a small fire. The chief studied them briefly, then motioned Beckwith to his left—the seat of honor—and Newell to his right. As the mountain men complied, Rotten Belly hauled out a cutting board, wedged it between his knees, and began chopping tobacco with deft strokes of his knife. Once it was minced to his satisfaction, he mixed the tobacco with a pinch of willowbark and commenced loading a long ceremonial pipe.

Throughout the ritual, Rotten Belly neither spoke nor acknowledged the trappers' presence in any way. Tall and strongly built, like most Crows, he was somewhat advanced in age, and it was apparent that he attached much significance to this thing of the pipe. His chiseled, hawklike features were wholly preoccupied with the task at hand; there seemed small doubt that here was a man whose values in life were proscribed and ordered beyond all measure.

Beckwith found no particular fascination with the pipe, though he knew the Indians were real sticklers for such hocus-pocus, and he took the opportunity to inspect the lodge. While it belonged to a chief, he couldn't see that it differed much from other Indian dwellings he had entered on occasion. There were the same rank, musky odor, somewhat like that found in a wolf's den, bed robes back toward the rear, and a jumble of camp gear near the front. Seated off to the side were a couple of sober-faced squaws, who kept so still they might have been carved from wood. All things considered, the whole shebang seemed pretty common.

Just another gut-eater, who doubtless scratched his ass and dipped meat from the pot with the same hand. The same as any other gut-eater.

Rotten Belly at last got the pipe working and made

quite a show of offering it to the earth, the sky, and the four winds. Then, after he had puffed on it a while, he let Beckwith have a turn and finally passed it over to Newell. The trappers had only a dim awareness of the meaning behind this ancient ritual, but the time didn't seem exactly right for asking questions. They both breathed a little easier when the chief emptied the pipe and returned it to an intricately quilled buckskin pouch.

With formalities out of the way, Rotten Belly finally got down to the business at hand. After establishing that Newell spoke a smattering of Crow, he launched into a long harangue about the horse raid and the ensuing fight with the Blackfeet. Whenever he came to a particularly difficult passage, the chief resorted to sign language, allowing Newell time to translate and provide a running commentary for Beckwith's benefit. After some ten minutes of general drift seemed to be that he lauded their courage as warriors and was deeply grateful they had avenged the death of his sister.

Hesitating at that point, Rotten Belly appeared to consider for a moment, then went into a shortened discourse with his hands. Newell's broad features erupted in a spontaneous grin and he leaned forward for a better look at the black man.

"Goddamn me, Jim, this ol' booger jest made us rich men. Whut it biles down to is that we fixed it so's he could lift the ha'r offen four Blackfeet. To sorta square things he's gonna give us eight ponies, pick o' the litter. Says he figgers a Blackfeet scalp is worth a couple of ponies anytime."

Beckwith nodded and smiled, indicating his thanks, but got no reaction whatever from Rotten Belly. Thus far the chief had centered his attention on Newell, though both trappers were aware that the black man had been seated in the place of honor. Some moments passed while the Crow leader stared intently into the fire, and the lodge grew still as a tomb. Only the crackle and spit of the flames broke the silence, and for a time the mountain men thought he had finished with them.

Then, quite abruptly, Rotten Belly roused and his hands once again went to work. After some preliminary sign, the chief touched his breast and made a sweeping motion over the crown of his head, then extended his left forefinger and chopped across it with his other hand.

Newell's expression clouded over about midway through the exchange and when it finished his jaw was set in a tight line. "Gut-eaters is tricky bastards, Jim. Seems like they allus come at a thing from the hindside. Case ye didn't catch it, that last leetle part there with the cut finger meant Cheyenne. 'Pears this ol' coon has heard 'bout yore ma bein' stole from the Crows and mated with a Cheyenne. Wants to know if that's the straight goods 'bout how ye was whelped."

Beckwith had steeled himself for just this question, but he waited, allowing some moments to pass as though considering it at length. "Doc, tell 'im I ain't right sure. Lay it out that the best I recollect is bein' taken in a raid from some tribe or t'other by the Commanch. Afterwards I was swapped off to the Mex'cans, which long way 'round is how I come to be in the fur trade. Say the onliest thing I recollect 'bout my ma was her bein' taller than other women, and that ever'body allus come to her when they wanted fancy quillwork done."

Newell bobbed his head and began translating, awkwardly at first but gathering speed as his hands fell into the sign motions. What his hands implied was lost on no one, least of all Rotten Belly. Crows were taller than any tribe on the plains, their women included. Moreover, if the men were noted as superb horse thieves, Crow squaws were unmatched as artisans in fine quillwork on ceremonial clothing. The conclusion was obvious, if not altogether credible.

Still, Rotten Belly was agreeably impressed with the

fact that Beckwith had made no outright claims. While the man was overly dark, and bore no resemblance whatever to the Crows, he was just ugly enough to have been sired by a dung-eating Cheyenne. Life taught many lessons, perhaps the most profound being that men seldom appear in the guise one expects. Whatever his birthright, he was a man of courage. Along the way it might also be revealed whose blood he possessed, and how his birth had come to pass.

The chief's gaze swung around, hard and impassive, centering on Beckwith without a flicker of emotion. His hands spoke, darting and jabbing like birds in flight, eloquent beyond mere words.

"Jim, ye got 'im hooked." Newell's voice was low-pitched with awe. "Says he wants ye to come see *Absaroka* and live a while with the Sparrowhawk People. That's what they call theirselves and them mountains where they live. Says ye ain't got to stay if ye don't like it and no hard feelin's either way. But he's mighty keen fer ye to give it a try."

The black man held Rotten Belly's gaze for what seemed a very long time. Then the corners of his mouth lifted in a tight smile and he nodded. Just once.

"*Ai!*" The chief grunted with satisfaction, and across his eyes a mellowing came and passed quickly away. Motioning sharply, he signaled the squaws huddled off to the side of the lodge. Like lumps of clay suddenly fused with life, they scrambled erect and waddled forward. Without a word being spoken, one produced a battered trade kettle while the other arranged cooking poles over the fire.

When the flames hit the pot, and the stew began to warm, a faint sweetish odor drifted over the lodge. Beckwith's face remained stolid, betraying nothing, but at last he knew his hunch had paid off.

They were having dog for supper. The feasting dish.

CHAPTER 2

Wild honeysuckle belled softly in a faint breeze, bright petals aflame in the noonday sun. Tufted redbirds flitted among the wolfberry bushes on the slope ahead, while overhead bluebirds swept from the sky in flat, shallow dives. Below, in the willows along the river bank, redwings scolded and chirred, darting scarlet flashes against the leafy green. Yet overpowering it all, erasing sight and sound from the mind, came the cloyed scent of honeysuckle. So sweet it hung in a man's nostrils, thick and vapid, surfeiting in its very essence.

Beckwith sucked it into his lungs, gorging himself on the nectar like some sable-thatched bee. Seated astride a barrel-chested pinto, the black man's eyes roved out across an immense plain, where the Wind River traced a turbulent ribbon along its southward course. Low clouds nestled gently atop the peaked Big Horns to the east, and before him the mighty Wind River mountains thrust awesomely skyward from the basin floor.

Absaroka. Land of the Sparrowhawk People.

Rotten Belly turned his pony and brought it to a halt, regarding the black man's wonder with a knowing look. After a moment his gaze also swept the towering ranges before them. Though it was the land of his ancestors, a land where every gully and stream and mountain meadow was as one with his soul, he could understand Beckwith's spellbound expression.

Whenever he himself returned, it was as if he were seeing it again for the first time. The enormousness of its lush, snowcapped grandeur always left him humbled, yet curiously undiminished. As if Absaroka meant only to remind a man of his insignificance, and having done so, let him pass on undaunted, perhaps even stronger than if he had never been there at all.

"It is a good land," Rotten Belly observed, acknowledging Beckwith's presence with only a slight cant of his head. *"Axace* chose wisely when he gave it to the Sparrowhawk People. While a man remains here he will fare well. When he leaves he wants only to return."

Beckwith and the chief had established communications of a sort. Between simple words and elaborate hand signs they could converse readily enough. Now Rotten Belly signed toward the direction of the four winds. "When a man rides south, there is barrenness and bad water. Should he go north, the winters are long and bitter, with no grass. West of the great mountains, the people are poor and dirty, and eat only fish. Those who dwell to the east must drink muddy water, of such filth that not even a dog would wet his muzzle."

Rotten Belly paused, allowing his words to take effect on the black man. Some moments elapsed before he spoke again, then his hands flashed, burnished copper in the warm sun. "Here, in the land of the Sparrowhawk People, we have snowy mountains and sunny plains. When summer scorches the prairies we move to the mountains, where the air is sweet and cool, the grass fresh, and the streams clear. There we can hunt elk and deer, and higher still the great bear and white sheep. Then, in the Leaf Fall Moon, when the ponies are strong and fat, we go down onto the plains and hunt buffalo to make meat for the cold time ahead. Before snow comes we take shelter in wooded valleys where there are branches for our fires and cottonwood bark for our horses."

The Crow leader nodded to himself, as if his words revealed an elemental truth which, once spoken, could be grasped by any man. "Absaroka is in exactly the right place. Where *Axace* meant it to be. Here the People have everything they want, more than the poorest among us could ever need."

"*Ai!*" Beckwith's Crow talk was limited, but his response brought a look of approval from the chief. Haltingly, the black man set dark hands to motion, intermingled with guttural, woofing sounds he had come to know as words. "The *batsetse* of the Sparrowhawk People has described that which every man seeks. Some find it on earth, but most believe it is to be attained only in the afterlife. Those who live among these mountains are perhaps more fortunate than they know."

"On that you will decide in your own time." Rotten Belly's tone was not unpleasant, but there was a certain terseness to his words. "Do not deceive yourself about the People. Men have come among us before, and most, such as the black robes, were allowed to go in peace. Others, who had foolhardy ways, took advantage of the People. Sooner than they expected, they crossed over to the other life. Now that I think on it, there was one whose coloring seemed much the same as yours."

Beckwith's jaw popped open. "The one the white-eyes called Rose?"

"*Tibo* names come hard to the tongue. Yet now that I hear it spoken, there is something familiar about that one."

"But the one called Rose was reported taken by the Rees." Beckwith made the sign of death, one palm erasing life from the other. "How could that happen if he was rubbed out by the Sparrowhawk People?"

"Perhaps it was the Rees. The truth of such things is often unclear." The chief frowned, shaking his head at the complexity of men's affairs. "Still, it is of no consequence. The one who has crossed over cares only that his hair has been taken. Who took it matters little, if at all."

Rotten Belly signed that the talk was ended and kneed his pony about. Beckwith tapped his pinto in the ribs and fell in behind, but his head felt like someone had thumped him with a good-sized rock. The beady-eyed bogger the same as said the Crows had rubbed out Ed Rose. All the same, where did the straight goods leave off and the horseshit begin? Rotten Belly like as not was just trying to throw a scare into him. Hell, for all anyone really knew, Ed Rose could still be alive. Which didn't mean a thing where his own problem—namely Rotten Belly—was concerned. The chief had clearly warned him to watch his step while in Absaroka. That much was plain as a diamond in a goat's ass. What wasn't quite so clear was exactly how much Rotten Belly suspected. Worse yet, if he did suspect something, why had he gone ahead with their deal? Why hadn't he just called the whole thing off before they ever left Rendezvous?

One thing was for goddamned sure, though. Rotten Belly wasn't like no gut-eater he'd ever run across before. The sonovabitch was a sure enough riddle, even if he did slick his hair down with bear grease.

Beckwith's puzzlement about the Crow leader was compounded in no small part by the Sparrowhawk People themselves. Since departing Rendezvous a fortnight past, he had seen contradiction heaped upon contradiction. Theories commonly accepted by mountain men regarding Indians of whatever tribe had been exploded with dizzying regularity. The first bubble had been pricked almost before the Crows rounded Bear Lake and struck north from the trade fair.

The white encampment was hardly out of sight when the stoic, sobersided Crows dropped all pretense and reverted to their real selves. Staring on in near stupefac-

tion, the black man discovered that the fabled Sparrowhawk People were nothing but a bunch of clowns.

Among themselves they were marathon talkers, jabbering like children as they tried to outshout one another. Fully three days passed, during which the column
swung west and headed north along the Snake River,
before the banter slackened off and the Crows quit telling stories about the incredible antics of the mountain
men.

Then the fun really started. While still recovering
from his opening shock, Beckwith awoke to the fact that
he had joined forces with a band of tireless, and highly
sophisticated, practical jokers. Crow humor tended
toward the vulgar—the raunchier the better, it
seemed—and they had a childlike relish for mixing violence with embarrassment. Apparently nothing was held
sacred once the pranksters got started, and the days
evolved into an endless round of elaborate, sometimes
wanton jokes.

Their fifth day on the trail, Beckwith himself had
fallen victim to the Crows' humor. As the sun came
high, and the midday heat grew stronger, he noticed a
particularly foul odor dogging his steps. The hotter it
got the worse the stench became, and only after considerable sniffing did he discover that the smell came directly from his horse's rump. Before he could dismount
and investigate, two warriors rode up alongside. The
one closest wrinkled his nose with disgust, and eyed the
black man's horse critically.

"Black one, that beast you ride breaks wind as if he
has been eating rotten grass."

"*Ae,* that is so," the other warrior agreed. "Perhaps
you should braid his tail with wild flowers before the
carrion eaters come expecting a feast."

The braves kicked their ponies into a trot, and it was
only then that Beckwith saw everyone laughing at him
behind their hands. Later, after being teased mercilessly

throughout the afternoon, he learned that the pranksters had spent an hour before dawn saturating his
pinto's tail with fresh dung.

The People had chuckled about it for days afterward,
imitating the sound of a pony breaking wind whenever
they rode near.

Curiously, there was even something called *iwatkusu,*
an ancient, ritualized, joking relationship. Every Crow
had a special joking relative, whose duty was to ridicule
and insult and jeer at him in public for the slightest
shortcoming. Though it was devilish entertainment for
everyone else, the game became raw, inescapable humiliation for the one being harassed. By tribal custom he
was allowed to display neither resentment nor anger.

Still, Beckwith's introduction to the Sparrowhawk
People had only just begun.

After passing the fluted spires of the Tetons they had
turned east at the Buffalo Fork of the Snake and as-
cended To-gwo-tee-a Pass. There, in a matter-of-fact
manner, as though it were some trivia hardly worth the
mention, Rotten Belly informed him that the crow nation was comprised of two separate, and very distinct,
bands. The largest, ruled by Rotten Belly himself, was
called *Acaraho,* Where-the-Many-Lodges-Are, more
commonly known as the Mountain Crow. The other
hand, governed by someone named Long Hair, was
called *Minesepere,* Dung-on-the-River Banks. Without
elaboration, Rotten Belly explained that they were
called the River Crow, since their territory roughly embraced the lower Yellowstone and its confluence with
the Missouri.

Reflecting back on his many surprises, Beckwith was
hard put to say which had come as the greatest shock.
Then, as Rotten Belly led the column over a rise in their
descent to the Wind River valley, the black man had his
answer. Spread out along the tree-studded banks of the
mighty river were better than a thousand lodges, con-

taining upwards of five thousand souls, every one of them red as a chigger.

The Sparrowhawk People.

Beckwith's first few days among the Crow had been filled with discovery and an overwhelming sense of bemusement. Nothing was as he had expected. Rarely, in fact, was anything as it seemed. He had taken for granted that Rotten Belly's skepticism would be reflected in the People themselves, particularly after those who had attended Rendezvous spread their own version of his tale. Instead, the Crow had welcomed him with warmth and dignity, and a guileless, childlike fascination for the tale itself. They found the story both incredible and bewitching and were utterly captivated by the tragic imagery of a young boy being wrenched from his mother and sold into slavery. Though appalled that even Comanche barbarians would do such a thing, they saw it as merely the opening verse in a saga of heroic proportions. The black man's ultimate struggle to free himself—what seemed to them his instinctive return to the land of his ancestors—this was the stuff of legends.

Temporarily quartered in Rotten Belly's lodge, Beckwith spent the better part of two days seated out front recounting his story. Early each morning clusters of warriors began to gather, jockeying for seats which afforded the best view, while squaws clutching round-eyed children assembled toward the rear. Once the story had been told, most of the crowd drifted off to discuss it at greater length among themselves. Some remained behind to ask simple, tactfully phrased questions, never once attempting to entrap the mountain man in falsehood or distortion, and almost before one group had walked away, another appeared to take its place. Beckwith's embellishment of the sketchy facts became much like a litany after the first morning. Before long he assumed overtones of a venerated oracle relating folklore to swarms of bedazzled youngsters. Black hands working to bolster his mangled grasp of Crow, he would begin as every fairy tale is customarily opened.

"Once, long ago, when I was but a mere boy, I lived with a woman of great generosity and good. She was my *igya*, the one whose milk gave me life and strength. Though we were not unhappy, neither were we contented, for we lived among a strange people who treated us poorly. Yet there was much joy in our lodge at times, for my mother was renowned for her work with quills, and people came from afar to . . ."

The story unfolded with a heartrending pathos that never failed to bring sniffles to the squaws. By the close of the second day Beckwith had told the bizarre tale so often he almost came to believe it himself. While it was pure hokum, it could have happened just that way, and the outpouring of compassion from his audience made him wish it were somehow more truth than fabrication.

The stunner, though, came on the morning of the third day. Wholly unexpected, it rocked the black man back on his heels with the force of a sharp rap in the mouth.

Strikes-Both-Ways, a shrunken gnome of more than threescore years, appeared at the Lodge of Rotten Belly shortly after sunrise and requested an audience with *Batse*. Since the Sparrowhawk People couldn't quite handle Beckwith, they had decided to call him simply "the man" until something more appropriate revealed itself. After being seated near the fire, Strikes-Both-Ways proceeded to talk in circles for a full half-hour. Among other things he related that he had once been a mighty warrior of the Dog Soldier society, was now a much respected maker of sheep-horn bows, and had been awake all night praying to *Axace* for guidance. Introductions out of the way, he at last came to the purpose of his call.

"I am alone and old now. Yet many snows past I was a man of great riches. Not that I am without horses, for even today I have considerable. But in the days of which

I speak my greater wealth was in my woman and our *barakbia.* This daughter was all any man could ask, tall and graceful, skilled with her hands. One any warrior would have been proud to court and take as wife. Then, on a day when the men of my village were off on a hunt, the Cut-Fingers came. They killed many women, my wife among them, and took several young girls captive. When I returned my woman was dead and my daughter had been taken from me for all time. The Cheyenne trail was cold, and though we killed our horses in the chase, we came back empty-handed."

Strikes-Both-Ways grew silent, his rheumy eyes clouding over with what once had been and was no more. Then he gathered himself, straightening his hunched shoulders, and his gaze cleared. When he spoke it was as though Rotten Belly had ceased to exist. Only he and the black man were there, come now to this thing his medicine spirits had counseled him to do.

"I have listened for two days while you talked of your youth and those parts easily recalled. There is much you have said which makes me consider. Though you are unlike my daughter in looks, you might still be her son. I have no way to know. I can only follow what a tired heart tells me, and hope that the One Above guides me well.

"Should you find it acceptable, I wish to adopt you as my *bacbapite.* My grandson. I have no illusions, nor should you. I am old and carry my life on my fingernails. I wish only to see my blood carried on, and for that I would risk the uncertainty of whose womb gave you life. I have spoken."

Beckwith couldn't have been more astonished if the old man jerked out his pud and pissed all over him.

There was a long silence while the black man struggled to collect his wits. His cock-and-bull story had been good—the slickest whopper he'd ever spun, in fact—but he sure as hell hadn't expected anything like this. Maybe grudging belief in his tale, eventually even acceptance into the tribe. But not a grandaddy!

Offhand he couldn't think of a thing to say. Flabbergasted as he was, he'd be better off simply to keep his mouth shut. Just stay downwind till things ripened up a little more.

The tension grew more oppressive by the moment and it was Rotten Belly who finally spoke. Looking from one to the other, his eyes came to rest at last on Beckwith. "Consider wisely. Strikes-Both-Ways is much respected by the People. Should you deceive him it would go hard with you."

The black man had an inkling that Rotten Belly wasn't exactly his best friend. Leastways, that being the case, he damn sure didn't need any enemies. Still, what the chief had meant as a warning was mighty fine advice all the same. Just the thing he'd needed to nudge him over the hump.

Studying on it a moment longer, he decided, and met the old man's waiting gaze. "Strikes-Both-Ways honors me with his kindness. Perhaps we are of the same blood. Perhaps not. This is a thing neither of us can say. Yet it comes to me that we are of one mind. Like spirit, if not of like blood. I accept your offer, Grandfather. But only so long as you would have it remain so. That is my one condition."

The bowmaker's leathery face wrinkled in a smile and he nodded. "Agreed. From this day forward you become the *bacbapite* of Strikes-Both-Ways. Now that we have settled this thing I would feel better to have you under my own lodge. There we will begin your instruction in the ways of the Sparrowhawk People." The old man's smile widened, as if some small jest had been revealed only to him. "The way is long, and there is much to learn, but you have long legs."

Beckwith grinned right back, not at all sure what the old goat meant. Still, it mattered little. Just now he wanted out from under Rotten Belly's thumb, and this deal seemed made to order. Of course, that powerful strong talk he'd been making for two days hadn't hurt any. Made 'em come to medicine, it did, even if the catch wasn't nothing but a prune-faced bag of bones that liked to toot his own whistle.

Later that afternoon Beckwith found out that Strikes-Both-Ways wasn't the sort to let any grass grow under his feet. The old man had no sooner put out the word that he had a new grandson than a delegation from the Tobacco Planters' society showed up. They had a slight problem, and now that the black man was a certified Crow, they thought he might be willing to lend a hand.

The Sparrowhawk People centered major powers of the universe in tobacco, believing that so long as they continued to preserve the seed they would sustain themselves as a nation. Should the seed disappear, then they, too, would perish from the face of the earth. The Tobacco Planters, who ranked high among the order of medicine men, were endowed with the power to bring rain, avert pestilence, control the wind, conquer disease, and produce bountiful herds of game. Even the Sun Dance paled in significance beside the Tobacco Planting ceremony. Each summer the entire tribe gathered at the foot of Wind Mountain to observe this ancient ritual. There the holy men supervised planting of the seed and then, as an added safeguard, made offerings to Old Woman in the Moon and her grandson, the North Star.

Curiously, the Tobacco Planters' problem centered on the very start of the ceremony. After the field had been hoed with buffalo shoulder-blades, great stacks of dried brush were laid across the plot. Then two people, a man and a woman, were required to light the ceremonial fire. But it was tribal law that the girl be a virgin and that the man swear he had never bedded any of his relatives' wives. The girl had proved no problem. Someone named Pine Leaf had already been selected. Thus far, though, the Tobacco Planters had been unable to find a man willing to test the wrath of the Gods. Apparently there wasn't a grown male in all the Crow Nation who could swear that he had never sampled forbidden fruit. Which made Beckwith a rare find indeed.

Strikes-Both-Ways agreed to the request immediately, viewing this as a signal honor for his new grandson, and the Tobacco Planters departed with their holiness assured for another year.

Now the seed could be planted, and the Gods appeased.

Batse, the mulatto mountain man turned Crow, wasn't sure he liked any part of this deal. Somehow, in a way he didn't exactly comprehend, he had a notion Strikes-Both-Ways had greased the skids and set him afloat. Sort of sink or swim all in one stroke.

Early next morning, though, the black man's skepticism was scattered to the winds. Led forward by medicine men flanked on either side, he was handed a firebrand and wedged into position beside a young girl in white buckskins.

When he turned to look at her, he failed to see that the girl also held a torch. What he saw was delicate beauty and virginal innocence, ripe and ready for plucking, the fantasy of every man who has laid with whores while dreaming of unsullied young girls.

Then, as though a bolt of lightning had been fired up his rectum, he shuddered, felt his palms go moist and his mouth dry. Like legions of men before him, he had been struck by a feverish malady: the raw, unvarnished lust of a boar grizzly trailing a sow in heat.

The Sparrowhawk People called it The Moon of Fat Horses. But for Beckwith the opening days of June were perhaps the most intolerable of his life. There was only one thing on his mind—Pine Leaf—and the intoxication of her image left his head reeling and his senses numbed. Strikes-Both-Ways was a master of the symptoms, though. Over his sixty-odd winters he had seen dozens of young men blinded to all about them by the swollen throbbing between their legs.

The cure was work, learning, endless distractions to cool a man's blood and engage his thoughts elsewhere. Strikes-Both-Ways was also accomplished at the art of misdirection, hard-driving at times, perhaps even a bit merciless, but thoroughly skilled in making things appear not as the viewer saw them, but rather as the old curmudgéon wanted them seen.

Strikes-Both-Ways organized a program of educational lectures, shrewdly set into motion the morning after the Tobacco Planting ceremony. Chattering like a magpie, he gave the black man little opportunity for conversation, and even less for uninterrupted thought.

Beckwith's first lesson as a fledgling Crow was in the field of economics. Sparrowhawk men were obliged to serve as both hunters and warriors, yet their greater preoccupation in life was the sport of stealing horses. Viewed in the larger perspective, the honor of their tribe was also at stake. Across the plains the Crows were uncontested as the most peerless of horse thieves, envied for this skill by even the Sioux and the Blackfeet. Tradition demanded that each generation surpass their fathers, and their fathers' fathers, in this highly refined pastime, and it made for lively rivalry indeed.

Still, as Strikes-Both-Ways was quick to point out, this in no way hindered the individual in feathering his own nest. Wealth was measured solely in terms of horses, for unlike white men, the Crow had no concept of owning land. How could one own the Earth Mother, sacred womb of all living things? It defied belief.

Even beaver pelts and otter skins, which could be traded for marvelous things at Rendezvous, were of minor value. Beads and woolen blankets were fine, that much was granted. But horses were forever, foaling each spring so that a man might accumulate even vaster wealth. Besides, those with any sense valued quillwork and buffalo robes far more than the fragile trappings of white men.

Thus it was that horses alone denoted wealth, and it was not uncommon for a Sparrowhawk warrior to own upwards of a hundred ponies. *Ai!* Men were considered poor if their herd amounted to less than twenty horses. For obvious reasons then, the Crows spent most of their time raiding enemy camps, and an accomplished horse thief carried equal standing with the bravest of warriors.

It was the way. The old man felt no need to elaborate further. Waving his wrinkled paw, he pointed with a mischievous grin to the surrounding countryside. Along the grassy river meadows, and across the broad sage-covered plain, upwards of ten thousand horses grazed contentedly on the lushness of Absaroka.

The Crows were indeed among the mightiest of horse thieves.

After the noonday meal Strikes-Both-Ways gave the black man an introduction into the rudiments of warriorhood. While it was essential that older boys undertake a vision quest before being recognized as men, their training as hunters and warriors began at a very early age. Thus, when the day came that they must stalk the buffalo brother, or face a Cutthroat Sioux, their skill with weapons would be equal to the task.

Clamorous packs of copper-skinned youngsters played out their war games along the outskirts of the village. Strikes-Both-Ways halted beneath a shady cottonwood for a moment's observation, allowing the youths themselves to illustrate his point. Close by, a group of boys had divided into sides and were shooting arrows at a bundle of grass tied with sinews to resemble a man. The target was a good twenty yards away, and despite the clumsiness of their toy bows, rarely did an arrow fall short. Being their fathers' sons, they had quite naturally devised a means of combining gambling with sport. The side with the most hits got to keep all the arrows.

Some distance apart a crowd of older boys took turns firing at a buffalo chip target. The hardened platter-like dung was first pierced in the middle, then rolled along the ground at whistling speed in the manner of a wheel. The stakes again were arrows, the winner being the boy who shot through the center, or came closest. While only one youngster actually hit the bullseye, not a single arrow failed to skewer the buffalo chip.

Watching them, Beckwith understood at last why Indians could perform remarkable feats with bows. Even children were deadly accurate, and amazingly fast at releasing a string of arrows within the space of a few heartbeats. Though he much preferred his Hawken—its half-ounce ball struck with the impact of a bull moose—the accuracy of the youngsters and their bows was a point worth remembering. Never let a gut-eater catch you with an unloaded rifle, not unless you wanted to finish the waltz looking like a pincushion.

Strikes-Both-Ways was pleased that his new grandson seemed duly impressed. That was as it should be, for the Sparrowhawk People were unquestionably a lordly race. Yet with the wisdom born of age, he had saved the best for last: something certain to cool a young man's ardor, better even than a plunge in an icy stream.

Strolling through the encampment early next morning, the bowmaker paused and stood watching a group of women at work. Beckwith knew by now that Strikes-Both-Ways wasn't the sort to waste time on idle lallygagging. There was a lesson here somewhere, and clearly the leathery old rascal was waiting for him to sniff out the scent. The black man inspected the scene carefully, but for the life of him, all he saw was a bunch of squaws softening hides with a mixture of fresh brains and bear grease. Then he blinked.

One of those squaws wasn't a squaw. Not a woman squaw, leastways. The sonovabitch was a man!

Thoroughly delighted with himself, Strikes-Both-Ways explained to his unnerved protege as they strolled on through the village. Among the Sparrowhawk People there were those known as *berdaches*. Generally indistinguishable from male infants at birth, by some freak of nature they grew up with the soft body and the weak voice of a girl. Despite the fact that they dressed and lived as squaws, the strange ones suffered no loss of dignity. They were thought merely to be obeying medicine revealed in their visions. Many enjoyed the reputation of great skill in women's crafts, and it wasn't uncommon at all for a *berdache* to pretend that he had a sweetheart among the warriors.

Chortling lecherously, the old man remarked that certain warriors found *berdaches* far more satisfying than a squaw. Not only more hot-blooded beneath the robes, but eager to perform the most outrageous acts, strange frolicsome things that a squaw would never dare consider.

Among those who had reason to know, he concluded, it was said that a man should never choose a wife until he had sampled at least one *berdache*.

Whatever Strikes-Both-Ways hoped to accomplish with his ribald humor, it fell short of the mark. Quite rapidly, in fact, he discovered that the past two days had been little more than an exercise in futility. Upon entering the lodge after their morning stroll, Beckwith nailed him with a lynx-eyed stare.

"*Axeisake*—grandfather—there is a thing I would do which needs your advice. I wish to take the maiden Pine Leaf to wife, but I am ignorant of how such matters are arranged."

This was a common practice among mountain men, though Beckwith had never yet succumbed to the temptation. Trappers took squaws to wife as casually as they swapped horses, perhaps even more so, since a fast pony was often the difference between a full head of hair and a scalp knife. Generally it was a cut-and-dried arrangement. The mountain man got a cook and someone to warm his robes, and in return, the squaw got all the

gewgaws she could carry at summer Rendezvous. When
the trapper tired of her he simply packed the squaw off
with a load of trade goods and she returned to her village a wealthy woman.

Sometimes, though, a man got carried away by lust. In
the heat of the moment, wanting only to bed the squaw,
he was blind to anything save the rutting instinct.
Strikes-Both-Ways saw this very thing in Beckwith's
face: the look of one whose judgment has been clouded
by hot juices and a stiffened pole.

The old man's reply was raspy, barely concealing his
anger. "You are a fool even to consider such a thing.
Pine Leaf's family is among the wealthiest in the
Acaraho band. Only a warrior who has counted many
coup, or one very rich, would presume to court this girl.
Her father will humiliate you before the village, leave
you crawling on your belly for all to see."

Beckwith chose to ignore the testy outburst. "Then
the accepted custom is that I must court her. That is the
way?"

Strikes-Both-Ways merely scowled at him for a moment. This arrogant young pup could well use a lesson
in humility. Perhaps then he would be more receptive to
the wisdom of his elders. Snubbing his temper, he
shrugged and let a benign expression creep over his
face.

"Since you are determined, I will instruct you. There
are many ways a suitor may win a girl to wife. The first,
while rarely effective, is to play a love flute outside her
lodge four nights running. Then, when she goes for water the next evening, you follow and persuade her to
ride off with you."

"Your words lead me to believe there is a better way."

"*Ae,* that is true. There is a custom among us known
as *biakusirau*—talking toward a woman—in which you
select a man of some standing to act as your emissary.
He speaks for you, approaching the girl's father in your
place."

Beckwith had never been keen on letting other men do his dirty work. Besides, the only upstanding Crow he knew was Rotten Belly. So that put the quietus to that. "There is still another way, perhaps? One with more honor. The custom a warrior might employ?"

Like a sly old snake who waits patiently for his prey to blink, Strikes-Both-Ways nodded, chuckling inwardly with great relish. "That is so, my *bacbapite*. The traditional courting, certainly the most honorable of all, is for the man to offer horses to the girl's family. This is to compensate them for their loss, and demonstrate that their prospective son-in-law is of generous heart."

The black man pondered on it only a moment, then smiled. "Thank you, my *axeisake*. This is how I would see it done. The girl is deserving of the right way."

"*Ae*, she is truly deserving," the bowmaker agreed. "Doubtless her father will raise that very point."

Strikes-Both-Ways didn't elaborate on his cryptic observation and Beckwith let it pass as the prattling of an old man. Already his mind was racing ahead, planning what must be done, and how. The latter especially occupied his thoughts. The *how* of the courting ritual.

Late that afternoon, as the sun dipped westward in a mushy ball of fire, Beckwith halted before the lodge of Yellowtail. Trailing behind him on a rawhide tether were the four ponies Rotten Belly had presented him after the Bear Lake fight. The mulatto was freshly scrubbed, decked out in his best buckskins, and solemn as a constipated owl.

Pine Leaf was squatted before an outside cooking fire, yet she made no move to rise, nor did she so much as glance in his direction. She had seen him coming and felt herself flush knowing why he had come, but then went cold with the shame he brought to her lodge door.

Four ponies was what a man paid for a *biawarax*, a woman already defiled.

Yellowtail came through the door flap and halted

dead in his tracks, flicking hooded glances between his daughter and Beckwith. Then he folded his arms and waited, eyeing the black man with a stony expression.

Beckwith met the stare straight on, wracking his brain for the right words. "Yellowtail, I have come to ask for your daughter as my *bua*. The ponies you see are but a token demonstrating the generous nature of her intended husband."

Yellowtail would have laughed had the insult not been so great. *"Baste,* you are new among our people, and ignorant of our ways, so I will not berate you. Instead I will tell you that Pine Leaf is a *bawuroke*—a virgin—and as such worth no less than twenty fine ponies." He paused, glancing at the girl, and a sly smile touched the corners of his mouth. "I am an indulgent father and have no wish to see my daughter unhappy. While it is not customary, I will let her state her own marriage price. If you are the man she wants, I will accept your ponies."

Pine Leaf came to her feet and stepped forward as Yellowtail moved aside. Her beauty was such that Beckwith felt his loins prickle, and the faint swishing of buckskin against her body made his mouth go thick with spit. She stopped before him, tiny speckles of fire dancing in her black eyes.

"It is said that you are a brave man, and that is good. For only a man with the courage of the great bear will become my *batsire.* I want no beggar for a husband. Nor do I want a mere stealer of horses. The man who shares my wedding couch will be the greatest warrior ever known among the Sparrowhawk People."

Beckwith nodded, hearing yet not hearing. Spellbound by the closeness of her, the fragrance of her body, the way her black hair shimmered with flecks of rust. Like the glint of a raven's wing in a bright sun. The need for her set his pulse to hammering and clogged his throat with a lump that wouldn't go down. When his words came, they seemed hollow and distant, as if spoken by someone far away.

"You aim high, but that is good. I, too, have goals beyond those of most men."

"You have farther to go than you suspect, *Batse.*" The girl raised her chin, and gave him a slow, scornful smile. "The marriage price I set is one hundred scalps taken from the enemies of our people. Let him who can meet this condition be the first to wait before my father's lodge."

Her eyes crackled defiantly, daring him to take up the challenge. Holding his gaze a moment longer, she spun on her heel and walked away. Without looking back, she disappeared into the lodge, jerking the door flap closed.

Beckwith slowly came back to life, a tingling sensation spreading to every joint in his body. Never had he seen a woman so devasting in her beauty, so regal in a moment of anger. She was the dream conjured up by all mountain men on cold wintry nights when they lay shivering and alone beneath their robes. She was a meteor flashing through a darkened sky, the North Star, the very thing every man in the dreary tedium of life has declared unattainable.

Leaving Yellowtail to stare after him, the black man turned and trudged away with the ponies at his heels. As he walked, his reason returned in fits and starts, and he suddenly came face to face with a very blunt fact. Pine Leaf might be all the things he had said, perhaps more, but she was going to be damned expensive to bring to bed.

Great crippled Christ. A hundred scalps.

Just the thought of it shriveled a man's innards tighter'n a dog passing peach seeds. Yet a fellow couldn't rightly back off. Not now. Not if he meant to save face with the Crows.

Beckwith was scarcely humbled by his encounter with Pine Leaf. While a Crow warrior might have been dis-

graced, he appeared heedless to the tawdry gossip being
spread by squaws. The black man's casual arrogance,
bulwarked by a natural bullheadedness, left him wholly
indifferent to the opinion of others. Instead of being
shamed, he merely became angry, and more determined
than ever.

Pine Leaf had had the last word, for now. But her day
would come, and a damn sight sooner than she expected.

Waugh! Once he got his horse between her shafts
she'd learn why birds flushed and bees stung. Virgin,
hell! One night under the robes and he'd have her begging for it morning, noon, and night, like a wild hog
rooting for acorns.

Of course, there was that little matter of a hundred
scalps. But that wasn't nothing that couldn't be overcome. Just a passing irritation. Like gnats, or a dose of
the trots.

With the matter comfortably relegated to the back of
his mind, Beckwith set about wooing the Sparrowhawk
People in earnest. Ashley's instructions had been clear.
"Bring the Crows to heel and deliver them into the
camp of Rocky Mountain Fur." That being the case, it
was time he buckled down to learning something about
his adopted tribe. Much the same as beaver, a man had
to get the hang of people's quirky little ways before he'd
know what bait to use.

Strikes-Both-Ways seemed ripe as a gourd, now that
he'd proved right about Pine Leaf, and the black man
decided to tap him while his spirits held. It would require a bit of meekness on his part, but that was no
problem. Shit fire! Wouldn't hardly be a contest even.
Niggers learned early on that white folks could be
played easier than a bull fiddle. Wasn't no reason a'tall
he couldn't strum a tune on some bare-assed gut-eater.

The old man was seated before his lodge fashioning a
sheephorn bow when Beckwith returned from his morning trip to the bushes. Glancing up from his work,

Strikes-Both-Ways allowed a toothless grin as the black man lowered himself to the ground. "Well, my son, you appear refreshed and eager to face the day. Obviously your awakening ritual passed without mishap."

"*Ae, axeisake.* All went well. Like my brothers, I have bathed thoroughly in the great river, and behind the bushes stands a mound of dung that would bring pride to the buffalo himself."

Strikes-Both-Ways paused and lighted his short pipe with a coal from the fire. These days, it seemed that the simple things most often brought him sorrow. No longer could his aching joints withstand the cold mountain waters, and so the ancient custom of a chill morning bath was lost to him forever. Even his bowels had grown reluctant with age, like a dog gone deaf to its master's command.

Ai! Youth was truly wasted on the young. Only a man grown weary and old could fully appreciate the wonderous gift of loose bowels.

"*Axeisake*"—the younger man's words brought him out of his reverie—"I have come again seeking your advice. There are things I would know of our people, and no longer is my mind clouded to your wisdom."

"I am listening." Strikes-Both-Ways didn't look up but a faint smile played over his mouth. Perhaps the mating dance had served its purpose after all.

"Where should I begin, grandfather? I know nothing of how our people are governed. Even their beliefs are strange to me. Nor am I yet sure how one ceases to be merely a man and becomes a warrior. My ignorance is so great that all about me appears as seen through muddy water."

"Admission of ignorance is the first step toward wisdom, my son. Still, that which is learned in a lifetime cannot be taught in a day."

The old man fell silent, puffing on his pipe as he worked over the bow. Earlier he had boiled the sheephorn in water until it became malleable, and then

cut it into strips of suitable width and length. Later the
strips had been spliced and glued together, forming the
shape of a backward double curve. Once the joints set,
the rough horn had been painstakingly scraped and filed
until it glistened with opaque smoothness. Now, with
painstaking care, he was performing the last step. Starting at the middle and moving to both ends, he tightly
bound the entire frame with slender threads of damp-
ened sinew. When this outer wrapping dried, the bow
would be stronger and more durable than iron itself.
Throughout Absaroka the bows of Strikes-Both-Ways
were much-honored possessions.

Setting aside his pipe, the ancient one regarded Beckwith briefly, then went on wrapping the bow. "Let us
begin where all things begin. With *Axace*—the One
Above. For it is through him that all else comes to
pass."

What must be accepted from the outset, he counseled, was that among the *Apsahrokee,* the Sparrowhawk
People, divine power was not centered in a supreme
ruler. Rather the power was diffused over the universe,
shared to varying degrees by Old Man Coyote, the
Morning Star, even Thunder. Yet over all others stood
Axace—the Sun—the One Above. The apparent dominance of *Axace* must not be overstated, though. While
the Sun was the father and the Earth the mother, each
person received through his vision quest a guardian
spirit. It was to this patron—his personal medicine—
that each man prayed during moments of hardship and
danger.

Beckwith found the going a little muddled, but he
kept still as the old man rambled on.

Four was the mystic number, with magic in its power.
The Sparrowhawk People had been taught this through
the creation of Earth. Three birds had swam to the
depths at Old Man Coyote's direction, seeking enough
mud to construct the earth. Finally the helldiver went
below and returned with the needed mud. Old Man

Coyote commended him, saying, "To every undertaking there are always four trials."

Still, one must not be deceived by Old Man Coyote's role in the creation. The Trickster had always been the incorrigible buffoon and unscrupulous lecher. Had he not feigned death to marry his own daughter, and perpetrated a vile hoax to seduce his mother-in-law? Grossness and low cunning were ever his way, and he flouted all notions of decency. On the other hand, Old Man Coyote could never be taken lightly either. His power was indisputable.

The bowmaker paused to let that sink in, pleased that he had been able to explain this matter of the spirit beings so clearly. Beckwith thought it over for a minute, now thoroughly confused, then tried to frame a question that wouldn't make him sound like a nitwit.

"Grandfather, your words are clear, except on one point, perhaps. If the Sun is the father, and the Earth the mother, then how is it that Old Man Coyote came to create the earth? That would seem to give him greater power than the Sun, the One Above."

Strikes-Both-Ways smiled wisely and shook his head. "Your confusion is understandable, my son. Let me answer with a parable. Perhaps in this way you will come to see the distinctions of which I speak."

Once the earth was infested with monsters, he began, who roamed the land destroying all creatures. The One Above chose a Sparrowhawk girl as his mate and sometime later she gave birth to a son. This boy, the son of the Sun, was then adopted by a very shrewd old woman, and he became known as Old Woman's Grandchild. After the old woman instilled in the boy all her wisdom and power, he went forth and slaughtered the monsters. The One Above rewarded them by transforming the old woman into the Moon and the boy into the Morning Star. Clearly then, it could be seen that while Old Man Coyote created the earth it was *Axace,* the One Above, who protected it.

The black man saw all right, despite the fact that he was more befuddled than ever. These Crows just had their own batch of mumbo jumbo like everyone else. Looking at it crosswise, this stuff about the Sun, and his kid Morning Star, wasn't much different from the voodoo witchcraft his Grandmam had practiced back on the plantation. That old mammy had rubbed out a few monsters in her time, too, and cast enough spells to last clean into Judgment Day. Speaking of which, the white folks were just as convinced that their blue-eyed Savior was the he-wolf of all time. Hell, everybody had some kind of thunder and lightning working for them. The Crows had just got things all sorted out their own way, naturally making themselves the chosen people, and the fact that it sounded like a crock of shit to anyone else didn't budge them in the least.

Beckwith knew the old man was watching him out of the corner of his eye, waiting for some response. While it galled him, the trapper decided to play it cagey. "Grandfather, I would consider this at length so that we might discuss it another day. Perhaps you could enlighten me on other matters for a time, such as the manner in which the Sparrowhawk People are governed."

Strikes-Both-Ways grunted, looking up from the bow with a smirk. "You have much to learn, my *bacbapite*. The *Apsahrokee* are not governed. They are free. Each man his own master, answerable to none but himself. Could you govern the wind, or the clouds in the sky?" The old man's eyes came alive and he laid aside the bow. "Now I will tell you a story: the story of Absaroka, and why none but the free dwell here."

Beckwith listened raptly as the bowmaker swung into a lecture on the politics of the Crows. The chief of the Mountain Crow, in this case Rotten Belly, was a far cry from a monarch. He controlled the destiny of his people only so long as his judgments proved correct, and not a moment longer. Moreover, even a chief of demonstrated wisdom was powerless to act unless supported by the tribal council. Among the *Acaraho* band there were seven clans. The elected chief sat as representative of his own clan and the six elders from the remaining clans comprised the main body of council. It was an ancient system of checks and balances that had existed beyond the memory of man, and rarely had it failed the People.

Yet there was an even greater safeguard, which prevented either the chief or the council from becoming all-powerful. The Mountain Crow were organized into eight warrior societies, the Kit Foxes, Ravens, and Dog Soldiers among them, and each of these factions was free to support, or ignore, the council as its membership decreed. This code of freedom extended even to the individual. Warriors were obligated to no one, neither clan nor council nor chief, and they obeyed edicts from above only if it suited their whims. Granted, they might be ridiculed, even banished, if their actions endangered the tribe. But they were nonetheless free to do exactly as they pleased whenever it took their fancy.

As for chiefs, they usually ended up poor men. Charity, along with war honors, was the means of attaining high standing. Once in power a leader could maintain his position only by lavish generosity to the unfortunate, especially widows and children. Sometimes, at the cost of self-impoverishment, a chief gave away all he had, and like a common warrior, was forced to conduct raids in order to replenish his wealth.

It was the way.

When Strikes-Both-Ways finally ran out of wind, Beckwith had all he could do to hide a grin. Matter of fact, he was feeling downright smug. The Sparrowhawk People might be free as the breeze, but their loose-jointed way of running things was made to order for a fellow who knew how to stir up a hornet's nest.

Especially if he was mean and hairy and didn't have no more scruples than a tomcat.

* * *

Strikes-Both-Ways, said the people, had been reborn,
galvanized with the energy of a man half his years.
Among those in the Wind River camp none walked
straighter, held his head higher, or stung more readily
with the vulgar jests so loved by the *Apsahrokee*.
Granted, Batse, his newly found grandson, had shamed
himself with the clumsy courting of Pine Leaf. Still, in
the days since, it had grown apparent that the dark-
skinned one was hardly an oaf. Unwise in the ways of
women, perhaps, but far shrewder than anyone had first
suspected.

Batse had become not only a willing pupil of Sparrowhawk ways, mastering ancient legends and tribal cus-
toms with remarkable ease, he was rapidly gaining fame
as a *biraxdeta*.

The one who fills the pot.

Under Strikes-Both-Ways' guidance, Batse had
proved a hunter of surpassing cleverness. The black
man now spent his days roaming the wooded mountain
slopes and lying in wait at distant water holes. Seldom
would the day pass that he failed to return with meat,
and his generosity seemingly knew no bounds. Each
night, the greater share of his kill was quietly left before
lodges without men of their own. Many hunters would
have flaunted both their skill and their charity for all to
see; even among the Sparrowhawk People such an uncanny feel for wild things was considered a rare gift.

Yet Beckwith seemed oblivious to the whole affair,
displaying no recognition whatever of his growing fame.
Calmly he went about the business of hunting, rigidly
sticking to a plan he had devised with utmost care.

The first step, sapping Strikes-Both-Ways of a lifetime's accumulated knowledge, had proved the simplest.
The old man now envisioned himself as a sage, an ancient expounding the wisdom of the ages, and he was
possessed with the idea of transforming his grandson
into a walking storehouse of Sparrowhawk lore. Effort-
lessly, with little more than a nudge, the black man

could set him to lecturing on virtually any scrap of Ab-saroka life.

The bowmaker had warmed to the subject of hunting immediately, for in his prime he had been known as a *biraxdeta* of extraordinary skill.

"There are secrets of the wild things," he chortled gleefully, "known only to a few men. These I will reveal to you, my grandson, just as my father told them to me. While a great hunter is obligated to share his kill with the less fortunate, it must be agreed that these words will go no further. Meat is one thing. Secrets of the hunt belong solely to the man himself."

When Beckwith nodded he went on. "Hunting, next to war, is man's greatest responsibility. Without it, there would be nothing to eat, no horn cups or spoons, no hides or robes or lodge covers, not even containers for the boiling of meat."

So it was that the Sparrowhawk People twice each year surrounded the buffalo herds on fleet ponies. Sometimes they even arranged a grand drive of deer and antelope, expertly forcing the animals into hidden enclosures where they might be slaughtered at will. These tribal hunts yielded enormous quantities of meat, which was then made into jerky or pemmican for the winter to come. Yet there was small personal honor in such hunts, for any fool could kill a buffalo from astride a horse.

The man who would be called *biraxdeta* hunted alone, afoot, off in distant places where his medicine could be made to charm the wild things. Only then would the people remark on his prowess, or respect him as one who fills the pot.

Strikes-Both-Ways then launched into a discourse on but a few of the secrets hinted at before. Let these be mastered and in time he would reveal even more. Beck-with had been in the mountains seven winters, but as the old man talked, it came to him that he had much left to learn about stealth and cunning.

The man who would hunt alone must first grasp one essential truth. He is a predator, like the great bear or the wolf or the tawny lion. Therefore he must train himself to think like the meat-eaters. Better yet to think of himself as a wild thing, patterning his actions after those of a wildcat, or perhaps a stealthy fox, creeping, moving slowly with infinite patience, sweeping before and behind with ever-restless eyes. Bushes and trees, the stones themselves, must be used to conceal movements, and never could the man allow haste to cloud his judgment. What all meat-eaters know instinctively, he must school himself to accept: Better a day spent in cautious stalking than a night spent in hunger.

Next he must learn the creature warnings. Without that his prey would be alerted long before he was even within stalking distance. Many things gave signals in the wilderness—magpies and crows, chipmunks and squirrels, the kingfisher and wren—and a man who studied their ways became as one with them. Then, and only then, could he move through the woods as silently and unnoticed as a falling leaf.

Finally he must enlighten himself on the habits of his prey: where they feed, their favorite watering holes, the paths they use both in flight and when unalarmed. For like man himself, wild things were but creatures of habit, lazy and given to ways which require the least thought, pleasured by that which demands the least exertion.

When these things had been mastered, the man was at last ready to hunt. Then could he smear himself with scent from the toes of deer and stalk the great bucks at their watering holes and in their bedgrounds. Or conceal himself at the scrapes where bucks paw leaves aside and urinate in rutting season to attract the does. Perhaps, after his skills had grown, he might even seek out the silver-tipped bear and ambush the ugly one while he gluts himself on ripening berries.

When that day came—when each secret in turn had

been mastered—then would a man become known as a *biraxdeta.*

Beckwith had listened well and taken to heart the old man's counsel. Once in the woods he remembered, and like a morning fog lifting, all became clear. Creature warnings were there for the one who listened. Sign was everywhere for the eyes to see. Every secret of the wild was revealed to the man who moved and thought as a predator.

Selecting the wily bobcat as his image, he studied it in the hunt. Watching from a distance, he observed what Strikes-Both-Ways had told him to look for: how the wild one went cautiously, alert to sound and wind, pausing often in a moment of frozen watchfulness. How he lifted one paw at a time, lowering it again to the ground with a padded softness that disturbed neither leaf nor twig. Then, having become a shadow in a forest of shadows, how the bobcat advanced unseen, step by step, and pounced at last on his unsuspecting prey.

Afterwards, remembering what he had seen, the black man moved through the wilderness without sound, drifting from tree to rock to bush like a light breeze. Elk, deer, and great bear fell before his gun, and within a week he had successfully stalked and killed his first mountain lion.

The Sparrowhawk People murmured words of respect when he returned each evening with fresh meat. Many came forward and engaged him in conversation, often using his rifle as an excuse to talk. While the Hawken was bored for .53 caliber, and murderously accurate, it was by no means their reason for seeking him out. Like the curious of whatever persuasion, they wished only to say that they had talked with the man who possessed the gift.

For Beckwith was no longer known as Batse. He was called The Hunter.

The black man was quite pleased with himself. From a simple clod, who shamed virgins with scandalous offers, he had neatly boosted himself into a position of respect and no little envy. That done, he was ready for the next step.

After the bowmaker had stuffed himself one evening on plump young antelope, Beckwith broached the subject of war. "Tell me, grandfather, how is it that a man becomes a war leader? I often see men raising raiding parties, but never have I seen Rotten Belly lead them against our enemies."

"That is true," Strikes-Both-Ways agreed. "War is not the concern of the chief alone, or even the council, it is the concern of the tribe as a whole. Do not girls as well as boys derive their names from the exploits of great warriors? Even squaws who dance at feasts wear scalps taken by their men to show honor. If you would goad men to join a vengeance raid you must do no more than show them a woman who grieves for a slain son. The lesson, my *bacbapite,* is that the Sparrowhawk People war constantly and with ancient purpose. Only so long as we carry the fight to our enemies will Absaroka be passed on to our sons, and their sons after them."

"Ae, that I understand. But how is it that mere warriors are permitted to mount a raiding party?"

"You miss the point, my son. They are not mere warriors. They are *araxtsiwice.* Men of Honor." Beckwith started to speak but the old man waved him silent. "Listen and your question will be answered. Among our people there are four deeds which bring honor. The first is to count coup—to touch an enemy without killing or wounding him. The second is to capture an enemy's bow or gun when fighting him at close quarters. Next is the theft of a war pony picketed outside its owner's lodge in a hostile camp. This is a much coveted honor indeed, for the danger of discovery and torture is great. Lastly, there is the honor of being selected as pipe-holder—the one chosen to plan raids. When a man has attained these four deeds, he is considered a chief. But only a war chief. He has no position on the council. Of course, should the tribal chief cross over—Rotten Belly, let us say—then one of the *araxtsiwice* would be selected as the new leader."

The black man kept his voice casual, toying absently with a stick in the fire. "Then a man who has performed the first three deeds could begin mounting raids. There is nothing to prevent him from forming war parties of his own?"

"My son, nothing is as simple as it appears. Not only must this man you speak of be selected as a pipe-holder, he must also bring to pass a vision which foretells victory in the fight to come. Otherwise the raid would be doomed before it starts. From our discussion of the spirits you can see that it would be unwise to ignore such omens. Clearly none would follow a man with bad visions. For if they smoke the pipe, signifying their willingness to ride with him, it would surely mean their death."

"Ai! You speak the truth, grandfather." Beckwith snapped the stick in half and flung it into the fire. "Nothing is as it appears."

Strikes-Both-Ways smiled and settled deeper into his willow backrest. "Curb your patience. As with stalking deer, haste brings nothing but regrets." The old man closed his eyes and was silent a long while. When he spoke again it was little more than a sigh, somehow filled with weariness. "You have learned well, my son. Yet there is one lesson the young rarely heed. Perhaps it is the most profound ever taught by the ancient ones. The earth and sky last forever, but men should die. Old age is a scourge and death in battle a blessing."

Beckwith found nothing profound about it. Dead was dead, and praise for getting killed in a burst of glory sounded like asinine dribble to him. Maybe it suited some folks—them that couldn't make their mark any other way—but he still had too much to do. Far too much.

Like teachin' the Crows which way the stick floats.

Waugh! Not to mention takin' the kinks out of that she-wolf with the sassy eyes, goddamn her little brown ass, anyway.

Between her and her hundred scalps, and the Crows hidebound way of doing things, a man wouldn't hardly have time to spit.

CHAPTER 3

The Moon of Fat Horses had proved a time of plenty in the lodge of Strikes-Both-Ways. Yet there was more to it than a full meat rack or the savory odors of a bubbling stew pot. For the old bowmaker was basking in a glow of newfound eminence unlike anything he had known since the long-ago days of his warrior youth. Among the Sparrowhawk People, there was much talk of his sly and crafty manner, likening him to a grey-muzzled fox of untold winters. The tribal elders chose loftier words, speaking of his wisdom and the keenness of his judgment.

Whatever their means of flattery, though, the People were of one accord. Strikes-Both-Ways was shrewd beyond measure, for while others pondered and debated, it was he who had brought the dark-skinned one into his lodge.

The old man merely smiled and applied himself with renewed vigor to the task of fashioning sheephorn bows. Talk was for gossipy squaws and bone-weary skeptics, many of them the same ones who had laughed at him behind their hands when he adopted Baste. Now, with the Moon of Fat Horses half gone, they chattered another tune, and their scorn had come full circle to taunt them.

His grandson, The Hunter, had seen to that.

The black man had indeed become a hunter of uncommon skill. But that alone accounted for only part of
the praise being heaped upon Strikes-Both-Ways. What
astounded the Sparrowhawk People even more was that
the bowmaker's *bacbapite* had adapted himself so completely to the Crow way, all within a matter of weeks.

Which led the skeptics to ruminate even further.
Clearly *Apsahrokee* blood flowed in the dark one's veins.
Otherwise there was no reckoning with his stark, and
somehow mystical, transformation.

The most noticeable change in Beckwith was of an
outward nature. He no longer wore the fringed buckskins favored by mountain men both winter and summer. Like his copper-skinned brothers, his attire now
consisted of breechclout and moccasins, the simple garb
worn by men of reason in the time of heat and sudden
rains. Though his hair was scandalously short, he had
also made some effort in that direction. Braided in tight
strands, his hair hung down the side of his neck, leaving
only a loose topknot swept forward from the crown of
his head. This forelock he had combed and greased in
the accepted manner, letting it stand as a challenge to
the scalp knife of all Sparrowhawk enemies. The part
down the backside of his skull had been painted a deep
vermilion, which flamed brilliantly against the ebony of
his hair, and except for the darkness of his skin, he appeared not unlike other men of the *Acaraho* band.

When he strode through the village of an evening
with a gutted buck over his shoulder, there were even
those who claimed he no longer looked quite so dark.
Not a red man by any means, but not so black either.

Still, it was his offhand manner and light banter which
ultimately turned the trick. Returning from a long hunt
toward sunset one day, he was stopped by a group of
squaws. One of the more brazen inspected him critically, without a trace of a smile, while the others engaged him in conversation. Then she stung him with a
coarse joke.

"Hunter, perhaps you would solve a riddle for us. Some say you are dark because you were fathered by a Cheyenne, but others argue you were sired by a *shua* stallion. Which would you have us believe?"

Beckwith grinned and appraised her plump figure with a mocking eye. "*Makukata*—my sister—you pose a riddle which requires no answer. Among the People, it is said that your mother also foaled after being mounted by this black stallion. Though of different clans, that would seem to make us kin nonetheless."

After the story was repeated throughout the village with much zest, there were few doubters left. The Hunter must be one of their own! Granted he was dark, but only a man of the Sparrowhawk could employ sharp wit with such ease.

Much to the outspoken squaw's embarrassment—and to Beckwith's growing fame—she became known widely as *Shua-Barakbia,* Daughter of the Black Horse.

The mulatto mountain man was hardly surprised, then, when the leader of the Dog Soldiers appeared at Strikes-Both-Ways' lodge one evening. For better than a fortnight, he had spared no effort in making himself over into a Crow, from dress to speech to behavior, and it stood to reason that one of the warrior societies would take the bait with raiding season in full swing.

Beckwith and the old man were seated around the fire, gnawing elk ribs, when a discreet cough sounded from outside. Among the Sparrowhawk People this was the polite way of informing a man that he had visitors. While vulgar humor was much appreciated, it was thought improper to catch the host under his robes with a squaw. Particularly since there was every likelihood she might belong to someone else.

Strikes-Both-Ways wiped the grease off his chin and called loudly, "Enter. There is meat to spare and warmth against the night wind."

The doorway filled as a man stepped through. When he straightened, they saw it was White Bear. The leader of the Dog Soldiers was tall and lithely built, with the angular features and high cheekbones of his people. Though cunning after a fashion, he was far from a shrewd man, and thus he had never been considered for a seat on the tribal council. Yet it was said that in battle he fought with inhuman ferocity. Which made him the perfect *batsetse* for the Dog Soldiers, the most widely feared of all Sparrowhawk warrior societies.

"*Kahe,* White Bear," the old bowmaker greeted him. "Join us. You are just in time for the fat ribs of a cow elk my grandson killed this morning."

"Another time, old one." White Bear's words were stilted, somewhat formal. Even after taking a seat beside them he appeared a bit stiff, almost brusque in manner. "I have come to speak of certain matters with your grandson."

The black man tossed a half-eaten rib on a pile of bones near the door and wiped his hands across his chest. "We are honored that White Bear seeks out our lodge. I am listening."

White Bear acknowledged the token of respect with a nod and let a moment pass before he spoke. "Last night I fasted and sought a vision. While asleep it was revealed to me that there was a village far to the south of this place." He paused, extending his forefinger, then laid it alongside his nose. The Cut-Nose sign. "The lodges shown to me were Arapahoe, and outside the village I saw many fine horses. The vision told me that it is there I would find a white mare, and that among the warriors I lead, one will kill an Arapahoe with but one thumb."

The Dog Soldier *batsetse* withdrew a ceremonial pipe from a quilled bag attached to his breechclout and held it before him. "It is said that you are a brave man. If that is so, I would see it for myself. There are none braver than the Dog Soldiers, and among them a man finds the true test. I ask you to take the pipe and join my *duxia* against the Arapahoe."

White Bear extended the pipe, watching the black man with a cold, stony gaze. Beckwith accepted it gravely, knowing that with the honor came a direct challenge to his courage. Selecting a stick from the fire, he lit the pipe, signifying his willingness to follow White Bear on the raid. After completing the ritual, he returned the pipe to the war leader.

"I will not fail you, or the Dog Soldiers. Whatever my part, it will be done."

"*Ai!* Let it be so, Hunter. Your grandfather was once a Dog Soldier, and wherever he walked, our enemies trembled. See that you bring no discredit to his lodge." White Bear saw no need to add that his offer honored the old man as much as the grandson. It was clear without words. Climbing to his feet, he returned the pipe to its bag and gave the black man a solemn look. "Remember all that the ancient one has taught you and you will do well. We leave before first light. Make yourself ready."

Turning, White Bear went through the door hole as silently as he had entered. Strikes-Both-Ways let out a huge sigh, as though he had been holding his breath. Then his face wrinkled in a leathery grin. The pipeholder of the Dog Soldiers in his lodge, extending the pipe to his very own grandson! It surpassed all expectations.

A rare honor indeed. One that few men lived to see.

Beckwith was no less overwhelmed himself, though perhaps for different reasons. Every move he had made since joining the Crows had been pointed toward this one moment, and all along he had felt reasonably confident it would come. Now that it was here, though, a sense of unease settled over him. White Bear's warning had been plain to read: Fail this test and there would be no more offers. He would remain a mere hunter while others went off to make war.

Strikes-Both-Ways cocked his head, noting the younger man's pensive look. "My son, it is given that we can learn from all things, even the little bug who breaks the darkness with flashes of light. Among the ancients, it is said that because this bug lights from behind, he gains a better view of where he has been than where he goes. It is a lesson well taken by a man who contemplates his first horse-stealing raid."

Beckwith grunted deep in his chest, heeding the wisdom that only recently he had come to understand. *Ai!* It was indeed a lesson to be reflected upon in the days to come.

Those who dwelled in the past seldom found their way along the path ahead. The hunter who would become a warrior might do well to study the lightning bug closely, especially if he had any notion of keeping his topknot rooted in place.

White Bear brought his party to a halt just before sunset along the headwaters of a large river. The *tibos* called this stream the North Platte, but to the Sparrowhawk warriors, it was a landmark, even a sign of warning. It meant they were a day's march from the lands of the Arapahoe.

The breeze had slackened and the air was very still. Overhead the cottonwood leaves hung limp, and as the raiders set about making camp, the only sound came from the gentle rush of the river. Later the night winds would sweep down from the north and the chill of the high plains would awaken them long before dawn. But for now, it was the quiet time of evening, when nothing moved. As if the Earth Mother, tired and weary, had paused to rest, breathing deeply before moving on into darkness.

Beckwith sunk down on the riverbank and swilled water till he thought his gut would burst. He was hot, covered with grime, and thoroughly disillusioned with the business of horse stealing. Somehow it had never occurred to him that the Crows would walk when they set out to raid an enemy pony herd. Even now, after a long-winded explanation by Strikes-Both-Ways and three days on the trail, it still failed to make any sense. Should they get caught afoot on these open plains, they were as good as dead. Even mounted, it would be damn ticklish to outfox a large war party, for there was no place to hide and a horse could only run so far. All of which plainly didn't mean a hill of beans to the Crows. When questioned they merely shrugged and gave him the same old skullduster.

It was the way.

The black man eased back on his haunches and began working on a piece of jerky. Then he grunted with disgust. Jerky and water and sore feet. Some raid! Hardly what a man would have expected from the mighty Dog Soldiers.

Still, in the back of his mind, Beckwith grudgingly admitted that the Dog Soldiers were tougher than boiled owl. Much as it grated on the bone, he even had to admit that they might be tougher than him, leastways till he got his second wind.

Over the past three days they had covered better than a hundred miles, all on shank's mare, hoofing it across some of the most hostile country he had ever seen. Once clear of the Wind River, they had struck due east through the barrens, a hard uncompromising land sparsely covered with buffalo grass and prickly pear. The dusty, rolling plains stretched onward beyond the horizon, broken only by parched coulees and an occasional treelined creek. Bald nobs speckled with a scattering of trees appeared now and then, yet these stunted heights offered small relief. Somehow they seemed to accentuate the utter desolation of the land itself.

As he munched on the jerky, Beckwith's eyes drifted longingly to the towering spine of the westward mountains. Coolness and shade and sparkling water had never before seemed quite so precious. Somewhere up there, the mountain brigades were moving along slow and easy, just taking life one day at a time, while he

tagged along behind a bunch of raggedy-assed Crows.
On foot! Christ, it was enough to shrivel a man's balls.

Chewing furiously, he slewed a look back at the silt-
bottomed river. The stream ran in snaky turns from the
sunset and disappeared into a murky green haze in the
east. As rivers went, it wasn't much. Just as the land
itself was something less than inviting.

The black man swallowed and ripped off another
hunk of jerky. Maybe the Arapahoes had fine horses,
but they'd sure as hell squatted on slim pickin's when
the land got handed out. From what he'd seen of the
country so far, the Cut-Nose ponies weren't eating
much better than White Bear's raiding party.

Reflecting on that a moment, he chuckled sourly to
himself. Shit! Compared to the Dog Soldier scouts, he
was doing just fine. Living in the lap of luxury.

The morning they left the Wind River encampment,
White Bear had sent two scouts on ahead. They were to
reconnoiter the country through which the raiding party
would pass and alert the *duxia* leader to any signs of
danger. While the raiders moved at a fast walk, the
scouts were obliged to trot in order to cover enough
ground for a day's march and return by evening.

Not that they were allowed into camp. Until the enemy was sighted they were sworn to fast and maintain
constant vigilance over the raiding party. Only after they
brought word of the Arapahoe pony herd would they be
allowed to eat.

Worse yet, custom demanded that during the entire
sortie they must wear wolfskin capes, which included
the wolf's skull pate, pointed ears and all. Fasting was
bad enough, but wolfskins in the scorching plains heat
had to be the next thing to torture itself. When Beckwith had asked the obvious question, he got the same
old shrug.

It was the way.

Still and all, there was at least a spark of sense to this
thing of wolf skins. Impersonating a wolf, a scout might

just sneak through unseen in a tight spot. But there was another little riddle that didn't make any sense whatever. Matter of fact, so far as the black man was concerned, it was plain goddamned foolishness.

The way Strikes-Both-Ways had explained the deal, it was considered meritorious to kill and scalp an enemy. Undeniably, that took a degree of courage. But the lightest tap with a coup-stick, performed on a live and armed opponent, was reckoned an even higher honor. Anyone could kill, and somewhere throughout their lives most warriors did. To count coup, though. There was an act of courage!

Beckwith didn't see it quite so much courageous as just plain crazy. The best he could figure out, the idea was not to annihilate a hostile force but to execute some sort of stunt, every man for himself, playing a game according to whimsical rules, instead of fighting together and handing the other gang a real licking. While it gave an individual the chance for plenty of honor, it seemed a strange way to keep Absaroka safe from its ancient foes.

The black man had kept these thoughts to himself, though. Better to coast along and play by the rules for the moment. But if things worked out just right, he might yet show these Crows a trick or two about fighting. *Waugh!* None of that piddling coup stuff, but real blood and thunder. The way white men fought.

Thinking about the gewgaws coup-strikers were entitled to wear—ermine skins, wolf tails, and the like—put him in mind of another absurdity Strikes-Both-Ways had unloaded with dead earnestness. Every now and then an especially brave Dog Soldier was offered the top honor a warrior could attain. He alone, amongst all the Sparrowhawks, was entitled to wear the sacred bear skin belt and a cap of dried bear guts painted red. Bear guts were particularly symbolic since they were supposed to give the man selected both the strength and the ferocity of a grizzly, which he dearly needed.

According to the old bowmaker, the man tapped for this honor was expected to lead the advance on an enemy force, and under no circumstances could he retreat, regardless of the danger. The *akducire,* as such men were called, was expected to die in any event, so to return alive was to become a laughingstock. Understandably, even the mightiest of warriors hesitated a long time before accepting this post.

The latter statement hadn't surprised Beckwith in the least. There was something damned dubious about the honor of being forced to commit suicide. Not that it didn't get the troops whipped up into a frenzy, which was the purpose right from the start, for it doubtless accomplished that in fine fashion. All the same, it was a little rough on the man leading the parade.

The corker, though, was a peculiar bunch called the Crazy Dogs. These were men who, for reasons of their own, had an aversion to life. Initiation rites into the club were simple and direct: they had merely to swear an oath to die in battle. While Beckwith had yet to meet one, he understood that Crazy Dogs were easy enough to recognize. They talked crosswise—said exactly the opposite of what they meant—and they deliberately courted death. Their goal was to be killed within a single raiding season; whenever battle was joined they recklessly dashed toward the enemy chanting their death song. Old women cheered them lustily, and young boys ran after them, but the adulation bestowed on Crazy Dogs was not altogether due to respect. It was well known that men who had renounced life would inflict the utmost damage on an enemy, and in warfare the fearlessness of this handful had often turned the tide for the Sparrowhawk People.

So far as Beckwith could tell, they had been aptly named. Crazy as rabid dogs. He had seen the same thing among whites, and niggers, too: men who purposely set out to tease Old Scratch, so anxious to die that they just naturally killed everybody around them.

Puzzling over it, the black man came to the conclusion that the Crow attitude toward war was a queer blend of vanity, foolhardiness, and raw courage, not to mention a peculiar temptation to flirt with death. The more he learned about the Sparrowhawk People and their ways, the more he came to understand perhaps the oddest of Strikes-Both-Ways' many sermons: "old age is a scourge and death in battle a blessing."

All of which brought his thoughts back to White Bear. The *duxia* leader was even then spreading his medicine bundle on the ground. Looking closely, Beckwith could see a hunk of dried buffalo dung, a small quantity of kinnikinnick, some braided sweet grass, and a fetish made of an eagle claw and an old, blackened arrow point. Same old voodoo-hoodoo he'd seen a hundred times back on the plantation. Now, if things went according to plan, the mumbo jumbo would come next.

Sure enough, White Bear lifted his head to the deepening twilight and began a plaintive chant to his guardian spirits. This was the ritual prayer for success in a raid, summoning the forces of the netherworld on the night before warriors crossed over into enemy lands. Without missing a note White Bear pulled out his knife and started slicing strips of skin from his forearm. These he placed atop the medicine bundle, and with each bloody offering, his mournful howl became all the louder.

The rest of the warriors were subdued, watching with a kind of reverent fascination. But for the black man, it was strictly old hat, just another numbskull practicing his own brand of witchcraft. Climbing to his feet, he started off downstream to empty his bladder. Suddenly White Bear's chant missed a beat and Beckwith froze in midstride.

Damn! He'd clean forgot the warning revealed in White Bear's vision. Should anyone pass on his right side before the raid took place, some unspeakable horror would befall the entire party.

Grunting and snorting like a sore-tailed old bear, Beckwith swerved and passed the Dog Soldier leader on his left side. Headed downstream in the fading light, he had to resist the rumbling urge to laugh.

The things a man wouldn't do just to piss in peace!

The raiders moved in a crouch along the arroyo, advancing step by step as they tested each foot of ground before them. White Bear led the way, with Beckwith close on his heels and the remainder of the party strung out in single file behind. They moved without sound, disturbing nothing in their passage, like great bronzed cats padding softly on furred paws. The *duxia* leader stopped now and again to test the faint breeze, satisfying himself that they were still downwind. This was caution born of habit, though, for the pungent smell of horse dung grew stronger with each step forward.

While there was no moon, the sky was a glittery sprinkle of stars, casting a dim light over the shadowy figures. Dawn was still hours away, and except for the night noises, a dewy stillness cloaked the land. The scent of chokecherries and wild plums lay heavy and sweet in the arroyo, and along its walls a scattering of white blooms glistened in the dusky starlight. Far off, nearer the river and the Cut-Nose village beyond, the men could make out the purling sound of crickets and the lively, if somewhat feeble, croak of tiny tree frogs.

Suddenly the ravine flattened out, merging with the valley floor, and White Bear bellied down at the lip of the draw. The warriors behind folded silently to the ground, scarcely daring to breathe as they waited for the Dog Soldier *batsetse* to survey their next move. Ahead lay a vast meadow, and in the distance bordering the river, a stand of cottonwoods arched skyward against the silvery night. Along the lower fringes of the line of trees could be seen the coned spires of the Arapahoe lodges, dark and somehow foreboding in the gloomy stillness. All of this White Bear covered in a sweeping

glance then he grunted softly and his gaze settled once
more on the meadow.

Grazing contentedly, unaware of the Dog Soldier's
scrutiny, was the pony herd he had come to steal.

Beckwith craned his neck for a better look over
White Bear's shoulder, slowly scanning the scene below.
This was the river he knew as the South Platte, and he
judged they were some hundred miles below where it
joined with the main stream. Carefully he committed
every landmark, each roll and dip of the terrain to memory, letting his eyes rove and search as he glutted his
mind with the sense of this place.

For what was to come, there could be no mistakes.
Even the slightest miscalculation and he was finished
with the Dog Soldiers. Nothing. Double-ought zero.

Perhaps that was what White Bear had intended all
along. To see him humiliated and shamed before the
Sparrowhawk People. Why else would the *duxia* leader
have picked a tyro like himself to silence the night
guard?

Why indeed?

Then again, perhaps such skulduggery was but another of his own farfetched notions. It wouldn't be the
first time he'd pulled a boner where the Crows were
concerned. Not by a damnsight. He seemed to have a
natural-born gift for misjudging gut-eaters and their
ways, and the Sparrowhawk variety in particular. Could
be he was again seeing things, not as they were, but as
his skepticism made them appear. Maybe White Bear
intended nothing more than what he had said earlier in
the night, that the Hunter would now be allowed to
stalk more dangerous game, and take the first step in
becoming a warrior.

The scouts had returned to the raider encampment
shortly after sundown that evening. On the way in they
let go a chorus of wolf-like howls to signify that the
Arapahoes had been sighted. White Bear had listened
to their report with solemn concentration, questioning

each one in turn about the map they had drawn on the ground beside the fire. Afterwards, satisfied that he could find the Cut-Nose village, he ordered them to eat and rest themselves for the journey ahead.

Their fast had lasted seven days.

When the scouts had filled their bellies and curled up to sleep, the Dog Soldier leader gathered his warriors and explained how it would be done. Tracing in the dirt with his knife, he outlined the salient features of the ground they must cover under full darkness. The arroyo and grazing meadow. The winding, tree-lined river. And the village, to be avoided at all costs. Then, with a final stroke of his knife, White Bear sketched in their escape route. Through the valley along the river, then a sharp swing north where they would rejoin the scouts, and afterwards a hard day's ride to the granite canyon below Lodgepole Creek.

Speaking in measured tones, detailing precisely what it was he wanted done, the *batsetse* instructed each man in his part. Some half-dozen of the warriors were ordered to disguise their scent with sweet-grass and flowers, for they had been chosen to steal the horse herd. Four others were delegated to hang back and fight a delaying action, should the Arapahoes organize a pursuit. One, a hollow-eyed man much given to silence, was assigned to kill the night guard.

Squatted close by, Beckwith nearly toppled over when the man acknowledged his orders.

"My leader, I reject the offer not to kill the Cut-Nose snake who watches over these ponies."

The man was a Crazy Dog. One of those who spoke crosswise, sworn to die in battle before first snow.

Beckwith was so fascinated with the Crazy Dog that for a moment he lost track of things. While he was staring bug-eyed after the man, the other warriors had scattered around the fire and commenced daubing themselves with war paint. Only when White Bear spoke to him was the black man jolted from his funk.

"Hunter, I have saved your part in this until last, for the success of our raid will depend much on what you do."

Beckwith took a sharp hold on himself and edged closer. "I am listening, *batsetse.*"

"Were you versed in the matter of horse stealing," White Bear informed him, "you would know that the Arapahoes always station two night guards over their herd. Never three, or one, or any other number. Always two. The Cut-Noses are not clever, as you can see. Perhaps it also comes to you that I have designated only one man to kill two guards."

"*Ae*, that is so. That one who speaks crosswise."

"You are observant, Hunter, and that is good. Yet tonight your gift for the stalk will be tested to the fullest. I want you to silence the second night guard. The one who will most surely be hidden in the trees along the stream."

Beckwith hardly needed to be told that of the two guards, the one along the river would be the most difficult to stalk. The map in the dirt at his feet told the tale. It would mean a long approach across the meadow, and one slip could abort the entire raid. Yet he found the idea highly tantalizing, even though White Bear's words were little more than an outright dare. Just the thing to make an ol' mountain coon shine his best.

"You honor me, White Bear. It will be as you have directed."

Walking away, the black man added to himself that the honor was one of the double-edged variety. Since he was a greenhorn at this business, killing the night guard could give him a real boost among the Crow, maybe even get him an invite to join the Dog Soldiers as a regular member. Should he fail, on the other hand, he would most likely wind up the butt of many a joke back in Absaroka.

Thinking about it now, Beckwith decided that hindsight wasn't much better than hind tit. White Bear and

the Dog Soldiers had played it pretty square throughout
the whole trip, never once scoffing at his sore feet or his
ignorance about their method of doing things. Matter of
fact, there wasn't nothing the least bit standoffish about
them. It was sort of like keeping company with a bunch
of amiable bears. All things considered, he might do
well to take them at their word and see if he couldn't
come out of this deal with a name for himself.

White Bear hissed and motioned flat-handed for their
attention. Jerking his thumb at Beckwith and the Crazy
Dog, he signaled them to get on with the business of the
night guards. Both men snaked forward on their bellies
and disappeared into the knee-high grass, then headed
in opposite directions.

The black man moved with deliberate speed across
the meadow, scuttling forward on his elbows and knees
at a crab-like pace. The tall grasses swayed gently in the
night breeze, cushioning the sound of his movements
with a lush softness. So long as he stayed downwind of
the ponies, he had little fear of being detected, which
left only the Crazy Dog to worry about. If the bastard
got his bloodlust up and struck too fast, it might easily
as not spoil the whole game. Cautioning himself against
undue haste, Beckwith set a dead reckoning for the riverbank.

After what seemed a lifetime, the rustling of wind
through the cottonwoods alerted him that he was nearing the stream. Sinking to his belly, he crawled to the
edge of the meadow and parted the grass. Then he
froze.

The crickets had fallen silent—a warning for anyone
bright enough to catch it.

Just as quickly, though, their chirring started up again
and he damned himself for being so jumpy. Glancing up
and down the treeline, he saw nothing that didn't belong
there, which meant that the night guard had to be
staked out somewhere in the cottonwoods. More to the

point, it meant he had to cross the open ground straight ahead and get into the woods without being spotted.

Steeling himself to the task, he hugged the ground and wormed across the clearing a foot at a time. Presently he caught the sound of the river, and a moment later he slithered into the welcoming darkness of the cottonwood grove. Standing, he flattened against a tree and started taking quick peeks downstream. Unless he was wide of the mark, that was where the night guard would be found, closer to the village.

Suddenly an owl hooted directly overhead and Beckwith came within a hair of dirtying his breechclout.

When his heart quit hammering he moved off through the trees, cursing all night things for the sneaky bastards they were, owls most particularly. The earth was soft underfoot, deadening his step, and he glided from shadow to shadow with no more sound than a whisper. Then, without quite knowing why, he stopped. Something was out there. Nothing he'd seen as yet, or even heard. More like a thing he felt, a presence he somehow sensed without actually being aware of its direction or form.

Within the blink of an eye, Beckwith spotted him leaning back against a tree deep in the shadows, watching the herd with the lazy nodding of a man too long on his feet. Easing his knife from its scabbard, Beckwith began the stalk, moving with greater stealth than he had ever employed in hunting wild things. Step by step, testing the ground with his toe before putting his foot down, he crossed the grove like a wraith on a faint wind. The nearer he came, the slower he moved, until at last, without hardly realizing it, he stood but an arm's length from the Cut-Nose guard.

Not unlike a coiled snake, he tensed, every fiber of his body galvanized toward a single moment. Then he struck, locking his arm around the night guard's throat in an iron embrace. Steel flashed and he drove the blade up to the hilt in the man's spine. The Arapahoe shuddered convulsively, uttering a hoarse death rattle, then went limp as Beckwith tightened his stranglehold.

The black man lowered the body to the ground, jerking his knife free in the same movement. Bending, he made a quick circle around the base of the topknot with his blade, and yanked. The scalp came off with a mushy snap, darkly crimson in the filtered starlight. Holding it to the skyline, he inspected it a moment, letting some of the gore drip off. Abruptly a wide grin split his face and a suppressed chuckle rumbled up from his gut.

"Spread yore legs, li'l she-cat. The red nigger's gainin' ground and movin' strong."

Then, in the faint light, something caught his eye. The dead Arapahoe was missing a thumb on his left hand. That had been part of White Bear's vision, that one of his warriors would kill an enemy with only one thumb. Kneeling again, he jerked his knife and quickly severed the night guard's hand.

Judas Priest! Wouldn't that give ol' White Bear something to chaw on, sure enough.

Tucking both the hand and the scalp in his belt, he came to his feet and headed toward the meadow. Even as he quit the treeline, he could see indistinct forms moving quietly through the herd. The ponies snorted and milled around some at first. But none spooked, and curiously enough, there wasn't so much as a whicker raised in protest. Clearly the Crows knew horse talk, or else they had some juju working for them he hadn't yet heard about. Hunched low, moving more swiftly now, he saw ponies being led from the herd and mounted. The grin returned, and this time there was no holding back the chuckle.

Like the man said, Sparrowhawk People were just natural-born horse thieves.

Suddenly two ponies loomed up out of the darkness. Astride one sat the Crazy Dog, looking for all the world like he was thoroughly mortified to still be among the living. Beckwith vaulted aboard the second pony without a word and kneed him back toward the grassy plain. Moments later the Crow warriors raised their voices in an ungodly howl and stampeded the entire herd up the westward slope of the narrow valley.

Thundering along in their wake, Beckwith threw back his head and bayed like a laughing wolf making song to the moon. Lawd God A'mighty, but weren't it sweet!

He'd made'em shine. Yessireee! Made'em shine.

They rode north out of the granite canyon just before sunrise next morning. White Bear was pushing them mercilessly, yet there was neither complaint nor resentment from the warriors. The Dog Soldiers *batsetse* demanded more of himself than he did any man, and none among them could fault the wisdom of his leadership. The gauge of his judgment trotted before them: something over a hundred Cut-Nose ponies, horses enough to make each of them a man of substance. And a white mare was among them! Let none forget that. For as it had been foretold, so it had come to pass: the fulfillment of White Bear's vision.

Ai! The People would greet them with acclaim and respect, and their raid would be recounted many times over around winter campfires.

White Bear's strategy was simple, if somewhat zealous. The day before, they had cut out nearly a hundred ponies from the Arapahoe herd and driven them off. These were the weaklings, short of wind and long in tooth, and had no place among the fine herds of Absaroka. Still, they were horses, no matter how puny. Though unlikely, it was possible the Cut-Noses might recapture some of the loose ponies and organize a pursuit. Moreover, the raiding season was in full bloom, and the country they must now cross was an ancient passageway for war parties of every tribe on the plains.

Speed alone would reduce the risks they faced. Grueling though it might prove, they would travel night and day, pausing only long enough to graze and water the horses.

Accordingly, they pointed the herd northwest and made a beeline for the Sweetwater. While this stream was still a hard two days from the Wind River encampment, it was at least within the boundaries of Absaroka. The pace was set at a fast trot, and it was understood that anyone who fell behind would be left to his own devices.

White Bear had gambled heavily to capture these ponies and he had no intention of losing them. Nor would he be slowed down by laggards, either man or beast.

The Dog Soldiers switched to fresh horses with uncommon regularity, and throughout the day the blistering pace never once slackened.

Beckwith had no bones to pick about the forced march—being mounted again had done wonders for his bruised feet—but he was sulking and just a bit nettled all the same. While he hadn't expected handstands exactly, he'd thought the Dog Soldiers would make some comment on his part in the raid, or recognition, no matter how slight, of the fact that he had pulled it off. Granted, any of them could have done the job, probably in half the time. But they hadn't, goddamnit! He was the one that had skewered that Cut-Nose peckerhead.

What really grated, though, was White Bear's offhand indifference about the whole affair. Like he had assigned the task, and it had been carried out, and that was that. Little things, like a pat on the head, or a kindly word, evidently weren't the Dog Soldier way. Which didn't set well with the black man at all. Not that he'd never killed anybody before. But, by God, it *was* his first scalp. And it was he who had got the one-thumbed man. Which, as visions went, was a damn sight harder to pull off than scaring up some old fleabag of a white mare. Somebody could have said something. Anything! Just so long as they let him know he'd pulled his share of the load.

Naturally, it wasn't as if he had done them any favors. After all, he would get a share of the captured herd the same as everyone else, and in a sense he'd been feathering his own nest the same as everyone else. But still, they could have said something, the tight-lipped bastards!

Beckwith's sulk came to an abrupt halt along about midday, when the sun had peaked and started on the downgrade. The scouts, mounted now but still decked out in their wolfskins, came roaring in making the Cut-Finger sign. Cheyennes! Just over a low ridge to the north, and evidently a whole lot of them, from the way the wolf-men were jabbering.

When White Bear finally got them calmed down and talking straight, it appeared things weren't so perilous after all. Under stiff questioning, the scouts admitted that there were only six Cheyenne, and poorly armed at that. From all indications it was a small war party out on a vengeance raid, for they were mounted and carrying lances as well as battle shields. Still, they were riding in a westerly direction, which meant it was the Sparrowhawk People they intended to raid.

White Bear's scowl deepened at that and he soon had the scouts down in the dirt drawing a map of the country ahead. After considerable grunting and ear-tugging, he finally got a plan formulated and turned to face his warriors.

The Dog Soldiers were honor-bound to stop the Cut-Fingers here, before they reached Absaroka.

That seemed to suit everyone well enough, so White Bear went on. Ahead there was a fault in the earth, narrow defiles like the fingers of a hand feeding westward into a main ravine, which then sloped upward to again rejoin the high plains. The Cheyenne would enter the ravine from one of the northern defiles. This they must do. Otherwise it meant a long ride to circle around the great fault. When they emerged into the ravine, the Dog Soldiers would be waiting in the southernmost defile. The attack would come from the rear and the Cut-

Fingers would be killed or scattered. Either way they would pose no further threat to Absaroka.

Four warriors were left behind to guard the pony herd and White Bear rode off with the others hard on his trail. Among them was the black man, and his glowering look had now been replaced by a broad, and somewhat smug, grin, much like a cat with a mouthful of feathers.

Something less than an hour later, the Dog Soldiers waited quietly in a sandy, rock-strewn defile. One of the scouts was posted at the head of the draw as lookout, but the warriors kept a wary eye on their mounts nonetheless. At the first flicker of an ear, each man would squeeze down firmly on his horse's nostrils; more than one ambush had been spoiled by a frisky pony snorting just at the wrong moment. Beckwith was seated astride a barrel-chested *eshoo-shebit*—a light buckskin that had taken his eye—and like the others, he was watching the pony's ears for some telltale sign. But his main concern, and one he seemed unable to set aside, was the Crazy Dog. Perhaps it was just a hunch, yet something warned him that the man was set to make a foolhardy play. The moment the Cheyenne showed, he was going to bolt out of the gully and tackle them single-handed. If he wanted to die, it made sense. Trouble was, he'd pretty well destroy anybody else's chances at the gravy, and that put a severe crimp in Beckwith's own little scheme, for today he meant to show these coons what fighting really looked like.

Between eyeballing the Crazy Dog and watching his pony, Beckwith failed to see the scout scampering back toward them. But he did see the Crazy Dog stiffen, and that was warning enough. Slamming his heels into the buckskin's ribs, he rocketed out of the defile in a clattering one-man charge. Caught flatfooted, White Bear and the Dog Soldiers could only stare after him in pop-eyed astonishment.

"Hooo-ki-hi! Wrrooow!"

The Crow war cry back-to-back with the roar of an

enraged grizzly was unnerving in itself. But when the Cheyenne saw a wild-eyed black man in full war paint bearing down on them, they froze stone-cold in a moment of panic. In the space of a heartbeat Beckwith drove the buckskin into their midst. Before anyone could move, he lightly tapped three of them with the muzzle of his Hawken.

Then, as the petrified Cut-Fingers came to life, he thrust the rifle under the nose of their head man and pulled the trigger. The Hawken roared and the upper half of the Cheyenne's skull gushered skyward in a frothy spray of bone and gore. Whirling the *eshoo-shebit,* the black man reversed the rifle in his hand and charged back through their ranks. He howled at the top of his lungs, swinging the Hawken like a scythe, and clubbed one warrior from the saddle. Then he grunted, jarred by the impact as his buckskin rode another horse and rider into the ground and trampled them underhoof.

Sawing the reins madly, he jerked the pony about and started back, but he was too late. White Bear and the Dog Soldiers had joined the fight at last, swarming over the remaining Cheyennes like a nest of hornets. Out of the cloud of dust and men and thrashing horses came the flash of war club and tomahawk, and within moments the screams of the dying were but echoes along the craggy ravine walls.

The six Cut-Fingers had been chopped to pieces under the Dog Soldiers' onslaught. Yet none would deny that the black man alone had accounted for three of the dead. Not to mention counting coup on an equal number while they were armed and very much alive.

White Bear reined in beside Beckwith and regarded him with a wooden look. "You fight well, Hunter, but you are rash. Take care that it does not one day cause you much grief. Go now and collect your scalps. We are finished here."

Beckwith merely nodded and slid from the buckskin,

jerking his knife as he walked toward the littered bodies. But as he knelt and took hold of the first topknot, he spotted the Crazy Dog standing off to one side. The warrior's expression was one of unbearable sadness, and his gaze clung to the dead with a hurt, wistful look, almost as if he longed to accompany them on their journey. Perhaps even despised them for not having fought harder to snuff out his own life.

The black man looked away and went to work with his knife, somehow diminished himself by the Crazy Dog's desolation. That any man would want to die, instead of sucking life dry of its sweet juices, was a mystery so profound that he had no way of comprehending it. There seemed to be only one answer, though that in itself posed yet another riddle.

It was the way.

Things were moving a little too fast for Beckwith. When the raiders had ridden into the Sparrowhawk camp that morning, whooping the war cry, their faces painted black in sign of victory, driving before them the herd of Cut-Nose ponies, they had been greeted by shouts and cheers that quickly drew a crowd from all parts of the village. Not just women and children either. Even the rival warrior societies turned out, praising them as loudly as everyone else. The Bulls and Prairie-Foxes, Ravens and Lumpwoods, Stone Hammers, and Kit Foxes. Rotten Belly came running, along with the rest, and back on the edge of the crowd, Beckwith caught sight of Pine Leaf among the squaws. Her eyes glistened with excitement, and she boldly held his stare, flirting outrageously with a teasing smile.

These things the black man understood. Like the Dog Soldiers, he accepted the tumult and praise as the due of returning warriors, particularly in light of their audacious feat. For seldom in the Sparrowhawks' long history of horse stealing had a raiding party captured an enemy camp's entire herd.

But what happened next left Beckwith stunned and Strikes-Both-Ways positively gibbering with glee. White Bear had stilled the crowd and informed them of the black man's extraordinary performance: Three coups and four scalps in one raid. That very night, the *duxia* leader declared, the Hunter would be initiated into the Dog Soldier society as a full-fledged warrior.

"Hooo-ki-hi! Hooo-ki-hi!"

The mighty throng had roared their approval and swarmed around Beckwith in a wild melee, wanting only to touch this dark one whose medicine had proved so strong. Jerked off his buckskin, the astounded black man was paraded through camp atop their shoulders, and deposited at last in front of Strikes-Both-Ways' lodge. There the squaws had teased him unmercifully, giggling and poking at him as they made obscene gestures with their hands. Pine Leaf had best prepare herself, they snickered wickedly. The Hunter was now four steps closer to her bed.

Ai! What a marriage night that would be.

This brought a squall of delight from the crowd, and Beckwith could see that the fun had only just started. Finally, when the squaws began grabbing at his breechclout, clamoring to see the joys awaiting Pine Leaf, he smiled and waved and beat a hasty retreat inside the lodge. Even then some of the bolder ones hung around outside for a while, making lewd remarks and laughing uproariously at the thought of Pine Leaf hoisted aloft on the dark one's shaft. At last, when they saw he wasn't going to take the bait, the squaws had drifted off.

Once the commotion subsided, Beckwith was able to sort out his thoughts, and attempt to make some reason out of this dizzying turn of events. What baffled him most was White Bear's wholly unexpected announcement. Since the fight with the Cheyennes, some three days back, the Dog Soldier leader had been aloof and coldly distant. Hardly looked at him, much less said anything. Now, out of absolute nowhere, he jumps up and

commences telling everybody what a holy terror the
dark one is when the fur starts to fly. No warning. No
handshakes. Nothing. Just pops up like the risen dead
and unloads the good news.

Jesus! There simply weren't no way to figure a gut-
eater.

When Beckwith put the question to Strikes-Both-
Ways, the old bowmaker merely shrugged and trotted
out his inscrutable look. "My son, you continue to think
like a *tibo.* Remember our lessons, and let your mind
accept as reality not what it sees, but rather that which
must be. Among the Sparrowhawk People, a man's
worth is measured in ancient ways, not in the petty
words another might use to extol his greatness."

That wasn't exactly the answer Beckwith was looking
for, but it was all he got. Strikes-Both-Ways let the matter rest there, and the black man was left to worry over
it like a dog with a new bone, which was exactly what he
did the remainder of the afternoon. By nightfall he was
as confused as ever, yet his earlier astonishment had
slowly given way to a thudding, lighthearted jubilation.
Before the night was out he would be a Dog Soldier. A
warrior! The first real, honest-to-God step in his quest
to manage the Crows.

That made'em come! Throwed'em dead center just as
he had meant to do all along. As for the rest, while he
didn't understand half of what these gut-eaters said or
did, he was damned well resigned to accepting things as
they were.

It was no longer *the* way. From now on it was the *only*
way. If you couldn't whip'em, then join'em. And by the
bleedin', crucified Christ, that was exactly what he intended to do.

The Dog Soldiers were ready and waiting when he arrived at the club lodge later that evening. Beckwith was
given the seat of honor across from the door flap, and
Strikes-Both-Ways, as his grandfather and sponsor, was

seated next to him. Just for a few moments, those in the lodge watched him without expression, their faces still as bronzed masks. Then several older men began a slow, measured beat on the drums.

White Bear, seated now on the black man's right side, nodded and the warriors who had participated in the raid stepped forward to form a circle around the fire. The tempo of the drums increased slightly and the men began a shuffling dance. Their movements cast eerie, distorted shadows on the sloping hide walls, like darkened specters leaping fitfully to life. One after another, the two scouts stepped from the circle and chanted the song of their ordeal in flat, dissonant tones. Then, in turn, each warrior broke ranks to tell of his part in the raid. When all were done a stout pole was brought forth and jammed into the dirt floor. Around it was tied a moth-eaten buffalo robe, and dangling from this was a Cheyenne battle shield and three fresh scalps. Each man again left the circle, performing a ritualistic enactment of his role in the brief fight. This drew murmurs of approval from the onlookers, and when the last warrior had struck his blow, they circled the fire only four times more. The throb of the drums ebbed and the dancers again slowed their pace to a shuffle, until on some silent command they simply halted in mid-stride and resumed their seats.

There was a moment of silence and then a sharp intake of breath from the assemblage as a bucket of raw dog meat and three dog skulls were brought forward and placed in front of Beckwith. White Bear rose and moved around to face the black man, grasping in his hand a forked stick wrapped with wolf tails and festooned on one end with a cluster of feathers and scalps. The drumbeat gathered strength once more, and in a singsong monotone, the Dog Soldier *batsetse* began relating Beckwith's feats during the horse raid and in his lone assault on the Cheyenne. Each time a scalp was lifted or a coup struck White Bear rapped the dog skulls a sharp blow with his stick. With successive raps on the leering skulls the spectators grew more restive, and when the number had mounted to seven, their muttered expressions of awe swept through the lodge.

Halting, White Bear jerked three eagle feathers from his stick and wedged them firmly into the black man's hair, one for each of the coups he had counted. Then the war leader jabbed his forked stick into the dog meat and lifted a bloody hunk to his mouth. Grasping it in his teeth, he tore off a bite and chewed it thoroughly before swallowing. Extending the stick to Beckwith, he nodded solemnly, indicating what must be done.

The black man faltered only a moment, then he clamped down hard on the meat, working his jaws, and ripped off a whole mouthful. Chewing slowly, his gaze never left the face of White Bear, and when he swallowed an imperceptible smile flickered at the corner of his mouth.

White Bear grunted approval and intoned a litany as he offered the dog meat to the Earth, and Sky, and the Four Winds.

"Kan di bare hawak. Bare karaxtasa. Now you are one of us. Do not forget. The Dog Soldier's way is hard, yet so long as he survives, the Sparrowhawk People will live on. From this day to that you are sworn to protect the old, and feed the hungry, and destroy those who would violate the sacred earth of Absaroka."

Laying aside the stick, the *batsetse* thrust his hand in the bucket of dog meat until it was drenched with blood. Squatting, he brought his hand forward, spreading the fingers wide, and placed it over Beckwith's face. When he leaned back the imprint of a hand was etched in blood across the black man's features. Rising to his full height, White Bear extended his arm overhead, making offering once more to the gods. Then his voice filled the lodge, deep and resonant, charged with the power of the spirit beings who sanctified this rite.

"Hereafter let all the People hear my words. While

this man walks among us, he will be known as Bloody Hand. *Bicitse-Wiak*. He who slays with his hand gone red. I have spoken."

Beckwith licked his lips and the taste was good, faintly sweet, somehow exhilarating. The blood trickled down his throat, infusing him with a curious atavistic force, magically exorcising all that had gone before. When he came to his feet, the mulatto named Jim Beckwith had ceased to exist.

There was only a warrior. A Dog Soldier of the Sparrowhawk People.

Bloody Hand.

CHAPTER 4

Like most mountain men, Will Sublette and Doc Newell had borrowed a trick from the Indians when it came to raiding an enemy camp. While almost intolerable, they imposed on themselves a stolid patience that was wholly uncharacteristic of their breed. It had been acquired through bitter experience, and wasn't so much a virtue as reluctant acceptance of an elementary tenet.

Survival in the wilderness, more often than not, boiled down to getting the jump on the other fellow. The unwary seldom got a second chance, and the one who walked away with his topknot intact was generally conceded to have taken top prize.

Sublette and Newell were squatted in a copse of aspen trees and hadn't spoken for the last three hours. The sky glittered with a profusion of stars, and below, along the fringe of the aspen grove, the campfire they watched was slowly diminishing into a bed of coals. The men around that fire had taken to their robes only within the past hour. Though all appeared quiet, the booshway and his burly companion were resigned to waiting a while longer. Soon the night guard would grow bored, heavy-lidded, and it was then they would strike.

Raiding an American Fur camp wasn't as risky as tangling with gut-eaters, but it was something a man didn't rush all the same. Meantime, there was a certain savor to this matter of waiting. It gave a man a chance to muse on all manner of things.

Such as leaving the porkeaters below stranded and afoot in a wilderness crawling with the devil's own. Bug's Boys. The hair-hungry Blackfeet.

Sublette had had ample time to ponder the precarious and highly vulnerable position of Rocky Mountain Fur. The Bear Lake Rendezvous was two months past, yet that last war council with Ashley remained fresh and all too vivid in the back of his head. The trader had lectured him and Jackson and Smith much like a schoolmaster patronizing backward children. While the three partners hadn't much liked his tone, they'd cared even less for his message. Ashley had gambled a sizeable fortune on the belief that Rocky Mountain Fur could maintain its hold on the mountain beaver trade. His words had left no doubt whatever that he was willing to declare war in order to prevent further encroachment by the opposition.

Hudson's Bay, according to Ashley's latest intelligence, was slowly branching out along the Salmon and Snake rivers, spreading eastward from their main trading post at Fort Vancouver. There was evidence to suggest that a party of voyageurs had already surveyed a site for a new fort only three days' ride northwest of Bear Lake. Which meant, given time and lack of stiff resistance by Rocky Mountain Fur, the Englishmen would gradually infiltrate the western slope of the Rockies just as they had the Pacific Northwest.

Sublette and his partners had received this bit of information with the gravity of three owls on a rotten limb, and with good reason. Dr. John McLoughlin, who ruled the Hudson's Bay empire, was hardly an adversary to be taken lightly. Something of a despot, as well as a shrewd tactician, he had shown how monopoly of the fur trade in the Pacific Northwest could be made to pay handsomely. Hudson's Bay in effect farmed the fur country, maintaining a steady market and a fixed price for pelts. The result was a stabilized bartering system and an assured yield with high profits for the company. McLoughlin enforced rigid discipline on his voyageurs and extended the same harsh demands to the Indians, governing them with a code of wilderness law which meant severe punishment for the slightest infraction. The company name alone struck terror in the Pacific Northwest tribes, and Hudson's Bay men could travel the vast empire at will, with never a thought for their own safety.

The handwriting was on the wall, plain enough for anyone to read. Hudson's Bay was a formidable rival. Should they gain a foothold in the Rockies, it would be only a matter of time until they worked the same spell over the mountain tribes. Afterwards, just as he had done in the Pacific Northwest, McLoughlin would ruthlessly and very deftly eliminate all forms of competition, Rocky Mountain Fur coming at the head of the list.

While the Hudson's Bay threat was distressing in itself, Ashley's commentary on the American Fur Company sobered the three partners even more. Since the days of Lewis and Clark, nearly three decades back, the Blackfeet had constantly warred on white trappers, and not just in their own territory up and around the Three Forks of the Missouri, either. Even when raiding their ancestral enemies, the Crows, Bug's Boys went out of their way to track down mountain men and lift a few added scalps. But from all accounts, this hadn't deterred John Jacob Astor in the slightest.

Back in St. Louis, it was common knowledge that Astor had sent his right-hand man, Kenneth McKenzie, up the Missouri to conclude a trade pact with the Blackfeet. According to reliable sources, McKenzie's orders were to win over the Blackfeet with rum and promises of firearms, and establish a trading post somewhere near the Great Falls of the Missouri. Moreover, McKenzie was reportedly sending agents south, along the Musselshell and the Yellowstone, to court outflung bands of the Blackfeet nation. Should American Fur form an alliance with the Blackfeet, it required little effort to imagine what would happen next.

Shortly, if not sooner, there would be a bounty on the scalp of every trapper in the mountain brigades. Then, when the Blackfeet had done the dirty work for them, Astor and McKenzie would simply pick up where Rocky Mountain Fur had been chopped off.

What it amounted to, Ashley had informed the somber-faced partners, was that they were besieged on all sides by treacherous and thoroughly unscrupulous rivals. Their only alternative was to fight fire with fire. Throughout the coming season, the brigades were to probe deeply into the lands of the Blackfeet, Flatheads, and Rees, and carry the fight to American Fur and Hudson's Bay on their own home ground. Each party would travel in strength, searching out prime beaver country. Those Indians who greeted them in peace were to be wooed and won over. Those who came looking for a fight must get a dose of trouble they would never forget. Whenever and wherever possible, as often as the opportunity presented itself, the brigades were to raid competitor's camps without mercy, send them packing back where they came from, and teach them to fear Rocky Mountain Fur no less than the wrath of God.

Let them understand, once and for all, that when they ventured into the remote fastness of the high mountains, there was every likelihood they would never return.

The meeting had concluded with Ashley railing that he was not a man to be outdone by either a Yankee interloper or a pack of English snobs. If the opposition wanted a fight, they could damn well have it, and he expected the mountain brigades to give them more than they could handle.

Sublette had departed the Bear Lake Rendezvous under a great cloud of gloom. While he was hardly a man to turn the other cheek, he had little taste for Ashley's declaration of war. Killing Indians was one thing. That was forced on a man. Simply to stay alive in the mountains he had to become more Indian than white, which meant fighting them with the same savagery with which they fought each other. But killing white men in cold blood was another matter entirely. That went against the grain.

Then again, it seemed pretty clear that Hudson's Bay and American Fur weren't above some dirty tactics themselves. If Ashley was to be believed—and with what he had at stake, there was every reason to take it as gospel—this deal looked to be dog eat dog from the very outset. That being the case, it came down to a matter of sheer survival. Either Rocky Mountain Fur went under without a whimper, or else it reared up on its hind legs and fought back. Given the circumstances, it was no choice at all. Dr. McLoughlin and Mr. Astor were in for some hard times.

Still, there were ways and there were ways, and not all of them were as permanent as others.

Sublette had worked his brigade north along the Snake, moving slowly as the mood struck him. Summer pelts were mostly ratty anyway, and with no reason to hurry, he had plenty of time to think out the problem. After trapping Henry's Fork for about thirty miles, he led the brigade east over the Tetons and into Jackson's Hole. There he turned north along the valley of the Snake and followed it to its headwaters above Jackson Lake. Three times in the course of a month, they were surprised by roving bands of Blackfeet, and it was this constant skirmishing that finally settled the issue for Sublette. Bug's Boys were ornery enough all on their own. Anybody that had ideas of feeding them raw meat laced with gunpowder deserved whatever he got.

Heading north from the Snake, Sublette and his men crossed the mountain range and dropped down the far slopes into Colter's Hell. This freak of nature, situated at the southern edge of Yellowstone Lake, was thought to be a place of evil spirits by the Indians. While the mountain men weren't that taken with haunts and spirit beings, they could respect another man's superstitions. Particularly when the place looked as though it had been spawned by Lucifer himself.

Colter's Hell was a land of upheaval and turbulence. Boiling underground springs erupted from mounds of earth resembling mush pots, shooting geysers of water and pinkish-colored clay far into the sky. Steam clouded the area in thick layers, and vaporous sulphur gases combined with the heat and boiling mud to form a sickening stench. Watching it, a man had a feeling that the very bowels of the earth might explode at any moment, destroying everything in its path in a giant, volcanic holocaust.

All things considered, it was a good place to avoid, which was exactly what the mountain men did. Sublette circled his brigade around the southern rim of the lake and set a course northwest for Targhee Pass. Shortly before sundown, though, they sighted smoke far in the distance. The billowing plume told its own tale, and Sublette knew that they had at last stumbled onto an American Fur encampment. Only a *mangeur de lard* fresh out of St. Louis would have built a bonfire in the middle of Indian country.

Sublette had ordered the brigade to make a cold camp, allowing neither a fire nor any noise much above a whisper. After dark he had selected Doc Newell to accompany him, and they struck off on foot toward the porkeaters' encampment.

Their hours of waiting had now come to an end, though. With dew fallen and the night guard drowsy, Sublette decided it was time to move. After working their way through the aspen grove, the trappers went to earth and bellied across a small meadow bordering the treeline. There, grazing placidly on the lush mountain grass, were three saddle horses and four pack animals. Undisturbed by the appearance of two strange white men, the horses went right on cropping grass while the raiders cut their hobbles and knotted lengths of rawhide through their halters. Within ten minutes Sublette and Newell were leading the horses back in the direction they had come, moving slowly and quietly as they melted foot by foot into the darkness.

Once out of earshot Newell couldn't hold back his excitement any longer. "Whoooiieee! Them coons is gonna be madder'n switched cats when they wakes up and finds out some booger man done stole their hoss-flesh."

"Serves 'em right!" Sublette growled. "Tell ye the truth, Doc, I've been half-frozen to get my hooks into them bustards someway. Course, they don't mean it'll end here. They'll likely find their way north and get their booshway all riled up agin' us."

"Whyn't ye jest kill'em then? Been a whole lot simpler all the way round."

"Killin' white men ain't my style. Lessen it's them that starts it. That bein' so, I calculate we'll have plenty of chances to get in our licks."

They walked along in silence for a while until at last Newell couldn't resist the question. "Will, the boys've been doin' a heap of talkin', sayin' we got a real war on our hands. Ye reckon thar's anything to it?"

"More'n likely, Doc. More'n likely. What it biles down to is eat shit and run, or stand and fight. Ain't much of a choice the way I see it."

Newell's massive brow screwed up in a frown and he grunted. *"Waugh!* How ye reckon that's gonna make the stick float fer ol' Beckwith, him bein' off with the Crows like he is?"

Sublette chuckled sardonically. "Doc, I'd feel a whole heap better if I knew the answer to that. Come rendezvous next y'ar, that black hunk of bear bait might be the only thing twixt us and a hole in the ground. Leastways if'n he gets them Crows broke to halter."

They didn't say much after that, but they were both

thinking on it as they strode on through the night. Somewhere back in the Wind Rivers, there was a dingy mulatto roaming around who didn't have no more idea than a bumblebee that Rocky Mountain Fur had latched onto his shirttail.

It looked to be a long winter, long and mighty risky for them that was partial to their hair.

The Moon of Black Cherries had been a time of honor for Bloody Hand.

Among the Sparrowhawk People, it was now said that the dark one must surely be the *bacbapite* of Strikes-Both-Ways, who himself had been a great warrior in his youth. There was no other explanation. The blood of the grandfather had been passed on to the grandson, for in the space of two brief moons, the fledgling Dog Soldier had outstripped battle-scarred warriors half again his age.

Bloody Hand had taken many desperate chances over the summer, not the least of which was his willingness to join every *duxia* leader who offered the pipe. This in itself was considered remarkable, for wiser heads knew that a warrior's prestige could be maintained with no more than two or three raids each season. But it was the ferocity with which Bloody Hand fought that left the People stunned. Even the pipe-holders themselves, selected as leaders for their exceptional bravery, were appalled by his reckless disregard for danger. The dark one, it was said when warriors gathered, seemed possessed by some demon spirit, driven to foolhardy acts of courage like a Crazy Dog. Yet different somehow, for his savagery and daring were strangely calculated, as though he knew precisely the bounds separating madness from raw courage, and past certain limits some deeper instinct held him back.

While the raid on the Arapahoes had brought him much fame, it was during the Moon of Black Cherries that Bloody Hand's gift for warfare became apparent.

Steadily he had risen through the ranks of the Dog
Soldiers, acquiring the coveted warrior honors in rapid
succession. On only his second raid he had slithered
through a Sioux village late at night and emerged leading a fine war pony. This, the stealing of a pony tethered
outside an enemy lodge, was perhaps the most highly
prized of all honors among a nation of horse thieves.
There were warriors who crossed over to the Faraway
Land without ever accomplishing this feat. Among the
Apsahrokee it was now accepted that Bloody Hand had
few equals as a thief of horses, and not without reason.
In but four raids, his herd had grown to something over
fifty ponies.

It was on the last of these raids that Bloody Hand had
gained the third honor. Locked in a hand-to-hand death
struggle with a Shoshone, he had broken his opponent's
arm with the ease with which some men might snap a
twig. Then, as many about him would later recount, the
dark one had bashed in the Shoshone's brains with his
own war club. Though his manner of wresting a weapon
from an adversary was somewhat irregular—first breaking the man's arm—it was nonetheless regarded with
mild awe by the Sparrowhawk warriors. There was nothing in tradition that dictated how an enemy must be
disarmed, nor was there any obligation to kill him afterwards. Bloody Hand had done both, scalping the man in
the process, and the honor was somehow lent stature by
the brute strength he employed so casually.

Yet, for all the wealth and accumulated honors of
Strikes-Both-Ways' grandson, the most indelibile aspect
of his fame lay in the icy savagery he exhibited during
battle. With the raiding season half gone, he had already
collected seventeen scalps, more than all but a handful
of braves had taken after many snows on the war trail.
When the dark one was engaged in a fight, he became
something not quite human, a death machine of sorts.
His every move had about it a catlike quality, so smooth
and economical that the onlooker's eye could scarcely

follow it. Nothing was wasted, whether a load from his Hawken or the blow of a war club. Like a thunderbolt loosed among men, he struck without excess or lost motion, dispatching victims with the clean swiftness of a born killer. Those who witnessed it later spoke of him with hushed reverence, describing a man so formidable that none but the foolhardy would dare provoke his wrath.

The Sparrowhawk People weren't alone in their awe. Across the plains, the seed of a legend had taken root, for their enemies were also talking of the black warrior who rode with the Dog Soldiers. Already he had collected scalps from the Arapahoe, Cheyenne, Sioux, Shoshone, and Cree, not to mention more than half a hundred of their finest ponies. Though few had seen him and lived to tell of it later, there was much discussion of the dark one. The name Bloody Hand had somehow become known, circulating from camp to camp, and among the plains tribes there was a rash of speculation as to his kinship with the Crows.

Still, with his fame spreading and glory enough for any warrior, the one called Bloody Hand was far from satisfied. While he had made a place for himself in Absaroka, garnering the right to wear ermine skin and wolf tails and scalplocks dangling from his shirt, it simply wasn't enough. Even the fact that he had made headway in Ashley's plan to subjugate the Crows gave him only passing comfort. Somehow Rocky Mountain Fur no longer seemed important, if it mattered at all. The mountain men and their struggle to dominate the fur trade were now so distant from his thoughts that it came to him only as a childhood dream returns, in bits and snatches. Nor was he fulfilled in any great sense by his spectacular climb within the Dog Soldiers. These honors doubled and doubled again wouldn't have sufficed, for the dark one's lodestone had become like the desire of the moth for the star.

He was obsessed with doing what no outsider had

ever done, being selected as a pipe-holder, a *batsetse,*
leading the Sparrowhawk People in war.

Desire and reality, though, had little in common.
Those who aspired to leadership, whether as raid planner or war chief, were first obligated to acquire a medicine bundle of great strength. Otherwise they would
never be selected as a pipe-holder simply because no
one would follow them. The contents of a medicine
bundle, as Bloody Hand well knew, were generally revealed to a warrior in his vision quest. Atop some high
cliff, alone with the One Above, the warrior deprived
himself of food and water for four days, making offerings to the spirit beings the entire time. There, if the
gods were willing, his vision would come, and through it
a revelation of the medicine that would watch over him
all his days on earth.

Bloody Hand had converted himself into a Sparrowhawk through sheer will power and a burgeoning taste
for fame. Yet beneath the war paint and braids, he was
still the black skeptic, a nonbeliever. Even among hea-
thens, he remained the greatest heathen of them all.
Having rejected the white man's Christ and the black
man's witchcraft, it came quite natural to reject the red
man's befuddling array of gods, which meant that seeking a vision was out of the question.

The gods would reveal nothing to him, whether he
fasted four days or forty. They couldn't, for in his mind
they simply didn't exist.

After considerable thought he had tactfully broached
the subject with Strikes-Both-Ways, inquiring if Sparrowhawk tradition made allowances for those unable to
bring about a vision. The old bowmaker's answer was a
revelation in itself, setting out his path more clearly
than a clash of thunder and the booming voice of Jehovah himself.

Failing inspiration of his own, the warrior could apply
to a holy man for help in devising a medicine bundle.
Likewise based on a vision, albeit that of the holy man,

the medicine bundle would become the dwelling place of the warrior's guardian spirits. Moreover, it was considered no less powerful than one he might have arranged for himself. The fee for this service, though, was outrageously high: generally three ponies.

Bloody Hand didn't laugh but he came close. If it worked, it would be cheap at ten times the price.

Early next morning he appeared at the lodge of Braided Tail, who was conceded to be the most powerful shaman in all of Absaroka. Instead of three horses, he brought four, the magic number. When the ancient one saw this, he agreed immediately to intervene with the spirits on Bloody Hand's behalf. Once inside his tent, the holy man seated the warrior opposite him, then sprinkled some evil-smelling powder in the fire, and breathed deeply of the fumes. Moments later his eyes glazed over with the unblinking stare of one in a trance, and in a toothless whisper he began chanting medicine songs. The spell lasted only a few minutes when suddenly the chant stopped and the shaman began to grunt and nod his head, as if listening intently to a voice that only he heard. After a while his gaze cleared and he graced Bloody Hand with a benign smile.

"You are fortunate, my son. The spirit beings were receptive to our plea, for it is ordained that you will be a great man once you have your medicine bundle. Through their wisdom and generosity has been revealed the guardian spirits who will guide you in the days to come."

Scampering about the lodge, the holy one began gathering odds and ends, which he placed on a parfleche laid out before the warrior. When all was in readiness, he again took his seat.

"My son, this is your medicine bundle. Watch closely and hear my words well. The bag of herbs you see will replenish your horse's wind in flight or in the chase." One by one he selected objects and held them up for inspection. "An eagle's head to give your eyes faraway power. A dried swallow for the elusiveness to evade your enemies. The claw of an eagle to give you swiftness and strength in the attack. And most powerful of all . . ."

The shaman opened a small buckskin bag and dumped four rattlesnake heads on the coals of the fire. Covering the snake heads with a piece of bull liver, he sat back to watch. The liver slowly shriveled to a crisp while the rattlesnake heads sizzled and popped. Their jaws gaped wide, fangs exposed, as if searching for something to bite even in the fiery coals. Braided Tail at last scooped the liver from the fire with a stick and placed it in the buckskin bag. Holding it out, he waited for Bloody Hand to take it.

"That, my son, is your personal medicine, an amulet to be worn at all times, even in sleep. The meat has now assumed the poison of the deadly ones. It will ward off evil wherever you ride, and if you believe strongly enough, it will even give you the power to stare men into their graves."

Bloody Hand accepted the little bag solemnly and tied the rawhide thongs around his neck. Then, quite abruptly, his amusement with Braided Tail's incantations and hocus-pocus was hauled up short. While he heard the shaman's words clearly enough, he wasn't quite sure he believed his own ears.

"There is one last thing, *barakbatse.* You must wear a necklace made from the claws of the great bear. So long as it is around your neck, you will have the strength and ferocity of the sullen one himself. Yet the spirits have decreed that you must slay this bear yourself, and remove his claws with your own knife. Only then will the medicine be strong."

The holy man paused, expecting some reaction, but Bloody Hand just stared at him with a wary scowl. Shrugging, the shaman ended with a prophesy that sent a tingling jolt down the warrior's spine.

"Shortly before sunset you must go to the bend in the

river below the village. The great bear will come to meet you there. When he roars and stands like a man, you will kill him and take his claws. I have spoken."

Bloody Hand left the lodge moments later, feeling he had just struck a bargain with the devil himself. Certainly the medicine bundle and the liver would have been enough. This foolishness about the bear was carrying things a mite too far. It could easily spoil the whole deal unless he was able to scare up a silvertip somewhere.

Along about sundown, Bloody Hand charged his Hawken with a fresh load and struck off toward the river. While he had little doubt that it was a wild-goose chase, he couldn't very well ignore the holy man's instructions. Word of Braided Tail's prophesy had made the rounds during the day, and as he strolled through the village, a pack of warriors fell in some distance behind. Whatever happened, it was sure to make a good story, and they had no intention of missing the show. All of which left Bloody Hand's temper a little frayed around the edges. Bad enough that he had to go through with the old faker's scheme, but now he was forced to make an ass of himself right out in public.

Had the Virgin Mary materialized on Wind River that afternoon, Bloody Hand would have been no less astounded. Grumping around the riverbank, as if merely awaiting his arrival, was the biggest grizzly he had ever laid eyes on. Somewhat in a daze, the warrior boldly stepped forward, and faithful to his own role in this business, the grizzly promptly reared up on his hind legs and let go a thundering roar.

Bloody Hand set the trigger and brought the Hawken to his shoulder. When the rifle cracked, a splotch of red blossomed over the bear's heart, but he merely swatted at the wound and lumbered forward. The warrior jerked his wiping stick and started reloading, though it was plainly clear that he was fresh out of time. The silvertip

was closing fast, and from the look in his eye he meant
to make a meal on dark meat well before sunset.

Later, looking back on it, Bloody Hand couldn't recall
what had possessed him. Yet at that last instant, when
the grizzly drew back his paw for the mortal blow, the
warrior somehow knew that he was dead on his feet.
Slashing out with the wiping stick, he dealt the bear a
stinging rap across the snout.

The grizzly whimpered like a scolded child, then staggered and fell dead at the black man's feet. Just for a
moment Bloody Hand couldn't quite believe that it was
real, that he wouldn't awaken in a cold sweat and find it
was only an outlandish nightmare. But the yipping howls
of the warriors brought him to his senses, and without
warning his knees turned to water and his hands began
to shake.

Fearing those behind him would see the cold terror
written across his face, he didn't dare look around.
Sucking up his gut, he took a long draught of fresh air
and exhaled it very slowly. Then he pulled his knife,
lowered himself gratefully to the ground, and went to
work on the grizzled monster's claws.

As he slipped the blade under the skin, and probed
for the joint, he reminded himself to present Braided
Tail with another pony. Anybody that could conjure up a
whole grizzly bear was damn well worth getting on the
good side of.

Waugh! That old coon made strong medicine. Even if
it was a little hard on the nerves.

Bloody Hand awoke with a start. Outside he could hear
Strikes-Both-Ways scraping a sheephorn bow, but he
had long since become accustomed to the grating sound,
hardly a noise to disturb a man's sleep. Then, in a warm
glow of discovery, he remembered.

Lifting one eyelid in the merest slit, he watched as the
young girl knelt before the firehole and stirred the ashes
with a stick. She was still naked, shivering a little in the

damp chill, and the rose-tipped nipples of her breasts stood erect and hard. She found a glowing ember in the ashes and covered it with a tuft of dried grass, then leaned forward and blew softly. Tiny flames shot up, like the lapping of a kitten's red tongue, and she scattered a handful of twigs over the fire. When the flames grew, she fed in several large sticks, nursing the fire along until she had a cheery blaze crackling. Satisfied, she stood and swung the cooking pot into position over the flames. This kettle was her treasure of treasures, for only the wealthy could afford the price demanded by white traders. It spoke well of her husband that he had brought one with him when he came to live among the *Apsahrokee.*

The black man liked to spy on her in the mornings when she first slipped from the robes. Yet he had a sneaking hunch that she wasn't wholly unaware of his little game. Trotting around naked like that, it was almost as if she were teasing him, pleased somehow that the sight of her could arouse him from even a deep sleep. The thought brought a silent chuckle up from his gut.

The copper-skinned little vixen knew how to light the spark well enough. Jesus! After three nights on the wedding couch, his pecker felt like it had been wrung through a sausage grinder.

Her name was Still Water, which in Sparrowhawk talk came out a hoarse cough with a grunt thrown in on the side. Bloody Hand had bought her for ten ponies, and next to his medicine bundle, figured it was about the best trade he'd ever made. The things she knew about greasing a man's pole weren't exactly what he had expected of a virgin, but he was satisfied that she'd never been gigged before. That little furball of hers was too damn tight to be anything but the real article. More than likely her mama had just been a good teacher. Crow women were like that, leastways before they got hitched: real keen on virtue and coy smiles, but regular chain lightning once they got beneath the covers.

Still sneaking peeks at her, he watched as she wiggled into a tanned doeskin dress. The skirt came just below her knees, hemmed with a fringe of tiny bells, so that when she walked a delicate tinkling seemed to follow her around. The dress was tightly girdled at the waist with a wide belt, which bore intricate quillwork of a brightly colored geometric design. Opening one eye a bit wider, the black man admired her legs as she pulled on ornately quilled moccasins. It amused him that she wore nothing underneath the dress, and simplified things no end when one of those sudden urges came over him.

After dressing, she scented her hair with pomatum and stroked it with a porcupine tail brush till it gave off a glossy black sheen. Next she plaited her hair in long braids, then dabbed her neck, arms, and legs with a bouquet of pulverized wild flowers and horsemint. With her toilette completed she was ready to meet the day—and her man.

Moving to the kettle, which was now bubbling with a savory aroma of hump meat, she gave it a light tap with a horn spoon. This was the way she had been taught to awaken a man: dressed, perfumed, looking her best, with a bowl of hot food to warm his belly, and open his eyes, so that he might better appreciate how she had prepared herself.

Bloody Hand stretched and knuckled the sleep from his eyes, perfectly willing to act out this morning ritual if it pleased her. Still Water's face lighted with a smile and she handed him a bowl of steamy meat mixed with crushed pine nuts and elderberries.

"Good morning, my *batsire*. You slept well?"

This, too, was part of the ritual. The warrior selected a hunk of meat thick with fat, chewed it for a moment, and smacked his lips appreciatively. Then he nodded. "The night passed quickly, my *bua*. And for you?"

Still Water scooted around behind him with the porcupine tail brush, somehow managing to rub her breast against his shoulder in the process. "With your seed to warm me, my *batsire,* I dreamt only of good things." She loosened his skimpy braids and began to brush them out. Then she paused, leaned down, and playfully bit him on the neck. "Had I known Bloody Hand would present me with a toy all my own, I would have grown to womanhood sooner."

The black man merely chortled, saying nothing. Though he was accustomed to the vulgar humor employed by Crow women, he wasn't yet fully at ease with his bride's suggestive remarks. There was always a jesting lilt to her voice, and he wasn't quite sure whether she was bragging on his manhood or complaining that she didn't get enough of it. Either way, though, it swelled his chest just the way she meant it to. Except that, for the life of him, he could never think of a snappy comeback.

When he didn't speak she went right on brushing his hair. Nor did she allow his silence to hobble her own tongue. Sparrowhawk women chattered constantly, and Still Water was no exception. While she stroked with the brush, working the kinks and knots from his hair, she talked of anything that came to mind. Dreams, tribal gossip, even legends of ancient demons. All of it spiced with the dizzy proverbs of the *Apsahrokee,* which to her contained the wisdom of the world. Some of what she said could have raised blisters on a lodgepole, for whatever the subject, it was fair game for the coarse humor of her people.

As she talked she also searched his hair for lice. Upon finding an offender she would cluck scoldingly and pop it between her fingernails. Then, with hardly a pause for breath, she was off and running again. The scandalous ways of Old Man Coyote. The fall hunting dance soon to be held. And most importantly, whose wife was currently the lover of which warrior.

It was woman's talk. Light, generally irrelevant to the task at hand, but thoroughly entertaining. Bloody Hand didn't mind it in the least. Besides, in these one-sided chats with Still Water, he had acquired many juicy tidbits of village life, all of which, in one way or another, might be made to serve some useful purpose in days to come.

Once Still Water finished braiding his hair, she bustled about the lodge sweeping the floor and dragging sleeping robes outside to air. That done, she collected several leather buckets for berry gathering, gave him a promising smile, and set off to work. Though a bride of only three days, she was a hard worker, and he had a feeling the older squaws would have a tough time matching her in the berry patch.

Then he chuckled. Hell, he had his hands full keeping up with her himself. The fact that she couldn't be a day over fourteen didn't mean a hill of beans. The Crows believed in bedding them young, before they were spoiled, and lack of experience hadn't seemed to cramp her style none a'tall. Matter of fact, he didn't begrudge her daddy them ten ponies in the least. There were plenty more where they came from.

The thought gave his spirits a lift, though his mood hardly needed boosting. Things had been going pretty well lately, just about as good as a fellow could ask for. After that little fracas with the bear, folks hereabout sort of thought he'd hung the moon. *Waugh!* Not everybody had clouted Old Grizzletip across the snout and walked away to tell the tale.

What with that, and word of his medicine bundle being mighty potent stuff, there was already talk of him getting the nod as a pipe-holder. Once that happened, and he started leading some raids himself, he'd just introduce these Crows to what real fighting looked like. Not to mention the little eye-openers he had in store for them what lived on the wrong side of *Absaroka*.

Still, much as he hated to admit it, things weren't all

pattycake and roses. The raw spot in particular was Pine Leaf. He had twenty-three scalps hanging outside his lodge now, but that didn't cut no ice with her. Wanted all hundred, she did. All or nothin', by God! Yet here lately the temptation to get between her legs had got to be like the temptation to bite down on a sore tooth. Way things were headed, he might have got carried away and just hauled her off to the bushes anyway, scalps or no scalps! Which was exactly why he'd made the deal for Still Water. With that little wildcat trimming his wick regularlike things had sort of eased off. Not that he was going to back off on Pine Leaf. Shit! Weren't nobody about to beat him to that piece of fluff. It was just that now he could do it without gritting his teeth every time something in skirts walked by.

Christ! Even the *berdaches* had got to lookin' good there for a while.

Meantime, Still Water would do very nicely indeed. She was pretty, cute as a button, and had a way of laughing about things that just naturally kept a man's spirits floating high and wide. Maybe a little young, but what the hell! He'd just raise her up to suit himself. Besides, it was sort of nice having somebody to make him soft moccasins and tan all the hides he brought in. And the cooking. Judas Priest! She had Strikes-Both-Ways beat seven ways to Sunday. The little she-devil was just a natural-born scavenger. Wild plums, juicy yellow currants, hazelnuts, acorns, chokecherries: weren't nothing she overlooked. With winter drawing close, it was a good thing, too. She could just work them tiny fingers to the bone making jerky and pemmican so everybody'd stay fat and sassy through the snows ahead.

All the same, married life took some getting used to. Like not being able to talk to his own mother-in-law, except through somebody else. Not that he wanted to talk to the old crone especially. She was ugly as a toad and her breath was enough to make a dragon back off. But it was mighty damn curious how the Crows had put the taboo on a man getting neighborly with his wife's mama. Maybe it had something to do with Old Man Coyote putting the pole to his own mother-in-law. One of these days when he didn't have nothing better to do he'd have to ask Strikes-Both-Ways about that.

Course, the strangest thing of all was when a woman's time of the month came around. Not being married, he'd never paid it much mind before. But now, with Still Water in the lodge, it would get to be sort of a regular thing. When the moon hit the gong, she'd have to take off to that little hut out at the edge of the village and wouldn't be allowed to come out for seven days, and couldn't touch anything, not even her own food. She had to be fed by the old women. Couldn't even scratch herself, for Chrissakes. Beat anything a man ever heard tell of.

Yes sir, it was powerful strange living among the gut-eaters. Seemed like every time a fellow thought he had them figured out, they pulled something new that jarred him clean down to the roots, even if he was struttin' around with a bear claw necklace and feathers in his topknot.

Heavy gray clouds scudded low across the mountains, obscuring the northern sky in a thick, roiling overcast. Along the lower slopes, great stands of aspens, smitten gold by autumn frosts, cast off their leaves in bright, swirling flurries. Scoured by chill winds and crisp nights, cottonwoods throughout the river valley rattled like old bones in a dance of death.

It was the Moon of Scarlet Plums, time for the fall hunt, and a scattering of the *Apsahrokee* to their distant winter camps.

The wind came up strong in the biting cold before false dawn, and overhead a plaintive moan whistled through the smokehole. Still Water unknowingly snuggled closer to her man, touched by the sudden chill which filled the lodge. There was something warm and comforting in his ropy hardness, as if in her drowsy slumber the gristle and sinew of his body somehow generated heat beneath the furry robes. They slept with their feet to the fire, yet the coals had long ago faded into ash, and the girl cuddled in around his lean flanks like a moth drawn to flame.

Bloody Hand came awake slowly, arching his rump to meet the girl as her arms came over his chest and tightened in close embrace. Just for a moment the dull torpor of sleep tugged him back into darkness, but the low whine in the smokehole was like a dogged beckoning in his ear. Then, senses alerted, he sat bolt upright.

It wasn't the wind that had awakened him. It was the *eshoo-shebit*—his buckskin gelding—picketed just outside the lodge.

Even as he slid from the robes, the pony snorted again. The sound was unmistakable. Fear. The skittish alarm of a horse spooked by something or someone whose smell meant danger.

An outsider.

Grabbing his Hawken from its wall rest, he moved soundlessly across the lodge and eased through the door flap. The wind stung his body with icy needles, penetrating clean to the marrow. Yet, in some curious way, it also sharpened his senses to a razor edge. Crouching, he advanced a couple of steps and cautiously poked his head around the side of the lodge. What he saw brought the rifle to his shoulder.

Walleyed with fright, the buckskin was jerking back on its tether as a Blackfoot warrior squirmed along the ground toward the picket stake.

The Hawken barked, rending the night with a sheet of flame, and the Blackfoot slammed backwards into the earth. The half-ounce lead ball had gutted him, and he died with only a slight tremor from one leg.

Lifting his voice to the sky, Bloody Hand sounded the warning. *"Ikye!* Blackfeet! *Hooo-ki-hi!"*

Whirling, he hurried back inside the lodge and began

throwing on clothing. Heedless of the frantic questions from Strikes-Both-Ways and Still Water, he slung powder horn and shot pouch over his shoulders, stuck a war axe in his belt, and darted once again through the door hole. Jerking the picket line free, he swung aboard the gelding and set off at a dead lope for the horse herds downriver.

Blackfeet were savage fighters, but they seldom rode alone. They traveled in packs, like wolves. Where there was one, there was a dozen. Or more. And unless he was wide of the mark, they were raiding the Sparrow-hawk herds right at that very moment.

Snorting and pawing, the Dog Soldier ponies waited restlessly under a hazy autumn sun. Yet the horses were no less restless than the men who rode them. White Bear had pulled his warriors off to one side while they awaited some decision from Rotten Belly. As yet, though, the Sparrowhawk chief seemed disinclined to take action, or even discuss it. Mounted astride a pinto stud, he appeared motionless and still, like a centaur carved from frozen stone. Alone on a grassy plain north of the creek, where he had sat without uttering a word for the last hour, the *Acaraho* leader stared pensively at the nearby mountain, almost as though he were communing with the Blackfeet, willing them to come out and fight.

Earlier, as false dawn broke over the mountains, the village had been aroused by Bloody Hand's warning cry. Warriors boiled from their lodges, mounting ponies staked out for just such an emergency, and galloped off in the black man's wake. Upon reaching the horse herds, they sighted the Blackfeet raiding party in the distance, driving close to a hundred ponies in headlong flight toward the north. The Sparrowhawk warriors gave chase, savagely quirting their mounts to greater speed, and by full light the gap had closed to within rifleshot. The Blackfeet abandoned the stolen horses at that point and concentrated solely on escape. But the enraged *Apsahrokee* weren't to be denied so easily. When Bloody Hand brought down a Blackfoot warrior with a lucky shot from his Hawken, the raiders lost all hope of escape and quickly sought shelter.

The chase ended at Elder Creek, some ten miles upstream from the Wind River encampment. There the Blackfeet made their stand at the base of a mountain, taking cover behind a granite outcropping that formed a natural barrier some ten feet in height. This jagged depression where the mountain sloped to meet the rocky upheaval made a superb fort. From behind their wall of stone the raiders were well protected, and all but invisible except when they popped up to take a shot. Unlimbering their fuses and short war bows, they laid down a withering fire that drove the Sparrowhawks back to the treeline along the creek.

Over the next three hours, Rotten Belly had ordered repeated charges against the rocky fortress. Several times the attackers came near scaling the wall, only to be routed at the last moment by a flurry of arrows and lead. Though the Blackfeet force was comprised of barely thirty warriors, which left them outnumbered ten to one, their position appeared impregnable. After watching his braves break and retreat for the fifth time, Rotten Belly had ordered them back into the cottonwoods bordering Elder Creek.

The Sparrowhawks had lost eleven killed and double that number wounded. Clearly, it was time to regroup and devise some greater strategy, a time to wait and think and ponder all manner of crafty things.

That was where it stood even now. Rotten Belly was still waiting, and presumably still thinking. Though to all appearances, he and his pinto stud had taken root on the grassy plain. He simply sat and stared at the mountain.

While the Dog Soldiers evidenced no overwhelming compulsion to charge the Blackfoot fortress again, there was nonetheless much grumbling among their ranks. Just as there was throughout the other warrior societies huddled abjectly in the cottonwood grove. The respect accorded a Sparrowhawk chief had little to do with age or wisdom, or even the paternal benevolence with which he governed his people. It was determined solely by the showing made in his last fight. Right now Rotten Belly wasn't doing too well, and his aloof silence had the warriors thoroughly puzzled. There were some who went so far as to suggest that he had lost his gift for making war, and several derisive jeers had already been hurled at his back from those crowding the creek bank.

Unless something happened fast, the *Acaraho* leader might well find himself with no one to lead, deposed of rank and title, reduced again to a mere warrior.

It was the way. Most especially for those whose medicine had gone sour.

Bloody Hand watched and listened but said nothing. He was fuming with impatience, wanting to get on with the fight. Yet there was nothing to be gained in muttered insults. In fact, it suited his purpose very nicely to hold himself above the backbiting and jeers. For in some remote corner of his mind a sly, if not outright insidious, plan had slowly begun to take form.

These Crows were a superstitious lot. Everything from the paint on their faces to their childish behavior in battle was ruled by signs and portents. So far as he could see, spirit beings were little more than an outlandish figment of paganism and witchery. Yet these supernatural forces dictated tribal custom with an iron hand. Even a warrior's battle shield bore talismanic symbols. Applied under the incantations of some toothless holy man, these paintings and ornaments were thought to deflect the death sting of enemy weapons by magic. When all the time it was two-inch thick bullhide, baked over a slow fire to the toughness of steel, which turned aside arrows, lances, and balls of lead chunked out from ancient trade muskets.

Still, there was much to be said for magic battle shields and guardian spirits. In the hands of the right man—someone who saw it for what it was—this superstition could be made to work wonders. Particularly if he wore a bear claw necklace and possessed a medicine bundle unrivaled for sheer potency. Not to mention a little bag of liver infused with snake juice, which according to rumor gave him the power to cast an evil spell over all who defied his will.

The black man had never been one to ignore a hunch. Much as spirit beings ruled the lives of the Crows, so did instinct govern his own actions. Seldom had these inner premonitions failed him. When a hunch gripped him with the clarity of the one now racketing through his brain, he could do no less than back it to the hilt.

Slamming his heels into the buckskin's ribs, he set out at a trot toward Rotten Belly. Throughout the cottonwood grove, a hush settled over the warriors, and only the drumbeat of his gelding's hooves shattered the morning stillness as he crossed the grassy meadow. The Sparrowhawks were stunned by his effrontery, for it was unheard of that anyone less than a pipe-holder would test the wrath of a chief. But they merely gawked and looked on in wonder, thoroughly fascinated by the dark one's never-ceasing boldness.

Bloody Hand reined to a halt beside the chief, gesturing toward the enemy stronghold with his rifle. "The Blackfeet await us, my leader. Would you have it known that the *Apsahrokee* cowered before such filth?"

"You overstep yourself, *Batse*. Return to the woods." The dismissal was curt, and failure to address the black man by his new name came much as a slap in the face.

"Perhaps you are right, that I take too much on myself. Yet my medicine is strong, and should I ride toward those rocks, there are many who would follow." The implication of his threat was clear, but lest it be taken lightly, he added a direct challenge. "There are those waiting in the trees who say you ride a stallion because your own manhood has shriveled with fear. Beware, Rotten Belly. Sparrowhawk warriors do not heed the commands of an *ipia-reksua.*"

The insult was larded with contempt. Only a fool or one of great bravery would dare tell a Sparrowhawk chieftain that he impersonates the lowly magpie. Rotten Belly's head jerked around and he studied the black man through hooded eyes. "Your arrogance will one day bring you grief, dark one. Now spare me your barbed tongue and say what it is you have to say. Or did you ride out here merely to try my patience?"

Briefly, in clipped, precise tones, Bloody Hand outlined the plan he had in mind. As he talked he pointed with the muzzle of his Hawken, tracing salient features of the distant mountainside. When finished, he waited in silence while the chief considered his words. Rotten Belly declined to meet his gaze. Instead he looked without emotion at the Blackfoot fortress, as if resigned to a moment that could no longer be avoided.

"It is a good plan," he said at last. "Sometimes it comes to me that war is for the young. Old age is a scourge, Bloody Hand. It weakens a man with the longing to grow yet older." He fell silent for a moment, then looked around with his chin held proudly. "Youth and courage are precious things, dark one. Use them wisely when you are chosen pipe-holder. Now return to the Dog Soldiers and await my instructions."

The black man started to say something, then he whirled the buckskin and rode off. Rotten Belly waited until he had disappeared into the trees before reining his own pony about and heading back toward the creek. When a short distance from the treeline, he pulled the horse to a halt, sitting erect and stern-faced as he raised his voice for all to hear.

Bloody Hand, he informed the warriors, had brought to him a sound plan for defeating the accursed Blackfeet. The Sparrowhawk forces would be split into two parties. The first, to be formed of the Dog Soldiers,

Lumpwoods, and Kit-Foxes, would depart now and take their orders directly from Bloody Hand. The remainder would delay a short while and then ride in a charge on the Blackfeet, a charge that he personally would lead. Rotten Belly rode back and forth before the treeline, exhorting the warriors to battle, insulting their manhood should they allow the Blackfeet to turn their charge again. As the Sparrowhawks' anger mounted his tirade grew even more heated. Slowly, with the skill that had won him fame, he provoked them to howls of bloodlust which made the very earth tremble with its savage beat.

Less than an hour later Bloody Hand and his war party crouched below a shallow bank where the creek made a sharp bend and skirted the mountain's lower slope. Leaving their horses behind, they had waded noiselessly and unseen to a point no more than thirty yards from the westerly edge of the Blackfoot stronghold. There they had remained hidden, listening with mounting excitement as Rotten Belly harangued his followers.

When the charge came the black man hissed a warning and motioned his men to stay out of sight. Waiting for the mounted warriors to cross the open meadow was almost unbearable for those secreted beneath the creek bank. But it was a wait their leader's dark scowl forced them to endure. While they knew little or nothing of discipline in battle, they somehow sensed that the dark one would exact a terrible price from any man who sacrificed the element of surprise.

Then, as the Sparrowhawk charge struck headlong into the granite outcropping, Bloody Hand led his warriors out of the creek. They covered the open ground in a wild rush, striking for the unguarded flank, and the black man's lungs swelled with exaltation. The plan had worked! The Blackfeet had been faked out completely. Scrambling to defense of the forward wall, they had left themselves naked to attack from the side.

Bloody Hand scaled the fortress wall, gaining the top,

and lifted his voice in a savage war cry. *"Hooo-ki-hi!"*
With a war axe in one hand and a knife in the other, he
plunged down the far side and waded full tilt into the
embattled Blackfeet. Behind him swarmed the Dog
Soldiers, and on their heels came the Lumpwoods and
Kit-Foxes.

The fight was brief and bloody. Slashing and dodging,
crunching a head with his war axe, then swerving to
open a gut with his knife, the black man cut a swath of
carnage and death through the Blackfoot ranks. Enveloped by Sparrowhawks clambering over the front
wall, and Bloody Hand's warriors from the side, the defenders were doomed from the start.

Within the space of a single minute, the Blackfeet
horse thieves had been killed to a man.

When it was over, Bloody Hand moved among the
littered bodies and collected the four scalps that were
rightfully his. Afterwards, as the Sparrowhawk warriors
began mutilating the dead, he climbed to the top of the
front wall and took a seat. Slicing a strip of buckskin
from his leggings, he bound up a gash in his arm, then
turned to look out over the grassy plain.

Suddenly he started, uttering a hoarse oath. Along
the forward slope of the wall lay Rotten Belly. The
Sparrowhawk chief's skull had been crushed like a brittle leaf, splattering brains and splintered bone across
the rocks around his head.

Bloody Hand blinked, shook his head, and looked
again. Nothing changed. The king was dead.

The scaffold had been erected for Rotten Belly's journey to the Faraway Land. Henceforth the chief would be
spoken of in conversation as *koresa*, the one who is not
here, for it was sacrilege to mention the name of a dead
person. But in these last moments, there was no shame
in speaking of him as he had been, and his deeds of
valor were eulogized in a keening chant as the funeral
procession wound its way to the burial ground.

Rotten Belly was to be laid to rest on a tall scaffold beside that of his son, who had been killed in a raid by the Sioux some years back. Leading the procession was the pinto stud, the chief's favorite war pony, covered now with the painted red blotches signifying mourning. Behind came a horse and travois pulling the dead man's body, followed by his wife and daughter and a long line of those come to honor him at this final rite. Both women had gashed their faces and legs with knives, hacked their hair short, and as was fitting, the wife had lopped off a finger from each hand. Their sorrowful wails were like the cry of a wild thing in mortal agony, piercing and wretching, rising in grief above the death chant of the praise singers.

Yet wailing and grief were hardly strangers atop the high burial hill that day. Not including the chief, the Sparrowhawk warriors lost in the Blackfeet raid numbered fifteen, and the mournful dirge of widows and kin laid a pall of gloom over the windswept knoll.

The funeral cortege came to a halt at the base of the scaffold, which had been lashed securely to four upright poles. Gently, Rotten Belly's remains were lifted from the travois and hoisted overhead to the platform. The body had been wrapped in several layers of water-soaked buffalo hide and bound tightly from head to foot with rawhide thongs. Within days the sun would shrink the moist hides by half, clutching the dead man in a steely embrace for all time. After the body had been lashed tightly to the scaffold, a holy man stepped forward and placed alongside it the chief's weapons, his pipe and tobacco, and enough food to last him on the journey ahead. Next a stout pole was raised over the platform; from this dangled Rotten Belly's lance, war shield, and medicine bundle. Finally, the pinto stud was led forward and a warrior slashed its throat. The horse made no sound whatever, merely wobbling about weakly for a moment and then falling dead beneath the scaffold.

Now the fabled chief of the *Apsahrokee* had all he needed for the journey to the Faraway Land. His shadow soul—the *aparaaxe* of those departed—could cross over in peace.

When all was completed, Bloody Hand suddenly emerged from the back of the procession and strode forward. Solemn-faced and staring straight ahead, he walked deliberately to the scaffold, gripped one of the poles with his left hand, and drew his knife. There was a startled gasp from the onlookers as comprehension flooded over them. Though they knew what he intended, it was an unheard-of act of tribute for anyone outside the dead man's family to perform the rite of sacrifice.

The black man wasn't anywhere near that certain of his own motives. Perhaps it was tribute to a great chief, the man who had given him refuge in Absaroka. But then again, perhaps it was merely atonement for an unwarranted insult made to a courageous man.

Or, if Jim Beckwith, the mulatto mountain man, could still separate himself from Bloody Hand, the Sparrowhawk warrior, perhaps it was yet another device to further bedazzle the Crows. Somehow, though, neither the mountain man nor the warrior really cared what it was that drove him to do it.

The black man hefted the knife and slowly severed the little finger from his left hand. The finger dropped to the earth beneath the scaffold, only inches from the pinto stud's head, and the dark one stood for a moment looking down on it. In some curious way, it seemed fitting that a part of him should accompany Rotten Belly when he crossed over to the other life.

Then, trailing blood from the mutilated stump, he turned and walked back down the hill.

Late that evening Bloody Hand received a summons to appear at the Dog Soldier lodge. Strikes-Both-Ways and Still Water said nothing, but their apprehension was plain to see. Already the story of his insolence in yesterday's fight with the Blackfeet was common gossip throughout the village. The Dog Soldiers were not noted for their leniency toward warriors who overstepped themselves, and it was speculated that the dark one would be severely chastised. Boldness was a virtue among warriors, but arrogance was frowned upon as a weakness, one seldom tolerated simply because it endangered the lives of all. Earlier, while cauterizing the black man's butchered stump, Strikes-Both-Ways had commented on this very thing.

The meek rarely lived out their life span, but among the ancients it had been said that an arrogant man rode with death throughout all his days.

Walking along in the chill night, Bloody Hand had reason to ponder the old bowmaker's words. Perhaps there was something to be said for humble men, after all, the ones who quietly went about their business without flaunting their honors, or imposing their will on others with small regard for the aftermath.

Only that afternoon the tribal council had elected White Bear *Batsetse* of the Sparrowhawk People. The *Acaraho* band needed a chief, and while the Dog Soldier leader wasn't noted for his mental agility, the elders believed him to be a man of reason, one who could lead the People in war, yet recognize his own shortcomings enough to be swayed by the wisdom of the council. Which said something about the affairs of men. And gut-eaters, too.

It wasn't always the best man, or even the most capable man, who wound up sporting the crown. It was the man of reason and a modicum of humility, the one who could be persuaded to the will of those who pulled the strings. There were perhaps a half dozen Crows better suited to the task, regular mental wizards compared to White Bear. But they hadn't gotten the nod. Old sobersides himself now ruled the roost.

Enough said about cock-of-the-walk and bull-of-the-woods. Politics was politics, even in Absaroka, and the

frog who croaked the loudest generally finished dead
last.

Long live the king. And God help the people.

When Bloody Hand entered the Dog Soldier lodge,
he found White Bear and the warriors seated in a circle
around the fire. White Bear indicated his position on
the far side of the fire, and the black man lowered himself to the ground. There was a strange feel to the place,
something he couldn't quite put his finger on. Slewing a
glance around the circle, he searched the warriors' faces
for some telltale sign. But their expressions revealed
nothing. Like stuffed owls, they merely sat and watched,
unblinking.

After a moment of silence, White Bear nailed him
with a beady look. "Bloody Hand, it is said that you are
a man of arrogance and great pride."

The black man didn't flinch. He had decided to take
his licks and try not to get skinned up too bad in the
process. "Pride in itself is not bad. As a man grows in
wisdom he learns to rule it with a firmer hand."

There was a murmur of assent from the warriors.
They were proud men themselves, and they found merit
in the answer. White Bear digested that and decided to
move on. "It is also said that you provoked the one who
is not here and caused him to hasten his own death."

"Perhaps. Yet his last words to me were that age
weakens a man, making him long to grow older. He died
as he had lived, a warrior. Would any here say that he
chose the wrong path?"

"*Ae,* what you say is true, dark one. But do you deny
that you shamed him before the People?"

"Where is the shame in leading the People to great
victory? Will we venerate him less for having died in
defense of Absaroka? I think not."

"Yet it was you who rode out from the trees, you who
took it upon yourself to advise a *batsetse.*"

"I did nothing that any man here had not thought of
before me. *Ae,* it was my plan. Yet it brought the *Ap-*

sahrokee victory over the Blackfeet, and it gave the one who is not here a death of honor. Think on it a moment. He could have refused my plan, but he did not. You heard his words yourself. Not only did he acknowledge the plan as good, he chose me to lead the circling attack. Those were not the actions of a shamed man. It was the course taken by a leader of wisdom, one not too proud to take the advice of a lowly warrior."

The statement was greeted with muttered approval from the Dog Soldiers. What the dark one said was true. Had they not lost eleven warriors in senseless charges on the Blackfoot stronghold? Would not they have lost many times that number except for his plan? They might even have been defeated instead of coming away with a great victory and many scalps. *Ai!* The dark one was possessed of much pride, well enough. But it was not the false pride of a braggart and fool. It was the pride of cunning and great skill in battle, hardly a thing for which a man should bow his head and look on others with downcast eyes.

White Bear listened to their words closely, and for all his slowness, he sensed a change in the wind. After a while he motioned flat-handed for silence. When the murmuring died down, he started at one side of the circle and looked each warrior squarely in the face. As his eyes moved from man to man around the lodge, each Dog Soldier nodded in turn. Come full circle at last, his gaze returned to the black man.

"Bloody Hand, you are aware that this day the tribal council appointed me *Batsetse?*"

"*Ae,* my leader. All are aware of your honor."

"Perhaps you are not aware that the law allows no man to serve as a pipe-holder while he sits as chief of the *Apsahrokee.*"

"This I did not know."

"These things I tell you so that you may understand what comes next. You were brought here tonight so that all might hear your words. Some among us were of a mind to dismiss you from the Dog Soldiers, while others felt you should be selected the new pipe-holder. But it is our way that the will of one must be the will of all. Now the Dog Soldiers have spoken, and they are in accord."

White Bear came to his feet, holding the sacred pipe in the crook of his arm. "Rise, Bloody Hand."

The black man stood, nerves strung tight and his mouth gone dry. White Bear crossed around the fire and halted in front of him, extending the pipe.

"I pass on to you, Bloody Hand, the ancient pipe of the Dog Soldiers. The burden of pipe-holder is not a light one, but it carries much honor. Let wisdom guide you, so that in all that follows, the spirits will walk closely in your shadow. From this day forward you hold the glory of the Dog Soldiers in your hands."

Bloody Hand held the pipe before him, staring at it in wonder. But he didn't speak, for the words wouldn't come. Only the pipe existed, and the moment, and the searing flame deep in his gut.

Waugh! It had come to pass.

CHAPTER 5

The Leaf Fall Moon had come and gone. With its passing, the Sparrowhawk People had separated once more into tribal bands and journeyed to their ancient winter campgrounds, the *Minesepere* along the headwaters of the Yellowstone and the *Acaraho* to a broad valley deep in the Wind River mountains. Shortly after the fall buffalo hunt, the Sparrowhawks had struck their lodges and departed the summer encampment. There had been much jesting, and long, ceremonious rounds of farewell, for the One Above had been generous that year. They took with them sufficient jerky and pemmican to see the People through the snowstorms and frozen stillness of the hard time to come.

The band led by White Bear had returned to the high mountain park revered beyond memory as their ancestral home. The camp was situated on Long Grass Creek, in a valley rimmed by the bluffs and ridges of surrounding mountains. When Bloody Hand first saw it, he understood at last the Crows' profound awe for the land called Absaroka.

The remote valley was some four miles in breadth and half again as long, split by a latticework of streams that tumbled down the rocky slopes and fed into the main tributary. Toward the western rim was a thundering waterfall, cascading downward to form the headwaters of Long Grass Creek. The streams were bordered with clumps of aspen and cottonwood, and the valley floor resembled a long bronzed carpet where the autumn grasses had cured out pale russet. Speckled orange and gold against the somber green of the high spruce forest were snatches of deadened leaves that still survived the morning frost.

It was the high country, a land of solitude and overwhelming stillness, where wind blew lonely and clouds played hide-and-seek atop fluted spires, where snow fell with deafening quietness and rose skyward in swirling drifts higher than the tallest saplings. A land that dwarfed man, made him puny beside its towering grandeur, yet somehow gave him a dimension of strength and tolerance he had never before possessed.

Exploring it from end to end, Bloody Hand was struck by the wisdom of whoever had first selected this as the *Acaraho*'s winter camp. Cradled beneath high northern peaks, the valley was sheltered from blustery winds, and provided forested mountainsides where abundant game could be found even in the coldest months. There was water, plenty of wood, and ample forage for the horses. Thick clumps of spruce and evergreen offered the livestock protection during storms, and when the grass finally played out, cottonwood bark would sustain them till spring melt-off. While he had wintered in many fine campsites with the mountain brigades, he had never seen one exactly like this.

It was all a man could ask—and more. The horn of plenty sought by all, but thought to exist only in the minds of snowbound dreamers.

Winter comforts aside, the black man's many hours of wandering the valley and surrounding mountains hadn't focused on scenery alone. He was looking for signs of the master builder, the iron-jawed beaver, and he found telltale markings galore. Tree cuttings, stripped twigs, mound-shaped dams, all far exceeding his wildest estimates. The land was swarming with beaver. Infested.

Every body of water larger than a trickle was diverted, plugged up, or altered in some fashion. More significant yet, the Crows had scarcely skimmed off the cream.

There were beaver enough in this remote mountain fastness to set William Ashley slobbering with greed. Not to mention a mulatto woods colt masquerading as a born and bred gut-eater. Just a few seasons trapping in *Absaroka* could make rich men of them all.

The Crows included.

Bloody Hand kept his own counsel and said nothing of what he had seen. After a suitable time had elapsed, and the village was settled in for the winter, he requested a meeting with the tribal elders. This was his right as leader of the Dog Soldiers, and without delay the council granted his petition. Perhaps even more speedily than normal, for in the month since assuming office as pipe-holder, the black man had become a figure of influence and power among the *Apsahrokee*.

The day after accepting the sacred pipe—two days after Rotten Belly's death—he had announced that the Dog Soldiers would ride in retaliation against the Blackfeet. This was not a horse-stealing raid, but instead a lightning sortie to exact retribution for the killing of a Sparrowhawk chief. Bloody Hand let it be known that while tribal honor was at stake, the raid was no less a final tribute to the one who had crossed over, something he could speak of with pride in the Faraway Land.

This proved to be a masterful stroke. White Bear was stymied from organizing a raid of his own, and the other warrior societies were simply left in the lurch. By reason of prior claim, the revenge of Rotten Belly's death became the sole property of the Dog Soldiers. Bloody Hand was lauded throughout the village as a leader of bold spirits, who in one fell swoop had stolen the march on his rivals. The Sparrowhawk People held audacity in high esteem, almost as much as the trait of generosity. When the dark one rode out at the head of his warriors, the People took considerable delight in chiding the leaders left behind.

Less than a fortnight later, the war party returned with more than a dozen scalps and a fine herd of ponies that had incidently come into their possession. The black man alone had accounted for three slain Blackfeet, and across the rump of his gelding was the highest mark of distinction in all of *Absaroka:* an imprint of a bloody hand, the symbol of a warrior who had killed an enemy with his bare hands.

Word of the raid swept through camp—along with the tale of how Bloody Hand had broken the neck of a Blackfoot warrior—and there was an outcry of acclaim for the new Dog Soldier leader. White Bear rewarded the raiders by appointing them to the coveted role of tribal police during the fall buffalo hunt. The fame of the dark one and his Dog Soldiers had become so compelling that no one dared to cross them. For the first time in many years, not one man attempted to break through the lines and charge the browsing herd in a moment of glory. The slaughter had been monumental, producing more meat than anyone could recall, and the Dog Soldiers were loudly praised for giving the people full bellies in the winter to come.

Through it all, Bloody Hand had withstood the temptation to flaunt his exploits in true mountain-man style. Instead he behaved in the prescribed manner of Sparrowhawk leaders. Without ceremony, he gave away his share of horses taken in the raid, and accepted the praise heaped upon him with uttermost humility. When the tribe split for the winter, the People had many stories worthy of retelling on cold nights around lodge fires. Yet on the lips of every warrior was the name of a single man, a name spoken with something akin to awe.

Bloody Hand.

The black man was thoroughly pleased with himself. Not unlike the Shakesperian troupes he'd heard tell of back in Missouri, he felt he'd brought it off with a very convincing performance. All the same, there was a part of it he hadn't quite come to grips with as yet. Nothing he could put a name to especially. Just a foggy sort of notion that maybe it wasn't all play-acting. That maybe he liked being called Bloody Hand and tromping around in war paint, and even admired the Crows in some odd way that remained hazy and ill-defined around the edges. After all, it wasn't as if they were the garden variety run-of-the-mill gut-eaters. They had style. And balls, too. Regular fire-eaters when it came down to a rock and a hard place.

More importantly, they had Absaroka. Not that he had any delusions about becoming King of the Hill. Or even wanted to. But it was a mighty fine place to stake out a claim just the same. A man could do worse. A hell of a lot worse.

These were thoughts much on his mind the day he met with White Bear and the elders in the council lodge. What he meant to propose wasn't exactly in the spirit of benevolence, for he still had a pact to fulfill with Ashley. But that didn't rule out brotherhood altogether. The Crows had been damned decent to him, and in a manner of speaking, he was just returning the favor, and might even make them rich in the bargain. Along with himself, of course.

When everybody was seated, and they had puffed on the pipe a while, White Bear finally got down to business. "Bloody Hand asked to speak with the council, and we gladly granted his request. The leader of the Dog Soldiers has earned great honor among the *Apsahrokee,* and we will listen to his words with open ears."

"Aho, batsetse," Bloody Hand responded formally. "What I wish to speak of has to do with the People. Here in Absaroka we want for little. *Axace* smiles on the Sparrowhawk, giving them warmth and full bellies. But there are things we lack, things which would not only make us stronger as a nation, but would pleasure the People at the same time. I speak of better guns, more

powder, fine knives, and the black kettles so prized by the women."

"Ae, that is so," White Bear agreed. "Yet these are things the *tibo* traders sell dearly. Would Bloody Hand have us exchange our ponies merely to pleasure the squaws?"

"Not ponies, my leader." The black man felt his heart thud as the word rolled off his tongue. "Beaver."

"Beaver?" White Bear stared at him as if dumbstruck. "It would be easier to give up the ponies. Stealing horses is small work measured against robbing the beaver of his pelt."

"The difficulty is less than it would seem, *batsetse.* I spent many snows among the white-eyes and their secrets became as my own. I would share these secrets with the People, so that they, too, might outwit the dambuilder."

There was an interval of absolute silence while the council stared at him in disbelief. Then Looks-at-Bulls, an elder of the Whistling Water clan, fixed him with a harsh glare. "You would have the Sparrowhawks become lowly trappers, Bloody Hand? Cease stealing horses and stop making war so that they might own these trifles the *tibos* dangle in front of us. You make a poor jest."

"Grandfather, I make no jest. Nor would I have the people deny their traditions. The raiding season is done, and now we wait only for winter. The People grow bored when they are idle, as each of us here today knows. Otherwise why would they have turned so quickly to the wife-abduction rivalry?"

The council again fell silent. Bloody Hand had made a telling point. The Sparrowhawk People normally enlivened dull winters with a custom known as *batsuarau.* This was a spirited contest between warrior societies to abduct one another's wives. The single rule was that a warrior must have been a woman's lover previous to marriage to claim her in the abduction rites. That being the case, he had simply to appear at her lodge and she was obliged to follow and share his bed. While a certain degree of honor was expected to prevail, some men alleged an intimacy that had never existed, and wrongfully carried off the helpless squaw. This was made all the easier due to an ancient code which held that jealousy was beneath a husband's dignity.

Once a man's wife was abducted it was considered a disgrace for him to take her back. Even if he attempted to visit her in secret he lost caste and was ridiculed unmercifully. If actually caught in the act by members of the rival society, he was thrown to the ground and smeared with a liberal coating of dog dung. Not without reason, the wife-abduction contests created longstanding frictions between the warrior societies.

Though Bloody Hand was not personally involved, since it was known that Still Water came to the wedding couch a virgin, he meant to use it as a wedge in influencing the council.

"Forgive my blunt speech, Grandfather." His eyes dropped respectfully before Looks-at-Bulls, then leveled and roved over the remaining elders. "Yet I speak only that which every Sparrowhawk leader knows. This business of wife-abduction cuts deep and leaves permanent scars among our people. Perhaps trapping beaver would divert their minds from such games. The pelts are considered prime from before first snow to just after spring thaw, though it is difficult to trap in the deep snow time. Still this would occupy much of the winter and might well reduce the discord brought on by boredom."

White Bear grunted skeptically. "Your words bear a certain truth, Bloody Hand. Yet perhaps we should ask your part in this. Where is your reward in bringing harmony to the People?"

The black man's eyes dulled in a flat stare. "I seek nothing for myself, if that is what you suggest. I am a pipe-holder, and my thoughts are for the People. What I

propose will give us better guns, and powder, so that
when the Moon of Fat Horses come again we will be
stronger than our enemies. Then will I find my reward,
in collecting the scalps of those who would threaten Absaroka."

The elders muttered among themselves, nodding,
their weathered faces enlivened by his thought. White
Bear nodded as well, and his frown gave way to an expression of feigned disinterest.

"The council will study your words, Bloody Hand.
When we have decided you will be called. In the meantime, it would be best if you spoke of this to no one."

The black man rose to his feet, again letting his gaze
touch on each elder down the line, and then turned and
walked from the lodge.

When the door flap closed behind him, there was
nothing said, either of him or his proposal. But among
the Sparrowhawk Council there was a common thought,
unstated, yet plainly felt nonetheless.

The Dog Soldier pipe-holder was a man who would
bear watching. Ambition in one so young was exceptional, even commendable. But only in moderate
amounts.

When the council acted, it was in a way universal to all
men of power. They moved cautiously, while making
themselves appear bold, and they were at great pains to
protect their hindsides. Though Bloody Hand was given
credit for the idea, they did it in a manner that relegated
him to the role of teacher. The honor of announcing the
plan, and organizing it throughout the tribe, they reserved for themselves.

The black man wasn't surprised in the least. Nor did
he resent their highhanded pilfering of his idea. The
scheme had been sanctioned by the council and that was
all he had hoped for from the outset. Still, he wasn't
fooled by their crafty methods. Should the idea prove
successful, the council meant to take full credit for

bringing prosperity to the Sparrowhawks. But, if it were to fail, they had their goat staked out and ready for sacrifice. White Bear and the elders would simply claim that they had been deceived and skillfully shift all blame to the pipe-holder of the Dog Soldiers.

As it happened, the scheme came very near failing even before it started.

Instead of announcing the plan openly to the people, the council called the leaders of the eight warrior societies into a meeting. There they outlined the proposal, using much the same arguments employed earlier by the black man. Bloody Hand merely sat back and watched, speaking only when a question was posed to him directly. For it was obvious that the council intended to muffle his part in the undertaking. What followed was stormy and not without bitterness. Only one pipe-holder, the leader of the Bulls, found merit in the idea. The rest denounced it in the harshest possible terms, ridiculing the thought of Sparrowhawk warriors lowering themselves to become mere trappers. After several heated exchanges, it was decided that the pipe-holders could advise their warriors as they saw fit. The council supported the plan, and for those who accepted it, Bloody Hand stood ready to instruct them in the secrets of *tibo* trappers.

The meeting ended on that note. The pipe-holders talked from the council lodge congratulating themselves heartily. Once again, they told one another, it had been demonstrated that a Sparrowhawk owed allegiance to no man, and least of all to the conniving elders who sat on the tribal council. *Ai!* It had been a good day. There would be much jest directed at the old tricksters when the story became known.

Bloody Hand was irked, not by the council's attempt to use him, but rather by the pathetic results obtained. Yet he was far from discouraged. Tribal politics were involved here, as he well knew. The elders were elected from the family clans that comprised the *Acaraho* band, while the pipe-holders represented the warrior societies. It was a system of checks and balances that prevented either side from gaining unlimited power. Quite naturally, it fostered jealousy, and a certain amount of stiff-necked animosity among the leaders themselves. But there were ways and there were ways. When a man came up against a mountain too steep to climb, he simply went around it.

Bloody Hand had little trouble convincing the Dog Soldiers that beaver pelts were but a means to an end. They liked the idea of better guns, unlimited supplies of powder, and the keen-edged knives offered by *tibo* traders. Such things would multiply their prowess in war and horse stealing, and lead to greater prestige, set them apart from other warrior societies and mark them as men of distinction.

More significantly, they accepted the idea because it was the wish of their leader. Though mortal man, with his flaws and weaknesses, could never acquire the power of spirit beings, the dark one came as close as any man could in their eyes. They believed his medicine bundle destined him to become a war leader of great renown. With him to guide them, they saw much glory for the Dog Soldiers in days to come.

Before long it became a common sight to see Bloody Hand and his warriors set out each morning for the creek. There he conducted a school in the fine art of beaver trapping. Since he had packed in a gross of traps from the Bear Lake Rendezvous, there were more than enough to go around. The Dog Soldiers treated it as a new game of sorts, and within a matter of days they had obtained considerable practice under the dark one's watchful eye.

The technique was simple enough in theory, but complicated in practice by the wary habits of the beaver. Along streams and creeks these industrious workers built their dams, displaying what seemed an irresistible impulse to stop flowing water. The beaver lodge, like the dam, was built of small branches, with a half-foot plastering of mud for the roof and walls. Inside, about a foot above water level, was the main chamber, where the beaver lived. Leading off from this were two underwater exits, tunnels which had been dug through the dam to the streambed above. There, weighted down with snags and mud, was the beaver's hoard of food, saplings and branches whose bark would sustain him through the winter.

The Indians were accustomed to hunting pelts by blocking off the tunnels, chopping through the roof, and digging out the beaver. The white man's way was considerably less work, employing a degree of trickery that appealed greatly to the Dog Soldiers.

The bait was castoreum, called medicine by the mountain men, carried in a plugged horn vial at the belt. It was a musky secretion taken from the beaver's preputial gland and gave off a highly pungent odor. The trap itself was a spring affair with an attached five-foot steel chain. After selecting a spot some distance from the beaver lodge, the trap was anchored below the waterline by driving a stout pole through a heavy ring on the end of the chain. Then a bit of castoreum was smeared on a twig which was stuck in the shoreline just over the trap.

When the beaver emerged from his lodge he scented the medicine and came straightaway to investigate. The trap was sprung when he scrambled up to examine the bait. Without fail, the beaver instinctively headed for the bottom and there his fate was sealed. The trap and stake held him below water and he drowned. Should his struggles unmoor the trap, the heavy pole, called a float stick by mountain men, would rise to the surface and show where the carcass lay.

The most important step in outfoxing the beaver, though, was in eliminating the man scent. The trapper waded into the stream some distance from the selected spot, and after baiting the trap, waded out again. While they understood the need, this part never sat well with the Dog Soldiers. Mountain streams in late fall left a man's teeth chattering, and long before running his trap line, he felt chilled to the very marrow.

Normally the traps were set before dusk and raised shortly after sunrise. The beaver was skinned on the spot, and the pelt, along with the medicine gland, was taken back to camp. The tail, which was something of a delicacy when boiled, was also collected. Later, the hide was scraped free of flesh and stretched on a willow frame. When dried the pelt became a plew, and with enough of them, a man could buy all manner of fascinating things at the summer Rendezvous.

This thought alone kept the Dog Soldiers wading icy streams, for their nights were spent in long discussions of guns and shiny knives, the *tibo* weapons that would be theirs when the Cold Maker departed again for his lodge in the north. Their leader, the dark one, had other ideas, though. The Dog Soldiers were collecting plews, well enough, but they had hardly made a dent in the beaver colonies close at hand. Not to mention those farther back in the mountains. Clearly what was needed was more trappers. The problem was how to ignite a spark of greed within the Sparrowhawks, something that would overcome the warriors' inborn aversion to labor of any description.

The solution came to Bloody Hand one night as he lay with Still Water beneath their robes.

The squaws!

What better way to move a man off his rump than to light a fire under his woman. It had been there all the time, right before his nose. Instead of horsing around with the council, he should have gone to the squaws at the outset. It would have been simpler, and a damn sight more effective. He spent the rest of the night in thoughtful restlessness, formulating exactly how it should be done. By morning his scheme was perfected, and he wasted no time in setting a spark to the tinder.

Still Water started it off. Then it was quickly picked up by squaws of the other Dog Soldiers. From there it spread like wildfire throughout the village, touching first the squaws, then their men, and through them the warrior societies.

It was a simple story, yet one with a certain feminine appeal. For the most part it dealt with bright beads, coffee, woolen blankets, pepper, and the highly treasured black kettles. All the foofaraw and gewgaws so dear to a squaw's heart.

More to the point, it started their jaws working, and their tongues wagging, and set their mercenary little minds to calculating how many plews it would take to buy a black kettle. And a bag of beads. And a couple of woolly blankets. And some of the coarse brown sweetness. Before nightfall the shrill screech of nagging squaws could be heard throughout the camp, and in every lodge warriors bent like reeds before a strong wind, helpless when set upon by the most formidable creature of them all: an aroused squaw.

Quite shortly, Bloody Hand became the most sought-after man in the village. Humble now, the warrior societies came begging the *tibo* secret of catching beaver. Generously he acceded to their requests, taught them all he knew, and even supplied them with traps.

When it was done, the dark one's life became a time of quiet gratification. Stepping to the door of his lodge each morning, with the hoarfrost glittering in the first rays of dawn, he watched as the Sparrowhawk warriors marched off to check their traplines.

Sometimes he even allowed himself a soft chuckle.

Strikes-Both-Ways had much to be thankful for. Before the dark one came to Absaroka he had been nothing but a bowmaker, respected for his craft, even honored as an artisan of sorts, yet an aged warrior nonetheless, one whose days of glory had long since faded in the minds of the People. But all that had changed with his adoption of Bloody Hand. Now he was the grandfather of a celebrated war leader, the elder in a lodge where honor once more dwelled. Others came to him seeking counsel, his words were repeated throughout the village, and wherever he walked, the People greeted him as a revered ancient.

Strikes-Both-Ways' heart was full. While many men his age subsisted on the charity of others, he basked in the glory of his *bacbapite*, and grew fat in a lodge of warmth and plenty. It called for a gesture, celebration, and thanksgiving: a Medicine Stone festival.

Though hardly a politician, the old bowmaker was not without a certain flair in the manipulation of men and things. Strikes-Both-Ways had never been the sort to develop close friendships with other men, and it pleased him that his grandson was also something of a lone wolf. Such men led the pack rather than run with it. Therefore, the customary obligation to entertain family and friends at a Medicine Stone festival was easily shunted aside. Instead, with devilish tact and cleverness, the old man invited those who might further the interest of his grandson: White Bear, chief of the *Acaraho* band, and Sitting Elk, council elder of Bloody Hand's ancestral clan.

The Medicine Stone festival was celebrated only on occasions of unusual significance. While there was no set time for it to be held, it was traditionally an act of thanksgiving and generally came sometime after the fall buffalo hunt. Unlike the Sun Dance and the Tobacco Planting ceremony, it was not a tribal event. The individual fortunate enough to have inherited one of the fabled Medicine Stones invited guests of his own choosing. Some years the feast wasn't staged at all, particularly if the buffalo hunt had gone poorly, and it was considered a great honor to be on hand when the Medicine Stones were displayed in ceremonial rites.

When Strikes-Both-Ways announced the forthcoming celebration, and made known his guests, Still Water immediately went into a frenzy of preparation. The girl had never attended a festival of such importance, much less been allowed to gaze upon the Medicine Stones. But if it were to be held in *her* lodge, it would be a feast long remembered by those in attendance, and widely discussed by those who were not.

The staple around which she built her feast was pemmican. Yet for this occasion, it must be a special pemmican, one not found in every lodge. From her winter stores she selected a parfleche containing a loaf blended and set back for just such an event. This particular pemmican was a mouth-watering concoction of pulverized hump meat, huckleberries, arrowroot jelly, and cherries. All of which, after being blended by hand and shaped into a loaf, had been covered with a thick layer of melted hump fat.

After much cajoling and wheedling, she next sent Bloody Hand off in search of a fat young doe. Not a buck, or an old doe, or even a yearling. None of those would do. She wanted only a young doe larded with fat. When he lugged it in two days later, Still Water went into a small fit of rapture. From it they would have broiled roasts, steaks fried in deep tallow, and a savory stew. This latter dish was her masterpiece, and for it, she began dragging out little treasures hoarded from the summer past. Onion bulbs, dried mushrooms, and a great variety of wild herbs. Simmered slowly, with chunks of fat doe meat, it would create an aroma no less tempting than ambrosia itself.

The crowning treat, though, would be her most highly guarded delicacy, tiny finger-like slices of rich hump fat, sun-cured with care and great patience until it had formed golden-brown slivers that melted on the tongue.

Somehow, between cooking up a storm and ordering the men about like small boys, Still Water even found time to make them new shirts for the festival. Selecting choice skins, soft and tanned a deep mahogany, she quilled them with ornate, brightly colored patterns

across chest and back. As befitted a warrior of Bloody
Hand's stature, she attached tufts of hair from each of
his thirty-four scalplocks along the outside seam of his
shirtsleeve. Then, when all was in readiness at last, she
brought out her white doeskin dress and cleansed it with
great care.

The night of the celebration was brisk and filled with
stars, and the guests arrived bearing small gifts for the
feast-giver. Strikes-Both-Ways greeted them with proper
solemnity and very tactfully seated everyone according
to rank: White Bear and his squaw on the left, and Sitting Elk, who was a widower, on the right. Bloody Hand
sat next to the council elder, and Still Water across from
him beside White Bear's woman.

The last to arrive, timing his entrance to the proper
moment, was Braided Tail. The holy man had been
asked by Strikes-Both-Ways to make a brief appearance
and bless the event. Braided Tail's fee for this service
was costly—a fine pony sound in wind and limb—but
the guests were suitably impressed that a shaman of his
eminence had agreed to perform a relatively minor rite.
The holy one stood just inside the door hole, on the
near side of the fire, waiting for Strikes-Both-Ways to
open the ceremony.

The old bowmaker produced a magnificently quilled
buckskin bag and opened it with the utmost care. From
inside the bag he withdrew a large bundle wrapped in
several layers of rawhide. These he peeled back one at a
time, with an air of great reverence, until before them
sat the *bacroritsitse.*

The Medicine Stone.

Somewhat ebony in color, the stone gave off a faint,
luminous glow. Though near the fire, it seemed to reflect nothing of the flames, generating a curious source
of energy and light all its own. Squat and broad, perhaps
half the size of a man's head, it was shaped roughly in
the image of a buffalo bull. Small knobs of rock thrust
upward from the crown to form blunted horns, and the

forward part bore a distinct resemblance to the massive brow of a full-grown buffalo. Suspended from a rawhide thong around its neck were three elk's teeth, an eagle's claw, and a strip of ermine skin.

These fabled stones, each shaped in the form of some animal, were thought to be the earthly embodiment of spirit beings. While never as strong as a man's medicine bundle, the rocks were believed to possess great power in staving off famine, as well as bestowing good fortune on its owner as a warrior and a stealer of horses. Curiously, the stones grew heavier in weight over the winter, and in the coldest months a film of frost covered their entire surfaces. The Sparrowhawk People believed that this was the breath vapor of the spirit being who lived inside. It was said that if the owner made certain offerings, especially the incense of wild carrot and sweetgrass, the one inside would reveal itself in an experience equivalent to the most powerful vision.

Strikes-Both-Ways rested his fingertips on top of the stone and lifted his eyes to the holy man. *"Waxpe,* I am no longer young. My bones grow brittle and my body weary. I am in the twilight time, and in the gaze of others I see that my days are numbered. This night we gather to make offering for a bountiful summer, yet before another snow passes, I feel the need to pass on to my grandson that which is rightfully his by birth."

Those around the fire exchanged startled glances, for, in fact, Strikes-Both-Ways looked healthy as a horse. Moreover, a Medicine Stone ceremony seemed a queer place for a man to reveal his impending death. Strikes-Both-Ways let the pause lengthen, thoroughly enjoying his moment. *Ai!* After tonight none among them would dare deny his grandson. Not White Bear. Or the council. Or the entire Sparrowhawk nation.

"I ask your blessing, holy one. For on this night of thanksgiving, I give all I possess to my *bacbapite.* I have already given him my blood and the wisdom of my years. Now I pass on to him my horses, my name, and all worldly things. And finally, in the knowledge that it will serve him well, I pass on this, my Medicine Stone."

There was an instant of stunned silence as White Bear and Sitting Elk gaped in disbelief. No man had ever before passed on his Medicine Stone before death. It was an ominous sign, what this old one did. Among the Sparrowhawk in days to come, the medicine of Bloody Hand would stand alone, unsurpassed in its strength.

The black man was a little surprised himself. He had heard about the medicine stones, and how they were considered pretty potent stuff, but it had never occurred to him that he might someday own one. Even now he had a sneaking hunch about this whole business. Strikes-Both-Ways looked just a mite too pleased with himself, like maybe he planned to live another hundred years, and this deal was just his idea of a huge joke on the rest of the tribe.

Braided Tail exhibited neither surprise nor shock. He was merely being paid to do a job, and if the old man wanted a blessing, that was exactly what he would get. Squatting before the fire, he emptied a bag of fresh owl dung on the ground. Then he pulled out a horn vial of dog blood and poured this over the owl dung. Mixing them together with the tip of his finger, he poked around in the mess for a minute, studying it intently. After a while he grunted to himself and looked up at his audience.

"The signs are very good. That Strikes-Both-Ways had done this thing on a night of thanksgiving pleases the spirits highly. What I read here is a message of great importance." Glancing down, he traced a chain of swirls with his finger in the crimsoned dung. "It says Bloody Hand will bring great glory to the Sparrowhawk People. Before his day is through, he will walk as a giant throughout Absaroka."

The holy man rose, chanting a low incantation as he

lifted his dung-smeared hand in offering to the One
Above. With his other hand, in a gesture so slight it
could have been the twitching of a finger, he sprinkled a
pinch of finely granulated powder into the fire. There
was a blinding flash, brighter than a thunderbolt on a
dark night, and on its heels came a thick cloud of sulfu-
rous smoke.

When the smoke cleared away Braided Tail had disappeared.

Bloody Hand ducked his head and struggled to hold
back a laugh. It was the oldest trick in the book. Keep
everybody busy watching one hand while the other hand
did its magic. Back in the mountain brigades, the old
faker would have been run out of camp for insulting
everybody's intelligence.

Suddenly the hunting cry of a predatory night owl
sounded in the smokehole overhead. The black man's
head jerked back, then he froze as a drop of owl dung
splattered on the earth at his feet.

Swirled through it were tiny flecks of blood.

The black man trudged on through the snow, casting
ahead with quick looks as he watched the tracks out of
the corner of his eye. The sky was gray and overcast,
working itself up for another storm, and the light was
fading fast. He would have to hurry now and chance
spooking the elk. That or abandon the hunt altogether,
which didn't make a hell of a lot of sense. Not when
he'd spent most of the day up to his crotch in snow.

Scanning ahead, he saw the tracks skirt the edge of a
spruce forest. Even elk liked the easy way when they
weren't pushed. He set a faster pace and headed
straight for the woods.

Winter had come to the high country. The blue skies
of fall were gone, and it was shivering cold even when
the sun came high, if it came at all. Most days, the sun
was just a dull glow somewhere above the murky clouds.
Dawn wasn't much, either. Not these days. When the

sun topped the mountain rims, it seemed to come later each morning, and it had none of the fiery splendor of earlier months. The light was darker now, slate-colored like the rocky peaks, and the afternoon shadows had become deeper and more pronounced, somber somehow. Yet there was a certain chilled witchery about the mountains in winter. Along the creeks there was a thin glaze of ice, and hoarfrost sparkled throughout the spruce forests like spun glass. The earth seemed to stand still, lost in slumber under a soft white blanket, and after a snowstorm it was as if the world had been frozen in an interlude of crystal brilliance.

Just at the moment, though, Bloody Hand would have traded it all for a warm lodge and a pair of dry moccasins. He was chilled clean to the bone, and getting colder with every step. All of which set him to wondering what the hell he was doing out here anyway. Back in that warm lodge, he had enough meat to feed half the Crow nation, with their dogs thrown in on the side. There was just no need for him to be out tromping around in the slush like some bushytailed greenhorn, except that he had a wild hair up his ass and couldn't rightly think straight anymore.

What with one thing and another, he ought to be about the most contented man in *Absaroka* these days. But he wasn't. He was sorely troubled, and despite some pretty strong ruminating over it, he hadn't been able to come to grips with what was bothering him. Worse yet, he couldn't bring himself to speak of it to anyone—not even Still Water—for it didn't figure to make any more sense in words than it did in his head. Besides which, there were some things a man just couldn't unload on his wife.

Especially when part of it had to do with another woman.

The more he thought about it—and he had thought about it plenty in the last month or so—the trouble seemed to stem from Strikes-Both-Ways. Matter of fact, he had a pretty strong hunch it got started that night the old devil had given him the Medicine Stone. Not that his conscience was bothering him, or anything like that. Shit! He'd cut enough throats in his time that a few more wouldn't make a jingle's worth of difference.

But it worried him all the same, festering inside like a boil that wasn't quite ripe enough to lance.

Somehow Strikes-Both-Ways' gift had dealt him a blow right where it hurt most, back in that little soft spot, the one he'd spent so many years burying beneath layers of indifference and skepticism. Of course, it wasn't like he could feel nothing at all. Every now and then somebody came along—like Doc Newell—who stirred up things that hadn't seen the light of day in a coon's age. Generally, though, the corrosion had thickened around his soft spot enough that it couldn't be flaked with a hammer and chisel.

Still, he'd felt a mighty sharp twang the night Strikes-Both-Ways gave him that shiny rock. Maybe not right off, but it had come to him later, when everybody was bedded down and he'd had time to think it out. The old rascal hadn't had any reason on earth to hand over his most prized possession. Except one. Perhaps the only reason that made any sense.

He wanted to help—make his grandson so strong that nobody would stand taller—and the only way he could do it was to part with the Medicine Stone.

Sure, he'd talked about his miseries, but that business of him being on the way to the promised land was nothing but a big crock. Christ Almighty, that old coon would outlive the whole bunch half again and more. Nor did he have any axe to grind with White Bear and the council. Naturally he was just ornery enough to like the idea of rubbing their noses in it. But that wasn't the reason either, no more than him being poorly.

The old man hadn't had a damn thing on his mind

except making a certain red nigger the he-wolf in all of Absaroka.

Didn't make no never mind how hard a man was, a gesture like that just naturally reamed him right down to the core. Couldn't fail, unless his soft spot had withered plumb down to nothing.

Bloody Hand broke through the spruce forest only a few steps ahead of the elk. As the rifle settled against his shoulder, it occurred to him that the cow looked downright mortified. She'd known he was back there, well enough. But she hadn't thought anybody—man or beast—would wade through hip-deep snowdrifts just to cut her off. When the Hawken cracked the elk collapsed like a stone church. She thrashed around a bit, snorting bright gouts of blood across the snow, then she stiffened and keeled over with her legs thrust straight out.

The black man finished reloading and circled around her cautiously. After assuring himself that she was dead, he laid the rifle across his shoulder and pulled his knife. Gauging a line between hip and tailbone, he began cutting on a hindquarter, taking care not to puncture any sacs that would spoil the meat. One haunch was about all he could manage in the deep snow, which made a day's hunting hardly worth the effort. Still, the meat wouldn't go to waste. When winter claimed the mountains there were lots of hungry things around. Warm meat would draw a crowd in no time a'tall.

As he worked, his mind returned to Strikes-Both-Ways. Or more precisely, the effect the old man's gift had had on his attitude about things in general, and Crow most particular. While he didn't fathom it completely, he had a fair notion that the bowmaker's generosity had forced him to come face-to-face with what he was doing. The Crows had treated him damned decently. Like as not, there were any number that didn't swallow the story of how he'd been whelped. But nobody had made any bones. They'd taken him in, shown him their ways, and taught him how to play the game.

Moreover, they seemed tickled pink when he earned his warrior honors, and so far as he could tell, nobody had kicked a lick when he got to be a pipe-holder. Even if he was black as the ace of spades.

Fact of the matter was, it seemed like everybody had clean forgot about his being a different color, if they had ever cared to start with. They just accepted him as a man. Black or red didn't appear to make a damn. They liked his style, and that was that. The proof of the pudding was his being made leader of the Dog Soldiers. Nobody climbed that high so long as he remained an outsider. The Sparrowhawks considered him one of their own. Otherwise he'd never have made it. They had adopted him, plain and simple. Just like they were stone-cold color-blind.

Which was a hell of a lot more than he could say about the mountain brigades. Not that they hadn't allowed him to live and let live. In their own way they had accepted him, too. But then, the mountain men were different than other whites. Renegades of sort. They lived in the wilds, among Indians and beasts, because they didn't like civilization or its ways. Yet even among them he was still looked upon as a nigger. A mulatto woods colt who was tolerated for his skills and the fact that he wouldn't take sass off of anyone. Back east, though, that wouldn't work. He'd learned that lesson the hard way, learned it every day for nearly twenty years. Back there he was nothing. Less than nothing. Double ought zero. Just an uppity nigger.

Which sort of brought him full circle. Back to the Crows. What he felt wasn't exactly guilt, but it came pretty damn close. He hadn't betrayed their trust—not anywhere near that—yet he hadn't paid them back in kind, either. It was more like he had taken advantage of a bunch of guileless children. Duped them. Tricked men born as warriors into becoming greedy trappers, no better than the mountain men they ridiculed in vulgar jests.

Perhaps it was shame he felt. Lately he had forgotten that he was a nigger, and started thinking of himself as a Sparrowhawk. Or something even more. A Sparrow-hawk warrior. Commenced believing it, like some kind of fairytale come to life. That's what the Crows had done for him. Made him believe. What he had done in return was to convert them into something less than they were, workers instead of warriors. Which was al-most as bad as the black robes trying to take away their spirit beings. Not quite, but almost.

So maybe what he felt was shame. The shame of all Sparrowhawk warriors who mucked about in icy streams trapping beaver.

Still, there wasn't much he could do about it. Least-ways, not till after Rendezvous. What began as a beaver harvest had now turned into an intense rivalry between the warrior societies. Everybody was out to beat every-body else, and the squaws bellyaching for fancy gewgaws had made it a matter of honor. Whoever rode away from Rendezvous with less loot than his neighbor would never hear the end of it, especially from his joking rela-tives and his squaw.

The thought made him grunt. Seemed like everybody was having trouble with their squaws these days. Him-self included. Lately he'd started thinking a lot about Pine Leaf. Whenever he saw her around the village, she went out of her way to tease him, looked him over with those saucy eyes, and switched her tail like a mare in heat. Feeling plumb safe, she was, knowing that he only had thirty-four scalps. It was enough to shrivel a man's innards.

Among other things.

That was what had Still Water stalking around the lodge here lately. Those other things. There hadn't been much horseplay under the robes in a while, and she was getting real testy about it. Just as she had every right. All the same, a man couldn't perform those little stud tricks when his mind was on another woman. Not that

Still Water had lost her bloom, or anything like that. She was ripe as ever. It was just that she was there, handy like, and a man didn't always want what he had closest to hand.

Funny thing about it was, she wouldn't have minded in the least if he brought Pine Leaf in to share the lodge. The Sparrowhawks were great believers in a man having more than one wife. But it got her fur riled having to compete with a woman who wasn't there. Or what was worse, a man's fantasies about another woman.

Maybe she had a point there. He'd sure as hell been plagued with fantasies the last few weeks. Dreams, too. The kind that brought a man awake with the hot sweats.

But then, that's what life was all about. Things a fellow had and couldn't have. People he didn't want to hurt and couldn't help hurting. Trading off one thing against another, and trying his damnedest to justify it somehow, when he knew all the time he couldn't.

Hefting the elk haunch over one shoulder, he stuck the Hawken under his arm and started the long trek back to the village.

It was a sorry day, and getting sorrier all the time.

Bloody Hand's struggle within himself grew no worse in the days that followed. Nor did it grow better. Like a canker it merely fed upon itself, refusing to go away, as it gnawed steadily at his insides. Throughout the time of the Cold Maker, though, he became moodier, and lapsed into long silences where his thoughts turned inward, looking at himself. What he saw was neither disturbing nor comforting. It was merely confusing.

What he wished for most was an end to winter. The howling mountain blizzards, hurled down out of the north on icy winds, had kept him chained to the lodge. Unable to move about freely in the deep snows, he felt caged, trapped in a musky cave with Strikes-Both-Ways and Still Water. Especially Still Water. While her tantrums had simmered down—out of sheer boredom he had resumed their nightly wrestling matches—there remained between them an unspoken tenseness. Though the matter was never broached openly, they both knew the name that preoccupied his thoughts. The phantom one, whose presence was felt if not seen. Pine Leaf.

He longed for Rendezvous, the drinking and brawling, something to ease the strain, make him forget. But more than that, he longed for Rendezvous to be over and done with, and the raiding season begun. Then there would be no time for brooding. The Dog Soldiers must be led, and in the stealing of horses and reprisal raids, it was to him they would look for guidance. At heart he wasn't suited to probe within himself, and the raiding season dangled before him like some glittering jewel. There, once again, he would become simply and completely the *duxia* leader of the Dog Soldiers.

Yet there was a bewilderment even to that. Sometimes, when his thoughts turned to Rendezvous, he was filled with recollections of the mountain brigades, the good times, their fights with gut-eaters, the tricks they pulled on one another, the drunken, sweaty marathons with rented squaws every summer at the trade fair. That life held out a lure he had never fully escaped. While the good times hadn't been all that many, and the mountain men had never really considered him one of the clan, it tugged at him all the same. There was something wild and free, wholly unfettered about that life. No obligations. No strings attached. No sticky involvements that kept a man mired down in responsibility and duty. Just the mountains and the beaver and a full gut. Those things alone claimed him. But only on his own terms.

Still, there was as much to be said for life in Absaroka, and as the furies of winter raged outside his lodge, the black man found himself wavering between two worlds. Jim Beckwith, mountain man, and Bloody Hand, Sparrowhawk pipe-holder. Much like a cloth rent in half, he was torn between the best in both worlds. Knowing full well, as he whipsawed back and forth, that no man in his right mind could lead a double life, least of all a man who paid homage to nothing save himself, earthly or otherwise.

Someday, soon perhaps, the choice would have to be made. What bewildered him most was not when he would choose, or even how. Instead he pondered the greater irony. What would sway him—which aspect of these two worlds he had created for himself—when the time came at last to decide?

Curiously, the dark one's struggle was not his alone. Strikes-Both-Ways watched and fretted and struggled silently right alongside him. The bowmaker's greatest struggle, though, was to keep his mouth shut. Not unlike times past, it was a losing fight from the outset. While he wasn't sure of what lay beneath Bloody Hand's dour moods, he knew that the solution wouldn't come with brooding and meditation. Straight talk, in its own way, was a purgative of rare qualities. Especially if administered by one of subtlety and tact.

Strikes-Both-Ways undertook the cure one morning when Still Water had gone out to gather wood. Seating himself on the other side of the fire, where he could watch the dark one's eyes, he tried first for shock. "Well my son, how is it these days with you and the Moon Beings?"

"Moon Beings?" the black man repeated dully.

"*Ai!* One who acts so strangely must surely have been touched by the Moon Beings." The old man pursed his lips, then shrugged. The gesture was exquisitely done, suggesting both mockery and puzzlement, shadowed with the merest fleck of contempt.

Bloody Hand roused from his funk long enough to retaliate. "You prattle like an old squaw. If I were crazy it would not be the work of your Moon Beings. Or can you call them down as the great Braided Tail makes himself disappear?"

Strikes-Both-Ways cocked his head, smiling slyly. "So! I detect the voice of a cynic. Could it be that the famed Dog Soldier has renounced belief in the spirits?"

"I believe in nothing except myself."

"Not even your medicine bundle?"

The dark one glared back at him, saying nothing, his eyes flat and guarded.

"Perhaps you believe not even in yourself," Strikes-Both-Ways observed.

"What riddle do you hand me now?"

"The simplest of all riddles. How can a man believe in himself when he has lost belief in the One Above?"

"What if there is no One Above, old man? Give that a moment's thought. Have you considered that these spirit beings might well be fables handed down from ancient times? The inventions of shabby fakers like Braided Tail."

"*Ae,* it is true that the holy men employ certain devices." The bowmaker raised a wrinkled hand, pointing at the bear claw necklace around Bloody Hand's neck. "Yet you have reason to know that he possesses powers unnatural to other men."

"Perhaps. Even granting you that, it was still my gun which killed the bear."

"That also is true. It is said, my son, that each soul must meet the morning light and the Great Silence alone. There is an essential difference, however, in being alone and being by one's self. Even when a man is alone, the One Above walks in his shadow. The man who walks by himself is a man who has not bothered to study life and his place in the scheme of things."

"Grandfather, I have no wish to offend you, but spare me your parables. If you must speak, then speak of things that are real."

"Very well. You have been among the *Apsahrokee* now for nine moons. In all that time have you seen a Sparrowhawk kill another Sparrowhawk? Or seen theft practiced? Or witnessed any man deny charity to one in need?"

Bloody Hand had the distinct feeling he was about to be ensnared, but he couldn't refuse to answer. "No, my *axeisake*. I have seen none of those things."

The old man fixed him with a penetrating stare. "Have you ever bothered to wonder why it is so?"

"Wondered, yes. But my curiosity centered on other things."

"Yet my question now arouses a different curiosity, so let me satisfy it. From childhood, a Sparrowhawk studies the habits of the wild things around him. The One Above has taught us that there are valuable lessons to be learned from the beasts: courage, endurance, cunning, and strength. When the warrior's guardian spirit is revealed to him in a vision, they are not strangers. The warrior knows the ways of his guardian and can take them as his own. Thus he is held safe from harm, and acquires wisdom beyond that of other people."

Strikes-Both-Ways paused, again indicating the black man's necklace. "The proof hangs from your neck. The great bear is venerated for many reasons, the most important being that he is invulnerable to the attack of other animals. You have counted many coup, and taken nearly two score scalps, yet you have never been harmed. Would you deny that those claws have added power to your medicine, kept you safe when all around you men were being killed?"

Bloody Hand smiled, acknowledging the old man's sly entrapment. "How can a man dispute his own survival? But the point of this escapes me. What do the wild things—your spirit beings—have to do with the virtues of the Sparrowhawks?"

"That is my point!" Strikes-Both-Ways crowed. "The Sparrowhawk is a part of all about him, the wild beasts and the clouds above, the green earth and the eternal rocks. He moves in harmony with the earth and its creatures, and in doing so he is blessed with a very rare inner peace: the peace you seek, my son, and have not found."

"*Ae,* but you evade my question, Grandfather. What role do the spirit beings play in all this?"

"The spirit beings are but a part of the whole, guardians who lead us along the paths of harmony. True peace is found within the shadow souls of men. It comes when they realize their oneness with the universe and *all* its powers, when they know that the One Above is at its center, and that this center is to be found within each of us."

The black man frowned and shook his head. "Among the white-eyes, it is also said that true peace comes only through the One Above. They, too, have protectors like the spirit beings. Only their protectors are in human form. Perhaps you will understand my skepticism better when I tell you that they have holy men who also practice trickery and deceit to rob the faithful."

Strikes-Both-Ways' watery gaze softened. "There are no perfect men, my *bacbapite,* whatever their color. Whatever their beliefs. Evil is often practiced in the name of good, and sometimes there is no justice to be found in the hearts of the holy. You ridicule these things, perhaps with reason, yet I would ask you a question. Is it the men you scorn, or the spirits they worship?"

Bloody Hand flinched, as though struck between the eyes. His jaw opened as if to speak, then closed. There was nothing he could say. Not then. Perhaps never. For within that confounding instant, the bowmaker had driven a shaft of doubt straight to the root of his own skepticism.

After a moment, Strikes-Both-Ways stood and walked to the doorhole. Then he turned, suddenly infused with the very thought he had been searching for throughout their talk. "My son, a man is unfit to grapple with wisdom while his scorn is being inscribed in stone."

The black man shivered as a chilling gust of air swept

through the doorhole. When the flap swung shut, leaving him alone with his thoughts, there seemed nothing left to ponder.

It had all been said.

CHAPTER 6

The Green River Rendezvous got off to a peppery start. Before the brigades hardly had time to unload their packs a man was dead, killed in a row over a squaw. The winner, a short-fused bruiser named Micah Johnson, gave the loser a rousing, if somewhat hasty, funeral. This slight interruption had no effect whatever on the fun and games, and things boiled along at a lively pace. Everybody agreed, though, that it was a damned sorry way for a fellow to go under. Seemed a shame, somehow. What with squaws being so plentiful this year, it was hardly worth a man getting himself killed.

That sounded like sensible advice to most of those present. Particularly since a man could spit in any direction and hit at least three squaws. Evidently word of Rendezvous was spreading, for the place seemed to be crawling with gut-eaters of every description: Nez Perce, Bannock, Flathead, Shoshone, not to mention a handful of Utes. Spread out along the banks of the Green, their lodges already covered the better part of two miles. And the Crows hadn't even shown yet.

It promised to be just about the wildest trade fair anybody could recollect, and the trappers didn't waste a moment getting the festivities underway. There was nothing that stimulated mountain men like a fresh audience, and Ashley had brought a flock of *mangeurs de lard* out from St. Louis. The pork-eaters were green as sap—chock full of tales about the mountain brigades they had come to join—and they looked on with enormous wonder. The veterans performed like a herd of frisky bears, sometimes astonishing even themselves with the stunts trotted out to impress their spectators.

They lied and bragged, spinning long, hair-raising windies about their experiences over the winter. Then, after consuming a snootful, the challenges began: horse races, wrestling matches, card games, and prolonged shooting contests that never failed to draw a crowd. They shot at charred Xs scratched on trees, twigs forking off from branches, and when the firewater had them feeling potent, they even shot at one another. The game was childishly simple, if hardly a sport for the fainthearted. The challenger and his opponent took positions fifty paces apart. They then placed some item on top their heads, usually a tin cup but in a pinch a fair-sized rock would do nicely. Lest there be some ulterior motive at work, the man challenged always got the first shot. The game was as much a test of raw nerve as of accuracy with a rifle, and it was considered no small disgrace to decline a challenge. The man who sent the cup flying was judged the winner; if both men rang the bell it was considered cause for a major celebration.

The presence of so many greenhorns was enough to fire the pride of anyone worth his salt, and the men of the mountain brigades weren't about to let their reputation suffer. They proceeded to demonstrate their skills in a spree of whiskey-soaked violence, leaving the newcomers goggle-eyed at the old timers' grisly idea of fun. Oddly enough, only one man was killed the first day, and according to the trappers, that didn't hardly count, not when he had got himself rubbed out over some mangy squaw.

Things started to slack off a bit late that afternoon. There was sort of a lull so everyone could gather a second wind for the night ahead. Then a cry swept through camp from upstream.

"The Crows. The Crows are coming!"

This roused the mountain men and brought them running, for it was eagerly awaited news. The Nez Perces had spotty-rumped ponies to trade, and the other tribes had brought along plenty of women. But only the Crows would have softly tanned buckskins and fine moccasins and the best of all buffalo sleeping robes.

Not to mention that every man in camp had a sizeable bet riding on a real skullduster. Was Beckwith still kicking, or had the Crows lifted his hair over the winter? Opinion was divided, and the odds about even, though few would have been surprised to see his topknot dangling from a scalp stick.

What they saw instead was the largest batch of Crows ever to attend Rendezvous. The column stretched practically half a mile upstream, trailed by an enormous pony herd. Yet that held the mountain men's attention only a moment. Their gaze was drawn to the advance scouts leading the column, and a man who was unmistakable, despite his Indian regalia.

It was Bloody Hand at the head of the Dog Soldiers.

The black man wore a gaudy, heavily quilled war shirt, with markings to indicate both the raids he had led and the number of scalps he had lifted. Along his sleeves hung wispy hairlocks instead of fringe, and waving defiantly from the crown of his head were three coup feathers. Though his face was unpainted, the buckskin gelding he rode had bands of white around its eyes, thunderbolts along its forelegs, and bloody handprints on its rump. Cradled in his arm was the Hawken, and from his belt hung a stag-handled scalping knife and a heavy war axe. From a distance he looked like any other warrior, darker perhaps, but with nothing to make him stand out. Up close the effect was worse, menacing somehow, for he was clearly a black man gone savage. The trappings of war were worn with an air of pride, arrogance even, and the look in his eye defied anyone to laugh.

Far from laughing, the mountain men stood slackjawed as he led the Crows to a campsite downstream. They watched him ride by, looking as if he had been nailed to the saddle, and not a man among them uttered the first word. Plain to see, the mulatto hadn't just survived. He was thriving like a weed in a berry patch. The bastard had actually led that bunch into Rendezvous! Which wasn't no small honor, the way guteaters figured things.

The Crows circled into their campgrounds like a well-organized, highly disciplined military formation. Everybody knew exactly where to go, and there wasn't a moment's hesitation or confusion in their actions. Squaws started unlashing skins and lodge poles, and within minutes a village began to spring erect where before there had been only bare earth. There was no wasted motion to be seen anywhere, and as the squaws worked, knots of warriors gathered at the cardinal points. While no command had been given, it was apparent that the warriors formed a loose, yet highly mobile, striking force in the event of attack. Normally an Indian village being erected was a scene of mass confusion, more vulnerable to a sneak raid than at any other time. The fact that the Crows were no longer vulnerable wasn't lost on any of the onlookers, white or otherwise.

Which was exactly the impression Bloody Hand had meant to create. Before leaving Absaroka he had convinced White Bear to experiment in training the Sparrowhawks along military lines. Considering the fortune in beaver plews they were packing, the *batsetse* felt the advice well taken, and allowed the dark one to instruct the People accordingly. The Dog Soldiers were assigned the role of tribal police, and every evening when the column halted, they guided the lodges into previously assigned spots. The trip had consumed close to a fortnight, which proved entirely adequate for what Bloody

Hand had in mind. They had drifted down the eastern slope of the Wind River, crossed the mountains at South Pass, and headed due west toward the headquarters of the Sandy. There they had turned southwest and followed the Sandy to its junction with the Green, the river known to the Sparrowhawks as *Seedskeedee.*

Bloody Hand had drilled the People firmly, but with a jesting manner that removed the sting from his words. By the time the column pulled into the trade fair, there was great pride in what they had accomplished. That they were well organized and working together had been closely observed, and the word would pass from tribe to tribe. While it wouldn't halt the raiding entirely, it would make their enemies think twice before entering Absaroka. This was precisely the reason the Dog Soldier leader had chosen Rendezvous to demonstrate the Sparrowhawks' unusual new spirit of watchfulness.

When the Crow lodges were nearly erected, the black man wheeled his pony and rode toward the mountain men. They had gathered at the edge of the white encampment, drinking and lazing about on the ground as they watched the village take shape. A puzzled murmur swept over them as he drew nearer, then fell silent when he pulled the gelding to a halt in front of Doc Newell.

The black man smiled, thoroughly enjoying himself. "Doc, long time, no see. How's yore stick floatin'?"

"Jim, it talks like ye, but damn me if'n it don't look like some funny breed of Injun we ain't never seen a'fore. Ye sure ye ain't some gut-eater that done stole ol' Jim's talk-box?"

"This chile? When'd ye ever see an Injun blacker'n a bear's ass? Ye got a short memory, ol' man, and a gut that's swelled some since I last seen ye."

"Great smokin' Jesus!" Newell bellowed. "Boys, it's him in the flesh. Done rize from the dead like Lazarus hisself."

Newell jerked him down off the gelding and clapped him into a smothering bear hug. Then the other trappers ganged around in a boisterous swarm, jostling and shoving as they shouted questions and edged closer to get a touch of his gaudy skins.

"Where in the hell d'ye get them feathers?"

"What's them signs thar on ye shirt?"

"Gawd Awmighty, is that ha'r, boy, real ha'r?"

The black man didn't even try to answer. They were shouting one another down, and nothing less than a bull moose could have made himself heard. Anyway, from the looks of things, all they really wanted was to grab hold and make sure he was real.

Waugh! If a man didn't have any better sense, it would've seemed sort of like a homecoming.

That night Pete Spence got himself baptized with fire. Not that he intended to, by any means. Nor had the mountain men meant to carry things that far. It was just a prank. Leastways, that's how it started out. But the trappers would be a long time forgetting how it ended.

The Indians wouldn't have much trouble on that score, either. They had never before seen a human torch.

The drinking had started in earnest shortly after sunset. Like most summer evenings in the high country, it was pleasantly cool, and the mountain men had gathered around fires in the center of the encampment. Nights at Rendezvous were devoted to gambling and swapping yarns, though if a squaw happened to take a man's eye, he was perfectly justified in a trip to the bushes. Indian bucks were always around, parading their wives and daughters for inspection, and a trapper had only to wait until something came along that suited his fancy.

Pete Spence, whose appetite for squaws was fast becoming legendary, had just returned from his third session of the evening. The trappers were feeling no pain at that point, and there was considerable joshing about Spence's staying power. Bill Williams, who was only slightly drunker than the others, scrambled to his feet clutching a kettle filled with whiskey. Cackling crazily, he upended the pot and sloshed its contents over Spence.

"I christen ye Bull's Balls!" Tottering unsteadily, he made the sign of the cross. "In the name of the Father, Son, and Holy Spook."

Drenched in alcohol, Spence sputtered and cursed as he struggled to his feet. But as he stood, the man seated next to him playfully grabbed a stick from the fire and touched it to his pantsleg. There was a fiery *whoosh* as the whiskey-soaked buckskins ignited, and Spence just seemed to burst into flames. Everybody froze for a moment, too stunned to move. But when the burning man let out a terrified scream and took off running, they all came to life. Grabbing sleeping robes, pack saddles, anything that came to hand, they threw him to the ground and began beating out the flames. Everyone pitched in to help and within moments the flames had been extinguished. Between the burning and beating, though, Spence was in pretty bad shape. The trappers coated him good with bear grease, which seemed about the only remedy close to hand. Then someone remembered an old witch doctor down in the Shoshone camp, and the whole crowd trooped off with the latest casualty in tow.

Spence survived, and oddly enough, didn't hold any grudge against Bill Williams. But for sometime afterwards, he looked like a greased pig that had been charred on an open spit.

Curiously, according to certain grim humorists among the brigades, William Ashley had also started using alcohol to fight fire with fire. While his methods were less crude, he had nonetheless kindled a blaze which was certain to be felt throughout the mountains.

Competition with Hudson's Bay and American Fur had become a matter of cut-throat and devil-take-the-hindmost. When the other companies introduced alcohol into the fur trade, Ashley had had little choice but to follow suit. Still, over the years he had restricted the amount of firewater dispensed to Indians at summer Rendezvous. His policy had been to give them a mere sampling, just enough to keep them coming back each year, but no more. Now the worm had turned. Hudson's Bay and American Fur were trading whiskey outright for Indian furs as an inducement to lure the mountain tribes away from Rendezvous. Ashley had countered by packing in four barrels of raw alcohol to the Green River trade fair.

While there were half a dozen Indian tribes and some hundred mountain men at Rendezvous, the four barrels proved adequate to slake their thirst. Adequate, that is, when doctored with William Ashley's special recipe. The alcohol was first diluted at a ratio of three parts river water to one part spirits. Afterwards a handful of tobacco was thrown in for color, ginger was added to give it flavor and a bunch of red peppers stirred in for good measure. The peppers had lent substance to the concoction's nickname, firewater, but the mountain men wouldn't have had it any other way. Not without some justification, they swore the devil's brew would kill a man, except that the bite of the peppers managed to keep his heart beating.

The whiskey trade was unusually profitable, as Ashley was discovering fully for the first time. Raw alcohol cost twenty cents a gallon in St. Louis. Doctored with the Ashley formula, it sold for one plew per pint in the mountains. The equivalent of five dollars. It didn't require a wizard to see that the twenty-cent gallon had been parlayed into a very respectable $160. Four barrels at the same rate meant that Green River was going to be the most profitable Rendezvous yet.

More significantly, at least from a tactical standpoint, it would keep the mountain tribes cross-eyed and happy.

This latter assumption proved only partially correct. The firewater kept the tribes cross-eyed, well enough, but far from happy. Unlimited trade of whiskey had a devastating effect on the Indians. Warriors lacked the white man's tolerance for alcohol, and under the influence they became holy terrors. They fought and killed one another, beat their squaws bloody, and behaved generally like some low form of animal. When sober again, suffering from a thunderous hangover, they gladly bartered their furs, their horses, even their women for another ration of the fiery whiskey.

It was profitable for Ashley, yet diabolic beyond measure in its aftermath among the Indians.

Bloody Hand had seen the consequences for himself within hours after reaching Rendezvous: warriors reduced to puking, slobbering hogs, their year's catch of furs, and all else they owned, gone in a spasm of muddled drunkenness. Perhaps his own fondness for popskull, the memory of countless mornings when he awoke remembering nothing of the night before, gave him an instinctive dread of this new threat. Plain to see, there could be only one result. The Indians would become slaves to their thirst, chained to the white man's whiskey barrel like trained bears.

Hurrying back to the Sparrowhawk encampment, he had taken White Bear aside and given him a stiff lecture on the evils confronting their people. Though the *batsetse* knew little of whiskey, he had come to trust the dark one's judgment, particularly in matters dealing with the *tibos*. The herald was summoned and sent through the village announcing White Bear's order.

The Sparrowhawks would not trade for firewater. Anyone caught exchanging furs for drink would be punished severely by the Dog Soldiers.

While each warrior society was represented at Rendezvous, those attending chose not to defy the ban. They were under no obligation to White Bear—before leaving Absaroka their members had authorized them to trade the furs as they saw fit—but they had an abiding respect for the Dog Soldiers. Bloody Hand would enforce the *batsetse*'s order, of that they were certain, and none among them cared to test the dark one's wrath.

That night, shortly after Pete Spence got himself baptized with fire, the black man went looking for Doc Newell. They talked for a while with members of Newell's brigade, rehashing the latest rumors about the fur trade war, but it was obvious the old trapper was uneasy about something. It was equally clear that the man they called Beckwith didn't ask for a cup of whiskey from the brigade kettle. Nor did anyone invite him to drink. When the conversation waned, Newell suggested a walk along the river, and the black man readily agreed. Somehow the homecoming hadn't worked out just the way he thought it would. He felt strangely uncomfortable among the mountain men, almost like a foreigner.

They walked in silence down to the river and took seats along the grassy bank. Both men felt the tension between them, and it was as if neither cared to broach the matter openly. Instead they listened to the night sounds, tree frogs and crickets, the mewling ripple of mountain water rushing through the streambed. Overhead a falling star flashed against the inky sky, disappearing in a silvery streak. The black man grunted and let his gaze rove about the heavens.

"When ye see a star like that, the Sparrowhawks believe it's somebody in the Faraway Land tryin' to come back to life. Sort of a purty way of lookin' at things, ain't it? 'Ceptin' I guess nobody's yet made it back."

Newell didn't say anything for a moment, watching the skies. "Sounds like ye been gettin' yoreself a heap of l'arnin'. Notice ye don't even call'em Crows no more."

"That's what their enemies call'em, Doc. They call theirselves *Apsahrokee*. The Sparrowhawk People."

"Meanin' which? Ye ain't their enemy? Or yore one of the Aspa—whatever ye called it?"

The black man's eyes swung around, meeting Newell's gaze. "Meanin' both, I reckon."

"That why ye ain't let'em trade fer liquor? Don't say it warn't ye that done it. Ever'body in camp knows it fer a fact."

"It was my doin', well enough. I see what's what with them other gut-eaters, and I ain't fixin' to let it happen to the Sparrowhawks."

Newell cocked his head in an owlish frown. "Them other gut-eaters? Ye mean to say they don't all look alike to ye anymore?"

"That's about what she biles down to, Doc. If ye was much on readin' sign, and ye took a keerful squint at this shirt I'm wearin', ye'd see I'm pipe-holder of the Dog Soldiers. That means I lead'em on raids. They picked me apurpose fer the job, 'cause I l'arned their ways and added a few tricks of my own."

"Now I suppose yore gonna tell me all them hanks of ha'r means ye been give'em lessons in skulpin', too."

"I ain't a critter to brag." The black man raised his arms and the hairlocks shimmered in the starlight. "So fur I only got me thirty-four. But raidin' season's comin' up and it looks to be good pickin's."

"Thirty-four, ye say?" Newell's mouth worked like a fish sucking bubbles. "Jesus Horatio Christ!"

"Oh, that ain't nothin' to what's comin', Doc. Thar's a little gal back in the Wind Rivers jest eatin' her heart out till I get a hunnert. Done promised she'll show me what she's sittin' on soon's I get'em all collected."

"I knowed it! I told the boys it warn't so, but I knowed it the minute I seen ye ride in with'em. Yore set on goin' back acrost the mountains, and winterin' with them gut-eaters agin."

"Doc, I don't know as I'd have it nary another way. Case I ain't mentioned it, I got me a woman over in the village and I 'spect she'd take it mighty unkindly if I was to up and leave her."

"Bearshit!" Newell exploded. "Thar warn't ary a

woman this side of hell ye couldn't walk away from if'n ye set yore mind to it."

"Mebbe. Mebbe not." The black man's brow furrowed in a quizzical look. "What ails ye, Doc? Cain't a feller follow his nose without ye gettin' yore bowels in an uproar?"

"It ain't my bowels. Nosireee! Don't ye fret yoreself none about my bowels a'tall. It's them fellers back in camp. They're sayin' ye done gone Injun on us. Talkin' it around that ye got yoreself high and mighty, and ain't got no more use fer sech as them."

"Never said I had much use fer'em to start with. 'Ceptin' you and a couple of others. Jest goes to show ye, though. All that palaver and horseshit they give me when I rode in warn't nothin' but pure swill."

"Yore wrong thar, Jim. Plumb wrong. Them boys was gladder'n all git out ye made it back with yore ha'r. But they was put out some that ye helt the Crows back from tradin' fer liquor. Figgered what's good enough fer them ort to be plenty good enough fer a gut-eater."

"Doc, ye don't believe that no more'n I do. Mebbe they're the least mite jealous 'cause I done somethin' they would've lost their topknot tryin'. That's got a better ring to it. But them bein' soured 'bout this liquor business jest won't hold water."

"Now is that a fact?" The trapper reared back and glowered down his nose. "Ol' coon, ye jest wait till Ashley hisself gets ye set down fer a do-si-do. That liquor business has got him foamin' at the mouth, and when he yells frog that's lots of folks around hyar that squats."

"Doc, Ashley don't know fat cow from pore bull. Give him a choice 'tween his ass and a hole in the ground and he's liable to shit all over hisself. What I'm sayin' is, it's me that's got holt of the short ha'rs, and I reckon he's already feelin' the pinch."

"I don't know nothin' one way or t'other 'bout that." Newell pulled a clump of grass from the earth and shredded it with his horny paws. "Jest watch yore hind-

sides, Jim. Thar's ill feelin' toward ye, and the reason
don't much matter. Like I l'arn't ye, sleep light and keep
yore sniffer to the wind."

The black man understood perfectly. What Newell
had left unsaid made the warning all the more urgent,
which was exactly why the old trapper had chucked his
whiskey for a stroll to the river. Somebody in camp—
and that could mean just about anybody—had a bone in
his throat.

When he spit it up, it wouldn't surprise nary a soul to
see that he'd gone got himself choked on dark meat.

William Ashley sometimes thought the Good Lord had
given him a mighty cross to bear, surrounded him with
idiots, as it were, and let the scum of the earth snapping
at his heels. Thieves and savages, backstabbers and
scoundrels: they were all there, poaching on an empire
he alone had snatched from the wilderness. Like some
great buffalo bull encircled by snarling wolves—an image of himself that seemed appropriately regal—he was
beseiged on all fronts, even in his own camp.

Seated in his tent, awaiting Beckwith's arrival, it occurred to him that life was often inequitable toward
those who shouldered the load. The caprice of God and
man alike seemed at times more than he could bear. A
crown of thorns he hardly deserved.

There were certain compensations, to be sure: power
and money, a sprawling plantation outside St. Louis,
and a promising political career should he play his cards
right. The very things he sought in life, and to no small
degree, had already realized. Yet the road seemed littered with obstacles, each more irksome that the last,
and he sometimes wondered if the toil and turmoil
weren't too stiff a price for what he sought.

Smith, Jackson, and Sublette were a case in point.
Bad enough that he was constantly badgered by Hudson's Bay and American Fur. But this sterling trio was
an aggravation he hardly needed. Smith and his brigade

were off galavanting around in California, for no reason anyone had yet been able to discover, except that Smith wanted to see what was on the other side of the mountains, and had lost a full year's trapping merely to satisfy his curiosity. It defied belief!

Not that the other partners were any better. Sublette had notions of becoming a great entrepreneur, flitting back and forth between St. Louis and the mountains like a molting butterfly. Then there was Davey Jackson, the workhorse, the fairhaired boy of Rocky Mountain Fur, except when his bloodlust was aroused, which seemed to occur with increasing regularity. This year it had been directed at the Blackfeet, with admirable results. Not many beaver, but loads of dead Blackfeet.

That was the trouble with this threesome in a nutshell. Not many beaver. They appeared to look upon trapping as a hobby, a pastime to be pursued when there was nothing better to do, like exploring California or playing the great tycoon or chasing off on some bloody vendetta. Rather than partners operating a business, they were three very dissimilar individuals leading their brigades when and where it suited their fancy.

All of this was something he should have foreseen years ago when he sold them the company. At the time, it had seemed a very shrewd gambit on his part. The great profits were in trade goods, so he would concentrate his energies on that end of the business. Let them run the trapping operation, which they had done from the start anyway, and each spring he would reap another harvest of pelts. There was only one thing he had overlooked. The missing link, and perhaps the most important element of all: leadership.

Without someone to guide them and divert them from their own follies, they had simply reverted to what they were the day he hired them on the St. Louis wharves. Misfits. Vagabonds. Backwoods riffraff, who had no ambition beyond their next meal, and lacked even the vision of the lowly pack rat. Granted, they made superb mountain men when led by someone with a strong hand. But left to their own devices they were like small children in a candy store, unable to decide which flavor looked best, they merely gorged their eyes and departed no wiser for the experience.

The proof could be found in black and white in the company ledgers. The partners had seen lots of geography in the last year but they hadn't trapped many beaver: seventy packs between the three brigades. Less than a hundred plews per man. Roughly $35,000 market value in St. Louis.

To be sure, that meant close to $14,000 in his own pocket, but it wasn't enough, not nearly enough if he was to fight the likes of Astor and Hudson's Bay. Wars cost money, and he was rapidly discovering that defending an empire drained the treasury faster than building one. The firm of Smith, Jackson & Sublette was in for a rude awakening. While he didn't resent masterminding the war, he was damned if he meant to fight it single-handed. They could start pulling their own chestnuts out of the fire and trapping beaver in earnest, instead of gawking about the mountains as though tomorrow would never come. Otherwise he might just wash his hands of the whole mess and enter politics a bit sooner than he had planned.

Reflecting further, Ashley decided there were any number of people about to get their ears boxed, particularly a mulatto upstart who had gotten too big for his britches. Some things a man could overlook in subordinates. Lack of vision and whimsical attitudes were common flaws of character. But insolence could not be tolerated. When a commander issued an order, there was no discussion. Nor any argument, either. And by the great God Jehovah, when William Ashley said the Indians would drink whiskey, that meant all Indians, Crows included.

The most unusual Crow of them all walked through the door right at that moment. Ashley had heard about

Beckwith's startling appearance, but even then, he wasn't quite prepared for the effect it created in person. Somehow it put him in mind of a traveling tent show. That was it! Some sort of glorified freak, the mulatto had obviously come unhinged. At the very least, gone eccentric. Living among the Indians apparently had its drawbacks, even for a colored man.

"Have a seat, Beckwith." The trader's tone was firm but not patronizing. "You seem to have changed somewhat since our last meeting."

The black man lowered himself to the ground, flourishing the hairlocks with a sweep of his arm. "Cap'n, I reckon there's a whole heap o' people got that feelin'."

Ashley blinked in spite of himself. The surly bastard still refused to address him by his proper rank. There was no end to the man's insolence. More than that, he was flaunting himself like an ignorant savage. "Perhaps you misunderstood me last summer. My orders were to bring the Crows into our camp. I said nothing about you becoming an Indian."

"Well, ye know what the wise ol' owl said, Cap'n. If ye wants to beat'em, there ain't no better way than to jine'em."

The trader bit off his reply. Something was askew here. Beckwith wasn't just insolent. He was cocky, very sure of himself for some reason. It was written all over him: the smirk on his face, his offhand manner. Whatever the cause, his wings would have to be clipped in short order.

"Beckwith, before we go any further, let's get a few things straight. First and foremost, like every man in the brigades, you are obligated to the company for its protection and support. Without the company you couldn't exist. That means, whether you like it or not, you will take orders just like everyone else. Now, as to this matter of the Crows. From your attitude, and the few things I've heard, you have evidently done a good job. Don't let it go to your head, though. Otherwise you might find yourself back on the docks wrestling cotton bales. There are any number of men in the brigades who could take your place with the Crows. And do just as good a job, if not better. Perhaps that's something you should consider before it's too late."

The black man chuckled, shaking his head. "Cap'n, ye done got a bear by the tail and ye don't even know it. Whyn't ye try sendin' another man over to the Crows? See what happens to him. I 'spect it'd turn out to be quite a race."

"What is that supposed to mean?"

"Why, jest that they'd skin him alive, lessen he could outrun'em. Leastways they would if'n it looked like somebody was holdin' me over here against my will. Y'see, they've sort of taken a shine to me. Don't that beat all, though, the way Injuns get to likin' a man!"

"Don't bank too much on that, Beckwith. I heard how they adopted you into the tribe, but Crows are just like other Indians. If I offered them a few trinkets, they wouldn't bat an eyelash over you. Throw in a few blankets and they might even offer to skin you themselves."

"Wal, Cap'n, if ye really think that, then I reckon ye oughta try it. Might make the most spectacular Rendeevous any of us ever seen."

Ashley chewed his lip for a minute, considering it. Then he backed off. Something warned him that the mulatto wasn't bluffing. "Perhaps your influence is greater than I suspected. At least I assume the stories are true. That it was you who stopped the Crows from trading for whiskey?"

"Yep. That was my doin', right enough. They'll trade, but it won't be fer no sore head and a rotten gut."

"Suppose I ordered you to trot back over there and tell them the whiskey barrel is open to all comers? That might put a different light on things, mightn't it?"

The black man smiled lazily, and stretched himself like a big cat. "Cap'n, ye said somethin' else awhile ago that needs dustin' off. That part 'bout me takin' orders like ever'body else. Y'see, that ain't the way it is no more. I ain't exactly givin' orders, ye understand, but I ain't exactly take'em neither."

"In other words, you're no longer working for the company. You're working for the Crows."

"Wouldn't say that neither. Fact is, I'm workin' fer myself. Figger that way I can do us all some good. You, me, and the Crows."

Ashley took a tight rein on his temper and then made another stab at gaining the upper hand. "Beckwith, has it ever occurred to you that I might just refuse to trade with the Crows on any terms? Now, tell me, what would that do for your standing? Sort of put you in a bad spot, wouldn't it?"

"Cap'n, lemme ask ye somethin'. How many packs of fur did the brigades bring in this time?"

"Just to be blunt about it, that's none of your business."

"What if I told ye I already know? Seventy packs. Nary a plew more."

"I would still say it's none of your business."

"What if I told ye the Crows have got fifty-three packs waitin' acrost the way? Think that'd interest ye?"

"I . . . I" The trader was nonplussed. But his mind still functioned, and it clicked out a figure that nearly doubled the year's profits.

"Now, what if I told ye the Crows'll only deal through me? Jest me. Wouldn't that make ye feel a heap better 'bout the way things is headed?"

"Jim, I don't know what to say." Ashley shrugged and smiled sheepishly, trying his best not to look the fool. "Obviously I have misjudged you. I mean . . ."

"Naw, ye ain't misjudged me, Cap'n. I'm workin' fer me first, and you and the Crows is runnin' a close second."

Ashley's smile faded, and a guarded look came over his eyes. "I see. Exactly what is it you want?"

"I want all the trade muskets ye packed in this trip."

"All! That's impossible. I wouldn't have any left for the other tribes."

"That's what she biles down to, Cap'n. Sure 'nough. And next Rendeevous I want a load of rifles. Not fusees, ye understand. Rifles."

The trader studied him intently for a moment. "Yes, I do understand. You've got some idea of making the Crows more powerful than the other tribes. Am I correct?"

"Somethin' like that. Leastways strong enough to hold what's their own."

"What about the ten percent I promised you? Let's see, on fifty-three packs—assuming they're prime, of course—that would come to almost three thousand dollars."

The black man grinned, just a hint of embarrassment showing in his eyes. "Count what needs be toward the fusees, with enough powder and lead to last the winter. Use what's left for them rifles. Make 'em good rifles, too, Cap'n. Not Hawkens especially, but good all the same."

Ashley matched his grin. "Yes, I see it quite clearly now. Very shrewd. The Crows are free to trade their own plews, and the muskets are a present from you. Which makes you their benefactor, correct?"

"I dunno. But if that means they owe me, then I 'spect it's close to the mark."

The trader nodded. Things clearly weren't as they should be. Certainly not as he would have liked. Still, with just the right tack, he might yet salvage what was needed most.

"Beckwith, I congratulate you on playing your hand with skill. I have a feeling the Crows will do very well under your influence. Very well, indeed. But let me remind you that we still face a common danger, one which could destroy your standing with the Crows just as quickly as it could Rocky Mountain Fur. I refer to our opposition generally, but to American Fur most specifically. Now listen closely."

The danger outlined by Ashley needed little exaggeration. American Fur had penetrated deeply into the mountains, far deeper than anyone could have suspected a year back. Their factor, Kenneth McKenzie, had already signed a trade pact with the Blackfeet and built a fort downstream from the Great Falls of the Missouri. Even now, another fort was under construction some miles above the mouth of the Yellowstone. Which meant that John Jacob Astor's tentacles were spreading surely and inevitably into the heart of the mountains. According to Ashley's spies, plans were afoot for yet a third trading post. This one to be erected next spring where the Big Horn emptied into the Yellowstone. Square in the country of the Crows! How American Fur meant to reconcile that with the Crows was anyone's guess. But of one point there was no uncertainty whatever. Unless American Fur was stopped, and stopped hard, their greed would consume everything and everyone south of the Missouri.

Ashley concluded with a scheme that had occurred to him even as he talked. The perfect solution to their problem. "We need each other, Beckwith, and despite what you've said, I feel you still have a spark of loyalty for the company. Now what I'm going to propose isn't stated as an order. Let's say it is more in the form of a suggestion. Something which will serve our mutual interests. I would like for you to influence the Crows—persuade them if need be—that they have good reason to raid the fort on the Yellowstone. Burn it to the ground and scatter the ashes. That's the only language American Fur understands. Of course, as I said, it's merely a suggestion. The choice is yours. But I remind you again, unless strong action is taken now, everyone in the mountains, the Crows included, will wind up on Astor's string."

The black man didn't say anything for a long while.

Instead he took the idea apart and examined it inside
and out. Though it galled him, he finally had to admit
that Ashley was right. There was no other solution. Not
for him or the Sparrowhawks.

"Cap'n, I reckon we got ourselves a deal. Ye scratch
my back and I'll burn yore fort. 'Pears to me, that's sort
of how the stick floats."

Rendezvous was nearing its end. The trading was done,
the whiskey barrels were empty, and the mountain men
had gone wobbly in the knees. Swilling firewater and
whoring among the squaws had taken its toll, no question about it. But it was the brawling and roughhouse
games that finally laid the trappers low. Every man in
camp seemed to be sporting a busted head, along with
an assortment of cuts, bruises, and oddly discolored
lumps. The general feeling was that everybody could
stand a little rest. The trade fair had been a whopping
success, maybe the best ever, but there was a time to call
it quits. One more day of such hilarity and men were
liable to start keeling over like flies.

While the mountain men would depart Rendezvous
with a sackful of recollections—old Pete Spence getting
himself fried to a crisp was pretty good for openers—
there was one story that would be told and rehashed
over every campfire of every brigade in the long winter
to come. It was the tale of Jim Beckwith, former mountain man, lately turned red nigger. Not that everyone
called him that to his face. But it was the term they used
openly among themselves. Particularly after they got
wind of his Crow name, and a loose translation of what
it meant: someone who has killed with his bare hands.
Which in itself sort of paled up next to the scalplocks
jangling on his sleeves.

Then there was the matter of those muskets. Beckwith became something pretty close to genuine, dyed-in-
wool nobility when he presented the Crows with fifty
spanking new fusees. From the looks of things—the

dance and the big feast they held in his honor—the Crows weren't far short of setting him at the right hand of White Bear himself. But the rest of the tribes were burned to a cinder. When they found out the Crows had made some underhanded deal for all the muskets in camp, it came near touching off a war. Ashley had finally cooled them down by promising a whole caravan of fusees at next year's Rendezvous, but it had left a sour taste in everybody's mouth.

The mountain men were just as sore over the deal as anybody else, though for reasons all their own. They resented the Crows deeply, and had since the fur trade started. Trappers weren't allowed in Absaroka, and over the years those who had defied the ban simply disappeared like Ed Rose, never to be heard from again. The Crows weren't exactly hostile, but then they weren't the friendliest of creatures either. They just meant business, and in an eerie sort of way they made their word stick.

Beckwith's adoption by the Crows had merely added fuel to the fire. What he had pulled off was something no other mountain man would even attempt—not sober anyway—and it grated on them to be put in the shade by a colored. They begrudged him his nerve and were rankled by his cool arrogance, the way he flaunted those scalplocks and all the gut-eater doodads he'd hung on himself. Then there was that little matter of the whiskey. It wasn't just the Crows that weren't drinking. Neither was Beckwith. He flat refused to touch the stuff, even when somebody got to feeling mellow and offered him a cup. Which wasn't very damned often, not the way he turned them down cold, like maybe he was too good for such as them, leastways since he'd become some kind of high muckamuck with the Crows. All in all, it was bitter as bear piss, and just about as hard to swallow.

But the last straw had been the pony, the one he bought for his squaw.

Word had got around that Beckwith had himself a woman down in the Crow village, but nobody thought anything about it at first. Lots of mountain men had squaws, and if that's how a fellow's stick floated then it was his own lookout. Then the trappers finally got a gander at Still Water one day and it fairly set them back on their heels.

Unlike other tribes, the Crows wouldn't sell their women to mountain men, either as whores or wives. Trappers were accustomed to sleeping with some pretty ripe meat—the pug-nosed brutes invariably offered for hire at Rendezvous—and up beside them Still Water looked like a fairy princess. She was trim and small, just a girl actually, but round in all the right places. Her face was a bright little oval, with a button nose and the devilish eyes that put thoughts in a man's head. She was clean and neat, always decked out in snazzy doeskins, and wherever she walked there lingered behind a faint scent of horsemint and wild flowers.

She was what every mountain man dreamed about on cold wintry nights. Huddled alone beneath the robes, just him and his aching pud, she was the picture he conjured up to take the edge off his miseries. What bothered the trappers about Still Water wasn't that she actually existed outside their dreams, or even that they couldn't have her. Their hackles came up because the black man had burst the bubble on yet another of their illusions.

Their resentment went deep on this, not that he was forking her, necessarily, but simply that he had her. Their dream. Somehow things would never be the same again at Rendezvous.

To be sure, the gut-eaters would still pack in the hogmeat they rented out by the hour. Whoring was an institution with the Indians, part of their economy. Wives and daughters were brought to Rendezvous by the master of the lodge the same as he brought his furs, for trade. The trinkets men paid for a few minutes' humping and pumping—a handful of beads, some awls or bells—meant no more than the act itself. When they got up and walked away, it had no more meaning than if they had splattered their seed on the ground. Later was what counted. Those winter nights, when they could evoke the dream and imagine how it would have been with her. But now there wasn't any dream. Beckwith had her.

The pony had merely compounded their envy, somehow rubbing salt into the wound. The Nez Perce bred a special kind of horse, known throughout the mountains as a Pelouse. It was solid in color, except for the distinctive spotted rump, and highly prized by Indians and whites alike. So one of these animals didn't come cheap. The Nez Perce bartered off only so many ponies each year, and the price they asked was closely akin to a pound of flesh. Nobody else bred horses such as this, and since the Nez Perce refused to sell a stallion, probably nobody ever would. That meant the western tribe could pretty well dictate its own terms, and to buy one of these spotty-rumped ponies generally took a man's catch for the entire year. It was hardly a decision to be made lightly.

Beckwith bought one for his woman. The kind of horse any man would have traded his soul to own, the mulatto gave to his squaw with the casual generosity of a trapper throwing trinkets to the whores. While the mountain men didn't understand it fully, they sensed that in some way they had been shamed, very likely on purpose. Just another little trick to make Beckwith look like a boar grizzly among a bunch of sheep. Everybody knew, of course, that the sheep were the white ones.

The lid blew off the last afternoon of Rendezvous. Everyone knew that everybody had to take a crack at Beckwith. Any man who set himself up that high was bound to draw flies, and trouble. The only real question was who among them had balls enough to tangle with the sledge-shouldered mulatto. Hardly anyone was surprised when it turned out to be Micah Johnson.

The black man had walked over to the company encampment to invite Doc Newell to supper. The Crows were pulling out in the morning and it somehow seemed right that this last evening should be spent with the old trapper. Clusters of mountain men were lolling about on the ground, nursing the last of their whiskey, and the talk fell off as he came into view. When he stopped in front of Newell, the trapper gave him the high sign, trying to warn him, but it was too late.

"Hey thar, boy. Ye in the fancy skins. The red niggah."

The black man turned and found Micah Johnson watching him with a grinning sneer. "Ye talkin' to me, Johnson?"

"Shore, I'm talkin' to ye. Ain't no other red niggah hereabouts. Now what I wanted to say is that I been watchin' that squaw of yores."

"That a fact?"

"That's a fact. Looks real ripe, she does. Though this bein' the last night and all, I'd jest rent her out fer the whole dang night. What d'ye think of that?"

The black man smiled, glad to have it out in the open at last. Johnson was big and strong, a bruising scrapper, grained clear through with a mean streak, the kind who enjoyed punishing other men and went out of his way to cripple them. The mountain men walked easy around Johnson, for given half an excuse, he would just as soon kill as fight. Which meant he would do very nicely. He was just the sort to demonstrate what the black man had in mind.

"Crow women ain't fer hire."

"Aw, shit! Don't be bashful, boy. C'mon, now. How much ye want to let me flush the birds out o' that little gal's nest?"

"Tell ye what, Johnson. She's yores when ye get past me. Any special way ye want yore whippin'?"

Johnson laughed and scrambled to his feet. "Why, niggah boy, whatever way ye can dish it out suits me jest fine."

"How 'bout knives and hatchets?"

"Waugh! The red niggah wants to play fer keeps." Johnson's smile slackened for just a moment, then came back as if plastered across his mouth. "That makes this chile shine, ol' coon. Makes him shine!"

"Whooiieee! Waugh! Waugh! Waugh!" Doc Newell jumped up and began a lumbering dance around the other trappers. "Ye bird-brained bastards wouldn't listen to me, would ye? Now yore gonna see what makes 'em come. Red nigger, huh! Ye know what that boy is? He's a nest of hornets and a grizzly b'ar all stirred up in the same pot. Sting ye to death and eat ye whole, that's what he does. Get ready to meet yore maker, Johnson! When he gets through gnawin' on yore bones ye won't know whether to spit, shit, or swaller."

The old trapper's bellowings attracted mountain men and Indians from every quarter, and within minutes a large crowd had formed around the antagonists. Both men stood ready, facing one another, their weapons in hand. Now it was only a matter of who made the first move.

The black man felt loose and easy, with not a nerve in his body. Clasped in his right hand was a ten-inch shaft of steel, honed to a razor edge on both sides. The war axe was held in his left hand, to be used mainly in blocking the other man's blows. Micah Johnson was partial to the hatchet—he liked the crunching sound when the blade struck bone—and his weapons were reversed. Axe in the right hand, knife in the left.

They began circling, looking for an opening. Suddenly the black man made a crosswise swipe with his knife, striking for the gut. Johnson gave ground, then realized too late that the blow had been only a feint. The blade was streaking upwards toward his throat. The trapper jerked his head back at the last instant and the razored tip traced a shallow arc across his chest. First blood had been drawn.

The circling began again, each man moving clockwise in a slow shuffle.

Johnson swung his hatchet for the head, followed quickly with a knife thrust, and in a blur of motion brought the axe around in an overhead chop. The black man shifted and dodged, avoiding the first two blows. But his own axe came up too late to fully deflect the third and Johnson's hatchet laid his forehead open to the bone. Blood spurted, slinging a red veil over his left eye. Instinctively he attacked, before Johnson could press the advantage. Thrusting out with the knife, he drove for the throat, forcing the other man to retreat. They backed off, both dripping blood, then circled and closed again.

Johnson rushed once more, his arms windmilling the air as he cunningly reversed the pattern. First came the knife, trailed by a feint with the axe, and on its heels came the knife again. The black man gave ground, warding off blows, completely blinded now in one eye. Before he could regain his stance, Johnson switched and led off with the hatchet. Off-balance, stumbling backwards, the black man took a glancing blow on the hip, but with such impact that it dropped him to his knees. Even as he went down he felt the trapper's knife pass within a whisker over his topknot and saw the hatchet being swung high for the death blow.

The black man thrust his war axe overhead and felt the clash of steel on steel as Johnson's downward chop was blocked. Then, ducking low, all in one motion, he ripped out and across with the knife. Something warm and sticky flooded over his arm, and he heard Johnson scream. The trapper dropped his weapons and staggered backwards, clutching at his gut. The blade had opened him clean across the middle, rib to rib, and his intestines began slipping through his fingers like long gray worms. His eyes bulged, veined through with shock, and his mouth worked in a hoarse rattle.

"Finish me, ye fuckin' niggah. Finish me!"

The black man struggled to his feet, switching the war axe to his right hand. Stepping forward, he calmly swung the axe in a gleaming arc and sunk it to the haft in Johnson's neck. The stench came as the trapper's bowels voided, and he toppled to the earth in a pool of offal and blood.

Staring down at him, the black man's chest heaved as he sucked in a great draught of air. Then he wiped the blood from his eyes and looked around at the hushed mountain men. After a moment he grunted, and his voice came in a woozy benediction.

"He should've had better luck."

Newell came to his side, supporting him under the shoulders with a strong arm, and a path opened before them through the crowds. They moved off, staring straight ahead, walking slowly toward the Crow lodges in the distance. Behind them the shadows deepened, and the sun went down over the river in a watery splash of orange and gold.

Rendezvous on the Green had come—and gone.

Bloody Hand and his Dog Soldiers led the People north, scouting ahead of the column as it wound along the banks of the Sandy. Despite the protest of Still Water and White Bear, he had refused to lay over at the Rendezvous site. Their arguments had fallen on deaf ears, countered by the black man's dogged logic. To postpone departure from the Green would only delay the Tobacco Planting ceremony, which in turn would steal time from the raiding season. The welfare of no individual, least of all a pipe-holder, should be allowed to disrupt the Sparrowhawks' ancient rites. Besides, his wounds would mend just as fast on the trail, perhaps even faster since his nostrils would no longer be offended by the *tibo* stench.

Still Water had obediently followed his directions. The gash on his forehead and the deeper wound on his hip had been stitched closed with an awl and sinew thread. Afterwards, the girl mixed a poultice of herbs and moist tobacco, and bound it over the cuts with clean rabbit skin. Next morning the black man mounted his pony as if nothing had happened and rode off with the Dog Soldiers. Like finely tempered steel, his body proved resilient and tough, and whatever pain he suffered remained his own secret.

The first day's march had been hard on Bloody Hand, more than he cared to admit. The wound in his hip was particularly sensitive on horseback, and several times he had been forced to grit his teeth against the pain. Sometime after midday, he began cursing his own stubborn pride, and wishing for a soft bed of robes to ease his tortured rump. Sundown seemed further away with each jouncing stride of his pony, and never before had the comforts of a lodge appeared so inviting. Still, he would make it through somehow, out of pure cussedness if nothing else. Tomorrow would be easier, and the day after easier yet. There was no doubt in his mind whatever that it would be just so, for each step northward took him that much closer to Absaroka.

The thought alone was a balm, easing the discomfort enough so that his hours in the saddle became bearable, if not pleasant. Oddly enough, he felt like a man going home, as though he had been on a long, grueling trip, and now, his errand accomplished, was returning to the land of his people. Stranger still, he found nothing the least bit queer about the idea. Absaroka was his home, perhaps the only one he had ever known, the home he had searched for across half a continent and the span of a decade.

Behind he left nothing worth the claiming, neither his place among the mountain men nor the identity of the one called Beckwith. *Waugh!* Above all else, it was good to leave that mulatto woods colt behind. Maybe forever, and high time, too. Across the shiny mountains, in the land of the Sparrowhawks, he was somebody else, the man he wanted to be. Perhaps the man some greater power had intended him to be all along.

The image that leaped to mind made him chuckle. Some grand old man of the spooks—God or the One Above or whatever name he went by—taking the bother to arrange things nice and neat for a lone black man. Not very likely. Yet not altogether impossible, either, despite what he might once have thought. Some things, as he had learned from Strikes-Both-Ways, couldn't be explained. Only accepted.

Still and all, such riddles were best left to the ancients. They had a fondness for the mysteries and miracles and holy hocus-pocus that couldn't be explained. What he believed in was facts. Certainties.

The greatest certainty of all was that Jim Beckwith hadn't departed the Green River Rendezvous. He had been left behind. If not in body, at least in spirit. Now there was only Bloody Hand, the Dog Soldier pipeholder, a Sparrowhawk returning gratefully and none too soon to his people, to Absaroka.

The dark one's ruminations came to an end as a warrior appeared from the east and rode toward him. It was Charges Strong, sub-leader of the Dog Soldiers. Bloody Hand reined in, thankful for a moment's respite from the fiery throb in his rump.

"Kahe, Charges Strong," he called in greeting. "Your smile would have me believe that all goes well."

"Kahe, my leader." The warrior's smile broadened as he halted his pony alongside the gelding. "I have ridden with our scouting parties on both flanks and to the front. There was Shoshone sign to the west, but very old. Otherwise nothing."

"That is good, but to be expected. Raiding season is not yet upon us."

Charges Strong grinned in the joking way. "The Dog Soldiers thought that also, my leader. Until they saw your raid of yesterday on the *tibo* camp."

The dark one chuckled softly at the jest. "Fighting

merely to kill is tiresome business. What honor is there in that for a warrior? As you can see, brother, I collected not even a strand of hair for my trouble."

"Still, it was a fight the Sparrowhawks will recount with much pride, my leader." The warrior's gaze filled with respect, and a moment elapsed before he spoke again. "You will see for yourself very soon. The People will sing praises of the Dog Soldier leader. They will say your medicine is second to none in all of Absaroka."

Bloody Hand was staring north, toward the high country, almost as if he had heard only the last word spoken. "*Ae.* It will be good to see home again."

The dark one reined his pony about and Charges Strong fell in alongside. Like burnished flecks of metal drawn to some distant lodestone, they rode toward the mountains.

CHAPTER 7

Bloody Hand was merely an observer at the Tobacco Planting ceremony, but an honored observer, for the rite itself was somehow overshadowed by his very presence. The dark one was now hailed as a leader of leaders among the *Apsahrokee,* second only to White Bear himself.

Never before had the People enjoyed such wealth. Though it was measured in *tibo* foofaraw rather than horses, they were nonetheless elated. Upon returning from Rendezvous, the trading party had distributed great quantities of trade goods amongst the warrior societies: Knives and fancy tomahawk-pipes for the men, black kettles and fuzzy wool blankets for the squaws, beads and bells and vermilion. Coffee and salt, and that rarest of all treats, sugar. There was laughter and merriment in every lodge. Like children presented with a treasure of gifts, the Sparrowhawks were beside themselves with joy. Even the warriors strutted about the village, making a great show of their new finery. Forgotten now were the months of wading icy streams, and the drudgery of tending traplines, for every man in the *Acaraho* band was suddenly rich, in a way he had never before imagined.

Yet it was Bloody Hand's gift that dazzled the People most.

Fifty muskets, along with many packloads of lead and powder, were distributed equally among the warrior societies. While the dark one could have claimed all the weapons for his Dog Soldiers, he chose instead to share them in a spirit of harmony and good will. The grandeur of the gesture left the Sparrowhawks dazed, for it was at once magnanimous and equitable.

Some said it was akin to a man giving away his entire pony herd, and throughout the village there was much talk of Bloody Hand's sense of loyalty, not to clan, or warrior society, or even self, but to the people as a whole. Until his gift, there had been less than a hundred muskets scattered amongst the men of the *Acaraho* band.

Still, it was the squaws, even more than the warriors, who sang the dark one's praises. The gewgaws and trade goods brought back from Rendezvous lent an added sparkle to their otherwise drab and toilsome lives. Wherever they gathered, the women spoke of him in terms normally reserved for the fathers of their children. Or, if there was small likelihood of being overheard, they employed words better suited to their lovers. Almost as if he had come among them one by one, in the dark of night, and left their lodges filled with gifts. Just as a secret admirer might do.

It made a pleasant daydream, though one not without substance in the minds of many squaws. Had Bloody Hand played the love flute some moonlit night, there were more than a few who would have followed without a backward glance.

Yet of all the women in the village, the one least captivated by the black man's charm was Pine Leaf. Not that she was any less susceptible than the others, or any less impressed with his rise to prominence. She simply had too much pride to let it show. She had set her own marriage price, though in looking back it now seemed an act of childish spite, and she would hold to it regardless. Even if it meant ending her days as a *makukata*.

One of the juiceless old crones never able to snare a man.

Which was exactly where it might end, unless Bloody Hand was prompted to speed things along. Clearly there wasn't another warrior in Absaroka who had any intention of courting her. The risks attached to collecting a hundred scalps apparently outweighed whatever reward she might bring to the wedding couch. That being true, it was Bloody Hand or nothing. Already she had sixteen snows behind her, and with but a few more, she would be too old to demand even twenty ponies, much less fivescore hairlocks.

Reflecting on it, she decided it might be well to give the dark one a bit of encouragement. Particularly since he already had one wife, and could afford another whenever the mood struck him. Virgins were scarce but hardly unobtainable. As evidenced by the fact that a girl from the *Minesepere* band had been elected by the Tobacco Planters this year. Perhaps that, more than anything else, goaded her to action. The morning after the field-burning ceremony, she arranged to pass along the riverbank just as Bloody Hand finished his bath.

The black man stepped from the water and stopped, staring at her with a quizzical smile. While the Sparrowhawks paid little attention to nakedness, he was acutely aware of his condition, somewhat unnerved that his pecker might react and start doing tricks. But he just stood there, waiting for her to make the first move. Plainly she had come this way on purpose, and he wasn't about to jump into his breechclout like some *tibo* greenhorn.

Pine Leaf took her time about looking him over. Though she appeared poised and remote as a star, her mind was awhirl with wonder. *It* was bigger than anything the squaws had imagined in their vulgar jests. Much bigger. Thick and long like the pole of a stallion. The sight of it brought a wetness between her legs, and it was all she could do not to stare. His smile somehow made the moment even worse, and it bothered her that he hadn't said anything, not even a greeting. Then it dawned on her. He intended to make her speak first.

"I was on my way to gather berries when I saw you bathing."

He just nodded, still smiling.

"I stopped only to thank you for the good you have brought to the *Apsahrokee*. The People honor Bloody Hand and sing his praises."

"And does Pine Leaf honor me also?"

There was a hint of mockery in his voice, but she couldn't be sure. "All in Absaroka honor you. Could a mere girl do less?"

"Ai! It is a good question." The black man cocked his head and studied her a moment. "Today you call yourself a mere girl, yet one snow past, you felt yourself worth the lives of a hundred warriors. There is a contradiction in that. Or have you grown humble with age?"

"Bloody Hand jests with me. That I honor you does not mean I have changed. I am the same."

"The same? If that were so, it would mean you honored me the day I sought you for wife."

"Perhaps it is so. Do you find that strange?"

"Ae. Strange indeed. You sent me away and set a price on yourself that no man in memory has paid."

"Perhaps the price itself was the honor. Would Bloody Hand be content with a woman any warrior could buy? I thought you more than a simple stealer of horses."

He grunted, no longer smiling. "Then you still consider yourself worth a hundred scalps?"

Her gaze fell, clung for a moment to his groin, then lifted again to his face. "It is a question you must decide for yourself. I have much to give, but the man who would be my *batsire* must be worthy of it."

The dark one felt a stiffening between his legs, knowing even as it happened that her eyes had lingered on him for just that purpose. The girl's boldness had caught him off-guard, her look touching him with the warmth of a caress. He fought against it, gritting his teeth, and the hardness slowly turned inward upon itself, softening.

"Pine Leaf talks in riddles. Would a man be more worthy because he brings a hundred scalps to the wedding couch instead of twoscore?"

She looked away, suddenly unable to meet his stare. "Let Bloody Hand answer his own question. Would he cheapen himself before the People? Have them say that he was not warrior enough to fulfill the vow?"

"*Ai!* You strike deep for a mere girl." The black man pursed his lips and shrugged. "Still, there is truth in your words. I would not change this thing between us, even if you willed it so."

"When the squaws tease me, my reply is the same. That Bloody Hand is not a man to weaken when the path grows steep."

"Yet what if I were to go under along the way? There is no certainty that the next man, or even the last, will not claim my scalplock. What then?"

"Then we would both have lost. For on that day, I too would begin to wither as the leaves in the Geese-Going Moon."

"Perhaps we should not risk all on such a hazardous sport."

"I do not understand."

The black man's smile returned. "It comes to me that we should perhaps sample what the other has to offer. Then, should misfortune overtake me, we would have that much at least to carry with us."

Pine Leaf laughed, and her eyes flashed wickedly. "Why should a man trade for a pony when he can ride free?" The pink tip of her tongue played across her lips. "Hurry, Bloody Hand. There are things you have never known which await our wedding night. But take care." Her eyes flicked downward, again caressing him in warmth. "Such a prize should not be lost even before it is won."

Then she was gone, swinging her hips shamelessly as she marched off down the river trail. The dark one watched after her, tiny needles of fire prickling his body as her buttocks jounced and swayed beneath the soft buckskin.

Waugh!

Before the swelling throb could stiffen further, he stepped into his breechclout and took off toward the village.

Enough was enough, leastways for one day anyhow.

The Dog Soldiers gathered in their lodge as darkness settled over the Wind River encampment. It was The Moon of Fat Horses, symbolic heralding of raiding season. Since ancient times it had been so, and throughout Absaroka the warrior societies were organizing as had their fathers and their father's fathers before them.

It was the way, and none among the Sparrowhawk doubted its wisdom.

Nor were the Dog Soldiers unprepared for Bloody Hand's summons. While it was a few days earlier than customary—the half-eaten moon had not yet shown—they came expecting talk of war. The dark one was restless, as everyone knew, and he wasn't a man to be curbed by tradition.

Among themselves the Dog Soldiers joked in a lighter vein. Their leader's impatience was that of a bull scenting a cow in heat. Raiding season was short, and the pipe-holder must hurry if he was to collect the needed scalps. *Ai!* His hunger for the maiden would bring much sorrow to Sparrowhawk enemies. It was truly the rage of a rutting bull, who attacked even the butterfly.

But as they entered the lodge, their jests fell silent. The dark one was not without humor, yet there were some things that ruffled his fur the wrong way. Tonight he would speak of war, and on that subject he was deadly serious. Where the glory of the Dog Soldiers was at stake, he frowned upon levity. Which was as it should be. He was the pipe-holder.

Bloody Hand waited till all were seated before he brought out the sacred pipe. He offered it first to the One Above, then the Earth, and lastly to the Four Winds. The ritual completed, he laid the pipe on a quilled bag before him and looked at the warriors. Charges Strong was seated on his left, and a full gathering of the Dog Soldiers, some forty in number, were ringed around the fire.

After looking at each man in turn, he began. "I have called you together to talk of the raiding time ahead. There is a thing which needs doing, a thing much on my mind of late. All here tonight know how fully our people honor the Dog Soldiers. The council has chosen us time and again to serve as tribal sentinels, and none among you can walk through the village without praise words being spoken. Yet it is not enough. The respect of the *Apsahrokee* for the Dog Soldiers must be increased manyfold. That is what I would see done."

The warriors glanced at one another, nodding their heads with approval. This was what they had come to hear: words of the glory days ahead, and a greater role in tribal affairs.

The Dark One hesitated only a moment before resuming. "It is no secret that the Kit-Foxes and the Ravens and all other warrior societies envy the Dog Soldiers. Even as we talk, their leaders scheme on ways to put dust in our faces, to capture the honored place we hold with the People. It is in my mind that we will strike first, while they are still haggling amongst themselves like squaws. That we will leave them choking in the dust of Dog Soldier ponies."

The words brought a swell of excitement from the warriors, but Bloody Hand motioned flat-handed for silence.

"I counsel that we set aside tradition, that we ride before the half-eaten moon rises. But it is not enough

that we ride first. We must strike a blow that will bring
wonder to the People, a blow which none but the Dog
Soldiers would dare."

With the fingers of his right hand extended and
joined, he made a slicing motion across his throat: the
Cut Throat sign.

"We must attack the Sioux!"

The Dog Soldiers muttered hoarse exclamations,
shaken by their leader's cold and somewhat unsettling
audacity. The Cut Throats were the most powerful of all
plains tribes. Their lodges easily outnumbered the Sparrowhawks two to one. To attack them as raiding season
commenced was a slap in the face. An insult which
placed them on the level of the lowly Pawnee, or the
Utes. The Cut Throats would swarm from their lodges
like angry hornets, and their pursuit would be relentless.
Only the very fortunate, or those graced by the spirit
beings, would have any hope of escape.

Kicking Bird, a coup-striker of two feathers, at last
managed to outshout his brothers. "My leader, I would
ask you a question. It is ten sleep's march to the land of
the Cut Throats. Is that not so?"

Bloody Hand nodded, just once. "That is my plan."

"That means, then, we will strike at the full of the
moon."

"That also is true."

"I ask you then, my leader, how will we escape the
Cut Throats? They will pursue us night and day. In the
time of the full moon their plains are without darkness.
We would be run to earth like crippled buffalo."

"The Cut Throats' pursuit will be short-lived. We will
lose them in the *Paha Sapa.*"

The Dog Soldiers gaped at him in stunned silence.
The Black Hills were the Holy Ground of the Sioux,
where monsters dwelled and the living dead roamed the
earth, the mountainous burial place where not even a
Cut Throat dared venture once the sun had set.

A storm of protest erupted from the warriors. Their

shouts were riddled through with disbelief, and something that bore passing similarity to fear. The lodge filled with a guttural jumble of words, like the buzzing of bees, and for a moment it was as if each man talked only to himself. Then, in a brief lull, Little Wolf overrode their angry murmuring. He was chief scout of the Dog Soldiers, a man of resourcefulness and great bravery, and they fell silent as he addressed himself to Bloody Hand.

"Batsetse, I am not afraid to die. None of us here tonight would shirk because death rides to meet us. But this thing you ask is not of the real world. It is of the other side. How can we, who are of flesh and blood, be expected to defy the unearthly ones who roam *Paha Sapa?"*

The dark one understood, perhaps better than the Dog Soldiers realized. Tales of haunts and the walking dead were hardly limited to Indians alone. Many people feared ghosts, and no more so than the blacks of his youth. It was an obstacle he had foreseen in advance.

"Little Wolf, I would answer your question with a question. Do you believe that the power of a Sparrowhawk holy man is less than that of the Cut Throat spirit beings?"

"No, my leader, I do not."

Bloody Hand let his eyes flick around the circle. "Does any man here believe that Sparrowhawk medicine can be tainted by the undead?"

The question was met with rapt silence.

"That is good, for now you have nothing to fear. This morning I sought a vision with Braided Tail, and all was made clear. The spirits of my medicine bundle directed me to lead the Dog Soldiers on a raid against the Sioux. They showed me a passage through *Paha Sapa* and assured me of great victory for the Dog Soldiers. There will be no pursuit by the Cut Throats."

Halting, he tapped the amulet dangling from his neck. Every warrior in the lodge knew what the rawhide bag contained: liver poisoned by the fanged ones, a talisman to ward off evil, and the power to stare a death sign on those who would do him harm.

"You have seen the strength of my medicine. Now you have heard my vision. Yet you are under no obligation to follow me. Those who have no wish to smoke the pipe should return to their squaws. This is not a raid for weaklings. I want only Dog Soldiers of the true faith to walk in my tracks."

Stillness fell over the lodge, broken only by the spit and crackle of the fire. Not a man moved.

Bloody Hand took up the pipe and lit it. He puffed, letting the smoke trail from his mouth, and again made offering to the spirit begins. Then, fingering the amulet for all to see, he passed the pipe to Charges Strong.

The black man was quite pleased with himself. Everything had gone off without a hitch. Just about the way he'd expected. His only regret was the extra pony Braided Tail had charged to include *Paha Sapa* in the vision.

But, what the hell! Pipe-holders weren't supposed to wind up rich anyway, just powerful. And damned hard to put in the shade.

When he stepped through the doorhole, Strikes-Both-Ways and Still Water were seated in front of the fire. The old man shot him a quizzical glance, then shrugged, waving his hand in an idle gesture.

"There is no need to tell me. I see it written across your face. The Dog Soldiers have smoked the pipe."

Bloody Hand gave him a lynx-eyed smile. "We leave with first light."

Still Water rose without a word and started gathering his war gear. Watching her, he felt a tingling glow along his spine. Tonight looked to be one long tussle once they crawled under the robes. Not that he minded. When a man went off to fight, a freshly greased pecker just naturally did something for his spirits.

Strikes-Both-Ways cocked one eye in an owlish frown

and scratched his armpit. "Your stride has quickened, my *bacbapite.*"

"The night grows late for riddles, grandfather."

"Ai! Perhaps later than you know. It is said that a spider who weaves his web too tightly catches no flies."

The black man smiled, refusing the goad. "I have no taste for flies. Have you forgotten that you taught me to think like the meat-eaters?"

"That is true. But the hunger is of your own making. The ancients tell us that men *tibo* have been known to devour themselves."

"Do you speak of greed?"

"No, my son. Ambition."

"I find that strange indeed. Unless my mind wanders, it was you who counseled me in the path to follow."

The old bowmaker scowled and shook his head. "I prepared you to become a pipe-holder. Now I see a man who hungers to become chief."

"Of the Sparrowhawks? You prattle like one touched by the moon beings."

"Are you unaware that a wedge has been driven between our bands? That Long Hair of the *Minesepere* daily grows more jealous of White Bear? Of the success our band has had with the *tibo* traders?"

Bloody Hand shrugged, fingers drifting to the deep scar on his forehead. "Let Long Hair teach his people to trap beaver."

"That is a shallow answer, unfit for a pipe-holder."

"White Bear needs no help from me." The black man snorted with disgust, glowering at Strikes-Both-Ways. "Do you believe I would attempt to bring disunity among the Sparrowhawks?"

"I would sooner cross over than believe that." The old man placed a hand on his shoulder and squeezed hard. "I want only what is good for you, my son. Whatever it is, then that too will bring me gladness. But there are those who say you aim too high, that you have rid the *Acaraho* of one chief and now you would rid us of another."

"They speak out of both sides of their mouths!"

"*Ae,* my son. I believe you. Yet even now, you break tradition by raiding before it is time. What will the forked-tongued ones say when they learn of that?"

"Let them say what they will. What I do is for the Dog Soldiers. Nothing more."

"Not for yourself? Some will say you seek only your own glory."

"What I seek," the dark one growled, "is a hundred scalps."

Still Water raised up from the food stores and gave him a cold glare. Her look said that things might not be so snuggly under the robes after all.

Strikes-Both-Ways muttered something under his breath and spit in the fire. "Take care that you do not get yourself killed over the taunts of a girl. If you must cross over, let it be for a greater cause than the hurt between your legs."

Bloody Hand grunted. "Rest easy, grandfather. The man who would lift my topknot has yet to be born."

Still Water hissed between her teeth and slung a bag of jerky in the direction of his war gear. Then she flounced across the lodge, ripped off her dress, and without so much as a look, crawled between the robes. The message was lost on no one, least of all the black man.

It was going to be a frosty night, like sleeping with a chilled rock.

Dawn of the sixth day found the raiders breaking camp along the Dry Fork of the Cheyenne. Bloody Hand took the lead and set a blistering pace. They had covered something more than thirty miles a day since departing the village, roughly tracing the Sweetwater to the head-waters of the North Platte and later swinging northward toward the Cheyenne. The warriors had grown paunchy and short of wind over the winter, and many of the older ones were hard pressed to keep up. But the black man never once slackened his stride. Hard walking under a broiling sun, would soon melt the suet off of them, restore the muscle to their guts and the wind to their lungs. Which was exactly what he had intended from the outset.

When the Dog Soldiers tangled with the Sioux they would need all the endurance and strength they could muster. He meant to see that they had plenty of both, even if it forced some of the weaker ones to fall by the wayside.

It was a thought that had been much on his mind while planning the raid. Looking back, viewing it now from the standpoint of a leader, he saw the wisdom of this ancient custom. Walking toughened a man, sharpened his reflexes and made him alert, gave him that slight edge which might save his own life and perhaps the lives of his brothers in a hard fight. Moreover, it was based on the oldest law known to man and animal alike: the fit survived, while the halt and lame fell victim to their own weakness.

Somewhere, untold generations in the past, a wise man had watched and learned from the wild things. Wolves never attacked the strong. Whether hunting deer or elk or buffalo, they surrounded the weak and the crippled, pulled them down and ate them, not because the wolves were invincible, but because their prey was weak. Mountain lions and wildcats and coyotes killed in the same way. Even the demoniac *carcajou*— the wolverine—liked to have his meals killed for him. Rather than hunt for himself, he would raid a trapline and leave behind a bloody garbage. Yet it was known that bears regularly gave ground when they crossed paths with this fierce little predator.

It was the way, both for wild things and their red brothers. The hardy survived, watching the lesson unfold before their eyes as the wolf preached from a pulpit of bones.

Bloody Hand saw it clearly now. The Sparrowhawks walked to a horse raid for a reason, perhaps the best of all reasons. The strong lived on, while the weak went under like whimpering pups.

Over the winter, in fact, many things had come clear. Not that enlightenment came easy. The Sparrowhawk way was so steeped in tradition and mysticism that it was like a mountain path shrouded in fog. Understanding dawned only when a man looked beneath what he saw, and groped instead for the cause, what had brought it about, the origin.

Like this thing of the scouts. Even now Little Wolf and his scouts ranged far ahead of the main body. They would fast until the Cut Throats were sighted, just as generations of Sparrowhawk scouts before them had fasted. But to a purpose! That was the thing Bloody Hand now saw, the reason he no longer meddled with custom.

The scout had but one goal, sighting the enemy. As long as he had sleep and water, he could function. The hunger for food passed with the second day. But with its passing came a sharpening of senses: keener eyesight, better smell, a clearing of the mind so acute it was as if he stood outside himself. Every nerve and fiber of his body was attuned to the world about him. He vibrated with intensity, strung as tight as catgut. The will of his mind focused solely on the next bush, the faraway hill, a faded track in the dust. Like the winter-gaunt wolf searching for field mice, he missed no sign, no movement, not the least scent. He had become as one with the wolf cape and skullpate he wore, a predator.

Somewhere over the winter, the black man had decided that hindsight, after all, had its place in the scheme of things. Leastways if a fellow was willing to learn from his backtrail. Not unlike most men, he mechanically rejected on first encounter the strange and unknown. But upon reflection, he had slowly grasped the most essential tenet of all. The Sparrowhawks, much like wild things, seldom did anything without purpose. Whether born of instinct or rational thought, there was some governing reason underlying even the queerest of their notions.

Some things, though, he still couldn't accept. Not that he rejected them necessarily. It was just that he hadn't figured them out as yet, and until that was done, they couldn't be accepted as gospel. The Sparrowhawk gods were a case in point. On the face of it, the whole thing was ridiculous, childish superstition fed and fostered by conniving medicine men. Yet for all their holy hocus-pocus, the witch doctors had a few tricks that left him completely befuddled.

Like Braided Tail making that grizzly appear on the riverbank. Or the screech of an owl in the smokehole and a bloody drop of dung splattering at his feet. Not to mention the fact that he had killed thirty-eight men in the past year and suffered only minor wounds in the process, almost as if the bear claw necklace, or the snake juice hanging around his neck, was watching over him after all, just as Braided Tail had foretold.

Granted, it could have been luck or coincidence or even skill, where the killings were concerned. But that left a mess of things unexplained, lots of ifs and a whole heap of maybes.

Now there was the matter of this raid. Braided Tail had sneaked the part about *Paha Sapa* into the vision only with great reluctance, even weaseled another pony for himself before he'd agree to give it a try. Yet his trance had been the real live article, just like before. After sprinkling powder in the fire and sniffing the fumes he'd floated off and had himself quite a talk with somebody. Then, when he came back, he hadn't hedged none at all. Just spit it right out, like he'd got the goods straight from the horse's mouth.

Somehow a path would be revealed through the Black

Hills. On the night of the raid, the spirit beings would loose thunder and lightning on the Cut Throats. One man among the Dog Soldiers would be killed, but his passing would be a thing of joy for all.

That last part had been a real puzzler. But then, the whole thing was enough to discombobulate a man something fierce. How the hell could the old faker be so certain? It was almost as if he had himself a window that opened up and showed all there was to know about the future. More baffling yet, what sort of spooks was he talking to when his eyes went glassy? Or was he just talking to himself? Putting on a performance in exchange for a bunch of fat ponies?

The black man would like to have believed that, except he couldn't forget the bear or the owl dung or the fact that he was still walking around full of piss and vinegar, with hardly more than a few scratches and a couple of scars as souvenirs. It wasn't that he believed Braided Tail's mumbo-jumbo, so much as he just couldn't refute it. He didn't necessarily believe, but then he didn't exactly disbelieve either.

It was confusing.

All the more so since the Sparrowhawk way left a man no choice but to play the cards dealt him. To be sure, not every step along the way was dictated by the spirit beings. But it came damn close. Too close for comfort sometimes.

Still and all, it wasn't as though a man's hands were tied. There were ways and there were ways. Some of which changed the odds more than others.

Bloody Hand was convinced that walking to a horse raid had its purpose. But wandering around on the plains afoot also had its drawbacks. Especially if a party of mounted hostiles happened to take them unawares. While the Dog Soldiers weren't too keen on the idea, he had started drilling them in a tactic employed by white men as a matter of course.

First thing in the morning, and again after the noon-

day halt, he had the warriors break column and form a
double circle. The outer ring, comprised of men armed
with bows, was required to kneel in place. The inner
circle stood, and this group was made up of warriors
who owned muskets. The idea was simple enough, but
quite effective if men on foot were attacked by a
mounted force. The warriors with muskets fired first,
and while they were reloading, the bowmen laid down a
storm of arrows. Between the seesaw waves of lead and
broadheads it generally discouraged even the most determined horsemen.

The Dog Soldiers were slightly embarrassed by the
whole affair. It wasn't the Sparrowhawk way of fighting,
and somehow smacked of *tibo* trickery. While it might
keep a man alive, it brought him little honor. Which, as
everyone knew, was the sole purpose of war. Yet their
pipe-holder persisted, and they went through the drills
with grudging listlessness. Had it been anyone but
Bloody Hand, they would have hooted him out of camp
and promptly selected another leader. That they didn't
was attributable not so much to the dark one's strength
of character as to the strength of the amulet hanging
from his neck.

Shortly after the day's march commenced, Charges
Strong moved up to walk alongside the black man. The
warriors were strung out behind in a loose column, and
from their low muttering it seemed apparent they hadn't
cared much for the morning's drill.

Charges Strong kept pace awhile, glancing at the
pipe-holder out of the corner of his eye. At last he felt
compelled to speak. "My leader, the Dog Soldiers
grumble."

"All soldiers grumble," Bloody Hand observed. "It is
their nature."

"*Ae*, that is so." Charges Strong mulled it over for a
few steps, then tried another tack. "They say this new
way brings them dishonor. That our enemies would

laugh behind their hands if they saw Sparrowhawks bunch together like frightened quail."

"Let the Cut Throats catch us afoot and the Dog Soldiers will see the wisdom of my teachings. This new way will keep them alive to fight another day. Better that, than for their spirit souls to wander the afterlife without hair."

"Batsetse, your words fall wisely on my ears. Yet the warriors are of a different mind. They say a man can not count coup when he is locked arm in arm with his brother."

"Can a dead man count coup?"

"No, my leader. A dead man can count nothing. He is only dead."

Bloody Hand pointed off in the direction they were headed. "We near the land of the Cut Throats. There the Dog Soldiers will find all the glory they seek. I have spoken, and it will be as I have said."

"Ai! I hear your words, my leader."

Charges Strong lifted his hand, as if to affirm his loyalty by gripping the dark one's shoulder. The black man leaped aside, glaring at him coldly. Charges Strong mumbled sheepish apologies, eyes downcast, and fell back to join the warriors.

Almost too late, Charges Strong had remembered the ominous warning that ended Braided Tail's prophecy. Before the raid no man must touch the dark one. Otherwise their attack on the Cut Throats would be doomed.

Charges Strong gave thanks to the One Above. The Dog Soldiers were indeed fortunate to have a leader in such close communion with the spirit beings.

The path was faintly lighted by a three-quarter moon. Ahead, the scouts led the way, seldom ranging more than a mile out front. The column moved now in single file, for the trail was narrow and overgrown with brush from disuse. Meandering eastward along a series of high ridges, it afforded a view in every direction of the bleak and foreboding landscape. Steep ravines, cut through by shallow streams, separated the ridges with maddening regularity. The path would drop abruptly into scrub-choked thickets that tore at the warriors with thorny claws. The scouts were forced to use their axes, slashing and chopping as they cleared a way through the tangled undergrowth. Then, almost magically, the path appeared again, climbing upward toward the next ridge.

It was a hostile land, *Paha Sapa*, the holiest of holy places to the Sioux.

Little Wolf had found the path. Returning to camp before dawn of the eighth day, he reported that an old, poorly marked trail wound upward from the Cheyenne into the Black Hills. He had scouted it for a distance of some miles, and though it was hard traveling, the path clearly led eastward through the mountains. Bloody Hand had asked only one question.

Was it a path suitable for use on horseback?

Little Wolf had considered a moment before observing that it would be no harder on horses than on men afoot. The scout's comment had set the Dog Soldiers to chattering excitedly. It was just as the vision had foretold! A path through *Paha Sapa* had been revealed. The horses they came to steal could be brought back over the same trail, and the Cut Throats would not dare to follow. Truly, Bloody Hand's medicine was strong beyond measure.

The black man was perhaps the least surprised of anyone in the raiding party. Though the admission came hard, he saw clearly for the first time that he had never seriously doubted the holy man's prophecy. Somehow he had known the path would be there.

Another time, perhaps only a summer past, he would have chalked his conviction off to other things. Indians had blazed trails through the western mountains for centuries. A man had only to follow the slope of the land, keeping his eye open for forage, water, and natural passes below timberline, and he was sure to find a path. Just as wild things always sought the easiest route, so it was with their Indian brothers, and game trails were frequently used by man and beast alike. Moreover, Indians seemed to have some sixth sense about direction. Never had he known a gut-eater to become lost. Plopped down in a stretch of wilderness never before seen, they would gawk around a while, then take off, walking with a certainty of direction that defied belief. Curiously, they neither understood nor questioned this gift. It was something every man was born with, like his nose, and represented no strange phenomenon whatever. They simply started off, whether horseback or afoot made no difference, and by some baffling process always wound up where they were headed.

Little Wolf might have found the path through *Paha Sapa* in just this manner, by instinct perhaps, or by a lifetime's accumulated knowledge of enemy habits, or by blind luck, even. But the black man believed none of these things.

The trail had been revealed in Braided Tail's vision with clarity, and an eerie sense of accuracy. Though the Cheyenne forked, circling the Black Hills north and south, he had said the path would be found along the lower fork. Which it was. Yet, in some way that remained unfathomable, Bloody Hand had been convinced even before his scouts found the trail. He no longer doubted the holy man's union with the supernatural.

He merely accepted it for what it was: the way.

The raiders traveled at night now, for it was known that the Cut Throats never ventured into *Paha Sapa* after dark. It was their burial grounds, revered since ancient times, yet it was also a place of evil spirits. Monsters roamed these craggy slopes, horrible beastlike creatures who devoured men whole and with great relish. Among the Sioux it was said that these fiends came forth from their caves and burrows when the sun went down, and anyone so foolish as to defy the spirits of darkness would be eaten alive, bones and all.

The more terrible fate, though, was to be caught by the living dead. These were Sioux warriors who had been mutilated in battle. Their scalps had been cut away, along with hands and eyes and sex organs, and they were consigned to walk the earth throughout eternity. Only by mutilating a living being, taking a scalp or nose or whatever part they had lost, could the undead release their spirit souls for deliverance to the Faraway Land. They stalked *Paha Sapa* in the hours of darkness, moaning the agonized wail of the risen dead. The flesh hung from their bones, and the grinning leer of death's skull marked them for what they were. It was said that when the moon was full they could be seen atop the high ridges, knives whetted, waiting to butcher their next victim.

These were thoughts much on the Dog Soldiers' minds as they themselves moved along those same ridges. While they feared nothing mortal, they had a healthy respect for another man's superstitions, and an abiding terror of the ghouls and flesh-eaters who lurked unseen in this evil place. Hacking their way through the brush-choked ravines, scrambling hand-over-hand to gain the next ridge, they rushed along the trail as if the living dead were marching them stride for stride.

Then, as the night wind stilled in the hours before false dawn, they were brought to a halt as the very earth itself trembled beneath their feet. Bunched in a tight knot, scarcely daring to breathe, they watched as a mountain to the north shuddered in violent upheaval. Within the space of a heartbeat, the mountaintop erupted in a fiery explosion, and molten jets of lava were hurled skyward in a thunderous roar. From deep within the earth came a rumbling quaver, unlike anything they had ever heard. Suddenly the mountaintop buckled and flaming geysers spewed fountains of sizzling gold down the forward slopes. Great billows of smoke leaped from the jaws of the volcano and across *Paha Sapa* came a searing blast of heat. Just as quickly as it had begun, the fiery holocaust subsided, and the Dog Soldiers felt their hackles rise as a whistling moon drifted over the high ridges.

It was the Hill of Thunder, dwelling place of the Great White Giant.

According to Sioux legend, the first white man to transgress on tribal lands had been pressed beneath the volcanic rocks as punishment. The spirit beings had imprisoned him for all time within the thunderous mountain as an example to other *tibos:* a warning that the holy ground of the Sioux should never again be violated. There he had fed on the fire and lava, until finally he became a giant so monstrous that his voice alone made the earth tremble and heave. The towering smoke cloud was said to be the White Giant's breath, rising from his burial place underneath the mountain. Strange noises in the night were thought to be his moans, as the molten rocks crushed his chest and forced life from his lungs. On occasion he was known to arise from the volcanic fires, clambering forth from the bowels of the mountain, and bathe his singed body in the winter snows. Ancient ones among the Cut Throats had seen his tracks, more than twenty feet in length, where he strode across the scarred landscape in search of some brief respite.

It was said that even the living dead and the beastlike fiends who roamed *Paha Sapa* sought refuge when the Great White Giant shook the earth.

All things considered, it was sound advice.

The Dog Soldiers, led by their pipe-holder, hurried along the ridgeline at a faster pace. While none of them doubted the strength of Bloody Hand's medicine, there seemed little to gain by putting it to the test. Better to pass on and leave the evil ones to their own business.

Ai! Far better indeed. The Cut Throats were barbarians, as all men knew. But they at least didn't belch fire.

* * *

The night was a bell jar of silence. Low clouds scudded across the sky, obscuring the full moon in a veiled overcast. Along the northern rim of the mountains, billowing thunderclouds darkened the horizon, rolling onward from ridge to ridge in relentless advance. The smell of rain swept in on a freshening wind, and the air suddenly chilled with a clammy dampness.

Bloody Hand squatted at the edge of a sheer cliff, watching the Cut Throat village below. He hadn't moved for the last hour, patiently waiting for the brewing storm to gather strength and move southward. The early hours of darkness had been spent in scouting the face of the cliff, and the narrow goat trail that led to the plains below. Then, the moon had been bright and full, a mellow globe bathing the countryside in a soft glow. The Dog Soldiers had hung back, muttering ominously among themselves. The moon was an omen, they whispered, a sign telling them that they had offended the evil spirits, warning them to be gone from this place before the unseen ones claimed them in some dread manner.

The black man had never for a moment doubted what the night would bring. Just as Braided Tail had foretold, the storm would come, laying down a cloak of thunder and lightning to cover their attack on the Sioux encampment. Moving among the Dog Soldiers, he had reassured them, calming their fears, and urged them to wait a while longer. Soon it would happen, exactly as the holy man had prophesied. Undue haste would gain them nothing. Wait and let the spirit beings work their will.

Far below the village dogs awoke, barking and growling before lifting their muzzles to the sky in a howling chorus. Bloody Hand listened, one eye cocked toward the gathering storm, and the corners of his mouth lifted in a tight smile. That was the second serenade of the night. Even without the storm, the village would now remain quiet until first light. Indian dogs instinctively

awakened twice during the night, raising an ungodly
racket. But once asleep they were notoriously poor sentinels. Staring down at the darkened village, the black
man grunted softly to himself. *Ai!* The Cut Throats
would long remember this night.

The dark one's plan of attack was daring, if somewhat
unorthodox. It centered on his certainty that the Sioux
would never expect raiders to materialize from the
Black Hills, or be so foolish as to retreat into *Paha Sapa*
in the dark of night. Earlier, when he outlined how it
would go, the Dog Soldiers themselves had been somewhat taken aback. They admired his boldness, had even
come to expect it of him. But this surprise he had
hatched for the Cut Throats was almost as unnerving on
the one who must execute it.

Thinking back to the startled looks on their faces,
Bloody Hand chuckled quietly. Still and all, he had no
qualms that they would come through when things got
down to the crunch. They were Dog Soldiers.

The wind suddenly slackened, then stopped altogether. Stillness settled over the mountainside, and the
chill air turned curiously hot and vapid. Standing, the
black man looked to the north and saw the rolling
cloudbank moving in fast. Already the sky had darkened
and the moon was but a thin silver disk high above the
murky haze. Then, off in the distance, came the low
rumble of thunder.

It was time.

Striding back to where the Dog Soldiers waited, he
motioned them in close. When they gathered around he
spoke in a clipped, guttural whisper. "Brothers, the
spirit beings have brought us our storm. We must leave
now so as to be in position when the time comes. Remember my instructions, and forget not even for a moment that you are Dog Soldiers. All in Absaroka will
praise us for this night's work. Move swiftly now, but
with caution. The Cut Throat ponies await us below."

Charges Strong and some thirty warriors moved off

toward the north, where the cliff jutted out at a height of perhaps a thousand feet. They were to descend the narrow trail, which switchbacked around several massive outcroppings, and make their way to the grassy plains far below. This great prairie stretched fifty miles to the eastward, ending at the edge of the Badlands. But the raiders had only to cover a mere fraction of that distance. The Cut Throat pony herd grazed peacefully less than a mile from the base of the mountain. Charges Strong and his party were to steal as many horses as they could manage, and drive them back up the winding, rocky path.

Bloody Hand, trailed by six warriors, struck out toward the southernmost slope of the mountain. The land dropped off rapidly in this direction, ending at a sheer granite cliff some two hundred feet above the basin floor. There, along the banks of a shallow stream, lay the Cut Throat village. According to Little Wolf and his scouts, it was a band of Oglala Sioux numbering something more than a hundred lodges.

The dark one's small force was comprised of men specially chosen for their fearlessness. Kicking Bird, a coup-stricker second only to Bloody Hand himself, was among them. Another was the Crazy Dog who had ridden with the black man on his very first raid, the night they had silenced the Arapahoe horse guards early last summer. Though the Crazy Dog was now in disgrace, having failed his vow of death in the raiding season past, Bloody Hand had selected him with no hesitation whatever. The man was a murderous fighter, as evidenced by the fact that he was still alive, a distinction of sorts for one who had actively sought death for more than a year. All of which meant he would be worth his weight in wildcats if someone stirred the Sioux out of their nests.

The black man led the way over the cliff. Their descent would be slow and dangerous, for one misstep could send a man hurtling to his death. Yet the element of surprise far outweighed the risks. The night guards

stationed around the Cut Throat village would hardly
expect an assault from the steep precipice at their backs.

But then, who would? Not even the Dog Soldiers relished a job better suited to mountain goats.

The face of the cliff was almost vertical, rising in a
straight plain from the ground below. But the rocky wall
was broken and cracked, riddled with faults from some
bygone age of violent unheaval. Grasping ridges and
cracks, anything he could get his hands on, the black
man lowered himself one step at a time. After gaining a
foothold he swung his off leg in a slow arc, feeling with
his toe for another support. Then he went down one
more step and again began searching blindly with his
toe. All the while he concentrated on keeping his body
plastered to the wall. Even without looking down, he
knew that if he leaned back so much as an inch, he
would topple over like a lead weight. Directly above
him, the Dog Soldiers came on one by one, cautiously
following his lead to each handhold and footrest in turn.
Their pace was torturously slow, and like dusky bronzed
snails they inched down the cliff in a race with death
itself.

The horse guards had been stalked and silenced and
even now the larger body of raiders was moving among
the pony herd. Charges Strong stood only a few paces
from a magnificent sorrel gelding. The horse was skittish, eyeing him warily. Snorting, it backed off a couple
of steps, then stopped and pawed the ground. Charges
Strong stooped, gathering a handful of clover, and
crushed it between his fingers. Slowly, careful of making
any sudden moves, he extended his hand. The sweet
scent of clover drifted off his fingers and the sorrel snuf-
fled, wrinkling his nostrils.

The horse came back a step, then another, stretching
his neck to reach the clover.

Charges Strong grunted deep in his chest and began
making horse talk, low muffled sounds that soothed and

lulled like a friend's greeting. The gelding nibbled at the clover, its skittishness forgotten now. The Dog Soldier advanced so slowly he appeared never to move, talking all the while in a series of soft, muted grunts. Then, as if they were of one spirit, he was standing beside the horse.

The sorrel finished eating the clover and nibbled with his lips at the lingering scent of the man's hand. Rubbing the velvety muzzle, Charges Strong leaned forward and blew softly into the gelding's broad nostrils. The horse whickered gently, eyelids fluttering, as if bewitched by this strange creature that had come to comfort him. With an imperceptible movement of his hands, Charges Strong slipped a war bridle over the sorrel's lower jaw and drew it tight. Still in a daze, the horse merely looked at him, rooted in its tracks.

Charges Strong sprang to the gelding's back, and as his knees locked in place, a white-hot shaft of lightning split the sky.

Bloody Hand drove his knife to the hilt in the night guard's spine, locking his other arm in a stranglehold over the man's windpipe. The Cut Throat thrashed and kicked for a moment, then just as suddenly slumped forward and went limp in the dark one's grip. Bloody Hand lowered the body to the ground and knelt, razoring the topknot with his knife. When he yanked, the scalp came away with a mushy pop, followed instantly by a blinding flash of light.

The lightning bolt slammed through the murky overcast and struck a nearby cottonwood with a jolting *baroom!* The pungent odor of ozone filled the air and the tree burst into flames. Suddenly a gale force wind swept down out of the north, staggering the black man. Trees along the creek bowed, then bent double, and crashed to the ground with a grinding roar. Lightning struck again and again, rending the night with a thunderous ear-splitting rumble. Rain began to fall in deafening torrents as the wind tore and shrieked through the Sioux encampment. Lodges were buffeted about like pine cones, slammed one against another, and many toppled over to leave Cut Throat families standing naked in the deluge. The fired tree near Bloody Hand sizzled and steamed, then went dead as the rain extinguished its flames.

The black man took off in a crouched run, twisting and dodging as he headed toward the path on the distant cliffside. Dim shapes began appearing out of the night, and by the time he had skirted the village, Kicking Bird, the Crazy Dog, and the remaining warriors had joined him once more. Ahead they spotted mounted Dog Soldiers yipping and howling as they drove a herd of ponies up the winding mountain trail. Bloody Hand sprinted into a dead lope, then slammed to a halt as a jagged streak of lightning bathed the earth in a brilliant silvery glow. Charges Strong loomed up directly in front of him astride the sorrel gelding, leading six ponies on rawhide war bridles.

The dark one and his men scrambled onto the horses and kicked them into a gallop toward the steep path. Somewhere behind, the muffled rattle of muskets sounded and lead whistled past them. Ducking low, Bloody Hand glanced back over his shoulder and saw a swarm of Cut Throat braves pounding after them. The Sioux were afoot, churning and pumping across the sodden prairie at a soggy pace. But they were within rifle range, and would be until the raiders hit the first switchback on the mountain trail.

The Dog Soldiers slammed their ponies in the ribs and hit the path in a thundering rush. The narrow trail forced them to ascend single file, and the steep grade slowed their mounts to a lurching upward plunge. Lead balls splattered all about them now, ricocheting off the cliff with the hissing whine of angry wasps. Kicking Bird slumped, blood spurting from his shoulder, and for a moment his pony faltered to a walk. Then he straightened, kicking the horse viciously, and the column again picked up speed. Moments later they rounded the switchback and disappeared from view.

But as they did so, Bloody Hand slid his pony to a halt, staring intently at the retreating forms.

Something was out of kilter.

There were only six horses in front of him. Not seven. Then, in a sudden jolt of comprehension, he knew. Sawing the reins, he jerked the pony around and started back.

Just as he cleared the switchback a colossal bolt of lightning streaked earthward and plowed into the Sioux village with a shuddering roar. The explosion rocked the mountain, setting off a landslide farther downhill, and for an instant the world was lighted in an eerie shimmer not unlike the faint gloaming of early dawn.

Musket fire erupted hard on the heels of the lightning, and it was then that Bloody Hand saw the Crazy Dog. Whipping his horse into a churning gallop, the warrior came down off the mountain path and charged headlong into a howling pack of Cut Throats. The light held for only a moment, but in its flickering glow Bloody Hand saw the Crazy Dog's war axe rise and fall no less than three times. Then the light faded and a moment later the flash of a dozen muskets split the night.

After that there was only silence.

The black man hesitated, reluctant to leave, yet knowing that it was finished. Only as he turned his pony back uphill did it come to him: the last of Braided Tail's prophecy, the part that had baffled him.

"One among the Dog Soldiers would be killed, but his passing would be a thing of joy for all."

Ai! It was a mystery no longer. Nor would the slain man be mourned. The Dog Soldiers would rejoice, for their brother's vow had now been fulfilled.

The Crazy Dog had crossed over at last.

CHAPTER 8

The Moon of Fat Horses again brought much praise to Bloody Hand and his Dog Soldiers. While their raid on the Sioux left the other warrior societies disgruntled, there was no gainsaying the magnitude of the deed. Nor would anyone dispute the dark one's cunning as a *duxia* leader. The dread Cut Throats had been devastated, with the loss of only one Dog Soldier. The daring march through *Paha Sapa,* along with thunderbolts loosed by spirit beings, made for a compelling tale. When the story became known, the People spoke of Bloody Hand in awed whispers.

Not only had he defied the evil spirits of the Black Hills. He had summoned forth the fury of Sparrowhawk gods in a way all but unimaginable to mere warriors.

Truly, the dark one's medicine was unsurpassed.

Yet the dark one himself was mildly galled by the whole affair. To be sure, the Dog Soldiers had stolen better than fifty ponies. Moreover, at least a score of Cut Throats had been killed in the stormy raid. All of which left him in a sullen mood.

He had taken only one scalp. One lousy scalp! After marching across hell and back, he was hardly better off than when he had started.

The feasting and victory dances were no sooner done with than he arranged another session with Braided Tail.

This time the holy man conjured up a vision better suited to the dark one's needs. He foresaw a great battle with the Blackfeet, not just a horse raid, but a bloody engagement that would leave a green meadow littered with dead. Though it cost him two fine ponies, it was a vision more to the black man's liking.

Next morning, the Dog soldiers started north, toward the Upper Missouri, and the lands of their most ancient foes.

Bloody Hand's mood brightened the moment they departed the Wind River encampment. With any luck they could collect a bundle of scalps and be back in plenty of time for *axkicirua,* the Sun Dance. Not that he meant to be anything more than a spectator. Wooing the spirit beings and lugging around a medicine bundle was one thing. Letting a witch doctor stick wooden skewers through your chest was just plain damn foolishness.

Even some of the Sparrowhawks said as much. Maybe not outright, but they hinted at their thoughts.

The *axkicirua* ceremony dated back past tribal paintings on the holy skins. It was a vengeance rite, conducted generally during the Moon of Black Cherries, and open to any warrior who felt the need to purge himself. Through it, a man whose kinsman had been slain by Sparrowhawk enemies could obtain a vision of revenge. While effective, it was perhaps the most arduous means of evoking a vision. Holy men cut slits through the chest muscles of the vengeance-seeker and pushed skewers underneath the flesh. Rawhide thongs were then connected from the skewers to a tall pole and the warrior danced in a circle until exhaustion and staring into the sun brought on a trance. When the flesh ripped away, freeing him from the skewers, the ceremony was complete.

All that remained was the month or so required for his chest to knit back together.

The black man had observed the Sun Dance last summer, shortly after being adopted into the Dog Soldiers. Certain of his warriors had already announced their intention of participating in the ceremony this year. He was obligated to have them back from the raid in time for the four days of preparation rites. But he felt no compulsion whatever to join them in self-mutilation. There were easier ways to drum up a vision, namely Braided Tail, and his evil-smelling powder.

Three days north along the Bighorn, Bloody Hand was musing on the holy man's latest prophecy when a series of wolf calls abruptly sounded: the warning signal. He motioned the Dog Soldiers into a cottonwood grove bordering the river, and had them fan out in an ambush formation. Crouched behind a tree, he marveled that Braided Tail's forecast had come about so easily. Only a short jaunt from the home camp. While the old devil hadn't mentioned it—and that seemed a little queer—his vision had apparently revealed a Blackfeet war party headed toward Absaroka.

Moments later Little Wolf and his scouts trotted into view. The black man exposed himself and waved them into the trees. They had evidently had a long run, and while Little Wolf was winded, there was nothing wrong with his hands. Like copper birds in flight, his hands darted and flashed even as he sucked in a great draught of air.

Hand flattened and stiff, he swept it across his forehead. *Tibos!* Then he drew a crooked forefinger toward his body, and followed by closing his fist, leaving the little and third fingers erect, and made a downward twisting motion with his wrist.

Twenty white men coming down the river!

Just for a moment Bloody Hand was too dumbfounded to speak. Then he found his voice. "White-eyes in Absaroka? That seems unlikely, old one. Are you certain it was not Blackfeet you saw?"

Little Wolf looked pained by the question. *"Ae, batsetse,* I am certain. My eyes see what they see. Nothing less." He paused, breathing heavily, and again filled his lungs. "They are *tibos* beyond doubt, and they lead many horses heavily loaded. We sighted them some distance above Gray Bull creek. They ride slowly, but with purpose toward the Sparrowhawk encampment."

The dark one had Little Wolf relate everything he had seen, sparing no detail. When the scout finished there were a number of things readily apparent. The white men were undoubtedly an American Fur brigade. Otherwise they wouldn't be moving into Absaroka from the north. Moreover, it clearly wasn't a trapping party, not in June or leading that many pack horses. Leastways if Little Wolf's eyes could be trusted. They were here for another purpose: nosing out the lay of the land, or perhaps trying to make contact with the Crows.

Suddenly a dim recollection jogged his mind. Ashley had said American Fur meant to establish a trading post next spring where the Bighorn joined the Yellowstone. But he had also wondered aloud how Astor's people meant to reconcile that with the Crows. Plainly they intended to get on the Crows' good side well in advance, with a bargeload of trade goods. That would explain so many pack horses, as well as their meandering through Absaroka as if they'd been invited to supper.

Waugh! Them coons was in for a shock. Like getting a little cayenne dusted in their eyes.

The black man glanced at the sun, now settled over the western rim of the mountains. Then he motioned the Dog Soldiers to gather in close. "You have all heard Little Wolf's words. The *tibos* dare to violate Sparrowhawk lands. This must not be allowed. For if one white-eye comes, others will follow, until they crawl over Absaroka like fleas on a dog."

Turning back to Little Wolf, he signed upriver. "You will return and become as a shadow to the *tibo* filth. When they camp for the night, you will send a scout to lead us to them. When dark turns to light we will attack. But only those who resist must be killed. We have need of captives, as you will see. Listen well, and hear my words. I have spoken."

Little Wolf nodded acknowledgment, then turned and trotted off with the scouts at his heels.

They left the dark of the trees, stepping softly, silent as hunting owls in flight. The morning sky was a cloudless slate, with streamers of umber and gold faintly lighting the horizon. Moving step by step, bows strung and muskets cocked, the Dog Soldiers slowly tightened in a circle around the *tibo* camp. They came on deliberately, unmindful of time, like wild things stalking the forest in the still moments before dawn.

The night guard sat cross-legged beside a smoldering bed of ashes, dozing peacefully, chin tucked against his chest. Around him men were sprawled on the ground in sleep, their heavy breathing and snores a calliope of brutish sounds. Saddles and packs were strewn about the camp, and off to one side, in a small meadow near the river, close to forty horses grazed contentedly. The ripple of water over a rocky streambed came softly, almost unheard, drifting in on a breeze so light not even the leaves stirred.

Suddenly the night guard tottered, nearly falling over, and his head jerked erect. Just for a moment his eyes remained half-closed, fighting sleep, then they popped open with a look of chilled terror. What he saw wasn't a dream, or even a nightmare. It was real, and drawing closer with each breath. Unthinking, acting out of blind reflex, he scrambled to his feet. At last his mouth opened, making pitiful bleating noises, and he swung the rifle to his shoulder, so unnerved he forgot to pull back the hammer.

The sharp twang of a half-dozen bowstrings jarred the stillness, and his body seemed to sprout a bright cluster of feathered shafts. The last arrow took him full in the throat, and a gurgled death rattle spilled out in a gout of blood. Like a felled tree, he stiffened and toppled forward into a batch of kettles near the fire. The clatter seemed almost deafening in the morning calm, and the camp abruptly came alive as sleeping men roused from their blankets.

"Freeze! First man that moves is dead."

The black man's barked command brought all movement to a halt. After a quick look around none of the trappers seemed inclined to argue. They were completely surrounded, outnumbered two to one, and the warriors would have plainly relished an excuse to open fire.

Bloody Hand strode forward and stopped beside the dead man. "Which one of ye coons is the booshway?"

There was an instant of stunned silence while the trappers gawked at him in disbelief. Though they could hardly credit their eyes, they had to admit it was real. A nigger decked out like a Crow! Finally a wiry, feisty man sprang to his feet, face purpling with rage.

"By god, mister, you'll pay for this. We come here in peace, and you got no call to go around killin' people."

The dark one looked him over with a wolfish smile. "Ye talk mighty big fer such a little feller. What's your name?"

"John Fitzpatrick. And in case you aren't aware of it, this is an American Fur brigade."

"Is that a fact? Wal, I allus did want to see what ye critters looked like. Where ye bound with all them packs?"

Fitzpatrick drew himself up another notch and stuck his chin out. "Not that it's any of your business, but we've come to council with the Crow. American Fur has authorized me to work out a trade pact with 'em."

"The Crows don't want no trade pact."

"If it's all the same to you, I'll wait and talk with them about that."

The black man's eyes went stony. "Ye are talkin' to 'em, ol' coon. So fur as your outfit's concerned, I am the

Crow, and I say ye ain't welcome south of the Yellowstone."

"That's . . ." Fitzpatrick sputtered, "that's insane. You're no more a Crow than I am."

"Don't ye believe it, booshway. I'm bull-of-the-woods around these hyar parts, and I say we done palavered enough. Now ye and yore boys jest haul yore ashes and start makin' tracks back to the Yellowstone. Jest leave all yore gear where it lays. We'll look after it fer ye."

"That's robbery! By God, I'll have you . . ."

"Booshway, I don't keer to argue 'bout it one way or t'other. Ye'd best get while the gettin's good. And pass the word along to the rest of yore bunch. Next time anybody wanders down here, I'll let the Crows start liftin' ha'r. They're sorta partial to scalps, case ye ain't heard."

John Fitzpatrick wasn't a man to push his luck when faced with a long shot, which he clearly faced just at that moment. Things being what they were, the walk back to the Yellowstone was by far the lesser of two evils. Within minutes he had his men formed and trudging upstream. Thankful they had gotten off so lightly, not one of them so much as looked back.

The Dog Soldiers went wild, tearing into the packs like excited children. Never before had they won such a victory. With such ease! A herd of fine ponies and more trade goods than any among them had ever seen. Without the loss of even one warrior! The Sparrowhawk People would honor them, sing their praises and make feasts. They were men of substance now, rich beyond measure.

Ai! Never had there been such a raid. The dark one's medicine was truly a thing of wonder. Not even the *tibos* could stand before him.

Bloody Hand was hard pressed to share their exuberance. Staring down at the prickly corpse of the dead trapper, he could only grunt with disgust.

It was some raid, sure enough. Two ponies for a vision

and he hadn't collected the first scalp. Hadn't even got a sniff, which seemed to be the way the stick floated.

Next time out somebody'd probably get his hair.

The honor bestowed on the Dog Soldiers was everything they had expected, and perhaps more. When the raiders rode into the village, only six days after departing, the People were astounded. That a raid could be conducted so swiftly was a marvel in itself. That it could result in capture of both a pony herd *and* a treasure in *tibo* trade goods simply defied belief.

Yet the proof was there for all to see. Unloaded before the Dog Soldier lodge, the trade goods made a mound taller than a man could stretch. The People came at first in bunches to stand and stare. Then, as the story spread, whole crowds formed, and throughout the day a steady throng filed past for a look at the Dog Soldiers' latest triumph. Some came again and again, shaking their heads in wonder, as if the packs were an illusion that might disappear like the morning mist. Their mood was hushed, almost reverent, and among themselves they spoke not so much of the trade goods as of the dark one himself.

Whatever lingering skepticism they might have harbored was now swept away in a flood of childlike awe. The Spirit beings walked in Bloody Hand's shadow. Whether it was his medicine bundle or the Medicine Stone presented him by his *axeisake* was a moot point. But on one matter they were all agreed.

The One Above somehow watched over the Dog Soldier leader, graced him with power and cunning unlike any Sparrowhawk had ever before possessed.

This latest feat merely confirmed what many had said all along. Bloody Hand was hardly a god, but he was something more than a man. Exactly what, they weren't sure. Yet it was something that set him apart, made him different and certainly more formidable, than those about him.

Bloody Hand seemed preoccupied with other matters, though evincing little awareness of the People's
spellbound manner. His thoughts centered not on gods,
or even godlike men, but on politics. The rout of the
tibo brigade brought to a head a great many things he
had shunted aside in days past, the foremost being his
bargain with William Ashley to destroy the American
Fur trading post on the Yellowstone. That promise
could no longer be discharged at his leisure. Waylaying
Fitzpatrick's pack train was tantamount to a declaration
of war, particularly since the trappers had come in
peace, seeking an accord with the Crow nation. Whatever the Sparrowhawks might have done had the caravan reached the Wind River encampment mattered
little now. The Dog Soldiers raid had in effect committed all of Absaroka to a course of hostility.

Which meant that he would have to move faster than
originally planned. No longer did he have time to win
the People over, slowly nurturing ill will toward American Fur. The council must somehow be persuaded to
act. Through whatever arguments he could muster, they
had to be convinced that the fort on the Yellowstone
represented a direct threat to Absaroka itself.

Like hornets goaded from their nest, the thought
brought yet another that carried its own sting. Would
the rival warrior societies support his plan, even if the
council sanctioned it? The People's fascination with the
Dog Soldiers had stirred up great jealousy. The Kit
Foxes and the Bulls had been particularly outspoken
about special honors accorded the dark one's warriors.
Perhaps of greater significance, the pipe-holders themselves were grumbling about his sudden influence within
the tribe. They resented his cool manner, and the fact
that the Sparrowhawks attributed much of the tribe's
recent good fortune to his bold and nervy leadership.
They also envied his staggering array of battle honors,
both as a warrior and a pipe-holder. It overshadowed
their own accomplishments, made them look bad in the

eyes of their followers. More than anything else, they begrudged him the recklessness and daring with which he led the Dog Soldiers.

All in all, it was a sorry kettle of fish. He damned both Ashley and American Fur for inflicting themselves on his life just at this time. Now, instead of tending to his own knitting, which had to do with scalps rather than empires, he was forced to finagle and sweet-talk like some oily bible-thumper.

For all his stewing, though, the black man was given little time to formulate a plan of action. Hardly before he had time to satisfy the curiosity of Strikes-Both-Ways and Still Water, an *aciperirau* arrived summoning him to a meeting in the council lodge.

The moment he came through the doorhole, he knew that something unusual was afoot. Seated next to White Bear was Long Hair, chief of the *Minesepere* band. That the leader of the River Crow would attend an *Acaraho* council meeting was an ominous sign. Worse yet, he had a hunch the whole affair was being staged strictly for his benefit, and not to pass out any honors, either.

White Bear motioned him to a seat and went straight to the heart of the matter. "Bloody Hand, a serious charge has been brought against you by Long Hair. As a chief of the Sparrowhawk People, he is within his rights, even though you are of another band."

The black man instinctively knew where they were headed, and why. He glanced sideways at the *Minesepere* leader, wondering if the man was any brighter than he appeared. Long Hair was tall and slim-hipped, but he had a ponderous belly that gave him the look of an aging and somewhat overfed bullfrog. His eyes were large and bulging, and the waist-length braids from which he derived his name gave off the rank smell of bear grease and lice. After a moment the dark one turned his gaze back to White Bear.

"I am listening, *batsetse.*"

White Bear clearly had no taste for this business, but

his actions from this point onward were proscribed by tribal law. "Long Hair charges that you have endangered the *Apsahrokee* nation by attacking the white-eyed party. Choose your words carefully, dark one. Should this charge prove true, the council is obligated by ancient code to banish you from Absaroka."

The black man realized quite suddenly that he was treading in deep water. But it was hardly the time to go humble. Lifting the corner of his lip in a sneer, he looked directly at Long Hair. "Since when do Sparrowhawks tremble before *tibo* filth! Or have I been misled? Do the *Minesepere* count themselves less than warriors?"

"Watch your tongue!" Long Hair growled. "It is you who stands charged with placing personal gain before the good of the People."

"Watch your own tongue, old man." Bloody Hand half rose from his seat. "Not even a *batsetse* can accuse me of betraying the People and walk away unharmed."

"Enough!" White Bear commanded. "I will have no threats spoken in the council lodge. We come to talk of justice. Nothing more." Glowering first at Long Hair, he waited until the chief's gaze lowered, then looked back at the black man. "Long Hair contends that your attack on the white-eyes will turn them against us and cause them to join our enemies. He says your raid had no motive but to enrich yourself and the Dog Soldiers. I would hear your words on this."

"That is easily answered. The Dog Soldiers will keep the ponies, which is as it should be. But I have ordered that the trade goods are to be shared equally among the warrior societies. Even now the distribution is being made."

White Bear allowed himself a faint smile. "The Dog Soldiers must have groaned loudly at their pipe-holder's generosity."

"*Ae,* it is so. Yet they saw the wisdom of sharing such wealth with the People." The dark one paused, letting his gaze drift around the circle of elders. Then, without warning, he leveled down on Long Hair. "I would ask the chief of the *Minesepere* a question. What do you know of these *tibos* from the north?"

"I know that they are our friends," Long Hair snapped. "They wish only to trade for our furs. Or at least that was their wish until you robbed the peace-makers they sent among us."

"Have not they already sent peace-makers with gifts of trade goods among your band?"

It was a shrewd guess, one that made Long Hair blink and dart a quick glance at the elders. "That is true, but I have not attempted to hide it."

"Yet you speak of it only when prompted. I would ask you another question. Does not their fort on the Yellow-stone pose a threat to Absaroka?"

"Threat? I see no harm in men of good heart who wish only to trade. What they offer are the things our people need."

"*Ai!* Perhaps such an arrangement will make even Long Hair look stronger in the eyes of the *Minesepere.* I hear it said that your people frown on you because White Bear's band has discovered the secret of the bea-ver."

"The gossip of jealous squaws. Nothing more. Only a fool would believe such lies."

"Lies? That is strange, for it is also said that the *tibos* have offered you great wealth to allow them to send trappers into Absaroka."

This was another wild guess, but it struck home like a thunderbolt. Long Hair paled visibly, and beads of sweat broke out on his forehead. White Bear and the elders watched him in grim silence, waiting for him to refute the charge.

When he said nothing, Bloody Hand tried another long shot. "Have they also told you that after the snows, in the Moon of First Eggs, they intend to build another fort where the Bighorn joins the Yellowstone?"

Long Hair's bulging eyes glistened like those of a cornered rat. "They said nothing about a fort within Absaroka. That I swear. They agreed to come south of the Yellowstone only to trap. Never to build."

"*Ae,* I can believe that. These are devious men, as are all *tibos.* They say one thing today and another thing tomorrow. Clearly they mean to invade Sparrowhawk lands by dividing the *Acaraho* and the *Minesepere.* Then, when we are at one another's throats, they would rule us as a man rules his dog."

Long Hair eyed him shrewdly. "You speak with great authority. How is it you know so much of the *tibos'* plans?"

"I make it my business to know. I lived among the white-eyes for many snows, and their treacherous ways hold no mystery for me. I have ears in many camps, Long Hair. Even yours."

The *Minesepere* chief just stared at him, unable to respond. Plainly the dark one spoke the truth. Or else the medicine that had brought him fame as a warrior also enabled him to read minds. Long Hair's gaze fell to the amulet around the black man's neck, and his silence held. While he scoffed at the idea that Bloody Hand had the power to cast a death curse, he decided not to test it further. Already he had been disgraced before the council, which in itself was perhaps a warning from the spirit beings.

White Bear grunted and gave him a dour look. "Long Hair, the words spoken here will not go outside this council lodge. Were we to make known the things you have done, your people would choose themselves a wiser leader. But it is Absaroka we must concern ourselves with now. Your bungling will remain a secret between those here."

Turning back to the black man, his gaze softened. "Bloody Hand, your words are those of a wise man. More than that, they are the words of a true Sparrowhawk. The council would hear you speak now as the pipe-holder of the Dog Soldiers. How must this *tibo* threat be met?"

The dark one's mouth tightened in a grim line. "It should be done the way a man rids his lodge of snakes. They must be driven from the Yellowstone and their fort burned. Only then will Absaroka be safe."

White Bear exchanged glances with the elders, listening closely to their muttered comments. While they had no taste for fighting white-eyes, there seemed no alternative to the dark one's angry response. After a few moments of counseling among themselves the elders fell silent, and White Bear again met the black man's stare.

"The wise man would be the first to admit his own weaknesses. I am a warrior of many snows, Bloody Hand, but I know nothing of attacking forts."

Bloody Hand's face was inscrutable. *"Batsetse,* I will advise you. The way it must be done is a thing I know well."

The black man took a deep breath, waiting for their reaction. The fact was, he had never been inside a fort, much less laid siege to one. But now was not the time for holding back. It was bluff and be damned, or see Absaroka slip from his grasp.

There was a moment of tomblike silence. Then White Bear nodded, his face cold as chiseled stone.

"So be it. Two suns from now the Sparrowhawk will ride north to the Yellowstone. I have spoken."

Bloody Hand let out his breath in a long sigh, and an imperceptible smile ticked at the corner of his mouth.

Like the man said, so be it.

The earth shimmered under the glaring shafts of a midday sun. Suddenly a ray of light splintered away and became a glistening span of feathers. Then it emerged in a slow glide, dropping below the blinding gaze, and took the shape of a hawk. Sweeping the river in lazy circles, it caught an updraft and again disappeared into the sun.

Watching it, Bloody Hand grunted to himself. It was a good omen, the first he had seen in some days. Out of the corner of his eye he saw that Little Wolf had no interest in hawks. The scout's attention centered on the fort below, and the gleaming brass cannons that bristled along its walls. His gaze moved slowly, scanning the fort foot by foot, committing every detail to memory as if carved in stone.

They were bellied down in a pine grove on a hill overlooking the fort. Under cover of darkness the night before, the Sparrowhawk war party had swum the Missouri, pulling behind them hastily constructed rafts loaded with weapons and food. The main force had kept hidden downriver while Little Wolf and Bloody Hand came ahead to scout the fort. Their morning had been spent drifting through the tree-studded hills that encircled the trading post on three sides. The fourth side, where the main gate was located, fronted on the river. What they saw were high walls commanding a view of all sides of a vast meadow which separated the fort from the wooded hills. Whoever built the fort had known his business.

It could be attacked only across open ground, and every approach was covered by intersecting cannon fire.

Bloody Hand had stared at the fort until his eyeballs felt numb. But no matter how hard he looked, nothing changed. If the timbered stockade had a weakness he couldn't find it. It was plain to see that anyone who attacked across the meadow would be shredded whole by grapeshot long before they reached the walls. While there appeared to be no more than thirty men in the fort, numbers counted for little. The canon changed the odds past all calculation.

That was another thing William Ashley had forgot to mention: the cannon. Thinking back on it, the black man saw now that Ashley had actually had only the vaguest of notions about the fort. He hadn't even known where it was located. Back at Rendezvous, the trader had fixed the fort at the mouth of the Yellowstone. Yet here it was on the Missouri, close to five miles upstream from the Yellowstone. And on the north bank! Still, finding it had been the simplest part.

Taking it looked to be a chore that would separate the men from the boys.

The Sparrowhawks, some two hundred strong, had left the Wind River encampment a fortnight past. Bloody Hand had advised White Bear against organizing a larger force. The number chosen was sufficient to the task and more would only complicate matters. Though the pipeholders raised an ungodly howl, White Bear selected three warrior societies from each of the tribal bands. Long Hair himself had quietly knuckled under, remaining behind to watch over the village. The Dog Soldiers had been appointed to the coveted post of scouts, and the war party rode out to the tumultuous cries of the People. Their march had roughly traced the Bighorn to the Yellowstone to the Missouri, a distance of some five hundred miles as the crow flies. Now their horses were hidden downstream across the river, and the warriors were busy painting themselves for the battle to come.

Just at the moment, though, the black man wasn't too sure there would be any battle. From the way things shaped up, they had ridden five hundred miles only to sit and stare at a hornet's nest. The hell of it was, the more a man looked at it, the worse it got.

Nudging Little Wolf, he crawled back deeper in the trees and came to his feet. Neither of them said anything, but then words really weren't necessary. The look they exchanged said it all. With the scout bringing up the rear, they took off in a dog trot toward the Sparrowhawk camp.

Twenty minutes later the dark one stood before White Bear. His breathing was even and unlabored, and the short run had given him time to collect his thoughts. Which was just as well, considering what he faced in the next few moments. His report on the fort must be worded with utmost care if he was to retain the confidence of the Sparrowhawk chieftain.

"It is a large fort, *batsetse.* Perhaps the length of four lodgepoles and half that in width. There are few men, no more than forty, and they appear well armed. They are of no consequence, though. Our problem is of a greater nature."

Squatting, he pulled his knife and drew a sketch of the fort in the dirt. "There are thunder guns mounted at each corner of the walls. They can be turned so that the fire of one connects with the fire of those on each side." Jabbing with the knife, he pocked the earth around his drawing. "There are hills on all sides except where the river flows. Between the hills and the fort is a meadow the width of a long rifleshot."

White Bear studied the sketch for a long while in silence. At last he squatted and pointed at the meadow. "Were we to attack across here, their thunder guns would stare down our throats."

"Ae, that is so."

"Yet the only other way is across the river. This would put us even more at their mercy."

"That also is true, *batsetse.*"

"What is it you say, Dark One? That we must turn around and ride back to Absaroka?"

"No, not that." Bloody Hand's eyes fell to the sketch, tracing the outline of the walls, as if seeing them again from the hilltop. "The *tibos* are always more vigilant at dawn. They believe that is the time favored by red men for attack. I would attack instead just at dusk, when the sun is gone and darkness approaches. They will be less watchful then, and if we come at them from three sides perhaps they will not have time to mount a defense."

White Bear nodded, digesting that. Then he studied the drawing again, rubbing his jaw in thought. Finally he looked up. "It is a good plan. But if the *tibos* are alert. If our attack should fail, what then?"

"Then we will have lost the advantage of surprise, *batsetse.* Once they know we are here, it would be the same as killing oneself to attack across the open ground."

"The circle grows tighter, Bloody Hand. Are you counseling that all is lost should we fail in the first attempt?"

"Not lost. But it would then become a game of the fox and the rabbit. We would be forced to encircle the fort from the hills and starve them from their hole."

The chief grimaced, shaking his head. "That is not the Sparrowhawk way. Our warriors have no taste for waiting. They came to fight."

"Better to wait and win, my leader, than to cross over having lost." The black man dismissed the thought with a casual gesture. "Time enough to consider that if we fail. The sun grows high and there is much to do if we are to attack before nightfall."

White Bear grunted, pondering it a moment longer, then sent a runner to fetch the other pipe-holders. Waiting for the war council to begin, Bloody Hand did a bit of pondering himself.

For a man who didn't know what the hell he was talking about, he was giving a lot of advice. Come dark, he had a hunch the Sparrowhawks were going to need all the medicine they could muster, and then some.

His hand went to the amulet hanging from his neck, and he fingered it, thinking of what the holy man had said. Maybe the old devil was right, after all. Maybe if he concentrated hard enough he could put a hex on the bastards.

Light faded fast after the sun dipped below the westward mountains. The smell of cooking fires drifted out from the fort, and in the silty twilight smoke funneled skyward in dark spirals. Even from the hills the sound of men talking and laughing came clear in the still air. Around the catwalk, high inside the log stockade, a lone sentry paced the walls. Every now and then he stopped, pausing to look out over the river or a stretch of meadow, then the pacing resumed. From a distance he appeared slack-shouldered and listless, as if bored by the monotony of it all. With the deepening of shadows, his pauses came more frequent and his pacing less.

Hidden behind the bole of a tall pine, Bloody Hand had watched the man's every move for the past hour. That was what it all boiled down to in the crunch: one man. If he was alert and watchful, the Sparrowhawks were in for a hard time. But if he grew careless, or stopped just at the right time to gaze out over the river, or maybe even paused for a quick catnap back in a dark corner, that would do it, give them time to cross the meadow and scale the walls.

The distance wasn't far, hardly more than a hundred yards from the base of the hills to the stockade walls. Crouched low, running fast, a man could cross it in half a minute at the outside, and never be seen. But if the men inside that fort ever got their cannons unlimbered, the distance might as well be ten miles. For that matter, even the last ten feet could become the road to hell.

Glancing about, the black man saw that it was almost time. Darkness was falling quickly now, and the signal would come at any moment. Across the way the Kit Foxes and the Shaved Heads would attack from the east. White Bear would lead the Ravens and the Stone Hammers from the north. Back in the trees, the Dog Soldiers and the Lumpwoods waited for him to take them against the west wall. Every warrior had his war bridle of plaited rawhide with a noose fashioned on one end. If only one in three managed to snag a loop on the stockade posts, they would be over the walls in no time at all, swarming through the fort like ants in a honeycomb.

Suddenly the screech of a hunting night owl sounded from the north.

Bloody Hand came to his feet and headed downhill in the fading light. When he hit the edge of the clearing, the Dog Soldiers and Lumpwoods were right on his heels. Lengthening his stride, he took off at a dead lope across the grassy meadow. The only sound was the rush of wind in his ears, and the pad of moccasined feet on soft earth.

Out of the twilight an orange flash appeared on the stockade walls, and the crack of a rifle shot drummed back off the sloping hills. The black man heard someone behind him grunt, almost in surprise, and in the next instant there came the thud of a body striking the ground.

Then the voice of the sentry seemed to fill the night. "Injuns! Get to the walls! Y'hear me, Injuns! They're comin' fast!"

The Sparrowhawks never faltered, pumping ever harder as they raced toward the fort. But along the wall heads began to bob in the gleaming light, and the steady spat of rifle fire grew in volume. Another warrior fell, and yet another, but the angry hiss of lead only seemed to quicken the stride of those remaining. They had covered half the distance, perhaps more. Just another few seconds, a brief sprint, and they would be at the walls. Somewhere in the back a Dog Soldier raised the ancient war cry.

"Hooo-ki-hi!"

Almost in challenge came a blinding flash as the four corners of the fort erupted in sheets of flame. The hollow roar of cannon thundered across the meadow and the night filled with death as grapeshot whistled through the air. Warriors were flung backwards, slammed to the earth, as if they had run headlong into a stone wall. Before the Sparrowhawks covered another twenty paces, the cannons belched flame again, exploding a hailstorm of lead right in their faces. From the catwalks the sharper crack of rifles beat a steady tattoo, and all about them, the raiders seemed enveloped in a churning swarm of deadly wasps.

Bloody Hand skidded to a halt and turned, stumbling

over the body of a Dog Soldier who had fallen almost at his heels. The murderous cannon fire was winnowing their ranks like a giant thresher. The stockade walls loomed directly ahead, but to go on was to embrace death itself. Lurching to his feet, he shouted the order to withdraw, waving the Sparrowhawks back. Only when he was standing did he realize that he was alone with the dead.

The living had fled.

The black man broke into a sizzling, dust-kicking sprint. He concentrated solely on speed, resisting the temptation to dodge and twist. Darkness had fallen now and the stockade defenders were firing blindly. Death was everywhere, and whatever direction he swerved might be more fatal than the next. It was better just to pucker tight and run like hell. Pumping harder, he took off in a beeline for the distant hills.

As he pounded along, it came to him in a grisly sort of way that the men had been separated from the boys after all, like chaff from wheat.

Dawn of the third morning found the Sparrowhawks and the fort's besieged defenders locked in a stalemate. The raiders couldn't get in and the white men couldn't get out, which made it a fairly miserable predicament for everyone involved. Not unlike the rabbit and the fox, those inside lived in constant dread, and those outside stewed in a broth of frustration and ever-increasing anger.

The Sparrowhawks had spent the past two days sniping at the fort from the surrounding hills. But for all the good it had done they might as well have chunked rocks. Their trade muskets threw lead with feeble accuracy, and their fire had done little more than harass the defenders. Bloody Hand's Hawken was the only weapon equal to the range and he had put it to good use. Moving about through the hills, changing positions often, he had killed three trappers since the seige began. Yet he couldn't be everywhere at once. The best he could manage was to work on one wall at a time, and those inside the fort quickly learned to take cover when the Hawken barked.

Aside from being deadlocked in a sniping contest, the Sparrowhawks had a more immediate problem. Their supply of powder and lead was running dangerously low. They had ridden north expecting to storm the fort in a brief fight and reduce it to ashes within a single day. None of them, Bloody Hand included, had ever tangled with a fortified, well defended stockade. The business of laying siege was more than they had bargained for, and something they were ill equipped to sustain for any length of time.

White Bear, at the black man's suggestion, had ordered an end to the sniping toward sundown of the second day. Their fast-dwindling supply of powder and lead must be conserved for another time, when they could somehow breach the walls, or devise some strategy for luring the *tibos* from their fort.

That night Bloody Hand had led a diversionary attack against the west wall. The plan was to fool the trappers into believing it was a full-scale assault, while a second party crept in and stacked brushwood against the east wall. Once the brushwood was set afire, it was hoped that the entire fort would go up in flames. Though the plan was sound enough, it floundered in a sea of grapeshot. The defenders simply opened fire with their cannons, raking the meadow in every direction, and the Sparrowhawks were again forced to retreat.

Clearly the trappers had power and lead to spare. The liberal doses spewed from their cannon left no doubt on that score. Moreover, there were few slouches among them with a rifle, and in the sniping contest, they had inflicted heavy losses. Muskets against rifles were hardly a match, and in two days they had killed or wounded more than twenty warriors.

This, along with the aborted night raid, pushed the *Minesepere* pipe-holders into open rebellion.

Shortly after sunrise of the third day, they stalked into White Bear's camp like three constipated owls. Their message was terse and acrimonious. This was a fight brought on by the *Acaraho* band alone, the work of White Bear and Bloody Hand. Already more than thirty warriors had died before the *tibos'* thunder guns, and of that number, more than half were *Minesepere.* Sparrow-hawks were not meant to war in this manner. They had come here to fight men, not walls. Unless White Bear could lead them to victory by nightfall they and their warriors would ride back to Absaroka. With that the pipe-holders turned and marched off.

Their ultimatum was a matter of no small conse-quence. Should the *Minesepere* forces pull out, there was every chance that White Bear's pipe-holders would re-volt as well. Certainly Bloody Hand could control the Dog Soldiers, but their strength was hardly equal to the task at hand. Afterwards, talking it over, White Bear and his black advisor came face to face with a blunt and rather unsavory truth.

The Sparrowhawks had no taste for siege warfare. They wanted open battle, where a man could win glory and honor. Without that, there was every likelihood the warriors would simply quit the fight and return to Ab-saroka.

Bloody Hand and the *batsetse* were pondering this latest development when a runner appeared from the forward slope of the hill. Astounded, they listened as the man rattled off something about a signal from the fort. Though his words were a bit muddled, they gath-ered that the defenders were waving a white cloth and shouting *tibo* gibberish. Bloody Hand led them in a wild scramble back down the hill, and as astonishing as it seemed, the warrior was right. The trappers were wav-ing a white flag.

Bloody Hand worked down to the edge of the trees and lifted his voice in a shout. "Hallo the fort!"

There was a moment of silence, then a faint cry came back. "Beckwith, is that you?"

The black man blinked a couple of times on that. Somebody in there knew his name! "It's me, awright. What d'ye want?"

"We want to parley. We're willin' to talk with the head wolf of your bunch."

The dark one smiled. Sure they did. Get White Bear out in the open and shoot him down. Then the Sparrow-hawks would turn tail and scoot home. Even pork-eaters knew that's the way Indians were. Once their chief's medicine went sour, it took the fight clean out of them.

"No dice! Ye can talk with me or nobody. I'm the one callin' the shots here anyways."

There was another long pause, then the voice drifted back. "It's a deal. We'll meet you halfway. No tricks, though. Our boys'll have you covered."

"Same here!" Bloody Hand shouted. "Only double!"

Briefly the black man related the gist of the agreement to White Bear. Just as an afterthought, he added that it could well be a *tibo* trick. In that event the Sparrowhawks were to fire, regardless of the danger to him personally. The important thing then would be to kill whoever came out from the fort.

Then he turned, stepped out in the open away from the trees, and waited. When he saw two men come around the corner of the fort carrying a white flag, he struck out across the meadow. The gap closed rapidly and he was startled to recognize one of the men as John Fitzpatrick, the booshway he and the Dog Soldiers had robbed down below Gray Bull creek. Then his jaw popped open.

The second man was Samuel Tullock, former booshway for Rocky Mountain Fur, Ashley's right-hand man in the first brigade that came out from St. Louis. Christ on a crutch! It beat all, for a fact.

Fitzpatrick and Tullock came to a halt about halfway out from the fort. The black man stopped some ten feet off and smiled, shaking his head.

"Sam, how ye be? I sorta wondered how anybody in thar knew me by name."

Tullock grinned, jerking his head at the brigade leader. "When Fitz here told me about some black Injun skinnin' him down on the Bighorn, I had a fair to middlin' notion it might be you."

Bloody Hand nodded, looking from one to the other. " 'Pears yer keepin' bad company, Sam. Yore partner almost lost his ha'r not knowin' when to button his lip."

Fitzpatrick's face mottled in an astringent expression. "Your day's comin', Beckwith. Renegades can't hide forever, and I got a long memory. 'Specially for red niggers."

The black man's eyes narrowed, flecked through with a pale opal coldness. "Lemme tell ye somethin', runt. I done killed one man fer callin' me that, and I ain't got no objection a'tall to yore bein' second."

Fitzpatrick ground his teeth in quiet fury, darting a glance at the Hawken cradled over the dark one's arm. Before it could go any further, Tullock broke in. "Boys, I allow as how you're just gonna have to let it lay awhile. We got more important things to iron out right now."

"Yeh, I was wonderin' 'bout that," Bloody Hand said, cocking his head for a look at the white flag. "Ye fellers figger it's time to call it quits?"

"Surrender?" Tullock laughed and spit, shifting his tobacco cud to the off cheek. "Jim, you oughta know me better'n that. We come out here to see if there wasn't some way to work out a deal with the Crows. Y'know, this fightin' ain't gettin' nobody anywhere. We'd a sight rather trade with you than fight you."

"Don't doubt it fer a minute, Sam. 'Cept it's like I told the runt here. Ye fellers ain't welcome in this neck of the woods. I ain't one to bury ol' friends, though, so if yer willin' to skedaddle, I'll keep the Crows off yore necks. Otherwise I reckon we'll jest have to starve ye out. Course, ye understand, I couldn't guarantee what my bunch'd do then. Yore ha'r would pretty much be yore own lookout."

Fitzpatrick bristled at the black man's arrogance, and he shook his fist in the air. "Mister, it's your hair you'd better start worryin' about. Couple of more days and there'll be more Blackfeet around here than you can shake a stick at. We're not wet behind the ears, y'know. Not by a damn sight!"

The booshway's heated outburst came to an abrupt halt as Tullock elbowed him in the ribs. After blistering Fitzpatrick with a sharp look, he turned back to the black man. "Seein' as Fitz let the cat out of the bag, I reackon there's no harm done in givin' you the low-down. That first night we sent a man up river for help. Y'see, I ain't exactly what you'd call the he-wolf of American Fur. I run this fort, but there's another one further upstream."

"So I heard tell." The dark one's tone was offhand, almost disinterested. "Up around the Great Falls, ain't it?"

"That's right. Fellow name of McKenzie runs it. Fact is, he runs the whole shebang out here, which sort of works around to what I'm tryin' to tell you. He's a real piss-cutter, meaner'n a teased rattler. When he gets wind that you and the Crows has got us boxed in, he'll fill them Blackfeet full of snake juice and send'em down here huntin' your scalp. They won't stop here, neither. They'll chase you to hell and gone."

Tullock paused, working on his cud. Then he spit and wiped his mouth. "The only reason I'm tellin' you this is 'cause of what you said a while ago. I ain't one for buryin' old friends, neither. Why'nt you and the Crows hightail it out of here, and I'll see if I can't keep Bug's Boys likkered up enough so's they won't trail after you."

"Sam, I take that mighty kindly of ye. Course, as y'know, Injuns is democratic as all get out. I'll tell'em what ye said and let'em put it to a vote. If'n ye don't see us come sunup, ye'll know we done lit out."

The black man started off, then he looked back, "Say, maybe I ort to mention it. Ever' gun in them hills is laid right on your backs. Any of yore boys gets an itchy finger 'fore I hit them trees, I 'spect ye two'll be cold meat. Like ye said, Sam. Ain't no need in *compadres* buryin' one another."

Grinning, he turned and walked off at a leisurely pace. Just for a minute he almost broke out whistling. Tullock's little story was the best news he'd had since crossing the Missouri. Once them *Minesepere* pipe-holders got wind of Blackfeet on the way there weren't nothing on God's green earth that'd make them quit and run. They'd stick to the last, and fight like bee-stung bears. Yessir, it just went to prove. Sometimes a shit storm turned out to be rose water all along.

Then he grunted, remembering, and deep in his gut a chuckle shook loose. It was just like the old witch doctor had said after all: a great battle with the Blackfeet and a green meadow littered with dead.

Waugh! Now wouldn't that be some medicine to whip on the Sparrowhawks!

The ambush site had been chosen with great care. Some three miles upstream from the fort, the Missouri made a sharp bend around a stunted hill. The river trail veered off to skirt the base of this knoll, and for perhaps a distance of twenty rods the path was flanked on either side by wooded hills. Then it emerged again in a faint, dusty ribbon stretching eastward. It was within this narrow hollow, embraced on all sides by steep, forested hills, that the Blackfeet would be ambushed, where there was no retreat, and nowhere to run, except into the waiting arms of the Sparrowhawks.

White Bear and Bloody Hand had selected the spot in the first light of false dawn, just hours after listening to Little Wolf's account of how and where the Blackfeet would attack. The Dog Soldiers' scouts had returned during the night with their eagerly awaited report, which in the telling created a mild puzzlement. The enemy had camped for the night some ten miles upstream. They were making medicine and preparing for battle. Apparently they meant to approach along the river trail, for they were mounted and scouts had observed them painting their war ponies. Yet, and Little Wolf himself had expressed amazement on this point, there were barely a hundred warriors in the party.

This startling bit of news had set the pipe-holders to jabbering amongst themselves. Were the Blackfeet fools? Or were they so scornful of the Sparrowhawks that they sent only a few to kill many? Perhaps it was a cunning trap. The Blackfeet were known for their sly and barbarous ways. Could there be more warriors circling in from another direction? Some plan to dupe the Sparrowhawks and attack them front and rear?

Little Wolf thought not. The Dog Soldiers had scouted the four winds for a distance of a day's march. There was no enemy activity except, as he reported, the lone encampment upstream. Perhaps other warriors followed. That was possible. But if so, they would arrive much too late for the battle.

Bloody Hand was inclined to agree with him. It was a queer twist that McKenzie would send only a hundred Blackfeet. Yet there were any number of reasonable answers. Perhaps the couriers from the fort had underestimated the Sparrowhawk force. After all, it had been dark the night of their first attack, and Tullock could well have misjudged what he faced. For that matter, maybe McKenzie didn't have as much influence with the Blackfeet as everyone thought. Or perhaps a hundred warriors were all near to hand when the message arrived. It was raiding season, and it stood to reason that not many Blackfeet would be loafing around a fort.

Whatever the reason, though, it had turned into a juicy plum for the Sparrowhawks. With any luck at all, what shaped up as a battle might just wind up a massa-

cre, which was sort of what Braided Tail had foretold in
the first place.

After selecting the ambush site, White Bear had
counseled with the black man as to how it should be
done. Lately the *batsetse* had come to rely on Bloody
Hand's judgment in matters pertaining to war. Under
White Bear's leadership, in times past, the Dog Soldiers
had been widely respected. But never had they won victories such as those engineered by their new pipe-
holder, the dark one. Nor was the chief unaware that
Bloody Hand had transformed the Dog Soldiers into an
organized, highly disciplined fighting unit, something he
himself had never been able to accomplish. Moreover,
the dark one had planned and executed a skillful attack
on the walled stockade. Granted, many warriors had
been lost, and the Sparrowhawks had small liking for
such tactics. But then, they had never before fought the
tibos on their own ground.

Whether it was the power of Bloody Hand's medicine
at work or merely his broader grasp of warfare itself
mattered little to White Bear. The fact remained that in
battle the dark one was unsurpassed for his cleverness,
and had an uncanny instinct for the enemy's soft spot.

Never was this more evident than in the way Bloody
Hand had prepared the ambush. The device by which he
meant to ensnare the Blackfeet was to the *batsetse* a
marvel in itself, a thing of great simplicity, yet a stratagem that wouldn't have occurred to White Bear had he
stared at the wooded hollow from dawn till dusk. Truly,
the Blackfeet would think the spirits themselves had
taken a hand in this fight.

Bloody Hand waited on a knoll at the mouth of the
draw, flattened out on a high rock where he could see
from one end of the wooded slopes to the other. The
Sparrowhawks lined both sides of the hollow, hidden in
the shadowed depths of the pine forest. Already the
black man had passed the word to the pipe-holders, who
in turn were charged to warn their followers. The signal

to open fire would be the distinct crack of Bloody Hand's rifle. Should any warrior spoil the surprise by firing sooner, he would answer personally to the Dog Soldiers.

Not a man among them, even those of the *Minesepere* band, doubted the deadliness of his warning. The dread talisman hung from the dark one's neck was sufficient alone to hold them in check.

Shortly after sunrise, the black man stiffened and peered intently toward the foot of the draw. The Blackfeet scouts had come into view, slowing their ponies to a walk as they entered the forested hills. Clearly they were suspicious. It was the perfect spot for a trap to be sprung, the kind of place to raise the hackles on any scout worth his powder. Yet as they moved along the trail, scrutinizing the wooded slopes with a wary eye, nothing in their actions indicated alarm. Bloody Hand's pulse thudded as he watched from above, waiting for what seemed a small lifetime as they rode through the draw. Then, like frozen statues suddenly sparked to motion, they went past and emerged onto the river trail.

Less than a quarter hour later, the Blackfoot column entered the draw. They held their horses to a prancing walk and rode strung out in loose bunches. While there was little talk, and some of them scoured the hills with their eyes, it was plain that they suspected nothing this far from the fort. The warriors were decked out in full battle regalia, their shields glistening and their warpaint a garish array of colors in the early morning sun. Three horsemen rode somewhat apart at the head of the column, and one of these wore a feathered war bonnet that trailed down over his back: clearly a chief, or failing that, a pipe-holder of great standing.

Bloody Hand laid his sights on the leader's chest and waited. The entire column was now within the draw, and as the chief passed below the black man slowly squeezed the trigger. When the Hawken barked the Blackfoot leader jerked upright, flailing the air with his arms, and

toppled backwards over his pony's rump. There was an
instant of dead silence as the Blackfeet warriors stared
on in disbelief, and then the slopes on either side of
them erupted in a volley of musket fire. This was followed only a split second later by a shower of arrows,
and in the space of a dozen heartbeats fully half the
Blackfoot force had been wiped from their saddles. The
survivors gigged their ponies and took off at a gallop
toward the head of the draw. Suddenly a groaning
screech filled the air, drowning out even the sound of
gunfire. Towering pine trees on either side of the hollow
listed ponderously as Sparrowhawk warriors slashed the
rawhide ropes anchoring them in place. The trees had
been chopped through past the core, and as the ropes
gave way, they slammed downhill in a grinding crash.
When the dust and debris settled, the mouth of the
draw had been sealed tight as a crypt.

The Blackfeet spun their horses and started back in
the other direction, only to see trees topple forward and
close off the lower entrance like a giant gate. Then the
enraged roar of a grizzly thundered out over the hollow
and on its heels came the Sparrowhawk war cry. Looking up, the Blackfeet saw a wild-eyed apparition hurtling down at them, brandishing a war axe in one hand
and a foot-long blade in the other. The bear claw necklace around his neck jangled with each leaping stride,
and as he came on they saw that he was somehow
darker than the others. Suddenly, in a moment of
numbing clarity, they knew him.

Bloody Hand!

The black man tore into them like a crazed ox, ripping and slashing and shattering skulls in a frenzy of
destruction. Before the Blackfeet could recover their
wits, every tree in the hollow seemed to sprout a Sparrowhawk warrior. Wherever they turned there were
clubs and knives and hatchets. Hands clawed at them,
dragging them off their horses, and they were swept
down in a maelstrom of bright steel. The circle closed

tighter and tighter, like the jaws of death itself, and at its center Bloody Hand bludgeoned and carved until he was bathed in slime of gore. The Blackfeet fought back gamely, unlimbering war axes and tomahawks with the desperation of the doomed. But they never had a chance. The Sparrowhawks swarmed over them with all the mercy of ravenous wolves.

Five minutes after the dark one's opening shot, it was over. The grassy floor of the draw was littered with the dead and the dying. The Blackfeet had been wiped out to a man. All that remained was the scalping and the mutilation.

Some hours later, as the midday sun hung suspended in the sky, Samuel Tullock looked on grimly as his men climbed aboard a barge at the river landing. Beside him, the black man observed their preparations with what amounted to a gloating smile. Surrender of the fort, along with the five scalps dangling from his belt, had made it a day he wouldn't soon forget.

Tullock worked his cud and squirted a nearby rock in disgust. "Jim, this ain't the end of it, y'know. After what you done today, you're gonna have McKenzie and the Blackfeet huntin' your topknot."

"Everybody's stick floats different," the dark one replied. "Now me, I ain't much fer killin' white men, even them that flies the wrong flag. Y'know, I could've let the Crows roast yore boys alive if I'd been a mind to."

Yipping war cries broke out from the fort and a tendril of smoke drifted skyward. Within moments flames appeared along the west wall, quickly gathering strength as the dried logs went up like kindling. There was garbled laughter and much shouting from inside the walls, and moments later the Sparrowhawks crowded through the front gate. They were carrying an odd assortment of blankets, trade goods, powder kegs, and several bolts of bright-patterned cloth.

Bloody Hand grinned, glancing sidewise at the trader. "Say, when ye see this hyar McKenzie feller, tell him

I'm shore obliged fer all them rifles yore boys let us
have. And the powder and lead, too. Seems a shame to
let them cannon get all melted up, but I don't rightly
know as the Crows'd ever put'em to much use."

Tullock frowned, unamused. "I'll tell you fair, Jim. I
wouldn't want to be standin' in your tracks. McKenzie'll
put a bounty on your head, sure as hell. And folks are
gonna be nosin' your trail in bunches."

The black man's eyes glinted with yellowish flecks.
"Tell'em they better stay clear of Absaroka. This fort's
my last warnin'. White or red, any man I ketch down
thar goes under without his ha'r. Now I reckon ye'd best
haul yore ashes, Sam. My boys might jest up and decide
they ain't had enough devilment fer one day."

The trader gave him a dour look, then walked off
toward the landing. When he stepped aboard the barge
the trappers shoved off and began poling up river.
Bloody Hand watched them for a minute and then
turned back to the fort. The flames were crackling and
leaping, and great billows of smoke mushed upwards in
a dark cloud.

He smiled, nodding absently to himself.

That finished it, the deal with Ashley, and whatever
else he owed the mountain brigades. It was done with.
Absaroka was closed to *tibos* for all time.

Then a warm glow bubbled up in his gut as it struck
him in a sudden rush. He was free, free at last.

CHAPTER 9

Strikes-Both-Ways was boiling sheep horn when the dark one returned from his morning bath. The old bow-maker paused long enough to greet him, then went back to dropping hot stones into a bull-hide vessel. This was the critical stage, heating the water to a temperature-where the horn became malleable but not spongy. Weilding two forked sticks, Strikes-Both-Ways lifted another rock from the fire and plopped it into the pear-shaped skin container, which was suspended from stout poles. The rock hit the water with a sizzling hiss and a vaporous cloud filled the air with steam. The old man tested the water with his finger and nodded, satisfied. Another half hour and he would be able to shape the horn and cut it to suitable lengths.

Bloody Hand grinned, shaking his head with mild wonder, and walked on toward the lodge. The old devil was his own man, no two ways about it. The fact that his grandson was the most honored war leader among the *Apsahrokee* hadn't fazed him in the least. Nor was he visibly impressed that the dark one's herd now numbered some two hundred sleek, fat ponies. These things were not of his doing, and while he might bask in his *bacbapite's* fame, he wasn't about to set aside his own craft. Other men, their joints stiff with time, would have been content to rest from their labors and spend their days bragging among the ancient ones. But not Strikes-Both-Ways. He was a bowmaker, an artisan, respected in a manner few had attained. So long as the People wanted his bows, he would continue to ply his skills. Gossip and lazing around in the warm sun was for those whose stones had shriveled with age. Strikes-Both-Way's juices ran strong, and he accepted charity from no man, not even his grandson. Instead he made bows for yet another generation of Sparrowhawk warriors.

When the black man came through the doorhole, he was surprised to find Still Water in the lodge. Earlier she had aired the bed robes after performing the regular morning chores, and it was unusual for her to still be fussing about. With berries in season she normally joined the other squaws and remained gone most of the morning. It was a special time for the women, when they could exchange gossip and chatter among themselves about things that held no interest for men. That she had stayed behind was revealing in itself. Bloody Hand wasn't exactly sure what it revealed, but he had no doubt she would enlighten him in short order. Unlike Strikes-Both-Ways, she considered her husband's honors her own, and lately her tongue had grown as sharp as a cactus spine, perhaps too sharp, leastways for one man's peace of mind.

Bloody Hand mulled that over, watching her out of the corner of his eye as he started collecting his hunting gear. He had awakened with a taste for deer meat, and all the while he was bathing his thoughts had been on a high meadow where the plump ones came out to feed late in the day. Grumping to himself, he silently promised the girl a good switching if she spoiled his mood.

Her words brought his head around. "My *batsire*, there is a thing I would speak of, but only if it does not interfere with your day's hunt."

The submissive tone put him on guard. Clearly the little spitfire wanted something, and was trying to come up on his blind side. "The deer will not leave their beds till the One Above sinks low. I am listening."

Still Water's chin lowered, eyes downcast. "My time of the moon has come again."

The black man gave her a keen, sidewise scrutiny. There was something fishy here. Before, whenever the mouse popped out of the hole, she had just gone on about her business without a fare-thee-well. "I understand. Will you go to the cleansing hut this morning?"

"Yes. Until my time passes."

"I will miss you. But I find it strange that you choose to speak of it. Never have you done so before."

She glanced at him, then her gaze fluttered and fell again to the ground. "No, my husband, I have not. But the moon has circled now twelve times since I came to your bed."

"That is so. Yet the meaning of your words eludes me."

She still couldn't look at him. "When I am clean again, I wish you to take a second wife."

"Ungh!" Bloody Hand grunted as if he had been kicked in the belly. "What madness is this? Are you so overworked that you need a helper?"

The girl shook her head and a tear rolled down her cheek. "Not that, *batsire*. I have disgraced you, and the women laugh behind their hands. Unless you take a second wife, they will ridicule you as well."

"Disgraced me?" The black man's eyes narrowed. "In what way?"

Still Water turned away, tears spilling over in a rush as she caught her breath. "My barrenness brings disgrace to your lodge. The women joke and say the bull wastes his seed on a dry cow."

Bloody Hand blinked and his head recoiled with a snap. Just for a moment he wasn't quite sure he had heard right. Then comprehension seeped through and he began to get the gist of where they were headed.

"Ai! It comes to me now. You are without child and the women make light of you."

"It is not myself I worry about. It is you, my husband. A great warrior must have sons, and the People will say you weaken if you fail to take another wife."

"Why did you wait until now to speak? Did the women not laugh before?"

"Oh, no." The girl brushed away her tears and looked at him, aware for the first time that he hadn't known. "They would not dare laugh before the twelfth moon. Only then is it certain that a woman is barren."

The black man nodded, digesting that. Plainly she spoke the truth. Twelve months without a baby and a woman was considered barren. It was the way, just as all things among the Sparrowhawks were governed by ancient custom. Yet, in a queer sort of way, it rocked him back on his heels. Not once in the past year had the thought of a kid even passed through his mind. Fact was, he'd never exactly pictured himself as the family type. The idea of a bunch of snotty-nosed brats underfoot all the time made him wince. His stick just didn't float that way, and the fact that Still Water hadn't given birth didn't mean a hill of beans. While it had never occurred to him before, he could see now that he should have been counting his blessings all along.

Lifting the girl's chin, he smiled and kept his voice gentle. "Let us have no more tears. You have made me a good *buá,* and you please me just the way you are. When I am ready to have a child, I will tell you."

She sniffled and blinked uncertainly. "I do not understand, *batsire."*

"Tell the squaws that my medicine forbids a child as yet. When the time is right, my spirit helpers will tell me, and then your belly will swell like a mother buffalo in calfing season."

"Truly?" the girl stared at him, fascinated by the thought.

"Truly. Until then any woman who makes jokes will

feel the sting of my medicine." He tapped the amulet dangling from his neck. "You tell them that."

"Oh, I will, my husband. I will." Her eyes danced wickedly and she threw herself against him in a fierce hug. But after a moment she withdrew, the devilish gleam replaced by a sober look. "You could take a second wife, even so, perhaps the one you think on so often."

"In time, little one. In time. There is a thing I must yet do."

"Is she so vain that she will not release you from the vow? You have greater honors than any warrior among the *Apsahrokee*. Such a woman must be a witch to demand . . ."

Bloody Hand spun the girl around and swatted her on the rump. "When I need your counsel, I will ask for it. Now, be off! The old crones await you in the hut."

Still Water knew better than to argue, but just before she went through the doorhole she giggled and threw a mischievous look over her shoulder. Outside he heard her speak briefly with Strikes-Both-Ways, then there was silence. After a moment he grinned, thinking back to her tears, and started gathering his gear.

Ai! She was a good wife, better than most men deserved, even if she was a temperamental little hellcat at times.

Strikes-Both-Ways entered the lodge and stood watching the dark one check his Hawken. When he spoke it was in the elder's tone, the one he reserved for lectures and unsolicited advice.

"My grandson grows wiser with time. Your words have driven the dark spirits from Still Water's shadow."

"*Ae, axeisake.* That is so." Bloody Hand set the rifle aside, then slung a powder horn over one shoulder and crossed a shot pouch over the other. "Yet I wonder if a man ever truly knows the mind of a woman. Often I think the ways of wild things are as a clear pool compared to the strangeness of the one who shares my bed."

The old bowmaker picked at his teeth with a taloned fingernail, then sucked a loose shred of meat into his mouth. "I have observed that a man is better off with a woman than without. Of course, whether two wives would make him doubly blessed is another matter. I chose to have only one woman, and am no judge of such things."

"That is a riddle I will solve for us both, grandfather." The black man flashed a pearly grin. "Perhaps before snow falls, if the One Above wills it so."

"Then you would still take Pine Leaf to wife?"

"Would you have it otherwise?"

"I only ask. The answer must be your own." Strikes-Both-Ways' rheumy eyes bored into the dark one. "What then, my *bacbapite?* After you have her?"

"There is a question beneath your question, old one. What is it you ask?"

"I ask only the obvious. After a man has climbed the mountain, what is there left? Unless to climb yet another mountain."

"Meaning?"

"That, too, is plain. You have gathered all honors the Sparrowhawks can bestow. Should you fulfill this vow of the scalps, you will have done something that no man has ever done. Will you then be content? Or will your eyes turn yet higher?"

"Grandfather, you are like one lost who walks in circles. I feel no urge to lead the *Apsahrokee.* I am the pipe-holder of the Dog Soldiers. That is enough."

"*Ai!* I speak not of the *Apsahrokee.*" The old man faltered, unsure now of what it was that troubled him. "There are times I sense in you the yearnings of a young eagle, as if, with each testing of your wings, you fly higher and higher, until one day you will simply fly away."

Bloody Hand laughed softly and clasped the bowmaker's shoulder. "It would be a foolish eagle who left such a nest as Absaroka. Yet if I let you twist my ear much longer, I will need the wings of an eagle to put meat in the pot tonight. Rest your fears, grandfather. I fly higher than most, but I always return to the same roost."

The black man hefted his rifle and ducked through the doorhole. Strikes-Both-Ways stepped to the entrance, and watched as he strode off toward the mountains. When the dark one disappeared into an aspen grove, the old man muttered to himself and again began picking at his teeth.

Beyond reckoning men had wished themselves eagles, flying high and free above the bonds of earth and mortal self. Even now it was so with the one who saw all about him, yet nothing of himself.

He was alone on a cliff, high above the village. The earth shimmered in the haze of a noonday sun, and below the camp seemed to sway with a gentle rocking motion. Smoke snaked up around the cottonwoods along the river, lifting skyward in fine wisps until it vanished in the still air. Farther out he could see the pony herds scattered across the grazing lands, their sleek hides burnished in the warm sun. The herds appeared motionless, separated in space and time by mere flecks of color. Bays, sorrels, an occasional flash of white, and the spotted horses, somehow more distinctive than the others. It was as if the earth had ground to a halt, and all before him fused to stone in the blink of an eye.

The Moon of Black Cherries was in its last days, and the dark one had come to this high place in search of solitude. There was much to dwell on, many things to ponder, and in the village of the *Apsahrokee* there was no peace for the man named Bloody Hand. Wherever he walked, the People gathered, clustering around, engaging him in conversation merely to say they had spoken with the dark one himself. Not even in his own lodge could he find sanctuary these days. Other pipeholders sought him out, their manner casual, but their questions incisive as they probed his mind on matters of war. Elders came, sometimes with a delegation from their clan, to talk of politics and sound him out on tribal affairs. Often fledgling warriors, young boys returned from their first vision quest, stood outside his lodge for days on end, waiting for a time when he emerged alone, so that they might seek hurried counsel about the path ahead.

Yet as the Moon of Black Cherries waned, the dark one seemed never alone. For he had become *Kambasakace,* the Lordly One, a war leader whose fame surpassed even the hallowed *batsetses* of ancient legend.

Events, beginning with the raid through Sioux holy land and culminating with the Blackfoot massacre, had given rise to a new legend, one which told of Bloody Hand, whose mysterious alliance with the spirit world would make the Sparrowhawks supreme among all nations. That the dark one had destroyed a fort and driven the *tibos* into flight lent even greater credence to the tale. Yet Bloody Hand had not stopped there. While another leader might have paused to bask in the People's adulation, the black man seemed never to rest, content somehow only in the thick of battle. Shortly after the Sun Dance he had led the Dog Soldiers in a great raid against the Pawnee. Then, in rapid succession, he had struck the Shoshone, the Cheyenne, and the Ree. With the raiding season not yet half gone, his Dog Soldiers had stolen nearly three hundred ponies, and not including the Blackfoot fight, had accounted for more enemy dead than all warrior societies lumped together.

Though the People were reluctant to joke about a man of such boldness, they nonetheless found grim humor in his murderous deeds. From the dark one's scalp-stick now hung forty-eight grisly trophies, and it was said that the enemies of the Sparrowhawks slept poorly, if they slept at all.

Ai! Truly there had never been a warrior the equal of Bloody Hand.

The black man's great popularity with the People, something bordering on reverence, was in no small part the reason he had escaped to the solitude of the high cliff. The demands being made on his time were not of his choosing, and it robbed him of precious days that could have been spent in raiding. Worse yet, it appeared that the council was even now hatching some plot to involve him further in tribal affairs. Only that morning his presence had been requested at a council meeting to be held tonight, and it required little foresight to see that some added demand would be made on his time.

The crux of his problem seemed to be White Bear. Since the day of the Blackfoot ambush and the resultant burning of the *tibo* fort, Bloody Hand had found himself cast in the role of advisor to the chief. White Bear openly sought his counsel, deferring to him on all matters pertaining to war. Whether the *batsetse* merely thought him infallible or had simply entrusted himself to the dark one's medicine seemed of little consequence. The fact remained that White Bear accepted his judgment over all others, and had taken to sulking like an old squaw every time Bloody Hand led the Dog Soldiers out on another raid. The chief wanted him near at hand, available for consultation day and night, almost like a resident witch doctor. All of which would have been bearable if White Bear hadn't suddenly turned into a magpie. Everywhere he went, the Sparrowhawk leader praised Bloody Hand with superlatives normally reserved for the One Above, or at the very least Old Man Coyote. Aside from the pleasure it gave him, for the black man halfway believed it himself, he found that it brought him no end of bother. Elders, pipe-holders, untried warriors, even squaws, thought nothing of laying their problems at his feet, almost as if Solomon, in all his wisdom, had suddenly been set down amidst the Sparrowhawks to solve their troubles.

Gazing out over the village, the dark one grunted sourly to himself. It was a pain in the ass, pure and simple. All he wanted was to collect some scalps and steal a few horses along the way. But apparently everybody else had it in their minds that he was some kind of lucky charm: just squeeze him like a bullfrog and out would croak the magic solution to ailments large and small.

Like Doc Newell used to say, horseturds dipped in honey still tasted like shit. Which, to the black man's way of thinking, was about all he was getting fed these days.

Bloody Hand's ruminations were interrupted abruptly by a pair of goldfinches. The birds swirled past his head and hovered over the delicate blue stems of a harebell bush. The male fluttered about like a plump yellow butterfly while his mate stuck her beak into the flower and drew nectar from deep within. Watching them, the black man decided that the little fellow had worked things out pretty much to suit himself. He just stood guard while his lady friend did all the work. When the molty-looking female had tapped all the flowers, the birds darted skyward in a bright yellow blur and winged off.

The dark one chuckled silently, struck by the absurdity of a grown man envying a bird. But then, when it came down to the crunch, that's what it was all about: rigging things to suit yourself, and not getting all bogged down in that holy horseshit of being your brother's keeper.

Suddenly the black man stiffened, and the hair on the back of his neck came up. It was a queer thing about living in the mountains. A man learned to sense the presence of any other living thing. Some instinct developed that relied on neither sound nor scent, and never on sight, either, for when a man's skin went prickly it was like as not the result of something unseen.

Slowly, with barely a trace of movement, he turned

his head and slipped his thumb over the hammer of the Hawken.

Pine Leaf giggled from behind a chokeberry bush and stepped into the open. "Oh, mighty warrior, spare me. I am but a poor maid who has strayed from the mountain path."

Bloody Hand flushed, feeling damned silly in the bargain. The girl had crept up on him like a soft breeze. Which was what came of a man ruminating so much instead of watching his business. It was a fine way to wind up without any hair.

"Pine Leaf stalks well, but she is a poor liar."

The girl came toward him, her lip stuck out in a teasing pout. "You are cruel to say such things. Any other warrior of the Sparrowhawk would see my distress and lead me safely back to the village."

He waited, aware that the look and the switching motion of her hips were meant to disarm him. When she stopped, glancing up at him with innocent doe eyes, he shook his head. "You have much to learn of men. Any other Sparrowhawk warrior, knowing you had followed him here, would pull you into the bushes. Had you thought of that?"

"I did not follow another. I followed you."

"Ai! Now the truth comes out. And why would a girl follow a man into the mountains?"

Pine Leaf blushed. "Not for that. I wanted only to talk with you."

"Talk?" The dark one leaned forward, resting his arms over the bore of the Hawken. "Very well, I am listening."

"Oh, you . . ." The word wouldn't come and the girl petulantly swatted his arm instead.

Her touch triggered something inside him. The rifle thudded to the ground as he released it and enfolded her in his arms. She melted, coming against him soft and limp, and her head turned upon his chest. Their eyes held for a moment, then his lips found hers in a long, probing kiss. She stiffened, uttering a little gasp of surprise. But in the next moment she clutched him around the neck, and her hips thrust into him, rubbing slowly and insistently as a soft moan escaped her lips. Then, as a wetness spread between her legs, she felt the force of his hardness throbbing against her belly.

Tearing her mouth from his, she pushed away from his chest, struggling to escape the powerful arms that held her. Neither of them said anything as they fought, but as quickly as it had begun, it suddenly stopped. The dark one let his arms go slack, releasing her. She stumbled back a step, breathing heavily, unable to meet his gaze.

"I am sorry. A woman should not tease a man in that way. My mother has told me this many times, but I do not always listen."

Bloody Hand's chest felt as if it were packed with hot coals, and there was a curious buzzing in his ears. He raised his hand in a gesture that seemed to have no meaning, then dropped it. "No, it was my fault. I knew you were only teasing, but your touch made me forget all else."

The girl darted a glance at him, then looked down. "I will not touch you again."

"That would be best. We have come so far on this road we travel that I have little will of my own."

"I will be more careful. I promise. We must not spoil this thing between us after waiting so long."

"*Ai.* A lifetime, or so it seems." He studied her a moment, letting the fires slowly quench. "What was it you wished to speak of?"

"I have forgotten." She frowned and her chin came up defiantly. "No, that is not true. I followed only to watch you. Is that so wrong, for me to enjoy watching you?"

"Perhaps you should watch from a safer distance."

She blushed again, nodding agreement, then turned to leave. After she had gone a few steps she stopped and looked back. "What is it called? This thing with the lips?"

The black man shrugged. "There is no word for it in Sparrowhawk. The *tibos* call it a kiss."

"K-i-s-s." The girl rolled the word slowly on her tongue and smiled. "It is a nice thing. Someday you must teach me how it is done."

Laughing, she ran off toward the path and was quickly lost among the trees. The dark one stared after her for a long while, thinking what it would have been like, lying with her on a bed of pine needles.

Then he grunted, changing it in his mind. Not what it *would* be like. What it *will* be like!

Absently he looked back over the wide plain below and started rubbing the amulet around his neck.

The black man knew something was in the wind late that afternoon. Word circulated through camp that there had been a meeting between White Bear and Long Hair. The leaders of the *Apsahrokee* bands seldom counseled with one another except on ceremonial occasions. There existed a sense of rivalry between them, and while the law forbade any one man to govern the Sparrowhawk nation, neither of them felt any compulsion to speak well of the other. Their only common goal was to preserve the ancient boundaries of Absaroka, and even then, jealousy and discord were not infrequent within the bands. That the tribal chiefs had smoked the pipe, and spent some hours in discussion, was an event not to be taken lightly. It was a portent of something momentous in the offing, or perhaps a crisis not yet revealed.

When Bloody Hand entered the council lodge early that evening, he sensed an atmosphere of strain and uneasiness. The elders were grim-faced and unusually quiet, which was something more than the somber visage they generally affected for the benefit of the People. It was apparent that for tonight, at least, they weren't acting the roles of venerable sages. They were nervous and apprehensive, and it showed.

He took a seat in the circle, near the door, and waited for White Bear to get the meeting underway. The chief seemed more preoccupied than shaky, but even that contrasted sharply with his normally phlegmatic detachment. The business of the pipe was dispatched with a swiftness that would have appeased few gods, but hardly anyone seemed to notice, or care. Clearly the spirit beings were getting short shrift tonight. The elders had something on their minds and they wanted to get on with it. Watching it unfold, the dark one was at some loss as to his own part in this little drama. Yet his bafflement was compounded, rather than tempered, by still another puzzler. He was the only pipe-holder present, which said a great deal yet told him nothing, all in the same breath.

White Bear laid the pipe aside and looked around the circle. "Elders of the council, we are here tonight to discuss a thing that affects all the People, perhaps the safety of Absaroka itself. I have summoned Bloody Hand to sit with us after counciling with certain among you. The reason for this will become clear in time."

The chief paused, permitting a moment for objections, should any exist. The elders merely stared at him, waiting, and after a brief interval he resumed. "This day has passed quickly, and as I saw no need to alarm the People, I have spoken only to a few of what it is we must discuss. Therefore, I will recount all I know, just as it happened, and you may judge for yourselves."

Again he halted, and again none of the elders spoke. Pursing his lips, he nodded, then continued. "Some of you are aware that the Kit Foxes departed many suns past to raid the Shoshone. Before first light this morning a warrior awakened me with a message from their leader, Lone Bull. What I tell you now is what was told to me."

The gist of the message, White Bear advised them,

was that an ominous threat to the Sparrowhawk People had been uncovered. After raiding the Shoshones, the Kit Foxes had ridden west to trade their stolen horses, for the spotted-rumped ponies of the Nez Perce. There the leader of the Kit Foxes had been told that the Blackfeet were mounting a large-scale vengeance raid against the Sparrowhawks. The Nez Perce had heard the tale from a *tibo* who belonged to the traders of the far northwest. According to this white-eyed man, the raid was meant as retaliation for the great defeat suffered by the Blackfeet outside the fort on the Missouri. While it was unclear as to when the Blackfeet would raid, it was stated as certainty that preparations were under way at this very moment.

The chief motioned with his hand that he had finished. "I will listen now to the counsel of the elders."

Muttered consternation erupted around the circle, but Sitting Elk's voice came loudest. "Why were we not told of this before? You take much upon yourself, White Bear. The council should have been called into session early this morning."

The chief started to answer, but Looks-at-Bulls overrode him. "Sitting Elk, it is well known that your tongue is faster than your mind. Yet never more so than now. Before this matter could be brought to the attention of the council there were things that first needed doing."

Sitting Elk's lip curled scornfully. "I would hear of these things."

"*Ai!* The *Uwutace* elder speaks for us all," Takes-the-Dead snapped. "There is a smell here which offends my nostrils. White Bear has seen fit to take some into his confidence and leave others as ignorant as blind pups."

White Bear sighed heavily and motioned flat-handed for silence. "Enough. Bickering among ourselves gains us nothing. I spoke with Looks-at-Bulls and Tall Crane only to affirm my own judgment of what must first be done. They agreed and afterwards I sat in council with Long Hair. While some of you here tend to forget, it bears repeating that the *Minesepere* band is also of the Sparrowhawk. It is not the *Acaraho* alone who are threatened, but the *Apsahrokee* nation as a whole."

The heat of his words quieted the elders for a moment, then Takes-the-Dead came back in the same waspish tone. "You talk much but say little, White Bear. Are we to hear of your meeting with Long Hair, or must that also remain a secret?"

The chief's jaw clenched, and he clamped down on his anger before answering. "Long Hair's thoughts were in accord with my own. We must act to protect the People, and drive all enemies from Absaroka. Even as we talk, Long Hair is meeting with the *Minesepere* council. Before the night is out they will elect the Stone Hammer warriors to serve as *akisate*. We must similarly choose from among our own warrior organizations. Their duty will be to guard against surprise, and warn the Sparrowhawks in time to prepare for the Blackfeet raid."

Bloody Hand grunted softly to himself. To be selected to serve as tribal sentinels was a high honor. The Dog Soldiers had been chosen *akisate* more often than any warrior society in the *Acaraho* band. The fog was lifting slightly, and he had a fair inkling of where this meeting was headed.

The elders were visibly impressed with White Bear's decisiveness, and he moved now to lead them into the next step. "We must never let it be said that the *Minesepere* are quicker to respond to the need of the People than are the *Acaraho*. That is why I summoned Bloody Hand to meet with the council. The Dog Soldiers have served well in the past, and it is my judgment that the elders should select them to serve again in the face of this new threat."

"White Bear speaks with wisdom and foresight," Looks-at-Bulls announced. "I, too, would cast my vote for the Dog Soldiers."

"And I," Tall Crane chimed in quickly.

It was apparent to the elders that the *Acaraho* chief

and his cohorts had laid their plans well. The way was greased for the swift, unimpeded selection of the Dog Soldiers. All eyes turned to Bloody Hand, waiting to see his part in this little conspiracy. The black man simply returned their stares, saying nothing. Sitting Elk, who was Bloody Hand's clan elder, at last broke the silence.

"My son, we would hear you speak. Never before have you been at a loss for words before the council."

That was true. The black man grudgingly admitted as much to himself. But never before had the council's wishes been so at odds with his own. Should he commit the Dog Soldiers to serve as *akisate,* it would close the damper on his own plans, which had to do with conducting raids rather than defending against them. Besides, the thought of the Blackfeet working up the nerve to raid Absaroka in strength was so far-fetched he could hardly keep from laughing. After the licking he'd handed Bug's Boys up on the Missouri, they weren't likely to come looking for another dose of the same. The only thing holding him back was how to worm out of it without making White Bear look like an ass. Silently, he cursed the chief for jumping at shadows.

"The council honors the Dog Soldiers." He let his gaze rove around the circle, and come to rest at last on White Bear. "But as pipe-holder, I must question the urgency of what we have heard here tonight. It is my belief that the Blackfeet have neither the will nor the courage to raid the Sparrowhawks."

The elders stared at him aghast. Though his words were plain enough, they couldn't believe the dark one would defy the will of White Bear, not after the chief had sung his praises to all who would listen. That Bloody Hand would rupture his closeness with the *Acaraho* leader left them thunderstruck. Aside from that, it also gave rise to grave doubts about White Bear's judgment. The Dog Soldier pipe-holder was without equal as a war leader. None among them disputed that. The man who took his council lightly might well find himself ridiculed by the People, or worse, disposed from the council by his clan for his own lack of judgment.

Takes-the-Dead found the situation much to his liking. "I would hear more of Bloody Hand's wisdom. This thing we do moves too swiftly to suit my tastes. Tell us why you question White Bear's plan."

"I do not question my *batsetse*'s plan." The black man's eyes flickered back to White Bear, but the chief's expression was like chilled granite. "I question instead what the Nez Perce ask us to believe. This tale, passed along from *tibo* trader to the Nez Perce to the leader of the Kit Foxes, could have grown much in the telling. What might have started out as a simple horse raid by the Blackfeet could easily have been expanded into a fullscale attack by the time it reached White Bear's ears."

"*Ae.* But you will not deny that the Blackfeet have reason to take revenge." Looks-at-Bulls pointed a wrinkled finger at him. "You above all others should know that they are unlikely to forget such a defeat."

"That is true, grandfather. I took five scalps that day. Yet I say to you that the Blackfeet are not fools. My Dog Soldiers have struck fear in the hearts of every tribe on the plains and none more so than the accursed ones who dwell along the Missouri. Would the Blackfeet dare to attack Absaroka when they know that they must answer to the Dog Soldiers? I think not."

The dark one's arrogance left them momentarily stunned. He was crediting the Dog Soldiers—and himself—with greater powers than the whole of the Sparrowhawk nation itself. Yet there was no denying that his words bore a kernel of truth. Never before had the People's enemies been so savaged as by Bloody Hand and his warriors.

Tall Crane snorted something under his breath and glowered at the black man. "Your pride is not unjustified, Bloody Hand, but I would ask you this. Have not we already been raided this season? If fear of your Dog Soldiers is so great, then how could such a thing happen?"

"Your snare is lightly set, old one. These raids were little more than a nuisance, like stinging flies. Let me instead pose another question. In the memory of all here, has Absaroka ever been raided so little as in this season? Think on it, and decide for yourselves why that is so."

"*Ai!* The dark one's words strike home." Sitting Elk made the sign for contempt, flinging it in the elder's face. "We tremble like nervous squaws over the merest rumor. I say Bloody Hand's words are as my own. Let us be done with this thing."

White Bear roused himself at last, scowling at those around the circle. "You prattle much of wisdom and truth. But it is the wise man who defends his own lodge before he rides off in search of honor. The *Minesepere* have promised warriors for the *akisate.* The *Acaraho* can do no less, whether the Dog Soldiers or another group is of no consequence. The threat may well be imagined. Bloody Hand is entitled to believe what he will. But so long as I am *batsetse* it is a threat that will not be ignored. I have spoken."

The lodge filled with an oppressive silence. White Bear had challenged the council to a vote of confidence. They must either accept his judgment or replace him as chief. There was no alternative in an impasse between the elders and the band leader. It was the way.

Bloody Hand saw where it was headed, and broke in before the elders could collect themselves. "My *batsetse,* let me propose a compromise. I will agree to keeping half the Dog Soldiers in camp at all times. This will leave the other half free to raid. If the council accepts, I will divide my warriors between Charges Strong and myself, and one of us will be on hand should this threat come to pass."

The council members looked around to one another,

murmuring agreement, and several made the sign of acceptance. The dark one's solution made sense, and it would surmount the greater problem of a bitter fight within the council. While White Bear was obstinate, and not the brightest of men, none of the elders had any real desire to see him removed as chief.

White Bear wasn't as dense as some of them believed. Though the meeting hadn't gone as planned, neither was it a complete loss. As in a battle, sometimes a leader was forced to give ground and regroup so that he might live to fight another day. Still, he could only grind his teeth in quiet fury at Bloody Hand's overbearing manner. It was an insult he would not soon forget.

Inscrutable, with no emotion whatever in his words, the *batsetse* nodded acceptance to the black man. "The council has spoken. So be it."

When he stepped through the doorhole of the lodge, Bloody Hand could still hear the elders congratulating themselves on having acted as reasonable men. But it was White Bear's darkly bland eyes that he felt on his back, boring holes clean through him, like the hollow sockets of a double-barreled greener with both hammers cocked.

They came in the dark, moments before false dawn. The pony herds were skirted and left undisturbed, for it was not horses they were after. Their force, some three hundred strong, had separated in the cold hours, when the dipper dropped low in the sky. Half their number had circled wide to the east, where they would strike from downstream. The others waited in a grove of cottonwoods to the west, within rifleshot of the village. When first light came they would attack, closing like the pincers of a crayfish on the sleeping Sparrowhawks.

It was the Moon of Short Grass and the camp guards had grown lax with time. The much heralded threat of a Blackfoot raid had occupied the *Apsahrokee's* thoughts for more than a fortnight. But when nothing happened, the People grew weary of the constant vigilance and the waiting. The story of how Bloody Hand had mocked the council spread through the village, and each day since had brought a lessening of fear. Truly, the People said amongst themselves, the dark one was right. Not even the dread Blackfeet would dare to attack Absaroka.

The night guards' ebbing watchfulness reflected the mood of the People, and they paid for it with their lives. The Blackfeet silenced them one by one, with the ruthless efficiency of great cats pouncing on mice. There was no cry of alarm, no warning. Just the chilled silence of dawn, and an occasional muffled gasp as a man felt a blade slide across his throat.

When darkness gave way to murky gray, the Sparrowhawks slumbered peacefully in their robes, unknowing, helpless, their defenses breached. The night guards had been killed to a man.

White Bear came awake with the first blood-curdling war whoop. Unlike many in the village at that moment, there wasn't the slightest doubt in his mind as to what came next, or who the raiders were. He knew.

Precious seconds were lost as he fumbled about the darkened lodge searching for his bow and quiver. Though his musket was close at hand, he gave it only passing thought. For what awaited him outside he would need more than one shot, and a weapon he could trust. Brushing through the door flap, he nocked an arrow and dropped to one knee. Mounted Blackfeet seemed to be everywhere, thundering through the village from all directions. He grunted, lifting the bow. There would be no scarcity of targets this day.

The bow came level on a passing Blackfoot and he swung it in a short arc, releasing the arrow as it aligned with the man's shoulder blades. The shaft went true to the mark and buried itself to the feathers in the raider's back. White Bear's mouth tightened in a grim smile as the Blackfoot collapsed and slid over the withers of his horse.

Something whistled past the chief's ear and in the next instant a bolt of fire toppled him backwards against the lodge wall. Righting himself, he saw an arrow protruding from his shoulder. When he took hold of it the pain brought beads of sweat to his forehead, but he steeled himself to what must be done. Grasping the arrow firmly, he broke it off near the skin line and cast it away.

Kneeling again, he withdrew an arrow from his quiver and nocked it. A mounted brave loomed up before him and he brought the bow level, closing his mind to the searing pain in his shoulder.

Strikes-Both-Ways was still groping around for his bow when Bloody Hand leaped through the door hole. Throwing the Hawken to his shoulder, the dark one fired, and saw a Blackfoot slammed from his pony by the half-ounce lead ball. It was incredible, a nightmare come to life. Yet the raiders' yipping war cries dinned against his ears, making it real. Then, in a moment of blinding clarity, his mind flooded with a single thought. He had sent Charges Strong and fully half the Dog Soldiers off to raid the Utes.

Fool! A lamebrained, muleheaded fool!

The rage he felt for the Blackfeet was like nothing to what he felt for himself. Swapping ends on the rifle, he swung it overhead as a mounted warrior bore down on him with an upraised war club. Twisting aside, he dodged the war club and put the weight of his shoulders behind a looping blow with the Hawken. The rifle butt caught the Blackfoot just above the breastbone, crushing his chest, and a gout of blood spewed from his mouth. The force of the blow stopped him in mid-air and his pony simply ran out from under him. He hung there a moment, suspended in death, then plummeted to earth in a bloody heap.

The rifle had been wrenched from the black man's hands, and as he stooped to recover it, another raider barreled toward him, whooping a shrill, gobbled cry, and brandishing a tomahawk. Bloody Hand leaped forward, ducking beneath the axe, and scooped the brave from his horse with a mighty heave. Grasping the man around the throat with one hand, and by the crotch with the other, he swung him overhead like a rag doll. Steadying himself, he brought the warrior hurtling down over an uplifted knee. The Blackfoot's spine snapped with a loud crack and he folded to the ground with his back twisted in a grotesque curve.

Bending low, the dark one snatched up the fallen tomahawk in his left hand and the war club in his right. Then he turned back to the fight and lifted his head to the sky.

"Hooo-ki-hi!"

Downstream, Long Hair and his band were fighting for their lives as the Blackfeet stormed through the lower village. The *Minesepere* leader was reeling drunkenly from a blow to the head, and blood streamed down over his face. But for all his conniving and greed, Long Hair was a warrior to the core, and he waded into the battle flailing blindly with his war club.

One-Who-Watches, pipe-holder of the Stone Hammers, was concerned not so much for his own life as for the shame he had brought to his warriors. The Stone Hammers had failed in their role as *akisate,* leaving the village open to surprise attack. Yet it was he who had committed them to serve as tribal sentinels, and it was on his shoulders the blame must fall. Then, in a moment of utter helplessness, his disgrace was compounded a hundredfold. Not ten feet away Long Hair went down under a horde of shouting Blackfeet.

Something came unhinged back in a dark corner of the pipe-holder's mind, and a low, chilling moan shook his body. Then he went berserk. Slinging his bow aside, he charged the throng of Blackfoot warriors with his bare hands. The urge to kill infused him with demonic strength, but it was hardly enough. A war club split his skull like a ripe plum, splattering brains in every direction, and he toppled to the earth beside his dead leader.

Bloody Hand had rallied a host of *Acaraho* warriors to a position in the center of the village. There in a shoulder-to-shoulder wedge they gave battle. Blackfeet braves circled and wheeled, driving their ponies in charge after charge against the Sparrowhawks. Raiders who had been unhorsed closed in from every side, a snarling pack of wolves rushing to the kill. The black man led the fight, slashing and carving like a thing gone wild as he moved from flank to flank. Wherever the action was the hottest, he would suddenly appear, springing from nowhere with the bellowing roar of an enraged grizzly.

"Wrooow! Wrooow! Wrooow!"

The war club and hatchet were instruments of death in his hands, leaving behind a swath of carnage as he spun and turned to meet the Blackfeet head on. Across the village he caught fleeting glimpses of women and children being hacked to pieces by raiders, and the rage within him swelled till his lungs all but burst. Yet the only hope for the defenseless ones was that his band of warriors could hold fast, present a challenge so tempting that the Blackfeet would be drawn to them from every quarter. Only then could the squaws and children make a run for it with any chance of living.

Every now and then the dark one caught sight of Strikes-Both-Ways back in the center of the wedge. Cool as ice, he stood there with a short war bow, loosing arrow after arrow into the Blackfeet ranks. The old man appeared to be enjoying himself immensely, and the spectacle of his courage sent renewed strength surging through Bloody Hand's battered and weary frame. Dripping blood from a dozen wounds, he let go a thundering roar, and lunged back into the fight.

Farther upstream White Bear had also gathered a mass of warriors about him. Fighting at close quarters, they were slowly being driven back toward the center of camp. Not a man among them was without wounds, and with each passing minute their numbers diminished. But for every brave they lost, at least one Blackfoot went down. The *Acaraho* leader took some satisfaction in that, yet he knew it couldn't last. His small band was vastly outnumbered, and it was only a matter of time until the raiders whittled them down to nothing. As he fought, he sensed that a greater battle must be raging somewhere downstream. The men alongside him were but a handful of Sparrowhawk forces. That the others were fighting, he never doubted for a moment. It seemed reasonable to assume that they had banded together more toward the center of the village.

Out of the corner of his eye the *batsetse* saw Sitting Elk stagger, clutching at an arrow buried in his chest. The elder's knees buckled and he disappeared beneath the swirling melee of men and horses. The sight somehow brought Bloody Hand to mind and White Bear's rage doubled and doubled again. He cracked a Blackfoot on the head and retreated another step. This was Bloody Hand's doing! Old men dying before their time, women and children being slaughtered like buffalo. His gorge filled with a brackish-tasting bile, and just for a moment he felt his head go dizzy with hate.

Then his eyes cleared and he became aware that the Blackfeet were breaking off the fight. Dumbfounded, he watched as the raiders circled around his own band and hurried toward the center of camp. Suddenly it dawned on him. They had been drawn away by a fiercer struggle, where the Sparrowhawks had gathered to make a stand.

Waving his battle axe overhead, he sounded the war cry and took off at a dead run after the Blackfeet.

The raiders had slowly converged in a pincer movement, coming together as planned in the middle of the village. But there the Blackfoot plan went awry. Instead of disengaging while they still held the advantage, the warriors were drawn irresistibly to the battle raging around Bloody Hand. The black man had been recognized, and the cry for his scalp swept through their ranks. There was the revenge they sought: the hair of the one who had slain their brothers on the Missouri!

Their leaders tried to turn them back, knowing that the Sparrowhawks outnumbered them twice over. The key to their raid had been in surprise, and with that gone, it was time to run. But the warriors had worked themselves into a frenzy and they couldn't be stopped. The black man was there and it was his scalplock they would claim.

The Blackfeet swarmed around Bloody Hand and his men like maggots on dead meat. The Sparrowhawks heard the clamor for the dark one's scalp and sensed the change in the raiders. They fought their way forward, surrounding the black man, shielding him with their own bodies. But Bloody Hand would have none of it. As quickly as they ganged around him, he would break out again, carrying the fight to the Blackfeet. Gradually, in this deadly game of seesaw, the raiders found themselves being forced to give ground, first in feet, then in yards, and at last in what amounted to open retreat.

The black man was crazed with rage, and he refused to pull back. Not even the cries of his own Dog Soldiers swayed him, and he lumbered forward, grunting savagely each time his war club struck bone. Then, in a sudden reversal, the Blackfeet saw that they were being cut off on all sides. From the lower end of the village the *Minesepere* were racing toward them, and from upstream White Bear's small force threatened to bottle them in completely.

What started as a withdrawal quickly became a rout, and the raiders who were still mounted kicked their ponies into a hard gallop toward the outskirts of the village. The Blackfeet who had lost their horses made a run for it, but it was too late. The Sparrowhawks converged on them in a mad rush, and the morning filled with the glint of steel and the screams of the dying.

The black man took no part in the final blood-letting. Arms dangling at his sides, rooted in his tracks, he merely stood and watched. Behind him, dawn broke, and a ball of fire burned its way up out of the earth's bowels. Golden streamers of light played across a scorched earth turned red with blood. The dark one awoke from a daze to see his shadow played over the body of a dead child.

He shuddered and flung his weapons in the dirt. Then he turned and slowly walked away.

It was a time of sorrow along the Wind River. The living mourned the dead and the keening wail of their grief filled the land. Hardly a family among the *Apsahrokee* had not lost a kinsman, and by rough count something over a hundred people had been killed in the raid. Of this number, more than half were women and children. Never in memory had the People suffered such a loss. On the holy skins it would be recorded as the most bitter defeat ever to befall the Sparrowhawk nation.

Throughout the village, long into the afternoon, people wandered aimlessly, numbed and hollow-eyed. They poked about the willows along the riverbank and the woodlands nearer the mountains, searching without hope for loved ones missing since morning. The encampment itself was devastated, a smoking ruin. Hundreds of lodges had been reduced to charred rubble; within the ashes lay the lifetime possessions of fully a third of the *Apsahrokee*. Yet the dead and the dying, and the desolated village, were but the more visible signs of their misery. The evil spirits, gods of retribution and suffering, had dealt them one final blow. Their pony herds had scattered to the winds while the battle raged. Staring blankly at the grazing lands, none doubted that the Cold Maker would be upon them before they could once again assemble the wealth of Absaroka.

But the remorse of the Sparrowhawks was no more heartfelt than that which claimed Bloody Hand. The

black man had lost no loved ones, that was true. Both
Still Water and Strikes-Both-Ways had come through
the holocaust unscathed. Yet the pipe-holder's shadow
soul was like a flayed beast, something raw and quivering that keened deep within his guts. That nearly threescore warriors had died weighed heavily on his
conscience, though in itself such a thing roused only
passing guilt. Warriors lived for battle, vowing death in
the fight more acceptable than the curse of old age.
Those who went under defending home and kin most
surely won a hallowed place for themselves in the Faraway Land. It was the way, and while he mourned them,
the black man was proud that they had died well, as
strong men should.

His torment, and with it a consuming shame, came
instead from the plight of the helpless ones, the ancients
and the women, and perhaps most of all, the children.
The innocents had been butchered in squealing horror
as they ran before the accursed Blackfeet. The thought
of it chilled the marrow in his bones, and as he heard
again their bleating cries for mercy, his innards shriveled into a knot of cold fury. Their wanton slaughter ate
at him like a nest of worms on putrid flesh, and in their
death he was diminished not just as a leader, but as a
man. Something of him had died with them, and the
part that remained left him filled with loathing for what
he had become.

Late that afternoon, when some semblance of order
had been restored, he requested a meeting with the
tribal council. It was granted without delay, and held in
the open, where all could see, for the council lodge had
been burned to the ground.

Bloody Hand appeared before them, not alone, as he
would have wished, but with a throng of onlookers
crowded around the meeting place. Word of his request
had spread quickly, and coming as it did, at such a
strange time, there was widespread speculation that the
dark one intended to mount a raid against the Black-

feet. Curiosity momentarily overcame the grief of the Sparrowhawks, and they gathered in large numbers to hear his words.

Not unlike the *Apsahrokee* themselves, the council had suffered heavily in the raid. Sitting Elk and Looks-at-Bulls, two of its most revered elders, had gone under fighting beside their people. The remaining elders looked haggard and drawn, old men who had lived to see their nation brought to its knees. White Bear's face was masked with ashen pallor, and he was obviously in much pain. Only hours before a *akbaria* had cut into his shoulder and removed the Blackfoot arrow. The wound had been covered with a poultice and his arm was cradled in a rawhide sling.

White Bear gave the black man a dour look. "You choose a poor time to talk, Bloody Hand. While none will deny that you fought bravely against the Blackfoot, the council has not yet forgotten your last words."

This veiled reference to his past arrogance went straight to the quick. The dark one didn't quite flinch, but it showed in his eyes. *"Batsetse,* I have little to say. My words to the council will be short, and require no discussion."

The elders merely stared back at him, withholding judgment. After a moment he gathered himself, summoning the grit to see it through. "I stand before you disgraced, a pipe-holder who has forsaken his vow to protect the weak and hold Absaroka safe from harm. Let all hear that the council must be held blameless for what the Sparrowhawks suffered this day. It was my counsel upon which they acted, and it is I who will bear the guilt."

Halting, he jerked the coup feathers from his topknot. Then he knelt, placing the feathers on the ground, and over them he laid the sacred pipe of the Dog Soldiers. The onlookers exchanged startled looks, and several gasped, unable to credit what they were seeing.

The black man came to his feet and lifted his hand to

the sky. "From where the sun now stands I renounce all claims as pipe-holder of the Dog Soldiers. I declare myself . . ."

There was a roar of protest from the crowd, and many of the Dog Soldiers surged forward, shouting frantically for him to wait, to reconsider. The dark one stared straight ahead, unmoving. Their cries rose to a feverish pitch, garbled and hoarse, entreating him to hold back. But he refused to look at them, or acknowledge their demands, and it became clear that he would not be swayed.

After a while the clamor died down and he again addressed himself to the council. "I declare myself unworthy even to be called a coup-striker. When the pony herds have been gathered, I ask the council to divide my horses among the women whose men were slain in today's fighting."

White Bear's eyes glistened with pride, and a moment passed before he could trust himself to speak. "It is an honorable thing you do, dark one. Yet I wonder if you do not judge yourself too harshly. Perhaps all of us here, myself included, share this guilt equally."

"No, my leader. The blood of our dead is on my hands alone. It was my arrogance, the flaunting of my deeds, which caused the council to ignore your warning. I would not have the People believe otherwise."

"Your words are charitable, Bloody Hand. It is a lesson we might all heed in the days ahead. But let us return for a moment to a thing that puzzles me. You have asked the council to distribute your horses among the widows. Would it not be more proper for you to do this thing yourself?"

"I will not be here, *batsetse*. My last act as pipe-holder of the Dog Soldiers is to banish myself from Absaroka."

Dead silence fell over the meeting place. The Sparrowhawks regarded them with open-mouthed shock, appalled that any man would sentence himself to exile. It was the punishment reserved for those who had killed a brother, or performed some unspeakable act of treachery against the *Apsahrokee,* a judgment so extreme that it required the full consent of the council before it could be enforced.

The black man raised his hands, spreading the fingers wide, and rapidly jabbed them together; the sign for war. "Let all the People hear, so that they might tell others. I have sworn a vow to wander the plains until every enemy of the Sparrowhawks has paid in kind for what befell us here today. However long it takes, vengeance will be exacted for the innocent ones who died to no purpose. I will return on that day when none would ever again dare attack Absaroka. Then, and only then, will my exile be ended."

Stiffening, shoulders squared, he looked directly at White Bear. "I have spoken."

Turning away, he walked off and a path opened before him through the crowd. Behind he left a void, as if the heartbeat of the people had abruptly come to a halt.

The lodge of Strikes-Both-Ways was unusually quiet. The old bowmaker and the girl watched Bloody Hand's every move, but there seemed nothing worth saying that hadn't already been said. Before the council meeting he had told them of his decision, and they had resigned themselves to what he must do. Yet their acceptance made it none the easier, for it was a thing which tore at their hearts.

The black man's preparations were finished and he stood at last before the door hole. The Hawken was cradled in his arm, and from his belt hung a war axe and scalping knife. Slung over his shoulders were shot pouch, powder horn, and a rawhide bag stuffed with jerky. Whatever else he needed would be stolen, or taken from those he killed.

Smiling, he clasped the old man's shoulder. "Look after yourself, grandfather."

Strikes-Both-Ways bobbed his head, hardly able to speak. "My son, I have never told you this, but it is a thing I have always felt. I am proud of you, honored that you are of my blood."

The bowmaker turned away, eyes glistening wetly. Bloody Hand tilted Still Water's chin and kissed her very slowly. When their lips parted he stroked her hair and smiled. "You are all things to me, little one. I will ask my spirit helpers to watch over you while I am gone."

The girl clutched him around the neck, smearing tears across his cheek. Then she stepped back and also turned away from him. If she did not watch him go, then the evil spirits could not follow his trail. Little as it was, it might somehow speed his return.

Bloody Hand moved through the door hole and strode quickly around the side of the lodge, where his gelding was picketed. Waiting for him, holding the reins, was Pine Leaf. Behind her the orange streamers of sunset glinted off her hair like rust on a raven's wing.

Their hands touched as he accepted the reins, but neither of them spoke. He swung into the saddle and sat watching her a moment. Then the merest suggestion of a grin touched the corners of his mouth.

"The path I follow is long, but *Axace* willing, it will bring me to this place again."

She smiled, and something deep and very bright flickered in her eyes. "I will be waiting."

Bloody Hand reined the gelding about, and kneed him into a trot. Dusk settled over the land as the last rays of sunlight fell behind the mountains, and along the riverbank crickets began their evening serenade.

It was the Moon of Short Grass, and a time of sadness in Absaroka.

CHAPTER 10

The moon came up soon after dusk, huge and orange, floating free of the earth. There was a bluish haze around its rim, and it cast a ghostly light across the dry land. An autumn wind, brisk and chill, rustled the leaves of the cottonwoods, and the murmuring waters of the stream became fainter as the breeze stiffened. It was the Moon of Leaves Turning Yellow, and the Cold Maker's first wintry breath drifted down over the southern plains.

Hunched around a small fire, Bloody Hand and his warriors waited for Little Wolf to return. Yesterday they had crossed the Sand Hills into the land of the Pawnees, and it was now but a matter of time until the scout located an enemy village. There was little talk among the warriors this night. The golden leaves stirring overhead and the cold breeze had turned their thoughts toward home. Absaroka. Already the Sparrowhawks would have split into bands and journeyed to their winter encampments. By now there was snow in the high country, and ice would have formed along the banks of Long Grass Creek. The People would be busy preparing for the hard days ahead, perhaps celebrating if the buffalo hunt had gone well. It would be a time of peace and quiet, when a man could reflect on the summer past and exchange tales with his brothers in the warmth of a snug winter lodge.

That was how it had always been, and how it should be now. Yet it was a thing which bothered the Dog Soldiers and made them wonder. Huddled around a cheerless blaze, in a strange land far from home, they couldn't be sure how the *Apsahrokee* had fared. If the pony herds had been gathered and the fall buffalo hunt had brought much meat, then the People would winter safe and warm, with full bellies. But if things had not gone well . . .

Ai! The Cold Maker would bring much suffering to Absaroka.

It was a thought the warriors pondered much these days. Two moons had passed since they departed the Wind River camp, and in all that time they had had no word of the People. Not that they regretted their decision to follow Bloody Hand. His was a worthy cause, even noble, one that a man could be proud to have joined. While he was no longer a pipe-holder, he was still their leader. The night he rode out on the vengeance path, every Dog Soldier in camp had ridden after him. But the dark one had turned them back, berating them for forsaking the People in a time of need. Yet the oath of brotherhood among the Dog Soldiers was stronger than he had reckoned. At last, after they refused to be dissuaded, he had compromised, allowing Little Wolf and nine warriors to ride with him. The others were to remain behind, and await the return of Charges Strong. They were then to choose a new pipe-holder, and erase from their minds the name of Bloody Hand. Though he had not taken a Crazy Dog vow, death would nonetheless stalk his shadow soul in the days to come. They must depend on him for nothing in the time ahead, least of all his return. Instead, they were to select another leader, one who would guide them with greater wisdom in protecting the *Apsahrokee.*

With that the dark one had ridden off, trailed by his

escort. In the days ahead he led them in lightning raids against the Ree, Arapaho, and Cheyenne. Each time they struck boldly, seeking neither captives nor horses. They were concerned solely with vengeance, and they fought with a savagery seldom matched in tribal warfare. Granting no quarter and asking none, they lived only to kill, like a wolf pack gone mad.

Slowly word of their murderous raids spread throughout the Great Plains. Somehow, in the way that bad news travels even among enemies, it became known that every tribe in turn would be hit by the dark one's fierce band. But none knew where he would strike next. The name of Bloody Hand shortly became a scourge, words to be spoken in a whisper, if at all.

It was said that he had taken scalps in less than two moons, fighting with the reckless abandon of a man who believes himself not yet marked for death. Those who had thus far escaped punishment could only wait apprehensively for the axe to fall. Like will'-o'-the-wisps, the Dog Soldiers struck where least expected, sometimes laying a deadly ambush, more often than not sweeping through a village just at dawn. Their raids were swift and merciless, leaving behind a trail of mutilated corpses. Then, as silently as they came, they faded into thin air, disappearing into the vast wilderness of the Great Plains.

But if the fear among certain tribes was profound, it was as nothing compared to that of the Blackfeet. For Bloody Hand occasionally took an enemy warrior captive and allowed him to live. Not out of mercy but only that he might carry a message. It was brief and always the same, and somehow diabolic in its chilling, calculated manner.

The Blackfeet, of all the Sparrowhawk enemies, would be the most brutally punished.

The dark one's purpose was that of a cat who toys with a mouse before killing it. The Blackfeet waited in dread, knowing only that he would strike, not when.

Their fear turned inward upon itself, breeding more fear, and as time passed an entire nation came to live in terror of a single man. Among the great and powerful tribes who roamed the plains, none doubted that this savage outcast would keep his promise, least of all the Blackfeet.

The dark one and his little band had gradually developed a sense of near-fatalism about the task before them. Living off the land, raising and killing for two moons now, they had been marked in a way known to few men. While some of them would die, enough would survive to see Bloody Hand's vow fulfilled. With death as their constant companion, they had come to share a certain contempt for life itself, almost as if they were resigned to the inevitability of what must touch them all, one by one. Yet their medicine was strong and the spirits were with them, and this thing they had undertaken was somehow more than simple revenge. It had about it all the compelling force of a holy quest, a thing not of men, but of the gods, sanctioned by the One Above: the sacrifice of a few so that the Sparrowhawks might live in peace throughout the tomorrows of their children and their children's children.

Still, as they squatted around their campfire as the moon rose high, the warriors' thoughts dwelt much on the more immediate fate of their people. Bloody Hand's concern was no less than that of his followers. The passing of time had done little to diminish his own sense of guilt, and that the Sparrowhawks might endure a harsh winter was a constant source of worry. Yet he never allowed it to preoccupy his mind, or to divert his energies from the job at hand. Given to the practical outlook, he knew there was nothing he could do to change the winter ahead. Over the long haul, though, there was a different matter. Already the enemies of the People had felt his sting, and before this thing was done with they would learn to curse his name. Even on that score he wasn't fooling himself. Nothing short of the second flood would stop Indians from stealing horses. However badly he punished the other tribes, the *Apsahrokee* would still have to watch over their pony herds. But every gut-eater on the plains, the Blackfeet especially, would learn that blood raids on Absaroka were a risky proposition, the kind that sent warriors to the Faraway Land before their time. Without their hair.

A wolf howl sounded nearby and without a word the Dog Soldiers faded back into the shadows. Moments later Little Wolf came trotting in out of the darkness, sweating lightly even in the chill wind. Clearly the scout had run some distance, and he filled his lungs, exhaling slowly as the warriors gathered again around the fire. When the black man squatted down across from him, Little Wolf nodded, smiling slightly, and made the sign for enemy.

"The Pawnee camp is not far, my leader, perhaps half a day's ride, no more. It is a small village, less than fifty lodges."

"Draw it for me," Bloody Hand said, "so that I might see it as you talk."

The scout sketched in the dirt with his finger. "They are camped near trees beside a stream. This stream is very wide but shallow."

The dark one grunted. That would be the Platte.

"The village is not spread out. All lodges are close together, in an open space where the trees end." Little Wolf jabbed pocks in the earth to show trees and drew a circle to indicate the cluster of lodges. "These are smart Pawnees. They stay out in the open where they can see far away."

"Tell me of their guards. How are they positioned?"

"*Ai!* They are heavily guarded, my leader, almost as if they expect attack. Each night warriors are stationed at the four winds. But they guard in pairs, never alone. This is strange to me. Never before have I seen such a thing."

"Not so strange, old friend." Bloody Hand grinned,

and the firelight reflected golden sparks off his teeth.
"They have heard of the Dog Soldiers."

The warriors nudged one another and chuckled,
warmed by his small joke. *Ai!* The Pawnees would know
even more of the Dog Soldiers before full light.

"Show me their pony herd," the black man said, serious now.

"Little Wolf scratched in the dirt, west of the village.
"Here, on an open grassland. There are perhaps two
hundred ponies and four guards. If you wish to steal the
ponies, an approach can be made from behind a small
hill farther to the west. This was the place from where I
watched. Even on horseback a man could advance without being seen."

"We will each steal a pony, but I think we have another use for this Pawnee herd."

Overhead a winged speck appeared, silhouetted
against the moon. Abruptly it folded into a feathered
shaft and hurtled toward them, enlarging swiftly as it
dropped earthward in whistling flight. Then, when it was
almost upon them, its wings fanned out and it swooped
up and away, rising gracefully into the night. From high
above came a shrill screech.

The scout listened for a moment, then glanced at
Bloody Hand. "The hawk watches over his people, my
leader. A good sign."

"*Ae.* A good sign, indeed." The dark one's gaze went
around the fire, touching each warrior. "Prepare yourselves. When all are ready I will explain how this thing is
to be done."

The Dog Soldiers acknowledged the order and
walked off to where the horses were picketed. Soon they
returned with small rawhide bags and again seated
themselves around the fire. There was no talk, and each
man had a look of solemn intensity as he began emptying the contents of his bag. Then, each in turn, they
started painting their faces with the personal medicine
signs that would protect them in the fight to come.

Bloody Hand gathered his own medicine bundle and walked off a ways, closer to the stream. There he opened the parfleche on the ground and arranged each item in its proper order, just as Braided Tail had shown him long ago. When everything was as it should be, he knelt before the medicine bundle and lifted his head to the sky.

"Bi-i-kya-waku. Di-qap-e-wina-tsiky."

The ancient chant began, summoning the spirit beings from the netherworld, imploring them to watch over his warriors in this thing they would do, asking that death and destruction be visited on the enemies of the Sparrowhawks.

Then, as the wail grew louder, the black man pulled his knife and began peeling tiny strips of skin from his forearm.

Light snow had fallen that morning, and already the orange and gold of the aspens had been carried away in bright flurries. Winter had come early to the high country, sooner than the Sparrowhawks expected. The ancients shook their heads, watching the sky, and agreed that a storm was building in the north. It was a bad sign, that the Cold Maker had come among them so soon. The time ahead would be harsh, with bitter winds and heavy snows, perhaps worse than anything the People had ever known.

Shortly after daybreak their speculation turned to certainty. A white snow owl flew over the village and disappeared south across the mountains. *Ai!* The Cold Maker himself had sent them a sign. A warning of what was to come.

Yet, as the shamans were quick to point out, it was but a part of the whole. The spirits were displeased with the Sparrowhawks, offended in some way as not yet revealed. Clearly the Blackfoot raid had shown it to be so. That the People had lost hundreds of their ponies in the aftermath and fared poorly in the buffalo hunt, were

signs that even the skeptics could not deny. This thing of
the owl merely confirmed all that had gone before.

The *Apsahrokee* had fallen from favor. Only when the
spirit beings had been appeased would life again return
to normal.

While Still Water had not seen the owl herself, she
hardly needed to be told that the Cold Maker was de-
scending upon them. That morning, when she had gone
for water, there had been a thin sheet of ice across the
width of the stream. Nor did she need holy men to tell
her that the Sparrowhawk People were besieged by
troubles. Within her own lodge there was trouble
enough for all, more than she dared admit even to herself.

She understood why her husband had banished himself from Absaroka. It was the honorable thing to do,
the only course open to a leader of his standing to restore himself in the eyes of the People. Not once had
she questioned his decision, and her heart had swelled
with pride the night he rode out from camp. But never
had she needed him so desperately as at this very moment.

The Dog Soldiers had been generous after the buffalo
hunt, Charges Strong had seen to it that each warrior
brought her a share of his kill. Yet there had been little
to share. The hunt was the worst in memory, and the
prayers of the holy men hadn't helped in the least. The
buffalo brothers had simply kept themselves hidden,
and despite the hunters' best efforts, the kill had fallen
far short of the People's needs. Now there was barely
enough meat in her lodge to last through the Geese
Going Moon. When it was gone, she would be depen-
dent on the charity of family and friends, and that in
itself presented a bleak prospect. Everyone, the Dog
Soldiers included, had their own families to care for,
and she could hardly expect more than scraps in the
cold time ahead. Perhaps she and Strikes-Both-Ways

wouldn't starve but it looked to be a lean and bitter winter.

At the moment, though, scarcity of meat was but one of her problems. It was Strikes-Both-Ways who worried her most, and more for his sake than her own, she wished desperately for Bloody Hand's quick return.

The dark one's disgrace and subsequent self-exile had been a cruel blow to the old man. Some essential part of him seemed to have withered and started to die the night Bloody Hand left Absaroka. Not that he wasn't proud of his grandson, or in any way believed the banishment to be justified. Even the wisest of men made mistakes, and it took a man of strong character to shoulder the folly of an entire nation. Strikes-Both-Ways saw this for what it was: the act of one who had come at last to place the good of all above self. Knowing that, his sorrow came not from shame or humiliation. It was a thing of the heart, for he had somehow convinced himself that his grandson would never live to fulfill the vow.

The old bowmaker had become morose and withdrawn. After bidding the dark one farewell, he had taken to his robes, and remained there ever since. Like a man whose juices have been sapped, he kept to the lodge, listless and given to long silences where he stared absently into space. Overnight he seemingly lost interest in all about him, even in his work, and perhaps this in itself was admission that his spirit had been drained to the marrow. The bows he made were works of art, each finer than the last, and for him to abandon his craft so casually was an ominous sign.

Watching him, Still Water sometimes had the feeling he had lost the will to live, as if in giving up all hope for his grandson he had also given up on himself. Resigned to it, he simply sat and waited, unable to summon the strength from either his gods or himself to fight on.

The wind whistled and cracked through the smoke hole, and the old man had moved closer to the fire, sitting hunched over with a bed robe thrown around his shoulders. He stared blankly at the flames, seeing nothing. Still Water had pulverized some jerky after returning from the stream and mixed it with herbs and water in the cooking pot. Soon the delicate aroma filled the lodge and she ladled out a portion in a horn drinking cup.

Kneeling beside Strikes-Both-Ways, she took his hand and gently placed his fingers around the cup. "Drink, grandfather. It is a fine broth to give you strength and warm your bones."

The bowmaker merely sat, staring at the steam rising from the broth. Then, like an obedient child, he took a sip. After a moment he took another sip, nodding as he glanced around at the girl. "It is a good broth, daughter."

"Then you must drink it all," she scolded lightly. "You have been very naughty these last few days. One would think my cooking sours your stomach, the way you refuse to eat."

"No, it is not that." He made a feeble gesture with his hand. "It is only that I have no taste for food." He paused and this time took a long drink. "*Ai!* This broth is different. Such warmth is welcome on a cold day."

"We will have many cold days. So you must drink it all and regain your strength for the hard times ahead."

"Do not concern yourself with me, daughter. I dreamt last night that I was in the Faraway Land with all my old friends. We were warriors again, just as in the days of our youth. They were happy to see me, and we went on a long hunt. Just before I awoke I saw myself killing a fine bull elk with but one arrow."

"That was a nice dream, grandfather, but only a dream." She dipped in the pot again and refilled his cup. "This broth will do more for you than a bull elk."

The old man's mouth crinkled in a leathery smile. "You coddle me, but there is no need. We both know what such dreams mean. The spirit helpers are talking to me and I have no fear of their words."

"You should be ashamed of yourself! What would your *bacbapite* think if he heard you talk of such things?" She twisted her face in a mock frown. "He would say, 'old man, you prattle like a squaw.' And that is what I say, too. Now, drink your broth, and let us hear no more of such dreams."

Strikes-Both-Ways sipped at the broth, watching her out of the corner of his eye. After a moment he stopped and looked up. "You would not hide things from me, would you, daughter?"

"I do not understand. What is there for me to hide from you?"

"Has there been any word of the boy?"

She clucked her tongue and wagged a finger at him. "You are a naughty old man. Truly! To think that I would do such a thing."

When his gaze drifted off her face softened and she placed her hand over his. "Grandfather, there is nothing to hide. You know that. The last word of him came before we left the river camp."

Still he didn't speak.

The girl sighed and squeezed his hand. "You torment yourself needlessly. We did not hear bad things. Only good. That he had raided many of our enemies and taken many scalps. That among all men none is so feared as your grandson. Now, I ask you, is that a thing to still your hunger and make you take to your robes?"

"Sometimes it is hard to know what is real and what is not." Strikes-Both-Ways' cheek twitched, as if a worm was wriggling beneath the skin. "There was more to my dream than I told."

"Now what did I say? No more about these foolish dreams."

"I saw your *batsire*. My grandson."

"You saw Bloody Hand?"

"*Ae.* Or someone who looked much like him. A dark man, only he was far away, so that his features were unclear. There was a great fight, with enemies coming at

him from both sides. He laughed and shook his fist at
them, and then . . ."

"Yes?" Still Water edged closer, looking into his face.
"And then? What happened, grandfather?"

"I do not know." The old man's watery eyes glazed
over, fixed on the lapping, golden flames in the fire.
"Everyone suddenly came together and there was much
screaming, and a great cloud of dust, and—then I saw
him no more. There was only the dust and the screams."

The girl studied him for a long while, certain now that
it had been no mere dream. Truly, he had been granted
a vision brought on by the spirit helpers while he slept.
But to what purpose? The vision had revealed nothing,
but told them only enough to raise their fears and make
their nights a time of quiet agony. Perhaps there would
be more, though, revealed in yet another dream. It was
said that the spirit beings often did that, returning again
and again until the vision had come clear.

The old man slumped forward, breathing heavily, and
she saw that his face was ashen. "Come, grandfather.
We must get you back to your robes. Then I will bring
you more hot broth and afterwards you can sleep
again."

"Let me just rest awhile, daughter. I am suddenly very
tired."

Strikes-Both-Ways accepted the girl's support and
made it to his bed on shaky legs. She helped him in
between the robes and then turned back to the kettle.
The bowmaker settled back into the furry warmth, letting the stiffness in his muscles fall away and start to
loosen. But he didn't close his eyes.

Whatever waited in sleep could wait a while longer.
Suddenly he didn't want to know.

The moon was a thin mallow disk on the far horizon
when the Dog Soldiers brought their ponies to a halt.
The low hill directly to their front blocked any view of
the Pawnee village, but it also screened their own pres-

ence. Dawn was less than two hours away and there was a sharp bite in the air. Soon the pale glow of moonlight would fade altogehter, and it was in this brief span of darkness before false dawn that Bloody Hand meant to silence the horse guards.

The black man tested the light breeze, assuring himself that they were still downwind, and then he dismounted and began stripping. His buckskins were tied forward of the saddle horn, where the Hawken hung from a rawhide sling, and his war axe was secured by its wrist thong so that it dangled over the opposite side. The only weapon he kept was the knife.

Shorn of clothing, garbed now only in breechclout and moccasins, the darkness of his skin became little more than a darkened shadow in the fading light. Hissing softly between his teeth, he signed for the warriors to hold their position, then turned and trotted off toward the hill. Within moments he disappeared into the night, a shadow among shadows, lost to sight.

Trotting along, the dark one grinned, resisting an outright chuckle. He could almost hear the Dog Soldiers muttering to themselves. After two months they still hadn't accepted this thing about night guards. Not that they resented it. There was killing enough for everyone, once they stormed a village. But they felt that it was foolish of him to take such risks unaided. Moreover, they made no bones of the fact that a leader should lead, not go off alone stalking night guards.

Under normal circumstances the black man would have agreed. But there was nothing normal about what they were doing. The vow was his, and his alone. That the Dog Soldiers had joined him made it better, but only in terms of enemy killed and greater havoc in the course of a raid. The responsibility was his, and he meant to share it with no one.

From the outset it had been a standing order that night guards were his special prey. Just his, without assistance from anyone. Since it was his game, the black man wasn't bound by tradition, and he made the rules to suit himself. Aside from his vow, which obligated him to assume the greater hazards in a raid, there was another reason that he persisted in this thing of the night guards. It was the most critical moment in a raid. If a warning were sounded and the element of surprise lost, then those stalking the night guards were sure to be killed. Should that happen, the waiting Dog Soldiers would have ample time to escape, and he could go under secure in the knowledge that no more Sparrowhawks had been sacrificed needlessly.

Besides, while he hadn't admitted as much to the Dog Soldiers, there was still another reason, perhaps the most personal of all. He needed the scalps. The count was seventy-three, going on seventy-seven if Little Wolf had been right about the number of horse guards.

Bellied down, he crawled the last few yards and poked his head over the crest of the hill. The scout had done his job well. Separated by perhaps a half-mile from one another, the night guards were stationed at the cardinal points. From the hilltop they looked like the tips of a rough-shaped diamond, sitting motionless astride their mounts in the biting cold. The herd they guarded, upwards of two hundred ponies, was spread out over a rolling prairie of sun-cured buffalo grass. The black man grunted to himself. They would be tired now, less watchful, and with the moon down he might even catch the Pawnees dozing. *Ai!* Before first light they would sleep forever. Testing the wind one last time, he started down the forward slope on his belly, moving with no more noise than a snail inching along the chilled earth.

The first guard went under without so much as a whimper. Bloody Hand had learned by trial and error, and by now he had his own personal method, one that never failed. Locking his arm around the man's throat, blocking off the windpipe, he drove the knife into the lower back. Ripping across and back again, the heavy blade severed the spinal column, and death came only an instant later. It was all so effortless and without commotion that the Pawnee's horse merely looked around, hardly more than curious, then returned gratefully to its nap.

After a long, painstaking stalk, the second guard, then the third, fell with equal ease. Murky streaks of gray had appeared in the sky by that time, and the black man had to rush the final kill more than he cared to. The Pawnee heard him coming and started to turn, but Bloody Hand was on him in a bounding leap that carried them off the horse's back. When they struck the earth the dark one had him in an iron embrace, and a moment later the knife had done its job. Kneeling, Bloody Hand deftly lifted the scalp and stuck it in his belt with the grisly trophies just collected. The Pawnee's mount was a fine broad-chested gelding, and it took only a few moments to coax him within reach. Gentling the pony with soothing horse talk, he caught the war bridle, scrambled aboard, and reined back toward the hill.

The Dog Soldiers were just where he had left them. Nobody said a word as he slammed the pony to a halt and dropped to the ground. They had endured similar waits while he butchered the night guards of other tribes, and none of them seemed particularly surprised that he had returned without so much as a scratch. Much to the contrary, they would have been shocked if it hadn't gone exactly as planned. The dark one's medicine was formidable stuff, and they had yet to see anything that could offer it a challenge.

Granted, Bloody Hand bore scars, more than most warriors collected in a lifetime of fighting. But he carried them as some men would a badge of honor. The jagged cleft in his forehead was testament to the fact. Though it was deep and marred his features, it served as a reminder that he had killed the *tibo* trapper who put it there. The same held true for all his scars. Each represented a dead man. Or perhaps many dead men. It was hard to tell. The number had grown so great that no-

body bothered keeping count any longer. What mattered was that never had there been a warrior with
bloodlust to match his. Few wild things had killed as
much as the dark one. Not the bear or the wolf, or even
the dreaded *carcajou*, the wolverine. Certainly no man.

Bloody Hand quickly donned his buckskins and re-
mounted the pinto. The captured gelding looked to be a
good horse, but in a fight he wanted his favorite war
pony, the *eshoo-shebit*, between his legs. After thrusting
the handle of the battle axe through his belt, he turned
to face the warriors.

"It is time. Remember all I have said. We make one
sweep through the camp. No more. When it is done
each man will capture a pony and ride west along the
river. Those who fail to take an extra pony may find
themselves left behind if we are pursued. Heed my
words, and let it be as I have said."

"Perhaps we could also capture a squaw, my leader?
Two moons without a woman sets a man's teeth to aching."

This remark came from Buffalo Calf, youngest of all
the warriors, but a man of daring and courage in a fight.
Looking at him, Bloody Hand was reminded of himself
not too long ago. He was brash, scornful of his elders,
and quick to test the pungency of his wit against others.

"Buffalo Calf, it comes to me that you should do this
thing. Then, in days to come, we will look back on the
one who stopped to take himself a squaw. *Ai!* It will
lighten our hearts to think of your stiffened shaft dangling from the smoke hole of a Pawnee lodge."

The Dog Soldiers chuckled softly behind their hands,
glancing from their leader to the youngster. Buffalo Calf
ducked his head and said nothing in response. Somehow
the ache in his teeth lessened at the thought of his rod
being hacked off and hung up for all to see.

Bloody Hand let the moment stretch out, then raised
his fist overhead. "The sun rises, Sparrowhawks. Let us

greet it among the Pawnee. *Di wace keetak.* It is a good day to die!"

The black man kicked his pony in the ribs and took off at a slow trot. The Dog Soldiers fanned out on a line, flanking him to either side, and moments later he led them over the crest of the hill. The pony herd came alert, eyeing them warily as they moved down off the forward slope. Bloody Hand signaled and the warriors on the extreme flanks split away, circling around the herd. When the horsemen were spread out in a crescent wall, the dark one kneed his pony to a gallop and lifted his head to the sky.

"Hooo-ki-hi!"

The Dog Soldiers took up the war cry, whooping and shouting as they drove their mounts at the pony herd. The Pawnee horses whirled in alarm and broke into a scrambling lope, headed toward the village. The warriors pressed them harder, yipping and screaming at the top of their lungs, and within moments the entire herd was thundering along at a dead gallop.

That was how they hit the encampment, bunched in a solid mass of horseflesh and hooves. The first glimmering rays of sunlight came over the horizon as the herd roared into the village. The effect of the stampede was not unlike that of a plains tornado. Lodges collapsed and toppled over. Some simply disappeared, pulverized in an instant as the terrified ponies crashed over anything barring their path. The Pawnees awoke to the horror of pounding hooves and raced outside only to be trampled underneath a flying wedge of death. Women and children scattered in every direction, running naked through the chill dawn. Screams rent the air, mixed with the shriller howl of dying dogs, and in a mere flicker of time an entire village was flattened to the ground.

The camp night guards fared no better. Dodging and twisting to get a clear shot, they were run down by the Dog Soldiers and killed to a man. Bloody Hand met two in a headlong crash, splattering the skull of one with his

war axe and pounding the other to the dirt beneath the
hooves of his gelding. Pawnee braves crawled from
the ruins of their lodges, searching desperately amid the
rubble for weapons of any sort. Many were killed where
they stood, clubbed down or shot by the screeching Dog
Soldiers. Those fortunate enough to salvage musket or
bow from the wreckage put up a stiff fight, but it was
strictly reflexive action, and availed them little. The
raiders were upon the village and through it, splashing
across the shallow waters of the Platte, before the Pawnees had time to organize more than token resistance.

Bloody Hand reined to a halt on the far side of the
river and was astonished to find that the gelding captured from the horse guard had followed them through
the entire attack. Bending low, he caught up the horse's
war bridle and looped it around his saddle horn. Looking around, he saw that the Pawnee herd had scattered
like quail over the prairie. The Dog Soldiers were
fanned out as well, chasing ponies in a mad dash until
they could snare them with rawhide ropes. Within minutes of fording the river, each of the warriors had himself an extra mount and was headed back to rejoin
Bloody Hand.

The black man turned and noted with grim satisfaction that the Pawnee encampment was devastated. Except for a dozen or so lodges off to one side, it was a
smoking ruin. Then he grunted and looked closer.

Across the way a Pawnee with a loud booming voice
was attempting to gather a force around him. Clearly he
meant to give chase, and that didn't suit the black man
at all. The Pawnees would have no trouble catching
their horses once things quieted down, and pursuit
wouldn't be long in forming. But a hunk of lead, judi-
ciously placed, might just slow them down a bit.

Steadying the pinto, he brought the Hawken to his
shoulder and sighted carefully. When the rifle cracked
the Pawnee with the loud voice spun around and

seemed to buckle in the middle. Then he folded over, slumping to the ground on his face, and lay still.

The dark one jerked his gelding around as the triumphant Dog Soldiers rode in with their captured mounts. Waving the rifle overhead, he sawed the reins and kneed his pony into a steady lope. The Pawnees looked on helplessly as the small band headed upstream, and back across the rolling plains came the jubilant Sparrowhawk cry.

"Hooo-ki-hi!"

The sun was a pale globe, obscured by a silty overcast that blanketed the land. Late that morning cloud formations had moved in from the north, scudding across the sky in roiling layers of mottled gray. There was a smell of snow in the air, borne in on a freshening wind. Farther west, toward the mountains, the sky had darkened in a purplish haze. Watching it, the Dog Soldiers had small doubt that a storm was raging throught the high country.

Bloody Hand had held the pace to an easy, ground-eating lope throughout the morning, putting distance between themselves and the Pawnees. That a pursuit had been organized, he never for a moment doubted. The Pawnees were a dogged and stubborn breed, not too bright, but mean fighters when aroused. Hardly the kind to slough off the outrage visited on them by the Sparrowhawks. Still, they had their work cut out for them. The Dog Soldiers had at least an hour's lead, perhaps more.

Toward noonday the black man halted to water the ponies and let his warriors wolf down a hasty meal of jerky. Gazing out over the backtrail, he decided that their lead might not be as significant as it appeared. The Pawnees were just the type to kill every horse they owned in order to overtake an enemy raiding party. The matter would be settled come evening, though. If they hadn't caught up by dark, then they never would. Meantime, there was little to be gained in fretting over it.

On the trail again, his thoughts turned from Pawnees to the storm and the days ahead. While he had no formulated plan, it was in his mind to strike the Utes on the next raid. Logic dictated that he hit the Cheyenne, whose lands were a few days' ride to the north, which was exactly why he had decided on the Utes. It was the illogical thing to do, what everyone would least expect. His small band had only one advantage—surprise. That being the case, it made sense to sting the Utes before they had even heard of the raid on the Pawnees, keep everybody guessing and wondering where he would turn up next. That way the Dog Soldiers would always have an edge.

But this storm to the west was giving him second thoughts. Winter looked to be long and hard, and before it was over his warriors would have a bellyful of bucking snow drifts. With that ahead of them, it seemed a bit senseless to ride straight into the teeth of the year's first norther. The Utes weren't going anywhere, and it wasn't as if they couldn't be trounced later on sometime. Perhaps it would be wiser to hit the Cheyenne after all. Then they could dose another band of Sioux and head south into Comanche country. Later they could swing around the lower Rockies, give the Utes and Shoshones a good lick, and head north to start the fracas with the Blackfeet. The more he thought about it, the better it sounded.

Early that afternoon the Pawnees made the decision for him. One of the Dog Soldiers acting as rearguard rode in with sobering news. A large body of horsemen was coming fast from the east. They were pushing their mounts hard, and it appeared certain they would close the gap before dark.

The black man was concerned, but not all that surprised. Evidently the Pawnees felt that a few dead ponies were a fair swap for some Sparrowhawk hair. Still, there was more to a race than speed. The Pawnees might just find themselves beating a dead horse, with nothing to show for their troubles.

Gathering the Dog Soldiers close around, he barked out a string of orders. The pace would be held to a lope, but hereafter the warriors were to change mounts every hour. With fresh ponies under them, they were almost certain to outdistance their pursuers. In the event the Pawnees' horses didn't drop dead, then it would be necessary to ride at a gallop, until nightfall, at any rate. His plan was to cut north from the Platte and make a forced march to the marshlands below the Niobrara River. There, even if by some miracle, the Pawnees managed to keep pace, they could be eluded with ease. Little Wolf was sent on ahead, and the Dog Soldiers were given a few minutes to switch saddles and water their mounts. There would be no stopping after this, Bloody Hand warned. Whatever needed doing had best be done now. The warriors took him at his word, and afterwards, astride their captured ponies, they rode north into a dismal, overcast day.

Bloody Hand reined to a halt late that afternoon, only moments after fording the South Loup. Little Wolf could be seen in the distance, quirting his horse savagely as he raced toward them. The scout barrelled in at a dead gallop, skidding to a stop only at the last instant. His pony was lathered with sweaty foam, heaving for wind in a hoarse, dry rattle.

Little Wolf leaped from the saddle and ran toward the black man. "Cheyennes! A large war party less than an hour's ride to the north."

The dark one dismounted, motioning the Dog Soldiers to do likewise. Then he turned back to the scout. "Slower, old friend. Now start again and tell me exactly what you saw."

"I told you. Cheyennes!" Little Wolf gave him an exasperated look, then stuck his hand up, three fingers extended, and made a circular motion to the left.

"Thirty warriors. They ride in this direction. But in no great hurry. Each man carries his battle shield, and they are well armed."

The significance of Little Wolf's words needed no exaggeration. The Dog Soldiers were in grave danger of being trapped between an angry band of Pawnee and a Cheyenne war party. While the Pawnee and Cheyenne warred on one another constantly, their hatred for the Sparrowhawks was particularly venomous. Should the Dog Soldiers become caught in the middle, they stood a good chance of being annihilated.

Bloody Hand glanced at the dull glow of the sun, noting its position. After a moment he looked back at the scout. "Little Wolf, think carefully on what I ask. You say they are riding slowly. Now, if that is so, where will they be when the sun touches the mountains?"

The scout's eyes flicked to the sky, and his brow wrinkled in concentration, judging time and distance. At last he nodded, satisfied with the calculation. "They will be at the middle stream, the one between this place and the main river. Clearly it is their intention to camp there for the night. The ford is easy, there are trees to break the wind, and grazing for their ponies. Even a dung-eating Cheyenne can nose out a good camp ground."

The black man grunted, suddenly taken with a notion that set his scalp to tingling. As well it might. If it worked, it would be something to behold. But if a hitch developed, there would be a whole passel of dead Sparrowhawks come nightfall. Still, it was sort of like the frying pan and the fire. The choices weren't all that many, and none of them what a man would exactly call good.

Motioning the Dog Soldiers in closer, he roughed out the idea in short order. Their eyes widened, and a couple gawked at him as if he had been touched by the moon beings. But for the most part it appealed to them. There was a certain cunning about it that couldn't be denied. Moreover, it provided an end that seemed wholly fitting for the likes of Pawnees and Cheyennes.

With much whooping and shouting, the Dog Soldiers scrambled aboard their ponies and turned back toward the Pawnees. If Bloody Hand was right, they wouldn't be far behind.

The black man's stratagem came very near working too well. While he had every intention of finding the Pawnees, things got a little out of hand just for a moment. It was the Pawnees who found him.

One second there was nothing but vast, empty plains, and in the next the Pawnees came boiling over a distant rise. Both parties slammed to a halt and sat staring at one another for the span of a half-dozen heartbeats. The distance separating them was perhaps a mile, certainly no more, and it occurred to the dark one that he had cut it very close indeed. The Pawnees were somewhat baffled themselves. They saw the Dog Soldiers clearly enough, knew it was the same band they had been chasing. Yet the Sparrowhawks were headed in the wrong direction!

It was confusing.

Bloody Hand played on that confusion to best advantage. Like a partridge feigning injury, he shouted and waved his arms, making a great show of getting the Dog Soldiers turned about. Then, with dust spurting from their ponies' hooves, the small band took off in headlong flight. They angled off to the north, somewhat west of where they had crossed the South Loup earlier. Quirting their ponies, pounding them over the rumps with bows and musket stocks, they gave every impression of terror-stricken raiders fleeing before a larger enemy force.

The Pawnees took the bait. Whipping their exhausted horses into a final burst of speed, they came on in a howling wedge. Since early morning they had been following an elusive trail, all but resigned to losing their chance for revenge. Now, at last, they had flushed the

Sparrowhawks on open prairie, so tantalizingly close
that it made their blood run hot, and brought their rage
boiling to the surface. Urging their ponies onward, they
came after the Sparrowhawks like wolves pursuing a
crippled elk.

The black man kept his gelding under tight rein, darting frequent glances over his shoulder. Plainly the Pawnee horses were almost spent. The object now was to
keep them in sight, luring them on in a game of fox and
hare. But if the pace were set too fast it might easily kill
their jaded ponies. On the other hand, he couldn't allow
the gap to close much more than it already had, not if
his little surprise was to work. Holding the pinto to a
slow gallop, he splashed through the South Loup for the
third time in the last hour, and led the Pawnees northward.

Something over an hour later the Dog Soldiers topped a
rise and stared down on the middle stream described by
Little Wolf. The sun was a fuzzy ball off to the west,
hovering low in the sky. In the fading light the warriors
could make out a grove of cottonwoods across the
stream. The trees thinned out to a narrow finger along
the western fringe, but downstream they stood tall and
thick, offering perfect cover. Bloody Hand scanned the
riverbank and trees, looking for signs of activity, but
nothing stirred. Just for a moment he thought that Little
Wolf had misjudged either the time or the Cheyennes.
Perhaps both.

Then he stiffened and rose in his stirrups. Off in the
distance, beyond the cottonwoods, he saw a body of
horsemen. Cheyennes, headed straight for the western
tip of the treeline, where the rolling prairie would offer
graze for their horses. Twisting in the saddle, he saw the
Pawnees approaching from the south, dogged as ever in
their pursuit. But he saw something else, too, perhaps
the luckiest break of all or a very timely gift from the
spirit beings. Once his warriors dropped down off the

rise into the wooded valley, their movements would be screened from Pawnee and Cheyenne alike.

Slamming his gelding in the ribs, he led the Dog Soldiers down the gentle slope toward the stream. They crossed the lowland at a hard gallop and made a beeline for the thick copse of trees to the east. Bloody Hand called a halt only when they were far back in the cottonwoods, hidden from view in all directions. Leaving their ponies tied, the Dog Soldiers hurried back through the woods and made it to the forward edge of the treeline just in time.

The Cheyennes came from the north, around the far end of the cottonwood grove, and the Pawnees came from the south, spilling down over the distant slope. Both parties jerked their mounts to a halt, and suddenly everything went very still. They sat there for a while, just staring at each other, completely nonplussed that they had met headlong in the middle of nowhere. Then a Cheyenne war cry split the air, and on its heels came the whooping howls of the Pawnees.

Both sides charged almost at the same instant, thundering across the valley at a full gallop. When they came together, solid walls of horseflesh cannonading into one another, the earth seemed to shudder with the impact. War clubs and bright steel axes flashed in the gloaming light, and the screams of the dying mingled eerily with the shrill, goggled cries of those who fought on. Within moments the battle was enveloped in a billowing dust cloud, and Cheyenne became indistinguishable from Pawnee. Riderless horses broke clear, scattering across the countryside, and behind, the killing ground became a small sea of gore. Raging and snarling like wild animals, the ancient plains enemies set about devouring each other in a fight to the death.

Bloody Hand and the Dog Soldiers were wholly engrossed by the spectacle. They had participated in many such battles, but never before had they witnessed one, been spectators. In a grim sort of way, they found it educational. But more than that, they found it amusing. Laughing and joking among themselves, thoroughly delighted with the frantic struggle taking place below, they agreed that the spirit beings had a choice sense of humor: Cheyennes and Pawnees slaughtering one another all for the benefit of the Sparrowhawks.

It was indeed a fine joke. One that would bear retelling again and again when they returned to Absaroka.

The fight was swiftly done with. A thing of perhaps a quarter-hour, no more. Like bears in rutting season, both sides had savaged one another, and now, as if by common consent, they withdrew to lick their wounds. The Pawnees retired, carrying their dead, the way they had come. Though heavily mauled, the Cheyennes claimed the battleground, if not the victory. Their force had been reduced by nearly half, and of those still living, four were unable to walk under their own power. After collecting their dead, the Cheyennes pulled back to the cottonwood grove, where it tapered out to a narrow spur. There they set about making camp, and by nightfall they had a fire built and their horses were grazing on the prairie to the west.

Bloody Hand and the Dog Soldiers had observed all of this from their vantage point downstream. Shortly after dark, they quietly withdrew into the woods where their ponies were tied. There was considerable talk of the fight, and many crude jests about the Cheyennes and Pawnees blundering onto one another. But the black man walked off a way, taking no part in the conversation. What was done was done, and now his thoughts turned to what lay ahead.

The Dog Soldiers had two moves open to them. They could pull out under cover of darkness, or they could make a cold camp and wait till the Cheyennes departed in the morning. One offered no more advantage than the other, yet curiously enough, the black man found neither choice to his liking. Instead, another thought was beginning to take shape in his mind.

He had turned north as much to raid the Cheyenne as to escape the Pawnee. Now, not a mile upstream, a Cheyenne war party was encamped for the night, battered and somewhat the worse for wear, but a war party nonetheless. Thinking about it, he decided that the spirit beings had a purpose in all things. The Cheyennes could have easily ridden off, just as the Pawnees had done. But they hadn't. They had camped right under his nose, and the reason was clear.

He had come north to raid Cheyennes and his spirit helpers had arranged the whole thing in a neat little package. It was just that simple.

Reflecting on it further, he was suddenly gripped by a perverse and somewhat unorthodox thought, a fitting end to an already extraordinary day, one which would give the Cheyenne nation a genuine case of the shakes. Not that what he had in mind would appeal to the Dog Soldiers. It wasn't exactly the Sparrowhawk way of doing things. Still, there were ways and there were ways. Especially if a man had the wrath of God dangling from his neck in a buckskin pouch.

Walking back to where the horses were tied, he called for quiet and had the Dog Soldiers gather around. They were still in a jocular mood, ready now for some food and a good night's sleep. His words rocked them back on their heels.

"It is in my mind to raid the Cut Finger war party tonight."

There was a moment of stunned silence and then Little Wolf spoke up. "While it is dark, my leader?"

"Ae. While it is dark," Bloody Hand replied. "Does that disturb you, old friend?"

"It is well known," the scout observed, "that the shadow soul of a man killed in the dark must roam the earth for all time. This is a grave thing, *batsetse,* for a man to be denied his journey to the Faraway Land."

"Grave indeed. Yet a man can fight in the dark and lose no more than a bit of sleep."

"*Ai!* That is so. But the risk is great all the same."

"Perhaps not so great. My spirit helpers have counseled me in this thing. They have shown me how it is to be done, and even in the dark, they will protect those who fight with me."

"That is enough for me," announced Buffalo Calf, clearly hoping to regain some of the ground he had lost earlier with the black man. "Whatever my leader's spirit helpers counsel is the thing I would do."

The other Dog Soldiers muttered reluctant agreement, and Bloody Hand looked directly at Little Wolf. "What about you, old friend? Will you join us?"

The scout snorted, grinning. "Who am I to oppose the spirits? I follow where you lead, dark one."

"Then we are agreed," Bloody Hand said, glancing around at the warriors. When no one objected, he went on. "Now this is how it has been revealed to me. After such a great battle the Cheyennes will be tired. There will be only one night guard, and I will silence him myself. Then we will encircle their camp and sneak in on them while they sleep. Their number is less than fifteen, and as you have seen, four of those are wounded. All will be killed, except one. And his sleep must not be disturbed."

The Dog Soldiers darted quick glances at one another, murmuring concern. The black man hissed, motioning flat-handed for silence. "My spirit helpers reveal that it is to be done just so. The one we spare will awaken to find that his brothers have been killed even as he slept. He will return to the Cheyennes with this tale, and henceforth their nation will quake at the mention of the Sparrowhawks. By allowing one to live, we strike fear in the hearts of all Cut Fingers."

There was a moment of utter stillness, then the warriors broke out in excited approval. Truly, the dark one's spirit helpers were bold beyond reckoning. To terrify an entire nation by sparing the life of one man! The cleverness of it surpassed anything yet.

"Remember all I have said," Bloody Hand cautioned them. "This thing must be done with great stealth, and absolute quiet. Otherwise the one who is to be spared will awaken, and all would be ruined. Only knives will be used, and no scalps are to be taken until all the killing is done. Walk softly, my brothers, and strike swiftly."

Fingering the amulet around his neck, he nodded soberly. "My spirit helpers would look with disfavor upon the one who spoils their plan. Take care that you make no noise. Be as the hungry cat, quiet in all things."

Bloody Hand tightened his stranglehold on the Cheyenne and felt his knife grate on bone. The guard sagged at the knees, then went limp, and the black man lowered him to the ground. The night was dark as pitch, overcast with low clouds, and it had taken longer to locate the guard than he expected. Glancing around, he grunted softly to himself. The Dog Soldiers were closing in, drawing the circle tighter around the Cut Fingers. He couldn't see them, but he sensed their presence.

Then, like a dream suddenly focused in the mind, he saw them, dim shapes outlined in the soft glow of coals from the smoldering campfire, worming along the ground on their bellies, moving noiselessly as snakes, and with no more sign of their passage. Entering the ghostly circle of light, they slithered from one sleeping form to another and began dispatching the Cheyennes.

The black man crawled forward to where three Cut Finger warriors slept side by side. Slowly, with the utmost care, he placed his hand over the first man's nostrils and mouth, then clamped down hard. When the warrior stiffened, he drove his knife into the neck, just behind his ear, and ripped down into the core of the spine. The body twitched, then went slack as its bowels voided. Moving quieter still, he eased over and killed the brave on the far side in exactly the same manner. The man in the middle he left untouched.

The thought appealed to him immensely. That this dung-eating Cheyenne would awaken at dawn to find the men on either side of him stone cold dead. *Waugh!* It was a nice touch.

After scalping the two warriors he crawled back and lifted the night guard's hair. Glancing around, he saw that the Dog Soldiers had come and gone, disturbing nothing. Laying his palm over the guard's raw skullpate, he soaked his hand in the warm, sticky wetness. Satisfied, he withdrew his hand and pressed it against the dead man's chest, leaving a bloody imprint for all to see. Then he uncoiled, coming to his feet, and faded silently into the night.

Behind, a lone Cheyenne slept on peacefully, his breathing even, and his dreams untroubled, secure in his slumber.

CHAPTER 11

Summer came slowly to Absaroka. It was the Moon of Fat Horses, yet the new grass still had pointed yellow tips and the wildflowers were late in blooming. Orange-breasted robins appeared as if borne on reluctant wings, somehow sluggish and lacking spirit as they searched the wooded riverbank for worms. Hummingbirds seemed to flutter in bright green listlessness among the late-budding flowers, and only within the last few days had the cry of the meadowlark been heard across the land. Winter had been long and harsh, assailing the very earth itself, and the mark of its icy grip could be felt by all things. The warming sun brought life and beauty and resurgent strength, but with a slowness that left creatures large and small in a state of numbed apathy.

There was no laughter in Sparrowhawk lodges as the Moon of Fat Horses came full. They had suffered cruelly throughout the winter, knowing cold and hunger as never before. The weakest among them, frail oldsters and undernourished babes, had died in great numbers. Women still painted their faces with ashes in mourning, and grief ran strong for those taken victim by the Cold Maker. What had always been their greatest time of joy, the tribe's reunion on Wind River and the Tobacco Planting ceremony, had instead brought the *Apsahrokee* together in lament for their dead. It was celebration of an ordeal ended rather than an offering to regenerate the tomorrows of a people.

Not even the *tibo* trade fair had given them respite from hard times. Winter had been devoted to hunting and staying alive instead of trapping. Their beaver catch had been small, hardly more than twenty packs, and without Bloody Hand to guide them in the trading, they had fared poorly at Rendezvous. The *tibo* chief had been disturbed with them at first, accusing them of having killed the dark one. Only after much argument was White Bear able to convince him that Bloody Hand was off raiding the enemies of the Sparrowhawks. But even then, the white-eyed leader tried to dupe them out of the rifles ordered a year past by Bloody Hand. White Bear threatened to withhold all Sparrowhawk furs and the *tibo* chief had finally relented.

Though the rifles were not the equal of a Hawken, they were far superior to the muskets normally offered at Rendezvous. The trader called them by a strange name, Pennsylvania Rifles, and had one of his men demonstrate that they were vastly more accurate than a musket, particularly at long ranges. When the *Apsahrokee* departed Rendezvous, they took with them a hundred of these fine rifles, along with enough powder and lead to see them through the winter. Yet they had taken little else, for the *tibo* leader dealt harshly with them in the trading. Had Bloody Hand been there, he could have haggled and cursed, bargaining in the white man's way, but as it was, they did well to come away with the rifles.

Now, with the raiding season upon them, the Sparrowhawks were preparing once again to go against their ancient enemies. But some essential force seemed to have vanished. While they were better armed than ever before, with rifles and muskets spread throughout the warrior societies, the spark that had fired them on in times past was curiously missing. Many blamed it on the hard winter, and others said the tribe had not yet recovered from the defeat handed them by the Blackfeet. Whatever their reasons, though, it was little more than talk. The wiser ones, particularly the council elders, saw it for what it was. With Bloody Hand's self-exile a malaise had fallen over the Sparrowhawks. They had once more reverted to what they were before his coming: magnificent horse thieves, but hardly lords of the plains. As if the heart had been plucked from a nation, they were diminished as warriors by the loss of his boldness and daring. It was the gauge against which all men had come to measure courage. Without it they had lost the goad which prompted them to test the limits of their own bravery, both as men and as warriors.

Yet of all Sparrowhawks, none had lost heart quite so much as Strikes-Both-Ways. The old bowmaker had somehow made it through the winter, more as the result of Still Water's nagging than anything else. She had badgered him incessantly, scorning his faith in his gods to spur him on one day at a time. The girl had slowly aroused a glimmer of hope in Strikes-Both-Ways, some faint spark of belief that his grandson might live to fulfill the vow. Though he remained bedridden and desperately ill, he had lived. Like a man groping blindly in the dark, he clung to the vibrancy of Still Water's voice, and on this slender thread had he survived.

But with the Moon of Fat Horses the girl came up against an obstacle not even she could surmount. White Bear had returned from Rendezvous with disheartening news: the dark one had failed to appear, as many thought he would. When Strikes-Both-Ways heard this, he began to sink rapidly. The old man had convinced himself that if his grandson was alive, he would have somehow attended the *tibo* trade fair. That he hadn't could mean only one thing: Bloody Hand was dead.

Still Water saw then that the bowmaker had settled on this as his one remaining hope. He had willed himself to live in the belief that his grandson would appear at Rendezvous. When he failed to materialize, all hope faded. Strikes-Both-Ways resigned himself to what had been averted throughout the time of the Cold Maker. He lay back in his robes and prepared to cross over to the Faraway Land.

The girl's bewilderment shortly turned to fear. She knew that people could will themselves to die, yet she didn't believe the bowmaker possessed the strength for such an act, not against the determination of her own will. She had staved off Death repeatedly, never once allowing it to enter the lodge of Strikes-Both-Ways, and she could do so again. But when she scolded and berated him the bowmaker didn't respond. His eyes were fixed and glassy, his breathing labored, and for the first time Still Waters felt the icy claws of panic clutching at her heart.

Hurriedly, she sent for Braided Tail.

The shaman arrived in short order, and to his credit he made no mention of a fee. His examination of Strikes-Both-Ways was thorough, if somewhat brief. Kneeling, he placed his ear to the old man's chest and listened first to the heart then to the lungs. After pondering that a moment, he lifted Strikes-Both-Ways' eyelids and peered deeply into the glazed eyes. Finally he thumped around on the bowmaker, much as one would rap a melon, and sat back to consider the results.

After a while he muttered something to himself and began rummaging around in his rawhide medicine bag. The parfleche he pulled from the bag was handled with the greatest care. He laid it on the floor and unwrapped it, revealing a mound of tiny, bright yellow leaves. He asked the girl for a horn cup and into this he crumpled a handful of the dried leaves. Then he poured hot water into the cup and waited for the mixture to brew. When it was ready he lifted Strikes-Both-Ways' head and gently forced the mixture down his throat.

Braided Tail went into his bag again and came out with an eagle head rattle and a bound thatch of sacred sage. Climbing to his feet, he began a slow, shuffling dance around the bowmaker. While he danced, he chanted an ancient healing song, shaking the rattle and waving the sage in a manner that seemed to accentuate each word of the chant. Four times he danced around the prostrate man, and then he stopped and again knelt down. Strikes-Both-Ways was clearly breathing easier, and the film over his eyes seemed to have dulled. The holy man nodded, smiling faintly, and settled back on his haunches to watch.

Suddenly the bowmaker's condition underwent a sharp reversal. His breathing became hoarse, almost a labored wheezing, and beads of perspiration appeared on his forehead.

Braided Tail grunted and turned back to the girl. "Listen well, and do not ask questions. I must have a kettle of boiling water and the skinned head of a freshly killed dog. Hurry, otherwise the old one's time is short."

Still Water grabbed a water bag and a knife and darted through the doorhole. When the flap swung shut the holy man carefully counted out ten of the yellow leaves, stuck them in his mouth, and slowly began munching.

Something more than an hour later Braided Tail stood before the simmering pot. He was bared to the waist and his eyes gave off a flat sheen as he stared at the boiling water. Then he blinked as a bone white dog skull popped to the surface, scalded clean of meat and tissue. It bobbed about on the roiling water for a moment and sunk again into the depths of the kettle. Twice more in the space of a minute the skull burst to the surface, almost as if it were trying to escape the steaming pot. When it disappeared for the third time, the holy man straightened and began an eerie, high-pitched chant.

Watching him, the girl gasped and covered her mouth as Braided Tail slowly lowered his arms into the boiling water. There was no expression whatever on his face, not the least sign of pain, and his shrill chant never once missed a beat. His arms moved and his hands seemed to grope about inside the pot. Then he stiffened and the veins in his arms became knotted cords as he pulled at something with all his might. Suddenly his hands exploded from the depths of the kettle, showering the lodge with scalding water, and in his palms was cupped the dog skull.

Lifting it overhead, he offered it to the four winds, chanting all the while. Still Water followed his every movement with a look of spellbound wonder. She could see that his arms were not scalded, nor did he evidence any pain at holding the steaming skull. Unable to stop herself, she gasped again as he turned and knelt beside the old bowmaker.

Braided Tail leaned forward and pressed the steaming skull to Strikes-Both-Ways' chest. Wispy tendrils of smoke rose in the air and there came the smell of scorched flesh. The holy man held the skull in place for several moments, pressing hard. Then, as the stench lessened and the smoke drifted away, he eased off and lifted the skull. The girl saw it clearly as he moved back, and she choked off a scream, burying her face in her hands.

Strikes-Both-Ways' chest bore no sign of a scald.

The holy man grunted and tossed the dog skull aside. Gathering his tools, he stuffed them into the bag and rose to his feet. With an air of detached interest he studied the bowmaker for several moments, then shook his head and looked around at the girl.

"There is nothing more to be done. The evil spirits refuse to come out. Sometimes it is this way. A man wills himself to die and medicine alone is not enough."

Braided Tail glanced once more at the old man, then turned and crossed to the doorhole. When the flap closed behind him, a tomblike stillness settled over the lodge.

The girl moved closer and knelt beside Strikes-Both-Ways. His breathing was shallow now, hardly more than small sighs, and the beads of sweat had been replaced by a cold pallor. Still Water pulled the bed robe up over his shoulders and tucked it under his chin. Her touch seemed to rouse him, and his eyes opened slowly in rheumy slits.

"Is that you, daughter?"

"Yes, grandfather. I am with you."

"My journey begins." He smiled, trying to focus on her face. "It is a peaceful thing. So easy to let go."

The girl's eyes filled with tears. "Please stay, grandfather. Only a little longer. Bloody Hand will return. I know he will. And if he finds you gone, his heart will break like dry earth under a pony's hooves."

"All things are possible to the One Above." There was a long silence and for a minute she thought he had slipped away. Then his lips moved in a guttural whisper. "If he returns, tell him I crossed over a proud man. Only my true *bacbapite* could have made it so."

The girl swallowed hard, fighting against a cry lodged in her throat. Hot tears streaked her cheeks and she brushed them away, leaning closer as his lips moved again.

"I go now, daughter. The spirit helpers have come to—"

Strikes-Both-Ways' words ended in a small rush of air. Then his eyes closed, and something like a smile touched his mouth.

He had crossed over at last.

The Dog Soldiers splashed through the stream, urged their mounts up the far bank, and set off at a gallop through a stand of aspens. Shortly the ground steepened and climbed upward toward a mountain pass, and their ascent slowed as they entered the pine forest. Scrambling and digging, their ponies carried them over the first bench, then tackled the higher slope in a series of lurching bounds. Using their quirts sparingly, the Dog Soldiers talked to their horses in the low-pitched way, and drove them to bursts of greater effort with little more than a touch of the heels.

Something less than an hour later, they gained the top of the divide. Bloody Hand reined in and signaled that the winded ponies were to be given a breather. Ahead lay a wide valley, dropping off slowly through the foothills to the south and emerging onto the sweeping grassland of the plains. The black man studied it a moment, fixing landmarks in his mind, then dismounted and walked back to the north side of the pass.

Below, in the valley they had just left, the ruins of a Blackfoot village smoldered in the early morning sun. From the mountaintop it looked like a smoking anthill as people and horses raced about in wild confusion. Watching, the dark one grunted approval. The raid had been well executed. Striking at first light, the Dog Soldiers had set fire to the lower village, killed a number of Blackfeet, and scattered the pony herd as they made good their escape. Now, a southern breeze had fanned the fire, spreading flames to the upper end of the camp. With only passing luck the entire village would be burned to the ground, which made it a good day's work. This was the largest Blackfoot encampment they had yet struck, numbering some three hundred lodges, and it seemed a fitting climax to all that had gone before.

Now they could go home. To Absaroka.

But the thought was a fleeting one, for the black man started and a frown wrinkled his brow. Below there was a sudden spurt of activity, and a great mass of horsemen gathered along the lower edge of the village. By rough count he judged it to be upwards of a hundred warriors. Apparently the Blackfeet were singed worse than he thought. They meant to give chase.

Little Wolf approached and stood beside him, watching the horsemen as they forded the stream. After a moment the scout snorted with disgust. "There are too many of the accursed ones for us to fight."

"*Ae,* that is so," Bloody Hand agreed.

"Even if we surprised them here in the pass their numbers would soon overpower us."

"That also is true, old friend."

"Yet you make no move to flee. If we are to outrun them, we must hold the lead your spirit helpers have given us."

"Their horses are fresh, while ours have ridden through the night. They would overtake us by midday."

"Then you did not expect them to pursue us?"

"Not this time. I thought the fire would claim their attention."

The scout smiled like a gray-muzzled wolf. "It is a fine way to die, fighting Blackfeet. A Sparrowhawk could ask no more."

The dark one turned, testing the wind, and the lynx-eyed look came over him. "No, old friend. It is Blackfeet who will die this day, not Sparrowhawks. Summon the warriors. Quickly!"

The Dog Soldiers came on the run at Little Wolf's call. By that time Bloody Hand was squatted over a pile of pine needles and twigs, striking sparks from his flint and steel. When the little mound caught fire he fed it brush and larger sticks until it was burning nicely. Then he explained what must be done, ordering the warriors to collect heavy branches that could be used as fire-brands. They clapped their hands with delight, thoroughly fascinated by the diabolic twists his mind took. Yipping and howling, they scattered to search for wood.

Within minutes the Dog Soldiers were rushing here and there across the mountaintop, setting their torches to dead trees, bushes, and the mounds of dried pine needles gathered at the base of nearly every tree. The fires started small but gained intensity with breathtaking quickness. The pass was like a funnel, and the south wind whisked through with considerable force, fanning the fires downward along the northern slope. Suddenly the entire mountainside seemed to ignite with a great whoosh as the flames crowned, leaping from tree to tree. Sped along by the south wind, a wall of flame grew higher and wider, raging downhill as its fiery tentacles spread outward on both flanks.

The Blackfeet were halfway up the mountain before they took alarm. The smell of smoke came first, puzzling them, but the towering lodgepole pines hid the growing conflagration from view. They pulled their ponies to a halt, jamming up in a large cluster on the steep incline. Then, with a suddenness that brought shrieks of terror from man and animal alike, the forest before them burst into flames. Those in the lead whirled their mounts, bowling over horsemen in the rear, and went plunging back the way they had come. Within seconds the mountainside became a hornet's nest of crazed ponies and screaming men, as they fled headlong before the flames. But they were pitted against the wind, and the race was lost even before it started.

The flames leaped ahead of them, crowning from treetop to treetop with lightning speed. They hadn't gone fifty yards when they found themselves encircled by a raging holocaust. Then, in the space of a blink, they were simply engulfed by flames. The roar of the blaze drowned out their screams, and in a matter of seconds the fire swept on downhill. Behind, it left only the charred shapes of man and beast, and the smoky rubble of a razed forest.

The Blackfeet had been fried to a cinder.

Watching it all from above, the Dog Soldiers danced with glee, whooping and shouting as the inferno devoured their enemies. They had seen many things since casting their lot with the dark one. Things so strange that only those who saw it with their own eyes could believe it had happened. But never had they seen anything to equal this. Perhaps no one had, or ever would again.

It was somehow enough. Like wolves slaughtering sheep, they had at last been sated with killing. Even the dark one's bloodlust had waned with the Moon of Fat

Horses. As he had said only last night, it was time to go home.

They gathered their ponies and mounted, and Bloody Hand led them down out of the pass. Little Wolf rode ahead to scout the valley, but even that seemed somehow different. They were no longer a band of exiled raiders looking for a fight. They were Sparrowhawk warriors returning to their homeland, bound at last for Absaroka.

The black man's thoughts were no less on home than those of the Dog Soldiers. Nearly a year had passed since he banished himself from the land of the *Apsahrokee*. In that time his hardy band had left a swath of suffering and desolation wherever they roamed. The best he could calculate, their odyssey had covered better than ten thousand miles, crisscrossing the plains and mountains like nomadic wanderers. But more to the point, they had wrought a bloodbath unlike anything known among the western tribes. Including this morning's little fracas, he figured they had accounted for somewhere around three hundred dead and half again that many wounded.

Their raids had become a thing of precision and swiftness, almost without flaw in the planning and execution. Over the months they had melded into a disciplined, well-coordinated fighting machine, like a pack of wolves grown accustomed to working with one another in the hunt. They struck where and when it suited them, and always against those who expected it least. They hit fast, left havoc in their wake, and evaporated with the morning mist, like a spectre of death.

Even the snows of the winter past had failed to halt their raids. Late in the time of the Snow Moon, Little Wolf had found a small band of Shoshones camped in a sheltered valley along the Snake. While the black man couldn't bring himself to kill women and children, the Dog Soldiers were not hindered by his squeamishness. Amid the deafening howls of a mountain blizzard, they had massacred the entire village. Afterwards they had jested about it, gently reminding him that Sparrowhawk enemies granted no mercy to the defenseless ones when they attacked. All of which was true, but the Shoshone raid somehow remained a night of horror he would sooner forget.

Still, he was proud of the Dog Soldiers in a way that few leaders are privileged to know. They had gone hungry, marched thousands of miles through blizzards and sand storms and scorching heat, and suffered deprivations that were harsh even by their own standards. But they had never complained, and in all their months together no man had talked of returning to home and family. They had sworn to follow the dark one until his vow was fulfilled, and none among them had ever voiced regret. They had fought and killed and endured hardship as if his vow were their own.

Not that the toll hadn't been heavy. Of the ten Dog Soldiers who rode out from Absaroka with him, only four remained. The price of what they had done was to flirt with death on an unending basis, and it had been paid in full.

Yet there was no sorrow for those who had fallen. They were warriors, and lived only that they might court death. It was the way, the code of all Sparrowhawks, accepted by every warrior in the days of his youth: old age was a scourge and death in battle a blessing.

Those who had been killed in the raids were the bravest of brave, honored above all men. They had given their lives not for horses or coup of another feather in their topknots, but in service to the vow of a brother. Their praises would be sung throughout all of Absaroka, and in days to come, wherever Sparrowhawks gathered, the stories of their courage would be retold in the honored way, the way reserved for those who had sacrificed all they possessed for the good of the People.

That was another vow Bloody Hand had made to himself many months back, when the snows were deep and his shivering little band had been reduced to eating horsemeat: Those who had taken up his cause, both the living and the dead, would be honored as no men before them.

It was little enough, and far less than they deserved.

The black man was reflecting on this very thing when Little Wolf came pounding back across the valley. The scout skidded his pony to a halt in a shower of dirt and began jabbering in the fast, guttural way that they had heard countless times over the year past.

"Blackfeet! A small band, where the valley narrows and opens onto the plains. They are driving many stolen horses this way."

"A small band, you say?" Bloody Hand cocked his head in an owlish frown. "After this morning's fight, old friend, tell me what it is you call small?"

The scout grinned. "Only ten warriors, my leader. But they have many ponies. A hundred. Perhaps more."

"I thought we were through with raiding. Was it not you who counseled me to back away from the fight on the mountain?"

"That is true, *batsetse.*" Little Wolf hung his head sheepishly. "But there is a difference. These men have horses."

The dark one grunted, holding back a smile. Never was a Sparrowhawk more serious than in a matter involving horses. War was one thing. But horses! As Little Wolf said, it made a difference.

Twisting in the saddle, he looked around at the warriors. "Which will it be, Dog Soldiers? Horses or home? Today I lead where you command."

Lame Deer, one of the older warriors, spoke up. "There are only ten Blackfeet, my leader. Perhaps we could persuade them to part with their horses, so that we do not return home empty-handed."

The Dog Soldiers laughed. *Ai!* Only ten Blackfeet, better odds than they had had in many moons. And so many fine horses. It was a rare opportunity, indeed.

Bloody Hand laughed also, blinking to hide the pride that welled up in his eyes. Waving the Hawken overhead, he gigged his pinto in the ribs and took off down the valley at a lope.

The Dog Soldiers topped the last rise into To-gwo-tee-a-Pass and brought the pony herd to a milling halt. Before them stretched the Wind River valley, now lush and green in the opening days of the Moon of Black Cherries. The grasslands were thick, swaying gently in a soft breeze, and tall as a man's knees. Along the river the great spangled leaves of the cottonwoods blended with the fringed plumes of slender willows. Golden shafts of sunlight sparkled off the water, reflecting the silver and green of the trees in a dizzying array of color. The mountains lifted upward from the earth in rocky, towered spires, and higher still, stark white clouds hung motionless against the soft blue muslin of the sky.

Nothing had changed. It was just as they remembered it, a land of warmth and plenty, eternal in its lavish grandeur.

Absaroka.

Bloody Hand swallowed around a lump in his throat, then he grinned, twisting in the saddle, and called out to the Dog Soldiers. "Brothers, our journey is ended! We have come home."

His words broke their trance, and like statues come to life they exploded with joy. Little Wolf and Lame Deer and the others laughed and babbled in a great clamor of pent-up emotion. Their eyes glistened, and the timbre of their voices was shrill, somehow shaky. Just for a moment they were no longer warriors, but little children come again and at long last to the land of their fathers.

The dark one turned and pointed to the only stranger among them, a blackfoot pipe-holder taken captive when they had ambushed the horse herd. The man rode with his arms bound behind him, and his feet lashed under his pony's belly. There was neither joy nor sorrow in his look, but merely the stony composure of one who must yet face the ultimate test.

"*Ai*, brothers!" Bloody Hand shouted. "Never let it be said that the Dog Soldiers return home without gifts for the People. There is a sight to warm the hearts of all!"

Amid garbled war cries and bellowed whoops of laughter, the black man led his warriors out of the pass and began the descent into the land of the Sparrowhawks.

Youngsters playing at the edge of the village spotted them first, and for a few seconds could only stare openmouthed. Then they raced ahead, darting through camp like copper butterflys, sounding the cry. "Bloody Hand! The dark one comes! Bloody Hand has returned!"

The name brought the village to a standstill. Squaws froze at their work and warriors turned to stare upstream, disbelieving. But their astonishment lasted only an instant. Suddenly an outcry went up, as the name ricocheted back and forth through camp, and pandemonium broke loose. People spilled from their lodges, howling dogs set off a deafening chorus, and a great wedge of women, children, and yipping warriors rushed toward the approaching Dog Soldiers. They came on by the tens, then the hundreds, until at last a thousand and then another thousand swarmed around in a milling crush. The racket they raised was an unintelligible din, laughing and shouting and crying, yet over it all, again and again, thundering the name. "Bloody Hand! Bloody Hand! Bloody Hand!"

Whatever his shortcomings in the past, it was clear that the dark one was now only a step removed from the spirit gods themselves. The People traced their suffering and hardships back to the very day he had left them. His departure had brought them grief and slack bellies and harsh winter. Like some dusky onyx talisman, they had built him up in their minds as a man above men, imbued by the spirits with some magical gift. It was he who had led them in their greatest victories, cast a charm over the buffalo brother so that their meat racks were full, taught them the ways of the beaver, and filled their lodges with the wonderous goods of *tibo* traders. They had prayed long and hard for the spirits to give him safe return, so that he might guide them in the hunt and lead them against their ancient enemies.

He belonged now to the People, to Absaroka. His medicine was no longer his own but a thing of the tribe. Power centered in one man for the good of all, to dispel evil and bring again to their land a time of plenty. Whatever doubts had been nurtured by skeptics in the past were long since gone. Now, truly, he was *Kambasakace*, the Lordly One.

Through the crowd Bloody Hand caught sight of White Bear, but search as he might he couldn't spot Strikes-Both-Ways. That Still Water wasn't here, he understood. A wife was expected to await her man in his lodge, where they had parted. But it puzzled him that the old man hadn't turned out. Then he had no more time for thought. The crowd pulled him from his horse as the chief strode forward to greet him.

White Bear clasped his shoulder in a rough grip. "The *Apsahrokee* welcome you, dark one. You have been gone from us too long."

"*Ae batsetse.* For too long. But it was a thing which needed doing."

"Your vow has been fulfilled, then?"

The black man nodded. "Only a fortnight past. We have raided the Blackfeet four times since the Moon of New Grass. They were the last, and we exacted full measure for the sorrow they brought to Absaroka."

"*Ai!* We have heard of your raids." White Bear grinned, cocking one eyebrow. "Our enemies sleep lightly these days. The tale is told among all tribes of how you mark the dead with a bloody handprint."

"The honor belongs not to me but to the Dog

Soldiers. As you can see, most of those who followed me have not returned. I would sing their praises to the People, for without them my vow would have been lost to the wind."

"I will arrange it myself." The chief glanced past Bloody Hand, regarding the Blackfoot captive a moment. "What is this? Something for the squaws?"

"Yes, my leader. They can vent their grief on this accursed one. It is little enough for what they have lost."

The people close around them overheard this and started muttering, casting dark looks at the Blackfoot. White Bear saw what was coming and moved to stop it. Holding his arms high, his voice floated out over the great throng.

"Hear me, Sparrowhawks. There will be a feast dance this night, to honor Bloody Hand and his warriors. They have brought us a Blackfoot captive, but he is not to be harmed. The law states that he must be turned over to the squaws, and that is how it will be, tonight, at the feast! Now go, and prepare yourselves for the long night ahead."

The Sparrowhawks went mad with excitement, hurling curses and shaking their fists at the Blackfoot. But they left him to his Dog Soldier captors, and began slowly drifting off. The law was a good thing, they told one another, and it was only right that all should see the fate of this accursed one. White Bear moved among them, hurrying along those whose curses seemed the loudest. When he finally turned back, he saw Bloody Hand disappearing through the crowd. People still swarmed around him, wanting only to speak his name and touch him, to welcome him back. Not to be distracted, he merely nodded and smiled, and kept on in a straight line toward his own lodge.

When he came through the doorhole, Still Water flung herself around his neck, sobbing and laughing in the same breath. She covered his face with kisses, squeezing harder and harder, and he squeezed right back. Their year apart had been a time of misery and need, and they strained against one another, as if nothing short of physical union would make it real, even now. Slowly, after a long while of caressing and soft endearments, they came apart. Then the black man saw her clearly for the first time, and he started.

Her face was coated with ashes.

"You are in mourning." It was a statement more than a question.

"Ae, my husband. Your grandfather has crossed over."

"When?" There was a peculiar ringing in his ears, and the words seemed far away, disembodied.

Still Water couldn't meet his gaze. "In the Moon of Fat Horses."

Hot flecks stung his eyes, and something thick and sour clogged his throat. A cry of rage came over him, stronger than anything he had ever known in a fight.

"Goddamn!" He whirled and slammed his fist into a lodge-pole with such force that the hide walls threatened to collapse. "Goddamn! Goddamn! Goddamn!"

The word flooded his mind, as if God alone could be cursed for having done this thing. Yet even as he damned and damned again, he knew it wasn't true. In the back of his mind, steely bright, was a greater truth. God had never killed anyone. He didn't have to. Men did it for him.

Suddenly his rage turned to grief and his body shuddered violently. Tears spilled down over his cheeks and a low, gurgling moan forced its way through his throat. His shoulders heaved, and helplessly, he just stood there, clenching and unclenching his fists.

Still Water didn't understand his words, but she was no stranger to sorrow. She came forward and tried to take him in her arms, but he turned away, withdrawing into himself like a wounded animal. She started to speak, then faltered, remembering a promise she had made to herself. Whatever happened, her man would never know how Strikes-Both-Ways had died. Or why.

At last, she touched him on the arm. "Your *axeisake* left a message, just before he crossed over he spoke, and his words were for you."

The black man's head swung around. His eyes were like dark, shimmering pits, but he slowly got hold of himself. "Tell me."

"He said, 'Tell the dark one I died a proud man. That only my true grandson could have made it so'."

Bloody Hand's mouth opened but nothing came out. His knees buckled and he sank to the ground, head bowed. The girl knelt beside him, and this time he didn't fight her. She took his head in her arms and laid it on her breast. Then she began to rock back and forth, slowly and with great tenderness, as if comforting a hurt child.

The speeches went on endlessly that night. White Bear spoke first, lauding the dark one and his Dog Soldiers. Then each of the council elders rose, and talked and talked as if their tongues had been coated with bear grease. Only when the People became restive did they give way and allow the Dog Soldiers themselves to speak. This in itself seemed to go on forever, but the crowd listened raptly to every word. Of the four surviving warriors, Little Wolf took the longest, relating every detail of every skirmish over the past year. But like the other raiders, he spoke not of himself, or his own deeds. He spoke instead of Bloody Hand, telling again and again of the dark one's cunning, of his resourcefulness, and above all, of his godlike courage. The onlookers seemed mesmerized by the scout's droning tale, but when he finally sat down they stirred and came to life. Now they would hear the dark one, the man all had come to see.

Bloody Hand uncoiled and came to his feet, gazing out over the crowd. It was the largest gathering of Sparrowhawks he had ever seen, greater even than at the Tobacco Planting ceremony. Their packed masses stretched endlessly into the night, and for the thousand lighted by the bonfire, fully three times that number were shadowed by darkness. He raised his fist overhead and an eerie stillness swept back across the spectators.

"I honor those who have spoken before me. And I honor those who are not here to speak for themselves. But I reject the glory Little Wolf and others would heap upon me. The vow I took was of my own doing, and courage had small part in either the decision or the act. The bravest of the brave are the ten who followed me. They took my vow as their own, and in that is the measure of true courage. Wherever Sparrowhawks gather from this day onward, let them honor these men above all others. They are the warriors of the People!"

The crowd roared their approval, but he held up his hands for silence, and after several moments their shouts died down. "Much had been said already, and in the days to come you will hear me speak more on the courage of those who rode with me. But tonight my heart is heavy for the one who is not here, the one who took me as his own and made his lodge mine. I mourn him as I would my own father, and on this night words come hard. Instead of talk, I offer something more: final retribution for those who died on this very ground at the hands of the accursed ones."

Turning, he called over his shoulder. "Let us have the Blackfoot!"

The Sparrowhawks burst into savage howls as the captive was led from the council lodge by two Dog Soldiers. Though naked, hands bound behind his back, he dismissed the crowd with a haughty look, staring out over their heads. He knew how he was to die, but he appeared calm and without fear. The Dog Soldiers pulled him forward to where a heavy stake had been driven into the ground some yards from the fire. They tied one end of a rawhide cord to his bonds and secured the other end to the post. Then they turned and walked away.

White Bear rose and strode forward to perform the opening rite. He stopped in front of the Blackfoot and pulled his knife. Suddenly he took hold of the man's nose and in one swift motion sliced it from his face. Blood spurted out of the gaping hole, splashing down across his chest in a scarlet stream, but the Blackfoot made no sound whatever. He continued to stare at some point beyond White Bear's head.

The hideous screams of the onlookers dropped off as the chief resumed his seat. Out of the crowd stepped some fifty warriors, armed with rifles and muskets. They marched forward and halted less than ten paces from the captive. Some of the spectators thought the execution was to end too swiftly and sent up a cry of protest. Then word passed that the weapons were loaded with extra-powerful charges of gunpowder but no balls.

The warriors raised their weapons, as if on unspoken command, and sighted carefully. The Blackfoot disdained even to look at them, turning his head aside with a slight sneer. In the next instant there was a thunderous volley as fifty muskets and rifles discharged at once. A dense cloud of gunsmoke blanketed the council ground, and from within its billowing layers came a low, bestial whimpering. Slowly, a light breeze carried the smoke away and the crowd could see that the Blackfoot had been knocked to the ground. His skin was peppered with grains of black powder, and deeper in the flesh, tiny coals of saltpeter continued to burn and sizzle. One blast had taken him in the face, and buried within the cavity that had once been a nose, a simmering pocket of blood bubbled and frothed. The other charges had struck him full in the groin. His penis and scrotum hung in bloody shreds, black and smoking as the last particles of gunpowder burned out.

Suddenly a squaw darted from the crowd. The knife in her hand glinted in the firelight, and with one sure stroke she cut away the Blackfoot's mangled penis. The stricken man jerked erect, eyes distended with pain, and a shrill, inhuman scream burst from his mouth. He rolled over on the ground, knees bent double, squeezing the raw stump between his legs. The squaw held aloft the blackened shreds of his manhood, for all to see, and the spectators hooted with savage delight as she pranced around the fire.

Then another squaw ran forward. Bending, she snatched a long, slender stick from the edge of the fire and whipped it through the air in a flaming arc. When it came to rest the flames had been extinguished, and she held in her hand a glowing spike. The crowd fell silent, hardly daring to breath, as she stalked the fallen man with slow catlike steps. He was still on his back, knees doubled up against his stomach in agony. Taking the last few steps in a rush, the squaw spread his buttocks wide and rammed the fiery point straight up his rectum.

The Blackfoot exploded to life with a strange, hair-raising animal shriek. One moment he was flat on his back and the next he was standing. The stick dangled from his rump, emitting little wisps of odorous smoke. Moaning pitifully, he began crow-hopping around the stake, tossing his backside high in the air like a bucking pony. The crowd went hysterical as he tried to shake the stick loose. Warriors bent double with laughter, and others fell to the ground clutching their sides, driven to choking spasms by the Blackfoot's wild antics.

While the captive was still jumping and stomping in his ghastly dance, some thirty squaws separated from the onlookers and walked forward. They were the widows of the warriors killed in last summer's raid, and by law it was their right to exact final vengeance. The women moved to the fire and each in turn selected a burning pole. As the squaw had before them, they whipped the firebrands through the air, snuffing out the flames. Then they spread out and surrounded the Black-foot.

Looking around, the trapped man suddenly forgot the stick planted in his rump. The circle tightened, and he found himself ringed in a steaming glow of orange-tipped spikes. He backed away, mutilated and dripping gore, but still very much alive. Then a squaw lunged, driving the cherry-red point of her stick into his chest. He lurched backwards, slamming into the stake, and the squaws from behind jabbed him in the legs and shoulders. Jerking away, he dodged around the post in a frenzied, shambling run. But wherever he turned, the women were there, drawing the net tighter and tighter. The glowing ends hissed and smoked whenever they touched his skin, and he flung himself in spastic convulsions from one side of the ring to the other. Suddenly a jarring moan shook his whole body as a squaw drove her stick into the grisly stump of his penis. Rearing back from the pain, he stumbled, and as he fell another squaw thrust a searing tip of fire straight into his eyeball.

The Blackfoot's scream was unearthly, a cry of terror beyond mere human suffering. He flopped to the ground and doubled up in a ball as the squaws closed in on him. Like a flock of magpies swarming over dead meat, they crowded around and began poking with their sticks. One jabbed him in the ear. Another thrust a fiery spike into the hole that had been his nose and forced it deep inside his head. Still others began burning his toes and the soles of his feet. They grunted and shoved and kept on jabbing, none of them uttering so much as a curse. Yet their eyes glistened brighter than the glowing sticks, and each convulsive jerk from the downed man brought a look of savage jubilation to their faces.

At last, the Blackfoot ceased to move. The women poked at him a minute then dropped their sticks and walked away. His entire body was pocked with blisters that had burst and curled up into charred crisps of skin. From all appearances, he looked dead as a roasted toad.

One of the squaws took a buffalo skull bowl and

scooped it full of live embers from the fire. Before anyone could detect her purpose, she returned to the Blackfoot, flipped the bowl over, and in one motion slammed it down on top of his head. His hair disappeared in a puff of flame, and as the coals began slowly frying his brains, his eyes opened in a numbed glaze. Groaning, he struggled to all fours, then somehow pushed himself erect. He wavered a moment, muttering crazed gibberish as the glowing embers tumbled down over his face and body. Several seconds passed before he turned and in a queer, beastlike shuffle walked to the stake. He wrapped his arms around the post and clung to it, staring sightlessly into the night.

The squaws quickly gathered faggots of brushwood from a pile stacked off to one side and ran back to the stake. The Blackfoot seemed unaware of what was happening, and remained motionless as the women began dumping their bundles at his feet. The mound of brushwood climbed steadily, and within moments there was nothing visible but his head and shoulders. Finished, the squaws again pulled flaming sticks from the fire and tossed them at the bottom of the pyre.

The dry wood kindled with a roaring whoosh and the Blackfoot seemed to melt before their very eyes. His skin burst and peeled back, and the globular tissue beneath crackled like dripping fat over an open spit. Then the flames arched skyward and he disappeared in a sizzling ball of fire.

The stench of charred flesh drifted over the council ground and seemingly snapped the onlookers out of their trance. They had been so engrossed with the squaws' handiwork that they could only look on with wide-eyed, gawking wonder. But the final act brought them surging forward, and even as the body shriveled into a hard, blackened knot, they began dancing around the stake. Their howls of triumph split the night, and the very earth shuddered with the stomp of their feet.

Bloody Hand exhaled a long sigh as the drums took

up the beat. He had watched the Blackfoot's ordeal with wooden detachment. Torture wasn't exactly his idea of sport, and even now his stomach felt a little queasy. But he had brought the captive back to Absaroka without misgivings of any sort. He knew what the man would face, and in his own mind, he was satisfied that the Sparrowhawks had every right to settle the score. Somehow, in a way he didn't fully understand, the grief and sorrow of widows was washed away in the act of torture, almost as if their souls had been freed from torment and they could now begin life anew. Like a clean slate, all the bad of the past had been wiped away and they had a whole new outlook toward what lay ahead.

Perhaps it was a little inhuman, but then, he'd seen white folks do things a lot worse than burn a man to death. Or, looking at it another way, maybe it was just the childlike side to the way Indians thought, like kids pulling the wings off flies, or squishing fat grub worms just to see them pop.

Whatever, it was the Sparrowhawk way. It worked for them, and so far as he was concerned, that was reason enough.

Thoughts of widows and death suddenly brought Strikes-Both-Ways to mind. But before he had time to carry that further, White Bear leaned over and grasped his arm.

"Dark one, the council has asked for a special meeting. They wish to speak with you before the feast begins."

The black man looked around and saw that the elders had disappeared. Apparently they were already waiting in the council lodge. He wasn't in any mood for talk, but offhand he couldn't think of an excuse to beg off.

He glanced back at White Bear. "My thoughts are elsewhere this night, but if the council feels it important . . ."

"Come. We will let you judge that for yourself."

They stood and walked toward the council lodge.

White Bear was silent for a few paces, then he snorted and jerked his head back over his shoulder. "The Blackfoot died poorly. Like a whimpering dog. Sometimes I think Sparrowhawks are the only ones who know how to meet death as a man should."

"*Ai!* That is true. Sparrowhawks die well."

White Bear looked at him curiously. "Your words seem bitter."

"Perhaps I have seen too many good men die. Or perhaps it is not death itself, but instead how they die. The one who mattered most was forced to cross over alone and unaided, while I . . ."

"While you were off avenging the People. You take too much upon yourself, Bloody Hand. All men die, some sooner than others. Only the earth and sky endure forever. Do not blame yourself for what the One Above demands of other men. It is the way."

"The way? If so, then it is a sorrowful way."

"Life is short and full of sorrow, dark one. You of all men should know that."

The council lodge loomed up before them and the black man had no chance to respond, which seemed just as well. White Bear's point had touched a nerve, but somehow it left him more confused than ever.

When he came through the doorhole the elders were seated and waiting. While a couple of new faces had been added, they seemed to have changed little, if at all, over the past year. White Bear motioned him to the guest seat, then crossed the lodge and took his position in the center of the council.

The chief glanced around at the elders and they nodded for him to begin. He cleared his throat and fumbled around a moment for the right words, and then his gaze swung back to the black man. "One snow past, in the Moon of Short Grass, you banished yourself from Absaroka. That was not the judgment of the council, but we respected your reasons for doing so. Now you have returned, and the People honor you above all men."

"I seek no honor." Bloody Hand broke in, unmindful that it was considered poor manners. "When a man looks back to where he has been, he sometimes sees truths that were not revealed before. I know now that what I did was not for the People. It was for myself, a purge of my own guilt."

"What you say may be true," White Bear admitted. "But that does not alter the facts as they are now. The People call you the Lordly One, and with reason. You have done a thing no mortal man would dare attempt."

"Have you forgotten that ten Dog Soldiers rode with me? Are they also godlike?"

White Bear appeared flustered, but in fact it was something more akin to amazement. The dark one had clearly matured during his self-exile. The old arrogance seemed to have fallen by the wayside. Curiously, it had been replaced by something a man was tempted to call wisdom. The word came hard, yet for the trait he saw displayed here tonight, none seemed to fit quite so well.

Before he could reply to the dark one's questions, Takes-the-Dead spoke up. "My son, we do not belittle the courage of your Dog Soldiers. We wish only to point out that the People have taken you to their hearts. Whether you approve or not, they have appointed you their guardian, and with that comes a grave responsibility."

Bloody Hand was both astonished and dismayed. "Grandfather, no man is worthy of such honor, none here, none in all of Absaroka. Least of all myself."

"There is truth in that," White Bear agreed. "But we are not talking of men or their worth. We are talking of the needs of the People. They need you, and for now, there is no other who can take your place."

Bloody Hand shook his head. "I ask nothing and want nothing, only to be left alone until I can sort out the path I must follow."

White Bear saw it suddenly and quite clearly, as if the dark one's mind had been revealed to him. Here was a

man who had fallen in his own eyes and had no wish to
fall again, a man who was not without arrogance even
yet, but one who had gained humility and wisdom in the
hardest of all ways. There would no longer be discord in
governing the tribe. Somewhere, between Bloody
Hand's brash schemes and the council's guiding hand,
would come a way for the People.

"Bloody Hand, there are times when a strong man
must serve the will of those weaker than himself. He
does so not for gain or power, but because in the wisdom granted him by the One Above he sees the obligation all men have to their brothers. This is true for none
so much as the man who possesses gifts his brothers
lack."

The black man sighed wearily. "My leader, what is it
you would have me do?"

"The council wishes you to again become pipe-holder
of the Dog Soldiers. We have reason to know that
Charges Strong will not oppose this move. He will step
aside so that you can once more ride as the *duxia* leader.
Further, it would be announced to the People that you
will sit as advisor to the council in all things, that your
wisdom and your medicine will forever serve the good
of Absaroka."

Bloody Hand was silent a long while. At last, he rose,
standing tall and straight before the elders, yet somehow humbled by the honor they had extended. "This is a
thing I must consider, *batsetse.* I will talk with my spirit
helpers and let them counsel me in the road to follow.
When that is done, I will give you my answer."

He started to say something more, then faltered. After a moment he turned and went through the doorhole.
The elders were left speechless, staring at one another
in bewilderment. Never had a man been offered such
power among the *Apsahrokee.* Yet never had a man
been so clearly reluctant to bear the burden.

It was strange. *Ai!* Stranger still, considering the man.

* * *

The black man sat before the buckskin bag, just staring at it, as if by loosening its drawstring he might unleash something he didn't want to see. Or, after all that had happened, something he simply couldn't contend with. He hadn't opened the bag since the night Strikes-Both-Ways gave it to him, never been curious enough even to look at it. For, in fact, this thing of spooks and mystic revelations had gradually won him over, yet with uncertainty and confusion, and a sense of delivering himself into the hands of a thing he couldn't comprehend, or perhaps even feared.

But now, he had no place else to turn. The blue-eyed god wasn't about to work any holy hocus-pocus for a nigger, especially a red nigger who wore bear claws and snake juice around his neck. Nor would one of Braided Tail's bought-and-paid-for visions turn the trick. The holy man had the gift, all right, but the spirits he summoned from the netherworld were oddly obliging. They had a knack for telling a man what he wanted to hear, more often than not leaving unsaid the things he most needed to know.

Yet the thing which disturbed the dark one most was that he needed help at all. A year ago, perhaps a bit longer, he would have scoffed at the whole idea. Just as he had always done, he would have tussled around with the problem till he saw what was best for him, and then acted accordingly. Now, he no longer felt so assured, or infallible. And though the admission came hard, he no longer felt so important. The notion was queer, somehow at odds with the man he had been. But there were things that had now become more important to him than just himself.

The death of Strikes-Both-Ways had dealt him a cruel blow back in that soft spot, the one the old man had wormed his way into with kindness, and understanding, and—there was no other word for it—love. It was an emotion the black man had never allowed himself. Nor had he allowed others to saddle him with their sticky sentimentality. Until Strikes-Both-Ways.

Looking back, he saw that it had all had its start with the old bowmaker. The generosity and selflessness—and love—of Strikes-Both-Ways had opened him up, wrenched his soft spot back out of its dark cave and fed it, enlarged it, even, made him vulnerable. Not so long ago, the death of a Sparrowhawk, or a hundred Sparrowhawks, wouldn't have fazed him in the slightest, Dog Soldiers included. Now he felt guilty. Responsible somehow.

Perhaps that troubled him above all else. The responsibility. This thing the council and the People wanted to saddle him with was to be their guardian and protector, the Lordly One who would hold them safe from harm and lead them on to greater conquests and make Absaroka an eternal Garden of Eden for Sparrowhawks alone.

It was too much, more than he could handle.

Something like that committed a man, tied him down permanent and final. Which was neither here nor there if that's what a man wanted. But what if it wasn't what he wanted? Or worse yet, what if he didn't know what he wanted?

This deal with the Sparrowhawks had started out as a lark, just another game to test his wits, almost like a dare one kid throws out to another. Somewhere along the line, though, he had gotten hooked. The Sparrowhawks had stopped being gut-eaters and had become real, live people. Warm and honest, and above all, tolerant. What they called "the way" had taken hold of him, made him better than he was, or ever had been, and taught him a code unlike any he had ever known. Crazier still, he even found himself believing in their spirit beings. Not because he could touch them or see them or hear them speak. But because it worked. Because something unworldly walked in his shadow, and gave him life where other men found only death.

Yet he had never meant to spend his life with the Sparrowhawks. A few years maybe, but no more, certainly not forever. There was too much he hadn't yet seen, the far side of the mountain. Something within him still cried out for that life. Granted, it was a world ruled by whites, full of injustice and hate and greed. But there was a freedom of sorts, too, living beholden to no man, never feeling obliged to become your brother's keeper. Which made it the greatest freedom of all—never being saddled with another man's lookout. That's what it all boiled down to, plain and simple: responsibility or freedom.

The black man grunted and blinked. The buckskin bag was still there. Slowly he loosened the drawstring and lifted the bundle from inside. Then he peeled back the layers of rawhide and let them fall away. The ebony glow seemed to reach out and touch him, generating some curious source of energy all its own. For a moment he just sat there and stared.

The medicine stone stared back. Squat and broad and faintly luminous, it watched him through unseen eyes. Waiting, as if it had survived the eons of time for this single moment.

Bloody Hand brought out a horn bowl and carefully began mixing the offering. Sweetgrass, wild carrot, and a handful of purplish leaves Braided Tail had given him. Earlier, after leaving the council lodge, he had paid a call on the holy man. There he had disclosed his wish to bring about a vision through the Medicine Stone. Braided Tail had listened attentively, asking few questions, then advised him in how it must be done. To gain a vision, a man must first be alone in his own lodge. Next, he must burn the sacred incense and make offering. After that, it was up to the medicine stone.

Perhaps some lingering shame over his failure to save Strikes-Both-Ways had prompted the holy man to go further. He had given the dark one ten of the precious purple leaves. This would make the offering stronger and more readily appease the medicine stone.

Now, the black man's preparations were almost complete. Still Water had been sent for the night to the lodge of her mother. The sacred incense had been pulverized and was ready for offering. The medicine stone waited, quietly watching.

Lifting the bowl, he held it over the coals at the edge of the fire. The heat slowly warmed the bottom of the bowl and after a while wisps of smoke began drifting up from the herbs and grass. He waited a moment longer, then placed the bowl in front of the medicine stone. Leaning forward, just as Braided Tail had told him to do, he breathed deeply of the incense. Its scent was at once musty and sweet, not at all unpleasant. He inhaled again, letting the fumes seep far down into his lungs. Then he sat back and once more exchanged stares with the medicine stone.

Some moments passed in silence, with nothing changed. Time seemed to slow, then stop altogether, and he gradually became aware that the Medicine Stone was dissolving before his eyes. The obsidian glow of the rock turned gray, then lighter still, and in a subtle transformation went from pale dinginess to a brilliant white incandescence.

It was a cloud, enormous and roiling, like a great thunderhead in a summer sky. It shifted and heaved, never still for an instant as it changed shape. Then, with frightening suddenness, a huge grizzly materialized in the center of the cloud. In the next moment a swift-flying hawk emerged from one side of the cloud and a snow-white dove appeared at the other. The grizzly reared up on its hind legs and let go a shuddering roar. The birds flew closer, never coming together or crossing paths, but darting nearer and nearer to the bear. Enraged, the grizzly showed its fangs, swatting first at the hawk and then at the dove. But somehow it was apparent that the monster meant them no harm. Strangely, it wasn't trying to strike them. It was trying to catch them.

Yet the birds were too swift. They dodged and looped and spiraled, and try as he might, the bear couldn't touch them. Suddenly the grizzly began to fade, roaring defiantly, and after a moment, both the hawk and the dove dissolved in thin air. The misty swirls of the cloud also faded, turning smoky, then gray, and finally a dark ebony which glowed softly.

Dizziness flooded over the black man, then receded in a rush. He blinked, shook his head, and blinked again. As when awakening, the fuzziness cleared from his head and he found himself staring once more at the Medicine Stone.

He just sat there, frozen, as if he himself had turned to stone, hardly daring to believe, yet unable to refute what he had seen. Then, in a moment of intense and numbing clarity, he knew. The vision had come.

One moment there was nothing. Then the sun seemed to burst from the earth, red as a clot of blood. Standing on the high cliff overlooking the village, the black man felt the first warming rays touch him. There was a chill in his bones, and in his heart, and the sun felt good. He had been standing there most of the night, staring off into the darkness. Thinking, wracking his brain, pondering what seemed a pitiful scarcity of alternatives. Now, with sunrise, came resolution. Looking into the ball of fire, he was blinded and yet enlightened. For one was of the body and the other was of the soul.

The decision brought with it inner warmth, and he felt the tenseness drain out of his muscles. He had wrestled with the problem all night, torn first one way and then another. But there had been nowhere to seek advice, none to make the choice for him. It was as Braided Tail had stated: before wisdom comes, a man must first know which things serve him and which things force him to serve them.

Earlier in the night the holy man had listened as

Bloody Hand revealed what was seen in his vision. Pondering on it at some length, the ancient one had appeared reluctant to offer any explanation. But when the black man persisted he had agreed to interpret the vision. The cloud quite clearly represented Absaroka, just as the bear was without doubt the dark one's spirit helper. The hawk was obviously the Sparrowhawk People. And the meaning of the dove was equally apparent: a manifestation of Bloody Hand's *tibo* past. Far from trying to kill the hawk or the dove, the great bear wanted only to catch one. To know at last where it belonged, with the *Apsahrokee* or with the *tibos*. Therein was the message from the dark one's spirit helper. He was torn between two worlds. Now, finally, he must decide what he was, red man or white. For truly, a man could not be both.

Bloody Hand grunted, his gaze shifting from the sun as the village came to life far below. *Ai!* The vision was clear, well enough. But there was a deeper irony overlooked by Braided Tail. That a black man could call himself either red or white seemed to mock them all. Still, it was a choice which could be shunted aside no longer. Having resolved that much, he knew now what must be done.

A footstep sounded behind him and he stiffened. Then, knowing somehow who it was, he smiled. "Pine Leaf should take lessons from the wild things if she means to stalk a man."

When he turned she was standing there, watching him from beneath lowered lashes. After a moment she smiled. "It is not you I stalk. I come here each morning to greet the One Above. I shame myself before him by asking that you be sent to claim me soon. But sometimes I think he does not hear my prayers."

With all his other problems the black man hadn't given much thought to the girl, or the arrangement between them. Suddenly it dawned on him that he had ninety-six scalps, only four shy of her marriage price.

Curiously, his only thought now was to marvel at himself. That he had ever undertaken such a thing seemed a case of supreme arrogance. Godlike, well enough, but in the way of Old Man Coyote.

"There is no shame in asking *Axace* to favor you. Nor does he turn a deaf ear to your prayers. It is only that He sees fit to delay this thing between us."

"Delay? I do not understand. Why would He hold us apart longer?"

"Through my spirit helpers He has directed me to return to the land of the *tibos*. There it will be revealed to me what I must know for the days ahead."

The girl looked at him a long while, and sadness crept over her eyes. "Will you return?"

"That is something the One Above will tell me. But only after I have journeyed among the *tibos*."

Her words were soft and tremulous, almost imploring. "Would you stay if I released you from your vow? I would do so gladly, without shame."

The black man chuckled, spreading his arms wide. "*Ai!* There is no end to a woman's cunning. Were you to release me from the vow I could never beat you or pull your ear when you are disobedient. You set a clever snare, but I will not take the bait."

Pine Leaf ducked her head, glancing at him sideways. "I am serious and you jest with me."

"There is too much seriousness this day." He put his arm around her shoulders and squeezed gently. "Come, let us watch together as *Axace* rises to greet the Sparrowhawks. We will both say a prayer for what lies ahead."

They walked forward, halting at the edge of the cliff, his arm still about her. Across the shining mountains the sun rose higher, golden now in its warmth, and gauzy streamers of light fell softly over the land.

Absaroka stirred and came forth to meet the day.

CHAPTER 12

The black man reined his gelding to a halt overlooking the Buffalo Fork of the Snake. Sitting there, he sorted through the alternatives and found himself still in a bit of a quandary. Somewhere in the mountains to the west he would find the brigades. Which one really didn't matter. The problem boiled down to where and how soon. If he took the wrong turn now, it might be a month, maybe longer, before he tracked them down. He could ride north, cross over the divide into Colter's Hell, and scout along the headwaters of the Yellowstone. That was good beaver country, and sooner or later the mountain men always got around to trapping it. Trouble was, what with it being the last days of the Moon of Black Cherries, it might be later instead of sooner.

Grunting, he chuckled to himself. That was another little problem. He couldn't hardly think like a white man no more. Ever since he rode off from the Wind River encampment, his Sparrowhawk had been getting in the way of his English, or vice versa. If he found the brigades and commenced talking about the Moon of Black Cherries, they'd think he was addled. It was July, and those were the terms he'd best start thinking in.

Something clicked, and one thought seemed to spark another. It was too early for anyone to be on the Yellowstone. The best bet was over in Snake country somewhere. This time of year there was always a brigade wandering around Pierre's Hole, and if he humped it, he could probably catch them before they headed north. Briefly, he calculated time and distance. Follow the Snake down through Jackson's Hole, cross over the Tetons, and head west toward Henry's Fork. The more he thought about it, the better it sounded. Wouldn't take more than five, maybe six days at the outside. Doubtless he'd find them squatted down in Pierre's Hole somewhere, grumbling about ratty plews and sting flies. Come to think of it, mountain men didn't have nothing else worth talking about in July. They just loafed along, waiting for the first cold snap, till furs turned prime again.

Settled now on where to head, he heeled the pinto into a trot and rode off toward the Buffalo Fork.

All of this wondering about the mountain brigades set him to ruminating. Not that he hadn't done plenty of that in the last few days. But now that he was getting closer, everything seemed to jell and sort of fall into place. Summer was a pretty good yardstick for the way men looked at things. Now the whites, they just poked along, taking it slow and easy, not doing much to work up a sweat. Then, come cold weather, they started wading icy streams and freezing their balls off, just so they could make a year's wages.

The Sparrowhawks had it gauged altogether opposite. They broke their backs raiding and hunting, so that come winter they could lay up in a warm lodge and spin whoppers about their fights. Maybe that's what made the difference—raiding season. Whites didn't have nothing like that. Stealing horses sort of went against the grain with them, and all this business about warrior honors was looked on as just plain foolishness. Not that whites didn't like to fight. It was just that they fought for different reasons, and honor generally had very little to do with it.

But then, in a way, that's what this little jaunt back to

the brigades was all about: the yardsticks men used to measure themselves against, and what it was they wanted out of life when it all wound down to that final turn of the screw. Strikes-Both-Ways had pretty well hit the mark with something he said a long time back— each man must find his own path, in his own way.

That made a lot more sense now than it had then. Truth to tell, nearly everything the old man had taught him had come to make a lot of sense. Yet back in some dark corner of his mind, there was always that inkling of doubt. The Sparrowhawk way had come to be his own, and he was drawn to it like a moth to flame. Something he couldn't articulate had taken hold of him, given his life reason and meaning for the first time, and the impulse to remain in Absaroka was all but irresistible.

Still, he would never know any peace until that smattering of doubt had been resolved. The freedom of a mountain man's life also held forth a certain fascination. It was the first real freedom he had ever known, until he became a Sparrowhawk. But there was a hitch. While the Sparrowhawks enjoyed greater personal freedom than the mountain men, they were also stuck with greater obligations, to family, clan, and tribe. Should he return to Absaroka, these would apply doubly to him. After considerable soul-searching, he knew that he could never remain among the Sparrowhawks and refuse the demands of White Bear and the elders. The People needed him, and if he stayed on there was no way to deny that need. Strikes-Both-Ways had taught him too well that a warrior exists to protect the weak and the defenseless.

That was the meaning behind the vision, and the reason he was riding west even now. Before cutting himself off completely from the white world, he had to see and talk with the mountain men again. Maybe he had gotten so wrapped up in the Sparrowhawk way that he had lost sight of what it meant to ride with the brigades. Seven years he had spent with the mountain men, and it had been a good time, better by a damn sight than any life he'd had before. Just maybe, it was a life that suited him better than the Sparrowhawk way. Somehow he had to find out.

There for a while, the night of his vision, he had thought about returning to St. Louis. That would have been the acid test. If St. Louis looked good, then Absaroka became a dead issue, over and done with. But he had discarded the idea out of hand. Twenty years had taught him all he needed to know about a black man's chances in a white man's game. Or, worse yet, the chances of a mulatto woods colt who never truly belonged to either side.

Looking back, he saw his life as a series of narrow and none too pleasant escapes. As each link in a chain binds itself to the whole, so was his life bound to a past that he had never fully been able to outdistance.

The white blood had been his own personal demon from the start, like a hex of some kind that dogged his footsteps wherever he went. Col. George Beckwith had bedded a quadroon slave, and in the normal course of things, a mulatto bastard came along nine months later. While his mother had died in childbirth and the baby had been given to an old mammy, nobody thought much about it one way or the other. Masters had always visited the slave quarters, and on the Beckwith plantation it was no different. Another light-skinned pickaninny hardly caused a ripple.

But with time, it became apparent that the one named James was unlike the others, smarter somehow, curious to learn, and with a boldness that was unbecoming in a slave. Later the boldness turned to insolence, and later still, the rebellious boy grew into an incorrigible troublemaker. As a youngster he kept the plantation in a constant state of turmoil, and spread unrest among the slaves. It was a dangerous situation. The elder Beckwith decided at last that perhaps he had too much white blood in his veins. Not enough to change his color, but enough to make him an uppity nigger, and an unrelenting source of embarrassment.

The youngster was apprenticed to a blacksmith, whom he came near killing with a hammer. Next he was sent to the mines outside Galena, where he touched off a riot and almost got himself killed. George Beckwith was not an unfeeling man, especially for his mulatto offspring, and he tried yet another tack. Perhaps the boy would be happier with a business of his own.

But the one named James wasn't interested. He had the wanderlust, and an itch to see something of the world. Col. Beckwith couldn't have been more relieved. He gave his bastard son $100 and his freedom papers, and sent him on his way. The money lasted less than twenty miles. Broke and hungry, but free, the youngster had wound up as a dockhand on the St. Louis wharves.

Then, in the boldest escape of all, he had joined William Ashley's overland expedition to the Rockies.

Reflecting on it now, with time and wisdom as a buffer, the black man could see that he had been luckier than most. The plantation was probably still there, and doubtless the senior Beckwith was still siring mulatto bastards in speckled litters. But few, if any, of them would escape. He had, step by step, and there was nothing to be gained in going back. Whatever was to be found on that plantation outside St. Louis was a thing of the past. It had held no answers then and could provide none now.

Nor did he have any need for civilization. Not now, not ever. Leastways not what white men called civilization. What lay west of the Missouri, the mountain wilderness and the endless plains, was tame enough for him. In fact, looking back across the span of a decade, he found nothing to regret. The life he had made for himself, give or take a few touchy moments, suited him just fine: nothing to crow about, but nothing to shame a man either. There wasn't a hell of a lot he'd change even if he could, except Strikes-Both-Ways.

Given the chance, there was much he would have changed there. Queer as the notion was, he figured the old bowmaker was about the closest thing he'd ever had to a father. Maybe it was Beckwith blood that had sired the boy, but it was Strikes-Both-Ways who had sired the man. The difference was about the same as lightning and a lightning bug, with the leathery old Sparrowhawk clutching a whole fistful of thunderbolts.

The black man kneed his gelding into a lope, hurried on by some curious sense of urgency. Ahead lay the snow-capped spires of the Tetons, and on the other side, perhaps, an answer that had eluded him much too long: sort of a riddle with the choice still to be made: Jim Beckwith or Bloody Hand.

The black man found their camp set back away from a small lake, some thirty miles upstream on Henry's Fork. Early that morning he had spotted their tracks where the smaller stream emptied into the Snake. The sign looked to be four, maybe five days old, but that hadn't bothered him. They would be moving slow, just loafing along in the drowsy summer heat. Most likely they were trapping the network of creeks branching off from Henry's Fork, but without any real eagerness. Summer was the time when mountain men put lard on their bones, beefing themselves up against the day when game was scarce and the land lay blanketed in snow.

Unlike the Sparrowhawks, the fur brigades had never acquired the knack of squirreling foodstuffs back for the hard times ahead. While they might jerk some meat before first snow, they seldom made any real preparations for winter. They merely endured it, growing lean as bark-fed ponies by the time of spring melt-off.

That was something else Strikes-Both-Ways had observed, and like so many things, it now seemed an obvious truth. The red man lived in harmony with the earth and its creatures, taking only what he needed to sustain himself and his brothers. The *tibos* hadn't yet learned this secret. They lived at odds with their surroundings, plundering it out of greed, but never knowing any real kinship with the wilderness. They sought to tame it rather than to let its bounty make them free. Oddly enough, they wound up as slaves to their own handiwork, and in the process became something less than they were, masters of all they surveyed, yet enslaved by the very thing they had tamed.

Such thoughts had been whipsawing through the black man's mind all day. Now, with the camp in sight, he brought the gelding to a halt in a stand of aspens. It suddenly occurred to him that he was no longer sure of why he had come. What he hoped to learn here wasn't as clear as it had been a week ago. Something of himself, perhaps? Or had it more to do with the mountain men themselves? Quite without warning, it all seemed a bit muddled, now that he was actually here.

More out of habit than anything else, he held the pinto in the trees and scanned the camp. After a year of raiding he had learned to move warily, like a wild thing alert to all around it, particularly the unseen. It had become a part of him, a trait so deeply ingrained that he was no longer aware of his own caution. Much like any predator, his stealth had become instinctive, the slight edge which separates the hunter from the hunted.

The leafy aspens screened him from sight, but he had a clear view of the camp: jumbled gear strewn about a small clearing between the woods and the lake, horses grazing in a meadow only a stone's throw upstream. A deer carcass hung from a high limb back in the trees. But he saw only one man, the booshway, Davey Jackson.

Twisting in the saddle, he checked the sun and had his answer. The trappers were out running their sets. Summer pelts, ratty or not, were better than no pelts at all. Most likely they would come drifting in along toward dusk, each trying to outgrumble the other about the slim pickings. He grunted, and a small smile played at the corners of his mouth. White men could never quite get the hang of loafing. They tried, but their hearts just weren't in it. Unlike the Sparrowhawks, they had never fully grasped one of life's essentials—that there were times when a man should do absolutely nothing, but just replenish himself and vitalize his energies toward the days ahead. Even with pelts hardly worth the skinning, *tibos* were still driven by some compulsion to work, almost like the beavers they trapped.

That was it! They were industrious, possessed by the furies of greed and accomplishment, but sorely limited in their outlook on life. A flower crushed underfoot evoked no sadness, and for them there was no beauty in the great bear. They found meaning only in what they could tame or kill. Or skin and sell.

He kneed the pony into a walk and slowly came out of the trees.

Davey Jackson was busy scribbling in a ledger. It was a chronicle he kept of the brigade's daily activities, perhaps the only meticulous endeavor he had ever undertaken in his life. When he heard the shuffling hoofbeats downstream, he dropped the quilled pen and made a dive for his rifle. Then he froze, mouth agape, looking at the black man as if he were something that had dropped out of a tree.

While the dark one was clothed in the grease-blackened buckskins of a mountain man, he was still something of a fright. His hair was plaited in short braids, with the topknot curled Sparrowhawk fashion, and the ridged scar across his brow seemed livid in the deepening sunlight. Something of the sun was also in his gaze, yellowish and bright. Yet the lynx-eyed stare he trained on the booshway was curiously devoid of warmth. Watching him ride closer, Davey Jackson had the sudden feeling of being stalked, as if he were somebody's supper, and the big meat-eater himself had just stepped out of the bushes.

The black man reined to a halt and nodded. "Davey. Long time no see."

" 'Tis, fer a fact." Jackson's mouth twitched in what passed for a smile. "Damn ye, Jim, thar fer a minute I thought a ghost'd rode in on me."

"Wal, I ain't no h'ant, if that's what's worryin' ye. Leastways not yet."

The booshway laughed nervously. "Course, ye ain't. Big as life and twice as ugly."

"Ye gonna ask me to step down?"

Jackson's laugh went hollow, then faltered altogether. "Why, sure. Light and turn yore horse out to graze. Boys'll be back 'fore long and we'll get some vittles cookin'."

The black man dismounted and dropped the reins to the ground. But he didn't unsaddle, and this point wasn't lost on Jackson. The pinto wandered off toward the meadow and began cropping grass.

"Don't reckon Doc Newell'd be with yore bunch this trip?"

"Yeah, he is, too. Ort to be stumblin' in here any minute now."

"Glad to hear it. Been a while since I seen him."

"That why ye come back? To see Doc, I mean."

"Nope. Not jest exactly, anyways."

There was a moment of stiff silence while Jackson waited for him to say more. The booshway blinked first. "Wal, like ye say, it's been a spell. We was sorta surprised ye didn't make a show at Rendezvous."

"Warn't much, to hear the Crows tell it. 'Sides, I had some business that needed tendin' to."

"We heared all about it." Jackson grinned mirthlessly. "Fact is, 'fore Rendezvous was over, nobody wasn't talkin' about nothin' else. Hell, the Shoshones even give ye a new name."

"Yeah, what's that?"

"The Widow Maker."

The black man smiled for the first time. "Cain't say as

they don't have reason. My boys worked'em over pretty good."

"Way they tell it, ye cleaned out a whole village, men, women, and kids."

"Tit fer tat, Davey. That's the way the Crows look at it."

"Meanin' nits make lice?"

"Somethin' like that. Course, the whole idee was to convince ever'body they oughta keep their nose whur it belongs."

"Out o' Crow territory, yore sayin'?"

"That's whut she biles down to."

Jackson stared at him a moment, then looked away. "Word drifted down that ye sorta put that same bee in McKenzie's bonnet."

"Ye talkin' about that fort up on the Missouri?"

The booshway nodded. "Way we got the story, ye burned it to the ground, lock, stock, and barrel."

"That's what Ashley wanted. My boys jest aim to please."

"Ashley?"

"Shore." The dark one cocked his head and one eyebrow lifted. "Ye mean to say he didn't tell ye nothin' about our deal?"

"Nary a goddamned word. What kind o' deal?"

"Why, I was to run American Fur off, and turn about, he was supposed to bring the Crows a load of rifles."

"Sorry, good-fer-nothin' sonovabitch!" Jackson's eyes burned fiercely and he kicked a stew kettle halfway across the camp.

"What's got ye riled? The deal worked out pretty fair all the way round."

"In a pig's ass! All it did was get McKenzie's dander up. He's got brigades workin' as far south as Bear Lake."

"Wal, I'm sorry to hear that, Davey. Course, I cain't say as we've seen any of'em over our way."

"Naw, they'll steer clear of ye fer awhile. Leastways 'til they get us cleaned out o' beaver."

The black man held back a grin. "Come next Rendezvous, I guess ye and Ashley'll have somethin' to palaver about."

"Not likely. The bastard's done sold out."

"Sold out? Who to?"

"Why, to us, that's who. Looks like he knew when the gettin' was good, and he's done got. Sublette's gonna be packin' in the trade goods from now on. Course, the way things is goin', thar ain't gonna be a hell of a lot to trade fer."

"Ashley warn't never one to ride a dead horse, that's a fact. What reason'd he give fer wantin' out?"

"Aw, he's got it in his head to run fer the Senate. Wants to go up to Washington and hobnob with the rest of them shitheels. They're all of a kind anyway, so I 'spect he'll feel right at home."

"Cain't say as I'm surprised he stung ye. Allus figgered him as the sort that'd skin a fart if'n it was wearin' fur."

"Looks that way, don't it?" Jackson grumped around a minute, kicking at camp gear and muttering to himself. Finally he cooled down and turned back, grinning sheepishly. "Wal, hell, that's enough about my troubles. What brings ye back this way, Jim? We'd sorta given ye up fer lost."

"Ye warn't fur off the mark, at that. Fact is, I jest got an itch to rove. Thought I'd wander over hyar and see how ye boys was makin' out. Even crossed my mind I might winter with ye."

The booshway gave him a startled look. "Jim, I ain't never been nothin' but straight out with ye, and I gotta tell ye, I don't allow as how that'd be a good idee."

"No?" The dark one's humor suddenly faded. "Why not?"

"Aw, Christ, I don't know. Jest a whole bunch of things all piled together, I guess. It started with ye killin'

Micah Johnson down on the Green. Then after yore Crows burned McKenzie's fort, the trouble shifted over our way, and the boys kind o' took that personal. Later we heard stories about ye and a bunch of mad dogs roamin' around killin' ever'body that warn't Crow. See what I mean? It's jest a whole lot o' things stirred up in the same pot."

"I ain't sure I got yore drift yet. Whyn't ye spell it out fer me?"

"Jest tryin' to give ye a friendly warnin', Jim. The boys don't trust ye no more. They sorta figger ye've gone renegade on'em. 'Specially since we ain't never got no invite to come trap Crow land."

The black man's hands clenched so hard his knuckles looked like polished stone. "What made ye think ye were gonna get an invite?"

"Why, that was the deal. That's what Ashley sent up thar fer, warn't it?"

"Maybe. Things sorta got out o' kilter, though."

"Meanin' ye got yoreself turned into a Crow."

"Somethin' like that."

"Then ye ort to see what I'm drivin' at. Why the boys taken ye to be a renegade. The way they figger it, ye stuck a knife in their back. Jest to be blunt about it, Jim, there ain't nothin' gone our way since the day ye took up with the Crows. Ye'll have to admit, that looks kind o' fishy, don't it?"

The dark one let out his breath in a sigh. "Wal, I guess I got the answer I come fer."

Jackson gave him a puzzled frown. "What answer was that?"

"Don't make no never mind. Jest a blister I had to get shet of. That's the way the Crow's talk, Davey. They call it a blister on a man's soul."

"Jim, I don't know what the hell yore talkin' about. But I'll tell ye somethin' fer true. If ye make that invite, ye'd sure enough shine with the boys. That'd make'em come! Wouldn't be no more talk o' renegade if they knew ye was gonna lead'em over the mountains into Crow territory."

The black man's jaw jutted out. "Davey, lemme give ye some friendly advice. Don't let nobody yore soft on wander over them mountains. They'll come back without their ha'r. If that ain't plain enough, I'll make it a warnin'. Stay out or get skulked. See what I mean?"

"Yeh, I see awright."

The two men were still glowering at each other when they heard voices from upstream. A moment later several trappers emerged from the trees and headed toward camp. They were laughing and seemed in good spirits, although it was apparent that none of them had taken the first plew.

Jackson gave the black man a sidewise scrutiny. "Jim, ye're welcome to spend the night. Jest try not to step on nobody's toes. I'm shorthanded as is, and I'd hate to see anyone get killed with no need."

"Fair enough. I'll have a little palaver with Doc and be gone by sunup."

The dark one turned and walked off toward his pony. Jackson started back to his ledger, then stopped, hardly able to credit his ears.

The bastard was whistling a tune.

Tension around the fire was oppressive, like a sultry night when the air becomes still and close. The mountain men lolled about on the ground, not saying much, just smoking and watching. They were in an ugly mood, and nothing made it more apparent than their glacial silence. Trappers were garrulous talkers, and nightfall was a special time in a brigade camp. It was reserved for swapping yarns and chewing the fat about the day past, and darkness generally brought on a lively gabfest.

That they weren't talking was an ominous sign.

Davey Jackson kept up a pretense of good humor, though it was clearly having no effect on the men themselves. Every now and then Joe Meek or Kit Carson would throw in a comment, but nobody paid them much mind. Either man could outtalk a split-tongue magpie, and they both had a fondness for their own chatter. They were just talking to hear themselves talk, and everybody knew it. The rest simply sat there, wooden-faced as a bunch of owls, trying to act as if they weren't watching the black man.

But they felt the strain. It was getting worse by the minute, and had been since supper. These men weren't hypocrites, and if they didn't like a man, they made no bones about it. Upon finding him in camp, some hadn't greeted him at all, and the others were just barely civil. They felt that he had betrayed them, turned his back on them once he got to be a he-wolf among the Crows. While they hadn't put it in so many words, it was generally agreed that he was profiting at their expense, that he had somehow rigged the deal out of spite, or maybe just plain greed, so that all the plews coming out of Crowlands fell on his side of the ledger, and they were left sucking hind tit. Otherwise he wouldn't have gone to such pains to keep them on their own side of the mountains. That was the way they saw it, and no one felt inclined to call it quits and let bygones be bygones.

They sucked on their pipes, kept to themselves, and continued to watch him out of the corner of their eyes. None of them particularly wanted to tangle with the sledge-shouldered mulatto, but if looks could have killed, their guest would have been stone cold and stiffening fast.

Doc Newell was caught in the middle. He felt like a man trying to straddle a chasm so wide that his legs wouldn't stretch. On one side were the mountain men, who at his age were the closest thing to family he'd likely ever have. They weren't exactly what a fellow would call gentle, and standing downwind of them could gag a buzzard off of dead meat. But they were loyal after their own fashion, and they weren't the kind to run out on a man when it got down to a rock and a hard place. Some of them had saved his own hair a couple of times along the way, and on occasion, the toss of the coin had made it his treat. They stuck together because they needed each other, and perhaps more important, because they liked one another.

All of which made his friendship for Beckwith a ticklish proposition. The black man stood alone, and always had. He wasn't the sort to run with the pack, and the mountain men had tolerated more than accepted him. Strangely enough, that was one of the reasons Newell felt drawn to him. The old trapper had an affinity for stray pups and broken-winged birds, and he'd known from the start that the black man was crippled in a way not exactly visible to the naked eye. But it wasn't the kind of thing he could rightly explain to the rest of the brigade, and they likely wouldn't have understood even if he'd tried.

The fix Beckwith found himself in now was one Doc Newell had seen coming way back. He'd known from the start, sensed it somehow, that the black man was searching for something within himself, almost as if there was a boil festering inside him, and it was only a matter of time and circumstance till something brought it to a head. This thing with the Crows had done just that. In his mind's eye, Newell saw it much like one of those tiny, worm-like creatures transforming itself into a butterfly. The black man had gone through stages in exactly the same way, sprouting wings, taking on color and character, until he had learned how to fly in a manner few men ever came to know.

Newell had sat beside the black man all evening, talking and joking as they always had, and he wasn't especially worried about what the other trappers would think. They were a manageable sort when a man put his mind to it. Nor was he overly concerned that anybody would try to pick a fight with Beckwith, not after the way he'd butchered Micah Johnson down on the Green. But Newell was a sorely troubled man nonetheless.

What bothered him most was this corkscrew twist the black man's life had taken. The queerest part was that Beckwith seemed to have brought it on himself.

Soon after the moon rose full, the old trapper nudged Beckwith and jerked his head downstream. The black man nodded, and without a word they climbed to their feet and strolled away from camp. Behind, no sooner than they were out of earshot, the mountain men started babbling like a flock of geese. Apparently everybody had something to say about the mulatto's sudden appearance, and quite likely, a few well chosen words as to where he should go next.

The black man and his burly friend walked along a ways without saying anything. They both knew this was probably the last time they would see each other, and words came hard. Newell finally broke the ice.

"Don't blame the boys too much, Jim. It's jest natural fer a feller to get his hackles up when he thinks somebody's takin' food out o' his mouth."

"Is that what I'm doin', Doc? Knifin' ever'body in the back? That's what Davey called it."

"Wal, that's carryin' things a mite too far. Let's jest say they're a leetle techy 'cause ye won't lead'em into the land of milk and honey."

"Meanin' Absaroka."

"Yeh. That's a good a name as any."

"Y'know, it beats the hell out o' me how some people will allus lay their troubles off on the other man. How long's that bunch been trappin' out here? Close to ten years, ain't it?"

"Some of'em more'n that, I'd guess."

"And in all that time they ain't never seen t'other side of the Crows' mountains. Ain't that a fact?"

"No, not to speak of. Leastways them that went over fer a look-see never got back to talk about it."

"Thar ye go! That's jest what I'm gettin' at. The Crows ain't never let nobody in thar. So what call they got to get down on me jest 'cause I won't open the gates?"

"Cain't rightly say. 'Ceptin' with McKenzie's bunch and Hudson's Bay movin' in on us, I reckon the boys jest figgered ye owed'em. What with that fort gettin' burned an' all, it's made things pretty tight in this neck o' the woods."

"Shit, I didn't take nobody to raise. They're full growed."

"That's a fact."

"Wal, far's I'm concerned, they can jest take their troubles and stick'em up their ass."

Newell snorted. "'Pears to me ye've already done that fer'em."

The black man chuckled, taken with the thought. "Yeh, it do look that way, don't it?"

They paced alongside the stream for some distance before Newell responded. "Ye goin' back acrost the mountains?"

"Jest like a streak, Doc. Jest like a streak."

"Fer good?"

The dark one seemed to consider a moment. "Offhand I couldn't think of nothin' short of Judgment Day that'd get me to come out again."

"Oughten ye to think on it some? I ain't ary a one to tell a man's he's wrong, but I wisht ye could see it 'nother way."

"What other way, Doc? Christ A'mighty, there ain't nothin' fer me with the brigades now."

"Mebbe not. But goddamnit, it jest don't seem fitten fer a man to go off and leave his own kind thataway."

"Awright, lemme ask ye one. What is my own kind?"

The trapper slewed a quizzical look at him. "Why, white men. What d'ye think I was talkin' about?"

The black man stopped, taking Newell's arm abruptly, and turned him around. "Doc, take a good look at me. Now, am I what ye'd rightly call a white man?"

Newell walked off a couple of paces and stared out

over the stream. "Mebbe it ain't no compliment to call ye white. I dunno about that. But I ain't never looked at ye as nothin' else."

"What about the others? Warn't it allus nigger this and nigger that when my back was turned?"

"I cain't rightly speak fer them. Nor jedge 'em, neither."

"But ye see what I'm drivin' at, don't ye?"

"Yeh, I reckon so."

"Then ye ort to know why I'm goin' back acrost the mountains."

Newell chewed that over for a while in silence, and then he looked around. "Thar's somethin' more to it, ain't thar? I mean, ye was with the brigades a long spell, and I don't recollect no such talk as this."

The black man grunted, falling silent himself. Then he chuckled, flashing a wide grin. "Allus was the foxy one, warn't ye?"

"Don't know about that," Newell laughed, "but it'll take more'n some bushy-tailed sprout to teach me to suck eggs."

"Waugh! Ye done caught this chile with his dauber hangin' out."

"Wal, ye gonna tell me, or do I have to pick ye up by yore heels and rattle yore gourd?"

"Think ye could still do it?"

"Woooiieee! Boy, I ain't so old I can't make 'em come. Who d'ye think l'arned ye to shine?"

"Are ye shore ye want to hear it? What I'm tryin' to say is that it ain't exactly the kind o' thing an ol' goat like ye could rightly get a holt on."

"Jest look at him, would ye! Got a mouthful o' hornets and cain't spit. C'mon, get it out 'fore ye swell up and burst."

The black man laughed and flecks of moonlight danced in his eyes. "Doc, I'm not right certain I can put it into words. Thar's things on t'other side of them mountains a growed man wouldn't swaller on a stack o'

Bibles. Ye can call it witchcraft or voodoo or whatever ye like. Thar ain't nary a way on earth to explain it. But I've seen it work. Hell, it's been workin' fer me fur more'n two years. How d'ye think I stayed alive all this time, doin' the kind o' things I been doin'?"

Newell scratched his head and frowned uncertainly. "Ye talkin' about some sorta god or other?"

"Naw, not a god exactly. I ain't never been right shore thar was such a thing. What I'm talkin' about is what the Sparrowhawks call spirit helpers. They're animal spirits that watch over a man and protect him. The Injuns call it medicine and some fellers has got more of it than others. What I've got is powerful, Doc, real powerful. Thar ain't never been nothin' like it."

"Sounds to me like what ye got is faith. What them Bible-thumpers is allus shoutin' about."

"Mebbe so. I dunno. I jest know it works. If it didn't, I would've gone under way back down the trail."

"Awright, since thar ain't nothin' better to call it, let's say ye got yoreself a god. Now, do I understand ye keerect? Is that why yore goin' back?"

"Not jest that. Don't y'see, it's what I can do with the medicine. It don't work jest fer me. It works fer ever'body. I got a chance to make things really good fer them people, Doc."

Newell got a crafty look in his eyes. "Why, shore, I see it now. What yore sayin' is that them Crows has put ye up on a throne. Sorta made ye a go-between twixt them and this god of theirs."

"Wal, somethin' like that. But there's a whole lot more to it. They accepted me, Doc. Jest took me in and made me one of'em. Never cared a lick whether I was red, green, or purple pokey-dotted. So fur's they're concerned, I'm jest a Sparrowhawk, one of the tribe. Don't y'see? I ain't out o' place. I belong."

"Yeh, I reckon I do see. Yore talkin' about the oldest thing in the book. What them Holy-Joe characters call brotherhood."

The black man opened his mouth but nothing came out. They stared at each other for several moments and at last, he nodded. "Doc, I think ye nailed it plumb sartain. That's not a word that ever come to me before, but it's jest exactly what I've been talkin' around. Now that I think on it, that's what the Sparrowhawks call one another. Brother."

Newell pursed his lips, rubbing the bearded stubble along his jawbone, and there was a scarcely perceptible sag to his shoulders. "Wal, it 'pears ye found yoreself a home. I'm glad fer ye, boy, glad as I can be. Mebbe somewheres along the line that's what we're all huntin' fer. I 'spect ye jest come to it sooner'n the rest of us."

"What're ye talkin' about, ye ol' grizzly b'ar? The only home ye know is these hyar mountains."

"Shore, but I been thinkin' some myself lately. I ain't gettin' any younger, y'know. Winters seem to get a lettle colder ever' y'ar. Way I figger it, I got mebbe five seasons left in me. Then I'm gonna call it quits."

"Hell, ye been spoutin' that line o' guff ever since I knowed ye."

"Naw, I'm plumb serious. Got an idee I might jest trail on back Missouri way. Buy a nice farm and sit out front in a rocker in the sun. Wouldn't be half bad, the way I got it figgered."

"Judas Priest! Now I heard ever'thing. Ye ain't no plowpusher, Doc. 'Sides, where're ye gonna get the money to buy this hyar farm?"

"Why, I guess I'll jest have to quit drinkin' whiskey and chasin' squaws. Reform myself, don't y'see. Listen, boy, Rendezvous don't mean a hill of beans to me, if'n I set my mind to it."

"Course it don't. Jest like a horse don't fart when he eats clover." The black man chuckled softly, shaking his head. "I got a better idee. When ye get ready to call it quits, ye come over the mountains. I'll interduce ye to some lettle Sparrowhawk squaws and 'fore ye know it, ye'll be up to yore armpits in snotty-nosed half-breeds."

"Ye mean in Absa—whatever the hell ye call it? I didn't calculate them Crows'd let another white man in there."

"What d'ye mean, another? They ain't let one in yet."

Both of them burst out chortling, and after a moment the dark one rapped Newell in the gut. "Don't let that stop ye, though. Jest c'mon. I'll even let ye hibernate in my lodge if'n ye can't get yoreself a squaw. Ye know them Sparrowhawk women ain't used to a miserable ol' chunk of bear-bait like ye. They likes their men full of piss and vinegar."

Doc Newell smote him across the shoulders with a great hairy paw and they went striding off toward camp. Upstream, the horses stood walleyed, and flared their nostrils in fright, as his booming laughter rumbled over the meadow. Even the mountain men spooked at first, but then they settled back as the figures emerged clearer in the moonlight. It wasn't a bear after all. It was only the old trapper, and his renegade friend.

The black man let the gelding set his own gait. The midday sun was warm, there was a scent of bluestem in the air, and he had all the time in the world. Ahead he saw a hummingbird, suspended on an invisible beat of wings as it hovered over a salmonberry bush. All things were a marvel this day, and he watched with heightened interest, fascinated by the tiny creature's aerial witchery. The bird never seemed to move, yet after feeding itself on seeds from the scarlet berries, it magically appeared over a white, flowery blossom and poked its beak deep within the petals. Then, having sipped of the nectar, it simply vanished in a brilliant green blur. The cheery whistle of a meadowlark seemed to accompany its departure, and the mewling ripple of the river was like a soft melody underscoring the song.

Ai! it was a good day to be alive and free and a man of the Sparrowhawk People.

There had been sadness at first, upon parting with

Doc Newell yesterday morning. But that had quickly passed. Once he hit the mouth of Henry's Fork, and turned his pony east along the Snake, it was as if a monstrous weight had been lifted from his shoulders, almost as though some unseen hand had snatched away his burden, swept the cobwebs from his mind, and in one final moment of grace, revealed to his inner eye all that he sought. The confusion disappeared, in a blink, as had the hummingbird, and in its place came the clear, sweet song of tempered certainty. It came over him swiftly, all in a rush, but somehow deep within, drilled to the very core of what he was and what he had never quite been. Curiously, his thoughts were not on himself at that moment, but instead on Strikes-Both-Ways. Something the old bowmaker had once said long ago.

That a Sparrowhawk was a part of all about him, that he moved in harmony with the earth and its creatures, that unlike others less fortunate, he was blessed with a very rare inner peace.

And so it was. For in that instant, as if a veil had lifted, he saw that he was neither black nor white. He was of the Sparrowhawk People.

His home, in some strange way, had always been Absaroka.

Now, one with the earth and the eternal rocks and the sky above, he was headed back to his people. There he would accept the will of the council, make himself an instrument of the *Apsahrokee*. Their life would be his life, and the good of all would prevail in his thoughts. Through them he would come to know himself as a man. The Sparrowhawk Way would guide him, and in time he might yet earn the honor given him by the People. *Kambasakace.* The Lordly One. But in all things, he would remain a kindred spirit with the least among them, a warrior and a Dog Soldier. Bloody Hand.

Nothing more.

The black man reined his pinto to a halt across stream from where the Salt Fork swept southward out of the Snake. Something had distracted him from his thoughts and he sat for a moment studying the far bank. Everything seemed in order, yet somehow not as it should be, as if some part of the whole had been moved from its proper place. Then he saw it.

A broken branch. Dangling crookedly from a tree limb no taller than a mounted man. Or perhaps many mounted men!

The dark one put his pony into the water and forded the Snake at a shallow, rocky narrows. Once across, he saw that the shoreline was covered with hoofprints of upward of thirty horses. But closer inspection revealed that only four of the animals had carried riders. Clearly somebody was driving a small herd of stolen ponies, yet driving them slowly. Which meant that the raiders had lost all fear of pursuit, or were perhaps already on home ground!

His hunch was confirmed several minutes later. Scouting the area, he found where a man had relieved himself against a tree. The moccasin prints tagged him as Indian rather than white, but it was the kind of prints that interested the dark one most. Swinging off the gelding, he knelt and scrutinized the tracks carefully. The seams were stitched in an irregular pattern. The inner part of the sole was cut on a straight edge. Yet the point was sewn in such a way as to make the man's stride appear pigeontoed.

Shoshone.

The tale was plain to read: four Shoshone braves returning from a horse-stealing raid, probably conducted against the Flatheads to the west. The pony tracks turned south from the Snake, roughly bordering the smaller stream. All of which meant that the raiders were returning home, for it was well known that the Shoshones favored the Salt Fork as a summer campground. Tiny insect marks in the hoofprints made the story complete. The raiders had passed this way during the night, and since they weren't being pursued, it was obvious they intended to enter their village at the honored time, sunrise. It was an important fact. The final piece in a dusty puzzle.

The Shoshone camp was less than a half-day's ride to the south, somewhere along the Salt Fork.

While he was ferreting out the Shoshones' passage, an idea began to form and take shape in his mind. Slowly he enlarged upon it, adding little embellishments, and a sly, cat-like smile creased his mouth.

Why not?

A one-man raid on the dung-eating Shoshone. He had the time and they had very generously presented him with the opportunity. The idea was spiced with a thought that made it all the more appealing. His original vow had been to raid the enemies of the Sparrowhawks alone and unaided. The Dog Soldiers had forestalled that plan, but now he had been handed another chance. One Sparrowhawk against an entire Shoshone camp. *Ai!* it had a good taste.

Besides, he needed four scalps.

Trotting back to the riverbank, he mounted and gigged his pony in the ribs. Moments later they disappeared downstream through a heavy stand of cottonwoods along the Salt Fork.

Dew had fallen when the dark one returned from scouting the enemy camp. Overhead the moon was full, casting a pale silvery glow across the land. The pinto raised his head and whickered softly in greeting, then went back to cropping grass. Bloody Hand checked the pony's hobbles, making low horse-talk as he satisfied himself that all was in order. Standing, he untied his medicine bundle, pulled it from behind the saddle, and walked off toward the stream.

Earlier he had removed his buckskins, stripping to breechclout and moccasins. Now moonlight rippled off the darkness of his skin, and there was something assured and quietly confident about his lithe movements.

Squatting, he loosened the rawhide thongs around the medicine bundle and unfolded it on the ground. Lifting the little buckskin pouch, he studied it intently, grunting to himself as he felt the power of the snake-juice flow out into his hands. After a moment, he smiled and strung the loop over his head, glad to have the bag snug against his chest again. Then he pulled out the bear claw necklace and fastened it around his neck, once more sensing the power of these holy things. Finally he stuck the three coup feathers in his topknot, anchoring them firmly in place.

Removing horn vials of vermilion and ochre from the medicine bundle, he slowly and very meticulously painted the holy symbols across his face. The thought crossed his mind that it somehow wasn't the same without Little Wolf and the Dog Soldiers. Then he paused, considering it, and it came to him that in some curious way it was perhaps better. Never before had he felt so close to his spirit helpers. After daubing paint over his face, he stoppered the vials and laid them aside.

At last he came to the medicine bundle itself.

Separating the contents, he spread each item in it in prescribed order: the bag of herbs to replenish his horse's wind, an eagle's head to give him faraway sight, a dried swallow to make him elusive if pursued, and finally, the claw of an eagle to bring him the swiftness and strength of the great hunter. Arranging them in the order of the four winds, he knelt before the sacred objects and lifted his head to the sky. Spreading his arms wide, he closed his eyes and began the chant.

"Bi-i-kya-waku. Di-wap-e-wima-tsiky."

The ancient words spilled out in a low wolflike howl. They came stronger and with greater force than ever before. He could feel the power sluicing through his body, and somehow he sensed the spirits' presence, summoned from the netherworld by his chant, gathering closer and closer, until he could almost feel them brushing against him.

Suddenly he heard the splatter of rain, beating down like liquid bullets, and the heavy rumble of thunder. But when his eyes popped open there was nothing. Just the moon and low clouds scudding across the starry sky.

It was a sign, the best of all signs. His spirit helpers were pleased. They had spoken at last.

After folding the medicine bundle closed, he drew the thongs tight and stood. Nothing about him had changed, but as he walked back to the pony, everything seemed bathed in an unearthly brilliance. Then he realized that this, too, was part of the sign. The spirits were lulling his enemies by lighting every tree and stone and blade of grass in the dead of night.

Lashing the medicine bundle to the saddle, he patted the pinto on the rump and took off at a dog-trot toward the Shoshone camp.

Bloody Hand burrowed deeper into the earth, burying his face in the tall grass. The Shoshone night guard was less than ten feet away from him now, leaning back against a tree watching the sky. One swift rush and he could have been on the man as silently as a night-hunting owl. But the dark one didn't move. Like the Shoshone, he was watching the sky and waiting.

The moon had become a chalky disk, glowing dimly behind a slate cloud bank. Streaks of lightning played about in the north and there was a smell of rain in the air. Soon the land would be washed in darkness, and not long afterwards would come the pelting deluge of a summer thunderstorm. Between darkness and rain he would strike, and come morning the gusting storm would have obliterated his trail.

This was the way, the sign revealed to him by his spirit helpers. They summoned the forces of earth and sky to protect him, and cautioned him to be patient in his hunt. Waiting was a hard thing, particularly with the Shoshone so close at hand, but he resisted the temptation to move too soon. There was another guard on the other side of the village, and two more watching over the pony herd. His spirit helpers had arranged this with uncanny cleverness. Four scalps quickly taken, and an escape under the cover of a mountain storm. It was too good to spoil with overeagerness, and as every Sparrow-hawk knew, there was great risk in defying the will of the spirit beings.

He curbed his impatience and waited.

Some minutes later it happened, just as he had been promised. The moon disappeared in the darkening clouds and an inky blackness fell over the land. Crouch-ing, he waited until lightning flashed in the north. There would be a moment now when the night guard was blinded by the silvery streak. Bending low, he crossed the open space in two strides, moving with the stealth of a great cat on soft pads. The Shoshone heard nothing and saw nothing. One moment he was alone, cursing the skies, and in the next a hairy band of steel locked around his throat. When the knife severed his spine he died with no more sound than a whining pup.

The black man lowered him to the ground, razored his topknot, and snapped it loose with a hard yank. Kneeling, he placed his hand over the raw wound, spread his fingers wide, and stamped a bloody imprint across the dead man's face. Climbing to his feet, he stuffed the scalp in his belt and moved off toward the far side of the village.

Lightning cracked in a fiery bolt and an instant later the black man faded into the night.

Bloody Hand rode into the Wind River encampment as the sun crested the mountains. Morning mist still clung to the ground, swirling around his pony's flanks, and tawny streamers of light fell over him in a spectral glow. His passage through the village brought a hush over the People. Squaws went rigid at their cooking fires and warriors stood transfixed in the river, their morning baths forgotten. Old and young alike stared on spellbound, for the deadened thud of his pony's hooves was muted to the ear, somehow unreal, as if the pinto disturbed neither earth nor stone but floated instead on the silty mist, while astride his back the dark one rode straight and tall, a ghostly apparition suddenly revealed on the illusive wings of sunrise.

It was *Kambasakace,* the Lordly One, borne along on the wind mists by the spirits themselves.

The People's awe-struck wonder was not without reason. All knew that Bloody Hand had returned to the land of the *tibos.* There were whispers of the vision granted him by the Medicine Stone. It was said that his spirit helpers were displeased with the Sparrowhawks, that he had been shown another way and been sent from Absaroka to punish the People for their shortcomings. According to the holy men, it was a sign from those who ruled the other side, a warning.

The Lordly One would not walk among them again until they had made themselves deserving of his protection, until they had offered him greatness exceeding all temptations the *tibos* could lay before him.

Yet the People saw another thing now, and it was not of the other world. It was a thing as real as the man himself, and what had come to symbolize his greatness as a warrior among warriors.

Hanging from his belt were four fresh scalps.

The black man felt their tenseness upon first entering the village, and it baffled him, for it was hardly the homecoming he had expected. Then, as he passed by, he heard the swelling murmur of their excitement, and again was puzzled that their mood could change so abruptly. But he looked straight ahead, acknowledging nothing. He had returned not as the Lordly One, nor did he expect glory and honor to be heaped upon his head. He had come back simply as a man, a Sparrowhawk weary of roaming and grateful to be once more among his people.

He rode directly to the lodge of White Bear and dismounted. Behind him, a crowd started to gather, and there was surprise in their whispered mutterings. That he had not gone first to his own lodge said much. It was known that he had renounced himself before the council, and there were rumors that he had turned his back on some curious offer the elders chose to keep secret from the tribe. Clearly, whatever had passed between the dark one and the council was to be revealed here at last. Shouts went up, and from all parts of the village people began scurrying toward the chief's lodge.

White Bear stepped through the door hole and stood for a moment staring at the black man. Then he strode forward, smiling broadly, and the two men clasped shoulders in greeting. The council leader searched the younger man's face, watching his eyes for some telltale sign, and was rewarded with more than he had hoped to find. They were the eyes of one who had made peace with himself, clear and untroubled and without regret.

"My heart smiles to look upon you once more, dark one."

"So it is with me, *batsetse.*"

"I see something in your gaze that tells me you have returned to the *Apsahrokee* for good."

"Ai! My journey is done with. I will wander no more."

"You found, then, what it was you sought?"

"Yes, my leader. I found the way."

White Bear seemed startled, but his mouth quirked in a smile and he nodded. "You are a fortunate man. Few among us are privileged to know the enlightenment from within."

"That is true. The one who is not here told me long ago that the journey would be difficult. Yet he never lost faith that I would one day find the way. It has happened just so, but it grieves me that he is not here to see it for himself."

"Perhaps he is, dark one. Having found the way, you should know that those on the other side often see more than we who have not yet crossed over."

"Ae, batsetse. It is a good thought. I will hold it close and take comfort in its knowledge."

"What of more worldly matters? Have you found resolution as a Sparrowhawk as well as a man?"

"That, too, has been granted me. I submit myself to the will of the council. Hereafter my enlightenment and my medicine will serve the People in all things."

The chief motioned to someone in the crowd and Charges Strong stepped forward. The black man went to meet him and they clasped shoulders.

"Welcome, my leader." Charges Strong honored him with lowered eyes, then grinned like a happy baby. "The Dog Soldiers will offer a feast dance for your safe return."

Bloody Hand smiled, but after a moment his gaze sobered. "Are you certain of this thing? I would gladly serve under you before bringing disunity to the Dog Soldiers."

Charges Strong shook his head. "No, my leader. It is you who are pipe-holder of the Dog Soldiers. Never has there been another. I stood for a time in your place, but only with great reluctance. Now you must come back as our *duxia* leader. It is the will of all, myself included."

"So be it." The dark one clasped his shoulder again, harder this time. "We will lead them together, as in times past."

"Ai!" Charges Strong exclaimed. "That brings gladness to my heart. Whom shall we raid first, my leader? The Cut Throats? Or perhaps the Arapahoe? They always have very good horses."

White Bear flung up his hand. "Enough! You would have Bloody Hand raiding even before his pony regains its wind. There are other matters to occupy his time. Have you forgotten that the Moon of Scarlet Plums approaches?"

The chief turned to the crowd and spread his arms wide for silence. "Hear me, *Apsahrokee!* from this day forward, let all know that Bloody Hand sits as my advisor on the council of elders. His wisdom will guide us in war, and his medicine will bring the People full bellies in the time of the Cold Maker. The buffalo hunt is almost upon us, and it is my command that the Dog Soldiers once more serve as *akisate*. With Bloody Hand to lead us our hunt will again bring abundance to your lodges. There will be meat for all, and a time of plenty for Absaroka!"

Laughing and shouting, the Sparrowhawks thundered their approval. The noise of their jubilant cries became deafening, but slowly a chant arose, gaining strength, and within moments the crowd was demanding in a single voice to hear Bloody Hand speak. Gradually the roar subsided and an air of expectancy swept back over the massed throng. When all were still, the dark one raised his clenched fist in salute, honoring them, and opened his mouth to reaffirm what they had heard.

Just then the crowd parted, revealing two squaws side by side, and the black man's jaws clicked shut. Standing before him were Still Water and Pine Leaf.

Astounded, he saw that Pine Leaf was carrying his scalp stick.

The girls advanced on him and halted a few paces off. The devilish gleam in their eyes told him all he needed to know. It was obvious to see that a conspiracy of sorts had been hatched in his absence. They smiled engagingly, and he had a sudden feeling of utter helplessness, like a sitting duck staring straight into the double whammy of a scattergun.

Motioning the girls forward, he took Still Water's hand and pulled her to his left side. The temptation to smile was great, but he held it back. This was a solemn occasion for both girls and they had clearly planned it with care. He jerked the scalps from his belt, nodding soberly, and handed them to Pine Leaf.

The girl took a moment to knot the hairlocks in with the others. Then she raised the scalp stick high overhead and with a great thrust jammed it into the earth.

When it stopped quivering, she calmly stepped forward, turned, and positioned herself at Bloody Hand's right side, the position befitting a second wife.

The dark one raised his hands and looked out over the crowd. *"Apsahrokee,* it would seem that you must await another day to hear me speak."

He brought his arms down, draping them over the shoulders of both girls. The onlookers went mad with excitement, dancing and shouting, their hands fluttering the air in a storm of obscene gestures. Squaws darted forward, shrieking lewd suggestions for the night ahead. Bolder still, the warriors yelled themselves hoarse with a string of crude jokes that left the spectators doubled over in fits of laughter. Even the children took part, their voices shrill and oddly discordant, for it was the ribald sport of the Sparrowhawks, a game all could play.

Bloody Hand started forward, his arms still about the girls, and the crowd opened a path before them. It was somewhat like running the gauntlet, but all in good fun, and the remarks hurled at them represented an amazing variety of vulgar humor. Soon they reached the outer fringes of the mob and moments later they were striding along in the direction of what was now a lodge of two wives.

The black man screwed up a mock frown, looking from one girl to the other. "It is well that I returned with four scalps. Otherwise the People would have laughed behind their hands at both of you."

Still Water batted her lashes, gazing up at him. "We had faith in you, *batsire."*

He grunted, saying nothing for a moment. Then he squeezed Pine Leaf's shoulders in a rough bear hug. "Well, little one, it seems your time has come."

The girl blushed, snuggling closer. "I am ready, great one. Still Water has instructed me in your desires and I know much of making babies."

"Is that so?" Undaunted, he turned back to Still Water. "And have you something further to offer, *bita?"*

The girls exchanged mischievous glances and broke out giggling. After they had gone a few paces more Still Water put her head against his chest. "My lord husband, I think it is as Old Man Coyote has taught us. The warrior who would take two young wives will be a stranger to sleep. Pine Leaf will give you babies and I will give you comfort. Between us you should grow old very soon."

Bloody Hand's rumbling laughter drifted back over the village and he hugged the girls in a fierce embrace. Then he threw his head to the sky and loosed a thunderous roar at the shining mountains.

"Waughhh!"

Absaroka had claimed its own. He was home to stay.